Tom

Since the phenomenal wo... *for Red October*, his con... first novel, Tom Clancy has become one of the world's fastest-selling authors. His bestselling novels, many of them featuring Jack Ryan, include *Red Storm Rising*, *Patriot Games*, *Clear and Present Danger*, *The Sum of All Fears*, *Without Remorse*, *Debt of Honour* and *Executive Orders*. He is also the author of the non-fiction books *Submarine*, *Armoured Warfare*, *Fighter Wing* and *Marine*.

Four of Tom Clancy's novels have been made into highly successful films: *The Hunt for Red October*, *Patriot Games*, *Clear and Present Danger* and, most recently, *The Sum of All Fears*.

THE CARDINAL OF THE KREMLIN

'It offers a marvellous portrait of the Soviet Union and Moscow – as good as anything in *Gorky Park*. As always this is an author who does a superlative job of clearly rendering a nearly unfathomable subject: the high-technology of modern warfare. Overall Clancy has performed a service rare in a popular novel, one that will read by millions: Tom Clancy has written a great spy novel.'

BOB WOODWARD, *Washington Post*

'Clancy has a genius for big, compelling plots, a passion for research, a natural narrative gift.' *New York Times*

'Fast and fascinating.' *Chicago Tribune*

'Clancy's done it again!' *New York Daily News*

TOM CLANCY

THE CARDINAL OF THE KREMLIN

HARPER

HarperCollins*Publishers*
77–85 Fulham Palace Road,
Hammersmith, London W6 8JB

www.harpercollins.co.uk

This paperback edition 2011
1

Previously published in paperback by Fontana 1989
(Special Fontana overseas edition 1989)
Reprinted six times

First published in Great Britain by
Collins 1988

First published in the USA by
G.P. Putnam's Sons 1988

Copyright © Jack Ryan Enterprises Ltd 1988

Photos by SPOT Satellite
© Space Media Network/CNES 1987
Contour maps courtesy of Space Media Network, Stockholm
Map redrawn by Lisa Amoroso

The Author asserts the moral right to
be identified as the author of this work

ISBN 978-0-00-789661-5

Set in Times

Printed and bound in Great Britain by
Clays Limited, St Ives plc

For Colonel and Mrs F. Carter Cobb

. . . Love is not love
Which alters when it alteration finds,
Or bends with the remover to remove.
O, no! it is an ever-fixèd mark
That looks on tempests and is never shaken;. . .

Sonnet 116
WILLIAM SHAKESPEARE

[T]he operations of spies, saboteurs and secret agents are generally regarded as outside the scope of national and international law. They are therefore anathema to all accepted standards of conduct. Nevertheless history shows that no nation will shrink from such activities if they further its vital interests.

FIELD MARSHAL VISCOUNT
MONTGOMERY OF ALAMEIN

The difference between a good man and a bad one is the choice of cause.

WILLIAM JAMES

Acknowledgments

If there was ever a case of casting pearls before swine, it is to be found in the efforts of numerous members of the scientific community who endeavoured to explain the theoretical and engineering aspects of strategic defense to this writer. To George, and Barry, and Bruce, and Russ, and Tom, and Danny, and Bob, and Jim I owe a great deal of thanks. But so does a country, and on one day to come, a world.

Special thanks, moreover, are due to Chris Larsson and Space Media Network, whose commercially generated 'overhead imagery' was good enough to make a few people nervous – and this is only the beginning . . .

PROLOGUE

Threats – Old, New, and Timeless

They called him the Archer. It was an honorable title, though his countrymen had cast aside their reflex bows over a century before, as soon as they had learned about firearms. In part, the name reflected the timeless nature of the struggle. The first of the Western invaders – for that was how they thought of them – had been Alexander the Great, and more had followed since. Ultimately, all had failed. The Afghan tribesmen held their Islamic faith as the reason for their resistance, but the obstinate courage of these men was as much a part of their racial heritage as their dark pitiless eyes.

The Archer was a young man, and an old one. On those occasions that he had both the desire and opportunity to bathe in a mountain stream, anyone could see the youthful muscles on his thirty-year-old body. They were the smooth muscles of one for whom a thousand-foot climb over bare rock was as unremarkable a part of life as a stroll to the mailbox.

It was his eyes that were old. The Afghans are a handsome people whose forthright features and fair skin suffer quickly from wind and sun and dust, too often making them older than their years. For the Archer, the damage had not been done by wind. A teacher of mathematics until three years before, a college graduate in a country where most deemed it enough to be able to read the holy Koran, he'd married young, as was the custom in his land, and fathered two children. But his wife and

11

daughter were dead, killed by rockets fired from a Sukhoi-24 attack-fighter. His son was gone. Kidnapped. After the Soviets had flattened the village of his wife's family with air power, their ground troops had come, killing the remaining adults and sweeping up all the orphans for shipment to the Soviet Union, where they would be educated and trained in other modern ways. All because his wife had wanted her mother to see the grandchildren before she died, the Archer remembered, all because a Soviet patrol had been fired upon a few kilometers from the village. On the day he'd learned this – a week after it had actually happened – the teacher of algebra and geometry had neatly stacked the books on his desk and walked out of the small town of Ghazni into the hills. A week later he'd returned to the town after dark with three other men and proved that he was worthy of his heritage by killing three Soviet soldiers and taking their arms. He still carried that first Kalashnikov.

But that was not why he was known as the Archer. The chief of his little band of *mudjaheddin* – the name means 'Freedom Fighter' – was a perceptive leader who did not look down upon the new arrival who'd spent his youth in classrooms, learning foreign ways. Nor did he hold the young man's initial lack of faith against him. When the teacher joined the group, he'd had only the most cursory knowledge of Islam, and the headman remembered the bitter tears falling like rain from the young man's eyes as their imam had counseled him in Allah's will. Within a month he'd become the most ruthless – and most effective – man in the band, clearly an expression of God's own plan. And it was he whom the leader had chosen to travel to Pakistan, where he could use his knowledge of science and numbers to learn the use of surface-to-air missiles. The first SAMs with which the quiet, serious man from *Amerikastan* had equipped the *mudjaheddin* had been the Soviets' own SA-7, known by the Russians as *strela*, 'arrow.' The first 'man-portable' SAM, it was not overly effective unless used with great skill. Only a few had such skill. Among

12

them the arithmetic teacher was the best, and for his successes with the Russian 'arrows,' the men in the group took to calling him the Archer.

He waited with a new missile at the moment, the American one called Stinger, but all of the surface-to-air missiles in this group – indeed, throughout the whole area – were merely called arrows now: tools for the Archer. He lay on the knife-edge of a ridge, a hundred meters below the summit of the hill, from which he could survey the length of a glacial valley. Beside him was his spotter, Abdul. The name appropriately meant 'servant,' since the teenager carried two additional missiles for his launcher and, more importantly, had the eyes of a falcon. They were burning eyes. He was an orphan.

The Archer's eyes searched the mountainous terrain, especially the ridgelines, with an expression that reflected a millennium of combat. A serious man, the Archer. Though friendly enough, he was rarely seen to smile; he showed no interest in a new bride, not even to join his lonely grief to that of a newly made widow. His life had room for but a single passion.

'There,' Abdul said quietly, pointing.

'I see it.'

The battle on the valley floor – one of several that day – had been under way for thirty minutes, about the proper time for the Soviet soldiers to get support from their helicopter base twenty kilometers over the next line of mountains. The sun glinted briefly off the Mi-24s glass-covered nose, enough for them to see it, ten miles off, skirting over the ridgeline. Farther overhead, and well beyond his reach, circled a single Antonov-26 twin-engine transport. It was filled with observation equipment and radios to coordinate the ground and air action. But the Archer's eyes followed only the Mi-24, a Hind attack helicopter loaded with rockets and cannon shells that even now was getting information from the circling command aircraft.

The Stinger had come as a rude surprise to the Russians, and their air tactics were changing on a daily basis as they struggled to come to terms with the new threat. The valley was deep, but more narrow than the rule. For the pilot to hit the Archer's fellow guerrillas, he had to come straight down the rocky avenue. He'd stay high, at least a thousand meters over the rocky floor for fear that a Stinger team might be down there with the riflemen. The Archer watched the helicopter zigzag in flight as the pilot surveyed the land and chose his path. As expected, the pilot approached from leeward so that the wind would delay the sound of his rotor for the few extra seconds that might be crucial. The radio in the circling transport would be tuned to the frequencies known to be used by the *mudjaheddin* so that the Russians could detect a warning of its approach, and also an indication where the missile team might be. Abdul did indeed carry a radio, switched off and tucked in the folds of his clothing.

Slowly, the Archer raised the launcher and trained its two-element sight on the approaching helicopter. His thumb went sideways and down on the activation switch, and he nestled his cheekbone on the conductance bar. He was instantly rewarded with the warbling screech of the launcher's seeker unit. The pilot had made his assessment, and his decision. He came down the far side of the valley, just beyond missile range, for his first firing run. The Hind's nose was down, and the gunner, sitting in his seat in front of and slightly below the pilot, was training his sights on the area where the fighters were. Smoke appeared on the valley floor. The Soviets used mortar shells to indicate where their tormentors were, and the helicopter altered course slightly. It was almost time. Flames shot out of the helicopter's rocket pods, and the first salvo of ordnance streaked downward.

Then another smoke trail came *up*. The helicopter lurched left as the smoke raced into the sky, well clear of the Hind, but still a positive indication of danger ahead; or so the pilot thought. The Archer's hands tightened on the launcher. The helicopter was sideslipping right at him now, expanding around the inner ring of the sight. It was now in

14

range. The Archer punched the forward button with his left thumb, 'uncaging' the missile and giving the infrared seeker-head on the Stinger its first look at the heat radiating from the Mi-24's turboshaft engines. The sound carried through his cheekbone into his ear changed. The missile was now tracking the target. The Hind's pilot decided to hit the area from which the 'missile' had been launched at him, bringing the aircraft farther left, and turning slightly. Unwittingly, he turned his jet exhaust almost right at the Archer as he warily surveyed the rocks from which the rocket had come.

The missile screamed its readiness at the Archer now, but still he was patient. He put his mind into that of his target, and judged that the pilot would come closer still before his helicopter had the shot he wanted at the hated Afghans. And so he did. When the Hind was only a thousand meters off, the Archer took a deep breath, super-elevated his sight, and whispered a brief prayer of vengeance. The trigger was pulled almost of its own accord.

The launcher bucked in his hands as the Stinger looped slightly upward before dropping down to home on its target. The Archer's eyes were sharp enough to see it despite the almost invisible smoke trail it left behind. The missile deployed its maneuvering fins, and these moved a few fractions of a millimeter in obedience to the orders generated by its computer brain – a microchip the size of a postage stamp. Aloft in the circling An-26, an observer saw a tiny puff of dust and began to reach for a microphone to relay a warning, but his hand had barely touched the plastic instrument before the missile struck.

The missile ran directly into one of the helicopter's engines and exploded. The helicopter was crippled instantly. The driveshaft for the tail rotor was cut, and the Hind began spinning violently to the left while the pilot tried to autorotate the aircraft down, frantically looking for a flat place while his gunner radioed a shrill call for rescue. The pilot brought the engine to idle, unloading his collective to control torque, locked his eyes on a flat space the size of a tennis court, then cut his switches and activated the onboard extinguishing system. Like most fliers he feared fire above all things, though he would learn the error soon enough.

The Archer watched the Mi-24 hit nose-down on a rocky ledge five hundred feet below his perch. Surprisingly, it didn't burn as the aircraft came apart. The helicopter cartwheeled viciously, the tail whipping forward and over the nose before it came to rest on its side. The Archer raced down the hill with Abdul right behind. It took five minutes.

The pilot fought with his straps as he hung upside down. He was in pain, but he knew that only the living felt pain. The new model helicopter had had improved safety systems built in. Between those and his own skill he'd survived the crash. Not his gunner, he noticed briefly. The man in front hung motionless, his neck broken, his hands limply reaching for the ground. The pilot had no time for that. His seat was bent, and the chopper's canopy had shattered, its metal frame now a prison for the flyer. The emergency release latch was jammed, the explosive release bolts unwilling to fire. He took his pistol from the shoulder holster and started blasting at the metal framework, one piece at a time. He wondered if the An-26 had gotten the emergency call. Wondered if the rescue helicopter at his base was on the way. His rescue radio was in a pants pocket, and he'd activate it as soon as he got away from his broken bird. The pilot cut his hands to ribbons as he prised the metal away, giving himself a clear path out. He thanked his luck again that he was not ending his life in a pillar of greasy smoke as he released his straps and climbed out of the aircraft to the rocky ground.

His left leg was broken. The jagged end of a white bone stuck clear of his flight suit; though he was too deeply in shock to feel it, the sight of the injury horrified him. He holstered his empty pistol and grabbed a loose piece of metal to serve as a cane. He had to get away. He hobbled to the far end of the ledge and saw a path. It was three kilometers to friendly forces. He was about to start down when he heard something and turned. Hope changed to horror in an instant, and the pilot realized that a fiery death would have been a blessing.

The Archer blessed Allah's name as he withdrew his knife from its sheath.

There couldn't be much left of her, Ryan thought. The hull was mainly intact – at least superficially – but you could see the rough surgery made by the welders as clearly as the stitches made on Frankenstein's monster. An apt-enough comparison, he thought silently. Man had made these things, but they could one day destroy their makers in the space of an hour.

'God, it's amazing how big they look on the outside . . .'

'And so small on the inside?' Marko asked. There was a wistful sadness in his voice. Not so long before, Captain Marko Ramius of the Voyenno Morskoi Flot had conned his ship into this very drydock. He hadn't been there to watch U.S. Navy technicians dissect her like pathologists over a cadaver, removing the missiles, the reactor plant, the sonars, the onboard computers and communications gear, the periscopes, and even the galley stoves for analysis at bases spread all over the United States. His absence had been at his own request. Ramius' hatred for the Soviet system did not extend to the ships that system built. He'd sailed this one well – and *Red October* had saved his life.

And Ryan's. Jack fingered the hairline scar on his forehead and wondered if they'd ever cleaned his blood off the helmsman's console. 'I'm surprised you didn't want to take her out,' he observed to Ramius.

'No.' Marko shook his head. 'I only want to say goodbye. He was good ship.'

'Good enough,' Jack agreed quietly. He looked at the half-repaired hole that the Alfa's torpedo had made in the port side and shook his head in silence. *Good enough to save my ass when that torpedo hit*. The two men watched in silence, separated from the sailors and Marines who'd secured the area since the previous December.

The drydock was flooding now, the filthy water from the Elizabeth River rushing into the concrete box. They'd take her out tonight. Six American fast-attack submarines were even now 'sanitizing' the ocean east of the Norfolk Navy Base, ostensibly part of an exercise that would also involve a few surface ships. It was nine o'clock on a moonless night. It would take an hour to flood the drydock. A crew of thirty was already aboard. They'd fire up the ship's diesel engines and sail her out for her second and final voyage, to the deep ocean trench north of Puerto Rico, where she would be scuttled in twenty-five thousand feet of water.

Ryan and Ramius watched as the water covered the wooden blocks that supported the hull, wetting the submarine's keel for the first time in nearly a year. The water came in more quickly now, creeping up the plimsoll marks painted fore and aft. On the submarine's deck, a handful of seamen wearing bright orange lifejackets for safety paced around, making ready to slip the fourteen stout mooring lines that held her steady.

The ship herself remained quiet. *Red October* gave no sign of welcome for the water. Perhaps she knew the fate that awaited her, Ryan said to himself. It was a foolish thought – but he also knew that for millennia sailors had imputed personalities to the ships they served.

Finally she started to move. The water buoyed the hull off the wooden blocks. There was a muted series of thuds, more felt than heard as she rose off them ever so slowly, rocking back and forth a few inches at a time.

A few minutes later the ship's diesel engine rumbled to life, and the line handlers on the ship and the drydock began to take in the lines. At the same time, the canvas that covered the seaward end of the drydock was taken down, and all could see the fog that hung on the water outside. Conditions were perfect for the operation. Conditions had to be perfect; the Navy had waited six weeks for them, a moonless night and the thick seasonal fog that plagued the

Chesapeake Bay region this time of year. When the last line was slipped, an officer atop the submarine's sail raised a hand-held air horn and blew a single blast.

'Under way!' his voice called, and the sailors at the bow struck the jack and put down the staff. For the first time, Ryan noticed that it was the Soviet jack. He smiled. It was a nice touch. On the sail's aft end, another seaman ran up the Soviet naval ensign, its bright red star emblazoned with the shield of the Red Banner Northern Fleet. The Navy, ever mindful of traditions, was saluting the man who stood at his side.

Ryan and Ramius watched the submarine start to move under her own power, her twin bronze propellers turning gently in reverse as she backed out into the river. One of the tugs helped her turn to face north. Within another minute she was gone from sight. Only the lingering rumble of her diesel came across the oily water of the navy yard.

Marko blew his nose once and blinked a half-dozen times. When he turned away from the water, his voice was firm.

'So, Ryan, they fly you home from England for this?'

'No, I came back a few weeks ago. New job.'

'Can you say what job is?' Marko asked.

'Arms control. They want me to coordinate the intelligence side for the negotiations team. We have to fly over in January.'

'Moscow?'

'Yes, it's a preliminary session – setting the agenda and doing some technical stuff, that sort of thing. How about you?'

'I work at AUTEC in Bahamas. Much sun and sand. You see my tan?' Ramius grinned. 'I come to Washington every two-three months. I fly back in five hours. We work on new quieting project.' Another smile. 'Is classified.'

'Great! I want you to come over to my house then. I still owe you a dinner.' Jack handed over a card. 'Here's my number. Call me a few days before you fly in, and I'll set things up with the Agency.' Ramius and his officers were under a very strict protection regime from CIA security officers. The really amazing thing, Jack thought, was that the story hadn't leaked. None of the news media had gotten word, and if security really was that tight, probably the Russians also didn't know the fate of their missile submarine *Krazny Oktyabr*. She'd be turning east about now, Jack thought, to pass over the Hampton Roads tunnel. Roughly an hour after that she'd dive and head southeast. He shook his head.

Ryan's sadness at the submarine's fate was tempered by the thought of what she'd been built for. He remembered his own reaction, in the sub's missile room a year before, the first time he'd been so close to the ghastly things. Jack accepted the fact that nuclear weapons kept the peace – if you could really call the world's condition *peace* – but like most of the people who thought about the subject, he wished for a better way. Well, this was one less submarine, twenty-six less missiles, and one hundred eighty-two less warheads. Statistically, Ryan told himself, it didn't count for much.

But it was something.

Ten thousand miles away and eight thousand feet above sea level the problem was unseasonable weather. The place was in the Tadzhik Soviet Socialist Republic, and the wind came from the south, still bearing moisture from the Indian Ocean that fell as miserably cold drizzle. Soon it would be the real winter that always came early here, usually on the heels of the blazing, airless summer, and all that fell would be cold and white.

The workers were mostly young, eager members of the Komsomol. They had been brought in to help finish a construction project that had been begun in 1983. One of them, a masters candidate at Moscow State University's school of physics, rubbed the rain from his eyes and straightened to ease a crick in his back. This was no way to utilize a promising young engineer, Morozov thought. Instead of playing with this surveyor's instrument, he could be building lasers in his laboratory, but he wanted full membership in the Communist Party of the Soviet Union, and wanted even more to avoid military service. The combination of his school deferment and his Komsomol work had helped mightily to this end.

'Well?' Morozov turned to see one of the site engineers. A civil engineer, he was, who described himself as a man who knew concrete.

'I read the position as correct, Comrade Engineer.'

The older man stooped down to look through the sighting scope. 'I agree,' the man said. 'And that's the last one, the gods be praised.' Both men jumped with the sound of a distant explosion. Engineers from the Red Army obliterating yet another rocky outcropping outside of the fenced perimeter. You didn't need to be a solider to understand what that was all about, Morozov thought to himself.

'You have a fine touch with optical instruments. Perhaps you will become a civil engineer, too, eh? Build useful things for the State?'

'No, Comrade. I study high-energy physics – mainly lasers.' *These, too, are useful things.*

The man grunted and shook his head. 'Then you might come back here, God help you.'

'Is this – '

'You didn't hear anything from me,' the engineer said, just a touch of firmness in his voice.

'I understand,' Morozov replied quietly. 'I suspected as much.'

'I would be careful voicing that suspicion,' the other said conversationally as he turned to look at something.

'This must be a fine place to watch the stars,' Morozov observed, hoping for the right response.

'I wouldn't know,' the civil engineer replied with an insider's smile. 'I've never met an astronomer.'

Morozov smiled to himself. He'd guessed right after all. They had just plotted the position of the six points on which mirrors would be set. These were equidistant from a central

21

point located in a building guarded by men with rifles. Such precision, he knew, had only two applications. One was astronomy, which collected light coming down. The other application involved light going up. The young engineer told himself that here was where he wanted to come. This place would change the world.

1

The Reception of the Party

Business was being conducted. All kinds of business. Everyone there knew it. Everyone there was part of it. Everyone there needed it. And yet everyone there was in one way or another dedicated to stopping it. For every person there in the St George Hall of the Great Kremlin Palace, the dualism was a normal part of life.

The participants were mainly Russian and American, and were divided into four groups.

First, the diplomats and politicians. One could discern these easily enough from their better-than-average clothing and erect posture, the ready, robotic smiles, and careful diction that endured even after the many alcoholic toasts. They were the masters, knew it, and their demeanor proclaimed it.

Second, the soldiers. One could not have arms negotiations without the men who controlled the arms, maintained them, tested them, pampered them, all the while telling themselves that the politicians who controlled the *men* would never give the order to launch. The soldiers in their uniforms stood mainly in little knots of homogeneous nationality and service branch, each clutching a half-full glass and napkin while blank, emotionless eyes swept the room as though searching for a threat on an unfamiliar battlefield. For that was precisely what it was to them, a bloodless battlefield that would define the real ones if their political masters ever lost control, lost temper, lost perspective, lost whatever it is in man that tries to avoid the profligate waste of young life. To a man the soldiers trusted none but one another, and in some cases trusted their enemies in different-colored uniforms more than their own soft-clothed masters. At least you knew where another soldier stood. You couldn't always say the same of politicians, even your own. They talked with one another quietly, always watching to see who listened, stopping occasionally for a quick gulp from the glass, accompanied by another look about the room. They were the victims, but also the predators – the dogs, perhaps, kept on leashes by those who deemed themselves the masters of events.

The soldiers had trouble believing that, too.

Third, the reporters. These could also be picked out by their clothing, which was always wrinkled by too many packings and unpackings in airline suitcases too small for all they carried. They lacked the polish of the politicians, and the fixed smiles, substituting for it the inquisitive looks of children, mixed with the cynicism of the dissolute. Mainly they held their glasses in their left hands, sometimes with a small pad instead of the paper napkin, while a pen was half-hidden in the right. They circulated like birds of prey. One would find someone who would talk. Others would notice and come over to drink in the information. The casual observer could tell how interesting the information was by how quickly the reporters moved off to another source. In this sense the American and other Western reporters were different from their Soviet counterparts, who for the most part hung close to their masters like favored earls of another time, both to show their loyalty to the Party and to act as buffers against their colleagues from elsewhere. But together, they were the audience in this performance of theater in the round.

Fourth came the final group, the invisible one, those whom no one could identify in any easy way. These were the spies, and the counterespionage agents who hunted them. They could be distinguished from the security officers, who watched everyone with suspicion, but from the room's perimeter, as invisible as the waiters who circulated about with heavy silver trays of champagne and vodka in crystal glasses that had been commissioned by the House of Romanov. Some of the waiters were counter-espionage agents, of course. Those had to circulate through the room, their ears perked for a snippet of conversation, perhaps a voice too low or a word that didn't fit the mood of the evening. It was no easy task. A quartet of strings in a corner played chamber music to which no one appeared to listen, but this too is a feature of diplomatic receptions and doing without it would be noticed. Then there was the volume of human noise. There were well over a hundred people here, and every one of them was talking at least half the time. Those close to the quartet had to speak loudly to be heard over the music. All the resulting noise was contained in a ballroom two hundred feet long and sixty-five wide, with a parquet floor and hard stucco walls that reflected and reverberated the sound until it reached an ambient level that would have hurt the ears of a small child. The spies used their invisibility and the noise to make themselves the ghosts of the feast.

But the spies were here. Everyone knew it. Anyone in Moscow could tell you about spies. If you met with a Westerner on anything approaching a regular basis, it was the prudent thing to report it. If you did so only once, and a passing police officer of the Moscow Militia – or an Army officer strolling around with his briefcase – passed by, a head would turn, and note would be taken. Perhaps cursory, perhaps not. Times had changed since Stalin, of course, but Russia was still Russia, and distrust of for-eigners and their ideas was far older than any ideology.

Most of the people in the room thought about it without really thinking about it – except those who actually played this particular game. The diplomats and politicians had practice guarding their words, and were not overly concer-ned at the moment. To the reporters it was merely amusing, a fabulous game that didn't really concern them – though each Western reporter knew that he or she was *ipso facto* thought an agent of espionage by the Soviet government. The soldiers thought about it most of all. They knew the importance of intelligence, craved it, valued it – and despised those who gathered it for the slinking things they were.

Which ones are the spies?

Of course there was a handful of people who fitted into no easily identified category – or fitted into more than one.

'And how did you find Moscow, Dr Ryan?' a Russian asked. Jack turned from his inspection of the beautiful St George clock.

'Cold and dark, I'm afraid,' Ryan answered after a sip of his champagne. 'It's not as though we have had much chance to see anything.' Nor would they. The American team had been in the Soviet Union only for a little over four days, and would fly home the next day after concluding the technical session that preceded the plenary one.

'That is too bad,' Sergey Golovko observed.

'Yes,' Jack agreed. 'If all of your architecture is this good, I'd love to take a few days to admire it. Whoever built this house had style.' He nodded approvingly at the gleaming white walls, the domed ceiling, and the gold leaf. In fact he thought it overdone, but he knew that the Russians had a national tendency to overdo a lot of things. To Russians, who rarely had enough of anything, 'having enough' meant having more than anyone else – preferably more than *everyone* else. Ryan thought it evidence of a national inferiority complex, and reminded himself that people who feel themselves inferior have a pathological desire to disprove their own perceptions. That one factor dominated all aspects of the arms-control process, displacing mere logic as the basis for reaching an agreement.

'The decadent Romanovs,' Golovko noted. 'All this came from the sweat of the peasants.' Ryan turned and laughed.

'Well, at least some of their tax money went for something beautiful, harmless – and immortal. If you ask me, it beats buying ugly weapons that are obsolete ten years later. There's an idea, Sergey Nikolay'ch. We will

26

redirect our political-military competition to beauty instead of nuclear weapons.'

'You are satisfied with the progress, then?'

Business. Ryan shrugged and continued to inspect the room. 'I suppose we've settled on the agenda. Next, those characters over by the fireplace have to work out the details.' He stared at one of the enormous crystal chandeliers. He wondered how many man-years of effort had gone into making it, and how much fun it must have been to hang something that weighed as much as a small car.

'And you are satisfied on the issue of verifiability?'

That confirms it, Ryan thought with a thin smile. *Golovko is GRU*. 'National Technical Means,' a term that denoted spy satellites and other methods of keeping an eye on foreign countries, were mainly the province of CIA in America, but in the Soviet Union they belonged to the GRU, the Soviet military intelligence agency. Despite the tentative agreement in principle for on-site inspection, the main effort of verifying compliance on an agreement would lie with the spy satellites. That would be Golovko's turf.

It was no particular secret that Jack worked for CIA. It didn't have to be; he wasn't a field officer. His attachment to the arms-negotiation team was a logical matter. His current assignment had to do with monitoring certain strategic weapons systems within the Soviet Union. For any arms treaty to be signed, both sides first had to satisfy their own institutional paranoia that no serious tricks could be played on them by the other. Jack advised the chief negotiator along these lines; when, Jack reminded himself, the negotiator troubled himself to listen.

'Verifiability,' he replied after another moment, 'is a very technical and difficult question. I'm afraid I'm not really that conversant on it. What do your people think about our proposal to limit land-based systems?'

'We depend on our land-based missiles more than you,' Golovko said. His voice became more guarded as they discussed the meat of the Soviet position.

'I don't understand why you don't place as much emphasis on submarines as we do.'

'Reliability, as well you know.'

'Aw, hell. Submarines are reliable,' Jack baited him as he reexamined the clock. It was magnificent. Some peasant-looking fellow was handing a sword to another chap, and waving him off to battle. *Not exactly a new idea*, Jack thought. *Some old fart tells a young kid to go off and get killed.*

'We have had some incidents, I regret to say.'

'Yeah, that Yankee that went down off Bermuda.'

'And the other.'

'Hmph?' Ryan turned back. It took a serious effort not to smile.

'Please, Dr Ryan, do not insult my intelligence. You know the story of *Krazny Oktyabr* as well as I.'

'What was that name? Oh, yeah, the Typhoon you guys lost off the Carolinas. I was in London then. I never did get briefed on it.'

'I think the two incidents illustrate the problem we Soviets face. We cannot trust our missile submarines as completely as you trust yours.'

'Hmm.' *Not to mention the drivers*, Ryan thought, careful not to let his face show a thing.

Golovko persisted. 'But may I ask a substantive question?'

'Sure, so long as you don't expect a substantive answer.' Ryan chuckled.

'Will your intelligence community object to the draft treaty proposal?'

'Now, how am I supposed to know the answer to that?' Jack paused. 'What about yours?'

'Our organs of State security do what they are told,' Golovko assured him.

Right, Ryan told himself. 'In our country, if the President decides that he likes an arms treaty, and he thinks he can get it through the Senate, it doesn't matter what the CIA and Pentagon think – '

'But your military-industrial complex – ' Golovko cut Jack off.

'God, you guys really love to beat on that horse, don't you? Sergey Nikolayevich, you should know better.'

But Golovko was a *military* intelligence officer, and might not, Ryan remembered too late. The degree to which America and the Soviet Union misunderstood each other was at one and the same time amusing and supremely dangerous. Jack wondered if the intelligence community over here tried to get the truth out, as CIA usually did now, or merely told its masters what they wanted to hear, as CIA had done all too often in the past. Probably the latter, he thought. The Russian intel agencies were undoubtedly politicized, just as CIA used to be. One good thing about Judge Moore was that he'd worked damned hard to put an end to that. But the Judge had no particular wish to be President; that made him different from his Soviet counterparts. One director of the KGB had made it to the top over here, and at least one other tried to. That made KGB a political creature, and that affected its objectivity. Jack sighed into his drink. The problems between the two countries wouldn't end if all the false perceptions were laid to rest, but at least things could be more manageable.

Maybe. Ryan admitted to himself that this might be as false a panacea as all the others; it had never been tried, after all.

'May I make a suggestion to you?'

'Certainly,' Golovko answered.

'Let's drop the shop talk, and you tell me about this room while I enjoy the champagne.' *It'll save us both a lot of time when we write up our contact reports tomorrow*.

'Perhaps I could get you some vodka?'

'No, thanks, this bubbly stuff is great. Local?'

'Yes, from Georgia,' Golovko said proudly. 'I think it is better than the French.'

'I wouldn't mind taking a few bottles home,' Ryan allowed.

Golovko laughed, a short bark of amusement and power. 'I will see to it. So. The palace was finished in 1849, at the cost of eleven million rubles, quite a sum at the time. It's the last grand palace ever built, and, I think, the best . . .'

Ryan wasn't the only one touring the room, of course. Most of the American delegation had never seen it. Russians bored with the reception led them around, explaining as they went. Several people from the embassy tagged along, keeping a casual eye on things.

'So, Misha, what do you think of American women?' Defense Minister Yazov asked his aide.

'Those coming this way are not unattractive, Comrade Minister,' the Colonel observed.

'But so skinny – ah, yes, I keep forgetting, your beautiful Elena was also thin. A fine woman she was, Misha.'

'Thank you for remembering, Dmitri Timofeyevich.'

'Hello, Colonel!' one of the American ladies said in Russian.

'Ah, yes, Mrs . . . .'

'Foley. We met at the hockey game last November.'

'You know this lady?' the Minister asked his aide.

'My nephew – no, my grand-nephew Mikhail, Elena's sister's grandson – plays junior-league hockey, and I was invited to a game. It turned out that they allowed an imperialist on the team,' he replied with a raised eyebrow.

'Your son plays well?' Marshal Yazov asked.

'He is the third-leading scorer in the league,' Mrs Foley replied.

'Splendid! Then you must stay in our country, and your son can play for Central Army when he grows up.' Yazov grinned. He was a grandfather four times over. 'What do you do here?'

'My husband works for the embassy. He's over there, shepherding the reporters around – but the important thing is, I got to come here tonight. I've never seen anything like this in my whole life!' she gushed. Her glistening eyes spoke of several glasses of something. Probably champagne, the

Minister thought. She looked like the champagne type, but she was attractive enough, and she had bothered to learn the language reasonably well, unusual for Americans. 'These floors are so pretty, it seems a crime to walk on them. We don't have anything like this at home.'

'You never had the czars, which was your good fortune,' Yazov replied like a good Marxist. 'But as a Russian I must admit that I am proud of their artistic sense.'

'I haven't seen you at any other games, Colonel,' she said, turning back to Misha.

'I don't have the time.'

'But you're good luck! The team won that night, and Eddie got a goal and an assist.'

The Colonel smiled. 'All our little Misha got was two penalties for high-sticking.'

'Named for you?' the Minister asked.

'Yes.'

'You didn't have those on when I saw you.' Mrs Foley pointed to the three gold stars on his chest.

'Perhaps I didn't take off my topcoat – '

'He always wears them,' the Marshal assured her. 'One *always* wears his Hero of the Soviet Union medals.'

'Is that the same as our Medal of Honor?'

'The two are roughly equivalent,' Yazov said for his aide. Misha was unaccountably shy about them. 'Colonel Filitov is the only man living who has ever won three in battle.'

'Really? How does someone win *three*?'

'Fighting Germans,' the Colonel said tersely.

'Killing Germans,' Yazov said even more bluntly. When Filitov had been one of the Red Army's brightest stars, he'd been a mere lieutenant. 'Misha is one of the best tank officers who ever lived.'

Colonel Filitov actually blushed at that. 'I did my duty, as did many soldiers in that war.'

'My father was decorated in the war, too. He led two missions to rescue people from prison camps in the Philippines. He didn't talk about it very much, but they

31

gave him a bunch of medals. Do you tell your children about those bright stars of yours?'

Filitov went rigid for a moment. Yazov answered for him.

'Colonel Filitov's sons died some years ago.'

'Oh! Oh, Colonel, I am so sorry,' Mrs Foley said, and she really was.

'It was long ago.' He smiled. 'I remember your son well from the game, a fine young man. Love your children, dear lady, for you will not always have them. If you will excuse me for a moment.' Misha moved off in the direction of the rest rooms. Mrs Foley looked to the Minister, anguish on her pretty face.

'Sir, I didn't mean – '

'You could not have known. Misha lost his sons a few years apart, then his wife. I met her when I was a very young man – lovely girl, a dancer with the Kirov Ballet. So sad, but we Russians are accustomed to great sadnesses. Enough of that. What team does your son play for?' Marshal Yazov's interest in hockey was amplified by the pretty young face.

Misha found the rest room after a minute. Americans and Russians were sent to different ones, of course, and Colonel Filitov was alone in what had been the private water closet of a prince, or perhaps a czar's mistress. He washed his hands and looked in the gilt-edged mirror. He had but one thought: *Again. Another mission.* Colonel Filitov sighed and tidied himself up. A minute later he was back out in the arena.

'Excuse me,' Ryan said. Turning around, he'd bumped into an elderly gentleman in uniform. Golovko said something in Russian that Ryan didn't catch. The officer said something to Jack that sounded polite, and walked over, Ryan saw, to the Defense Minister.

'Who's that?' Jack asked his Russian companion.

'The Colonel is personal aide to the Minister,' Golovko replied.

'Little old for a colonel, isn't he?'

'He is a war hero. We do not force all such men to retire.'

'I guess that's fair enough,' Jack commented, and turned back to hear about this part of the room. After they had exhausted the St George Hall, Golovko led Jack into the adjacent St Vladimir Hall. He expressed the hope that he and Ryan would next meet here. St Vladimir Hall, he explained, was set aside for the signing of treaties. The two intelligence officers toasted one another on that.

The party broke up after midnight. Ryan got into the seventh limousine. Nobody talked on the ride back to the embassy. Everyone was feeling the alcohol, and you didn't talk in cars, not in Moscow. Cars were too easy to bug. Two men fell asleep, and Ryan came close enough himself. What kept him awake was the knowledge that they'd fly out in another five hours, and if he was going to have to do that, he might as well keep tired enough to sleep on the plane, a skill he had only recently acquired. He changed his clothes and went down to the embassy's canteen for coffee. It would be enough to keep himself going for a few hours while he made his own notes.

Things had gone amazingly well these past four days. Almost too well. Jack told himself that averages are made up of times when things went well and times they went poorly. A draft treaty was on the table. Like all draft treaties of late, it was intended by the Soviets to be more a negotiating tool than a negotiating document. Its details were already in the press, and already certain members of Congress were saying on the floor how fair a deal it was – and why don't we just agree to it?

Why not, indeed? Jack wondered with an ironic smile. Verifiability. That was one reason. The other . . . was there another? Good question. Why had they changed their stance so much? There was evidence that General Secretary Narmonov wanted to reduce his military expenditures, but despite all the public perceptions to the contrary, nuclear arms were not the place you did that. Nukes were cheap for what they did; they were a very cost-effective way of killing people. While a nuclear warhead and its missile were expensive gadgets, they were far cheaper than the equivalent destructive power in tanks and artillery. Did Narmonov genuinely want to reduce the threat of nuclear war? But that threat didn't come from the weapons; as always it came from the politicians and their mistakes. Was it all a symbol? Symbols, Jack reminded himself, were far easier for Narmonov to produce than substance. If a symbol, at whom was it aimed?

Narmonov had charm, and power – the sort of visceral presence that came with his post, but even more from his personality. What sort of man was this? What was he after? Ryan snorted. That wasn't his department. Another CIA team was examining Narmonov's political vulnerability right here in Moscow. His far easier job was to figure out the technical side. Far easier, perhaps, but he didn't yet know the answer to his own questions.

Golovko was already back at his office, making his own notes in a painful longhand. Ryan, he wrote, would uneasily support the draft proposal. Since Ryan had the ear of the Director, that probably meant that CIA would, too. The intelligence officer set down his pen and rubbed his eyes for a moment. Waking up with a hangover was bad enough, but having to stay awake long enough to welcome it with the sunrise was above and beyond the duty of a Soviet officer. He wondered why his government had made the offer in the first place, and why the Americans seemed so eager. Even Ryan, who should have known better. What did the Americans have in mind? Who was outmaneuvering whom?

Now there was a question.

He turned back to Ryan, his assignment of the previous evening. Well along for a man of his years, the equivalent of a colonel in the KGB or GRU and only thirty-five. What had he done to rise so quickly? Golovko shrugged. Probably connected, a fact of life as important in Washington as in Moscow. He had courage – the business with the terrorists almost five years before. He was also a family man, something Russians respected more than their American counterparts would have believed – it implied stability, and that in turn implied predictability. Most of all, Golovko thought, Ryan was a thinker. Why, then, was he not opposed to a pact that would benefit the Soviet Union more than it benefited America? *Is our evaluation incorrect*? he wrote. Do the Americans know something we do not? That was a question, or better still: Did Ryan know something that Golovko did not? The Colonel frowned, then reminded himself what *he* knew that Ryan did not. That drew a half-smile. It was all part of the grand game. The grandest game there was.

'You must have walked all night.'

The Archer nodded gravely and set down the sack that had bowed his shoulders for five days. It was almost as heavy as the one Abdul had packed. The younger man was near collapse, the CIA officer saw. Both men found pillows to sit on.

'Have something to drink.' The officer's name was Emilio Ortiz. His ancestry was sufficiently muddled that he could have passed for a native of any Caucasian nation. Also thirty years of age, he was of medium height and build, with a swimmer's muscles, which was how he'd won a scholarship to USC, where he'd won a degree in languages. Ortiz had a rare gift in this area. With two weeks' exposure to a language, a dialect, an accent, he could pass for a native anywhere in the world. He was also a man of compassion, respectful of the ways of the people with whom he worked. This meant that the drink he offered was not – could not be – alcoholic. It was apple juice. Ortiz watched him drink it with all the delicacy of a wine connoisseur sampling new bordeaux.

'Allah's blessings upon this house,' the Archer said when he finished the first glass. That he had waited until drinking the apple juice was as close as the man ever came to making a joke. Ortiz saw the fatigue written on the man's face, though he displayed it no other way. Unlike his young porter, the Archer seemed invulnerable to such normal human concerns. It wasn't true, but Ortiz understood how the force that drove him could suppress his humanity.

The two men were dressed almost identically. Ortiz considered the Archer's clothing and wondered at the ironic similarity with the Apache Indians of America and Mexico. One of his ancestors had been an officer under Terrazas when the Mexican Army had finally crushed Victorio in the Tres Castillos Mountains. The Afghans, too, wore rough trousers under their loincloths. They, too, tended to be small, agile fighters. And they, too, treated captives as noisy amusements for their knives. He looked at the Archer's knife and wondered how it was used. Ortiz decided he didn't want to know.

'Do you wish something to eat?' he asked.

'It can wait,' the Archer replied, reaching for his pack. He and Abdul had brought out two loaded camels, but for the important material, only his backpack would do. 'I fired eight rockets. I hit six aircraft, but one had two engines and managed to escape. Of the five I destroyed, two were helicopters, and three were bombing-fighters. The first helicopter we killed was the new kind of twenty-four you told us about. You were correct. It did have some new equipment. Here is some of it.'

It was ironic, Ortiz thought, that the most sensitive equipment in military aircraft would survive treatment guaranteed to kill its crew. As he watched, the Archer revealed six green circuit boards for the laser-designator that was now standard equipment on the Mi-24. The U.S. Army Captain who'd stayed in the shadows and kept his mouth shut to this point now came forward to examine them. His hands fairly trembled as he reached for the items.

'You have the laser, too?' the Captain asked in accented Pashtu.

'It was badly damaged, but, yes.' The Archer turned. Abdul was snoring. He nearly smiled until he remembered that he had a son also.

For his part, Ortiz was saddened. To have a partisan with the Archer's education under his control was rare enough. He'd probably been a skilled teacher but he could never teach again. He could never go back to what he'd been. War had changed the Archer's life as fully and certainly as death. Such a goddamned waste.

'The new rockets?' the Archer asked.

'I can give you ten. A slightly improved model, with an additional five-hundred-meter range. And some more smoke rockets, too.'

The Archer nodded gravely, and the corners of his mouth moved in what, in different times, might have been the beginnings of a smile.

'Perhaps now I can go after their transports. The smoke rockets work very well, my friend. Every time, they push the invaders close to me. They have not yet learned about that tactic.'

Not a *trick*, Ortiz noted. He called it a *tactic*. *He wants to go after transports now, he wants to kill a hundred Russians at a time. Jesus, what have we made of this man*? The CIA officer shook his head. That wasn't his concern.

'You are weary, my friend. Rest. We can eat later. Please honor my house by sleeping here.'

'It is true,' the Archer acknowledged. He was asleep within two minutes.

Ortiz and the Captain sorted through the equipment brought to them. Included was the maintenance manual for the Mi-24's laser equipment, and radio code sheets, in addition to other things they'd seen before. By noon he had it all fully catalogued and began making arrangements to ship it all to the embassy; from there it would be flown immediately to California for a complete evaluation.

The Air Force VC-137 lifted off right on time. It was a customized version of the venerable Boeing 707. The 'V' prefix on its designation denoted that it was designed to carry VIP passengers, and the aircraft's interior reflected this. Jack lay back on the couch and abandoned himself to the fatigue that enveloped him. Ten minutes later a hand shook his shoulder.

'The boss wants you,' another member of the team said.

'Doesn't he ever sleep?' Jack growled.

'Tell me about it.'

Ernest Allen was in the VIP-est accommodations on the aircraft, a cabin set exactly atop the wing spar with six plush swivel chairs. A coffeepot sat on the table. If he didn't have some coffee he'd soon be incoherent. If he did, he'd be unable to go back to sleep. Well, the government wasn't paying him to sleep. Ryan poured himself some coffee.

'Yes, sir?'

'Can we verify it?' Allen skipped the preliminaries.

'I don't know yet,' Jack replied. 'It's not just a question of National Technical Means. Verifying the elimination of so many launchers – '

'They're giving us limited on-site inspection,' noted a junior member of the team.

'I'm aware of that,' Jack replied. 'The question is, does that really mean anything?' *The other question is, why did they suddenly agree to something we've wanted for over thirty years . . . ?*

'What?' the junior member asked.

'The Soviets have put a lot of work into their new mobile launchers. What if they have more of them than we know about? Do you think we can find a few hundred mobile missiles?'

'But we have surface-scanning radar on the new birds, and – '

'And they know it, and they can avoid it if they want to – wait a minute. We know that our carriers can and do evade Russian radar-ocean-recon satellites. If you can do it with a ship, you can damned sure do it with a train,' Jack pointed out. Allen looked on without comment, allowing his underling to pursue the line in his stead. A clever old fox, Ernie Allen.

'So, CIA is going to recommend against – damn it, this is the biggest concession they've ever made!'

38

'Fine. It's a big concession. Everyone here knows that. Before we accept it, maybe we ought to make sure that they haven't conceded something that they've made irrelevant to the process. There are other things, too.'

'So you're going to oppose – '

'I'm not opposing anything. I'm saying we take our time and use our heads instead of being carried away by euphoria.'

'But their draft treaty is – it's almost too good to be true.' The man had just proved Ryan's point, though he didn't see it quite that way.

'Dr Ryan,' Allen said, 'if the technical details can be worked out to your satisfaction, how do you view the treaty?'

'Sir, speaking from a technical point of view, a fifty-percent reduction in deliverable warheads has no effect at all on the strategic balance. It's – '

'That's crazy!' objected the junior member.

Jack extended his hand toward the man, pointing his index finger like the barrel of a gun. 'Let's say I have a pistol pointed at your chest right now. Call it a nine-millimeter Browning. That has a thirteen-round clip. I agree to remove seven rounds from the clip, but I still have a loaded gun, with six rounds, pointed at your chest – do you feel any safer now?' Ryan smiled, keeping his 'gun' out.

'Personally, I wouldn't. That's what we're talking about here. If both sides reduce their inventories by half, that still leaves five *thousand* warheads that can hit our country. Think about how big that number is. All this agreement does is to reduce the overkill. The difference between five thousand and ten thousand only affects how far the rubble flies. If we start talking about reducing the number to one thousand warheads on either side, then *maybe* I'll start thinking we're on to something.'

'Do you think the thousand-warhead limit is achievable?' Allen asked.

'No, sir. Sometimes I just wish it were, though I've been told that a thousand-warhead limit could have the effect of

39

making nuclear war "winnable", whatever the hell that means.' Jack shrugged and concluded: 'Sir, if this current agreement goes through, it'll look better than it is. Maybe the symbolic value of the agreement has value in and of itself; that's a factor to be considered, but it's not one within my purview. The monetary savings to both sides will be real, but fairly minor in terms of gross military expenditures. Both sides retain half of their current arsenals –and that means keeping the newest and most effective half, of course. The bottom line remains constant: in a nuclear war, both sides would be equally dead. I do not see that this draft treaty reduces the "threat of war", whatever that is. To do that, we either have to eliminate the damned things entirely or figure something to keep them from working. If you ask me, we have to do the latter before we can attempt the former. Then the world becomes a safer place – maybe.'

'That's the start of a whole new arms race.'

'Sir, that race started so long ago that it isn't exactly new.'

2

Tea Clipper

'More photos of Dushanbe coming in,' the phone told Ryan.

'Okay, I'll be over in a few minutes.' Jack rose and crossed the hall to Admiral Greer's office. His boss had his back to the blazing white blanket that covered the hilly ground outside the CIA headquarters building. They were still clearing it off the parking lot, and even the railed walkway outside the seventh-floor windows had about ten inches' worth.

'What is it, Jack?' the Admiral asked.

'Dushanbe. The weather cleared unexpectedly. You said you wanted to be notified.'

Greer looked at the TV monitor in the corner of his office. It was next to the computer terminal that he refused to use – at least when anyone might watch his attempts to type with his index fingers and, on good days, one thumb. He could have the real-time satellite photos sent to his office 'live', but of late he'd avoided that. Jack didn't know why. 'Okay, let's trot over.'

Ryan held open the door for the Deputy Director for Intelligence, and they turned left to the end of the executive corridor on the building's top floor. Here was the executive elevator. One nice thing about it was that you didn't have to wait very long.

'How's the jet lag?' Greer asked. Ryan had been back for nearly a day now.

'Fully recovered, sir. Westbound doesn't bother me very much. It's the eastbound kind that still kills me.' *God, it's nice to be on the ground.*

The door opened and both men walked across the building to the new annex that housed the Office of Imagery Analysis. This was the Intelligence Directorate's own private department, separate from the National Photographic Intelligence Center, a joint CIA-DIA effort which served the whole intelligence community.

The screening room would have done Hollywood proud. There were about thirty seats in the mini-theater, and a twenty-foot-square projection screen on the wall. Art Graham, the chief of the unit, was waiting for them.

'You timed that pretty well. We'll have the shots in another minute.' He lifted a phone to the projection room and spoke a few words. The screen lit up at once. It was called 'Overhead Imagery' now, Jack reminded himself.

'Talk about luck. That Siberian high-pressure system took a sharp swing south and stopped the warm front like a brick wall. Perfect viewing conditions. Ground temp is about zero, and relative humidity can't be much higher than that!' Graham chuckled. 'We maneuvered the bird in specially to take advantage of this. It's within three degrees of being right overhead, and I don't think Ivan has had time to figure out that this pass is under way.'

'There's Dushanbe,' Jack breathed as part of the Tadzhik SSR came into view. Their first look was from one of the wide-angle cameras. The orbiting KH-14 reconnaissance satellite had a total of eleven. The bird had been in orbit for only three weeks, and this was the first of the newest generation of spy satellites. Dushanbe, briefly known as Stalinabad a few decades earlier – *that* must have made the local people happy! Ryan thought – was probably one of the ancient caravan cities. Afghanistan was less than a hundred miles away. Tamurlane's legendary Samarkand was not far to the northwest . . . and perhaps Scheherazade had traveled through a thousand years earlier. He wondered why was it that history worked this way. The same places and the same names always seemed to show up from one century to the next.

But CIA's current interest in Dushanbe did not center on the silk trade.

The view changed to one of the high-resolution cameras. It peered first into a deep, mountainous valley where a river was held back by the concrete and stone mass of a hydroelectric dam. Though only fifty kilometers southeast of Dushanbe, its power lines did not serve that city of 500,000. Instead they led to a collection of mountaintops almost within sight of the facility.

'That looks like footings for another set of towers,' Ryan observed.

'Parallel to the first set,' Graham agreed. 'They're putting some new generators into the facility. Well, we knew all along that they were only getting about half the usable power out of the dam.'

'How long to bring the rest on-stream?' Greer asked.

'I'd have to check with one of our consultants. It won't take more than a few weeks to run the power lines out, and the top half of the powerhouse is already built. Figure the foundations for the new generators are already done. All they have to do is rig the new equipment. Six months, maybe eight if the weather goes bad.'

'That fast?' Jack wondered.

'They diverted people from two other hydro jobs. Both of them were "Hero" projects. This one has never been talked about, but they pulled construction troops off two high-profile sites to do this one. Ivan does know how to focus his effort when he wants to. Six or eight months is conservative, Dr Ryan. It may be done quicker,' Graham said.

'How much power'll be available when they finish?'

'It's not all that big a structure. Total peak output, with the new generators? Figure eleven hundred megawatts.'

'That's a lot of power, and all going to those hilltops,' Ryan said almost to himself as the camera shifted again.

The one the Agency called 'Mozart' was quite a hill, but this area was the westernmost extension of the Himalayan Range, and by those standards it was puny. A road had

43

been blasted to the very top – there wasn't a Sierra Club in the USSR – along with a helicopter pad for bringing VIPs out from Dushanbe's two airports. There were sixteen buildings. One was for apartments, the view from which must have been fantastic, though it was a prototypical Russian apartment building, as stylish and attractive as a cinderblock, finished six months before. A lot of engineers and their families lived in it. It seemed strange to see such a building there, but the message of the building was: The people who lived here were privileged. Engineers and academicians, people with enough skill that the State wanted to look after them and their needs. Food was trucked up the new mountain road – or, in bad weather, flown in. Another of the buildings was a theater. A third was a hospital. Television programming came in via satellite earth-station next to a building that contained a few shops. That sort of solicitude was not exactly common in the Soviet Union. It was limited to high Party officials and people who worked in essential defense projects. This was not a ski resort.

That was also obvious from the perimeter fence and guard towers, both of which were recent. One of the identifiable things about Russian military complexes was the guard towers; Ivan had a real fixation for the things. Three fences, with two ten-meter spaces enclosed. The outer space was usually mined, and the inner one patrolled by dogs. The towers were on the inner perimeter, spaced two hundred meters apart. The soldiers who manned the towers were housed in a better-than-average new concrete barracks –

'Can you isolate one of the guards?' Jack asked.

Graham spoke into his phone, and the picture changed. One of his technicians was already doing this, as much to test camera calibration and ambient air conditions as for the purpose Ryan intended.

As the camera zoomed in, a moving dot became a man-shape in greatcoat and probably a fur hat. He was walking a big dog of uncertain breed and had a Kalashnikov rifle slung over his right shoulder. Man and dog left puffs of vapor in the air as they breathed. Ryan leaned forward unconsciously, as though this would give him a better view.

'That guy's shoulder boards look green to you?' he asked Graham.

The reconnaissance expert grunted. 'Yep. He's KGB, all right.'

'That close to Afghanistan?' the Admiral mused. 'They know we have people operating there. You bet they'll take their security provisions seriously.'

'They must have really wanted those hilltops,' Ryan observed. 'Seventy miles overland are a few million people who think killing Russians is God's will. This place is more important than we thought. It isn't just a new facility, not with that kind of security. If that's all it was, they wouldn't have had to put it here, and they for damned sure wouldn't have picked a place where they had to build a new power supply and risk exposure to hostiles. This may be an R and D facility now, but they must have bigger plans for it.'

'Like what?'

'Going after my satellites, maybe.' Art Graham thought of them as his.

'Have they tickled any of 'em recently?' Jack asked.

'No, not since we rattled their cage last April. Common sense broke out for once.'

That was an old story. Several times in the past few years, American reconnaissance and early-warning satellites had been 'tickled' – laser beams or microwave energy had been focused on the satellites, enough to dazzle their receptors but not enough to do serious harm. Why had the Russians done it? That was the question. Was it merely an exercise to see how we'd react, to see if it caused a ruckus at the North American Aerospace Defense Command – NORAD – at Cheyenne Mountain, Colorado? An attempt to determine for themselves how sensitive the satellites were? Was it a demonstration, a warning of their ability to destroy the satellites? Or was it simply what Jack's British friends called bloody-mindedness? It was so hard to tell what the Soviets were thinking.

They invariably protested their innocence, of course. When one American satellite had been temporarily blinded over Sary Shagan, they said that a natural-gas pipeline had caught fire. The fact that the nearby Chimkent-Pavlodar pipeline carried mostly oil had escaped the Western press.

The satellite pass was complete now. In a nearby room a score of videotape recorders were rewound, and now the complete camera coverage would be reviewed at leisure.

'Let's have a look at Mozart again, and Bach also, please,' Greer commanded.

'Hell of a commute,' Jack noted. The residential and industrial site on Mozart was only one kilometer or so from the emplacement on 'Bach', the next mountaintop over, but the road looked frightful. The picture froze on Bach. The formula of fences and guard towers was repeated, but this time the distance between the outermost perimeter fence and the next was at least two hundred meters. Here the ground surface appeared to be bare rock. Jack wondered how you planted mines in that – or maybe they didn't, he thought. It was obvious that the ground had been leveled with bulldozers and explosives to the unobstructed flatness of a pool table. From the guard towers, it must have looked like a shooting gallery.

'Not kidding, are they?' Graham observed quietly.

'So that's what they're guarding . . .' Ryan said.

There were thirteen buildings inside the fence. In an area perhaps the size of two football fields – which had also been leveled – were ten holes, in two groups. One was a group of six arranged hexagonally, each hole about thirty feet across. The second group of four was arrayed in a diamond pattern, and the holes were slightly smaller, perhaps twenty-five feet. In each hole was a concrete pillar about fifteen feet across, planted in bedrock, and every hole was at least forty feet deep – you couldn't tell from the picture

46

on the screen. Atop each pillar was a metal dome. They appeared to be made of crescent-shaped segments.

'They unfold. I wonder what's in them?' Graham asked rhetorically. There were two hundred people at Langley who knew of Dushanbe, and every one wanted to know what was under those metal domes. They'd been in place for only a few months.

'Admiral,' Jack said, 'I need to kick open a new compartment.'

'Which one?'

'Tea Clipper.'

'You're not asking much!' Greer snorted. '*I'm* not cleared for that.'

Ryan leaned back in his chair. 'Admiral, if what they're doing in Dushanbe is the same thing we're doing with Tea Clipper, we sure as hell ought to know. Goddammit, how are we supposed to know what to look for if we're not told what one of these places looks like!'

'I've been saying that for quite a while.' The DDI chuckled. 'SDIO won't like it. The Judge will have to go to the President for that.'

'So he goes to the President. What if the activity here is connected with the arms proposal they just made?'

'Do you think it is?'

'Who can say?' Jack asked. 'It's a coincidence. They worry me.'

'Okay, I'll talk to the Director.'

Ryan drove home two hours later. He drove his Jaguar XJS out onto the George Washington Parkway. It was one of the many happy memories from his tour of duty in England. He loved the silky-smooth feeling of the twelve-cylinder engine enough that he'd put his venerable old Rabbit into semiretirement. As he always tried to do, Ryan set his Washington business aside. He worked the car up through its five gears and concentrated on his driving.

'Well, James?' the Director of Central Intelligence asked.

47

'Ryan thinks the new activity at Bach and Mozart may be related to the arms situation. I think he might be correct. He wants into Tea Clipper. I said you'd have to go to the President.' Admiral Greer smiled.

'Okay, I'll get him a written note. It'll make General Parks happier, anyway. They have a full-up test scheduled for the end of the week. I'll set it up for Jack to see it.' Judge Moore smiled sleepily. 'What do you think?'

'I think he's right: Dushanbe and Tea Clipper are essentially the same project. There are a lot of coarse similarities, too many to be a pure coincidence. We ought to upgrade our assessment.'

'Okay.' Moore turned away to look out the windows. *The world is going to change again. It may take ten or more years, but it's going to change. Ten years from now it won't be my problem*, Moore told himself. *But it sure as hell will be Ryan's problem*. 'I'll have him flown out there tomorrow. And maybe we'll get lucky on Dushanbe. Foley got word to CARDINAL that we're very interested in the place.'

'CARDINAL? Good.'

'But if something happens . . .'

Greer nodded. 'Christ, I hope he's careful,' the DDI said.

Ever since the death of Dmitri Fedorovich, it has not been the same at the Defense Ministry, Colonel Mikhail Semyonovich Filitov wrote into his diary left-handed. An early riser, he sat at a hundred-year-old oak desk that his wife had bought for him shortly before she died, almost – what was it? Thirty years, Misha told himself. Thirty years this coming February. His eyes closed for a moment. *Thirty years*.

Never a single day passed that he did not remember his Elena. Her photograph was on the desk, the sepia print faded with age, its silver frame tarnished. He never seemed to have time to polish it, and didn't wish to be bothered with a maid. The photo showed a young woman with legs like spindles, arms high over her head, which was cocked to one side. The round, Slavic face displayed a wide, inviting smile that perfectly conveyed the joy she'd felt when dancing with the Kirov Company.

Misha smiled also as he remembered the first impression of a young armor officer given tickets to the performance as a reward for having the best-maintained tanks in the division: *How can they do that?* Perched up on the tips of their toes as though on needle-point stilts. He'd remembered playing on stilts as a child, *but to be so graceful!* And then she'd smiled at the handsome young officer in the front row. For the briefest moment. Their eyes had met for almost as little time as it takes to blink, he thought. Her smile had changed ever so slightly. Not for the audience any longer, for that timeless instant the smile had been for him alone. A bullet through the heart could not have had a more devastating effect. Misha didn't remember the rest of the performance – to this day he couldn't even remember which ballet it had been. He remembered sitting and squirming through the rest of it while his mind churned over what he'd do next. Already Lieutenant Filitov had been marked as a man on the move, a brilliant young tank officer for whom Stalin's brutal purge of the officer corps had meant opportunity and rapid promotion. He wrote articles on tank tactics, practiced innovative battle drills in the field, argued vociferously against the false 'lessons' of Spain with the certainty of a man born to his profession.

But what do I do now? he'd asked himself. The Red Army hadn't taught him how to approach an artist. This wasn't some farm girl who was bored enough by work on the *kolkhoz* to offer herself to anyone – especially a young Army officer who might take her away from it all. Misha still remembered the shame of his youth – not that he'd thought it shameful at the time – when he'd used his officer's shoulder boards to bed any girl who'd caught his eye.

But I don't even know her name, he'd told himself. *What do I do?* What he'd done, of course, was to treat the matter as a military exercise. As soon as the performance had ended,

49

he'd fought his way into the rest room and washed hands and face. Some grease that still remained under his fingernails was removed with a pocketknife. His short hair was wetted down into place, and he inspected his uniform as strictly as a general officer might, brushing off dust and picking off lint, stepping back from the mirror to make sure his boots gleamed as a soldier's should. He hadn't noticed at the time that other men in the men's room were watching him with barely suppressed grins, having guessed what the drill was for, and wishing him luck, touched with a bit of envy. Satisfied with his appearance, Misha had left the theater and asked the doorman where the artists' door was. That had cost him a ruble, and with the knowledge, he'd walked around the block to the stage entrance, where he found another doorman, this one a bearded old man whose greatcoat bore ribbons for service in the revolution. Misha had expected special courtesy from the doorman, one soldier to another, only to learn that he regarded all the female dancers as his own daughters – not wenches to be thrown at the feet of soldiers, certainly! Misha had considered offering money, but had the good sense not to imply the man was a pimp. Instead, he'd spoken quietly and reasonably – and truthfully – that he was smitten with a single dancer whose name he didn't know, and merely wanted to meet her.

'Why?' the old doorman had asked coldly.

'Grandfather, she smiled at me,' Misha had answered in the awed voice of a little boy.

'And you are in love.' The reply was harsh, but in a moment the doorman's face turned wistful. 'But you don't know which?'

'She was in – the line, not one of the important ones, I mean. What do they call that? – I will remember her face until the day I die.' Already he'd known that.

The doorman looked him over and saw that his uniform was properly turned out, and his back straight. This was not a swaggering pig of a NKVD officer whose arrogant breath stank of vodka. This was a soldier, and a handsome young one at that. 'Comrade Lieutenant, you are a lucky man. Do you know why? You are lucky because I was once young, and old as I am, I still remember. They will start to come out in ten minutes or so. Stand over there, and make not a sound.'

It had taken thirty minutes. They came out in twos and threes. Misha had seen the male members of the troupe and thought them – what any soldier would think of a man in a ballet company. His manhood had been offended that they held hands with such pretty girls, but he'd set that aside. When the door opened, his vision was damaged by the sudden glare of yellow-white light against the near blackness of the unlit alley, and he'd almost missed her, so different she looked without the makeup.

He saw the face, and tried to decide if she were the right one, approaching his objective more carefully than he would ever do under the fire of German guns.

'You were in seat number twelve,' she'd said before he could summon the courage to speak. *She had a voice!*

'Yes, Comrade Artist,' his reply had stammered out.

'Did you enjoy the performance, Comrade Lieutenant?' A shy, but somehow beckoning smile.

'It was wonderful!' Of course.

'It is not often that we see handsome young officers in the front row,' she observed.

'I was given the ticket as a reward for performance in my unit. I am a tanker,' he said proudly. *She called me handsome!*

'Does the Comrade Tanker Lieutenant have a name?'

'I am Lieutenant Mikhail Semyonovich Filitov.'

'I am Elena Ivanova Makarova.'

'It is too cold tonight for one so thin, Comrade Artist. Is there a restaurant nearby?'

'Restaurant?' She'd laughed. 'How often do you come to Moscow?'

'My division is based thirty kilometers from here, but I do not often come to the city,' he'd admitted.

'Comrade Lieutenant, there are few restaurants even in Moscow. Can you come to my apartment?'

'Why – yes,' his reply had stuttered out as the stage door opened again.

'Marta,' Elena said to the girl who was just coming out. 'We have a military escort home!'

'Tania and Resa are coming,' Marta said.

Misha had actually been relieved by that. The walk to the apartment had taken thirty minutes – the Moscow subway hadn't yet been completed, and it was better to walk than to wait for a tram this late at night.

She was far prettier without her makeup, Misha remembered. The cold winter air gave her cheeks all the color they ever needed. Her walk was as graceful as ten years of intensive training could make it. She'd glided along the street like an apparition, while he gallumped along in his heavy boots. He felt himself a tank, rolling next to a thoroughbred horse, and was careful not to go too close, lest he trample her. He hadn't yet learned of the strength that was so well hidden by her grace.

The night had never before seemed so fine, though for – what was it? – twenty years there had been many such nights, then none for the past thirty. *My God*, he thought, *we would have been married fifty years this . . . July 14th.* My God. Unconsciously he dabbed at his eyes with a handkerchief.

Thirty years, however, was the number that occupied his mind.

The thought boiled within his breast, and his fingers were pale around the pen. It still surprised him that love and hate were emotions so finely matched. Misha returned to his diary . . . .

An hour later he rose from the desk and walked to the bedroom closet. He donned the uniform of a colonel of tank troops. Technically he was on the retired list, and had been so before people on the current colonel's list had been born. But work in the Ministry of Defense carried its own perks, and Misha was on the personal staff of the Minister.

That was one reason. The other three reasons were on his uniform blouse, three gold stars that depended from claret-colored ribbons. Filitov was the only soldier in the history of the Soviet Army who'd won the decoration of Hero of the Soviet Union three times on the field of battle, for personal bravery in the face of the enemy. There were others with such medals, but so often these were political awards, the Colonel knew. He was aesthetically offended by that. This was not a medal to be granted for staff work, and certainly not for one Party member to give to another as a gaudy lapel decoration. Hero of the Soviet Union was an award that ought to be limited to men like himself, who had risked death, who'd bled – and all too often, died – for the *Rodina*. He was reminded of this every time he put his uniform on. Beneath his undershirt were the plastic-looking scars from his last gold star, when a German 88 round had lanced through the armor of his tank, setting the ammo racks afire while he'd brought his 76mm gun around for one last shot and extinguished that Kraut gun crew while his clothing burned. The injury had left him with only fifty percent use of his right arm, but despite it, he'd led what was left of his regiment nearly two more days in the Kursk Bulge. If he'd bailed out with the rest of his crew – or been evacuated from the area at once as his regimental surgeon had recommended – perhaps he would have recovered fully, but, no, he knew that he could not have *not* fired back, could not have abandoned his men in the face of battle. And so he'd shot, and burned. But for that Misha might have made General, perhaps even Marshal, he thought. *Would it have made a difference?* Filitov was too much a man of the real, practical world to dwell on that thought for long. Had he fought in many more campaigns, he might have been killed. As it was, he'd been given more time with Elena than could otherwise have been the case. She'd come nearly every day to the burn institute in Moscow; at first horrified by the extent of his wounds, she'd later become as proud of them as Misha was. No one could question that her man had done his duty for the *Rodina*.

But now, he did his duty for his Elena.

Filitov walked out of the apartment to the elevator, a leather briefcase dangling from his right hand. It was about all that side of his body was good for. The *babushka* who operated the elevator greeted him as always. They were of an age, she the widow of a sergeant who'd been in Misha's regiment, who also had the gold star, pinned on his breast by this very man.

'Your new granddaughter?' the Colonel asked.

'An angel,' was her reply.

Filitov smiled, partly in agreement – was there any such thing as an ugly infant? – and partly because terms like 'angel' had survived seventy years of 'scientific socialism.'

The car was waiting for him. The driver was a new draftee, fresh from sergeant school and driving school. He saluted his Colonel severely, the door held open in his other hand.

'Good morning, Comrade Colonel.'

'So it is, Sergeant Zhdanov.' Filitov replied. Most officers would have done little more than grunt, but Filitov was a combat soldier whose success on the battlefield had resulted from his devotion to the welfare of his men. A lesson that few officers ever understood, he reminded himself. Too bad.

The car was comfortably warm, the heater had been turned all the way up fifteen minutes ago. Filitov was becoming ever more sensitive to cold, a sure sign of age. He'd just been hospitalized again for pneumonia, the third time in the past five years. One of these times, he knew, would be the last. Filitov dismissed the thought. He'd cheated death too many times to fear it. Life came and went at a constant rate. One brief second at a time. When the last second came, he wondered, would he notice? Would he care?

The driver pulled the car up to the Defense Ministry before the Colonel could answer that question.

Ryan was sure that he'd been in government service too long. He had come to – well, not actually to *like* flying, but at least to appreciate the convenience of it. He was only four hours from Washington, flown by an Air Force C-21 Learjet whose female pilot, a captain, had looked like a high-school sophomore.

Getting old, Jack, he told himself. The flight from the airfield to the mountaintop had been by helicopter, no easy feat at this altitude. Ryan had never been to New Mexico before. The high mountains were bare of trees, the air thin enough that he was breathing abnormally, but the sky was so clear that for a moment he imagined himself an astronaut looking at the unblinking stars on this cloudless, frigid night.

'Coffee, sir?' a sergeant asked. He handed Ryan a thermos cup, and the hot liquid steamed into the night, barely illuminated by a sliver of new moon.

'Thanks.' Ryan sipped at it and looked around. There were few lights to be seen. There might have been a housing development behind the next set of ridges; he could see the halolike glow of Santa Fe, but there was no way to guess how far off it might be. He knew that the rock he stood on was eleven thousand feet above sea level (the nearest level sea was hundreds of miles away), and there is no way to judge distance at night. It was altogether beautiful, except for the cold. His fingers were stiff around the plastic cup. He'd mistakenly left his gloves at home.

'Seventeen minutes,' somebody announced. 'All systems are nominal. Trackers on automatic. AOS in eight minutes.'

'AOS?' Ryan asked. He realized that he sounded a little funny. It was so cold that his cheeks were stiff.

'Acquisition of Signal,' the Major explained.

'You live around here?'

'Forty miles that way.' He pointed vaguely. 'Practically next door by local standards.' The officer's Brooklyn accent explained the comment.

He's the one with the doctorate from State University of New York at Stony Brook, Ryan reminded himself. At only twenty-nine years old, the Major didn't look like a soldier, even less like a field-grade officer. In Switzerland he'd be called a gnome, barely over five-seven, and cadaverously thin, acne on his angular face. Right now, his deep-set eyes were locked on the sector of horizon where the space shuttle *Discovery* would appear. Ryan thought back to the documents he'd read on the way out and knew that this major probably couldn't tell him the color of the paint on his living-room wall. He really lived at Los Alamos National Laboratory, known locally as the Hill. Number one in his class at West Point, and a doctorate in high-energy physics only two years after that. His doctor's dissertation was classified Top Secret. Jack had read it, and didn't understand why they had bothered – despite a doctorate of his own, the two-hundred-page document might as well have been written in Kurdish. Alan Gregory was already being talked of in the same breath as Cambridge's Stephen Hawking, or Princeton's Freeman Dyson. Except that few people knew his name. Jack wondered if anyone had thought of classifying *that*.

'Major Gregory, all ready?' an Air Force lieutenant general asked. Jack noted his respectful tone. Gregory was no ordinary major.

A nervous smile. 'Yes, sir.' The Major wiped sweaty hands – despite a temperature of fifteen below zero – on the pants of his uniform. It was good to see that the kid had emotions.

'You married?' Ryan asked. The file hadn't covered that.

'Engaged, sir. She's a doctor in laser optics, on the Hill. We get married June the third.' The kid's voice had become as brittle as glass.

'Congratulations. Keeping it in the family, eh?' Jack chuckled.

'Yes, sir.' Major Gregory was still staring at the southwest horizon.

'AOS!' someone announced behind them. 'We have signal.'

'Goggles!' The call came over the metal speakers. 'Everyone put on their eye-protection.'

56

Jack blew on his hands before taking the plastic goggles from his pocket. He'd been told to stash them there to keep them warm. They were still cold enough on his face that he noticed the difference. Once in place, however, Ryan was effectively blinded. The stars and moon were gone.

'Tracking! We have lock. *Discovery* has established the downlink. All systems are nominal.'

'Target acquisition!' another voice announced. 'Initiate interrogation sequencing . . . first target is locked . . . auto firing circuits enabled.'

There was no sound to indicate what had happened. Ryan didn't see anything – *or did I?* he asked himself. There had been the fleeting impression of . . . what? *Did I imagine it?* Next to him he felt the Major's breath come out slowly.

'Exercise concluded,' the speaker said. Jack tore off his goggles.

'*That's all?*' What had he just seen? What had they just done? Was he so far out of date that even after being briefed he didn't understand what was happening before his eyes?

'The laser light is almost impossible to see,' Major Gregory explained. 'This high up, there isn't much dust or humidity in the air to reflect it.'

'Then why the goggles?'

The young officer smiled as he took his off. 'Well, if a bird flies over at the wrong time, the impact might be, well, kind of spectacular. That could hurt your eyes some.'

Two hundred miles over their heads, *Discovery* continued toward the horizon. The shuttle would stay in orbit another three days, conducting its 'routine scientific mission,' mainly oceanographical studies this time, the press was told, something secret for the Navy. The papers had been speculating on the mission for weeks. It had something to do, they said, with tracking missile submarines from orbit. There was no better way to keep a secret than to use another 'secret' to conceal it. Every time someone asked about the mission, a Navy public-affairs officer would do the 'no comments'.

'Did it work?' Jack asked. He looked up, but he couldn't pick out the dot of light that denoted the billion-dollar space plane.

'We have to see.' The Major turned and walked to the camouflage-painted truck van parked a few yards away. The three-star General followed him, with Ryan trailing behind.

Inside the van, where the temperature might have been merely at freezing, a chief warrant officer was rewinding a videotape.

'Where were the targets?' Jack asked. 'That wasn't in the briefing papers.'

'About forty-five south, thirty west,' the General replied. Major Gregory was perched in front of the TV screen.

'That's around the Falklands, isn't it? Why there?'

'Closer to South Georgia, actually,' the General replied. 'It's a nice, quiet, out-of-the-way sort of place, and the distance is about right.'

And the Soviets had no known intelligence-gathering assets within three thousand miles, Ryan knew. The Tea Clipper test had been timed precisely for a moment when all Soviet spy satellites were under the visible horizon. Finally, the shooting distance was exactly the same as the distance to the Soviet ballistic missile fields arrayed along the country's main east-west railway.

'Ready!' the warrant officer said.

The video picture wasn't all that great, taken from sea level, specifically the deck of the *Observation Island*, a range-instrumentation ship returning from Trident missile tests in the Indian Ocean. Next to the first TV screen was another. This one showed the picture from the ship's 'Cobra-Judy' missile-tracking radar. Both screens showed four objects, spaced in a slightly uneven line. A timer box in the lower right-hand corner was changing numbers as though in an Alpine ski race, with three digits to the right of the decimal point.

'Hit!' One of the dots disappeared in a puff of green light.

'Miss!' Another one didn't.

'Miss!' Jack frowned. He'd half-expected to see the beams of light streaking through the sky, but that happened only in movies. There wasn't enough dust in space to denote the energy's path.

'Hit!' A second dot vanished.

'Hit!' Only one was left.

'Miss.'

'Miss.' The last one didn't want to die, Ryan thought.

'Hit!' But it did. 'Total elapsed time, one point eight-zero-six seconds.'

'Fifty percent,' Major Gregory said quietly. 'And it corrected itself.' The young officer nodded slowly. He managed to keep from smiling, except around the eyes. 'It works.'

'How big were the targets?' Ryan asked.

'Three meters. Spherical balloons, of course.' Gregory was rapidly losing control. He looked like a kid whom Christmas had taken by surprise.

'Same diameter as an SS-18.'

'Something like that.' The General answered that one.

'Where's the other mirror?'

'Ten thousand kilometers up, currently over Ascension Island. Officially it's a weather satellite that never made its proper orbit.' The General smiled.

'I didn't know you could send it that far.'

Major Gregory actually giggled. 'Neither did we.'

'So you sent the beam from over there to the shuttle's mirror, from *Discovery* to this other one over the equator, and from there to the targets?'

'Correct,' the General said.

'Your targeting system is on the other satellite, then?'

'Yes,' the General answered more grudgingly.

Jack did some numbers in his head. 'Okay, that means you can discriminate a three-meter target at . . . ten thousand kilometers. I didn't know we could do that. How do we?'

'You don't need to know,' the General replied coldly.

'You had four hits and four misses – eight shots in under two seconds, and the Major said the targeting system corrected for misses. Okay, if those had been SS-18s launched off of South Georgia, would the shots have killed them?'

'Probably not,' Gregory admitted. 'The laser assembly only puts out five megajoules. Do you know what a joule is?'

'I checked my college phyzzies book before I flew down. A joule is one newton-meter per second, or zero-point-seven foot-pounds of energy, plus change, right? Okay, a megajoule is a million of them . . . seven hundred thousand foot-pounds. In terms I can understand – '

'A megajoule is the rough equivalent of a stick of dynamite. So we just delivered five sticks. The actual energy transferred is like a kilogram of explosives, but the physical effects are not exactly comparable.'

'What you're telling me is that the laser beam doesn't actually burn through the target – it's more of a shock effect.' Ryan was stretching his technical knowledge to the limit.

'We call it an "impact kill",' the General answered. 'But, yeah, that's about it. All the energy arrives in a few millionths of a second, a lot faster than any bullet does.'

'So all that stuff I've heard about how polishing the missile body, or rotating it, will prevent a burn-through – '

Major Gregory giggled again. 'Yeah, I like that one. A ballet dancer can pirouette in front of a shotgun and it'll do her about as much good. What happens is that the energy has to go somewhere, and that can only be into the missile body. The missile body is full of storable liquids – nearly all of their birds are liquid fueled, right? The hydrostatic effect alone will be to rupture the pressure tanks – *ka-boom!* no more missile.' The Major smiled as though describing a trick played on his high-school teacher.

'Okay, now, I want to know how it all works.'

'Look, Dr Ryan – ' the General started to say. Jack cut him off.

'General, I am cleared for Tea Clipper. You know that, so let's stop screwing around.'

Major Gregory got a nod from the General. 'Sir, we have five one-megajoule lasers – '

'Where?'

'You're standing right on top of one of them, sir. The other four are buried around this hilltop. The power rating is per pulse, of course. Each one puts out a pulse-chain of a million joules in a few microseconds – a few millionths of a second.'

'And they recharge in . . .?'

'Point zero-four-six seconds. We can deliver twenty shots per second, in other words.'

'But you didn't shoot that fast.'

'We didn't have to, sir,' Gregory replied. 'The limiting factor at present is the targeting software. That's being worked on. The purpose of this test was to evaluate part of the software package. We know that these lasers work. We've had them here for the past three years. The laser beams are converged on a mirror about fifty meters that way' – he pointed – 'and converted into a single beam.'

'They have to be – I mean, the beams all have to be exactly in tune, right?'

'Technically it's called a Phased-Array Laser. All the beams have to be perfectly in phase,' Gregory answered.

'How the hell do you do that?' Ryan paused. 'Don't bother, I probably wouldn't understand it anyway. Okay, we have the beam hitting the downside mirror . . . .'

'The mirror is the special part. It's composed of thousands of segments, and every segment is controlled by a piezoelectric chip. That's called "adaptive optics". We send an interrogation beam to the mirror – this one was on the shuttle – and get a reading on atmospheric distortion. The way the atmosphere bends the beam is analyzed by computer. Then the mirror corrects for the distortion, and we fire the real shot. The mirror on the shuttle also has adaptive optics. It collects and focuses the beam, and sends it off to the "Flying Cloud" satellite mirror. That mirror refocuses the beam on the targets. Zap!'

'That simple?' Ryan shook his head. It was simple enough that over the previous nineteen years, forty billion dollars had gone into basic research, in twenty separate fields, just to run this one test.

'We did have to iron out a few little details,' Gregory acknowledged. These little details would take another five or more years, and he neither knew nor cared how many additional billions. What mattered to him was that the goal was now actually in sight. Tea Clipper wasn't a blue-sky project anymore, not after this system test.

'And you're the guy who made the breakthrough on the targeting system. You figured a way for the beam to provide its own targeting information.'

'Something like that,' the General answered for the kid. 'Dr Ryan, that part of the system is classified highly enough that we will not discuss it further without written authorization.'

'General, the purpose in my being here is to evaluate this program relative to Soviet efforts along similar lines. If you want my people to tell you what the Russians are up to, I have to know what the hell we're supposed to look for!'

This did not elicit a reply. Jack shrugged and reached inside his coat. He handed the General an envelope. Major Gregory looked on in puzzlement.

'You still don't like it,' Ryan observed after the officer folded the letter away.

'No, sir, I don't.'

Ryan spoke with a voice colder than the New Mexico night. 'General, when I was in the Marine Corps, they never told me that I was supposed to like my orders, just that I was supposed to obey them.' That almost set the General off, and Jack added: 'I really am on your side, sir.'

'You may continue, Major Gregory,' General Parks said after a moment.

'I call the algorithm "Fan Dance",' Gregory began. The General almost smiled in spite of himself. Gregory could not have known anything about Sally Rand.

'That's all?' Ryan said again when the youngster finished, and he knew that every computer expert in Project Tea Clipper must have asked himself the same thing: Why didn't I think of that! No wonder they all say that Gregory is a genius. He'd made a crucial breakthrough in laser technology at Stony Brook, *then* one in software design. 'But that's simple!'

'Yes, sir, but it took over two years to make it work, and a Cray-2 computer to make it work fast enough to matter. We still need a little more work, but after we analyze what went wrong tonight, another four or five months, maybe, and we got it knocked.'

'Next step, then?'

'Building a five-megajoule laser. Another team is close to that already. Then we gang up twenty of them, and we can send out a hundred-megajoule pulse, twenty times per second, and hit any target we want. The impact energy then will be on the order of, say, twenty to thirty kilograms of explosives.'

'And that'll kill any missile anybody can make . . . .'

'Yes, sir.' Major Gregory smiled.

'What you're telling me is, the thing – Tea Clipper works.'

'We've validated the system architecture,' the General corrected Ryan. 'It's been a long haul since we started looking at this system. Five years ago there were eleven hurdles. There are three technical hurdles left. Five years from now there won't be any. Then we can start building it.'

'The strategic implications . . .' Ryan said, and stopped. 'Jesus.'

'It's going to change the world,' the General agreed.

'You know that they're playing with the same thing at Dushanbe.'

'Yes, sir,' Major Gregory answered. 'And they might know something that we don't.'

63

Ryan nodded. Gregory was even smart enough to know that someone else might be smarter. This was some kid.

'Gentlemen, out in my helicopter is a briefcase. Could you have somebody bring it in? There are some satellite photos that you might find interesting.'

'How old are these shots?' the General asked five minutes later as he leafed through the photos.

'A couple of days,' Jack replied.

Major Gregory peered at them for a minute or so. 'Okay, we have two slightly different installations here. It's called a "sparse array". The hexagonal array – the six-pillar one – is a transmitter. The building in the middle here is probably designed to house six lasers. These pillars are optically stable mounts for mirrors. The laser beams come out of the building, reflect off the mirrors, and the mirrors are computer-controlled to concentrate the beam on a target.'

'What do you mean by optically stable?'

'The mirrors have to be controlled with a high degree of accuracy, sir,' Gregory told Ryan. 'By isolating them from the surrounding ground you eliminate vibration that might come from having a man walk nearby, or driving a car around. If you jiggle the mirrors by a small multiple of the laser-light frequency, you mess up the effect you're trying to get. Here we use shock mountings to enhance the isolation factor. It's a technique originally developed for submarines. Okay? This other diamond-shaped array is. . . oh, of course. That's the receiver.'

'What?' Jack's brain had just met another stone wall.

'Let's say you want to make a really good picture of something. I mean, *really* good. You use a laser as your strobe light.'

'But why four mirrors?'

'It's easier and cheaper to make four small mirrors than one big one,' Gregory explained. 'Hmph. I wonder if they're trying to do a holographic image. If they can really lock their illuminating beams in phase . . . theoretically it's possible. There are a couple of things that make it tricky, but the Russians like the brute-force approach . . . Damn!' His eyes lit up. 'That's one hell of an interesting idea! I'll have to think about that one.'

'You're telling me that they build this place just to take pictures of our satellites?' Ryan demanded.

'No, sir. They can use it for that, no sweat. It makes a perfect cover. And a system that can image a satellite at geosynchronous altitude might be able to clobber one in low earth orbit. If you think of these four mirrors here as a telescope, remember that a telescope can be a lens for a camera, or part of a gunsight. It could also make a damned efficient aiming system. How much power runs into this lab?'

Ryan set down a photo. 'The current power output from this dam is something like five hundred megawatts. But – '

'They're stringing new power lines,' Gregory observed. 'How come?'

'The powerhouse is two stories – you can't tell from this angle. It looks like they're activating the top half. That'll bring their peak power output to something like eleven hundred megawatts.'

'How much comes into this place?'

'We call it "Bach". Maybe a hundred. The rest goes to "Mozart", the town that grew up on the next hill over. So they're doubling their available power.'

'More than that, sir,' Gregory noted. 'Unless they're going to double the size of that town, why don't you assume that the increased power is just going to the lasers?'

Jack nearly choked. *Why the hell didn't you think of that!* he growled at himself.

'I mean,' Gregory continued, 'I mean . . . that's like five hundred megawatts of new power. Jesus, what if they just made a breakthrough? How hard is it to find out what's happening there?'

'Take a look at the photos and tell me how easy you think it would be to infiltrate the place,' Ryan suggested.

'Oh.' Gregory looked up. 'It would be nice to know how much power they push out the front end of their instruments. How long has this place been there, sir?'

'About four years, and it's not finished yet. Mozart is new. Until recently the workers were housed in this barracks and support facility. We took notice when the apartment building went up, same time as the perimeter fence. When the Russians start pampering the workers, you know that the project has a really high priority. If it has a fence and guard towers, we know it's military.'

'How did you find it?' Gregory asked.

'By accident. The Agency was redrawing its meteorological data on the Soviet Union, and one of the technicians decided to do a computer analysis of the best places over there for astronomical observation. This is one of them. The weather over the last few months has been unusually cloudy, but on average the skies are about as clear there as they are here. The same is true of Sary Shagan, Semipalatinsk, and another new one, Storozhevaya.' Ryan set out some more photographs. Gregory looked at them.

'They sure are busy.'

'Good morning, Misha,' Marshal of the Soviet Union Dmitri Timofeyevich Yazov said.

'And to you, Comrade Defense Minister,' Colonel Filitov replied.

A sergeant helped the Minister off with his coat while another brought in a tray with a tea setting. Both withdrew when Misha opened his briefcase.

'So, Misha, what does my day look like?' Yazov poured two cups of tea. It was still dark outside the Council of Ministers building. The inside perimeter of the Kremlin walls was lit with harsh blue-white floods, and sentries appeared and disappeared in the splashes of light.

'A full one, Dmitri Timofeyevich,' Misha replied. Yazov wasn't the man that Dmitri Ustinov was, but Filitov had to admit to himself that he did put in a full day's work as a uniformed officer should. Like Filitov, Marshal Yazov was by background a tank officer. Though they had never met during the war, they did know one another by reputation. Misha's was better as a combat officer – purists claimed that he was an old-fashioned cavalryman at heart, though Filitov cordially hated horses – while Dmitri Yazov had won a reputation early on as a brilliant staff officer and organizer – and a Party man, of course. Before anything else, Yazov was a Party man, else he would never have made the rank of Marshal. 'We have that delegation coming in from the experimental station in the Tadzhik SSR.'

'Ah, "Bright Star". Yes, that report is due today, isn't it?'

'Academicians,' Misha snorted. 'They wouldn't know what a real weapon was if I shoved it up their asses.'

'The time for lances and sabers is past, Mikhail Semyonovich,' Yazov said with a grin. Not the brilliant intellect that Ustinov had been, neither was Yazov a fool like his predecessor, Sergey Sokolov. His lack of engineering expertise was balanced by an uncanny instinct for the merits of new weapons systems, and rare insights into the people of the Soviet Army. 'These inventions show extraordinary promise.'

'Of course. I only wish that we had a real soldier running the project instead of these starry-eyed professors.'

'But General Pokryshkin – '

'He was a fighter pilot. I said a *soldier*, Comrade Minister. Pilots will support anything that has enough buttons and dials. Besides, Pokryshkin has spent more time in universities of late than in an aircraft. They don't even let him fly himself anymore. Pokryshkin stopped being a soldier ten years ago. Now he is the procurer for the wizards.' *And he is building his own little empire down there, but that's an issue we'll save for another day.*

'You wish a new job assignment, Misha?' Yazov inquired slyly.

'Not that one!' Filitov laughed, then turned serious. 'What I am trying to say, Dmitri Timofeyevich, is that the progress assessment we get from Bright Star is – how do I say this? – warped by the fact that we don't have a real military man on the scene. Someone who understands the vagaries of combat, someone who knows what a weapon is supposed to be.'

The Defense Minister nodded thoughtfully. 'Yes, I see your point. They think in terms of "instruments" rather than "weapons", that is true. The complexity of the project concerns me.'

'Just how many moving parts does this new assembly have?'

'I have no idea – thousands, I should think.'

'An instrument does not become a weapon until it can be handled reliably by a private soldier – well, at least a senior lieutenant. Has anyone outside the project ever done a reliability assessment?' Filitov asked.

'No, not that I can recall.'

Filitov picked up his tea. 'There you are, Dmitri Timofeyevich. Don't you think that the Politburo will be interested in that? Until now, they have been willing to fund the experimental project, of course, but' – Filitov took a sip – 'they are coming here to request funding to upgrade the site to operational status, and we have no independent assessment of the project.'

'How would you suggest we get that assessment?'

'Obviously I cannot do it. I am too old, and too uneducated, but we have some bright new colonels in the Ministry, especially in the signals section. They are not combat officers, strictly speaking, but they are soldiers, and they are competent to look at these electronic marvels. It is only a suggestion.' Filitov didn't press. He had planted the seed of an idea. Yazov was far easier to manipulate than Ustinov had ever been.

'And what of the problems at the Chelyabinsk tank works?' Yazov asked next.

Ortiz watched the Archer climbing the hill half a mile away. Two men and two camels. They probably wouldn't be mistaken for a guerrilla force the way that twenty or so would have. Not that this had to matter, Ortiz knew, but

68

the Soviets were to the point now that they attacked almost anything that moved. *Vaya con Dios*.

'I sure could use a beer,' the Captain observed.

Ortiz turned. 'Captain, the thing that allowed me to deal with these people effectively is that I live the way they do. I observe their laws and respect their ways. That means no booze, no pork; that means I don't fool with their women.'

'Shit.' The officer snorted. 'These ignorant savages – ' Ortiz cut him off.

'Captain, the next time I hear you say that, or even think it real loud, will be your last day here. These people are working for us. They're bringing us stuff that we can't get any place else. You will, repeat, *will* treat them with the respect they deserve. *Is that clear!*'

'Yes, sir.' *Christ, this guy's turned into a sand nigger himself.*

69

3

The Weary Red Fox

'It's impressive – if you can figure out what they're doing.'
Jack yawned. He'd taken the same Air Force transport
back to Andrews from Los Alamos, and was behind in his
sleep again. For all the times this had happened to him,
he'd never quite learned to deal with it. 'That Gregory kid
is smart as hell. He took about two seconds to identify the
Bach installation, practically word for word with the NPIC
assessment.' The difference was that the photointerpreters
at the National Photographic Intelligence Center had taken
four months and three written reports to get it right.

'You think he belongs in the assessment team?'

'Sir, that's like asking if you want to have surgeons in the
operating room. Oh, by the way, he wants us to infiltrate
somebody into Bach.' Ryan rolled his eyes.

Admiral Greer nearly dropped his cup. 'That kid must
watch ninja movies.'

'It is nice to know that somebody believes in us.' Jack
chuckled, then turned serious. 'Anyway, Gregory wants to
know if they've made a breakthrough in laser power output
– excuse me, I think the new term is "throughput." He
suspects that most of the new power from the hydroelectric
dam will go to Bach.'

Greer's eyes narrowed. 'That's an evil thought. Do you
think he's right?'

'They've got a lot of good people in lasers, sir. Nikolay
Bosov, remember, won the Nobel Prize, and he's been in
laser-weapons research ever since, along with Yevgeniy
Velikhov, noted peace activist, and the head of the Laser
Institute is Dmitri Ustinov's son, for God's sake. Site Bach

is almost certainly a sparse array laser. We need to know what kind of lasers, though – could be gas-dynamic, free-electron, chemical. He thinks it'll be the free-electron kind, but that's just a guess. He gave me figures to establish the advantage of putting the laser assembly on this hilltop, where it's above about half of the atmosphere, and we know how much energy it takes to do some of the things they want to do. He said he'd try to do some backwards computations to estimate the total power of the system. The figures will be on the conservative side. Between what Gregory said, and the establishment of the residential facilities at Mozart, we have to assume that this site is intended to go into formal test and evaluation in the near future, maybe operational in two or three years. If so, Ivan may soon have a laser that can snuff one of our satellites right out of business. Probably a soft kill, the Major says – it'll smoke the camera receptors and the photovoltaic cells. But the next step – '

'Yeah. We're in a race, all right.'

'What are the chances that Ritter and the Operations people can find out something inside one of those Bach-site buildings?'

'I suppose we can discuss the possibility,' Greer said diffidently, and changed the subject. 'You look a little ragged.'

Ryan got the message: he didn't need to know what Operations had in mind. He could talk like a normal person now. 'All this traveling around has been pretty tiring. If you don't mind, sir, I'd just as soon take the rest of the day off.'

'Fair enough. See you tomorrow. But first – Jack? I got a call about you from the Securities and Exchange Commission.'

'Oh.' Jack bowed his head. 'I forgot all about that. They called me right before I flew to Moscow.'

'What gives?'

'One of the companies I own stock in, the officers are being investigated for insider trading. I bought some of it right when they did, and SEC wants to know how I decided to buy it just then.'

'And?' Greer asked. CIA had had enough scandals, and the Admiral didn't want one in his office.

'I got a tip that it might be an interesting company, and when I checked it out I saw that the company was buying itself back. So what got me to buy in was that I saw they were buying in. That's legal, boss. I have all the records at home. I do all this by computer – well, I *don't* since I came to work here – and I have hard copies of everything. I didn't break any rules, sir, and I can prove it.'

'Let's try to settle that in the next few days,' Greer suggested.

'Yes, sir.'

Jack was in his car five minutes later. The drive home to Peregrine Cliff was easier than usual, taking only fifty minutes instead of the usual seventy-five. Cathy was at work, as usual, and the kids were at school – Sally at St Mary's and Jack at kindergarten. Ryan poured himself a glass of milk in the kitchen. Finished, he wandered upstairs, kicked off his shoes, and collapsed into bed without even bothering to take off his pants.

Colonel of Signal Troops Gennady Iosifovich Bondarenko sat across from Misha, straight of back and proud, as so young a field-grade officer should be. He did not show himself to be the least intimidated by Colonel Filitov, who was old enough to be his father, and whose background was a minor legend in the Defense Ministry. *So this was the old war-horse who fought in nearly every tank battle in the first two years of the Great Patriotic War.* He saw the toughness around the eyes that age and fatigue could never erase, noted the impairment to the Colonel's arm, and remembered how that had happened. It was said that old Misha still went out to the tank factories with some of the men from his old regiment, to see for himself if quality control was up to standards, to make certain that his hard blue eyes could still hit a target from the gunner's seat. Bondarenko was somewhat in awe of this soldier's soldier. More than anything else, he was proud to wear the same uniform.

'How may I serve the Colonel?' he asked Misha.

'Your file says that you are very clever with electronic gadgets, Gennady Iosifovich.' Filitov waved at the file folder on his desk.

'That is my job, Comrade Colonel.' Bondarenko was more than just 'clever', and both knew it. He had helped develop laser range-finders for battlefield use, and until recently had been engaged in a project to use lasers in place of radios for secure front-line communications.

'What we are about to discuss is classified Most Secret.' The young Colonel nodded gravely and Filitov went on. 'For the past several years the Ministry has been financing a very special laser project called Bright Star – the name itself is also classified, of course. Its primary mission is to make high-quality photographs of Western satellites, though when fully developed, it may be able to blind them – at a time when such action is politically necessary. The project is run by academicians and a former fighter pilot from Voyska PVO – this sort of installation comes under the authority of the air-defense forces, unfortunately. I would have preferred myself that a real soldier was running it, but – ' Misha stopped and gestured at the ceiling. Bondarenko smiled in agreement. *Politics*, they both communicated silently. *No wonder we never get anything done*.

'The Minister wants you to fly down there and evaluate the weapons potential of the site, particularly from a reliability standpoint. If we are to bring this site to operational status, it would be well to know if the damned-fool thing will work when we want it to.'

The young officer nodded thoughtfully while his mind raced. This was a choice assignment – much more than that. He would report to the Minister through his most trusted aide. If he did well, he would have the personal stamp of the Minister in his personnel jacket. That would guarantee him general's stars, a bigger apartment for his family, a good education for his children, so many of the things he'd worked all these years for.

'Comrade Colonel, I presume that they know of my coming?'

Misha laughed derisively. 'Is that the way the Red Army does it now? We *tell* them when they are to be inspected! No, Gennady Iosifovich, if we are to evaluate reliability, we do it by surprise. I have a letter for you here from Marshal Yazov himself. It will be sufficient to get you past security – site security comes under our KGB colleagues,' Misha said coolly. 'It will give you free access to the entire facility. If you have any difficulty at all, call me at once. I can always be reached through this number. Even if I am in the *banya*, my driver will come and fetch me.'

'How detailed an evaluation is required, Comrade Colonel?'

'Enough that a weary old tanker like me can understand what their witchcraft is all about,' Misha said humorlessly. 'Do you think you can understand it all?'

'If not, I will so inform you, Comrade Colonel.' It was a very good answer, Misha noted. Bondarenko would go far.

'Excellent, Gennady Iosifovich. I would much rather have an officer tell me what he does not know than try to impress me with a truckload of *mudnya*.' Bondarenko got that message loud and clear. It was said that the carpet in this office was rust-red from the blood of officers who'd tried to bullshit their way past this man. 'How soon can you leave?'

'This is an extensive installation?'

'Yes. It houses four hundred academicians and engineers, and perhaps six hundred other support personnel. You can take up to a week doing your evaluation. Speed here is less important than thoroughness.'

'Then I'll have to pack another uniform. I can be on my way in two hours.'

'Excellent. Off with you.' Misha opened a new file.

As was generally the case, Misha worked a few minutes later than his Minister. He locked his personal documents in secure files and had the rest picked up by a messenger

74

whose cart wheeled them to Central Files a few meters down the main corridor from his office. The same messenger handed over a note saying that Colonel Bondarenko had taken the 1730 Aeroflot flight to Dushanbe, and that ground transport from the civil airport to Bright Star had been arranged. Filitov made a mental note to congratulate Bondarenko for his cleverness. As a member of the Ministry's in-house General Inspectorate, he could have requisitioned special transport and flown directly to the city's military airfield, but the security office at Bright Star undoubtedly had some of its people there to report the arrival of such a flight. This way, however, a colonel from Moscow could just as easily be mistaken for what colonels in Moscow usually were – messenger boys. That fact offended Filitov. A man who had worked hard enough to attain the rank of a regimental commander – which really was the best job in any army – should not be a staff slave who fetched drinks for his general. But he was sure that this was a fact in any military headquarters. At least Bondarenko would have a chance to try out his teeth on the feather merchants down in Tadzhikistan.

Filitov rose and reached for his coat. A moment later, briefcase dangling from his right hand, he walked out of the office. His secretary – a warrant officer – automatically called downstairs for his car to be ready. It was waiting when Misha walked out the front door.

Forty minutes later, Filitov was in soft clothes. The television was on, broadcasting something mindless enough to have been imported from the West. Misha sat alone at his kitchen table. There was an open half-liter bottle of vodka beside his evening meal. Misha ate sausage, black bread, and pickled vegetables, not very different from what he'd eaten in the field with his men, two generations before. He'd found that his stomach dealt more easily with rough foods than the fancy ones, a fact that had thoroughly confused the hospital staff during his last bout of pneumonia. After every other bite, he'd take a brief sip of vodka, staring out of the windows, whose blinds were adjusted just so. The city lights of Moscow burned brightly, along with the numberless yellow rectangles of apartment windows.

He could remember the smells at will. The verdant odor of good Russian earth, the fine, green smell of meadow grass, along with the stink of diesel fuel and above all the acidic reek of propellant from the tank's guns that stayed in the cloth of your coveralls no matter how many times you tried to wash it out. For a tanker, that was the smell of combat, that – and the uglier smell of burning vehicles, and burning crews. Without looking, he lifted the sausage and cut off a piece, bringing it to his mouth atop the knife. He was staring out the window, but as though it were a television screen, what he saw was the vast, distant horizon at sunset, and columns of smoke rising along the perimeter of green and blue, orange and brown. Next, a bite of the rich, thickly textured black bread. And as always on the nights before he committed treason, the ghosts came back to visit.

We showed them, didn't we, Comrade Captain? a weary voice asked.

We still had to retreat, Corporal, he heard his own voice answer. *But, yes, we showed the bastards not to trifle with our T-34s. This is good bread you stole.*

Stole? But, Comrade Captain, it is heavy work defending these farmers, is it not?

And thirsty work? was the Captain's next question.

Indeed, Comrade. The corporal chuckled. From behind, a bottle was handed down. Not State-produced vodka, this was Samogan, the Russian bootleg liquor that Misha himself knew well. Every true Russian claimed to love the taste, though not one would touch it if vodka was handy. Nevertheless, for this moment Samogan was the drink he craved, out here on Russian soil, with the remains of his tank troop standing between a State farm and the leading elements of Guderian's panzers.

They'll be coming again tomorrow morning, the driver thought soberly.

And we'll kill some more slug-gray tanks, the loader said.

After which, Misha did not say aloud, *we'll withdraw another ten kilometers. Ten kilometers only – if we're lucky again, and if regimental headquarters manages to control things better than they did this afternoon. In either case, this farm will be behind German lines when tomorrow's sun sets. More ground lost.*

It was not a thought on which to dwell. Misha wiped his hands carefully before unbuttoning the pocket on his tunic. It was time to restore his soul.

A delicate one, the corporal observed as he looked over his Captain's shoulder at the photograph for the hundredth time, and as always, with envy. *Delicate like crystal glass. And such a fine son you have. Lucky for you, Comrade Captain, that he has his mother's looks. She is so tiny, your wife, how can she have had such a big boy as that and not be hurt by it?*

God knows, was his unconscious reply. So strange that after a few days of war even the most adamant atheist invoked the name of God. Even a few of the commissars, to the quiet amusement of the troops.

I will come home to you, he'd promised the photograph. *I will come home to you. Through all the German Army, through all the fires of hell, I will come home to you, Elena.*

Just then mail had come, a rare-enough occurrence at the front. Only one letter for Captain Filitov, but the texture of the paper and the delicate handwriting told him of its importance. He slit the envelope open with the bright edge of his combat knife and extracted the letter as carefully as his haste allowed so as not to soil the words of his love with grease from his battle tank. Seconds later he leaped to his feet and screamed at the stars in the twilight sky.

I will be a father again in the spring! It must have been that last night on leave, three weeks before this brutal madness began . . .

I am not surprised, the corporal observed lightly, *after the fucking we gave the Germans today. Such a man leads this troop! Perhaps our Captain should stand at stud.*

You are nekulturny, Corporal Romanov. I am a married man.

Then perhaps I can stand in the Comrade Captain's stead? he asked hopefully, then handed the bottle down again. *To another fine son, my Captain, and to the health of your beautiful wife.* There were tears of joy in the young man's eyes, along with the grief that came with the knowledge that only the greatest good fortune would ever allow him to be a father. But he would never say such a thing. A fine soldier Romanov was, and a fine comrade, ready for command of his own tank.

And Romanov had gotten his own tank, Misha remembered, staring at the Moscow skyline. At Vyasma, he'd defiantly placed it between his Captain's disabled T-34 and an onrushing German Mark-IV, saving his Captain's life as his own ended in red-orange flames. Aleksey Il'ych Romanov, Corporal of the Red Army, won an Order of the Red Banner that day. Misha wondered if it was fair compensation to his mother for her blue-eyed freckled son.

The vodka bottle was three-quarters empty now, and as he had so many times, Misha was sobbing, alone at his table.

So many deaths.

Those fools at High Command! Romanov killed at Vyasma. Ivanenko lost outside Moscow. Lieutenant Abashin at Kharkov – Mirka, the handsome young poet, the slight, sensitive young officer who had the heart and balls of a lion, killed leading the fifth counterattack, but clearing the way for Misha to extract what was left of his regiment across the Donets before the hammer fell.

And his Elena, the last victim of all . . . All of them killed not by an external enemy, but by the misguided, indifferent brutality of their own Motherland –

Misha took a long last swallow from the bottle. No, not the Motherland. Not the *Rodina*, never the *Rodina*. By the inhuman bastards who . . .

He rose and staggered toward the bedroom, leaving on the lights in his sitting room. The clock on the nightstand said quarter to ten, and some distant part of Misha's brain took comfort in the fact that he'd get nine hours' sleep to recover from the abuse that he inflicted on what had once been a lean, hard body, one that had endured – even thrived on – the ghastly strain of prolonged combat operations. But the stress Misha endured now made combat seem a vacation, and his subconscious rejoiced in the knowledge that this would soon end, and rest would finally come.

About a half hour later, a car drove down the street. In the passenger's seat, a woman was driving her son home from a hockey game. She looked up and noted that the lights in certain windows were on, and the shades adjusted just so.

The air was thin. Bondarenko arose at 0500, as he always did, put on his sweatsuit, and took the elevator downstairs from his guest quarters on the tenth floor. It took him a moment to be surprised – the elevators were operating. So the technicians travel back and forth to the facility round the clock. *Good*, the Colonel thought.

He walked outside, a towel wrapped around his neck, and checked his watch. He frowned as he began. He had a regular morning routine in Moscow, a measured path around the city blocks. Here he couldn't be sure of the distance, when his five kilometers ended. Well – he shrugged – that was to be expected. He started off heading east. The view, he saw, was breathtaking. The sun would soon rise, earlier than Moscow because of the lower latitude, and the jagged spires of mountains were outlined in red, like dragons' teeth, he smiled to himself. His youngest son liked to draw pictures of dragons.

The flight in had ended spectacularly. The full moon had illuminated the Kara Kum desert flatlands under the aircraft – and then these sandy wastes had ended as though at a wall built by the gods. Within three degrees of longitude, the land had changed from three-hundred-meter lowlands to five-thousand-meter peaks. From his vantage point he could see the glow of Dushanbe, about seventy kilometers to the northwest. Two rivers,

Kafirnigan and Surkhandarya, bordered the city of half a million, and like a man halfway around the world, Colonel Bondarenko wondered why it had grown here, what ancient history had caused it to grow between the two mountain-fed rivers. Certainly it seemed an inhospitable place, but perhaps the long caravan of Bactrian camels had rested here, or perhaps it had been a crossroads, or – He stopped his reverie. Bondarenko knew that he was merely putting off his morning exercise. He tied the surgical mask over his mouth and nose as a protection against the frigid air. The Colonel began his deep knee-bends to loosen up, then stretched his legs against the building wall before he started off at an easy, double-time pace.

Immediately he noticed that he was breathing more heavily than usual through the cloth mask over his face. The altitude, of course. Well, that would shorten his run somewhat. The apartment building was already behind him, and he looked to his right, passing what his map of the facility indicated to be machine and optical shops.

'Halt!' a voice called urgently.

Bondarenko growled to himself. He didn't like having his exercise interrupted. Especially, he saw, by someone with the green shoulder boards of the KGB. Spies – thugs – playing at soldiers. 'Well, what is it, Sergeant!'

'Your papers, if you please, Comrade. I do not recognize you.'

Fortunately, Bondarenko's wife had sewn several pockets onto the Nike jogging suit that she'd managed to get on the gray market in Moscow, a present for his last birthday. He kept his legs pumping as he handed over his identification.

'When did the Comrade Colonel arrive?' the sergeant asked. 'And what do you think you are doing so early in the morning?'

'Where is your officer?' Bondarenko replied.

'At the main guard post, four hundred meters that way.' The sergeant pointed.

'Then come along with me, Sergeant, and we will speak with him. A colonel of the Soviet Army does not explain himself to sergeants. Come on, you need exercise too!' he challenged and moved off.

The sergeant was only twenty or so, but wore a heavy greatcoat and carried a rifle and ammo belt. Within two hundred meters, Gennady heard him puffing.

'Here, Comrade Colonel,' the young man gasped a minute later.

'You should not smoke so much, Sergeant,' Bondarenko observed.

'What the hell is going on here?' a KGB lieutenant asked from behind his desk.

'Your sergeant challenged me. I am Colonel G.I. Bondarenko, and I am doing my morning run.'

'In Western clothing?'

'What the hell do you care what clothes I wear when I exercise?' *Idiot, do you think spies jog?*

'Colonel, I am the security watch officer. I do not recognize you, and my superiors have not made me aware of your presence.'

Gennady reached into another pocket and handed over his special visitor's pass, along with his personal identification papers. 'I am a special representative of the Ministry of Defense. The purpose of my visit is not your concern. I am here on the personal authority of Marshal of the Soviet Union D.T. Yazov. If you have any further questions, you may call him directly at that number!'

The KGB Lieutenant scrupulously read the identification documents to make sure they said what he'd been told.

'Please excuse me, Comrade Colonel, but we have orders to take our security provisions seriously. Also, it is out of the ordinary to see a man in Western clothes running at dawn.'

'I gather that it is out of the ordinary for your troops to run at all,' Bondarenko noted dryly.

'There is hardly room on this mountaintop for a proper regime of physical training, Comrade Colonel.'

'Is that so?' Bondarenko smiled as he took out a notebook and pencil. 'You claim to take your security duties seriously, but you do not meet norms for physical training of your troops. Thank you for that piece of information, Comrade Lieutenant. I will discuss that matter with your commanding officer. May I go?'

'Technically, I have orders to provide escort for all official visitors.'

'Excellent. I like to have company when I run. Will you be so kind as to join me, Comrade Lieutenant?'

The KGB officer was trapped, and knew it. Five minutes later, he was puffing like a landed fish.

'What is your main security threat?' Bondarenko asked him – maliciously, since he did not slow down.

'The Afghan border is one hundred eleven kilometers that way,' the Lieutenant said between wheezes. 'They have occasionally sent some of their bandit raiders into Soviet territory, as you may have heard.'

'Do they make contact with local citizens?'

'Not that we have established, but that is a concern. The local population is largely Muslim.' The Lieutenant started coughing. Gennady stopped.

'In air this cold, I have found that wearing a mask helps,' he said. 'It warms the air somewhat before you breathe it. Straighten up and breathe deeply, Comrade Lieutenant. If you take your security provisions so seriously, you and your men should be in proper physical shape. I promise you that the Afghans are. Two winters ago I spent time with a *Spetznaz* team that chased them over a half dozen miserable mountains. We never did catch them.' *But they caught us*, he didn't say. Bondarenko would never forget that ambush. . . .

'Helicopters?'

'They cannot always fly in bad weather, my young Comrade, and in my case we were trying to establish that we, too, could fight in the mountains.'

'Well, we have patrols out every day, of course.'

It was the way he said it that bothered Bondarenko, and

the Colonel made a mental note to check that out. 'How far have we run?'

'Two kilometers.'

'The altitude does make things difficult. Come, we will walk back.'

The sunrise was spectacular. The blazing sphere edged above a nameless mountain to the east, and its light marched down the nearer slopes, chasing the shadows into the deep, glacial valleys. This installation was no easy objective, even for the inhuman barbarians of the *mud-jaheddin*. The guard towers were well sited, with clear fields of fire that extended for several kilometers. They didn't use searchlights out of consideration for the civilians who lived here, but night-vision devices were a better choice in any case, and he was sure that the KGB troops used those. And – he shrugged – site security wasn't the reason he'd been sent down, though it was a fine excuse to needle the KGB security detail.

'May I ask how you obtained your exercise clothing?' the KGB officer asked when he was able to breathe properly.

'Are you a married man, Comrade Lieutenant?'

'Yes, I am, Comrade Colonel.'

'Personally, I do not question my wife on where she buys her birthday presents for me. Of course, I am not a *chekist*.' Bondarenko did a few deep knee-bends to show that he was, however, a better man.

'Colonel, while our duties are not quite the same, we both serve the Soviet Union. I am a young, inexperienced officer, as you have already made quite clear. One of the things that disturbs me is the unnecessary rivalry between the Army and the KGB.'

Bondarenko turned to look at the Lieutenant. 'That was well said, my young Comrade. Perhaps when you wear general's stars, you will remember the sentiment.'

He dropped the KGB Lieutenant back at the guard post and walked briskly back to the apartment block, the morning breeze threatening to freeze the sweat on his neck. He went inside and took the elevator up. Not surprisingly, there was no hot water for his shower this early in the morning. The Colonel endured it cold, chasing away the last vestiges of sleep, shaved and dressed before walking over to the canteen for breakfast.

He didn't have to be at the Ministry until nine, and on the way was a steam bath. One of the things Filitov had learned over the years was that nothing could chase away a hangover and clear your head like steam. He'd had enough practice. His sergeant drove him to the San-dunovski Baths on Kuznetskiy Most, six blocks from the Kremlin. It was his usual Wednesday morning stop in any case. He was not alone, even this early. A handful of other probably important people trudged up the wide marble steps to the second floor's first-class (not called that now, of course) facilities, since thousands of Moscovites shared with the Colonel both his disease and its cure. Some of them were women, and Misha wondered if the female facilities were very different from those he was about to use. It was strange. He'd been coming here since he joined the Ministry in 1943, and yet he'd never gotten a peek into the women's section. *Well, I am too old for that now.*

His eyes were bloodshot and heavy as he undressed. Naked, he took a heavy bath towel from the pile at the end of the room, and a handful of birch branches. Filitov breathed the cool, dry air of the dressing room before opening the door that led to the steam rooms. The once-marble floor was largely replaced now with orange tiles. He could remember when the original floor had been nearly intact.

Two men in their fifties were arguing about something, probably politics. He could hear their rasping voices above the hiss of steam coming off the hotbox that occupied the center of the room. Misha counted five other men, their heads stooped over, each of them enduring a hangover in grumpy solitude. He selected a seat in the front row, and sat.

84

'Good morning, Comrade Colonel,' a voice said from five meters away.

'And to you, Comrade Academician,' Misha greeted his fellow regular. His hands were wrapped tightly around his bundle of branches while he waited for the sweat to begin. It didn't take long – the room temperature was nearly one hundred forty degrees Fahrenheit. He breathed carefully, as the experienced ones did. The aspirins he'd taken with his morning tea were beginning to work, though his head was still heavy and the sinuses around his eyes swollen. He swatted the branches across his back, as though to exorcize the poisons from his body.

'And how is the Hero of Stalingrad this morning?' the academic persisted.

'About as well as the genius of the Ministry of Education.' This drew a painful laugh. Misha never could remember his name . . . Ilya Vladimirovich Somethingorother. What sort of fool could laugh during a hangover? The man drank because of his wife, he said. *You drink to be free of her, do you? You boast of the times you've fucked your secretary, when I would trade my soul for one more look at Elena's face.* And my sons' faces, he told himself. My two handsome sons. It was well to remember these things on such mornings.

'Yesterday's *Pravda* spoke of the arms negotiations,' the man persisted. 'Is there hope for progress?'

'I have no idea,' Misha replied.

An attendant came in. A young man, perhaps twenty-five or so and short. He counted heads in the room.

'Does anyone wish a drink?' he asked. Drinking was absolutely forbidden in the baths, but as any true Russian would say, that merely made the vodka taste better.

'No!' came the reply in chorus. No one was the least interested in the hair of the dog this morning, Misha noted with mild surprise. Well, it was the middle of the week. On a Saturday morning it would be very different.

'Very well,' the attendant said on the way out the door. 'There will be fresh towels outside, and the pool heater has been repaired. Swimming is also fine exercise, Comrades.

Remember to use the muscles that you are now baking, and you will be refreshed all day.'

Misha looked up. *So this is the new one.*

'Why do they have to be so damned cheerful?' asked a man in the corner.

'He is cheerful because he is *not* a foolish old drunk!' another answered. That drew a few chuckles.

'Five years ago vodka didn't do this to me. I tell you, quality control is not what it used to be,' the first went on.

'Neither is your liver, Comrade!'

'A terrible thing to get old.' Misha turned around to see who said that. It was a man barely fifty, whose swollen belly was the color of dead fish and who smoked a cigarette, also in violation of the rules.

'A more terrible thing not to, but you young men have forgotten that!' he said automatically, and wondered why. Heads came up and saw the burn scars on his back and chest. Even those who did not know who Mikhail Semyonovich Filitov was knew that this was not a man to be trifled with. He sat quietly for another ten minutes before leaving.

The attendant was outside the door when he emerged. The Colonel handed over his branches and towel, then walked off to the cold-water showers. Ten minutes later he was a new man, the pain and depression of the vodka gone, and the strain behind him. He dressed quickly and walked downstairs to where his car was waiting. His sergeant noted the change in his stride and wondered what was so curative about roasting yourself like a piece of meat.

The attendant had his own task. On asking again a few minutes later, it turned out that two people in the steam room had changed their minds. He trotted out of the building's back door to a small shop whose manager made more money selling drink 'on the left' that he did by dry-cleaning. The attendant returned with a half-liter bottle of 'Vodka' – it had no brand name as such; the premium Stolychnaya was made for export and the elite – at a little over double the market price. The imposition of sales restrictions on alcohol had begun a whole new – and extremely profitable – part of the city's black market. The attendant had also passed along a small film cassette that his contact had handed over with the birch branches. For his part, the bath attendant was also relieved. This was his only contact. He didn't know the man's name, and had spoken the code phrase with the natural fear that this part of the CIA's Moscow network had long since been compromised by the KGB's counterintelligence department, the dreaded Second Chief Directorate. His life was already forfeit and he knew it. But he had to do something. Ever since his year in Afghanistan, the things he'd seen, and the things he'd been forced to do. He wondered briefly who that scarred old man was, but reminded himself that the man's nature and identity were not his concern.

The dry-cleaning shop catered mainly to foreigners, providing service to reporters, businessmen, and a few diplomats, along with the odd Russian who wished to protect clothing purchased abroad. One of these picked up an English overcoat, paid the three rubles, and left. She walked two blocks to the nearest Metro station, taking the escalator down to catch her train on the Zhdanovsko-Krasnopresnenskaya line, the one marked in purple on the city maps. The train was crowded, and no one could have seen her pass the cassette. In fact, she herself didn't see the face of the man. He in turn made his way off the train at the next station, Pushkinskaya, and crossed over to Gor'kovskaya Station. One more transfer was made ten minutes later, this one to an American who was on his way to the embassy a little late this morning, having stayed long at a diplomatic reception the previous night.

His name was Ed Foley; he was the press attaché at the embassy on Ulitsa Chaykovskogo. He and his wife, Mary Pat, another CIA agent, had been in Moscow for nearly four years, and both were looking forward to putting this grim, gray town behind them once and for all. They had two children, both of whom had been denied hot dogs and ball games long enough.

It wasn't that their tour of duty hadn't been successful. The Russians knew that CIA had a number of husband-wife teams in the field, but the idea that spies would take their children abroad wasn't something that the Soviets could accept easily. There was also the matter of their cover. Ed Foley had been a reporter with the *New York Times* before joining the State Department – because, as he explained it, the money wasn't much different and a police reporter never traveled farther than Attica. His wife stayed home with the children for the most part – though she did substitute-teach when needed at the Anglo-American School at 78 Leninsky Prospekt – often taking them out in the snow. Their older son played on a junior hockey team, and the KGB officers who trailed them around had it written up in their file that Edward Foley II was a pretty good wingman for a seven-year-old. The Soviet government's one real annoyance with the family was the elder Foley's inordinate curiosity about street crime in their capital, which was at its worst a far cry from what he had written about in New York City. But that proved that he was relatively harmless. He was far too obviously inquisitive to be any kind of intelligence officer. They, after all, did everything possible to be inconspicuous.

Foley walked the last few blocks from the Metro station. He nodded politely to the militiaman who guarded the door to the grimly decorous building, then to the Marine sergeant inside before going to his office. It wasn't much. The embassy was officially described in the State Department's USSR Post Report as 'cramped and difficult to maintain'. The same writer might call the burned-out shell of a South Bronx tenement a 'fixer-upper', Foley thought. In the building's last renovation, his office had been remade from a storage room and broom closet into a marginally serviceable cubicle about ten feet square. The broom closet, however, was his private darkroom, and that was why the CIA station had had one of its people in this particular room for over twenty years, though Foley was the first station chief to be housed there.

Only thirty-three, tall but very thin, Foley was an Irishman from Queens whose intellect was mated to an impossibly slow heart rate and a pokerface that had helped him earn his way through Holy Cross. Recruited by CIA in his senior year, he'd spent four years with the *Times* to establish his own personal 'legend.' He was remembered in the city room as an adequate, if rather lazy reporter who turned out workmanlike copy but never would really go anywhere. His editor hadn't minded losing him to government service, since his departure made room for a youngster from Columbia's School of Journalism with hustle and a real nose for what was happening. The current *Times* correspondent in Moscow had described him to his own colleagues and contacts as a nebbish, and rather a dull one at that, and in doing so gave Foley the most sought-after compliment in the business of espionage: *Him? He's not smart enough to be a spy.* For this and several other reasons, Foley was entrusted with running the Agency's longest-lived, most productive agent-in-place, Colonel Mikhail Semyonovich Filitov, code name CARDINAL. The name itself, of course, was sufficiently secret that only five people within the Agency knew that it meant more than a red-caped churchman with princely diplomatic rank.

Raw CARDINAL information was classified Special Intelligence/Eyes Only-Δ, and there were only six Δ-cleared officials in the entire American government. Every month the code word for the data itself was changed. This month's name was SATIN, for which less than twenty others were cleared. Even under that title, the data was invariably paraphrased and subtly altered before going outside the Δ fraternity.

Foley took the film cassette from his pocket and locked himself in the darkroom. He could go through the developing process drunk and half-asleep. In fact, a few times, he had. Within six minutes, the job was done, and Foley cleaned up after himself. His former editor in New York would have found his neatness in Moscow surprising.

Foley followed procedures that had been unchanged for

nearly thirty years. He reviewed the six exposed frames through a magnifying glass of the type used to inspect 35mm slides. He memorized each frame in a few seconds, and began typing a translation on his personal portable typewriter. It was a manual whose well-worn cloth ribbon was too frayed to be of use to anyone, particularly the KGB. Like many reporters, Foley was not a good typist. His pages bore strikeovers and X-outs. The paper was chemically treated, and you couldn't use an eraser on it. It took nearly two hours for him to finish the transcription. When done, he made a final check of the film to guarantee that he hadn't left anything out, nor made any serious grammatical mistakes. Satisfied, but with a tremor that he never quite got over, he crumpled the film into a ball and set it in a metal ashtray, where a wooden kitchen match reduced the only direct evidence of CARDINAL's existence to ashes. He then smoked a cigar to disguise the distinctive smell of burning celluloid. The folded typescript pages went into his pocket, and Foley walked upstairs to the embassy's communications room. Here he drafted an innocuous dispatch to Box 4108, State Department, Washington: 'Reference your 29 December. Expense report en route via pouch. Foley. Ends.' As press attaché, Foley had to pick up a lot of bar bills for former colleagues who held him in contempt that he didn't bother returning; he had to do quite a few expense reports for the cookie-pushers at Foggy Bottom, and it amused him greatly that his press brethren worked so hard at maintaining his cover for him.

Next he checked with the embassy's courier-in-residence. Though little known, this was one aspect of life at the Moscow post that hadn't changed since the 1930s. There was always a courier to take the bag out, though nowadays he had other duties, too. The courier was also one of four people in the embassy who knew which government agency Foley really worked for. A retired Army warrant officer, he had a DSC and four Purple Hearts for flying casualties out of Vietnam battlefields. When he smiled at people, he did so in the Russian way, with the mouth but almost never the eyes.

'Feel like flying home tonight?'

The man's eyes lit up. 'With the Super Bowl this Sunday? You're kidding. Stop by your office around four?'

'Right.' Foley closed the door and returned to his office. The courier booked himself on the British Airways 5:40 P.M. flight to Heathrow.

The difference in time zones between Washington and Moscow virtually guaranteed that Foley's messages reached D.C. early in the morning. At six, a CIA employee walked into the State Department mail room and extracted the message forms from a dozen or so boxes, then resumed his drive to Langley. A senior field officer in the Operations Directorate, he was barred from any further overseas duty due to an injury sustained in Budapest – where a street hoodlum had fractured his skull, and been locked up for five years by the irate local police. *If only they'd known*, the agent thought, *they'd have given him a medal*. He delivered the messages to the appropriate offices, and went to his own office.

The message form was lying on Bob Ritter's desk when he got to work at 7:25. Ritter was the Agency's Deputy Director for Operations. His turf, technically known as the Directorate of Operations, included all of the CIA's field officers and all of the foreign citizens they recruited and employed as agents. The message from Moscow – as usual there was more than one, but this one counted the most – was immediately tucked into his personal file cabinet, and he prepared himself for the 8:00 brief, delivered every day by the night-watch officers.

'It's open.' Back in Moscow, Foley looked up when the knock came at the door. The courier stepped in.

'The plane leaves in an hour. I have to hustle.'

91

Foley reached into his desk and pulled out what looked like an expensive silver cigarette case. He handed it over, and the courier handled it carefully before tucking it into his breast pocket. The typed pages were folded inside, along with a tiny pyrotechnic charge. If the case were improperly opened, or subjected to a sudden acceleration – like being dropped to a hard floor – the charge would go off and destroy the flash paper inside. It might also set fire to the courier's suit, which explained his care in handling it.

'I should be back Tuesday morning. Anything I can get you, Mr Foley?'

'I hear there's a new *Far Side* book out . . .' That got a laugh.

'Okay, I'll check. You can pay me when I get back.'

'Safe trip, Augie.'

One of the embassy's drivers took Augie Giannini to Sheremetyevo Airport, nineteen miles outside of Moscow, where the courier's diplomatic passport enabled him to walk past the security checkpoints, and right onto the British Airways plane bound for Heathrow Airport. He rode in the coach section, on the right side of the aircraft. The diplomatic pouch had the window seat, with Giannini in the middle. Flights out of Moscow were rarely crowded, and the seat on his left was also vacant. The Boeing started rolling on schedule. The Captain announced the time of flight and destination, and the airliner started moving down the runway. The moment it lifted off Soviet soil, as often happened, the hundred and fifty passengers applauded. It was something that always amused the courier. Giannini pulled a paperback from his pocket and started reading. He couldn't drink on the flight, of course, nor sleep, and he decided to wait for dinner until his next flight. The stewardess did manage to get a cup of coffee into him, however.

Three hours later, the 747 thumped down at Heathrow. Again he was able to clear customs perfunctorily. A man who spent more time in the air than most commercial pilots, he had access to the first-class waiting rooms still allowed in most of the world's airports. Here he waited an hour for a 747 bound for Washington's Dulles International.

Over the Atlantic, the courier enjoyed a Pan Am dinner, and a movie that he hadn't seen before, which happened rarely enough. By the time he'd finished his book, the plane was swooping into Dulles. The courier ran his hand over his face and tried to remember what time it was supposed to be in Washington. Fifteen minutes later he climbed into a nondescript government Ford that headed southeast. He got into the front seat because he wanted the extra leg room.

'How was the flight?' the driver asked.

'Same as always: borrr-inggg.' On the other hand, it beat flying medivac missions in the Central Highlands. The government was paying him twenty grand a year to sit on airplanes and read books, which, combined with his retirement pay from the Army, gave him a fairly comfortable life. He never bothered himself wondering what he carried in the diplomatic bag, or in this metal case in his coat. He figured it was all a waste of time anyway. The world didn't change very much.

'Got the case?' the man in the back asked.

'Yeah.' Giannini took it from his inside pocket and handed it back, with both hands. The CIA officer in the back took it, using both hands, and tucked it inside a foam-lined box. The officer was an instructor in the CIA's Office of Technical Services, part of the Directorate of Science and Technology. It was an office that covered a lot of bureaucratic ground. This particular officer was an expert on booby traps and explosive devices in general. At Langley, he took the elevator to Ritter's office and opened the cigarette case on the latter's desk, then returned to his own office without looking at the contents.

Ritter walked to his personal Xerox machine and made several copies of the flash-paper pages, which were then burned. It was not so much a security measure as a simple safety precaution. Ritter didn't want a sheaf of highly flammable material in his personal office. He started reading the pages even before all the copies were done. As usual, his head started moving left and right by the end of the first paragraph. The Deputy Director for Operations walked to his desk and punched the line to the Director's Office.

'You busy? The bird landed.'

'Come on over,' Judge Arthur Moore replied at once. Nothing was more important than data from CARDINAL.

Ritter collected Admiral Greer on the way, and the two of them joined the Director of Central Intelligence in his spacious office.

'You gotta love this guy,' Ritter said as he handed the papers out. 'He's conned Yazov into sending a colonel into Bach to do a "reliability assessment" of the whole system. This Colonel Bondarenko is supposed to report back on how everything works, in layman's terms, so that the Minister can understand it all and report to the Politburo. Naturally, he detailed Misha to play gofer, so the report goes across his desk first.'

'That kid Ryan met – Gregory, I think – wanted us to get a man into Dushanbe,' Greer noted with a chuckle. 'Ryan told him it was impossible.'

'Good,' Ritter observed. 'Everybody knows what screwups the Operations Directorate is.' The entire CIA took perverse pride in the fact that only its failure made the news. The Directorate of Operations in particular craved the public assessment that the press constantly awarded them. The foul-ups of the KGB never got the attention that CIA's did, and the public image, so often reinforced, was widely believed even in the Russian intelligence community. It rarely occurred to anyone that the leaks were purposeful.

'I wish,' Judge Moore observed soberly, 'that somebody would explain to Misha that there are old spies and bold spies, but very few old *and* bold ones.'

'He's a very careful man, boss,' Ritter pointed out.

'Yeah, I know.' The DCI looked down at the pages.

Since the death of Dmitri Fedorovich, it is not the same at the Defense Ministry, the DCI read. *Sometimes I wonder if Marshal Yazov takes these new technological developments seriously enough, but to whom can I report my misgivings? Would KGB believe me? I must order my thoughts. Yes, I must organize my thoughts before I make any accusations. But can I break security rules . . .*

But what choice do I have? If I cannot document my misgivings, who will take me seriously? It is a hard thing to have to break an important rule of security, but the safety of the State supersedes such rules. It must.

As the epic poems of Homer began with the invocation of the Muse, so CARDINAL's messages invariably began like this. The idea had developed in the late 1960s. CARDINAL's messages began as photographs of his personal diary. Russians are inveterate diarists. Each time he began one, it would be as a Slavic *cri de coeur*, his personal worries about the policy decisions made in the Defense Ministry. Sometimes he would express concern with the security on a specific project or the performance of a new tank or aircraft. In each case, the technical merits of a piece of hardware or a policy decision would be examined at length, but always the focus of the document would be a supposed bureaucratic problem within the Ministry. If Filitov's apartment were ever searched, his diary would be easily found, certainly not hidden away as a spy was expected to do, and while he was definitely breaking rules of security, and would certainly be admonished for it, there would at least be a chance that Misha could successfully defend himself. Or, that was the idea.

When I have Bondarenko's report, in another week or two, perhaps I can persuade the Minister that this project is one of truly vital importance to the Motherland, it ended.

'So, it looks like they made a breakthrough on laser power output,' Ritter said.

'Throughput is the current term,' Greer corrected. 'At least that's what Jack tells me. This is not very good news, gentlemen.'

'Your usual keen eye for detail, James,' Ritter said. 'God, what if they get there first?'

'It's not the end of the world. Remember that it'll take ten years to deploy the system even after the concept is validated, and they haven't come close to doing that yet,' the DCI pointed out. 'The sky is not falling. This could even work to our benefit, couldn't it, James?'

'If Misha can get us a usable description of their breakthrough, yes. In most areas we're further along than they are,' the DDI replied. 'Ryan will need this for his report.'

'He's not cleared for this!' Ritter objected.

'He had a look at Delta information before,' Greer noted.

'Once. Only once, and there was a good reason for it – and, yes, he did damned well for an amateur. James, there's nothing here he can use except that we have reason to suspect Ivan has made a power – throughput? – break-through, and that Gregory kid already suspects it. Tell Ryan we've confirmed the suspicion through other assets. Judge, you can tell the President yourself that something's up, but it'll have to wait a few weeks. It shouldn't go any farther than that for a while.'

'Makes sense to me.' The Judge nodded. Greer conceded the point without argument.

There was temptation to voice the opinion that this was CARDINAL's most important mission, but that would have been too dramatic for any of the three senior executives, and besides, CARDINAL had provided CIA with a good deal of important data over the years. Judge Moore reread the report after the others had left. Foley had tagged onto the end that Ryan had literally bumped into CARDINAL after Mary Pat had given him the new assignment – and right in front of Marshal Yazov. Judge Moore shook his head. *What a pair, the Foleys.* And how remarkable that Ryan had, after a fashion, made contact with Colonel Filitov. Moore shook his head. It was a crazy world.

4

Bright Stars and
Fast Ships

Jack didn't bother asking which 'asset' had confirmed Major Gregory's suspicions. Field operations were something that he struggled – successfully for the most part – to keep at arm's length. What mattered was that the information was graded as Class-1 for reliability – CIA's newly adopted grading system used numbers 1–5 instead of letters A–E, surely the result of six months' hard work by some deputy-assistant-to educated at Harvard Business School.

'What about specific technical information?'

'I'll let you know when it comes in,' Greer replied.

'I got two weeks to deliver, boss,' Ryan pointed out. Deadlines were never fun. This was especially true when the document being prepared was for the President's eyes.

'I do seem to recall reading that somewhere or other, Jack,' the Admiral noted dryly. 'The people at ACDA are calling me every day for the damned thing, too. I think what we'll do is have you run over to brief them in person.'

Ryan winced. The whole point of his Special National Intelligence Estimate was to help set the stage for the next session of arms negotiations. The Arms Control and Disarmament Agency needed it also, of course, so that they'd know what to demand and how much they could safely concede. That was quite a bit of additional weight on his shoulders, but as Greer liked to tell him, Ryan did his best work under pressure. Jack wondered if maybe he should screw one up sometime, just to disprove that idea.

'When will I have to get over?'

'I haven't decided yet.'

'Can I have a couple of days' warning?'

'We'll see.'

Major Gregory was actually at home. This was fairly unusual; even more so, he was taking the day off. But that wasn't his doing. His General had decided that all work and no play were beginning to take their toll on the young man. It hadn't occurred to him that Gregory could work at home as well.

'Don't you ever stop?' Candi asked.

'Well, what are we supposed to do in between?' He smiled up from the keyboard.

The housing development was called Mountain View. It wasn't a rousing bit of originality. In that part of the country the only way not to see mountains was to close your eyes. Gregory had his own personal computer – a very powerful Hewlett-Packard provided by the Project – and occasionally wrote some of his 'code' there. He had to be careful about the security classification of his work, of course, though he often joked that he himself wasn't cleared for what he was doing. That was not an unknown situation inside government.

Dr Candace Long was taller than her fiancé at nearly five-ten, willowy, with short, dark hair. Her teeth were a little crooked because she'd never wanted to suffer through braces, and her glasses were even thicker than Alan's.

She was thin because like many academics she was so enthralled with her work that she often forgot to eat. They'd first met at a seminar for doctoral candidates at Columbia University. She was an expert in optical physics, specifically in adaptive-optics mirrors, a field she'd selected to complement her life-long hobby, astronomy. Living in the New Mexico highlands, she was able to do her own observations on a $5,000 Meade telescope, and, on occasion, to use the instruments at the Project to probe the heavens – because, she pointed out, it was the only effective way to calibrate them. She had little real interest in Alan's obsession with ballistic-missile defense, but she was certain that the instruments they were developing had all kinds of 'real' applications in her field of interest.

Neither of them was wearing very much at the moment. Both young people cheerfully characterized themselves as nerds, and as is often the case, they had awakened feelings in one another – feelings that their more attractive college fellows would have thought not possible.

'What are you doing?' she asked.

'It's the misses we had. I think the problem's in the mirror-control code.'

'Oh?' It was *her* mirror. 'You're sure it's software?'

'Yeah.' Alan nodded. 'I have the readouts from the Flying Cloud at the office. It was focusing just fine, but it was focusing on the wrong place.'

'How long to find it?'

'Couple of weeks.' He frowned at the screen, then shut it down. 'The hell with it. If the General finds out that I'm doing this, he might never let me back in the door.'

'I keep telling you.' She wrapped her hands around the back of his neck. He leaned back, resting his head between her breasts. They were rather nice ones, he thought. For Alan Gregory it had been a remarkable discovery, how nice girls were. He'd dated occasionally in high school, but for the most part his life at West Point, then at Stony Brook, had been a monastic existence, devoted to studies and models and laboratories. When he'd met Candi, his initial interest had been in her ideas for configuring mirrors, but over coffee at the Student Union, he'd noticed in a rather clinical way that she was, well, attractive – in addition to being pretty swift with optical physics. The fact that the things they frequently discussed in bed could be understood by less than one percent of the country's population was irrelevant. *They* found it as interesting as the things that they did in bed – or almost so. There was a lot of experimentation to do there, too, and like good scientists, they'd purchased textbooks – that's how they thought of them – to explore all the possibilities. Like any new field of study, they found it exciting.

Gregory reached up to grasp Dr Long's head, and pulled her face down to his.

'I don't feel like working any more for a while.'

'Isn't it nice to have a day off?'

'Maybe I can arrange one for next week . . .'

Boris Filipovich Morozov got off the bus an hour after sunset. He and fourteen other young engineers and technicians recently assigned to Bright Star – though he didn't even know the project name yet – had been met at the Dushanbe airport by KGB personnel who'd scrupulously checked their identity papers and photographs, and on the bus ride a KGB captain had given them a security lecture serious enough to get anyone's attention. They could not discuss their work with anyone outside their station; they could not write about what they did, and could not tell anyone where they were. Their mailing address was a post-office box in Novosibiirsk – over a thousand miles away. The Captain didn't have to say that their mail would be read by the base security officers. Morozov made a mental note not to seal his envelopes. His family might be worried if they saw that his letters were being opened and resealed. Besides, he had nothing to hide. His security clearance for this posting had taken a mere four months. The KGB officers in Moscow who'd done the background check had found his background beyond reproach, and even the six interviews that he'd gone through had ended on a friendly note.

The KGB Captain finished his lecture on a lighter note as well, describing the social and sport activities at the base, and the time and place for the biweekly Party meetings, which Morozov had every intention of attending as regularly as his work allowed. Housing, the Captain went on, was still a problem. Morozov and the other new arrivals would be placed in the dormitory – the original barracks put up by the construction gangs who'd blasted the installation into the living rock. They would not be crowded, he said, and the barracks had a game room, library, and even a telescope on the roof for astronomical observation; a small astronomy club had just formed. There was hourly bus service to the main residential facility, where there was a cinema, coffee shop, and a beer bar. There were exactly thirty-one unmarried females on the base, the Captain concluded, but one of them was engaged to him, 'and any one of you who trifles with her *will be shot!*' That drew laughter. It wasn't very often that you met a KGB officer with a sense of humor.

It was dark when the bus pulled through the gate into the facility, and everyone aboard was tired. Morozov was not terribly disappointed at the housing. All the beds were two-level bunks. He was assigned the top berth in a corner. Signs on the wall demanded silence in the sleeping area, since the workers here worked three shifts around the clock. The young engineer was perfectly content to change clothes and go to sleep. He was assigned to the Directional Applications Section for a month of project orientation, after which he'd receive a permanent job assignment. He was wondering what 'directional applications' meant when he drifted off to sleep.

The nice thing about vans was that lots of people owned them, and the casual observer couldn't see who was inside, Jack thought as the white one pulled into his carport. The driver was CIA, of course, as was the security man in the right seat. He dismounted and surveyed the area for a moment before pulling the side door open. It revealed a familiar face.

'Hello, Marko,' Ryan said.

'So, this is house of spy!' Captain First Rank Marko Aleksandrovich Ramius, Soviet Navy (retired), said boisterously. His English was better, but like so many Russian émigrés he often forgot to use articles in his speech. 'No, house of helmsman!'

Jack smiled and shook his head. 'Marko, we can't talk about that.'

'Your family does not know?'

'Nobody knows. But you can relax. My family's away.'

'Understand.' Marko Ramius followed Jack into the house. On his passport, Social Security card, and Virginia driver's license he was now known as Mark Ramsay. Yet another piece of CIA originality, though it made perfect sense; you wanted people to remember their names. He was, Jack saw, a little thinner now that he was eating a less starchy diet. And tan. When they'd first met, at the forward escape trunk of the missile submarine *Red October*, Marko – Mark! – had worn the pastry-white skin of a submarine officer. Now he looked like an ad for Club Med.

'You seem tired,' 'Mark Ramsay' observed.

'They fly me around a lot. How do you like the Bahamas?'

'You see my tan, yes? White sand, sun, warm every day. Like Cuba when I went there, but nicer people.'

'AUTEC, right?' Jack asked.

'Yes, but I cannot discuss this,' Marko replied. Both men shared a look. AUTEC – Atlantic Underwater Test and Evaluation Center – was the Navy's submarine test range, where men and ships engaged in exercises called miniwars. What happened there was classified, of course. The Navy was very protective of its submarine operations. So Marko was at work developing tactics for the Navy, doubtless playing the role of a Soviet commander in the war games, lecturing, teaching. Ramius had been known as 'the Schoolmaster' in the Soviet Navy. The important things never change.

'How do you like it?'

'Tell this to nobody, but they let me be the captain of American submarine for a week – the real Captain he let me do everything, yes? I kill carrier! Yes! I kill *Forrestal*. They would be proud of me at Red Banner Northern Fleet, yes?'

Jack laughed. 'How'd the Navy like that?'

'Captain of submarine and me get very drunk. *Forrestal* Captain angry, but – good sport, yes? He join us next week and we discuss exercise. He learn something, so good for all of us.' Ramius paused. 'Where is family?'

'Cathy's visiting her father. Joe and I don't get along very well.'

'Because you are spy?' Mark/Marko asked.

'Personal reasons. Can I get you a drink?'

'Beer is good,' he replied. Ramius looked around while Jack went into the kitchen. The house's cathedral ceiling towered fifteen feet – five meters, he thought – above the lush carpeting. Everything about the house testified to the money spent to make it so. He was frowning when Ryan returned.

'Ryan, I am not fool,' he said sternly. 'CIA does not pay so good as this.'

'Do you know about the stock market?' Ryan asked with a chuckle.

'Yes, some of my money is invested there.' All of the officers from Red October had enough money salted away that they'd never need to work again.

'Well, I made a lot of money there, and then I decided to quit and do something else.'

That was a new thought for Captain Ramius. 'You are not – what is word? Greed. You have no more greed?'

'How much money does one man need?' Ryan asked rhetorically.

The Captain nodded thoughtfully. 'So, I have some questions for you.'

'Ah, business.' Marko laughed. 'This you have not forgotten!'

'In your debriefing, you mentioned that you ran an exercise in which you fired a missile, and then a missile was fired at you.'

'Yes, years ago – was 1981 . . . April, yes, it was twenty April. I command Delta-class missile submarine, and we fire two rockets from White Sea, one into Okhotsk Sea, other at Sary Shagan. We test submarine rockets, of course, but also the missile defense radar and counterbattery system – they simulated firing a missile at my submarine.'

'You said it failed.'

Marko nodded. 'Submarine rockets fly perfectly. The Sary Shagan radar work, but too slow to intercept – was computer problem, they say. They say get new computer, last thing I hear. Third part of test almost work.'

'The counterfire part. That's the first we heard of it,' Ryan noted. 'How did they actually run the test?'

'They *not* fire land rocket, of course,' Marko said. He held up a finger. 'They do this, and you understand nature of test, yes? Soviets are not so stupid as you think. Of course you know that entire Soviet border covered with radar fence. These see rocket launch and compute where submarine is – very easy thing to do. Next they call Strategic Rocket Force Headquarters. Strategic Rocket Force have regiment of old rockets on alert for this. They were ready to shoot back three minutes after detecting my missile on radar.' He stopped for a moment. 'You not have this in America?'

'No, not that I know of. But our new missiles fire from much farther away.'

'Is true, but still good things for Soviets, you see.'

'How reliable is the system?'

That drew a shrug. 'Not very. Problem is how alert the people are. In time of – how you say? – time of crisis, yes? In time of crisis, everyone is alert, and system may work some of time. But every time system works, many, many bombs do not explode in Soviet Union. Even one could save hundred thousand citizens. This is important to Soviet leadership. Hundred thousand more slaves to have after war end,' he added to show his distaste for the government of his former homeland. 'You have nothing like this in America?'

'Not that I have ever heard about,' Ryan said truthfully.

Ramius shook his head. 'They tell us you do. When we fire our rockets, then we dive deep and race at flank speed, straight line in any direction.'

'Right now I'm trying to figure out how interested the Soviet government is in copying our SDI research.'

'Interested?' Ramius snorted. 'Twenty million Russians died in Great Patriotic War. You think they want to have this happen again? I tell you, Soviets are more intelligent about this than Americans – we have harder lesson, and we learn better. Someday I tell you about my home city after war, destruction of everything. Yes, we have very good lesson in protect *Rodina*.'

That's the other thing to remember about the Russians, Jack reminded himself. It wasn't so much that they had abnormally long memories; they had things in their history that no one would forget. To expect the Soviets to forget their losses in the Second World War was as futile as asking Jews to forget the Holocaust, and just as unreasonable.

So, a little over three years ago, the Russians staged a major ABM exercise against submarine-launched ballistic missiles. The acquisition and tracking radar worked, but the system failed due to a computer problem. That was important. But –

'The reason the computer didn't work well enough – '

'That is all I know. All I can say is was honest test.'

'What do you mean?' Jack asked.

'Our first . . . yes, our original orders were to fire from known location. But the orders were changed just as submarine left dock. Eyes-only to Captain, new orders signed by aide to Defense Minister. Was Red Army colonel, I think. Do not remember name. Orders from Minister, but Colonel sign them, yes? He wanted the test to be – how you say?'

'Spontaneous?'

'Yes! Not spontaneous. Real test should be surprise. So my orders sent me to different place and said to shoot at different time. We have general aboard from Voyska PVO, and when see new orders he is banana. Very, very angry, but what kind of test is it without no surprise? American missile submarines do not call on telephone and tell Russians day that they shoot. You either are ready or not ready,' Ramius noted.

'We did not know that you were coming,' General Pokryshkin noted dryly.

Colonel Bondarenko was careful to keep his face impassive. Despite having written orders from the Defense Minister, and despite belonging to a completely different uniformed service, he was dealing with a general officer with patrons of his own in the Central Committee. But the General, too, had to be wary. Bondarenko was wearing his newest and best-tailored uniform, complete with several rows of ribbons, including two awards for bravery in Afghanistan and the special badge worn by Defense Ministry staff officers.

'Comrade General, I regret whatever inconvenience I have caused you, but I do have my orders.'

'Of course,' Pokryshkin noted with a broadening smile. He gestured to a silver tray. 'Tea?'

'Thank you.'

The General poured two cups himself instead of summoning his orderly. 'Is that a Red Banner I see? Afghanistan?'

'Yes, Comrade General, I spent some time there.'

'And how did you earn it?'

'I was attached to a *Spetznaz* unit as a special observer. We were tracking a small band of bandits. Unfortunately, they were smarter than the unit commander believed, and he allowed us to follow them into an ambush. Half the team was killed or wounded, including the unit commander.' *Who earned his death*, Bondarenko thought. 'I assumed command and called in help. The bandits withdrew before we could bring major forces to bear, but they did leave eight bodies behind.'

'How did a communications expert – '

'I volunteered. We were having difficulties with tactical communications, and I decided to take the situation in hand myself. I am not a real combat soldier, Comrade General, but there are some things you have to see for yourself. That is another concern I have with this post. We are perilously close to the Afghan border, and your security seems . . . not lax, but perhaps overly comfortable.'

Pokryshkin nodded agreement. 'The security force is

KGB, as you have doubtless noted. They report to me, but are not strictly under my orders. For early warning of possible threats, I have an arrangement with Frontal Aviation. Their aerial-reconnaissance school uses the valleys around here as a training area. A classmate of mine at Frunze had arranged coverage of this entire area. If anyone approaches this installation from Afghanistan, it's a long walk, and we'll know about it long before they get here.'

Bondarenko noted this with approval. Procurer for wizards or not, Pokryshkin hadn't forgotten everything, as too many general officers tended to do.

'So, Gennady Iosifovich, exactly what are you looking for?' the General asked. The atmosphere was somewhat milder now that both men had established their professionalism.

'The Minister wishes an appraisal of the effectiveness and reliability of your systems.'

'Your knowledge of lasers?' Pokryshkin asked with a raised eyebrow.

'I am familiar with the applications side. I was on the team with Academician Goremykin that developed the new laser communications systems.'

'Really? We have some of them here.'

'I didn't know that,' Bondarenko said.

'Yes. We use them in our guard towers, and to link our laboratory facilities with the shops. It's easier than stringing telephone lines, and is more secure. Your invention has proven very useful indeed, Gennady Iosifovich. Well. You know our mission here, of course.'

'Yes, Comrade General. How close are you to your goal?'

'We have a major system test coming up in three days.'

'Oh?' Bondarenko was very surprised by that.

'We received permission to run it only yesterday. Perhaps the Ministry hasn't been fully informed. Can you stay for it?'

'I wouldn't miss it.'

'Excellent.' General Pokryshkin rose. 'Come, let's go to see my wizards.'

The sky was clear and blue, the deeper blue that comes from being above most of the atmosphere. Bondarenko was surprised to see that the General did his own driving in a UAZ-469, the Soviet equivalent of a jeep.

'You do not have to ask, Colonel. I do my own driving because we do not have room up here for unnecessary personnel, and – well, I was a fighter pilot. Why should I trust my life to some beardless boy who barely knows how to shift gears? How do you like our roads?'

Not at all, Bondarenko didn't say as the General speeded down a slope. The road was barely five meters wide, with a precipitous drop on the passenger side of the car.

'You should try this when it's icy!' The General laughed. 'We've been lucky on weather lately. Last autumn we had nothing but rain for two weeks. Most unusual here; the monsoon's supposed to drop all the water on India, but the winter has been agreeably dry and clear.' He shifted gears as the road bottomed out. A truck was coming from the other direction, and Bondarenko did all he could not to cringe as the jeep's right-side tires spun through rocks at the road's uneven edge. Pokryshkin was having some fun with him, but that was to be expected. The truck swept past with perhaps a meter of clearance, and the General moved back to the center of the black-topped road. He shifted gears again as they came to an upslope.

'We don't even have room for a proper office here – for me at any rate,' Pokryshkin noted. 'The academicians have priority.'

Bondarenko had seen only one of the guard towers that morning as he ran around the residential facility, and as the jeep climbed the last few meters, the Bright Star test area became visible.

There were three security checkpoints. General Pokryshkin stopped his vehicle and showed his pass at each of them.

'The guard towers?' Bondarenko asked.

'All manned round the clock. It is hard on the *chekisti*. I had to install electric heaters in the towers.' The General chuckled. 'We have more electrical power here than we know how to use. We originally had guard dogs running between the fences, too, but we had to stop that. Two weeks ago several of them froze to death. I didn't think that would work. We still have a few, but they walk about with the guards. I'd just as soon get rid of them.'

'But – '

'More mouths to feed,' Pokryshkin explained. 'As soon as it snows, we have to bring food in by helicopter. To keep guard dogs happy, they must eat meat. Do you know what it does for camp morale to have dogs on a meat diet when our scientists don't have enough? Dogs aren't worth the trouble. The KGB commander agrees. He's trying to get permission to dispense with them altogether. We have starlight-scopes in all the towers. We can see an intruder long before a dog would smell or hear one.'

'How big is your guard force?'

'A reinforced rifle company. One hundred sixteen officers and men, commanded by a lieutenant colonel. There are at least twenty guards on duty round the clock. Half here, half on the other hill. Right here, two men in each of the towers at all times, plus four on roving patrol, and of course the people at the vehicle checkpoints. The area is secure, Colonel. A full rifle company with heavy weapons on top of this mountain – to be sure, we had a *Spetznaz* team run an assault exercise last October. The umpires ruled them all dead before they got to within four hundred meters of our perimeter. One of them almost was, as a matter of fact. One pink-faced lieutenant damned near fell off the mountain.' Pokryshkin turned. 'Satisfied?'

'Yes, Comrade General. Please excuse my overly cautious nature.'

'You didn't get those pretty ribbons from being a coward,' the General observed lightly. 'I am always open to new ideas. If you have something to say, my door is never locked.'

Bondarenko decided that he was going to like General Pokryshkin. He was far enough from Moscow not to act like an officious ass, and unlike most generals, he evidently didn't see a halo in the mirror when he shaved. Perhaps there was hope for this installation after all. Filitov would be pleased.

'It's like being a mouse, with a hawk in the sky,' Abdul observed.

'Then do what a mouse does,' the Archer replied evenly. 'Stay in the shadows.'

He looked up to see the An-26. It was five thousand meters overhead, and the whine of its turbine engines barely reached them. Too far for a missile, which was unfortunate. Other *mudjaheddin* missileers had shot the Antonovs down, but not the Archer. You could kill as many as forty Russians that way. And the Soviets were learning to use the converted transports for ground surveillance. That made life harder on the guerrillas.

The two men were following a narrow path along the side of yet another mountain, and the sun hadn't reached them yet, though most of the valley was fully lit under the cloudless winter sky. The bombed-out ruins of a village lay next to a modest river. Perhaps two hundred people had lived there once, until the high-altitude bombers came. He could see the craters, laid out in uneven lines two or three kilometers in length. The bombs had marched through the valley, and those who had not been killed were gone – to Pakistan – leaving only emptiness behind. No food to be shared with the freedom fighters, no hospitality, not even a mosque in which to pray. Part of the Archer still wondered why war had to be so cruel. It was one thing for men to fight one another; there was honor in that, at times enough to be shared with a worthy enemy. But the Russians didn't fight that way. *And they call us savages.* . . .

So much was gone. What he had once been, the hopes for the future he'd once held, all of his former life slipped further away with the passage of every day. It seemed that he only thought of them when asleep now – and when he awoke, the dreams of a peaceful, contented life wafted away from his grasp like the morning mist. But even those dreams were fading away. He could still see his wife's face, and his daughter's, and his son's, but they were like photographs now, flat, lifeless, cruel reminders of times that would not return. But at least they gave his life purpose. When he felt pity for his victims, when he wondered if Allah really approved of what he did – of the things that had sickened him at first – he could close his eyes for a moment and remind himself why the screams of dying Russians were as sweet to his ears as the passionate cries of his wife.

'Going away,' Abdul noted.

The Archer turned to look. The sun glinted off the plane's vertical rudder as it passed beyond the far ridges. Even if he'd been atop that rocky edge, the An-26 would have been too high. The Russians weren't fools. They flew no lower than they had to. If he really wanted to get one of those, he'd have to get close to an airfield . . . or perhaps come up with a new tactic. That was a thought. The Archer started ordering the problem in his mind as he walked along the endless rocky path.

'Will it work?' Morozov asked.

'That is the purpose of the test, to see if it works,' the senior engineer explained patiently. He remembered when he'd been young and impatient. Morozov had real potential. His documents from the university had shown that clearly enough. The son of a factory worker in Kiev, his intelligence and hard work had won him an appointment at the Soviet Union's most prestigious school, where he had won the highest honors – enough to be excused from military service, which was unusual enough for someone without political connections.

'And this is new optical coating . . .' Morozov looked at the mirror from a distance of only a few centimeters. Both men wore overalls, masks, and gloves so that they would not damage the reflecting surface of the number-four mirror.

'As you have guessed, that is one element of the test.' The engineer turned. 'Ready!'

'Get clear,' a technician called.

They climbed down a ladder fixed to the side of the pillar, then across the gap to the concrete ring that surrounded the hole.

'Pretty deep,' he observed.

'Yes, we have to determine how effective our vibration-isolation measures are.' The senior man was worried about that. He heard a jeep motor and turned to see the base commander lead another man into the laser building. Another visitor from Moscow, he judged. *How do we ever get work done with all those Party hacks hanging over our shoulders?*

'Have you met General Pokryshkin?' he asked Morozov.

'No. What sort of man is he?'

'I've met worse. Like most people, he thinks the lasers are the important part. Lesson number one, Boris Filipovich: it's the mirrors that are the important part – that and the computers. The lasers are useless unless we can focus their energy on a specific point in space.' This lesson told Morozov which part of the project came under this man's authority, but the newly certified engineer already knew the real lesson – the entire system had to work perfectly. One faulty segment would convert the most expensive piece of hardware in the Soviet Union into a collection of curious toys.

5

Eye of the Snake –
Face of the Dragon

The converted Boeing 767 had two names. Originally known as the Airborne Optical Adjunct, it was now called Cobra Belle, which at least sounded better. The aircraft was little more than a platform for as large an infrared telescope as could be made to fit in the wide-bodied airliner. The engineers had cheated somewhat, of course, giving the fuselage an ungainly humpback immediately aft of the flight deck that extended half its length, and the 767 did look rather like a snake that had just swallowed something large enough to choke on.

What was even more remarkable about the aircraft, however, was the lettering on its vertical tail: U.S. ARMY . The fact, which infuriated the Air Force, resulted from unusual prescience or obstinacy on the part of the Army, which even in the 1970s had never shut down its research into ballistic- missile defense, and whose 'hobby shop' (as such places were known) had invented the infrared sensors on the AOA.

But it was now part of an Air Force program whose cover-all name was Cobra. It worked in coordination with the Cobra Dane radar at Shemya, and often flew in conjunction with an aircraft called Cobra Ball – a converted 707 – because Cobra was the code name for a family of systems aimed at tracking Soviet missiles. The Army was smugly satisfied that the Air Force needed its help, though wary of ongoing attempts to steal its program.

The flight crew went through its checklist casually, since

they had plenty of time. They were from Boeing. So far the Army had successfully resisted attempts by the Air Force to get its own people on the flight deck. The copilot, who was ex-Air Force, ran his finger down the paper list of things to do, calling them off in a voice neither excited nor bored while the pilot and flight engineer/navigator pushed the buttons, checked the gauges, and otherwise made their aircraft ready for a safe flight.

The worst part of the mission was the weather on the ground. Shemya, one of the western Aleutians, is a small island, roughly four miles long by two wide, whose highest point is a mere two hundred thirty-eight feet above the slate-gray sea. What passed for average weather in the Aleutians would close most reputable airports, and what they called bad weather here made the Boeing crew wish for Amtrak. It was widely believed on the base that the only reason the Russians sent their ICBM tests to the Sea of Okhotsk was to make life as miserable as possible for the Americans who monitored them. Today the weather was fairly decent. You could see almost to the far end of the runway, where the blue lights were surrounded by little globes of mist. Like most flyers, the pilot preferred daylight, but in winter that was the exception here. He counted his blessings: there was supposed to be a ceiling at about fifteen hundred feet, and it wasn't raining yet. The crosswinds were a problem, too, but the wind never blew where you wanted up here – or more correctly, the people who laid out the runway hadn't known or cared that wind was a factor in flying airplanes.

'Shemya Tower, this is Charlie Bravo, ready to taxi.'

'Charlie Bravo, you are cleared to taxi. Winds are two-five-zero at fifteen.' The tower didn't have to say that Cobra Belle was number one in line. At the moment, the 767 was the only aircraft on the base. Supposedly in California for equipment tests, it had been rushed here only twenty hours earlier.

'Roger. Charlie Bravo is rolling.' Ten minutes later the Boeing started down the runway, to begin what was expected to be yet another routine mission.

Twenty minutes later the AOA reached its cruising altitude of 45,000 feet. The ride was the same smooth glide known by airline passengers, but instead of downing their first drinks and making their dinner selections, the people aboard this aircraft had already unbuckled and gone to work.

There were instruments to activate, computers to recycle, data links to set up, and voice links to check out. The aircraft was equipped with every communications system known to man, and would have had a psychic aboard if that Defense Department program – there was one – had progressed as well as originally hoped. The man commanding it was an artilleryman with a masters in astronomy, of all things, from the University of Texas. His last command had been of a Patriot missile battery in Germany. While most men looked at airplanes and wished to fly them, his interest had always been in shooting them out of the sky. He felt the same way about ballistic missiles, and had helped develop the modification that enabled the Patriot missile to kill other missiles in addition to Soviet aircraft. It also gave him an intimate familiarity with the instruments used to track missiles in flight.

The mission book in the Colonel's hands was a facsimile printout from the Washington headquarters of the Defense Intelligence Agency (DIA) telling him that in four hours and sixteen minutes the Soviets would conduct a test firing of the SS-25 ICBM. The book didn't say how DIA had obtained that information, though the Colonel knew that it wasn't from reading an ad in *Izvestia*. Cobra Belle's mission was to monitor the firing, intercept all telemetry transmissions from the missile's test instruments, and, most important, to take pictures of the warheads in flight. The data collected would later be analyzed to determine the performance of the missile, and most particularly the accuracy of its warhead delivery, a matter of the greatest interest to Washington.

115

As mission commander, the Colonel didn't have a great deal to do. His control board was a panel of colored lights that showed the status of various onboard systems. Since the AOA was a fairly new item in the inventory, everything aboard worked reasonably well. Today the only thing currently 'down' was a backup data link, and a technician was working to put that back on line while the Colonel sipped his coffee. It was something of an effort for him to look interested while he had nothing in particular to do, but if he started looking bored, it would set a bad example for his people. He reached in the zippered sleeve pocket of his flight suit for a butterscotch candy. These were healthier than the cigarettes he'd smoked as a lieutenant, though not so good for his teeth, the base dentist liked to point out. The Colonel sucked on the candy for five minutes before he decided that he had to do *something*. He unstrapped from his command chair and went to the flight deck forward.

'Morning, people.' It was now 0004-Lima, or 12:04 A.M., local time.

'Good morning, Colonel,' the pilot replied for his crew. 'Everything working in back, sir?'

'So far. How's the weather in the patrol area?'

'Solid undercast at twelve-to-fifteen thousand,' the navigator answered, holding up a satellite photograph. 'Winds three-two-five at thirty knots. Our nav systems check out with the track from Shemya,' she added. Ordinarily the 767 operates with a crew of two flight officers. Not this one. Since the Korean Air 007 flight had been shot down by the Soviets, every flight over the Western Pacific was especially careful with its navigation. This was doubly true of Cobra Belle; the Soviets hated all intelligence-gathering platforms. They never went within fifty miles of Soviet territory, nor into the Russian Air Defense Identification Zone, but twice the Soviets had sent fighters to let the AOA know they cared.

'Well, we aren't supposed to get very close,' the Colonel observed. He leaned between the pilot and copilot to look out the windows. Both turbofans were performing well. He would have preferred a four-engined aircraft for extended over-water flight, but that hadn't been his decision. The navigator raised an eyebrow at the Colonel's interest and got a pat on the shoulder by way of apology. It was time to leave.

'Time to observation area?'

'Three hours, seventeen minutes, sir; three hours thirty-nine minutes to orbit point.'

'Guess I have time for a nap,' the Colonel said on his way to the door. He closed it and walked aft, past the telescope assembly to the main cabin. Why was it that the crews doing the flying now were so damned young? They probably think I *need* a nap instead of being bored to death.

Forward, the pilot and copilot shared a look. *Old fart doesn't trust us to fly the goddamned airplane, does he?* They adjusted themselves in their seats, letting their eyes scan for the blinking lights of other aircraft while the autopilot controlled the aircraft.

Morozov was dressed like the other scientists in the control room, in a white laboratory coat adorned with a security pass. He was still going through orientation, and his assignment to the mirror-control team was probably temporary, though he was beginning to appreciate just how important this part of the program was. In Moscow, he'd learned how lasers work, and done some impressive lab work with experimental models, but he'd never truly appreciated the fact that when the energy came out the front of the instruments the task had only begun. Besides, Bright Star had already made its breakthrough in laser power.

'Recycle,' the senior engineer said into his headset.

They were testing the system calibration by tracking their mirrors on a distant star. It didn't even matter which star. They picked one at random for each test.

'Makes one hell of a telescope, doesn't it?' the engineer noted, looking at his TV screen.

'You were concerned about the stability of the system. Why?'

'We require a very high degree of accuracy, as you might imagine. We've never actually tested the complete system. We can track stars easily enough, but . . .' He shrugged. 'This is still a young program, my friend. Just like you.'

'Why don't you use radar to select a satellite and track on that?'

'That's a fine question!' The older man chuckled. 'I've asked that myself. It has to do with arms-control agreements or some such nonsense. For the moment, they tell us, it is enough that they feed us coordinates of our targets via landline. We do not have to acquire them ourselves. Rubbish!' he concluded.

Morozov leaned back in his chair to look around. On the other side of the room, the laser-control team were shuffling about busily, with a flock of uniformed soldiers behind them whispering to themselves. Next he checked the clock – sixty-three minutes until the test began. One by one, the technicians were drifting off to the rest room. He didn't feel the need, nor did the section chief, who finally pronounced himself satisfied with his systems, and placed everything on standby.

At 22,300 miles over the Indian Ocean, an American Defense Support Program satellite hung in geosynchronous orbit over a fixed point on the Indian Ocean. Its huge cassegrain-focus Schmidt telescope was permanently aimed at the Soviet Union, and its mission was to provide first warning that Russian missiles had been launched at the United States. Its data was downlinked via Alice Springs, Australia, to various installations in the United States. Viewing conditions were excellent at the moment. Almost the entire visible hemisphere of the earth was in darkness, and the cold, wintry ground easily showed the smallest heat source in precise definition.

The technicians who monitored the DSPS in Sunnyvale, California, routinely amused themselves by counting industrial facilities. There was the Lenin Steel Plant at Kazan, and there was the big refinery outside Moscow, and there –

'Heads up,' a sergeant announced. 'We have an energy boom at Plesetsk. Looks like one bird lifting off from the ICBM test facility.'

The Major who had the duty this night immediately got on the phone to 'Crystal Palace,' the headquarters of the North American Aerospace Defense Command – NORAD – under Cheyenne Mountain, Colorado, to make sure that they were copying the satellite data. They were, of course.

'That's the missile launch they told us about,' he said to himself.

As they watched, the bright image of the missile rocket exhaust started turning to an easterly heading as the ICBM arced over into the ballistic flight path that gave the missile its name. The Major had the characteristics of all Soviet missiles memorized. If this were an SS-25, the first stage would separate right about . . . now.

The screen bloomed bright before their eyes as a fireball six hundred yards in diameter appeared. The orbiting camera did the mechanical equivalent of a blink, altering its sensitivity after its sensors were dazzled by the sudden burst of heat energy. Three seconds later it was able to track on a cloud of heated fragments, curving down to earth.

'Looks like that one blew,' the sergeant observed unnecessarily. 'Back to the drawing board, Ivan. . . .'

'Still haven't licked the second-stage problem,' the Major added. He wondered briefly what the problem was, but didn't care all that much. The Soviets had rushed the -25 into production and had already begun deploying them on railcars for mobility, but they were still having problems with the solid-fuel bird. The Major was glad for it. It didn't take a great degree of unreliability in missiles to make their use a very chancy thing. And that uncertainty was still the best guarantee of peace.

119

'Crystal Palace, we call that test a failure at fifty-seven seconds after launch. Is Cobra Belle up to monitor the test?'

'That's affirmative,' the officer on the other end replied. 'We'll call them off.'

'Right. 'Night, Jeff.'

Aboard Cobra Belle, ten minutes later, the mission commander acknowledged the message and cut off the radio channel. He checked his watch and sighed. He didn't feel like heading back to Shemya yet. The Captain in charge of the mission hardware suggested that they could always use the time to calibrate their instruments. The Colonel thought about that one and nodded approval. The aircraft and crew were new enough that everyone needed the practice. The camera system was put in the MTI-mode. A computer that registered all the energy sources the telescope found began to search only for targets that were moving. The technicians on the screens watched as the Moving-Target Indicator rapidly eliminated the stars and began to find a few low-altitude satellites and fragments of orbiting space junk. The camera system was sensitive enough to detect the heat of a human body at a range of one thousand miles, and soon they had their choice of targets. The camera locked on them one by one and made its photographic images in digital code on computer tape. Though mainly a practice drill, this data would automatically be forwarded to NORAD, where it would update the register of information of orbiting objects.

'The power-output breakthrough you've made is breathtaking,' Colonel Bondarenko said quietly.

'Yes,' General Pokryshkin agreed. 'Amazing how that happens, isn't it? One of my wizards notices something and tells another, who tells another, and the third says something that works its way back to the first, and so on. We have the best minds in the country here, and still the discovery process seems about as scientific as stubbing your toe on a chair! That's the odd part. But that's what makes it so exciting. Gennady Iosifovich, this is the most exciting thing I've done since I won my wings! This place will change the world. After thirty years of work, we may have discovered the basis of a system to protect the *Rodina* against enemy missiles.'

Bondarenko thought that was an overstatement, but the test would demonstrate just how much of an overstatement. Pokryshkin was the perfect man for this job, however. The former fighter pilot was a genius at directing the efforts of the scientists and engineers, many of whom had egos as large as a battle tank, though far more fragile. When he had to bully, he bullied. When he had to cajole, he cajoled. He was by turns the father, uncle, and brother to all of them. It took a man with a large Russian heart to do that. The Colonel guessed that commanding fighter pilots had been good training for this task, and Pokryshkin must have been a brilliant regimental commander. The balance between pressure and encouragement was so hard to strike, but this man managed it as easily as breathing. Bondarenko was watching how he did it very closely. There were lessons here that he could use in his own career.

The control room was separate from the laser building itself, and too small for the men and equipment it held. There were over a hundred engineers – sixty doctorates in physics – and even those called technicians could have taught the sciences at any university in the Soviet Union. They sat or hovered at their consoles. Most smoked, and the air-conditioning system needed to cool the computers struggled mightily to keep the air clear. Everywhere were digital counters. Most showed the time: Greenwich Mean Time, by which the satellites were tracked; local time; and, of course, Moscow Standard time. Other counters showed the precise coordinates of the target satellite, Cosmos-1810, which bore the international satellite designator 1986-102A. It had been launched from the Cosmodrome at Tyuratam on December 26, 1986, and was still up because it had failed to deorbit with its film. Telemetry showed that its electrical systems were still functioning, though its orbit was slowly decaying, with a current perigee – the lowest point in its orbit – of one hundred eighty kilometers. It was now approaching perigee, directly over Bright Star.

'Powering up!' the chief engineer called over the intercom headsets. 'Final system check.'

'Tracking cameras on line,' one technician reported. The wall speakers filled the room with his voice. 'Cryogen flows nominal.'

'Mirror tracking controls in automatic mode,' reported the engineer sitting next to Morozov. The young engineer was on the edge of his swivel chair, eyes locked to a television screen that was as yet blank.

'Computer sequencing in automatic,' a third said.

Bondarenko sipped at his tea, trying and failing to calm himself. He'd always wanted to be present for a space rocket launch, but never been able to arrange it. This was the same sort of thing. The excitement was overpowering. All around him machines and men were uniting into a single entity to make something happen as one after another announced the readiness of himself and his equipment. Finally:

'All laser systems are fully powered and on-line.'

'We are ready to shoot,' the chief engineer concluded the litany. All eyes turned to the right side of the building, where the team on the tracking cameras had their instruments trained on a section of the horizon to the northwest. A white dot appeared, coming upward into the black dome of the night sky. . . .

'Target acquisition!'

Next to Morozov, the engineer lifted his hands from the control panel to ensure that he wouldn't inadvertently touch a button. The 'automatic' light was blinking on and off.

Two hundred meters away, the six mirrors arrayed around the laser building twisted and turned together, coming almost vertical with the ground as they tracked after a target sitting above the jagged, mountainous horizon. On the next knoll over, the four mirrors of the imaging array did the same. Outside, alarm klaxons sounded, and rotating hazard lights warned everyone in the open to turn away from the laser building.

On the TV screen next to the chief engineer's console sat a photograph of Cosmos-1810. As the final assurance against mistakes, he and three others had to make positive visual identification of their target.

'That one's Cosmos-1810,' the Captain was telling the Colonel aboard Cobra Belle. 'Broken recon bird. Must have had a reentry-motor failure – it didn't come back down when they told it to. It's in degenerating orbit, should have about four more months left. The satellite's still sending routine telemetry data out. Nothing important, far as we can tell, just telling Ivan that it's still up there.'

'The solar panels must still be working,' the Colonel observed. The heat came from internal power.

'Yeah. I wonder why they didn't just turn it off . . . Anyway, the onboard temperature reads out at, oh, fifteen degrees Celsius or so. Nice cold background to read it against. In sunlight we might not have been able to pick out the difference between onboard and solar heating. . . .'

The mirrors in the laser-transmitter array tracked slowly, but the movement was discernible on the six television screens that monitored them. A low-power laser reflected off one mirror, reaching out to find the target . . . In addition to aiming the whole system, it made a high-resolution image on the command console. The identity of the target was now confirmed. The chief engineer turned the key that 'enabled' the entire system. Bright Star was now fully out of human hands, controlled wholly by the site's main computer complex.

'There's target lock,' Morozov observed to his senior.

The engineer nodded agreement. His range readout was rapidly dropping as the satellite came toward them, circling its way to destruction at 18,000 miles per hour. The image they had was of a slightly oblong blob, white with internal heat against a sky devoid of warmth. It was exactly in the center of the targeting reticle, like a white oval in a gunsight.

They didn't hear anything, of course. The laser building was fully insulated against temperature and sound. Nor did they see anything on ground level. But, watching the television screens in the control building, a hundred men balled hands into fists at the same instant.

'What the hell!' the Captain exclaimed. The image of Cosmos-1810 suddenly went as bright as the sun. The computer instantly adjusted its sensitivity, but for several seconds failed to keep pace with the change in the target's temperature.

'What in hell hit . . . Sir, that can't be internal heat.' The Captain punched up a command on his keyboard and got a digital readout of the satellite's apparent temperature. Infrared radiation is a fourth-power function. The heat given off by an object is the *square of the square* of its temperature. 'Sir, the target temperature went from fifteen-C to . . . looks like eighteen hundred-C in under two seconds. Still climbing . . . wait, it's dropping – no, it's climbing again. Rate of rise is irregular, almost like . . . Now it's dropping. What in the hell was that?'

To his left, the Colonel started punching buttons on his communications console, activating an encrypted satellite link to Cheyenne Mountain. When he spoke, it was in the matter-of-fact tone that professional soldiers save for only the worst nightmares. The Colonel knew exactly what he'd just seen.

'Crystal Palace, this is Cobra Belle. Stand by to copy a Superflash message.'

'Standing by.'

'We have a high-energy event. I say again, we are

124

tracking a high-energy event. Cobra Belle declares a Dropshot. Acknowledge.' He turned to the Captain, and his face was pale.

At NORAD headquarters, the senior watch officer had quickly to check his memory to remember what a Dropshot was. Two seconds later, a 'Jesus' was spoken into his headset. Then: 'Cobra Belle, we acknowledge your last. We acknowledge your Dropshot. Stand by while we get moving here. Jesus,' he said again, and turned to his deputy. 'Transmit a Dropshot Alert to the NMCC and tell them to stand by for hard data. Find Colonel Welch and get him in here.' The watch officer next lifted a phone and punched the code for his ultimate boss, Commander in Chief of North American Aerospace Defense Command, CINC-NORAD.

'Yes,' a gruff voice said over the phone.

'General, this is Colonel Henriksen. Cobra Belle has declared a Dropshot Alert. They say they have just seen a high-energy event.'

'Have you informed NMCC?'

'Yes, sir, and we're calling Doug Welch in also.'

'Do you have their data yet?'

'It'll be ready when you get here.'

'Very well, Colonel, I'm on the way. Get a bird up to Shemya to fly that Army guy down.'

The Colonel aboard Cobra Belle was now talking to his communications officer, ordering him to send everything they had via digital to NORAD and Sunnyvale. This was accomplished in under five minutes. Next the mission commander told the flight crew to return to Shemya. They still had enough fuel for two more hours of patrolling, but he figured that nothing else would be happening tonight. What had taken place to this point was enough. The colonel had just had the privilege of witnessing something that few men in human history ever saw. He had just seen the world change, and unlike most men, he understood the significance of it. It was an honor, he told himself, that he would just as soon have never seen.

'Captain, they got there first.' *Dear God.*

Jack Ryan was just about to take the cloverleaf exit off I-495 when his car phone rang.

'Yes?'

'We need you back here.'

'Right.' The line clicked off. Jack took the exit and stayed in the curb lane, continuing to take another of the sweeping cloverleaf exits back onto the Washington Beltway, and back to CIA. It never failed. He'd taken the afternoon off to meet with the SEC people. It had turned out that the company officers had been cleared of any wrong-doing, and that cleared him, too – or would, if the SEC investigators ever closed their file. He'd hoped to call it a day and drive home. Ryan grumbled as he headed back toward Virginia, wondering what today's crisis was.

Major Gregory and three members of his software team were all standing by a blackboard, diagramming the flow of their mirror-control program package when a sergeant entered the room.

'Major, you're wanted on the phone.'

'I'm busy; can it wait?'

'It's General Parks, sir.'

'His master's voice,' Al Gregory grumbled. He tossed the chalk to the nearest man and walked out of the room. He was on the phone in a minute.

'There's a helicopter on its way to pick you up,' the General said without any pleasantries.

'Sir, we're trying to nail down – '

'There'll be a Lear waiting for you at Kirtland. Not enough time to get you here on a commercial bird. You won't need to pack. Get moving, Major!'

'Yessir.'

*

'What went wrong?' Morozov asked. The engineer stared at his console, an angry frown on his face.

'Thermal blooming. Damn! I thought we'd put that one behind us.'

Across the room, the low-powered laser system was making another image of the target. The monocolor image was like a close-up black-and-white photograph, though what would have been black was maroon instead. The television technicians made up a split-screen image to compare before and after.

'No holes,' Pokryshkin noted sourly.

'So what?' Bondarenko said in surprise. 'My God, man, you melted the thing! That looks like it was dipped in a ladle of molten steel.' And indeed it did. What had been flat surfaces were now rippled from the intense heat that was still radiating away. The solar cells arrayed on the body of the satellite – which were designed to absorb light energy – appeared to be burned off entirely. On closer inspection, the entire satellite body was distorted from the energy that had blasted it.

Pokryshkin nodded, but his expression hadn't changed. 'We were supposed to have chopped a hole right through it. If we can do that, it would look as though a piece of orbiting space junk had impacted the satellite. That's the kind of energy concentration we were looking for.'

'But you can now destroy any American satellite you wish!'

'Bright Star wasn't built to destroy satellites, Colonel. We can already do that easily enough.'

And Bondarenko got the message. Bright Star had, in fact, been built for that specific purpose, but the power breakthrough that had justified the funding for the installation exceeded expectations by a factor of four, and Pokryshkin wanted to make two leaps at once, to demonstrate an antisatellite capability *and* a system that could be adapted to ballistic-missile defense. This was an ambitious man, though not in the usual sense.

Bondarenko set that aside and thought about what he'd

seen. What had gone wrong? It must have been thermal blooming. As the laser beams chopped through the air, they'd transferred a fractional amount of their power as heat in the atmosphere. This had roiled the air, disturbing the optical path, moving the beam on and off the target and also spreading the beam wider than its intended diameter.

But despite that, it had still been powerful enough to melt metal one hundred eighty kilometers away! the Colonel told himself. This was no failure. It was a giant leap toward a wholly new technology.

'Any damage to the system?' the General asked the project director.

'None, otherwise we'd not have gotten the follow-up image. It would appear that our atmospheric-compensation measures are sufficient for the imaging beam but not for the high-power transmission. Half a success, Comrade General.'

'Yes.' Pokryshkin rubbed his eyes for a moment and spoke more firmly. 'Comrades, we have demonstrated great progress tonight, but there is still more work to be done.'

'And that's my job,' Morozov's neighbor said. 'We'll solve this son of a bitch!'

'Do you need another man for your team?'

'It's part mirrors and part computers. How much do you know about those?'

'That is for you to decide. When do we begin?'

'Tomorrow. It'll take twelve hours for the telemetry people to organize their data. I'm going to catch the next bus back to my flat and have a drink. My family is away for another week. Care to join me?'

'What do you think that was?' Abdul asked.

They had just gotten to the top of a ridge when the meteor had appeared. At least, it had looked like a meteor's fiery track across the sky at first. But the thin golden line had hung there, and actually marched upward – very quickly, but it had been discernible.

A thin golden line, the Archer thought. The air itself had glowed. What made the air do that? He forgot where and who he now was for a moment, thinking back to his university days. *Heat* made air do that. Only heat. When a meteor came down, the friction of its passage . . . but this line could not have been a meteor. Even if the upward stroke had been an illusion – and he wasn't sure of that; eyes could play tricks – the golden line had lasted for nearly five seconds. Perhaps longer, the Archer reflected. Your mind couldn't measure time either. Hmph. He sat down abruptly and pulled out his note pad. The CIA man had given him that and told him to keep a diary of events. A useful thing to do; it hadn't ever occurred to him. He wrote down the time, date, place, and approximate direction. In a few more days he'd be heading back to Pakistan, and perhaps the CIA man would find this interesting.

6

One if by Land

It was dark when he arrived. Gregory's driver came off the George Washington Parkway toward the Pentagon's Mall entrance. The guard raised the gate, allowing the nondescript government Ford – the Pentagon was buying Fords this year – to proceed up the ramp, loop around the handful of parked cars, and drop him off at the steps right behind a shuttle bus. Gregory knew the routine well enough: show the guard the pass, walk through the metal detector, then down the corridor filled with state flags, past the cafeteria, and down the ramp to the shopping arcade lit and decorated in the style of a 12th-century dungeon. In fact, Gregory had played Dungeons and Dragons in high school, and his first trip to the dreary polygon of a building had convinced him that the authors' inspiration had come from this very place.

The Strategic Defense Initiative Office was beneath the Pentagon's shopping concourse (its entrance, in fact, directly under the pastry shop), a space about a thousand feet long that had previously been the bus and taxi stand – before the advent of car bombs had persuaded the nation's defense community that automobiles were not all that fine a thing to have under the E-ring. This portion of the building, therefore, was the newest and most secure office – for the nation's newest and least secure military program. Here Gregory took out his other pass. He showed it to the four people at the security desk, then held it against the wall panel that interrogated its electromagnetic coding and decided that the Major could enter. This took him through a waiting room to double glass doors. He smiled at the

130

receptionist as he went through, then at General Parks's secretary. She nodded back, but was annoyed to be staying so late and was not in a smiling mood.

Neither was Lieutenant General Bill Parks. His spacious office included a desk, a low table for coffee and intimate talks, and a larger conference table. The walls were covered with framed photographs of various space activities, along with numerous models of real and imagined space vehicles . . . and weapons. Parks was usually a genial man. A former test pilot, he'd marched through a career so accomplished that one would expect a bluff-hearty handshaker to have done it. Instead, Parks was an almost monkish person, with a smile that was at once engagingly shy and quietly intense. His many ribbons did not adorn his short-sleeved shirt, only a miniature of his command-pilot's wings. He didn't have to impress people with what he'd done. He could do so with what he was. Parks was one of the brightest people in government, certainly in the top ten, perhaps in the top one. Gregory saw that the General had company tonight.

'We meet again, Major,' Ryan said, turning. In his hands was a ring binder of perhaps two hundred pages that he was halfway through.

Gregory came to attention – for Parks – and reported-as-ordered, sir.

'How was the flight?'

'Super. Sir, is the soda machine in the same place? I'm a little dried out.'

Parks grinned for half a second. 'Go ahead, we're not in that much of a hurry.'

'You have to love the kid,' the General said after the door closed behind him.

'I wonder if his mom knows what he's doing after school.' Ryan chuckled, then turned serious. 'He hasn't seen any of this yet, right?'

'No, we didn't have time, and the Colonel from the Cobra Belle won't be here for another five hours.'

Jack nodded. That was why the only CIA people here

were himself and Art Graham from the satellite unit. Everyone else would get a decent night's sleep while they prepared the full briefing for tomorrow morning. Parks could have skipped it himself and left the work to his senior scientists, but he wasn't that sort of man. The more Ryan saw of Parks, the more he liked him. Parks fulfilled the first definition of a leader. He was a man with a vision – and it was a vision with which Ryan agreed. Here was a senior man in uniform who hated nuclear weapons. That wasn't terribly unusual – people in uniform tend to be rather tidy, and nuclear weapons make for a very untidy world. Quite a few soldiers, sailors, and airmen had swallowed their opinions and built careers around weapons that they hoped would never be used. Parks had spent the last ten years of his career trying to find a way to eliminate them. Jack liked people who tried to swim against the tide. Moral courage was more rare a commodity than the physical kind, a fact as true of the military profession as any other.

Gregory reappeared with a can of Coca-Cola from a machine near the door. Gregory didn't like coffee. It was time for work.

'What gives, sir?'

'We have a videotape from Cobra Belle. They were up to monitor a Soviet ICBM test. Their bird – it was an SS-25 – blew, but the mission commander decided to stay up and play with his toys. This is what he saw.' The General lifted the remote-control for the VCR and thumbed the Play button.

'That's Cosmos-1810,' Art Graham said, handing over a photograph. 'It's a recon bird that went bad on them.'

'Infrared picture on the TV, right?' Gregory asked, sipping at his Coke. 'God!'

What had been a single dot of light blossomed like an exploding star in a science-fiction movie. But this wasn't science-fiction. The picture changed as the computerized imaging system fought to keep up with the energy burst. At the bottom of the screen a digital display appeared, showing the apparent temperature of the glowing satellite.

132

In a few seconds the image faded, and again the computer had had to adjust to keep track on the Cosmos.

There was a second or two of static on the screen, then a new image began to form.

'This is ninety minutes old. The satellite went over Hawaii a few orbits later,' Graham said. 'We have cameras there to eyeball the Russian satellites. Look at the shot I gave you.'

'"Before" and "after", right?' Gregory's eyes flicked from one image to another. 'Solar panels are gone . . . wow. What's the body of the satellite made of?'

'Aluminum, for the most part,' Graham said. 'The Russians go in for ruggeder construction than we do. The internal frames may be made of steel, but more likely titanium or magnesium.'

'That gives us a top-end figure for the energy transfer,' Gregory said. 'They killed the bird. They got it hot enough to fry the solar cells right off, and probably enough to disrupt the electrical circuitry inside. What height was it at?'

'One hundred eighty kilometers.'

'Sary Shagan or that new place Mr Ryan showed me?'

'Dushanbe,' Jack said. 'The new one.'

'But the new power lines aren't finished yet.'

'Yeah,' Graham observed. 'They can at least double the power we just saw demonstrated. Or at least they think they can.' His voice was that of a man who had just discovered a fatal disease at work on a family member.

'Can I see the first sequence again?' Gregory said. It was almost an order. Jack noted that General Parks carried it out at once.

This continued for another fifteen minutes, with Gregory standing a bare three feet from the television monitor, drinking his Coke and staring at the screen. The last three times, the picture was advanced frame by frame while the young Major took notes at every one. Finally he'd had enough.

'I can have you a power figure in half an hour, but for the moment, I think they've got some problems.'

'Blooming,' General Parks said.

'And aiming difficulty, sir. At least, it looks like that, too. I need some time to work, and a good calculator. I left mine at work,' he admitted sheepishly. There was an empty pouch on his belt, next to his beeper. Graham tossed one over, an expensive Hewlett-Packard programmable.

'What about the power?' Ryan asked.

'I need some time to give you a good number,' Gregory said as though to a backward child. 'Right now, at least eight times anything we can do. I need a quiet place to work. Can I use the snack room?' he asked Parks. The General nodded, and he left.

'*Eight* times . . .' Art Graham observed. 'Christ, they might be able to smoke the DSPS birds. It's for damned sure they can wreck any communications satellite they want. Well, there are ways to protect them. . . .'

Ryan felt a little left out. His education was in history and economics, and he hadn't quite learned the language of the physical sciences yet.

'Three years,' General Parks breathed as he poured some coffee. 'At least three years ahead of us.'

'Only in power throughput,' Graham said.

Jack looked from one to another, knowing the significance of what they were worried about, but not its substance. Gregory came back in twenty minutes.

'I make their peak power output something between twenty-five and thirty million watts,' he announced. 'If we assume six lasers in the transmission assembly, that's – well, that's enough, isn't it? It's just a matter of racking enough of them together and directing them at a single target.

'That's the bad news. The good news is, they definitely had blooming problems. They only delivered peak power on target for the first few thousandths of a second. Then it started blooming out on them. Their average power delivery was between seven to nine megawatts. And it looks like they had an aiming problem on top of the blooming. Either the mounts aren't shock-mounted properly or they can't correct for the earth's rotational jitter. Or

134

maybe both. Whatever the actual reason, they have trouble aiming more accurately than three seconds of arc. That means they're only going to be accurate plus or minus two hundred forty meters for geostationary satellite – of course, those targets are pretty stationary, and the movement factor could count either way.'

'How's that?' Ryan asked.

'Well, on one hand, if you're hitting a moving target – and low-earth-orbit birds move across the sky pretty fast; something like eight thousand meters per second – there are fourteen hundred meters per degree of arc; so we're tracking a target that's moving about five degrees per second. Okay so far? Thermal blooming means that the laser is giving up a lot of its energy to the atmosphere. If you're tracking across the sky rapidly, you keep having to drill a new hole in the air. But it takes time for the bloom to get real bad – and that helps you. On the other hand, if you've got vibration problems, every time you change your aiming point, you add a new variable into your targeting geometry, and that makes things a lot worse. Shooting at a fairly stationary target, like a communications satellite, you simplify your aiming problem, but you keep shooting up the same thermal bloom until you lose almost all your energy into the air. See what I mean?'

Ryan grunted agreement, though his mind had again reached beyond its limit. He barely understood the language the kid was speaking, and the information Gregory was trying to communicate was in a field that he simply didn't understand. Graham jumped in.

'Are you telling me we don't have to worry about this?'

'No, sir! If you got the power, you can always figure out how to deliver it. Hell, we've already done that. That's the easy part.'

'As I told you,' the engineer told Morozov, 'the problem isn't getting the lasers to put the power out – that's the easy part. The hard part is delivering the energy to the target.'

'Your computer cannot correct for – what?'

'It must be a combination of things. We'll be going over that data today. The main thing? Probably the atmospheric-compensation programming. We'd thought that we could adjust the aiming process to eliminate blooming – well, we didn't. Three years of theoretical work went into yesterday's test. My project. And it didn't work.' He stared off at the horizon and frowned. The operation on his sick child hadn't quite been successful but, the doctors said, there was still hope.

'So the increase in laser output came from this?' Bondarenko asked.

'Yes. Two of our younger people – he's only thirty-two and she's twenty-eight – came up with a way to increase the diameter of the lasing cavity. What we still need to do, however, is come up with better control of the wiggler magnets,' Pokryshkin said.

The Colonel nodded. The whole point of the free-electron laser that both sides were working on was that one could 'tune' it much like a radio, choosing the light frequency that one wished to transmit – or that was the theory. As a practical matter, the highest power output was always in about the same frequency range – and it was the wrong one. If they'd been able to put out a slightly different frequency the day before – one that penetrated the atmosphere more efficiently – the thermal blooming might have been reduced by fifty percent or so. But that meant controlling the superconducting magnets better. They were called wigglers because they induced an oscillating magnetic field through the charged electrons in the lasing cavity. Unfortunately, the breakthrough that made the lasing cavity larger had also had an unexpected effect on their ability to control magnetic-field flux. There was no theoretical explanation for this as yet, and the thinking of the senior scientists was that there was a minor, though undiscovered, engineering problem in the magnet design. The senior engineers, of course, said that there was something wrong in the theorists' explanation for what was happening, because *they* knew the magnets worked properly. The arguments that had already rocked the conference rooms were spirited but cordial. A number of very bright people were struggling together to find Truth – the scientific kind that did not depend on human opinion.

Bondarenko's mind reeled at the details even as he scribbled down his notes. He'd thought himself knowledgeable on lasers – he had, after all, helped to design a wholly new application for them – but looking at the work that had been done here, he thought himself a toddling child wandering through a university laboratory and wondering at the pretty lights. The principal breakthrough, he wrote, was in the lasing-cavity design. It allowed the enormous increase in power output, and had been made over a table in the canteen when an engineer and a physicist had jointly stumbled across a piece of Truth. The Colonel smiled to himself. *Pravda* was actually the word they used. 'Truth' was the exact translation, and the two young academicians had spoken it so artlessly. Indeed, that was a word that had gained currency at Bright Star, and Bondarenko wondered how much of that was an inside joke of some sort or another. 'But is it *pravilno*,' they would ask of a fact. 'Is it truthful?'

Well, he told himself, one thing was truthful enough. Those two people who'd met to discuss their love life – Bondarenko had already heard the story in greater detail – over a canteen table had combined to make a colossal leap forward in laser power. The rest would come in good time, Bondarenko told himself. It always did.

'So it appears that your main problem is computer control, both of your magnetic flux field and the mirror array.'

'Correct, Colonel.' Pokryshkin nodded agreement. 'And we need some additional funding and support to correct these difficulties. You must tell them in Moscow that the most important work has already been done, and proven to work.'

'Comrade General, you have won me over.'

'No, Comrade Colonel. You merely have the intelligence to perceive the *truth*!' Both men had a good laugh as they shook hands. Bondarenko couldn't wait for the flight back to Moscow. The time had long passed when a Soviet officer needed to fear at the delivery of bad news, but the delivery of good news was always good for one's career.

'Well, they can't be using adaptive optics,' General Parks said. 'What I want to know is where their optical coatings came from.'

'That's the second time I heard about that one.' Ryan stood and walked around the table to get his circulation going. 'What's the big deal about the mirror? It's a glass mirror, isn't it?'

'Not glass – can't handle the energy. Right now we're using copper or molybdenum,' Gregory said. 'A glass mirror has its reflecting surface at the back. This kind of mirror, the reflecting surface is on the front. There's a cooling system on the back.'

'Huh?' *You should have taken more science courses at BC, Jack.*

'Light doesn't reflect off the bare metal,' Graham said. It seemed to Ryan that he was the only dummy in the room. And he, of course, was the one tapped to write the Special National Intelligence Estimate. 'It reflects off an optical coating. For really precise applications – an astronomical telescope, for example – what's on the face of the mirror looks like a skim of gasoline on a puddle.'

'Then why use metal at all?' Jack objected. The Major answered.

'You use metal to keep the reflecting surface as cool as possible. We're trying to get away from it, as a matter of fact. Project ADAMANT: Accelerated Development of Advanced Materials and New Technologies Group. We're hoping the next mirror will be made out of diamond.'

'*What*?'

'Artificial diamond made from pure Carbon-12 – that's an isotopic form of regular carbon, and it's perfect for us.

The problem is energy absorption,' Gregory went on. 'If the surface retains much of the light, the heat energy can blast the coating right off the glass, then the mirror blows apart. I watched a half-meter mirror let go once. Sounded like God snapping His fingers. With C-12 diamond you have a material that's almost a superconductor of heat. It permits increased power density, and a smaller mirror. General Electric just learned how to make gemstone-quality diamond out of Carbon-12. Candi's already working to see how we can make a mirror out of it.'

Ryan looked through his thirty pages of notes, then rubbed his eyes.

'Major, with the General's permission, you're coming up to Langley with me. I want you to brief our Science and Technology people, and I want you to see everything we've got on the Soviet project. Okay with you, sir?' Jack asked Parks. The General nodded.

Ryan and Gregory left together. It turned out that you needed a pass to get out of here, too. The guards had changed shifts, but looked at everyone just as seriously. On reaching the parking lot, the Major thought Jack's XJS was 'boss'. *Do they still say that?* Jack asked himself.

'How does a Marine get to work for the Agency?' Gregory asked as he admired the interior leather. *And where does he get the coin to afford this?*

'They invited me. Before that, I taught history at Annapolis.' *Nothing like being the famous Sir John Ryan. Well, I don't suppose they have me listed in any laser textbooks . . .*

'Where'd you go to school?'

'Bachelor's at Boston College, and I got my doctorate right across the river there, at Georgetown.'

'You didn't say you were a doctor,' the Major observed.

Ryan laughed at that. 'Different field, pal. I have a lot of trouble understanding what the hell you're up to, but they stuck me with the job of explaining what it all means to – well, to the people who do the arms negotiations. I've been

139

working with them on the intelligence side for the last six months.' This drew a grunt.

'That bunch wants to put me out of business. They want to trade it all away.'

'They have their job, too,' Jack allowed. 'I need your help to persuade them that what you do is important.'

'The Russians think it's important.'

'Yeah, well, we just saw that, didn't we?'

Bondarenko got off the plane and was agreeably surprised to find an official car waiting for him. It was a Voyska PVO car. General Pokryshkin had called ahead. The working day was over, and the colonel instructed the driver to take him home. He'd write up his report tomorrow and present it to Colonel Filitov and later, perhaps, brief the Minister himself. He asked himself over a glass of vodka whether Pokryshkin had handled – he didn't know the Western expression 'stroked' – him enough to create a false impression. Not enough, he told himself. The General had done quite a job of selling both his program and himself, but this was not mere *pokazhuka*. They hadn't faked the test, and they'd been honest in detailing their problems. All they were asking for was what was really needed. No, Pokryshkin was a man with a mission, willing to put his career – well, if not behind it, then at least alongside it; and that was all anyone could reasonably ask. If he was building his own empire, it was an empire worth building.

The pickup was made in a way that was both unique and routine. The shopping mall was quite ordinary, a roofed-over promenade of ninety-three shops, plus a cluster of five small-screen theaters. There were six shoe stores, and three for jewelry. In keeping with the western location of the place, there was a sporting-goods store that catered to sportsmen, and had a wall full of Winchester Model 70 hunting rifles, something one does not often see in the East. Three up-scale men's clothing establishments dotted the concourse, along with seven for women. One of the latter adjoined the gunshop.

That suited the owner of Eve's Leaves, since the gunshop had an elaborate burglar-alarm system; this, combined with the mall's own security staff, allowed her to maintain a sizable stock of exclusive women's fashions without an overly expensive insurance package. The shop had started shakily enough – the fashions of Paris, Rome, and New York do not translate well west of the Mississippi River, except perhaps along the Pacific Coast – but much of the academic community came from both coasts, and clung to their ways. It didn't take much exposure at the country clubs for Ann Klein II to become a hot item even in the Rocky Mountains.

Ann strolled into the shop. She was a very easy customer to fit, the owner knew. A perfect six, she put the clothing on only to see how it looked. She never needed any alterations, which made life easy on everyone and allowed the owner to discount what she bought by five percent. In addition to being easy to fit, she also spent a lot of her money here, never less than $200 per visit. She was a regular, coming in every six weeks or so. The owner didn't know what she did, though she looked and acted like a doctor. So precise, so careful about everything. Oddly, she paid cash, the other reason for the discount she got, since credit card companies got a percentage of the sales figure in return for a guarantee of payment. This returned the five percent to the owner, and then some. It was a pity, she thought, that all of her customers couldn't be like this. Ann had brown bedroom eyes and hair, the latter shoulder-length and slightly wavy. Willowy, with a petite figure. The other odd thing was that she didn't ever seem to use perfume of any kind; that's what made the owner think she was a doctor. That and the hours she came in – never when it was crowded, as though she were entirely her own boss. That had to be true, and the 'doctor' dressed the part. This appealed to the owner. Every time she moved about, you could see the purpose in her stride.

141

She picked up the skirt and blouse combination, leaving for the dressing rooms in the back. Though the store owner didn't know it, Ann always used the same dressing cubicle. While in there, she unzipped her skirt, unbuttoned her blouse, but before she put the new set on, she reached under the plain wooden shelf that you could sit on and removed a cassette of microfilm that had been taped there the evening before. This went into her purse. Next she dressed and paraded outside to the mirrors.

How can American women wear this garbage? Tania Bisyarina asked her smiling image in the mirror. A Captain in Directorate S of the First Chief (also known as the 'Foreign') Directorate of the KGB, she reported to Directorate T, which oversees scientific espionage and works in cooperation with the State Committee for Science and Technology. Like Edward Foley, she 'ran' a single agent. That agent's code name was Livia.

The cost of the outfit was two hundred seventy-three dollars, and Captain Bisyarina paid in cash. She told herself that she'd have to remember to wear this outfit the next time she came back, even if it did look like rubbish.

'See you soon, Ann.' the shop owner called to her. That was the only name by which she was known in Santa Fe. The Captain turned and waved back. The owner was a pleasant-enough woman, for all her stupidity. Like any good intelligence officer, the Captain looked and acted quite ordinary. In the context of this area, that meant dressing in what passed for a moderately fashionable way, driving a decent but not flashy car, and living in a style that denoted comfort short of actual wealth. In this sense, America was an easy target. If you had the right lifestyle, nobody questioned where it came from. Getting across the border had been almost a comic exercise. All the time she'd spent getting her documents and background 'legend' exactly right, and all the Border Patrol had done was to have a dog sniff the car for drugs – she'd come in over the Mexican border at El Paso – and wave her through with a smile. *And for that* – she smiled to herself eight months later now – *I actually got excited.*

It took forty minutes for her to drive home, checking as always to be sure that she didn't have anyone following her, and once there she developed the film and made her copies; not quite the same way Foley did, but close enough not to matter. In this case she had photographs of actual government documents. She placed the developed film in a small projector and focused the frame on the white paint of her bedroom wall. Bisyarina had a technical education, one of the reasons for her current assignment, and knew a little about how to evaluate what she'd just received. She was sure it would make her seniors happy.

The next morning she made her drop, and her photographs traveled across the border into Mexico on a tractor-trailer rig belonging to a long-haul concern based in Austin. It was delivering oil-drilling machinery. By the end of the day the photos would be in the Soviet Embassy in Mexico City. The day after that, in Cuba, where they would be placed on an Aeroflot flight direct to Moscow.

7

Catalysts

'So, Colonel, what is your assessment?' Filitov asked.

'Comrade, Bright Star may be the most important program in the Soviet Union,' Bondarenko said with conviction. He handed over forty handwritten pages. 'Here is the first draft of my report. I did that on the airplane. I'll have a proper copy typed today, but I thought that you'd – '

'You thought correctly. I understand that they ran a test . . .'

'Thirty-six hours ago. I saw the test, and I was allowed to inspect much of the equipment both before and after. I was profoundly impressed with the installation and the people who run it. If I may be permitted, General Pokryshkin is an outstanding officer, and the perfect man for the post. He is decidedly not a careerist, but rather a progressive officer of the finest type. To manage the academics on that hilltop is no easy task – '

Misha grunted agreement. 'I know about academicians. Are you telling me he has them organized like a military unit?'

'No, Comrade Colonel, but Pokryshkin has learned how to keep them relatively happy and productive at the same time. There is a sense of . . . a sense of mission at Bright Star that one rarely encounters even in the officer corps. I do not say this lightly, Mikhail Semyonovich. I was most impressed by all aspects of the operation. Perhaps it is the same at the space facilities. I have heard such, but having never been there, I cannot draw the comparison.'

'And the systems themselves?'

'Bright Star is not yet a weapon. There are still technical

difficulties. Pokryshkin identified and explained them at length to me. For the moment, this is still nothing more than an experimental program, but the most important breakthroughs have been made. In several years, it will be a weapon of enormous potential.'

'What of its cost?' Misha asked. That drew a shrug.

'Impossible to estimate. It will be costly, but the expensive part of the program, the research and development phase, is largely completed. The actual production and engineering costs should be less than one might expect – for the weapon itself, that is. I cannot evaluate the costs of the support equipment, the radars, and surveillance satellites. That was not part of my brief in any case.' Besides, like soldiers all over the world, he thought in terms of mission, not cost.

'And the system reliability?'

'That will be a problem, but a manageable one. The individual lasers are complex and difficult to maintain. On the other hand, by building more than the site actually needs, we could easily cycle them through a regular maintenance program, and always have the necessary number on-line. In fact, this is the method proposed by the chief project engineer.'

'So they've solved the power-output problem, then?'

'My draft report describes that in rough terms. My final paper will be more specific.'

Misha allowed himself a smile. 'So that even I can understand it?'

'Comrade Colonel,' Bondarenko replied seriously, 'I know that you have a better understanding of technical matters than you care to admit. The important aspects of the power breakthrough arc actually quite simple – in theory, that is. The precise engineering details are rather complex, but can easily be deduced from the redesign of the lasing cavity. As with the first atomic bomb, once the theory is described, the engineering can be worked out.'

'Excellent. You can finish your report by tomorrow?'

'Yes, Comrade Colonel.'

Misha stood. Bondarenko did the same. 'I will read over your preliminary report this afternoon. Get me the complete report tomorrow and I will digest it over the weekend. Next week we will brief the Minister.'

Allah's ways were surely mysterious, the Archer thought. As much as he'd wanted to kill a Soviet transport aircraft, all he had to do was return to his home, the river town of Ghazni. It had been only a week since he'd left Pakistan. A local storm had grounded Russian aircraft for the past several days, allowing him to make good time. He arrived with his fresh supplies of missiles and found his chieftain planning an attack on the town's outlying airport. The winter weather was hard on everyone, and the infidels left the outer security posts to Afghan soldiers in the service of the traitorous government in Kabul. What they did not know, however, was that the Major commanding the battalion on perimeter duty worked for the local *mudjaheddin*. The perimeter would be open when the time came, allowing three hundred guerrillas to attack straight into the Soviet camp.

It would be a major assault. The freedom fighters were organized into three companies of one hundred men each. All three were committed to the attack; the chieftain understood the utility of a tactical reserve, but had too much front to cover with too few men. It was a risk, but he and his men had been running risks since 1980. What did one more matter? As usual, the chieftain would be in the place of greatest danger, and the Archer would be nearby. They were heading for the airfield and its hated aircraft from windward. The Soviets would try to fly their craft off at the first sign of trouble, both to get them out of the way and allow them to provide defensive support. The Archer inspected four Mi-24 helicopters through his binoculars, and all had ordnance hanging on their stubby wings. The *mudjaheddin* had but a single mortar with which to damage them on the ground, and because of this the Archer would be slightly behind the assault wave to provide support.

146

There was no time to set up his usual trap, but at night this was not likely to matter.

A hundred yards ahead, the chieftain met at the appointed place with the major of the Afghan Army. They embraced and praised Allah's name. The prodigal son had returned to the Islamic fold. The Major reported that two of his company commanders were ready to act as planned, but the commander of Three Company remained loyal to the Soviets. A trusted sergeant would kill this officer in a few minutes, allowing that sector to be used for the withdrawal. All around them, men waited in the bone-chilling wind. When the sergeant had accomplished his mission, he'd fire off a flare.

The Soviet Captain and the Afghan Lieutenant were friends, which in reflective moments surprised them both. It helped that the Soviet officer had made a real effort to be respectful of the ways of the local people, and that his Afghan counterpart believed Marxism-Leninism was the way of the future. Anything had to be better than the tribal rivalries and vendettas that had characterized this unhappy country for all of remembered history. Spotted early on as a promising candidate for ideological conversion, he'd been flown to the Soviet Union and shown how good things were there – compared to Afghanistan – especially the public health services. The Lieutenant's father had died fifteen years before of infection from a broken arm, and because he had never found favor with the tribal chief, his only son had not led an idyllic youth.

Together the two men were looking at a map and deciding on patrol activities for the coming week. They had to keep patrolling the area to keep the *mudjaheddin* bandits away. Today the patrols were being handled by Two Company.

A sergeant entered the command bunker with a message form. His face didn't show the surprise he felt at finding two officers there instead of one. He handed the envelope over to the Afghan Lieutenant with his left hand. In his right palm was the hilt of a knife, now held vertically up the baggy sleeve of his Russian-style tunic. He tried to be impassive as the Russian Captain stared at him, and merely watched the officer whose death was his responsibility. Finally the Russian turned away to look out of the bunker's weapon slit. Almost on cue, the Afghan officer tossed the message on the map table and framed his reply.

The Russian turned back abruptly. Something had alerted him, and he knew that something was wrong before he'd had time to wonder why. He watched the sergeant's arm come up in a rapid underhand movement toward his friend's throat. The Soviet Captain dove for his rifle as the Lieutenant threw himself backward to avoid the first lunge. He succeeded only because the sergeant's knife caught in the overly long sleeve of his tunic. Cursing, he freed it and lunged forward, slashing his target across the abdomen. The Lieutenant screamed, but managed to grab the sergeant's wrist before the knife reached his vital organs. The faces of the two men were close enough that each could smell the other's breath. One face was too shocked to be afraid, the other too angry. In the end, the Lieutenant's life was saved by the cloth of an ill-fitting tunic sleeve, as the Soviet flipped the safety off his rifle and fired ten rounds into the assassin's side. The sergeant fell without a sound. The Lieutenant held a bloody hand to his eyes. The Captain shouted the alarm.

The distinctive metallic chatter of the Kalashnikov rifle carried the four hundred meters to where the *mudjaheddin* waited. The same thought rippled through everyone's mind: the plan had been blown. Unfortunately, there was no planned alternative. To their left, the positions of Three Company were suddenly alight with the flashes of gunfire. They were firing at nothing – there were no guerrillas there – but the noise could not help but alert the Russian positions three hundred meters ahead. The chieftain ordered his men forward anyway, supported by nearly two hundred Afghan Army troops for whom the change of side had come as a relief. The additional men did not make as much of a difference as one might expect. These new *mudjaheddin* had no heavy weapons other than a few crew-served machine guns, and the chieftain's single mortar was slow setting up.

The Archer cursed as he watched lights go off at the airfield, three kilometers away. They were replaced with the wiggling dots of flashlights as flight crews raced to their aircraft. A moment later parachute flares began turning night to day. The harsh southeast wind blew them rapidly away, but more kept appearing. There was nothing he could do but activate his launcher. He could see the helicopters . . . and the single An-26 transport. With his left hand the Archer lifted his binoculars and saw the twin-engine, high-wing aircraft sitting there like a sleeping bird in an unprotected nest. A number of people were running to it as well. He turned his glasses back to the helicopter area.

An Mi-24 helicopter lifted off first, struggling with the thin air and howling wind to gain altitude, as mortar rounds began to drop within the airfield perimeter. A phosphorus round fell within a few meters of another Hind, its searing white flash igniting the Mi-24's fuel, and the crew leaped out, one of them aflame. They'd barely gotten clear when the aircraft exploded, taking a second Hind with it. The last one lifted off a moment later, rocking backward and disappearing into the black night, its flying lights off. They'd both be back – the Archer was sure of that – but they'd gotten two on the ground, and that was better than he'd expected.

Everything else, he saw, was going badly. Mortar rounds were falling in front of the assault troops. He saw flashes of guns and explosives. Above the noises came the other sound of the battlefield: the battle cries of warriors and the screams of the wounded. At this distance it was hard to distinguish Russian from Afghan. But that was not his concern.

The Archer didn't need to tell Abdul to scan the sky for the helicopters. He tried using the missile launcher to search for the invisible heat of their engines. He found nothing, and returned his eyes to the one aircraft he could still see. There were mortar rounds falling near the An-26 now, but the flight crew already had the engines turning. In a moment he saw some lateral movement. The Archer gauged the wind and decided that the aircraft would try coming into the wind, then flare left over the safest portion of the perimeter. It would not be easy to climb in this thin air, and when the pilot turned, he'd rob his wings of lift in the quest for speed. The Archer tapped Abdul on the shoulder and began running to the left. He made it a hundred meters when he stopped and looked again for the Soviet transport. It was moving now, through the black showers of dirt, bouncing across the frozen, uneven ground as it accelerated.

The Archer stood to give the missile a better look at the target, and immediately the seeker chirped on finding the hot engines against the cold, moonless night.

'V-One,' the copilot shouted over the noise of battle and engines. His eyes were locked on the instruments while the pilot fought to hold the aircraft straight. 'V-R – *rotate!*'

The pilot eased back on the yoke. The nose came up, and the An-26 took a final bounce off the hard dirt strip. The copilot instantly retracted the landing gear to reduce drag, allowing the plane to speed up that much quicker. The pilot brought the aircraft into a gentle right turn to avoid what seemed to be the heaviest concentration of ground fire. Once clear, he'd come back to the north for Kabul and safety. Behind him, the navigator wasn't looking at his charts. Rather, he was deploying parachute flares every five seconds. These were not to help the troops on the ground, though they did have that effect. They were to fool ground-launched missiles. The manual said to deploy one every five seconds.

The Archer timed the flares carefully. He could hear the change in the seeker's tone when they fell clear of the aircraft's cargo hatch and ignited. He needed to lock on to the plane's left-side engine and to time his shot carefully if he wanted to hit his target. In his mind he had already measured the point of closest approach – about nine hundred meters – and just before reaching it, the aircraft ejected another flare. A second later, the seeker returned to its normal acquisition tone, and he squeezed the trigger.

As always, it was almost a sexual release when the launcher tube bucked in his hands. The sounds of battle around him vanished as he concentrated on the speeding dot of yellow flame.

The navigator had just released another flare when the Stinger impacted on the left-side engine. His first thought was one of outrage – the manual was wrong! The flight engineer had no such thoughts. Automatically, he punched the 'emergency-kill' switch to the number-one turbine. That shut down the fuel flow, cut off all electrical power, feathered the propeller, and activated the fire extinguisher. The pilot pushed the rudder pedal to compensate for left yaw induced by the loss of portside power and pushed the nose down. That was a dangerous call, but he had to measure speed against altitude, and he decided that he needed speed most of all. The engineer reported that the left-side fuel tank was punctured, but it was only a hundred kilometers to Kabul. What came next was worse:

'Fire warning light on number one!'

'Pull the bottle!'

'Already done! Everything's off.'

The pilot resisted the temptation to look around. He was only a hundred meters above the ground now, and couldn't allow anything to interfere with his concentration. His peripheral vision caught a flash of yellow-orange flame, but he shut it out. His eyes went from the horizon to his airspeed and altimeter and back again.

'Losing altitude,' the copilot reported.

'Ten degrees more flaps,' the pilot ordered. He reckoned that he had enough speed now to risk it. The copilot reached down to deploy them ten degrees farther, and so doomed the aircraft and its passengers.

The missile explosion had damaged the hydraulic lines to the left-side flaps. The increased pressure needed to change the setting ruptured both the lines, and the flaps on the left wing retracted without warning. The loss of left-lift nearly snap-rolled the aircraft, but the pilot caught it and leveled out. Too many things were going wrong at once. The aircraft started sinking, and the pilot screamed for more power, knowing that the right-side engine was already firewalled. He prayed that getting into the ground effect might save his bird, but just holding her straight was nearly impossible, and he realized that they were sinking too fast in the thin air. He had to put her down. At the last moment the pilot switched on his landing lights to find a flat spot. He saw only a field of rocks, and used his last vestige of control to aim his falling bird between the two biggest. A second before the aircraft hit the ground he snarled a curse, not a cry of despair, but one of rage.

For a moment the Archer thought that the aircraft might escape. The flash of the missile was unmistakable, but for several seconds there was nothing. Then came the trailing tongue of flame that told him that his target was fatally injured. Thirty seconds after that, there was an explosion on the ground, perhaps ten kilometers away, not far from the planned escape route. He'd be able to see what he'd done before dawn. But he turned back now, hearing the sputtering whine of a helicopter overhead. Abdul had already discarded the old launch tube and attached the acquisition/guidance package to a new tube with a speed that would have done a trained soldier proud. He handed the unit over, and the Archer searched the skies for yet another target.

Though he didn't know it, the attack on Ghazni was falling apart. The Soviet commander had reacted instantly to the sound of gunfire – the Afghan Army Three Company was still shooting at nothing at all, and the Soviet officer there couldn't get things going right – and gotten his men into their positions in a matter of two hectic minutes. The

Afghans now faced a fully alerted battalion of regular troops, supported by heavy weapons and hidden in protective bunkers. Withering machine-gun fire halted the attack wave two hundred meters from the Soviet positions. The chieftain and the defecting Major tried to get things going again by personal example. A ferocious war cry echoed down the line, but the chieftain stood directly into a line of tracers that transfixed him for nearly a second before he was thrown aside like a child's toy. As generally happens with primitive troops, the loss of their leader broke the heart of the attack. Word spread throughout the line almost before the radio call was received by the unit leaders. At once, the *mudjaheddin* disengaged, firing their weapons wildly as they pulled back. The Soviet commander recognized this for what it was, but did not pursue. He had helicopters for that.

The Archer knew something was wrong when the Russian mortars started deploying flares in a different place. Already a helicopter was firing rockets and machine guns at the guerrillas, but he couldn't lock on to it. Next he heard the shouts of his comrades. Not the reckless howls of the advance, they were the warning cries of men in retreat. He settled down and concentrated on his weapon. His services would really be needed now. The Archer ordered Abdul to attach his spare seeker unit to another missile tube. The teenager had it done in under a minute.

'There!' Abdul said. 'To the right.'

'I see it.' A series of linear flashes appeared in the sky. A Hind was firing its rocket pods. He trained his launcher on the spot and was rewarded with the acquisition sound. He didn't know the range – one cannot judge distances at night – but he'd have to risk it. The Archer waited until the sound was completely steady and fired off his second Stinger of the night.

The pilot of the Hind saw this one. He'd been hovering a hundred meters above the burning parachute flares, and pushed his collective control all the way down to dive among them. It worked. The missile lost lock and ran straight at one, missing the helicopter by a bare thirty meters. The pilot immediately pivoted his aircraft and ordered his gunner to salvo ten rockets back down the missile's flight path.

The Archer fell to the ground behind the boulder he'd selected for his perch. The rockets all fell within a hundred meters of his position. So it was man against man this time . . . and this pilot was a clever one. He reached for the second launcher. The Archer regularly prayed for this situation.

But the helicopter was gone now. Where would he be?

The pilot swept to leeward, using the wind, as he'd been taught, to mask his rotor noise. He called in for flares on this side of the perimeter and got a response almost instantly. The Soviets wanted every missile-shooter they could get. While the other airborne helicopter pounded the retreating *mudjaheddin*, this one would track down their SAM support. Despite the danger involved, it was a mission for which the pilot lusted. The missileers were his personal enemy. He kept clear of the known range of the Stinger and waited for the flares to light the ground.

The Archer was again using his seeker to search for the helicopter. It was an inefficient way to search, but the Mi-24 would be somewhere in an arc that his knowledge of Soviet tactics could easily predict. Twice he got chirps and lost them as the helicopter danced left and right, altering altitude in a conscious effort to make the Archer's job impossible. This was truly a skilled enemy, the guerrilla told himself. His death would be all the more satisfying. Flares were dotting the sky above him, but he knew that the flickering light made for poor viewing conditions as long as he kept still.

'I see movement,' the Hind's gunner reported. 'Ten o'clock.'

'Wrong place,' the pilot said. He brought his cyclic control to the right and slid horizontally as his eyes searched the ground. The Soviets had captured several of the American Stingers, and had tested them exhaustively to determine their speed, range, and sensitivity. He figured himself to be at least three hundred meters beyond its range, and if fired upon, he'd use the missile's track to fix his target, then rush in to get the missileer before he could shoot again.

'Get a smoke rocket,' the Archer said.

Abdul had only one of those. It was a small, finned plastic device, little more than a toy. It had been developed for the training of US Air Force pilots, to simulate the feel – the terror – of having missiles shot at them. At a cost of six dollars, all it could do was fly in a fairly straight line for a few seconds while leaving a trail of smoke. They'd been given to the *mudjaheddin* merely as a means to scare Soviet flyers when their SAMs had run out, but the Archer had found a real use for them. Abdul ran a hundred meters and set it up on the simple steel-wire launcher. He came back to his master's side, trailing the launching wire behind him.

'Now, Russian, where are you?' the Archer asked the night.

'Something to our front, something moved, I am sure of it,' the gunner said.

'Let's see.' The pilot activated his own controls and fired two rockets. They hit the ground two kilometers away, well to the Archer's right.

'Now!' the Archer shouted. He'd seen where the Russian had launched from, and had his seeker on the spot. The infrared receiver began chirping.

The pilot cringed as he saw the moving flame of a rocket, but before he could maneuver, it was clear that the missile would miss him. It had been launched close to where he'd fired before.

'I have you now!' he shouted. The gunner started pouring machine-gun fire at the spot.

The Archer saw the tracers and heard the bullets sprinkling the ground to his right. This one was good. His aim was nearly perfect, but in firing his own guns, he gave the Archer a perfect point of aim. And the third Stinger was launched.

'Two of them!' the gunner shouted over the intercom.

The pilot was already diving and veering, but he had no flares around him this time. The Stinger exploded against a rotor blade and the helicopter fell like a stone. The pilot managed to slow his descent, but still hit the ground hard. Miraculously there was no fire. A moment later armed men appeared at his window. One, the pilot saw, was a Russian captain.

'Are you all right, Comrade?'

'My back,' the pilot gasped.

The Archer was already moving. He had tested Allah's favor enough for one night. The two-man missile team left the empty launcher tubes behind and ran to catch up with the retreating guerrillas. If the Soviet troops had pursued, they might have caught them. As it was, their commander kept them in place, and the sole surviving helicopter was content to circle the encampment. Half an hour later he learned that his chieftain was dead. The morning would bring Soviet aircraft to catch them in the open, and the guerrillas had to reach the rockfields quickly. But there was one more thing to do. The Archer took Abdul and three men to find the transport that he'd killed. The price of the Stinger missiles was the inspection of every downed aircraft for items in which the CIA might have interest.

Colonel Filitov finished the diary entry. As Bondarenko had pointed out, his knowledge of technical material was far better than one might suspect from his academic credentials. After over forty years in the higher echelons of the Defense Ministry, Misha was self-taught in a number of technical fields ranging from gas-protection suits to communications-encryption equipment to . . . lasers. Which was to say that while he didn't always comprehend the theory as well as he might have wished, he could describe the working equipment as well as the engineers who assembled it. It had taken four hours to transcribe it all into his diary. This data had to go out. The implications were too frightening.

The problem with a strategic-defense system was simply

that no weapon had ever been 'offensive' or 'defensive' in and of itself. The nature of any weapon, like the beauty of any woman, lay in the eye of the beholder – or the direction in which it was pointed – and throughout history, success in warfare was determined by the proper balance of offensive and defensive elements.

Soviet nuclear strategy, Misha thought to himself, made far more sense than that of the West. Russian strategists did not consider nuclear war unthinkable. They were taught to be pragmatic: The problem, while complex, did have a solution – while not a perfect one; unlike many Western thinkers they acknowledged that they lived in an imperfect world. Soviet strategy since the Cuban Missile Crisis of 1962 – the event had killed Filitov's recruiter, Colonel Oleg Penkovskiy – was based on a simple phrase: 'Damage Limitation.' The problem wasn't destroying one's enemy with nuclear weapons. With nuclear weapons, it was more a question of *not* destroying so much that there would be nothing left with which to negotiate the 'war-termination' phase. The problem that occupied Soviet minds was preventing enemy nuclear weapons from destroying the Soviet Union. With twenty million dead in *each* of two world wars, the Russians had tasted enough destruction, and craved no more.

This task was not viewed as an easy one, but the reason for its necessity was as much political as technical. Marxism-Leninism casts history as a process: not a mere collection of past events, but a scientific expression of man's social evolution that will – must – culminate in mankind's collective recognition that Marxism-Leninism is the ideal form for all human society. A committed Marxist, therefore, believed in the ultimate ascendancy of his creed as surely as Christian, Jew, and Muslim believed in an afterlife. And just as religious communities throughout history have shown a willingness to spread their good news with fire and sword, so it was the duty of the Marxist to make his vision a reality as quickly as possible.

The difficulty here, of course, was that not everyone in

the world had the Marxist-Leninist view of history. Communist doctrine explained this away as the reactionary forces of imperialism, capitalism, the bourgeoisie, and the rest of their pantheon of enemies, whose resistance was predictable – but whose *tactics* were not. As a gambler who has rigged his gambling table, the communists 'knew' that they would win, but like a gambler, in their darker moments they reluctantly admitted that luck – or more scientifically, random chance – could alter their equation. In lacking the proper scientific outlook, the Western democracies also lacked a common ethos, and that made them unpredictable.

More than any other reason, that was why the East feared the West. Ever since Lenin had assumed control of – and renamed – the Soviet Union, the communist government had invested billions in spying on the West. As with all intelligence functions, its prime purpose was to predict what the West would and could do.

But despite countless tactical successes, the fundamental problem remained: Time and again the Soviet government had gravely misread Western actions and intentions; and in a nuclear age unpredictability could mean that an unbalanced American leader – and, to a lesser extent, English or French – could even spell the end of the Soviet Union and the postponement of World Socialism for generations. (To a Russian, the former was more grave, since no ethnic Russian wanted to see the world brought to Socialism under Chinese leadership.) The Western nuclear arsenal was the greatest threat to Marxism-Leninism; countering that arsenal was the prime task of the Soviet military. But unlike the West, the Soviets did not see the prevention of its use as simply the prevention of war. Since the Soviets viewed the West as politically unpredictable, they felt that they could not depend on deterring it. They needed to be able to eliminate, or at least degrade, the Western nuclear arsenal if a crisis threatened to go beyond the point of mere words.

Their nuclear arsenal was designed with precisely this task in mind. Killing cities and their millions of inhabitants would always be a simple exercise. Killing the missiles that their countries owned was not. To kill the American missiles had meant developing several generations of highly accurate – and hugely expensive – rockets like the SS-18, whose sole mission was to reduce America's Minuteman missile squadrons to glowing dust, along with the submarine and bomber bases. All but the last were to be found well distant from population centers; consequently, a strike aimed at disarming the West might be carried off without necessarily resulting in world holocaust. At the same time, the Americans did not have enough really accurate warheads to make the same threat against the Soviet missile force. The Russians, then, had an advantage in a potential 'counterforce' attack – the sort aimed at weapons rather than people.

The shortcoming was naval. More than half of the American warheads were deployed on nuclear submarines. The US Navy thought that its missile submarines had never been tracked by their Soviet counterparts. That was incorrect. They had been tracked exactly three times in twenty-seven years, and then never more than four hours. Despite a generation of work by the Soviet Navy, no one predicted that this mission would ever be accomplished. The Americans admitted that *they* couldn't track their own 'boomers', as the missile submarines were known. On the other hand, the Americans *could* track Soviet missile submarines, and for this reason the Soviets had never placed more than a fraction of their warheads at sea, and until recently neither side could base accurate counterforce weapons in submarines.

But the game was changing yet again. The Americans had fabricated another technical miracle. Their submarine-launched weapons would soon be Trident D-5 missiles with a hard-target-kill capability. This threatened Soviet strategy with a mirror-image of its own potential, though a crucial element of the system was the Global Positioning Satellites, without which the American submarines would be unable to determine their own locations accurately enough for their weapons to kill hardened targets. The twisted logic of the nuclear balance was again turning on itself – as it had to do at least once per generation.

It had been recognized early on that missiles were offensive weapons with a defensive mission, that the ability to destroy the opponent was the classical formula both to prevent war and achieve one's goals in peace. The fact that such power accrued to both sides had transformed the historically proven formula of unilateral intimidation into bilateral deterrence, however, made that solution unpalatable.

Nuclear Deterrence: preventing war by the threat of mutual holocaust. Both sides told the other in substance, *If you kill our helpless civilians, we will kill yours*. Defense was no longer protection of one's own society, but the threat of senseless violence against another. Misha grimaced. No tribe of savages had ever formulated such an idea – even the most uncivilized barbarians were too advanced for such a thing, but that was precisely what the world's most advanced peoples had decided – or stumbled – upon. Although deterrence could be said to work, it meant that the Soviet Union – and the West – lived under a threat with more than one trigger. No one thought that situation satisfactory, but the Soviets had made what they considered the best of a bad bargain by designing a strategic arsenal that could largely disarm the other side if a world crisis demanded it. In achieving the ability to eliminate much of the American arsenal, they had the advantage of dictating how a nuclear war would be fought; in classical terms that was the first step toward victory, and in the Soviet view, Western denial that 'victory' was a possibility in a nuclear war was the first step toward Western defeat. Theorists on both sides had always recognized the unsatisfactory nature of the entire nuclear issue, however, and quietly worked to deal with it in other ways.

As early as the 1950s, both America and the Soviet Union had begun research in ballistic-missile defense, the latter at Sary Shagan in southwestern Siberia. A workable Soviet system had almost been deployed in the late 1960s, but the advent of MIRVs had utterly invalidated the work of fifteen years – perversely, for both sides. The struggle for ascendancy between offensive and defensive systems always tended to the former.

But no longer. Laser weapons and other high-energy-projection systems, mated to the power of computers, were a quantum jump into a new strategic realm. A workable defense, Bondarenko's report told Colonel Filitov, was now a real possibility. And what did that mean?'

It meant that the nuclear equation was destined to return to the classic balance of offense *and* defense, that both elements could now be made part of a single strategy. The professional soldiers found this a more satisfying system in the abstract – what man wishes to think of himself as the greatest murderer in history? – but now tactical possibilities were raising their ugly heads. Advantage and disadvantage; move and countermove. An *American* strategic-defense system could negate all of Soviet nuclear posture. If the Americans could prevent the SS-18s from taking out their land-based missiles, then the disarming first strike that the Soviets depended upon to limit damage to the *Rodina* was no longer possible. And that meant that all of the billions that had been sunk into ballistic-missile production were now as surely wasted as though the money had been dumped into the sea.

But there was more. Just as the *scutum* of the Roman legionnaire was seen by his barbarian opponent as a weapon that enabled him to stab with impunity, so today SDI could be seen as a shield from behind which an enemy could first launch his own disarming first strike, then use his defenses to reduce or even eliminate the effect of the resulting retaliatory strike.

The view, of course, was simplistic. No system would ever be foolproof – and even if the system worked, Misha knew, the political leaders would find a way to use it to its greatest *dis*advantage; you could always depend on politicians for that. A workable strategic defense scheme would have the effect of adding a new element of uncertainty to the equation. It was unlikely that any country could eliminate all incoming warheads, and the deaths of as 'few' as twenty million citizens was too ghastly a thing to contemplate, even for the Soviet leadership. But even a rudimentary SDI system might kill enough warheads to invalidate the whole idea of counterforce.

If the Soviets had such a system first, the meager American counterforce arsenal could be countered more easily that the Soviet one, and the strategic situation for which the Soviets had worked thirty years would remain in place. The Soviet government would have the best of both worlds, a far larger force of accurate missiles with which to eliminate American warheads, and a shield to kill most of the retaliatory strike against their reserve missile fields – and the American sea-based systems could be neutralized by elimination of their GPS navigation satellites, without which they could still kill cities, but the ability to attack missile silos would be irretrievably gone.

The scenario Colonel Mikhail Semyonovich Filitov envisaged was the standard Soviet case study. Some crisis erupted (the Middle East was the favorite, since nobody could predict what would happen there), and while Moscow moved to stabilize matters, the West interfered – clumsily and stupidly, of course – and started talking openly in the press about a nuclear confrontation. The intelligence organs would flash word to Moscow that a nuclear strike was a real possibility. Strategic Rocket Force's SS-18 regiments would secretly go to full alert, as would the new ground-based laser weapons. While the Foreign Ministry airheads – no military force is enamored of its diplomatic colleagues – struggled to settle things down, the West would posture and threaten, perhaps attacking a Soviet naval force to show its resolve, certainly mobilizing the NATO armies to threaten invasion of Eastern Europe. Worldwide panic would begin in earnest. When the tone of Western rhetoric reached its culmination, the launch orders would be issued to the missile force, and 300 SS-18s would launch, allocating three warheads to each of the American Minuteman silos. Smaller weapons would go after the submarine and bomber bases to limit collateral casualties as much as possible – the Soviets had no wish to exacerbate the situation more than necessary. Simultaneously, the lasers would disable as many American reconnaissance and navigation satellites as possible but leave the communications satellites intact – a gamble calculated to show 'good' intent. The Americans would not be able to respond to the attack before the Soviet warheads struck. (Misha worried about this, but information from KGB and GRU said that there were serious flaws in the American command-and-control system, plus the psychological factors involved.) Probably the Americans would keep their submarine weapons in reserve and launch their surviving Minutemen at Soviet missile silos, but it was expected that no more than two to three hundred warheads would survive the first strike; many of those would be aimed at empty holes anyway, and the defense system would kill most of the incoming weapons.

At the end of the first hour, the Americans would realize that the usefulness of their submarine missiles was greatly degraded. Constant, carefully prepared messages would be sent via the Moscow-Washington Hot Line: WE CANNOT LET THIS GO ANY FURTHER. And, probably, the Americans would stop and think. That was the important part – to make people stop and think. A man might attack cities on impulse or in a state of rage, but not after sober reflection.

Filitov was not concerned that either side would see its defense systems as a rationale for an offensive strike. In a crisis, however, their existence could mitigate the fear that prevented its launch – if the other side had no defenses. Both sides, therefore, had to have them. That would make a first strike far less likely, and *that* would make the world a safer place. Defensive systems could not be stopped now. One might as easily try to stop the tide. It pleased this old soldier that intercontinental rockets, so destructive to the ethic of the warrior, might finally be neutralized, that death in war would be returned to armed men on the field of battle, where it belonged. . . .

Well, he thought, *you're tired, and it's too late for that sort of deep thinking.* He'd finish up this report with the date from Bondarenko's final draft, photograph it, and get the film to his cutout.

8

Document Transfer

It was almost dawn when the Archer found the wreckage of the airplane. He had ten men with him, plus Abdul. They'd have to move fast. As soon as the sun rose over the mountains the Russians would come. He surveyed the wreck from a knoll. Both wings had been sheered off at the initial impact, and the fuselage had rocketed forward, up a gentle slope, tumbling and breaking apart until only the tail was recognizable. He had no way of knowing that it had taken a brilliant pilot to accomplish this much, that getting the airplane down under any kind of control was a near miracle. He gestured to his men, and moved quickly toward the main body of wreckage. He told them to look for weapons, then any kind of documents. The Archer and Abdul went to what was left of the tail.

As usual, the scene of the crash was a contradiction. Some of the bodies were torn apart, while others were superficially intact, their deaths caused by internal trauma. These bodies looked strangely at peace, stiff but not yet frozen by the low temperature. He counted six who'd been in the after section of the aircraft. All, he saw, were Russians, all in uniform. One wore the uniform of a KGB captain and was still strapped in his seat. There was a pink froth around his lips. He must have lived a little after the crash and coughed up blood, the Archer thought. He kicked the body over and saw that handcuffed to the man's left hand was a briefcase. That was promising. The Archer bent down to see if the handcuff could be taken off easily, but he wasn't that lucky. Shrugging, he took out his knife. He'd just have to cut it off the body's wrist.

He twisted the hand around and started –

– when the arm jerked and a high-pitched scream made the Archer leap to his feet. Was this one alive? He bent down to the man's face and was rewarded by a coughing spray of blood. The blue eyes were now open, wide with shock and pain. The mouth worked, but nothing intelligible came out.

'Check to see if any more are still living,' the Archer ordered his assistant. He turned back to the KGB officer and spoke in Pashtu: 'Hello, Russian.' He waved his knife within a few centimeters of the man's eyes.

The Captain started coughing again. The man was fully awake now, and in considerable pain. The Archer searched him for weapons. As his hands moved, the body writhed in agony. Broken ribs at the least, though his limbs seemed intact. He spoke a few tortured words. The Archer knew some Russian but had trouble making them out. It should not have been hard – the message the officer was trying to convey was the obvious one, though it took the Archer nearly half a minute to recognize it.

'Don't kill me . . .'

Once the Archer understood it, he continued his search. He removed the Captain's wallet and flipped through its contents. It was the photographs that stopped him. The man had a wife. She was short, with dark hair and a round face. She was not beautiful, except for the smile. It was the smile a woman saved for the man she loved, and it lit up her face in a way that the Archer himself had once known. But what got his attention were the next two. The man had a son. The first photo had been taken at age two perhaps, a young boy with tousled hair and an impish smile. You could not hate a child, even the Russian child of a KGB officer. The next picture of him was so different that it was difficult to connect the two. His hair was gone, his skin tightly drawn across the face . . . and transparent like the pages of an old Koran. The child was dying. Three now, maybe four? he wondered. A dying child whose face wore a smile of courage and pain and love. *Why must Allah visit his anger on the little ones?* He turned the photo to the officer's face.

'Your son?' he asked in Russian.

'Dead. Cancer,' the man explained, then saw that this bandit didn't understand. 'Sickness. Long sickness.' For the briefest moment his face cleared of pain and showed only grief. That saved his life. He was amazed to see the bandit sheathe his knife, but too deeply in pain to react in a visible way.

No. I will not visit another death upon this woman. The decision also amazed the Archer. It was as though the voice of Allah Himself reminded him that mercy is second only to faith in the human virtues. That was not enough by itself – his fellow guerrillas would not be persuaded by a verse of scripture – but next the Archer found a key ring in the man's pants pocket. He used one key to unlock the handcuffs and the other to open the briefcase. It was full of document folders, each of which was bordered in multicolored tape and stamped with some version of SECRET. That was one Russian word he knew.

'My friend,' the Archer said in Pashtu, 'you are going to visit a friend of mine. If you live long enough,' he said.

'How serious is this?' the President asked.

'Potentially very serious,' Judge Moore answered. 'I want to bring some people over to brief you.'

'Don't you have Ryan doing the evaluation?'

'He'll be one of them. Another's this Major Gregory you've heard about.'

The President flipped open his desk calendar. 'I can give you forty-five minutes. Be here at eleven.'

'We'll be there, sir.' Moore hung up the phone. He buzzed his secretary next. 'Send Dr Ryan in here.'

Jack came through the door a minute later. He didn't even have time to sit down.

'We're going in to see The Man at eleven. How ready is your material?'

'I'm the wrong guy to talk about the physics, but I guess

Gregory can handle that end. He's talking to the Admiral and Mr Ritter right now. General Parks coming, too?' Jack asked.

'Yeah.'

'Okay. How much imagery do you want me to get together?'

Judge Moore thought that one over for a moment. 'We don't want to razzle-dazzle him. A couple of background shots and a good diagram. You really think it's important, too?'

'It's not any immediate threat to us by any stretch of the imagination, but it's a development we could have done without. The effect on the arms-control talks is hard to gauge. I don't think there's a direct connec – '

'There isn't, we're certain of that.' The DCI paused for a grimace. 'Well, we think we're certain.'

'Judge, there is data on this issue floating around here that I haven't seen yet.'

Moore smiled benignly. 'And how do you know that, son?'

'I spent most of last Friday going over old files on the Soviet missile-defense program. Back in '81 they ran a major test out of the Sary Shagan site. We knew an awful lot about it – for example, we knew that the mission parameters had been changed from within the Defense Ministry. Those orders were sealed in Moscow and hand-delivered to the skipper of the missile sub that fired the birds – Marko Ramius. He told me the other side of the story. With that and a few other pieces I've come across, it makes me think that we have a man inside that place, and pretty high up.'

'What other pieces?' the Judge wanted to know.

Jack hesitated for a moment, but decided to go ahead with his guesses. 'When *Red October* defected, you showed me a report that had to come from deep inside, also from the Defense Ministry; the code name on the file was WILLOW, as I recall. I've only seen one other file with that name, on a different subject entirely, but also defense-related. That makes me think there's a source with a rapidly changing code-name cycle. You'd only do that with a very sensitive source, and if it's something I'm not cleared for, well, I can only conclude that it's something closely held. Just two weeks ago you told me that Gregory's assessment of the Dushanbe site was confirmed through "other assets", sir.' Jack smiled. 'You pay me to see connections, Judge. I don't mind being cut out of things I don't need to know, but I'm starting to think that there's something going on that's part of what I'm trying to do. If you want me to brief the President, sir, I should go in with the right information.'

'Sit down, Dr Ryan.' Moore didn't bother asking if Jack had discussed this with anyone. Was it time to add a new member to the Δ fraternity? After a moment he delivered his own sly smile.

'You've met him.' The Judge went on for a couple of minutes.

Jack leaned back in his chair and closed his eyes. After a moment's thought, he could see the face again. 'God. And he's getting us the information . . . But will we be able to use it?'

'He's gotten us technical data before. Most of it we've put to use.'

'Do we tell the President this?' Jack asked.

'No. That's his idea, not ours. He told us some time ago that he didn't want the details of covert operations, just the results. He's like most politicians – he talks too much. At least he's smart enough to know that. We've had agents lost because presidents talked too much. Not to mention the odd member of Congress.'

'So when do we expect this report to come in?'

'Soon. Maybe this week, maybe as long as three – '

'And if it works, we can take what they know and add it to what we know . . .' Ryan looked out the window at the bare limbs of trees. 'Ever since I've been here, Judge, I've asked myself at least once a day – what's most remarkable about this place, the things we know or the things we don't?'

Moore nodded agreement. 'The game's like that, Dr Ryan. Get your briefing notes together. No reference to our friend, though. I'll handle that if I have to.'

Jack walked back to his office, shaking his head. He'd suspected a few times that he was cleared for things the President never saw. Now he was sure. He asked himself if this was a good idea and admitted that he didn't know. What filled his mind was the importance of this agent and his information. There were precedents. The brilliant agent Richard Sorge in Japan in 1941, whose warnings to Stalin were not believed. Oleg Penkovskiy, who'd given the West information on the Soviet military that might have prevented nuclear war during the Cuban Missile Crisis. And now another. He didn't reflect on the fact that alone in CIA, he knew the agent's face but not his name or code name. It never occurred to him that Judge Moore didn't know CARDINAL's face, had for years avoided looking at the photograph for reasons that he could never have explained even to his deputy directors.

The phone rang, and a hand reached out from under a blanket to grab it. 'H'lo.'

''Morning, Candi,' Al Gregory said in Langley.

Two thousand miles away, Dr Candace Long twisted around in her bed and stared at the clock. 'You at the airport?'

'Still in Washington, honey. If I'm lucky, I'll fly back later today.' He sounded tired.

'What's happening anyway?' she asked.

'Oh, somebody ran a test, and I have to explain what it means to some people.'

'Okay. Let me know when you're coming in, Al. I'll come out to get you.' Candi Long was too groggy to realize that her fiancé had bent a rule of security to answer her question.

'Sure. Love ya.'

'Love you, too, honey.' She replaced the phone and rechecked the clock. There was time for another hour's sleep. She made a mental note to ride into work with a

170

friend. Al had left his car at the lab before flying east, and she'd ride that one out to pick him up.

Ryan got to drive Major Gregory again. Moore took General Parks in his Agency limo.

'I asked you before: what are the chances that we'll find out what Ivan is doing at Dushanbe?'

Jack hesitated before answering, then realized that Gregory would hear it all in the Oval Office. 'We have assets that are working to find out what they did to increase their power output.'

'I'd love to know how you do that,' the young Major observed.

'No, you don't. Trust me.' Ryan looked away from the traffic for a moment. 'If you know stuff like that, and you make a slip, you could kill people. It's happened before. The Russians come down pretty hard on spies. There's still a story floating around that they cremated one – I mean they slid him into a crematorium alive.'

'Aw, come on! Nobody's that – '

'Major, one of these days you ought to get out of your lab and find out just how nasty the world can really be. Five years ago, I had people try to kill my wife and kid. They had to fly three thousand miles to do it, but they came anyway.'

'Oh, right! You're the guy – '

'Ancient history, Major.' Jack was tired of telling the story.

'What's it like, sir? I mean, you've actually been in combat, the real thing, I mean – '

'It's not fun.' Ryan almost laughed at himself for putting it that way. 'You just have to perform, that's all. You either do it right or you lose it. If you're lucky, you don't panic until it's all over.'

'You said out at the lab that you used to be a Marine . . .'

'That helped some. At least somebody bothered to teach me a little about it, once upon a time.' *Back when you were in high school or so*, Jack didn't say. Enough of that. 'Ever meet the President?'

'No, sir.'

'The name's Jack, okay? He's a pretty good guy, pays attention and asks good questions. Don't let the sleepy look fool you. I think he does that to fool politicians.'

'They fool easy?' Gregory wondered.

That got a laugh. 'Some of them. The head arms-control guy'll be there, too. Uncle Ernie. Ernest Allen, old-time career diplomat, Dartmouth and Yale; he's smart.'

'He thinks we ought to bargain my work away. Why does the President keep him?'

'Ernie knows how to deal with the Russians, and he's a pro. He doesn't let personal opinions interfere with his job. I honestly don't know what he thinks about the issues. It's like with a doc. A surgeon doesn't have to like you personally. He just has to fix whatever's wrong. With Mr Allen, well, he knows how to sit through all the crap that the negotiations entail. You've never learned anything about that, have you?' Jack shook his head and smiled at the traffic. 'Everybody thinks it's dramatic, but it's not. I've never seen anything more boring. Both sides say exactly the same thing for hours – they repeat themselves about every fifteen or twenty minutes, all day, every day. Then after a week or so, one side or the other makes a small change, and keeps repeating that for hours. The other side checks with its capital, and makes a small change of its own, and keeps repeating that. It goes on and on that way for weeks, months, sometimes years. But Uncle Ernie is good at it. He finds it exciting. Personally, after about a week, I'd be willing to start a war just to put an end to the negotiation process' – another laugh – 'don't quote me on that. It's about as exciting as watching paint dry, tedious as hell, but it's important and it takes a special kind of mind to do it. Ernie's a dry, crusty old bastard, but he knows how to get the job done.'

'General Parks says that he wants to shut us down.'

'Hell, Major, you can ask the man. I wouldn't mind finding out myself.' Jack turned off Pennsylvania Avenue, following the CIA limousine. Five minutes later, he and

Gregory were sitting in the west wing's reception room under a copy of the famous painting of Washington crossing the Delaware while the Judge was talking to the President's national security advisor, Jeffrey Pelt. The President was finishing up a session with the Secretary of Commerce. Finally, a Secret Service agent called to them and led the way through the corridors.

As with TV studio sets, the Oval Office is smaller than most people expect. Ryan and Gregory were directed to a small sofa along the north wall. Neither man sat down yet; the President was standing by his desk. Ryan noted that Gregory appeared a little pale now, and remembered his own first time here. Even White House insiders would occasionally admit to being intimidated by this room and the power it contained.

'Hello again, Jack!' The President strode over to take his hand. 'And you must be the famous Major Gregory.'

'Yes, sir.' Gregory nearly strangled on that, and had to clear his throat. 'I mean, yes, Mr President.'

'Relax, sit down. You want some coffee?' He waved to a tray on the corner of his desk. Gregory's eyes nearly bugged out when the President got him a cup. Ryan did his best to suppress a smile. The man who'd made the presidency 'imperial' again – whatever that meant – was a genius for putting people at ease. Or appearing to, Jack corrected himself. The coffee routine often made them even more uneasy, and maybe that was no accident. 'Major, I've heard some great things about you and your work. The General says you're his brightest star.' Parks shifted in his chair at that. The President sat down next to Jeff Pelt. 'Okay, let's get started.'

Ryan opened his portfolio and set a photograph on the low table. Next came a diagram. 'Mr President, this is a satellite shot of what we call sites Bach and Mozart. They're on a mountain southeast of the city of Dushanbe in the Tadzhik Soviet Socialist Republic, about seventy miles from the Afghan border. The mountain is about seventy-six hundred feet high. We've had it under surveillance for the past two years. This one' – another photo went down – 'is Sary Shagan. The Russians have had ballistic-missile-defense work going on here for the past thirty years. This site right here is believed to be a laser test range. We believe that the Russians made a major breakthrough in laser power here two years ago. They then changed the activity at Bach to accommodate it. Last week they ran what was probably a full-power test.

'This array here at Bach is a laser transmitter.'

'And they blasted a satellite with it?' Jeff Pelt asked.

'Yes, sir,' Major Gregory answered. 'They "slagged it down", as we say at the lab. They pumped enough energy into it to, well, to melt some of the metal and destroy the solar power cells entirely.'

'We can't do that yet?' the President asked Gregory.

'No, sir. We can't put that much power out the front end.'

'How is it that they got ahead of us? We're putting a lot of money into lasers, aren't we, General?'

Parks was uncomfortable with the recent developments, but his voice was dispassionate. 'So are the Russians, Mr President. They've made quite a few leaps because of their efforts in fusion. They've been investing in high-energy physics research for years as part of an effort to get fusion-power reactors. About fifteen years ago that effort was mated with their missile-defense program. If you put that much time and effort into basic research, you can expect a return, and they've gotten plenty. They invented the RFQ – the radio-frequency quadrapole – that we use in our neutral-particle beam experiments. They invented the Tokamak magnetic-containment device that we copied up at Princeton, and they invented the Gyrotron. Those are three major breakthroughs in high-energy physics that we know about. We've used some of them in our own SDI research, and it's for sure that they've figured out the same applications.'

'Okay, what do we know about this test they ran?'

It was Gregory's turn again. 'Sir, we know that it came

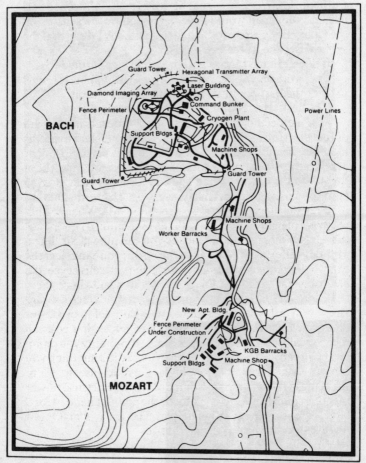

Detail of Dushanbe site

from Dushanbe because the only other high-energy laser sites, the one at Sary Shagan and Semipalatinsk, were under the visible horizon – I mean, they couldn't see the satellite from there. We know that it wasn't an infrared laser, because the beam would have been seen by the sensors on the Cobra Belle aircraft. If I had to guess, sir, I'd say that the system uses the free-electron laser – '

'It does,' Judge Moore noted. 'We just confirmed that.'

'That's the one we're working on at Tea Clipper. It seems to offer the best potential for weapons applications.'

'Can I ask why, Major?' the President asked.

'Power efficiency, sir. The actual lasing occurs in a stream of free electrons – that means they're not attached to atoms like they usually are, sir – in a vacuum. You use a linear accelerator to produce a stream of the electrons and shoot them into the cavity, which has a low-energy laser shining along its axis. The idea is that you can use electromagnets to oscillate the electrons crosswise to their path. What you get is a beam of light coincident with the oscillation frequency of the wiggler magnets – that means you can tune it, sir, like a radio. By altering the energy of the beam, you can select the exact light frequency you generate. Then you can recycle the electrons back into the linear accelerator and shoot them back into the lasing cavity again. Since the electrons are already in a high-energy state, you gain a lot of power efficiency right there. The bottom line, sir, is that you can theoretically pump out forty percent of the energy you pump in. If you can achieve that reliably, you can kill anything you can see – when we talk about high-energy levels, sir, we're speaking in relative terms. Compared to the electrical power that this country uses to cook food, the amount needed for a laser defense system is negligible. The trick is making it really work. We haven't done that yet.'

'Why not?' The President was interested now, leaning forward slightly in his chair.

'We're still learning how to make the laser work, sir. The fundamental problem is in the lasing cavity – that's where the energy comes off the electrons and turns into a beam of light.

We haven't been able yet to make a very wide one. If the cavity is too narrow, then you have such a high power density that you fry the optical coatings both in the cavity itself and on the mirrors that you use to aim the beam.'

'But they've beaten the problem. How do you think they did it?'

'I know what we're trying to do. As you draw energy into the laser beam, the electrons become less energetic, okay? That means you have to taper the magnetic field that contains them – and remember that at the same time you have to continue the wiggling action of the field, too. We haven't figured that out yet. Probably they have, and that probably came from their research into fusion research. All the ideas for getting energy out of controlled fusion are concerned with using a magnetic field to contain a mass of high-energy plasma – in principle the same thing we're trying to do with the free electrons. Most of the basic research in that field comes from Russia, sir. They're ahead of us because they've spent more time and money in the most important place.'

'Okay, thank you, Major.' The President turned to Judge Moore. 'Arthur, what does CIA think?'

'Well, we're not going to disagree with Major Gregory – he just spent a day briefing our Science and Technology people. We have confirmed that the Soviets do have six free-electron lasers at this place. They have made a breakthrough in power output and we're trying to find out exactly what the breakthrough was.'

'Can you do that?' General Parks asked.

'I said we're trying, General. If we're very lucky, we'll have an answer by the end of the month.'

'Okay, we know they can build a very powerful laser,' the President said. 'Next question: it is a weapon?'

'Probably not, Mr President,' General Parks said. 'At least not yet. They still have a problem with thermal blooming because they haven't learned how to copy our adaptive optics. They've gotten a lot of technology from the West, but so far they don't have that. Until they do, they can't use the ground-based laser as we have, that is, relaying the beam by orbiting mirror to a distant target. But what they have now can probably do great damage to a satellite in low-earth orbit. There are ways to protect satellites against that, of course, but it's the old battle between heavier armor and heavier warheads. The warhead usually wins in the end.'

'Which is why we should negotiate the weapons out of existence.' Ernie Allen spoke for the first time. General Parks looked over to him with unconcealed irritation. 'Mr President, we are now getting a taste – just a taste – of how dangerous and destabilizing these weapons might be. If we merely consider this Dushanbe place to be an antisatellite weapon, look at the implications it has for verification of arms-treaty compliance, and for intelligence-gathering in general. If we don't try to stop these things now, all we'll get is chaos.'

'You can't stop progress,' Parks observed.

Allen snorted. 'Progress? Hell, we have a draft treaty on the table now to reduce weapons by half. *That's* progress, General. In the test you just ran over the South Atlantic, you missed with half your shots – I can take out as many missiles as you can.'

Ryan thought the General might come off his chair at that one, but instead he adopted his intellectual guise. 'Mr Allen, that was the first test of an experimental system, and half of its shots did hit. In fact, *all* of the targets were eliminated in under a second. Major Gregory here will have that targeting problem beaten by summer – won't you, son?'

'Yes, sir!' Gregory piped up. 'All we have to do is rework the code some.'

'Okay. If Judge Moore's people can tell us what the Russians have done to increase their laser power, we have most of the rest of the system architecture already tested and validated. In two or three years, we'll have it all – and then we can start thinking seriously about deployment.'

'And if the Soviets start shooting your mirrors out of

space?' Allen asked dryly. 'You could have the best laser system ever made on the ground, but it won't do much more than defend New Mexico.'

'They'll have to find 'em first, and that's a much harder problem than you think. We can put 'em pretty high up, between three hundred and a thousand miles. We can use stealth technology to make them hard to locate on radar – you can't do that with most satellites, but we can do it with these. The mirrors will be relatively small, and light. That means we can deploy a lot of them. Do you know how big space is, and how many *thousands* of pieces of junk are orbiting up there? They'd never get them all,' Parks concluded with confidence.

'Jack, you've been looking at the Russians. What do you think?' the President asked Ryan.

'Mr President, the main force we're going against here is the Soviet fixation on defending their country – and I mean actually *defending* it against attack. They've invested thirty years of work and quite a pile of money in this field because they think it's something worth doing. Back in the Johnson administration, Kosygin said, "Defense is moral, offense is immoral." That's a Russian talking, sir, not just a communist. To be honest, I find that a hard argument to disagree with. If we do enter a new phase of competition, at least it would be defensive instead of offensive. Kind of hard to kill a million civilians with a laser,' Jack noted.

'But it will change the whole balance of power,' Ernest Allen objected.

'The current balance of power may be fairly stable, but it's still fundamentally crazy,' Ryan said.

'It works. It keeps the peace.'

'Mr Allen, the peace we have is one continuous crisis. You say we can reduce inventories by half – again, so what? You could cut Soviet inventories by two thirds and still leave them with enough warheads to turn America into a crematorium. The same thing is true of our inventory. As I said coming back from Moscow, the reduction agreement now on the table is cosmetic only. It does not provide any degree of additional safety. It is a symbol – maybe an important one, but only a symbol with very little substance.'

'Oh, I don't know,' General Parks observed. 'If you reduce my target load by half, I wouldn't mind all that much.' That earned him a nasty look from Allen.

'If we can find out what the Russians are doing different, where does that leave us?' the President asked.

'If the CIA gives us data that we can use? Major?' Parks turned his head.

'Then we'll have a weapons system that we can demonstrate in three years, and deploy over the five to ten years after that,' Gregory said.

'You're sure,' the President said.

'As sure as I can be, sir. Like with the Apollo Program, sir, it's not so much a question of inventing a new science as learning how to engineer technology we already have. It's just working out the nuts and bolts.'

'You're a very confident young man, Major,' Allen said professorially.

'Yes, sir, I am. I think we can do it. Mr Allen, our objective isn't all that different from yours. You want to get rid of the nukes, and so do we. Maybe we can help you, sir.'

Zing! Ryan thought with a hastily concealed smile. A discreet knock came at the door. The President checked his watch.

'I have to cut this one short. I have to go over some antidrug programs over lunch with the Attorney General. Thank you for your time.' He took one last look at the Dushanbe photo and stood. Everyone else did the same. They filed out by the side door, the one concealed in the white plaster walls.

'Nice going, kid,' Ryan observed quietly to Gregory.

Candi Long caught the car outside her house. It was driven by a friend from Columbia, Dr Beatrice Taussig, another optical physicist. Their friendship went back to undergraduate days. She was flashier than Candi. Taussig drove a

Nissan 300Z sports car, and had the traffic citations to prove it. The car fitted well with her clothes, however, and the Claircoled hairstyle, and the brash personality that turned men off like a light switch.

"Morning, Bea.' Candi Long slipped into the car and buckled the seat belt before she closed the door. Driving with Bea, you always buckled up – though she never seemed to bother.

'Tough night, Candi?' This morning it was a severe, not quite mannish wool suit, topped by a silk scarf at the neck. Long could never see the point. When you spent your day covered in a cheap white lab coat, who gave a damn what was under it – except Al, of course, but he was interested in what was under what was under, she thought to herself, smiling.

'I sleep better when he's here.'

'Where'd he go?' Taussig asked.

'Washington.' She yawned. The rising sun cast shadows on the road ahead.

'How come?' Bea downshifted as she accelerated the car up the freeway on-ramp. Candi felt herself pressed sideways against the seat belt. Why did her friend have to drive this way? This wasn't the Grand Prix of Monaco.

'He said that somebody ran a test, and he has to explain it to somebody or other.'

'Hmph.' Beatrice looked at her mirror and left the car in third as she selected a slot in the rush-hour traffic. She matched velocities expertly and slid into a space only ten feet longer than her Z-car. That earned her an angry beep from the car behind. She just smiled. The nondriving part of her psyche took note of the fact that whatever test Al was explaining hadn't been American. And there weren't too many people doing tests that this particular little geek had to explain. Bea didn't understand what Candi saw in Al Gregory. Love, she told herself, is blind, not to mention deaf and dumb – especially dumb. Poor, plain Candi Long, she could have done so much better. If only she'd been able to room with Candi at school . . . if only there were a way to let her know . . . 'When's Al going to be back?'

'Maybe tonight. He's going to call. I'll take his car. He left it at the lab.'

'Put a towel over the seat before you sit in it.' She chuckled. Gregory drove a Chevy Citation. The perfect car for a geek, Bea Taussig thought. It was filled with the cellophane wrappers from Hostess Twinkies, and he washed it once a year whether the car needed it or not. She wondered what he was like in bed, but stifled the thought. Not in the morning, not after you just woke up. The thought of her friend . . . involved with *that* made her skin crawl. Candi was just so naive, so innocent – so *dumb!* about some things. Well, maybe she'd come around. There was still hope. 'How's the work on your diamond mirror coming?'

'ADAMANT? Give us another year and we'll know. I wish you were still working with my team,' Dr Long said.

'I can see more on the administrative side,' Bea answered with remarkable honesty. 'Besides, I know I'm not as smart as you.'

'Just prettier,' Candi noted wistfully.

Bea turned to look at her friend. Yes, there was still hope.

Misha had the finished report by four. It was delayed, Bondarenko explained, because all the most-secret-cleared secretaries were busy with other material. It was forty-one pages long, including the diagrams. The young Colonel was as good as his word, Filitov saw. He'd translated all of the engineering gobbledygook into plain, clear language. Misha had spent the previous week reading everything he could find in the files on lasers. While he didn't really understand the principles of their operation all that clearly, he had the engineering details committed to his trained memory. It made him feel like a parrot. He could repeat the words without comprehending their significance. Well, that was enough.

He read slowly, memorizing as he went. For all his peasant voice and gruff words, his mind was an even sharper razor than Colonel Bondarenko believed. And as things turned out, it didn't have to be. The important part of the breakthrough appeared simple enough, not a matter of increasing the size of the lasing cavity, but of adapting its shape to the magnetic field. With the proper shape, size could be increased almost at will . . . and the new limiting factor became a part of the superconducting magnetic-pulse-control assembly. Misha sighed. The West had done it yet again. The Soviet Union did not have the proper materials. So, as usual, the KGB had secured them in the West, this time shipped through Czechoslovakia via Sweden. Wouldn't they ever learn?

The report concluded that the other remaining problem was in the optical and computer system. *I'll have to see what our intelligence organs are doing about that*, Filitov told himself. Finally, he spent twenty minutes going over the diagram of the new laser. When he got to the point at which he could close his eyes and recall every single detail, he put the report back in its folder. He checked his watch and punched the button for his secretary. The warrant officer appeared at the door in a few seconds.

'Yes, Comrade Colonel?'

'Take this down to Central Files – Section 5, maximum security. Oh, and where's today's burn-bag?'

'I have it, Comrade.'

'Get it for me.' The man went back to the anteroom and returned a moment later with the canvas bag that went daily to the document-destruction room. Misha took it and started putting papers into it. 'Dismissed. I'll drop this off on the way out.'

'Thank you, Comrade Colonel.'

'You work hard enough, Yuri Il'ych. Good night.' When the door closed behind his secretary, Misha produced some additional pages, documents that had not originated at the Ministry. Every week or so he took care of the burn-bag himself. The warrant officer who handled Filitov's clerical work assumed that it was because of his Colonel's kindness, and perhaps also because there were some especially sensitive papers to be destroyed. In any case, it was a habit that long predated his own service to the Colonel, and the security services viewed it as routine. Three minutes later, on the way to his car, Misha walked into the destruct room. A young sergeant greeted the Colonel as he might have greeted his grandfather, and held open the chute to the incinerator. He watched as the Hero of Stalingrad set down his briefcase and used his crippled arm to open the bag as the good arm elevated it, dumping perhaps a kilogram of classified documents into the gas-fed fire in the Ministry's basement.

He could not have known that he was helping a man destroy evidence of high treason. The Colonel signed off in the log for having destroyed the documents from his section. With a friendly nod, Misha left the burn-bag on its hook and walked out the door to his waiting staff car.

Tonight the ghosts would come again, Misha knew, and tomorrow he'd take steam again, and another package of information would go to the West. On the way to his apartment, the driver stopped off at a special grocery store that was open only to the elite. Here the lines were short. Misha bought some sausage and black bread, and a half-liter bottle of Stolychnaya vodka. In a gesture of comradeliness, he even got one for his driver. For a young soldier, vodka was better than money.

In his apartment fifteen minutes later, Misha extracted his diary from its drawer, and first of all reproduced the diagram appended to Bondarenko's report. Every few minutes he'd spend a second or two looking at the framed photograph of his wife. For the most part, the formal report had tracked with the handwritten one; he had to write only ten new pages, carefully inserting the critical formulae as he went. CARDINAL reports were always models of brevity and clarity, something that came from a lifetime of writing operational directives. When he was finished, he put on a pair of gloves and walked into the kitchen. Magnetically attached to the back side of the steel panel at the bottom of his West German-made refrigerator was a small camera. Misha operated the camera with ease, despite the inconvenience of the gloves. It took only a

185

minute for him to photograph the new diary pages, after which he rewound the film and extracted the film cassette. He pocketed this and replaced the camera in its hiding place before removing the gloves. Next he adjusted the window shades. Misha was nothing if not careful. Close examination of his apartment's door would show scratches on the lock, indicating that it had been picked open by an expert. In fact, anyone could make the scratches. When it was confirmed that his report had reached Washington – tire scuff marks on a predetermined section of curb – he'd tear the pages out of the diary, take them to the Ministry in his pocket, put them in the burn-bag, and dump them down the chute himself. Misha had supervised the installation of the document-destruction system twenty years before.

When the task was complete, Colonel Mikhail Semyonovich Filitov looked again at Elena's picture and asked if he'd done the right thing. But Elena merely smiled as she had always done. *All these years*, he thought, *and it still troubles my conscience*. He shook his head. The final part of the ritual followed. He ate sausage and bread while his long-dead comrades of the Great Patriotic War came to visit, but he couldn't bring himself to ask those who had died for their country if he was justified in betraying it. He thought they would understand even better than his Elena, but was afraid to find out. The half-liter of vodka didn't provide the answer either. At least it drugged his brain to insensibility, and he staggered off to bed just after ten, leaving the lights on behind him.

Just after eleven, a car drove by the wide boulevard that fronted the apartment block, and a pair of blue eyes checked the Colonel's windows. It was Ed Foley this time. He noted the shades. On the way to his own flat, another covert message was passed. A Moscow sanitation worker set up a collection of signals. They were innocuous things, a chalk mark on a lamp post, for example, each of which would tell a part of the cutout team to be at their assigned posts. Another member of the CIA Moscow Station staff would check the cues at dawn, and if anything was amiss, Foley himself could abort everything.

As tense as the job was, Ed Foley found many aspects of it amusing. For one thing, the Russians themselves had made it easier by giving CARDINAL an apartment on a heavily traveled street. For another, in making such a hash of the new embassy building, they prevented him and his family from living in the new compound, and that forced Foley or his wife to drive down this boulevard every night. And they were so glad to have his son on their hockey team. That was one thing he'd miss on leaving this place, Foley told himself as he got out of the car. He now liked junior-league hockey better than baseball. Well, there was always soccer. He didn't want his son to play football. Too many kids got hurt, and he'd never be big enough. But that was in the future, and he still had the present to worry about.

He had to be careful not to say things aloud in his own apartment. Every room in every flat occupied by Americans was assumed to be more heavily bugged than an ant farm, but over the years, Ed and Mary Pat had made a joke of that, too. After he came in and hung up his coat, he kissed his wife, then tickled her ear at the same time. She giggled in recognition, though both were thoroughly tired of the stress that came with this post. Just a few more months.

'So how was the reception?' she asked for the benefit of the wall microphones.

'The usual crap,' was the recorded answer.

9

Opportunities

Beatrice Taussig didn't make up a report, though she considered the slip Candi had made significant. Cleared for nearly everything that happened at Los Alamos National Laboratory, she hadn't been told about an unscheduled test, and while some SDI work was being done in Europe and Japan, none of it required Al Gregory as an interpreter. That made it Russian, and if they'd flown the little geek to Washington – and, she remembered, he'd left his car at the lab; so they'd sent him a helicopter, too – it had to have been something big. She didn't like Gregory, but she had no reason to doubt the quality of his brain. She wondered what the test was, but she wasn't cleared for what the Russians were up to, and her curiosity was disciplined. It had to be. What she was doing was dangerous.

But that was part of the fun, wasn't it? She smiled to herself.

'That leaves three unaccounted for.' Behind the Afghans, the Russians were sifting through the wreckage of the An-26. The man talking was a KGB major. He'd never seen an air crash before, and only the cold air on his face had kept him from losing his breakfast.

'Your man?' The infantry Captain of the Soviet Army – until very recently a battalion advisor to the puppet Afghan Army – looked around to make sure his troops were manning the perimeter properly. His stomach was as settled as it could be. Watching his friend nearly gutted before his eyes had been the greatest shock of his life, and he was wondering if his Afghan comrade would survive emergency surgery.

'Still missing, I think.' The aircraft's fuselage had broken into several pieces. Those passengers in the forward section had been bathed in fuel when the plane had hit the ground, and were burned beyond recognition. Still, the troops had assembled the pieces for nearly all the bodies. All but three, that is, and the forensic experts would have to determine who was surely dead and who was still missing. They were not normally so solicitous for the victims of an airline crash – the An-26 had technically been part of Aeroflot rather than the Soviet Air Force – but a full effort was being made in this case. The missing Captain was part of the KGB's Ninth 'Guards' Directorate, an administrative officer who'd been making a tour of the region, checking up on personnel and security activities at certain sensitive areas. His travel documents included some highly sensitive papers, but, more important, he had intimate knowledge of numerous KGB personnel and activities. The papers could have been destroyed – the remains of several briefcases had been found, burned to ashes, but until the death of the Captain could be confirmed there would be some very unhappy people at Moscow Center.

'He left a family – well, a widow. His son died last month, they tell me. Some kind of cancer,' the KGB Major noted quietly.

'I hope you will take proper care of his wife,' the Captain replied.

'Yes, we have a department to manage that. Might they have dragged him off?'

'Well, we know they were here. They always loot crash sites, looking for weapons. Documents?' The Captain shrugged. 'We're fighting ignorant savages, Comrade Major. I doubt that they have much interest in documents of any kind. They might have recognized his uniform as that of a KGB officer, then dragged him off to mutilate the body. You wouldn't believe what they do to captives.'

189

'Barbarians,' the KGB man muttered. 'Shooting down an unarmed airliner.' He looked around. 'Loyal' Afghan troops – that was an optimistic adjective for them, he grumbled – were putting the bodies, and the pieces, into rubber bags to be helicoptered back to Ghazni, then flown to Moscow for identification. 'And if they dragged my man's body off?'

'We'll never find it. Oh, there's some chance, but not a good one. Every circling vulture we see, we'll send a helicopter out, but . . .' The Captain shook his head. 'The odds are that you already have the body, Comrade Major. It will just require some time to confirm the fact.'

'Poor bastard – desk man. Wasn't even his territory, but the man assigned here is in the hospital with gallbladder problems, and he took this job in addition to his own.'

'What's his usual territory?'

'The Tadzhik SSR. I suppose he wanted the extra work to get his mind off his troubles.'

'How are you feeling, Russian?' the Archer asked his prisoner. They couldn't provide much in the way of medical attention. The nearest medical team, made up of French doctors and nurses, was in a cave near Hasan Khél. Their own walking casualties were heading there now. Those more seriously hurt . . . well, what could they do? They had a good supply of painkillers, morphine ampuls manufactured in Switzerland, and injected the dying to ease their pain. In some cases the morphine helped them along, but anyone who showed hope of recovery was placed on a litter and carried southeast toward the Pakistani border. Those who survived the sixty-mile journey would receive care in something that passed for a real hospital, near the closed airfield at Miram Shah. The Archer led this party. He'd successfully argued with his comrades that the Russian was worth more alive than dead, that the *Americastani* would give them much for a member of the Russian political police and his documents. Only the tribal headman could have defeated this argument, and he was dead. They'd given the body as hasty a burial as their faith permitted, but he was now in Paradise. That left the Archer now as the most senior and trusted warrior of the band.

Who could have told from his flint-hard eyes and cold words that for the first time in three years there was pity in his heart? Even he was bemused by it. Why had those thoughts entered his head? Was it the will of Allah? *It had to be*, he thought. *Who else could stop me from killing a Russian?*

'Hurt,' the Russian answered finally. But the Archer's pity didn't stretch that far. The morphine the *mudjaheddin* carried was only for their own. After looking to be sure that no one saw, he passed the Russian the photographs of his family. For the briefest instant his eyes softened. The KGB officer looked at him in surprise that overcame the pain. His good hand took the photographs, cupping them to his chest. There was gratitude on his face, gratitude and puzzlement. The man thought of his dead son, and contemplated his own fate. The worst thing that could happen, he decided within the cloud of pain, was that he'd rejoin his child, wherever he was. The Afghans could not hurt him worse than he already was in body and soul. The Captain was already to the point that the pain had become like a drug, so familiar that the agony had become tolerable, almost comfortable. He'd heard that this was possible, but not believed it until now.

His mental processes were still not fully functional. In his twilight state he wondered why he hadn't been killed. He'd heard enough stories in Moscow about how the Afghans treated captives . . . *and was that why you volunteered to handle this tour in addition to your own . . .?* He wondered now at his fate, and how he'd brought it about.

You cannot die. Valeriy Mikhailovich, you must live. You have a wife, and she has suffered enough, he told himself. *Already she is going through* . . . The thought stopped of its own accord. The Captain slid the photo into a breast pocket and surrendered himself to the beckoning unconsciousness as his body labored to heal itself. He didn't wake as he was bound to a board and placed aboard a travois. The Archer led his party off.

Misha woke with the sounds of battle reverberating through his head. It was still dark outside – the sun would not rise for some time – and his first considered action was to go into the bathroom, where he splashed cold water on his face and washed down three aspirin. Some dry heaves followed, over the toilet, but all that came out was yellow bile, and he rose to look in the mirror to see what treason had done to a Hero of the Soviet Union. He could not – would not – stop, of course, but . . . *but look what it is doing to you, Misha.* The once clear-blue eyes were bloodshot and lifeless, the ruddy complexion gray like a corpse. His skin sagged, and the gray stubble on his cheeks blurred a face that had once been called handsome. He stretched his right arm, and as usual the scar tissue was stiff, looking like plastic. Well. He washed out his mouth and trudged off to the kitchen to make some coffee.

At least he had some of that, also bought in a store that catered to the members of the *nomenklatura*, and a Western-made machine with which to brew it. He debated over eating something, but decided to stick with coffee alone. He could always have some bread at his desk. The coffee was ready in three minutes. He drank a cup straight down, ignoring the damaging heat of the liquid, then lifted his phone to order his staff car. He wanted to be picked up early, and though he didn't say that he wanted to visit the baths this morning, the sergeant who answered the phone at the motor pool knew what the reason was.

Twenty minutes later Misha emerged from the front of his building. His eyes were already watering, and he squinted painfully into the cold northwest wind that tried to sweep him back through the doors. The sergeant thought to reach out and steady his Colonel, but Filitov shifted his weight slightly to fight against the invisible hand of nature that held him back and got into the car as he always did, as though he were boarding his old T-34 for combat.

'The baths, Comrade Colonel?' the driver asked after getting back in front.

'Did you sell the vodka I gave you?'

'Why, yes, Comrade Colonel,' the youngster answered.

'Good for you, that's healthier than drinking it. The baths. Quickly,' the Colonel said with mock gravity, 'and I might yet live.'

'If the Germans couldn't kill you, my Colonel, I doubt that a few drops of good Russian vodka can,' the boy said cheerfully.

Misha allowed himself a laugh, accepting the flash in his head with good humor. The driver even looked like his Corporal Romanov. 'How would you like to be an officer someday?'

'Thank you, Comrade Colonel, but I wish to return to the university to study. My father is a chemical engineer and I plan to follow him.'

'He is a lucky man, then, Sergeant. Let's get moving.'

The car pulled up to the proper building in ten minutes. The Sergeant let his Colonel out, then parked in the reserved spaces from which he could see the doors. He lit a cigarette and opened a book. This was very good duty, better than tromping around in the mud with a motor-rifle company. He checked his watch. Old Misha wouldn't be back for nearly an hour. Poor old bastard, he thought, to be so lonely. What miserable luck that a hero should come to this.

Inside, the routine was so fixed that Misha could have done it asleep. After undressing, he got his towels, and slippers, and birch branches, and moved off to the steam room. He was earlier than usual. Most of the regulars hadn't shown up yet. So much the better. He increased the flow of water onto the firebricks and sat down to allow his pounding head to clear. Three others were scattered about the room. He recognized two of them, but they weren't acquaintances, and none seemed in the mood to talk. That was fine with Misha. The mere act of moving his jaw hurt, and the aspirin were slow today.

Fifteen minutes later the sweat poured off the white body. He looked up to see the attendant, heard the usual cant about a drink – nobody wanted one just yet – plus the line about the swimming pool. It seemed the likely thing for a man in this job to say, but what the precise wording meant was: *All secure. I am ready for the transfer*. By way of reply, Misha wiped the sweat off his brow in an exaggerated gesture common to elderly men. *Ready*. The attendant left. Slowly, Misha began counting to three hundred. When he got to two hundred and fifty-seven, one of his fellow alcoholics stood and walked out. Misha took note of this, but didn't worry about it. He had far too much practice. When he got to three hundred he rose with a jerking movement of his knees and left the room without a word.

The air was much cooler in the robing room, but he saw that the other man hadn't left yet. He was talking to the attendant about something or other. Misha waited patiently for the attendant to notice him, which he did. The young man came over, and the Colonel took a few steps to meet him. Misha stumbled on a loose tile and nearly fell. His good arm went forward. The attendant caught him, or nearly did. The birch sticks fell to the floor.

The young man swept them up in an instant and helped Misha to his feet. In another few seconds he'd given him a fresh towel for his shower and sent him on his way.

'Are you all right, Comrade?' the other man asked from the far end of the room.

'Yes, thank you. My old knees, and these old floors. They should pay more attention to the floor.'

'Indeed they should. Come, we can shower together,' the man said. He was about forty, and nondescript except for his bloodshot eyes. Another drinker, Misha observed at once. 'You were in the war, then?'

'Tanker. The last German gun got me – but I got him, too, at the Kursk Bulge.'

'My father was there. He served in the Seventh Guards Army under Konev.'

'I was on the other side: Second Tanks, under Konstantin Rokossovskiy. My last campaign.'

'I can see why, Comrade . . .'

'Filitov, Mikhail Semyonovich, Colonel of Tank Troops.'

'I am Klementi Vladimirovich Vatutin, but I am no one's hero. It is a pleasure to meet you, Comrade.'

'It is good for an old man to be shown respect.'

Vatutin's father had served in the Kursk Campaign, but as a political officer. He'd retired a colonel in the NKVD, and his son had followed in his footsteps, in the agency later redesignated KGB.

Twenty minutes later, the Colonel was off to his office, and the bath attendant had slipped out the rear door again and entered that of the dry-cleaners. The store manager had to be called from the machine room, where he'd been oiling a pump. As a matter of simple security, the man who took the cassette from his hand was supposed to know neither the man's name nor where he worked. He pocketed the cassette, passed over three half-liter bottles of liquor, and returned to finish oiling the pump, his heart rate up as it always was on these days. He was quietly amused that his cover assignment as a CIA 'agent' – a Soviet national working for the American intelligence agency – worked very much to his personal fiscal benefit. The under-the-counter marketing of alcohol paid him in 'certificate' rubles that could be used to buy Western goods and premium foodstuffs at the hard-currency stores. He balanced that against the tension of his assignment as he washed the machine oil off his hands. He'd been part of this line of cutouts for six months, and though he didn't know it, his work along this line would soon be ended. He'd still be used to pass along information, but not for CARDINAL. Soon thereafter the man at the baths would seek another job, and this link of nameless agents would be dissolved – and untraceable even to the relentless counterintelligence officers of the KGB's Second Chief Directorate.

Fifteen minutes later, a regular customer appeared with one of her English coats. It was an Aquascutum with the zippered-in liner removed. As always, she said something about taking special care to use the gentlest process on the coat, and as always he nodded and protested that this was the best cleaning shop in all of the Soviet Union. But it didn't have pre-printed check forms, and he wrote out three by hand on carbon-sets. The first was attached to the coat with a straight pin, the second went into a small box, and the third – but first he checked the pockets.

'Comrade, you've left some change. I thank you, but we do not need the extra money.' He handed this, and the receipt, over. Plus something else. It was so easy. Nobody ever checked the pockets, just as in the West.

'Ah, truly you are an honorable man,' the lady said with an odd formalism common in the Soviet Union. 'Good day, Comrade.'

'And to you,' the man replied. 'Next!'

The lady – her name was Svetlana – walked off to the Metro station as usual. Her schedule allowed for a leisurely walk in case of problems at either end of her exchange. The streets of Moscow were invariably crowded with bustling, unsmiling people, many of whom looked at her coat with brief glances of envy. She had a wide selection of English clothing, having traveled to the West many times as part of her job at GOSPLAN, the Soviet economics planning ministry. It was in England that she'd been recruited by the British Secret Intelligence Service. She was used in the CARDINAL chain because the CIA didn't have all that many agents in Russia who could be used, and she was carefully given jobs only in the center of the chain, never at either end. The data she herself gave the West was low-level economic information, and her occasional services as a courier were actually more useful than the information of which she was so proud. Her case officers never told her this, of course; every spy deems him- or herself to possess the most vital intelligence ever to make its way out. It made the game all the more interesting, and for all their ideological (or other) motivations, spies view their craft as the grandest of all games, since they must invariably outsmart the most formidable resources of their own countries. Svetlana actually enjoyed living on the jagged edge of life and death, though she did not know why. She also believed that her highly placed father – a senior Central Committee member – could protect her from anything. After all, his influence enabled her to travel to Western Europe two or three times a year, didn't it? A pompous man, her father, but Svetlana was his only child, the mother of his only grandchild, and the center of his universe.

She entered the Kuznetskiy Most station in time to see one train leave. Timing was always the tricky part. In rush hour, the Moscow Metro trains run a mere thirty seconds apart. Svetlana checked her watch, and again she had timed her arrival perfectly. Her contact would be on the next one. She walked along the platform to the exact spot for the forward door on the second car of that train, ensuring that she'd be the first one aboard. Her clothing helped. She was often mistaken for a foreigner, and Moscovites treated foreigners with deference ordinarily reserved for royalty – or the gravely ill. She didn't have to wait long. Soon she heard the rumble of an approaching train. Heads turned, as they always did, to see the lights of the lead car, and the sound of brakes filled the vaulted station with high-pitched noise. The door opened, and a rush of people emerged. Then Svetlana stepped in and took a few steps toward the back of the car. She grabbed the overhead bar – all the seats were filled, and no man offered his – and faced forward before the train lurched forward again. Her ungloved left hand was in her coat pocket.

She'd never seen the face of her contact on this train, but she knew that he'd seen hers. Whoever he was, he appreciated her slim figure. She knew that from his signal. In the crush of the crowded train, a hand hidden by a copy of *Izvestia* ran along her left buttock and stopped to squeeze gently. That was new, and she fought off the impulse to see his face. Might he be a good lover? She could use another one. Her former husband was such a . . . but, no. It was better this way, more poetic, more Russian, that a man whose face she'd never know found her beautiful and desirable. She clasped the film cassette between her thumb and forefinger, waiting the next two minutes for the train to stop at Pushkinskaya. Her eyes were closed, and a millimeter of a smile formed on her lips as she contemplated the identity and attributes of the cutout whose hand caressed her. It would have horrified her case officer, but she gave no other outward sign of anything.

The train slowed. People rose from their seats, and those standing shuffled about in preparation to leave. Svetlana took her hand out of the pocket. The cassette was slippery, whether from water or some oily substance from the cleaners she didn't know. The hand left her hip – a last, lingering trail of gentle pressure – and came upward to receive the small metal cylinder as her face turned to the right.

Immediately behind her, an elderly woman tripped on her own feet and bumped into the cutout. His hand knocked the cassette from Svetlana's. She didn't realize it for a moment, but the instant the train stopped, the man was on all fours grabbing for it. She looked down more in surprise than horror to see the back of his head. He was going bald, and the shroud of hair about his ears was gray – he was an old man! He had the cassette in a moment and sprang back to his feet. Old, but spry, she thought, catching the shape of his jaw. A strong profile – yes, he'd be a good lover, and perhaps a patient one, the best kind of all. He scurried off the train, and she cleared her mind. Svetlana didn't notice that a man sitting on the left side of the car was up and moving, exiting the car against traffic a second before the doors closed again.

His name was Boris, and he was a night-watch officer at KGB headquarters now on his way home to sleep. Ordinarily he read the sports newspaper – known originally as *Sovietskiy Sport* – but today he'd forgotten to get one at the kiosk in the headquarters building, and he'd accidentally happened to see on the dirty black floor of the subway car what could only be a film cassette, and one too small to come from an ordinary camera. He hadn't seen the attempted pass, and didn't know who'd dropped it. He assumed that the fiftyish man had, and noted the skill with which the man had retrieved it. Once off the car, he realized that a pass must have taken place, but he'd been too surprised to respond properly, too surprised and too tired after a long night's duty.

He was a former case officer who'd operated in Spain before being invalided home after a heart attack and set on the night desk in his section. His rank was major. He felt he deserved a colonelcy for the work he'd done, but this thought, too, was not in his mind at the moment. His eyes searched the platform for the gray-haired man in the brown coat. *There!* He moved off, feeling a small twinge in his left chest as he walked after the man. He ignored that. He'd quit smoking a few years before, and the KGB doctor said that he was doing well. He got within five meters of the man, and closed no more. This was the time for patience. He followed him through the crossover to the Gor'kovskaya Station and onto the platform. Here things got tricky. The platform was crowded with people heading to their offices, and he lost visual contact with his quarry. The KGB officer was a short man and had trouble in crowds. Could he dare to close further? It would mean pushing through the crowd . . . and calling attention to himself. That was dangerous.

He'd been trained in this, of course, but that was over twenty years behind him, and he frantically searched his mind for procedures. He knew fieldcraft, knew how to identify and shake a tail, but he was a First Directorate man, and the shadowing skills used by the ferrets of the Second Directorate were not part of his repertoire. *What do I do now?* he raged at himself. Such a chance this was! The First Directorate men naturally hated their counterparts in the Second, and to catch one of them at – but what if there might be a 'Two' man here? Might he be observing a training exercise? Might he now be the subject of curses from a 'Two' man who had a case running on this courier? Could he be disgraced by this? *What do I do now?* He looked around, hoping to identify the counterintelligence men who might be working this courier. He couldn't hope to discern which face it was, but he might get a wave-off signal. He thought he remembered those. Nothing. *What do I do now?* He was sweating in the cold subway station, and the pain in his chest increased to add another factor to his dilemma. There was a system of covert telephone lines built into every segment of the Moscow subway system. Every KGB officer knew how to use them, but he knew he didn't have time to find and activate the system.

He had to follow the man. He had to run the risk. If it turned out to be the wrong decision, well, he was an experienced field officer in his own right, and he *had* looked for the wave-off. The 'Two' people might tongue-lash him, but he knew he could depend on his First Directorate supervisors to protect him. The decision now made, the chest pain subsided. But there was still the problem of seeing him. The KGB officer wormed his way through the crowd, enduring grumbles as he did so, but finally finding his way blocked by a gang of laborers who were talking about something or other. He craned his neck to get a look at his quarry – *yes! still standing there, looking to the right* . . . The sound of the subway train came as a relief.

He stood there, trying not to look too often at his target. He heard the subway doors open with a hiss, heard the sudden change in noise as the people got off, then the rasping shuffle of feet as people crowded forward toward the doors.

The car was full! His man was inside, but the doors overflowed with bodies. The KGB officer raced to the rear door and fought his way in a moment before it shut. He realized with a chill that he might have been too obvious, but there was nothing he could do about that. As the train began moving, he worked his way forward. The people seated and standing noticed this untoward movement. As he watched, a hand adjusted a hat. Three or four newspapers rattled – any of these signals could be a warning to the courier.

One of them was. Ed Foley was looking away after adjusting his glasses with a right hand that wore one glove and held another. The courier turned back forward and went over his escape procedures. Foley went over his own. The courier would dispose of the film, first exposing it by pulling it out of the metal cylinder, then dumping it in the nearest trash receptacle. That had happened twice before that he knew of, and in both cases the cutout had gotten away cleanly. *They're trained how,* Foley told himself. *They know how.* CARDINAL would be warned, and another film would be made, and . . . but this had never happened on Foley's watch, and it took all of his discipline to keep his face impassive. The courier didn't move at all. He got off at the next stop anyway. He'd done nothing unusual, nothing that didn't appear normal. He would say that he'd found this funny little thing with the – *was it film, Comrade?* – stuff pulled out on the floor of the train, and thought it merely trash to be disposed of. In his pocket, the man was trying to pull the film out of the cassette. Whoever took it always left a few millimeters out so that you could yank all of it – or so they'd told him. But the cassette was slippery and he couldn't quite get a grip on the exposed end. The train stopped again and the courier moved out. He didn't know who was trailing him. He knew nothing other than he'd gotten his wave-off signal, and that signal also told him to destroy what he had in the prescribed way – but he'd never had to do it before. He tried not to look around, and moved out of the station as quickly as anyone else in the crowd. For his part, Foley didn't even look out of the train's windows. It was nearly inhuman but he managed it, fearing above all that he might endanger his cutout.

The courier stood alone on a moving step of the escalator. Just a few more seconds and he'd be on the street. He'd find an alley to expose the film, and a sewer to dump it in, along with the cigarette he'd just lit. One smooth motion of the hand, and even if he were picked up, there would be no evidence, and his story, drilled into his head and practiced there every day, was good enough to make the KGB wonder. His career as a spy was now over. He knew that, and was surprised at the wave of relief that enveloped him like a warm, comfortable bath.

The air was a cold reminder of reality, but the sun was rising, and the sky was beautifully clear. He turned right and walked off. There was an alley half a block away, and a sewer grate that he could use. His cigarette would be finished just as he got there, yet another thing that he'd practiced. Now, if only he could get the film out of the cassette and exposed to sunlight . . . Damn. He slipped off his other glove and rubbed his hands together. The courier used his fingernails to get the film. Yes! He crumpled the film and put the cassette back into his pocket, and –

'Comrade.' The voice was strong for a man of his age, the courier thought. The brown eyes sparkled with alertness, and the hand at his pocket was a strong one. The other, he saw, was in the man's pocket. 'I wish to see what is in your hand.'

'Who are you?' the courier blustered. 'What is this?'

The right hand jerked in the pocket. 'I am the man who will kill you, here on the street, unless I see what is in your hand. I am Major Boris Churbanov.' Churbanov knew that this would soon be false. From the look on the man's face, he knew that he had his colonelcy.

Foley was in his office ten minutes later. He sent one of his men – actually a woman – out on the street to look for the signal that the dump had been made successfully, and his hope was that he'd simply goofed, that he'd overreacted to a commuter who was trying too hard to get to work. But . . . but there was something about that face that had said *professional*. Foley didn't know what, but it had been there. He had his hands flat on the desk and stared at them for several minutes.

What did I do wrong? he asked himself. He'd been trained to do that, too, to analyze his actions step by step, looking for flaws, for mistakes, for . . . Had he been followed? He frequently was, of course, like all Americans on the embassy staff. His personal tail was a man he thought of as 'George'. But George wasn't there very often. The Russians didn't know who Foley was. He was sure of that. That thought caught in his throat. Being certain about anything in the intelligence business was the surest route to disaster. That was why he'd never broken craft, why he never deviated from the training that had been drilled into him at Camp Peary, on the York River in Virginia, then practiced all over the world.

Well. The next thing he had to do was predetermined. He walked to the communications room and sent a telex to Foggy Bottom. This one, however, went to a box number whose traffic was never routine. Within a minute of its receipt, a night-watch officer from Langley drove to State to retrieve it. The wording of the message was innocuous, but its meaning was not: TROUBLE ON THE CARDINAL LINE. FULL DATA TO FOLLOW.

They didn't take him to Dzerzhinskiy Square. KGB headquarters, so long used as a prison – a dungeon for all that happened there – was now exclusively an office building since, in obedience to Parkinson's Law, the agency had expanded to absorb all its available space. Now the interrogations were done at Lefortovo Prison, a block from the Sputnik Cinema. There was plenty of room here.

He sat alone in a room with a table and three chairs. It had never occurred to the courier to resist, and even now he didn't realize that if he'd run away or fought the man who'd arrested him, he might still be free. It wasn't the idea that Major Churbanov had had a gun – he hadn't – but simply that Russians, in lacking freedom, often lack the concepts needed for active resistance. He'd seen his life end. He accepted that. The courier was a fearful man, but he feared only what had to be. You cannot fight against destiny, he told himself.

'So, Churbanov, what do we have?' The questioner was a Captain of the Second Chief Directorate, about thirty years old.

'Have someone develop this.' He handed over the cassette. 'I think this man is a cutout.' Churbanov described what he'd seen and what he'd done. He didn't say that he'd rewound the film into the cassette. 'Pure chance that I spotted him,' he concluded.

'I didn't think you "One" people knew how, Comrade Major. Well donc!'

'I was afraid that I'd blundered into one of your operations and – '

'You would have known by now. It is necessary for you to make a full report. If you will accompany the sergeant here, he'll take you to a stenographer. Also, I will summon a full debriefing team. This will take some hours. You may wish to call your wife.'

'The film,' Churbanov persisted.

'Yes. I will walk that down to the lab myself. If you'll go with the sergeant, I'll rejoin you in ten minutes.'

The laboratory was in the opposite wing of the prison. The Second Directorate had a small facility here, since much of its work centered on Lefortovo. The Captain caught the lab technician between jobs, and the developing process started at once. While he waited, he called his Colonel. There was as yet no way to measure what this 'One' man had uncovered, but it was almost certainly an espionage case, and those were all treated as matters of the utmost importance. The Captain shook his head. That old war-horse of a field officer, just stumbling into something like that.

'Finished.' The technician came back. He'd developed the film and printed one blow-up, still damp from the process. He handed back the film cassette, too, in a small manila envelope. 'The film has been exposed and rewound.

I managed to save part of one frame. It's interesting, but I have no idea what it actually is.'

'What about the rest?'

'Nothing can be done. Once film is exposed to sunlight, the data is utterly destroyed.'

The Captain scanned the blow-up as the technician said something else. It was mainly a diagram, with some caption printed in block letters. The words at the top of the diagram read: BRIGHT STAR COMPLEX #1, and one of the other captions was LASER ARRAY. The Captain swore and left the room at a run.

Major Churbanov was having tea with the debrief team when the Captain returned. The scene was comradely. It would get more so.

'Comrade Major, you may have discovered something of the highest importance,' the Captain said.

'I serve the Soviet Union,' Churbanov replied evenly. It was the perfect reply – the one recommended by the Party. Perhaps he might leap over the rank of lieutenant colonel and become a full colonel . . .

'Let me see,' the chief debriefer said. He was a full colonel, and examined the photographic print carefully. 'This is all?'

'The rest was destroyed.'

The Colonel grunted. That would create a problem, but not all that much of one. The diagram would suffice to identify the site, whatever it was. The printing looked to be the work of a young person, probably a woman because of its neatness. The Colonel paused and looked out the window for a few seconds. 'This has to go to the top, and quickly. What is described in here is – well, I have never heard of it, but it must be a matter of the greatest secrecy. You comrades begin the debrief. I'm going to make a few calls. You, Captain, take the cassette to the lab for fingerprints and – '

'Comrade, I touched it with my bare hands,' Churbanov said ashamedly.

'You have nothing to apologize for, Comrade Major,

your vigilance was more than exemplary,' the Colonel said generously. 'Check for prints anyway.'

'The spy?' the Captain asked. 'What about interrogating him?'

'We need an experienced man. I know just the one.' The Colonel rose. 'I'll call him, too.'

Several pairs of eyes watched him, measuring him, his face, his determination, his intelligence. The courier was still alone in the interrogation room. The laces had been taken from his shoes, of course, and his belt, and his cigarettes, and anything else that might be used as a weapon against himself, or to settle him down. There was no way for him to measure time, and the lack of nicotine made him fidgety and even more nervous than he might have been. He looked about the room and saw a mirror, which was two-way, but he didn't know that. The room was completely soundproofed to deny him even the measure of time from footsteps in the outside corridor. His stomach growled a few times, but otherwise he made no sound. Finally the door opened.

The man who entered was about forty and well dressed in civilian clothes. He carried a few sheets of paper. The man walked around to the far side of the table and didn't look at the courier until he sat down. When he did look at him, his eyes were disinterested, like a man at the zoo examining a creature from a distant land. The courier tried to meet his gaze impassively, but failed. Already the interrogater knew that this one would be easy. After fifteen years, he could always tell.

'You have a choice,' he said after another minute or so. His voice was not hard, but matter-of-fact. 'It can go easily for you or it can go very hard. You have committed treason against the Motherland. I do not need to tell you what happens to traitors. If you wish to live, you will tell me now, today, everything you know. If you do not do this, we will find out anyway, and you will die. If you tell us today, you will be allowed to live.'

206

'You will kill me anyway,' the courier observed.

'This is not true. If you cooperate, today, you will at worst be sentenced to a lengthy term in a labor camp of strict regime. It is even possible that we can use you to uncover more spies. If so, you will be sent to a camp of moderate regime, for a lesser term. But for that to happen, you must cooperate, today. I will explain. If you return to your normal life at once, the people for whom you work may not know that we have arrested you. They will, therefore, continue to make use of you, and this will enable us to use you to catch them in the act of spying against the Soviet Union. You would testify in the trial against them, and this will allow the State to show mercy. To show such mercy in public is also useful to the State. But for all this to happen, to save your life, and to atone for your crimes, you must cooperate, today.' The voice paused for a beat, and softened further.

'Comrade, I take no pleasure in bringing pain to people, but if my job requires it, I will give the order without hesitation. You cannot resist what we will do to you. No one can. No matter how brave you may be, your body has its limits. So does mine. So does anyone's. It is only a matter of time. Time is important to us only for the next few hours, you see. After that, we can take all the time we wish. A man with a hammer can break the hardest stone. Save yourself the pain, Comrade. Save your life,' the voice concluded, and the eyes, which were oddly sad and determined at the same time, stared into the courier's.

The interrogator saw that he'd won. You could always tell from the eyes. The defiant ones, the hard ones, didn't shift their eyes. They might stare straight into yours, or more often at a fixed point of the wall behind you, but the hard ones would fix to a single place and draw their strength from it. Not this one. His eyes flickered around the room, searching for strength and finding none. Well, he'd expected this one to be easy. Perhaps one more gesture . . .

'Would you like a smoke?' The interrogator fished out a pack and shook one loose on the table.

The courier picked it up, and the white paper of the cigarette was his flag of surrender.

10

Damage Assessment

'What do we know?' Judge Moore asked.

It was a little after six in the morning at Langley, before dawn, and the view outside the windows matched the gloom that the Director and his two principal subordinates felt.

'Somebody was trailing cutout number four,' Ritter said. The Deputy Director for Operations riffled through the papers in his hand. 'He spotted the tail just before the pass was made and waved the guy off. The tail probably didn't see his face, and took off after the cutout. Foley said he looked clumsy – that's pretty strange, but he went with his instincts, and Ed's pretty good at that. He put an officer on the street to catch the shake-off signal from our agent, but it wasn't put up. We have to assume that he's been burned, and we have to assume that the film is in their hands, too, until we can prove otherwise. Foley has broken the chain. CARDINAL will be notified never to use his pickup man again. I'm going to tell Ed to use the routine data-lost signal, not the emergency one.'

'Why?' Admiral Greer asked. Judge Moore answered.

'The information he had en route is pretty important, James. If we give him the scramble signal, he may – hell, we've told him that if that happens he's to destroy everything that might be incriminating. What if he can't re-create the information? We need it.'

'Besides, Ivan has to do a lot to get back to him,' Ritter went on. 'I want Foley to get the data restored and out, and then – then I want to bust CARDINAL out once and for all. He's paid his dues. After we get the data, then we'll give him the emergency signal, and if we're lucky it'll scare him enough that we can get him to come out.'

'How do you want to do it?' Moore asked.

'The wet way, up north,' the DDO answered.

'Opinions, James?' Moore asked the DDI.

'Makes sense. Take a little time to set up. Ten to fourteen days.'

'Then let's do that today. You call the Pentagon and make the request. Make sure they give us a good one.'

'Right.' Greer nodded, then smiled. 'I know which one to ask for.'

'As soon as we know which, I'll send our man to her. We'll use Mr Clark,' Ritter said. Heads nodded. Clark was a minor legend in the Operations Directorate. If anybody could do it, he could.

'Okay, get the message off to Foley,' the Judge said. 'I'll have to brief the President on this.' He wasn't looking forward to that.

'Nobody lasts forever. CARDINAL's beat the odds three times over,' Ritter said. 'Make sure you tell him that, too.'

'Yeah. Okay, gentlemen, let's get to it.'

Admiral Greer went immediately to his office. It was just before seven, and he called the Pentagon, OP-02, the office of the Assistant Chief of Naval Operations (Undersea Warfare). After identifying himself, he asked his first question: 'What's *Dallas* up to?'

Captain Mancuso was already at work, too. His last deployment on USS *Dallas* would begin in five hours. She'd sail on the tide. Aft, the engineers were already bringing the nuclear reactor on line. While his executive officer was running things, the Captain was going over the mission orders again. He was heading 'up north' one last time. In the US and Royal navies, up north meant the Barents Sea, the Soviet Navy's backyard. Once there, he'd conduct what the Navy officially termed *oceanographic research*, which in the case of USS *Dallas* meant that she'd spend all the time possible trailing Soviet missile submarines. It wasn't easy work, but Mancuso was an expert at it, and he had, in fact, once gotten a closer look at a Russian 'boomer' than any other American sub skipper. He couldn't discuss that with anyone, of course, not even a fellow skipper. His second Distinguished Service Medal, awarded for that mission, was classified and he couldn't wear it; though its existence did show in the confidential section of his personnel file, the actual citation was missing. But that was behind him, and Mancuso was a man who always looked forward. If he had to make one final deployment, it might as well be up north. His phone rang.

'Captain speaking,' he answered.

'Bart, Mike Williamson,' said the Submarine Group Two commander. 'I need you there, right now.'

'On the way, sir.' Mancuso hung up in surprise. Within a minute he was up the ladder, off the boat, and walking along the blacktopped quay in the Thames, where the Admiral's car was waiting. He was in the Group Two office four minutes after that.

'Change in orders,' Rear Admiral Williamson announced as soon as the door was closed.

'What's up?'

'You're making a high-speed run for Faslane. Some people will be meeting you there. That's all I know, but the orders originated at OP-02 and came through SUBLANT in about thirty seconds.' Williamson didn't have to say anything else. Something very hot was up. Hot ones came to *Dallas* quite often. Actually, they came to Mancuso, but then, he was *Dallas*.

'My sonar department's still a little thin,' the Captain said. 'I've got some good young ones, but my new chief's in the hospital. If this is going to be especially hairy . . .'

'What do you need?' Admiral Williamson asked, and got his answer.

'Okay, I'll get to work on that. You have five days to Scotland, and I can work something out on this end. Drive her hard, Bart.'

'Aye, aye, sir.' He'd find out what was happening when he got to Faslane.

*

211

'How are you, Russian?' the Archer asked.

He was better. The previous two days, he'd been sure that he'd die. Now he wasn't so sure. False hope or not, it was something he hadn't had before. Churkin wondered now if there might really be a future in his life, and if it were something he might have to fear. Fear. He'd forgotten that. He'd faced death twice in a small expanse of time. Once in a falling, burning airplane, hitting the ground and seeing the instant when his life ended; then waking up from death to find an Afghan bandit over him with a knife, and seeing death yet again, only to have it stop and leave. Why? This bandit, the one with the strange eyes, both hard and soft, pitiless and compassionate, wanted him to live. Why? Churkin had the time and energy to ask the question now, but they didn't give him an answer.

He was riding in something. Churkin realized that he was lying on a steel deck. A truck? No, there was a flat surface overhead, and that, too, was steel. Where am I? It had to be dark outside. No light came through the gunports in the side of – he was in an armored personnel carrier! Where did the bandits get one of those? Where were they –

They were taking him to Pakistan! They would turn him over to . . . Americans? And hope changed yet again to despair. He coughed again, and fresh blood erupted from his mouth.

For his part, the Archer felt lucky. His group had met up with another, taking two Soviet BTR-60 infantry carriers out to Pakistan, and they were only too happy to carry the wounded of his band out with them. The Archer was famous, and it could not hurt to have a SAM-shooter protect them if Russian helicopters showed up. But there was little danger of that. The nights were long, the weather had turned foul, and they averaged almost fifteen kilometers per hour on the flat places, and no less than five on the rocky ones. They'd be to the border in an hour, and this segment was held by the *mudjaheddin*. The guerrillas were starting to relax. Soon they'd have a week of relative peace, and the Americans always paid handsomely for

212

Soviet hardware. This one had night-vision devices that the driver was using to pick his way up the mountain road. For that they could expect rockets, mortar shells, a few machine guns, and medical supplies.

Things were going well for the *mudjaheddin*. There was talk that the Russians might actually withdraw. Their troops no longer craved close combat with the Afghans. Mainly the Russians used their infantry to achieve contact, then called in artillery and air support. Aside from a few vicious bands of paratroopers and the hated *Spetznaz* forces, the Afghans felt that they had achieved moral ascendancy on the battlefield – due, of course, to their holy cause. Some of their leaders actually talked about winning, and the talk had gotten to the individual fighters. They, too, now had hope of something other than continued holy war.

The two infantry carriers reached the border at midnight. From there the going was easier. The road down into Pakistan was now guarded by their own forces. The APC drivers were able to speed up and actually enjoy what they were doing. They reached Miram Shah three hours later. The Archer got out first, taking with him the Russian prisoner and his wounded.

He found Emilio Ortiz waiting for him with a can of apple juice. The man's eyes nearly bugged out when he realized that the man the Archer was carrying was a Russian.

'My friend, what have you brought me?'

'He is badly hurt, but here is what he is.' The Archer handed over one of the man's shoulder boards, then a briefcase. 'And this is what he was carrying.'

'Son of a bitch!' Ortiz blurted in English. He saw the crusted blood around the man's mouth and realized that his medical condition was not promising, but . . . what a catch this was! It took another minute of following the wounded to the field hospital before the next question came to the case officer: *What the hell do we do with him?*

The medical team here, too, was composed mainly of Frenchmen, with a leavening of Italians and a few Swedes. Ortiz knew most of them, and suspected that many of them

213

reported to the DGSE, the French foreign intelligence agency. What mattered, however, was that there were some pretty good doctors and nurses here. The Afghans knew that, too, and protected them as they might have protected the person of Allah. The surgeon who had triage duty put the Russian third on the operating schedule. A nurse medicated him, and the Archer left Abdul to keep an eye on things. He hadn't brought the Russian this far to have him killed. He and Ortiz went off to talk.

'I heard what happened in Ghazni,' the CIA officer said.

'God's will. This Russian, he lost a son. I could not – perhaps I had killed enough for one day.' The Archer let out a long breath. 'Will he be useful?'

'These are.' Ortiz was already riffling through the documents. 'My friend, you do not know what you have done. Well, shall we talk about the last two weeks?'

The debrief took until dawn. The Archer took out his diary and went over everything he'd done, pausing only while Ortiz changed tapes in his recorder.

'That light you saw in the sky.'

'Yes . . . it seemed very strange,' the Archer said, rubbing his eyes.

'The man you brought out was going there. Here is the base diagram.'

'Where is it, exactly – and what is it?'

'I don't know, but it's only about a hundred kilometers from the Afghan border. I can show you on the map. How long will you be staying on this side?'

'Perhaps a week,' the Archer answered.

'I must report this to my superiors. They may want to see you. My friend, you will be greatly rewarded. Make a list of what you need. A long list.'

'And the Russian?'

'We will talk to him, too. If he lives.'

The courier walked down Lazovskiy Pereulok, waiting for his contact. His own hopes were both high and low. He actually believed his interrogator, and by later afternoon he'd taken the chalk that he used and made the proper mark in the proper place. He knew that he'd done so five hours later than he was supposed to, but hoped that his controller would put that off to the evasion process. He hadn't made the false mark, the one that would warn the CIA officer that he'd been turned. No, he was playing too dangerous a game now. So he walked along the dreary sidewalk, waiting for his handler to show up for the clandestine meet.

What he didn't know was that his handler was sitting in his office at the American Embassy, and would not travel to this part of Moscow for several weeks. There were no plans to contact the courier for at least that long. The CARDINAL line was gone. So far as CIA was concerned, it might never have existed.

'I think we're wasting our time,' the interrogator said. He and another senior officer of the Second Directorate sat by the window of an apartment. At the next window was another 'Two' man with a camera. He and the other senior officer had learned this morning what Bright Star was, and the General who commanded the Second Chief Directorate had given this case the highest possible priority. A leak of colossal proportions had been uncovered by that broken-down war-horse from 'One.'

'You think he lied to you?'

'No. This one was easy to break – and, no, it was not too easy. He broke,' the interrogator said confidently. 'I think we failed to get him back on the street quickly enough. I think they know, and I think they've broken off the line.'

'But what went wrong – I mean from their point of view, it might have been routine.'

'*Da.*' The interrogator nodded agreement. 'But we know that the information is highly sensitive. So, too, must be its source. They have therefore taken extraordinary measures to protect it. We cannot do things the easy way now.'

'Bring him in, then?'

'Yes.' A car drove up to the man. They watched him get in before they walked to their own vehicle.

Within thirty minutes they were all back in Lefortovo Prison. The interrogator's face was sad.

'Tell me, why is it I think that you have lied to me?' the man asked.

'But I have not! I did everything I was supposed to do. Perhaps I was late, but I told you that.'

'And the signal you left, was it the one to tell them that we had you?'

'*No!*' The courier nearly panicked. 'I explained all of that, too.'

'The problem, you see, is that we cannot tell the difference between one chalk mark and another. If you are being clever, you may have deceived us.' The interrogator leaned forward. 'Comrade, you *can* deceive us. Anyone can – for a time. But not a very long time.' He paused to let that thought hover in the air for a minute. It was so easy, interrogating the weak ones. Give hope, then take it away; restore it, and remove it yet again. Take their spirits up and down until they no longer knew which was which – and, lacking a measure of their own feelings, those feelings became yours to use.

'We begin again. The woman you meet on the train – who is she?'

'I do not know her name. She is over thirty, but young for her age. Fair hair, slim and pretty. She is always dressed well, like a foreigner, but she is not a foreigner.'

'Dressed like a foreigner – how?'

'Her coat is usually Western. You can tell from the cut and the cloth. She is pretty, as I have said, and she – '

'Go on,' the interrogator said.

'The signal is that I put my hand on her rump. She likes it, I think. Often she presses back against my hand.'

The interrogator hadn't heard that detail before, but he immediately deemed it the truth. Details like that one were never made up, and it fitted the profile. The female contact was an adventuress. She was not a true professional, not if she reacted like that. And that probably – almost certainly – made her a Russian.

'How many times have you met her like this?'

'Only five. Never the same day of the week, and not on a regular schedule, but always on the second car of the same train.'

'And the man you pass it to?'

'I never see his face, not all of it, I mean. He is always standing with his hand on the bar, and he moves his face to keep his arm between it and me. I have seen some of it, but not all. He is foreign, I think, but I don't know what nationality.'

'Five times, and you have never seen his face!' the voice boomed, and a fist slammed down on the table. 'Do you take me for a fool!'

The courier cringed, then spoke rapidly. 'He wears glasses; they are Western, I am sure of it. He usually wears a hat. Also, he has a paper folded, *Izvestia*, always *Izvestia*. Between that and his arm, you cannot see more than a quarter of his face. His go-ahead signal is to turn the paper slightly, as though to follow a story, then he turns away to shield his face.'

'How is the pass made, again!'

'As the train stops, he comes forward, as though to get ready to leave at the next station. I have the thing in my hand, and he takes it from behind as I start to leave.'

'So, you know her face, but she does not know yours. He knows your face, but you do not know his . . .' *The same method that this one uses to make his pickup. That's a nice piece of fieldcraft, but why do they use the same technique twice on the same line?* The KGB used this one too, of course, but it was harder than other methods, doubly so on the Metro's crowded, frantic rush-hour schedule. He was beginning to think that the most common means of transferring information, the dead-drop, wasn't part of this line. That, too, was very curious. There should have been at least one dead-drop, else the KGB could roll up the line – maybe . . .

They were already trying to identify the source of the leak, of course, but they had to be careful. There was always the possibility that the spy was himself (or herself?)

a security officer. That was, indeed, the ideal post for an intelligence agent, since with the job came access to everything, plus foreknowledge of any counterintelligence operations under way. It had happened before – the investigation of a leak had itself alerted a spy, a fact not discovered until some years after the investigation had been terminated. The other really odd thing was that the one photographic frame they had was not of a real diagram, but rather of a hand-drawn one . . .

Handwriting – was that the reason that there were no dead-drops? The spy could be identified that way, couldn't he? What a foolish way to –

But there was nothing foolish here, was there? No, and there wasn't anything accidental either. If the techniques on this line were odd, they were also professional. There was another level to this, something that the interrogator didn't have yet.

'I think that tomorrow, you and I will ride the Metro.'

Colonel Filitov woke up without a pounding in his head, which was pleasure enough. His 'normal' morning routine was not terribly different from the other sort, but without the pain and the trip to the baths. He checked the diary tucked away in the desk drawer after he dressed, hoping that he'd be able to destroy it, as per his usual procedure. He already had a new blank diary that he'd begin with when this one was destroyed. There had been hints of a new development on the laser business the previous day, plus a paper on missile systems that he'd be seeing the following week.

On entering the car, he settled back, more alert than usual, and looked out the window during the drive into work. There were a number of trucks on the street, early as it was, and one of them blocked his view of a certain piece of curb. That was his 'data-lost' signal. He was slightly annoyed that he couldn't see where it was, but his reports were rarely lost, and it didn't trouble him greatly. The 'transfer successful' signal was in a different place, and was always easy to see. Colonel Filitov settled back in his seat, gazing out the window as he approached the spot . . . there. His head turned to track on the spot, looking for the mark . . . but it wasn't there. Odd. Had the other marker been set? He'd have to check that on the trip home tonight. In his years of work for CIA, several of his reports had been lost one way or another, and the danger signal hadn't been set, nor had he gotten the telephone call asking for Sergey that would tell him to leave his apartment at once. So there was probably no danger. Just an annoying inconvenience. Well. The Colonel relaxed and contemplated his day at the Ministry.

This time the Metro was fully manned. Fully a hundred Second Directorate men were in this one district, most dressed like ordinary Moscovites, some like workmen. These latter were operating the 'black' phonc lines installed along with electrical service panels throughout the system. The interrogator and his prisoner were riding trains back and forth on the 'purple' and 'green' lines, looking for a well-dressed woman in a Western coat. Millions of people traveled the Metro every day, but the counterintelligence officers were confident. They had time working for them, and their profile of the target – an adventuress. She was probably not disciplined enough to separate her daily routine from her covert activities. Such things had happened before. As a matter of faith – shared with their counterparts throughout the world – the security officers held that people who spied on their homeland were defective in some fundamental way. For all their cunning, such traitors would sooner or later connive at their own destruction.

And they were right, at least in this case. Svetlana came onto the station platform holding a bundle wrapped in brown paper. The courier recognized her hair first of all. The style was ordinary, but there was something about the way she held her head, something intangible that made him point, only to have his hand yanked down. She turned and

219

the KGB Colonel got a look at her face. The interrogator saw that she was relaxed, more so than the other commuters who displayed the grim apathy of the Moscovite. His first impression was of someone who enjoyed life. That would change.

He spoke into a small radio, and when the woman got on the next train, she had company. The 'Two' man who got on with her had a radio earpiece, almost like a hearing aid. Behind them at the station, the men working the phone circuit alerted agents at every station on the line. When she got off, a full shadow team was ready. They followed her up the long escalator onto the street. Already a car was here, and more officers began the surveillance routine. At least two men always had visual contact with the subject, and the close-in duty rotated rapidly among the group as more and more men joined in the chase. They followed her all the way to the GOSPLAN Building on Marksa Prospekt, opposite the Hotel Moscow. She never knew that she was being followed, and never even attempted to look for evidence of it. Within half an hour, twenty photographs were developed and were shown to the prisoner, who identified her positively.

The procedure after that was more cautious. A building guard gave her name to a KGB officer who admonished him not to discuss the inquiry with anyone. With her name, a full identity was established by lunchtime, and the interrogator, who was now running all aspects of the case, was appalled to learn that Svetlana Vaneyeva was the child of a senior Central Committee member. That would be a complication. Quickly, the Colonel assembled another collection of photographs and reexamined his prisoner, but yet again he selected the right woman from a collection of six. The family member of a Central Committee man was not someone to – but they had identification, and they had a major case. Vatutin went to confer with the head of his directorate.

What happened next was tricky. Though deemed all-powerful by the West, the KGB has always been subservient to the Party apparatus; even the KGB needed permission to trifle with a family member of so powerful an official. The head of the Second Directorate went upstairs to the KGB Chairman. He returned thirty minutes later.

'You may pick her up.'

'The Secretary of the Central Committee – '

'Has not been informed,' the General said.

'But – '

'Here are your orders.' Vatutin took the handwritten sheet, personally signed by the Chairman.

'Comrade Vaneyeva?'

She looked up to see a man in civilian clothes – GOSPLAN was a civilian agency, of course – who stared at her oddly. 'Can I help you?'

'I am Captain Klementi Vladimirovich Vatutin of the Moscow Militia. I would like you to come with me.' The interrogator watched closely for a reaction, but got nothing.

'Whatever for?' she asked.

'It is possible that you can help us in the identification of someone. I cannot elaborate further here,' the man said apologetically.

'Will it take long?'

'Probably a few hours. We can have someone drive you home afterward.'

'Very well. I have nothing critical on my desk at the moment.' She rose without another word. Her look at Vatutin betrayed a certain sense of superiority. The Moscow Militia was not an organization that was lavished with respect by local citizens, and the mere rank of captain for a man of his age told her much of his career. Within a minute she had her coat on and the bundle under her arm, and they headed out of the building. At least the Captain was *kulturny*, she saw, holding the door open for her. Svetlana assumed from this that Captain Vatutin knew who she was – more precisely, who her father was.

A car was waiting and drove off at once. She was

surprised at the route, but it wasn't until they drove past Khokhlovskaya Square that she was sure.

'We're not going to the Ministry of Justice?' she asked.

'No, we're going to Lefortovo,' Vatutin replied off-handedly.

'But – '

'I didn't want to alarm you in the office, you see. I am actually *Colonel* Vatutin of the Second Chief Directorate.' There was a reaction to that, but Vaneyeva recovered her composure in an instant.

'And what is it that I am to help you with, then?'

She was good, Vatutin saw. This one would be a challenge. The Colonel was loyal to the Party, but not necessarily to its officials. He was a man who hated corruption almost as much as treason. 'A small matter – you'll doubtless be home for dinner.'

'My daughter – '

'One of my people will pick her up. If things run a little late, your father will not be upset to see her, will he?'

She actually smiled at that. 'No, Father loves to spoil her.'

'It probably won't take that long anyway,' Vatutin said, looking out the window. The car pulled through the gates into the prison. He helped her out of the car, and a sergeant held the door open for both of them. *Give them hope, then take it away.* He took her gently by the arm. 'My office is this way. You travel to the West often, I understand.'

'It is part of my work.' She was on guard now, but no more than anyone would be here.

'Yes, I know. Your desk deals with textiles.' Vatutin opened his door and waved her in.

'That's her!' a voice called. Svetlana Vaneyeva stopped dead, as though frozen in time. Vatutin took her arm again and directed her to a chair.

'Please sit down.'

'What is this!' she said, finally in alarm.

'This man here was caught carrying copies of secret State documents. He has told us that you gave them to him,' Vatutin said as he sat behind his desk.

Vaneyeva turned and stared at the courier. 'I have never seen that face in my life! Never!'

'Yes,' Vatutin said dryly. 'I know that.'

'What – ' She searched for words. 'But this makes no sense.'

'You've been very well trained. Our friend here says that his signal to pass on the information is that he runs his hand across your rump.'

She turned to face her accuser. '*Govnoed!* This *thing* said that! This' – she sputtered for another moment – 'worthless person. Rubbish!'

'So you deny the charge?' Vatutin inquired. Breaking this one would really be a pleasure.

'Of course! I am a loyal Soviet citizen. I am a Party member. My father – '

'Yes, I know about your father.'

'He will hear of this, *Colonel* Vatutin, and if you threaten me – '

'We do not threaten you, Comrade Vaneyeva, we ask for information. Why were you on the Metro yesterday? I know that you have your own car.'

'I often ride the Metro. It is simpler than driving, and I had to make a stop.' She picked her package up off the floor. 'Here. I dropped off the coat for cleaning. It is inconvenient to park the car, go in, and then drive on. So I took the underground. Same thing today, when I picked it up. You can check at the cleaners.'

'And you did not pass this to our friend here?' Vatutin held up the film cassette.

'I don't even know what that is.'

'Of course.' Colonel Vatutin shook his head. 'Well, there we are.' He pressed a button on his intercom set. The office's side door opened a moment later. Three people came in. Vatutin waved to Svetlana. 'Prepare her.'

Her reaction was not so much panic as disbelief. Svetlana Vaneyeva tried to bolt from the chair, but a pair of men grabbed her by the shoulders and held her in place. The third rolled up the sleeve on her dress and stuck a needle in her arm before she had the presence of mind to shout. 'You can't,' she said, 'you can't. . .'

Vatutin sighed. 'Ah, but we can. How long?'

'That'll keep her under for at least two hours,' the doctor replied. He and his two orderlies picked her out of the chair. Vatutin came around and got the parcel. 'She'll be ready for you as soon as I do the medical check, but I anticipate no problems. Her medical file is clean enough.'

'Excellent. I'll be down after I have something to eat.' He gestured to the other prisoner. 'You can take him away. I think we're done with him.'

'Comrade, I – ' the courier began, only to be cut off.

'Do not dare to use that word again.' The reprimand was all the harsher for its soft delivery.

Colonel Bondarenko now ran the Ministry's laser-weapons desk. It was by the decision of Defense Minister Yazov, of course, as recommended by Colonel Filitov.

'So, Colonel, what news do you bring us?' Yazov asked.

'Our colleagues at KGB have delivered to us partial plans for the American adaptive-optics mirror.' He handed over two separate copies of the diagrams.

'And we cannot do this ourselves?' Filitov asked.

'The design is actually quite ingenious, and, the report says, an even more advanced model is in the design stages right now. The good news is that it requires fewer actuators –'

'What is that?' Yazov asked.

'The actuators are the mechanisms which alter the contours of the mirror. By lowering the number of them you also reduce the requirements of the computer system that operates the mirror assembly. The existing mirror – this one here – requires the services of an extremely powerful supercomputer, which we cannot yet duplicate in the Soviet Union. The new mirror is projected to require only a fourth as much computer power. This allows both a smaller computer to operate the mirror and also a simpler control program.' Bondarenko leaned forward. 'Comrade

Minister, as my first report indicated, one of the principal difficulties with Bright Star is the computer system. Even if we were able to manufacture a mirror like this one, we do not as yet have the computer hardware and software to operate it at maximum efficiency. I believe we could do so if we had this new mirror.'

'But we don't have the new mirror plans yet?' Yazov asked.

'Correct. The KGB is working on that.'

'We can't even replicate these "actuators" yet,' Filitov groused. 'We've had the specifications and diagrams for several months and still no factory manager has delivered—'

'Time and funds, Comrade Colonel,' Bondarenko chided. Already he was learning to speak with confidence in this rarest of atmospheres.

'Funding,' Yazov grunted. 'Always funding. We can build an invulnerable tank – with enough funds. We can catch up with Western submarine technology – with enough funding. Every pet project of every academician in the Union will deliver the ultimate weapon – if only we can provide enough funding. Unfortunately there is not enough for all of them.'
There's one way in which we've caught up with the West!

'Comrade Minister,' Bondarenko said, 'I have been a professional soldier for twenty years. I have served on battalion and divisional staffs, and I have seen close combat. Always I have served the Red Army, only the Red Army. Bright Star belongs to another service branch. Despite this, I tell you that if necessary we should deny funds for tanks, and ships, and airplanes in order to bring Bright Star to completion. We have enough conventional weapons to stop any NATO attack, but we have nothing to stop Western missiles from laying waste to our country.' He drew back. 'Please forgive me for stating my opinion so forcefully.'

'We pay you to think,' Filitov observed. 'Comrade Minister, I find myself in agreement with this young man.'

'Mikhail Semyonovich, why is it that I sense a palace coup on the part of my colonels?' Yazov ventured a rare smile, and turned to the younger man. 'Bondarenko, within these walls I expect you to tell me what you think. And if you can persuade this old cavalryman that your science-fiction project is worthwhile, then I must give it serious thought. You say that we should give this program crash status?'

'Comrade Minister, we should consider it. Some basic research remains, and I feel that its funding priority should be increased dramatically.' Bondarenko stopped just short of what Yazov suggested. That was a political decision, one into which a mere colonel ought not stick his neck. It occurred to the CARDINAL that he had actually under-estimated this bright young colonel.

'Heart rate's coming up,' the doctor said almost three hours later. 'Time zero, patient conscious.' A reel-to-reel tape recorder took down his words.

She didn't know the point at which sleep ended and consciousness began. The line is a fuzzy one for most people, particularly so in the absence of an alarm or the first beam of sunlight. She was given no signals. Svetlana Vaneyeva's first conscious emotion was puzzlement. *Where am I?* she asked herself after about fifteen minutes. The lingering aftereffects of the barbiturates eased away, but nothing replaced the comfortable relaxation of dreamless sleep. She was . . . floating?

She tried to move, but . . . couldn't? She was totally at rest, every square centimeter of her body was evenly supported so that no muscle was stretched or strained. Never had she known such wonderful relaxation. *Where am I?*

She could see nothing, but that wasn't right, either. It was not black, but . . . gray . . . like a night cloud reflecting the city lights of Moscow, featureless, but somehow textured.

She could hear nothing, not the rumble of traffic, not the mechanical sounds of running water or slamming doors . . .

She turned her head, but the view remained the same, a

gray blankness, like the inside of a cloud, or a ball of cotton, or –

She breathed. The air had no smell, no taste, neither moist nor dry, not even a temperature that she could discern. She spoke . . . but incredibly she heard nothing. *Where am I!*

Svetlana began to examine the world more carefully. It took about half an hour of careful experimentation. Svetlana kept control of her emotions, told herself forcefully to be calm, to relax. It had to be a dream. Nothing untoward could really be happening, not to her. Real fear had not yet begun, but already she could feel its approach. She mustered her determination and fought to hold it off. *Explore the environment.* Her eyes swept left and right. There was only enough light to deny her blackness. Her arms were there, but seemed to be away from her sides, and she could not move them inward, though she tried for what seemed like hours. The same was true of her legs. She tried to ball her right hand into a fist . . . but she couldn't even make her fingers touch one another.

Her breathing was more rapid now. It was all she had. She could feel the air come in and out, could feel the movement of her chest, but nothing else. Closing her eyes gave her the choice of a black nothing over a gray one, but that was all. *Where am I!*

Movement, she told herself, more movement. She rolled around, searching for resistance, searching for any tactile feeling outside her own body. She was rewarded with nothing at all, just the same slow, fluid resistance – and whichever way she turned, the sensation of floating was the same. It mattered not – she could tell not –whether gravity had her up or down, left side or right. It was all the same. She screamed as loudly as she could, just to hear something real and close, just to be sure that she at least had herself for company. All she heard was the distant, fading echo of a stranger.

The panic started in earnest.

*

227

'Time twelve minutes . . . fifteen seconds,' the doctor said into the tape recorder. The control booth was five meters above the tank. 'Heart rate rising, now one-forty, respiration forty-two, acute anxiety reaction onset.' He looked over to Vatutin. 'Sooner than usual. The more intelligent the subject . . .'

'The greater the need for sensory input, yes,' Vatutin said gruffly. He'd read the briefing material on this procedure, but was skeptical. This was brand-new, and required a kind of expert assistance that he'd never needed in his career.

'Heart rate appears to have peaked at one seventy-seven, no gross irregularities.'

'How do you mute her own speech?' Vatutin asked the doctor.

'It's new. We use an electronic device to duplicate her voice and repeat it back exactly out of phase. That neutralizes her sound almost completely, and it's as though she were screaming in a vacuum. It took two years to perfect.' He smiled. Like Vatutin he enjoyed his work, and he had here a chance to validate years of effort, to overturn institutional policy with something new and better, that had his name on it.

Svetlana hovered on the edge of hyperventilation, but the doctor altered the gas mixture going into her. He had to keep a very close watch on her vital signs. This interrogation technique left no marks on the body, no scars, no evidence of torture – it was, in fact, not a form of torture at all. At least, not physically. The one drawback to sensory deprivation, however, was that the terror it induced could drive people into tachycardia – and that could kill the subject.

'That's better,' he said, looking at the ECG readout. 'Heart rate stabilized at one thirty-eight, a normal but accelerated sinus rhythm. Subject is agitated but stable.'

Panic didn't help. Though her mind was still frantic, Svetlana's body drew back from damaging itself. She fought to assert control and again felt herself become strangely calm.

Am I alive or dead? She searched all her memories, all her experiences, and found nothing . . . but . . .

There *was* a sound.

What is it?

Lub-dub, lub-dub . . . what was it . . .?

It was a heart! Yes!

Her eyes were still open, searching the blankness for the source of the sound. There was something out there, if only she could find it. Her mind searched for a way. *I have to get to it. I must grab hold of it.*

But she was trapped inside something that she couldn't even describe. She started moving again. Again she found nothing to grab, nothing to touch.

She was only beginning to understand how alone she was. Her senses cried out for data, for input, for *something*! The sensory centers of her brain were seeking sustenance and finding only a vacuum.

What if I am dead? she asked herself.

Is this what happens when you're dead . . . Nothingness . . .? Then a more troubling thought:

Is this hell?

But there was something. There was that sound. She concentrated on it, only to find that the harder she tried to listen, the harder it was to hear. It was like trying to grab for a cloud of smoke, it was only there when she didn't try to – but she had to grab it!

And so she tried. Svetlana screwed her eyes shut and concentrated all of her will on the repeating sound of a human heart. All she accomplished was to blank the sound out of her own senses. It faded away, until it was only her imagination that heard it and then that, too, became bored.

She moaned, or thought she did. She heard almost nothing. How could she speak and not hear it?

Am I dead? The question had an urgency that demanded an answer, but the answer might be too dreadful to contemplate. There had to be something . . . but did she dare? Yes!

Svetlana Vaneyeva bit her tongue as hard as she could. She was rewarded with the salty taste of blood.

I am alive! she told herself. She reveled in this knowledge for what seemed a very long time. But even long times had to end:

But where am I? Am I buried . . . alive? BURIED ALIVE!

'Heart rate increasing again. Looks like the onset of the secondary anxiety period,' the doctor observed for the recording. It really was too bad, he thought. He'd assisted in preparing the body. A very attractive woman, her smooth belly marred only by a mother's stretchmarks. Then they'd oiled her skin and dressed her in the specially made wetsuit, one made of the best-quality nomex rubber, so smooth that you could barely feel it when dry – and when filled with water, it hardly seemed there at all. Even the water in the tank was specially formulated, heavy in salt content so that she was neutrally buoyant. Her gyrations around the tank had twisted her upside down and she hadn't known. The only real problem was that she might tangle the air lines, but a pair of divers in the tank prevented this, always careful not to touch her or to allow the hose to do so. Actually, the divers had the hardest job in the unit.

The doctor gave Colonel Vatutin a smug look. Years of work had gone into this most secret part of Lefortovo's interrogation wing. The pool, ten meters wide and five deep, the specially salted water, the custom-designed suits, the several man-years of experimentation to back up the theoretical work – all these went to devise a means of interrogation that was in all ways better than the antiquated methods KGB had used since the revolution. Except for the one subject that had died of an anxiety-induced heart attack . . . The vital signs changed again.

'There we go. Looks like we're into the second stage. Time one hour, six minutes.' He turned to Vatutin. 'This is usually the long phase. It will be interesting to see how long it lasts with this subject.'

It seemed to Vatutin that the doctor was a child playing an elaborate, cruel game; as much as he wanted what this subject knew, part of him was horrified by what he watched. He wondered if it came from fear that one day it might be tried on him . . .

Svetlana was limp. Tremors from the extended hours of terrors had exhausted her limbs. Her breaths now came in shallow pants, like a woman holding off the urge to deliver her child. Even her body had deserted her now and her mind sought to escape its confines and explore on its own. It seemed to her consciousness that she was separated from the useless sack of flesh, that her spirit, soul, whatever it was, was alone now, alone and free. But the freedom was no less a curse that what had gone before.

She could move freely now, she could see the space around her, but it was all empty. She moved as though swimming or flying in a three-dimensional space whose limits she could not discern. She felt her arms and legs moving effortlessly, but when she looked to see her limbs, she found that they were out of her field of view. She could feel them move, but . . . they weren't there. The part of her mind that was still rational told her that this was all an illusion, that she was swimming toward her own destruction – but even that was preferable to being alone, wasn't it?

This effort lasted for an eternity. The most gratifying part was the lack of fatigue in her invisible limbs. Svetlana shut out her misgivings and reveled in the freedom, in being able to see the space around her. Her pace speeded up. She imagined that the space ahead of her was brighter than that behind her. If there were a light she would find it, and a light would make all the difference. Part of her remembered the joy of swimming as a child, something she hadn't done in . . . fifteen years, wasn't it? She was the school champion at swimming underwater, could hold her breath far longer than all the others. The memories made her young again, young and spry and prettier and better-dressed than all the others. Her face took on an angelic smile and ignored the warnings from the remaining shreds of her intellect.

She swam for days, it seemed, for weeks, always toward the brighter space ahead. It took a few more days to realize that the space never got any brighter, but she ignored this last warning of her consciousness. She swam harder, and felt fatigue for the first time. Svetlana Vaneyeva ignored that, too. She had to use her freedom to advantage. She had to find where she was, or better yet find a way out of this place. This horrible place.

Her mind moved yet again, traveling away from her body, and when it had reached a sufficient height, it looked back down at the distant, swimming figure. Even from its great height it could not see the edges of this wide, amorphous world, but she could see the tiny figure below her, swimming alone in the void, moving its spectral limbs in futile rhythm . . . going nowhere.

The scream from the wall speaker almost made Vatutin bolt from his chair. Perhaps Germans had heard that once, the scream of the victims of their death camps when the doors were shut and the gas crystals had sprinkled down. But this was worse. He'd seen executions. He'd seen torture. He had heard cries of pain and rage and despair, but he had never heard the scream of a soul condemned to something worse than hell.

'There . . . that ought to be the beginning of the third stage.'

'What?'

'You see,' the doctor explained, 'the human animal is a *social* animal. Our beings and our senses are designed to gather data that allow us to react both to our environment and our fellow human beings. Take away the human company, take away all sensory input, and the mind is totally alone with itself. There is ample data to demonstrate what happens. Those Western idiots who sail around the world alone, for example. A surprising number go insane, and many disappear; probably suicides. Even those who survive, those who use their radios on a daily basis – they often need physicians to monitor them and warn them against the psychological hazards of such solitude. And they can *see* the water around. They can see their boats. They can feel the motion of the waves. Take all that away . . .' The doctor shook his head. 'They'd last perhaps three days. We take everything away, as you see.'

'And the longest they've lasted in here?'

'Eighteen hours – he was a volunteer, a young field officer from the First Directorate. The only problem is that the subject cannot know what is happening to him. That alters the effect. They still break, of course, but not as thoroughly.'

Vatutin took a breath. That was the first good news that he'd heard here. 'And this one, how much longer?'

The doctor merely looked at his watch and smiled. Vatutin wanted to hate him, but recognized that this physician, this healer, was merely doing what he'd been doing for years, more quickly, and with no visible damage that might embarrass the State at the public trials that the KGB now had to endure. Then, there was the added benefit that even the doctor hadn't expected when he'd begun the program . . .

'So . . . what is this third stage?'

Svetlana saw them swimming around her form. She tried to warn it, but that would mean getting back inside, and she didn't dare. It was not so much something she could see, but there *were* shapes, predatory shapes plying the space around her body. One of them closed in, but turned away. Then it turned back again. And so did she. She tried to fight against it, but something drew her back into the body that was soon to be extinguished. She got there just in time. As she told her limbs to swim faster, it came up from behind. The jaws opened and enveloped her entire body, then closed slowly around her. The last thing she saw was the light toward which she'd been swimming – the light, she finally knew, that was never there. She knew her protest was a vain one, but it exploded from her lips.

'*No!*' She didn't hear it, of course.

She returned now, condemned to go back to her useless real body, back to the gray mass before her eyes and the limbs that could move only without purpose. She somehow understood that her imagination had tried to protect her, to get her free – and had failed utterly. But she couldn't turn her imagination off, and now its efforts turned destructive. She wept without sound. The fear she felt now was worse than mere panic. At least panic was an escape, a denial of what she faced, a retreat into herself, but there was no longer a self that she could find. She'd watched that die, had been there when it happened. Svetlana was without a present, certainly without a future. All she had now was a past, and her imagination selected only the worst parts of that . . .

'Yes, we're in the final stage now,' the doctor said. He lifted the phone and ordered a pot of tea. 'This was easier than I expected. She fits the profile better than I realized.'

'But she hasn't told us anything yet,' Vatutin objected.

'She will.'

She watched all the sins of her life. That helped her to understand what was happening. This was the hell whose existence the State denied, and she was being punished. That had to be it. And she helped. She had to. She had to see it all again and understand what she'd done. She had to participate in the trial within her own mind. Her weeping never stopped. Her tears ran for days as she watched herself doing things that she ought never to have done. Every transgression of her life played out before her eyes in fullest detail. Especially those of the past two years . . . Somehow she knew that those were the ones that had brought her here. Svetlana watched every time she had betrayed her Motherland. The first coy flirtations in London, the clandestine meetings with serious men, the warnings not to be frivolous, and then the times she had used her importance to breeze through customs control, playing the game and enjoying herself as she committed her most heinous crimes. Her moans took on a recognizable timbre. Over and over she said it without knowing.

'I'm sorry. . . .'

'Now comes the tricky part.' The doctor put on his headset. He had to make some adjustments on his control board. 'Svetlana . . .' he whispered into the microphone.

She didn't hear it at first, and it was some time before her senses were able to tell her that there was *something* crying out to be noticed.

Svetlana . . . the voice called to her. Or was it her imagination . . .?

Her head twisted around, looking for whatever it was.

Svetlana . . . it whispered again. She held her breath as long as she could, commanded her body to be still, but it betrayed her yet again. Her heart raced, and the pounding blood in her ears blanked out the sound, if it was a sound. She let out a despairing moan, wondering if she had imagined the voice, wondering if it was only getting worse . . . or might there be some hope . . . ?

Svetlana. . . . Slightly more than a whisper, enough to detect emotional content. The voice was so sad, so disappointed. *Svetlana, what have you done?*

'I didn't, I didn't – ' she sputtered, and still could not hear her own voice as she called out from the grave. She was rewarded with renewed silence. After what seemed an hour she screamed: 'Please, *please* come back to me!'

Svetlana, the voice repeated finally, *what have you done . . .?*

'I'm sorry . . .' she repeated in a voice choked with tears.

'What have you done?' it asked again. 'What about the film . . .?'

'Yes!' she answered, and in moments she told all.

*

'Time eleven hours, forty-one minutes. The exercise is concluded.'

The doctor switched off the tape recorder. Next he flicked the lights in the pool room on and off a few times. One of the divers in the tank waved acknowledgment and jabbed a needle into Subject Vaneyeva's arm. As soon as her body went completely limp, she was taken out. The doctor left the control room and went down to see her.

She was lying on a gurney when he got there, the wetsuit already taken off. He sat beside the unconscious form and held her hand as the technician jabbed her with a mild stimulant. She was a pretty one, the doctor thought as her breathing picked up. He waved the technician out of the room, leaving the two of them alone.

'Hello, Svetlana,' he said in his gentlest voice. The blue eyes opened, saw the lights on the ceiling, and the walls. Then her head turned toward him.

He knew he was indulging himself, but he'd worked long into the night and the next day on this case, and this was probably the most important application of his program to date. The naked woman leaped off the table into his arms and nearly strangled him with a hug. It wasn't because he was particularly good-looking, the doctor knew, just that he was a human being, and she wanted to touch one. Her body was still slick with oil as her tears fell on his white laboratory coat. She would never commit another crime against the State, not after this. It was too bad that she'd have to go to a labor camp. Such a waste, he thought as he examined her. Perhaps he could do something about that. After ten minutes she was sedated again, and he left her asleep.

'I gave her a drug called Versed. It's a new Western one, an amnesiac.'

'Why one of those?' Vatutin asked.

'I give you another option, Comrade Colonel. When she wakes up later this morning, she will remember very little. Versed acts like scopalamine, but is more effective. She will remember no firm details, and very little else that happened to her. It will all seem to be a fearful dream. Versed is also an hypnotic. For example, I can go back to her now and make a suggestion that she will not remember anything, but that she may never betray the State again. There is roughly an eighty-percent probability that both suggestions will never be violated.'

'You're joking!'

'Comrade, one effect of this technique is that she has condemned herself more forcefully than the State ever could. She feels more remorse now for her actions that she would before a firing squad. Surely you have read *1984*? It might have been a dream when Orwell wrote it, but with modern technology, we can do it. The trick is not breaking the person from without, but doing it from within.'

'You mean we can use her now . . .?'

11

Procedures

'He's not going to make it.' Ortiz had gotten the embassy doctor, an Army surgeon whose real job was to assist in the treatment of wounded Afghans. Churkin's lungs were too badly damaged to fight off the pneumonia that had developed during his transit. 'He probably won't last out the day. Sorry, just too much damage. A day sooner and maybe we might have saved him, but . . .' The doctor shook his head. 'I'd like to get a preacher to him, but that's probably a waste of time.'

'Can he talk?'

'Not much. You can try. It won't hurt him any more than he already is. He'll be conscious for a few more hours, then he's just going to fade out.'

'Thanks for the try, doc,' Ortiz said. He almost sighed with relief, but the shame of such a gesture stopped him cold. What would they have done with a live one? Give him back? Keep him? Trade him? he asked himself. He wondered why the Archer had brought him out at all. 'Well,' he said to himself, and entered the room.

Two hours later he emerged. Then Ortiz drove down to the embassy, where the canteen served beer. He made his report to Langley, then over the next five hours, sitting alone at a corner table he left only for refills, he got himself thoroughly and morosely drunk.

Ed Foley could not allow himself that luxury. One of his couriers had disappeared three days earlier. Another had left her desk at GOSPLAN and returned two days later. Then, only this morning, his man in the dry-cleaners had called in sick. He'd sent a warning to the kid at the baths, but didn't know if it had gotten to him or not. This was not mere trouble in his CARDINAL network, it was a disaster. The whole point of using Svetlana Vaneyeva was her supposed immunity from KGB's more forceful measures, and he'd depended on several days' resistance from her to get his people moved. Warning orders for the CARDINAL breakout had arrived but were still awaiting delivery. There was no sense in spooking the man before things were fully ready. After that, it should be a simple matter for Colonel Filitov to come up with an excuse to visit the Leningrad Military District headquarters – something he did every six months or so – and get him out.

If that works, Foley reminded himself. It had been done only twice that he knew of, and as well as it had gone before . . . there were no certainties, were there? *Not hardly*. It was time to leave. He and his wife needed time off, time away from all this. Their next post was supposed to be on the training staff at 'the Farm' on the York River. But these thoughts didn't help him with his current problem.

He wondered if he should alert CARDINAL anyway, warn him to be more careful – but then he might destroy the data that Langley was screaming for, and the data was paramount. That was the rule, a rule that Filitov knew and understood, supposedly as well as Foley did. But spies were more than objects that provided information, weren't they?

Field officers like Foley and his wife were supposed to regard them as valuable but expendable assets, to distance themselves from their agents, to treat them kindly when possible but ruthlessly when necessary. To treat them like children, really, with a mixture of indulgence and discipline. But they weren't children. CARDINAL was older than his own father, had been an agent when Foley was in second grade! Could he *not* show loyalty to Filitov? Of course not. He had to protect him.

But how?

*

Counterespionage operations were often nothing more than police work, and as a result of this, Colonel Vatutin knew as much about the business of investigation as the best men in the Moscow Militia. Svetlana had given him the manager of the dry-cleaning shop, and after two perfunctory days of surveillance, he'd decided to bring the man in for interrogation. They didn't use the tank on him. The Colonel still did not trust the technique, and besides, there was no need to go easy on him. It annoyed Vatutin that Vaneyeva now had a chance to remain free – free, after working for enemies of the State! Somebody wanted to use her as a bargaining chip for something or other with the Central Committee, but that was not the Colonel's concern. Now the dry-cleaner had given him a description of another member of this endless chain.

And the annoying part was that Vatutin thought he knew the boy! The dry-cleaner had soon told him of his suspicion that he worked at the baths, and the description matched the attendant whom he himself had talked to! Unprofessional as it was, it enraged Vatutin that he'd met a traitor that morning last week and not recognized him for what . . .

What was that colonel's name? he asked himself suddenly. The one who'd tripped? Filitov – Misha Filitov? Personal aide to Defense Minister Yazov?

I must have really been hung over not to make the connection! Filitov of Stalingrad, the tanker who'd killed Germans while he burned within a knocked-out tank. Mikhail Filitov, three times Hero of the Soviet Union . . . It had to be the same one. Could he be the –

Impossible, he told himself.

But nothing was impossible. If he knew anything, Vatutin knew that. He cleared out his mind and considered the possibilities coldly. The good news here was that everyone of consequence in the Soviet Union had a file at 2 Dzerzhinskiy Square. It was a simple thing to get Filitov's.

The file was a thick one, he saw fifteen minutes later. Vatutin realized that he actually knew little about this man. As with most war heroes, exploits performed in a brief span of minutes had expanded to cover a whole life. But no life was ever that simple. Vatutin started reading the file.

Little of it had to do with his war record, though that was covered in full, including the citations for all of his medals. As personal aide to three successive defense ministers, Misha had been through rigorous security screenings, some of which Filitov knew about, some of which not. These papers were also in order, of course. He turned to the next bundle.

Vatutin was surprised to see that Filitov had been involved in the infamous Penkovskiy case. Oleg Penkovskiy had been a senior officer in the GRU, the Soviet military intelligence command; recruited by the British, then 'run' jointly by the SIS and CIA, he'd betrayed his country as thoroughly as any man could. His penultimate treason had been to leak to the West the state of preparedness – or lack thereof – of the Strategic Rocket Forces during the Cuban Missile Crisis; this information had enabled American President Kennedy to force Khrushchev to withdraw the missiles that he'd so recklessly placed on that wretched island. But Penkovskiy's twisted loyalty to foreigners had forced him to take too many risks in delivering that data, and a spy could take only so many risks. He'd already been under suspicion. You could usually tell when the other side was getting just a little too clever, but . . . Filitov had been the one who provided the first real accusation. . . .

Filitov was the one who'd denounced Penkovskiy? Vatutin was astounded. The investigation had been fairly advanced at that point. Continuous surveillance had shown Penkovskiy to be doing some unusual things, including at least one possible dead-drop, but – Vatutin shook his head. *The coincidences you encounter in this business.* Old Misha had gone to the senior security officer and reported a curious conversation with his GRU acquaintance, one that might have been innocent, he'd said, but it made his antennae twitch in an odd way, and so he felt constrained to report it. On instructions from KGB, he'd followed it up,

241

and the next conversation hadn't been quite so innocent. By this time the case against Penkovskiy had been firmed up, and the additional proof hadn't really been needed, though it had made everyone involved feel a little better. . . .

It was an odd coincidence, Vatutin thought, but hardly one to cast suspicion on the man. The personal section of the file showed that he was a widower. A photo of his wife was there, and Vatutin took his time admiring it. There was also a wedding picture, and the Second Chief Directorate man smiled when he saw that the old warhorse had indeed been young once, and a raffishly handsome bastard at that! On the next page was information on two sons – both dead. That got his attention. One born immediately before the war, the other soon after it began. But they hadn't died as a result of the war . . . What, then? He flipped through the pages.

The elder had died in Hungary, Vatutin saw. Because of his political reliability he'd been taken from his military academy, along with a number of cadets, and sent to help suppress the 1956 counterrevolution. A crewman in a tank – following in his father's footsteps, he'd died when his vehicle had been destroyed. Well, soldiers took their chances. Certainly his father had. The second – also a tanker, Vatutin noted – died when the breech on the gun in his T-55 had exploded. Poor quality-control at the factory, the bane of Soviet industry, had killed the whole crew . . . and when had his wife died? The following July. Broken heart, probably, whatever the medical explanation had been. The file showed both sons had been models of young Soviet manhood. All the hopes and dreams that just have died with them, Vatutin thought, and then to lose your wife, too.

Too bad, Misha. I guess you used up all your family's good luck against the Germans, and the other three had to pay the bill . . . So sad that a man who has done so much should be . . .

Should be given a reason to betray the Rodina? Vatutin looked up, and out the window of his office. He could see the square outside, the cars curving around the statue of Feliks Dzerzhinskiy. 'Iron Feliks,' founder of the *Cheka*. By birth a

242

Pole and a Jew, with his odd little beard and ruthless intellect, Dzerzhinskiy had repelled the earliest efforts by the West to penetrate and subvert the Soviet Union. His back was to the building, and wags said that Feliks was condemned to perpetual isolation out there, as Svetlana Vaneyeva had been isolated. . . .

Ah, Feliks, what would you advise me right now? Vatutin knew that answer easily enough. Feliks would have had Misha Filitov arrested and interrogated ruthlessly. The merest possibility of suspicion had been enough back then, and who knew how many innocent men and women had been broken or killed for no reason? Things were different now. Now even the KGB had rules to follow. You couldn't just snatch people off the street and torture whatever you wanted out of them. And that was better, Vatutin thought. KGB was a professional organization. They had to work harder now to do their job, and that made for well-trained officers, and better performance . . . His phone rang.

'Colonel Vatutin.'

'Come up here. We're going to brief the Chairman in ten minutes.' The line clicked off.

KGB headquarters is an old building, built around the turn of the century to be the home office of the Rossiya Insurance Company. The exterior walls were of rust-colored granite, and the inside was a reflection of the age in which it had been built, with high ceilings and over-sized doors. The long, carpeted corridors of the building, however, were not terribly well lit, since one was not supposed to take too great an interest in the faces of the people who walked them. There were many uniforms in evidence. These officers were members of the Third Directorate, which kept an eye on the armed services. One thing that set the building apart was its silence. Those walking about did so with serious faces and closed mouths, lest they inadvertently let loose one of the million secrets that the building held.

The Chairman's office also faced the square, though with a far better view than Colonel Vatutin's. A male secretary rose from his desk and took the two visitors past the pair of

243

security guards who always stood in the corners of the reception room. Vatutin took a deep breath as he walked through the opened door.

Nikolay Gerasimov was in his fourth year as Chairman of the Committee for State Security. He was not a spy by profession, but rather a Party man who'd spent fifteen years within the CPSU bureaucracy before being appointed to a middle-level post in the KGB's Fifth Chief Directorate, whose mission was the suppression of internal dissent. His delicate handling of this mission had earned him steady promotion and finally appointment as First Deputy Chairman ten years earlier. There he had learned the business of foreign intelligence from the administrative side, and performed well enough to gain the respect of professional field officers for his instincts. First and foremost, however, he was a Party man, and that explained his chairmanship. At fifty-three he was fairly young for his job, and looked younger still. His youthful face had never been lined by contemplation of failure, and his confident gaze looked forward to further promotion. For a man who already had a seat both on the Politburo and the Defense Council, further promotion meant that he considered himself in the running for the top post of all: General Secretary of the Communist Party of the Soviet Union. As the man who wielded the 'sword and shield' of the Party (that was indeed the official motto of the KGB), he knew all there was to know about the other men in the running. His ambition, though never openly expressed, was whispered about the building, and any number of bright young KGB officers worked every day to tie their own fortunes to this rising star. A charmer, Vatutin saw. Even now he rose from his desk and waved his visitors to chairs opposite the massive oak desk. Vatutin was a man who controlled his thoughts and emotions; he was also too honest a man to be impressed by charmers.

Gerasimov held up a file. 'Colonel Vatutin, I have read the report of your ongoing investigation. Excellent work. Can you bring me up to date?'

'Yes, Comrade Chairman. We are currently looking for one Eduard Vassilyevich Altunin. He is an attendant in the Sandunovski Baths. Interrogation of the dry-cleaner revealed to us that he is the next step in the courier chain. Unfortunately he disappeared thirty-six hours ago, but we should have him by the end of the week.'

'I've gone to the baths myself,' Gerasimov noted with irony. Vatutin added his own.

'I still do, Comrade Chairman. I have myself seen this young man. I recognized the photograph in the file we're putting together. He was a corporal in an ordnance company in Afghanistan. His Army file shows that he objected to certain weapons being used there – the ones we use to discourage civilians from helping the bandits.' Vatutin referred to the bombs that were disguised as toys and designed to be picked up by children. 'His unit political officer wrote up a report, but the first verbal warning shut him up, and he finished his tour of duty without further incident. The report was enough to deny him a factory job, and he's floated from one menial assignment to another. Co-workers describe him as ordinary but fairly quiet. Exactly what a spy should be, of course. He has never once referred to his 'troubles' in Afghanistan, even when drinking. His flat is under surveillance, as are all of his family members and friends. If we don't have him very quickly, we'll know he's a spy. But we'll get him, and I will talk to him myself.'

Gerasimov nodded thoughtfully. 'I see you used the new interrogation technique on this Vaneyeva woman. What do you think of it?'

'Interesting. Certainly it worked in this case, but I must say that I have misgivings about placing her back on the street.'

'That was my decision, in case no one told you,' Gerasimov said offhandedly. 'Given the sensitivity of this case, and the doctor's recommendation, I think that the gamble is one worth taking for the moment. Do you agree that we shouldn't call too much attention to the case? Charges against her remain open.'

Oh, and you can use it against her father, can't you? Her disgrace is his also, and what father would want to see his only child in the GULAG? Nothing like a little blackmail, is there, Comrade Chairman? 'The case is certainly sensitive, and is likely to get more so,' Vatutin replied carefully.

'Go on.'

'The one time I saw this Altunin fellow, he was standing beside Colonel Mikhail Semyonovich Filitov.'

'Misha Filitov, Yazov's aide?'

'The same, Comrade Chairman. I reviewed his file this morning.'

'And?' This question came from Vatutin's boss.

'Nothing at all that I can point to. I hadn't known of his involvement in the Penkovskiy case . . .' Vatutin stopped, and for once his face showed something.

'Something is troubling you, Colonel,' Gerasimov observed. 'What is it?'

'Filitov's involvement in the Penkovskiy matter came soon after the death of his second son and his wife.' Vatutin shrugged after a moment. 'An odd coincidence.'

'Wasn't Filitov the first witness against him?' asked the head of the Second Directorate. He'd actually worked on the fringes of the case.

Vatutin nodded. 'That's right, but it was after we already had the spy under surveillance.' He stopped for another moment. 'As I said, an odd coincidence. We are *now* after a suspected courier who was running defense data. I saw him standing next to a senior Defense Ministry official, who was involved in another similar case almost thirty years ago. On the other hand, Filitov was the man who first reported Penkovskiy, and he is a distinguished war hero . . . who lost his family under unfortunate circumstances . . .' It was the first time he had strung all these thoughts together.

'Has there ever been a hint of suspicion against Filitov?' the Chairman asked.

'No. His career could scarcely be more impressive. Filitov was the only aide who stayed with the late Minister Ustinov throughout his career, and he's hung on there ever since. He functions as a personal inspector-general for the Minister.'

'I know,' Gerasimov said. 'I have here a request over Yazov's signature for our file on American SDI efforts. When I called about it, the Minister told me that colonels Filitov and Bondarenko are assembling data for a full report to the Politburo. The code word on that photographic frame you recovered was Bright Star, was it not?'

'Yes, Comrade Chairman.'

'Vatutin, we now have three coincidences,' Gerasimov observed. 'Your recommendation?'

That was simple enough: 'We should place Filitov under surveillance. Probably this Bondarenko fellow also.'

'Very carefully, but with the utmost thoroughness.' Gerasimov closed the file. 'This is a fine report, and it would seem that your investigative instincts are as sharp as ever, Colonel. You will keep me posted on this case. I expect to see you three times a week from now until its conclusion. General,' he said to the head of 'Two', 'this man will get all the support he needs. You may requisition resources from any part of the Committee. If you run into objections, please refer them to me. We may be certain that there is a leak at the highest level of the Defense Ministry. Next: this case is classified to my eyes and yours. No one – I repeat, *no one* will know of this. Who can say where the Americans have managed to place their agents? Vatutin, run this one to earth and you will have general's stars by summer. But' – he held up a finger – 'I think you should cease drinking until you are finished with this one. We need your head clear.'

'Yes, Comrade Chairman.'

The corridor was nearly empty outside the Chairman's office when Vatutin and his boss left. 'What about Vaneyeva?' the Colonel asked *sotto voce*.

'It's her father, of course. General Secretary Narmonov will announce his election to the Politburo next week,' the General replied in a neutral, quiet voice.

And it won't hurt to have another friend of the KGB at

court, Vatutin thought to himself. *Might Gerasimov be making some sort of move?*

'Remember what he said about drinking,' the General said next. 'I've heard that you're hitting the bottle very hard of late. That's one area of agreement between the Chairman and the General Secretary, in case no one ever told you.'

'Yes, Comrade General,' Vatutin replied. *Of course, it's probably the only area of agreement*. Like any good Russian, Vatutin thought that vodka was as much a part of life as air. It occurred to him to note that his hangover had encouraged him to take steam that morning and notice the crucial coincidence, but he refrained from pointing out the irony involved. Back at his desk a few minutes later, Vatutin took out a pad and began planning the surveillance on two colonels of the Soviet Army.

Gregory took usual commercial flights home, changing planes at Kansas City after a two-hour layover. He slept through most of the transit and walked straight into the terminal without having to chase after any baggage. His fiancée was waiting for him.

'How was Washington?' she asked after the usual welcome-home kiss.

'Never changes. They ran me all over the place. I guess they figure scientific types don't ever sleep.' He took her hand for the walk out to the car.

'So what happened?' she asked when they were outside.

'The Russians ran a big test.' He stopped to look around. This was a technical violation of security – but Candi was part of the team, wasn't she? 'They slagged down a satellite with the ground-based lasers at Dushanbe. What's left looks like a plastic model that got put in the oven.'

'That's bad,' Dr Long observed.

'Sure is,' Dr Gregory agreed. 'But they have optical problems. Blooming and jitter both. It's for sure they don't have anybody like you over there to build mirrors. They must have some good folks on the laser end, though.'

'How good?'

'Good enough that they're doing something we haven't figured out yet,' Al grumped as they reached his Chevy. 'You drive, I'm still a little dopey.'

'Will we figure it out?' Candi asked as she unlocked the door.

'Sooner or later.' He couldn't go any further than that, fiancée or not.

Candi got in and reached to unlock the right-side door. As soon as Al was seated and strapped in, he opened the glove compartment and extracted a Twinkie. He always had a stash. It was a little stale, but he didn't mind. Sometimes Candi wondered if his love for her resulted from the fact that her nickname reminded him of junk food.

'How's work on the new mirror going?' he asked after snapping down half of the Twinkie.

'Marv has a new idea that we're modeling out. He thinks we should thin out the coating instead of thickening it. We're going to try it next week.'

'Marv's pretty original for an old guy,' Al observed. Dr Marv Greene was forty-two.

Candi laughed. 'His secretary thinks he's pretty original, too.'

'He should know better than to fool around with somebody at work,' Gregory said seriously. He winced a moment later.

'Yeah, honey.' She turned to look at him, and they both laughed. 'How tired are you?'

'I slept on the flight.'

'Good.'

Just before reaching around her, Gregory crumbled the Twinkie wrapper and tossed it on the floor, where it joined about thirty others. He flew around quite a bit, but Candi had a sure cure for jet lag.

'Well, Jack?' Admiral Greer asked.

'I'm worried,' Ryan admitted. 'It was pure dumb luck that we saw the test. The timing was cute. All of our recon birds were well below the optical horizon. We weren't supposed

249

to notice – which is hardly surprising, since it's a technical violation of the ABM treaty. Well, probably.' Jack shrugged. 'Depends on how you read the treaty. Now you get into the "strict" or "loose" interpretation argument. If we pulled something like this, the Senate would go nuts.'

'They wouldn't like the test that you saw.' Very few people knew how far along Tea Clipper was. The program was 'black'. More classified than top secret, 'black' programs simply did not exist.

'Maybe. But we were testing the aiming system, not an actual weapon.'

'And the Soviets were testing a system to see if it was –' Greer chuckled and shook his head. 'It's like talking metaphysics, isn't it? How many lasers can dance on the head of a pin?'

'I'm sure Ernie Allen could give us an opinion on that.' Jack smiled. He didn't agree with Allen, but he had to like the man. 'I hope our friend in Moscow can deliver.'

12

Success and Failure

One of the problems with surveillance of any individual is that one must determine how he or she spends an ordinary day before one can establish what resources are needed for the operation. The more solitary the person or the activity, the harder it generally is to keep a covert eye on him. Already, for example, the KGB officers trailing Colonel Bondarenko hated him thoroughly. His daily jogging routine was an ideal activity for a spy, they all thought. He ran about entirely alone on city streets that were largely vacant – vacant enough that everyone out at that time was undoubtedly known to him by sight, and vacant enough that he would immediately notice anything out of the ordinary. As he ran around the residential blocks in this part of Moscow, the three agents assigned to keep an eye on him lost visual contact with him no less than five times. The sparse trees they might hide behind were bare of leaves, and the apartment buildings stood like tombstones on flat, open land. In any of those five times, Bondarenko might have stopped to retrieve something from a dead-drop or could have made one himself. It was more than frustrating, and added to this was the fact that this Soviet Army Colonel had a service record that was as immaculate as a field of freshly fallen snow: exactly the cover that any spy would contrive to acquire for himself, of course.

They spotted him again turning the corner for home, his legs pumping vigorously, his breath marked in the air behind him as small clouds of vapor. The man in charge of this part of the case decided that half a dozen 'Two' officers would be needed just to shadow the subject for his morning runs. And they'd have to be here an hour earlier than he was expected to run, enduring the dry, bitter cold of the Moscow dawn. People from the Second Chief Directorate never considered themselves fully appreciated for the hardships of their job.

Several kilometers away, another team of three was quite satisfied with their subject. In this case, an eighth-floor apartment in the building opposite the subject's was obtained – the diplomat who lived there was abroad. A pair of telephoto lenses was focused on Misha's windows, and he was not a man who troubled to lower his shades or even to adjust them properly. They watched him go through the morning routine of a man who'd had too much to drink the night before, and that was familiar enough to the 'Two' men who watched in heated comfort from across the street.

Misha was also sufficiently senior at the Defense Ministry that he rated a car and driver. It was an easy thing to reassign the sergeant and to substitute a shiny young face fresh from the KGB's counterintelligence school. A tap on his phone recorded his request for an early pickup.

Ed Foley left his apartment earlier than usual. His wife drove him over today, with the kids in the back of the car. The Soviet file on Foley noted with amusement that she kept the car on most days to run the kids around and generally socialize with the wives of other Western diplomats. A Soviet husband would keep the car for his own use. At least she wasn't making him take the Metro today, they observed; decent of her. The militiaman at the entrance to the diplomatic compound – he was really KGB, as everyone knew – noted the time of departure and the occupancy of the car. It was slightly out of the ordinary, and the gate guard looked around to see if Foley's KGB shadow was here today. He wasn't. The 'important' Americans got much more regular surveillance.

Ed Foley had a Russian-style fur hat, and his overcoat was sufficiently old and worn that it didn't look terribly foreign. A wool scarf clashed slightly with it, protecting his neck and hiding his striped tie. The Russian security officers who knew him by sight noted that, as with most foreigners, local weather was the great equalizer. If you lived through a Russian winter, you soon started dressing and acting like a Russian, even to the point of looking slightly downward when you walked.

First the kids were dropped off at school. Mary Pat Foley drove normally, her eyes flicking back and forth to the mirror every three or four seconds. Driving here wasn't all that bad, compared to American cities. Although Russian drivers could do the most extraordinary things, the streets weren't terribly crowded, and having learned to drive in New York City, she could handle nearly anything. As with commuters all over the world, she had a route composed of indirect shortcuts that avoided the handful of traffic bottlenecks and saved a few minutes each day at the cost of an extra liter or two of *benzin*.

Immediately after turning a corner, she moved expertly to the curb and her husband hopped out. The car was already moving as he slammed the door shut and moved off, not too quickly, toward the side entrance of the apartment block. For once Ed Foley's heart was beating fast. He'd done this only once before and didn't like it at all. Once inside, he avoided the elevators and bounded up the eight flights of stairs, looking at his watch.

He didn't know how his wife did it. It pained his male ego to admit that she drove so much more precisely than he did, and could place her car at any spot she wished with an accuracy of five seconds, plus or minus. He had two minutes to get to the eighth floor. Foley accomplished it with seconds to spare. He opened the fire door, and anxious eyes scanned the corridor. Wonderful things, corridors. Especially the straight, bare ones in high-rise apartment buildings. Nowhere for people to lurk with their cameras, with a bank of elevators in the middle, and fire stairs at both ends. He walked briskly past the elevators, heading toward the far end. He could measure the time with his heartbeats now. Twenty yards ahead, a door opened, and a man in uniform came out. He turned to set the lock on his apartment door, then picked up the briefcase and headed toward Foley. A passerby, if there had been one, might have thought it odd that neither man moved to avoid the other.

It was over in an instant. Foley's hand brushed against CARDINAL's, taking the film cassette and passing back a tiny rolled slip of paper. He thought he noted a look of irritation in the agent's eyes, but nothing more than that, not even a 'Please excuse me, Comrade', as the officer continued toward the elevators. Foley walked straight into the fire stairs. He took his time going down.

Colonel Filitov emerged from the building at the appointed time. The sergeant holding the door of his car noted that his mouth was working on something, perhaps a crumb of bread caught between his teeth.

'Good morning, Comrade Colonel.'

'Where's Zhdanov?' Filitov asked as he got in.

'He took ill. An appendix, they think.' This drew a grunt.

'Well, move off. I want to take steam this morning.'

Foley came out of the building's back entrance a minute later and walked past two other apartment blocks as he made his way to the next street over. He was just reaching the curb when his wife pulled over, picked him up almost without stopping. Both took a few deep breaths as she headed toward the embassy.

'What are you doing today?' she asked, her eyes still checking the mirror.

'The usual,' was the resigned reply.

Misha was already in the steam room. He noted the absence of the attendant and the presence of a few unfamiliar faces. That explained the special pickup this morning. His face gave nothing away as he traded a few friendly words with the regulars. It was a pity that he'd run out of film in his camera. Then there was the warning from

Foley. If he were under surveillance again – well, every few years some security officer or other would get a bug up his ass and recheck everyone at the Ministry. CIA had noticed and broken up the courier chain. It was amusing, he thought, to see the look on that young man's face in the corridor. So few people were left who knew what combat was like. People were so easy to frighten. Combat taught a man what to fear and what to ignore, Filitov told himself.

Outside the steam room, a 'Two' man was riffling through Filitov's clothing. In the car, his briefcase was being searched. In each case, the job was done quickly and thoroughly.

Vatutin himself supervised the search of Filitov's apartment. It was a job for experts whose hands were in surgical gloves, and they spent much of their time looking for 'telltales'. It could be the odd scrap of paper, a crumb, even a single human hair placed in a specific spot whose removal would tell the man who lived in the flat that somebody had been here. Numerous photographs were taken and rushed off for developing, and then the searchers went to work. The diary was found almost at once. Vatutin leaned down to look at the simple book that sat openly in the desk drawer to be sure that its placement wasn't secretly marked. After a minute or two, he picked it up and started reading.

Colonel Vatutin was irritable. He hadn't slept well the previous night. Like most heavy drinkers, he needed a few drinks to sleep, and the excitement of the case added to the lack of a proper sedative had given him a fitful night of tossing and turning; it showed enough on his face to warn his team to keep their mouths shut.

'Camera,' he said curtly. A man came over and started photographing the pages of the diary as Vatutin turned them.

'Somebody's tried to pick the door lock,' a major reported. 'Scratches around the keyhole. If we dismantle the lock, I think we'll see scratches on the tumblers also. Somebody's probably been in here.'

'I have what they were after,' Vatutin said crossly. Heads turned throughout the apartment. The man checking the refrigerator popped off the front panel, looked underneath the appliance, then put the panel back in place after the interruption. 'This man keeps a fucking diary! Doesn't anybody read security manuals anymore?'

He could see it now. Colonel Filitov used personal diaries to sketch out official reports. Somehow, someone had learned this, and got into his flat to make copies of . . .

But how likely is that? Vatutin asked himself. *About as likely as a man who writes out his memories of official documents when he could just as easily copy them at his desk in the Defense Ministry.*

The search took two hours, and the team left in ones and twos, after replacing everything exactly the way they'd found it.

Back at his office, Vatutin read the photographed diary in full. At the apartment he'd merely skimmed it. The fragment from the captured film exactly matched a page at the beginning of Filitov's journal. He spent an hour going through the photographs of the pages. The data itself was impressive enough. Filitov was describing Project Bright Star in considerable detail. In fact, the old Colonel's explanation was better than the brief he'd been given as part of the investigation directive. Tossed in were details of Colonel Bondarenko's observations about site security and a few complaints on the way priorities were assigned at the Ministry. It was evident that both colonels were very enthusiastic about Bright Star, and Vatutin already agreed with them. But Minister Yazov, he read, was not yet sure. Complaining about funding problems – well, that was an old story, wasn't it?

It was clear that Filitov had violated security rules by having records of top-secret documents in his home. That was itself a matter sufficiently serious that any junior or middle-level bureaucrat would lose his job for it, but Filitov was as senior as the Minister himself, and Vatutin knew all too well that senior people regarded security rules as inconveniences to be ignored in the Interest of the State, of which they viewed themselves as the ultimate arbiters. He wondered if the same were true elsewhere. Of one thing he was sure: before he or anyone else at KGB could accuse Filitov of anything, he needed something more serious than this. Even if Misha were a foreign agent – *Why am I looking for ways to deny that?* Vatutin asked himself in some surprise. He took himself back to the man's flat, and remembered the photographs on the walls. There must have been a hundred of them: Misha standing atop the turret of his T-34, binoculars to his eyes; Misha with his men in the snows outside Stalingrad; Misha and his tank crew pointing to holes in the side armor of a German tank . . . and Misha in a hospital bed, with Stalin himself pinning his third Hero of the Soviet Union medal to his pillow, his lovely wife and both children at his side. These were the memorabilia of a patriot and a hero.

In the old days that wouldn't have mattered, Vatutin reminded himself. *In the old days we suspected everyone.*

Anyone could have scratched the door lock. He'd leaped to the assumption that it was the missing bath attendant. A former ordnance technician, he probably knew how. *What if that is a coincidence?*

But if Misha were a spy, why not photograph the official documents himself? In his capacity as aide to the Defense Minister, he could order up any documents he wanted, and smuggling a spy camera into the Ministry was a trivial exercise.

If we'd gotten the film with a frame from such a document, Misha would already be in Lefortovo Prison . . .

What if he's being clever? What if he wants us to think that someone else is stealing material from his diary? I can take what I have to the Ministry right now, but we can accuse him of nothing more than violating in-house security rules, and if he answers that he was working at home, and admits to breaking the rule, and the Minister defends his aide – would the Minister defend Filitov?

Yes. Vatutin was sure of that. For one thing, Misha was a trusted aide and a distinguished professional soldier. For another, the Army would always close ranks to defend one of its own against the KGB. *The bastards hate us worse than they hate the West.* The Soviet Army had never forgotten the late 1930s, when Stalin had used the security agency to kill nearly every senior uniformed officer, and then as a direct result nearly lost Moscow to the German Army. No, if we go to them with no more than this, they'll reject all our evidence and launch their own investigation with the GRU.

Just how many irregularities are going to show up in this case? Colonel Vatutin wondered.

Foley was wondering much the same thing in his cubby-hole a few miles away. He had had the film developed and was reading it over. He noted with irritation that CARDINAL had run out of film and hadn't been able to reproduce the entire document. The part he had before him, however, showed that the KGB had an agent inside an American project that was called Tea Clipper. Evidently Filitov deemed this of more immediate interest to the Americans than what his own people were up to, and on reading the data, Foley was tempted to agree. Well. He'd get CARDINAL some more film cassettes, get the full document out, and then let him know that it was time to retire. The breakout wasn't scheduled for another ten days or so. Plenty of time, he told himself despite a crawly feel at the back of his neck that was telling him something else.

For my next trick, how do we get the new film to CARDINAL? With the usual courier chain destroyed, it would take several weeks to establish a new one, and he didn't want to risk a direct contact again.

It had to happen eventually, he knew. Sure, everything had gone smoothly the whole time he'd run this agent, but sooner or later something happened. Random chance, he told himself. Eventually the dice would come up the wrong way. When he'd first been assigned here and learned the operational history of CARDINAL, he'd marveled that the man had lasted so long, that he'd rejected at least three offers for breakout. How far could one man push his luck? The old bastard must have thought he was invincible. *Those whom the gods would destroy, they first make proud*, Foley thought.

He put it aside and continued with the task of the day. By evening, the courier was heading west with a new CARDINAL report.

'It's on the way,' Ritter told the Director of Central Intelligence.

'Thank God.' Judge Moore smiled. 'Now let's concentrate on getting him the hell out of there.'

'Clark's being briefed. He flies over to England tomorrow, and he meets the submarine the day after that.'

'That's another one who's pushed his luck,' the Judge observed.

'The best we got,' Ritter replied.

'It's not enough to move with,' Vatutin told the Chairman after outlining the results of his surveillance and search. 'I'm assigning more people to the operation. We've also placed listening devices in Filitov's apartment –'

'And this other colonel?'

'Bondarenko? We were unable to get in there. His wife does not work and stays home all day. We learned today that the man runs a few kilometers every morning, and some additional men have been assigned to this case also. The only information we have at present is a clean record – indeed, an exemplary one – and a goodly portion of ambition. He is now the official Ministry representative to Bright Star, and as you see from the diary pages, an enthusiastic supporter of the project.'

'Your feeling for the man?' The Chairman's questions were delivered in a curt but not menacing voice. He was a busy man who guarded his time.

'So far, nothing that would lead us to suspect anything.

He was decorated for service in Afghanistan; he took command of a *Spetznaz* group that was ambushed and fought off a determined bandit attack. While at this Bright Star place, he upbraided the KGB guard force for laxness, but his formal report to the Ministry explained why, and it is hard not to fault his reasons.'

'Is anything being done about it?' Gerasimov asked.

'The officer who was sent out to discuss the matter was killed in a plane crash in Afghanistan. Another officer will be sent out shortly, they tell me.'

'The bath attendant?'

'We are still looking for him. No results as yet. Everything is covered: airports, train stations, everything. If anything breaks, I'll report to you immediately.'

'Very well. Dismissed, Colonel.' Gerasimov went back to the papers on his desk.

The Chairman of the Committee for State Security allowed himself a smile after Vatutin left. He was amazed at how well things were going. The masterstroke was the Vaneyeva matter. It wasn't often that you uncovered a spy ring in Moscow, and when you did so, the congratulations were always mixed with the question: *Why did it take you so long?* That wouldn't happen this time. No, not with Vaneyeva's father about to be appointed to the Politburo. And Secretary Narmonov thought that he'd be loyal to the man who'd arranged the promotion. Narmonov, with all his dreams of reducing arms, of loosening the grip of the Party on the life of the nation, of 'liberalizing' what had been bequeathed to the Party . . . Gerasimov was going to change all that.

It wouldn't be easy, of course. Gerasimov had only three firm allies on the Politburo, but among them was Alexandrov, the ideologue whom the Secretary had been unable to retire after he'd changed allegiance. And now he had another, one quite unknown to the Comrade General Secretary. On the other hand, Narmonov had the Army behind him.

That was a legacy of Mathias Rust, the German teenager

260

who'd landed his rented Cessna in Red Square. Narmonov was a shrewd operator. Rust had flown into the Soviet Union on Border Guards Day, a coincidence that he could not explain – and Narmonov had denied KGB the opportunity to interrogate the hooligan properly! Gerasimov still growled about that. The young man had staged his flight on the only day in the year when one could be sure that the KGB's vast force of border guards would be gloriously drunk. That had got him across the Gulf of Finland undetected. Then the air defense command, Voyska PVO, had failed to detect him, and the child had landed right in front of St Basil's!

General Secretary Narmonov had acted quickly after that: firing the chief of Voyska PVO and Defense Minister Sokolov after a stormy Politburo session where Gerasimov had been unable to raise any objections, lest he endanger his own position. The new Defense Minister, D. T. Yazov, was the Secretary's man, a nobody from far down the numerical list of senior officers; a man who, having failed to earn his post, depended on the Secretary to stay there. That had covered Narmonov's most vulnerable flank. The complication it added now was that Yazov was still learning his job, and he obviously depended on old hands like Filitov to teach it to him.

And Vatutin thinks that this is merely a counterespionage case, Gerasimov grunted to himself.

The security procedures that revolved around CARDINAL data precluded Foley from sending any information in the normal way. Even one-time-pad ciphers, which were theoretically unbreakable, were denied him. So the cover sheet on the latest report would warn the Δ fraternity that the data being dispatched wasn't quite what was expected.

That realization lifted Bob Ritter right off his chair. He made his photocopies and destroyed the originals before walking to Judge Moore's office. Greer and Ryan were already there.

'He ran out of film,' the DDO said as soon as the door was closed.

'What?' Moore asked.

'Something new came in. It seems that our KGB colleagues have an agent inside Tea Clipper who just gave them most of the design work on this new gollywog mirror gadget, and CARDINAL decided that that was more important. He didn't have enough film left for everything, so he prioritized on what the KGB is up to. We only have half of what their laser system looks like.'

'Half might be enough,' Ryan observed. That drew a scowl. Ritter was not the least bit happy that Ryan was now Δ-cleared.

'He discusses the effects of the design change, but there's nothing about the change itself.'

'Can we identify the source of the leak on our side?' Admiral Greer asked.

'Maybe. It's somebody who really understands mirrors. Parks has to see this right quick. Ryan, you've actually been there. What do you think?'

'The test I watched validated the performance of the mirror and the computer software that runs it. If the Russians can duplicate it – well, we know they have the laser part down pat, don't we?' He stopped for a moment. 'Gentlemen, this is scary. If the Russians get there first, it blows away all the arms-control criteria, and it faces us with a deteriorating strategic situation. I mean, it would take several years before the problem manifests itself, but . . .'

'Well, if our man can get another goddamned film cassette,' the Deputy Director for Operations said, 'we can get to work on it ourselves. The good news is that this Bondarenko guy that Misha selected to run the laser desk at the Ministry will report to our man regularly on what's happening. The bad news –'

'Well, we don't have to go into that now,' Judge Moore said. Ryan didn't need to know any of that, his eyes told Ritter, who nodded instant agreement. 'Jack, you said you had something else?'

'There's going to be a new appointment to the Politburo Monday – Ilya Arkadyevich Vaneyev. Age sixty-three, widower. One daughter, Svetlana, who works at GOSPLAN; she's divorced, with one child. Vaneyev is a pretty straight guy, honest by their standards, not much in the way of dirty laundry that we know about. He's moving up from a Central Committee slot. He's the guy who took over the agricultural post that Narmonov held and did fairly well at it. The thinking is that he's going to be Narmonov's man. That gives him four full voting members of the Politburo who belong to him, one more than the Alexandrov faction, and –' He stopped when he saw the pained looks on the other three faces in the office. 'Something wrong?'

'That daughter of his. She's on Sir Basil's payroll,' Judge Moore told him.

'Terminate the contract,' Ryan said. 'It would be nice to have that kind of source, but that kind of scandal now would endanger Narmonov. Put her into retirement. Reactivate her in a few years, maybe, but right now shut her the hell off.'

'Might not be that easy,' Ritter said, and let it go at that. 'How's the evaluation coming?'

'Finished it yesterday.'

'It's for the President's eyes plus a few others, but this one's going to be tightly held.'

'Fair enough. I can have it printed up this afternoon. If that's all . . .?' It was. Ryan left the room. Moore watched the door close before speaking.

'I haven't told anyone yet, but the President is concerned about Narmonov's political position again. Ernie Allen is worried that the latest change in the Soviet position indicates a weakening in Narmonov's support at home, and he's convinced the boss that this is a bad time to push on a few issues. The implication of that is, if we bring CARDINAL out, well, it might have an undesired political effect.'

'If Misha gets caught, we get the same political effect,' Ritter pointed out. 'Not to mention the slightly deleterious effect it'll have on our man. Arthur, they are after him. They may have gotten to Vaneyev's daughter already –'

'She's back at work in GOSPLAN,' the DCI said.

'Yeah, and the man at the cleaners has disappeared. They got to her and broke her,' the DDO insisted. 'We have to break him out once and for all. We can't leave him flapping in the breeze, Arthur. We *owe* this man.'

'I cannot authorize the extraction without presidential approval.'

Ritter came close to exploding. 'Then get it! Screw the politics – in this case, screw the politics. There is a practical side to this, Arthur. If we let a man like this go down, and we don't lift a finger to protect him, the word will get out – hell, the Russians'll make a TV miniseries out of it! It will cost us more in the long term than this temporary political garbage.'

'Hold it for a minute,' Greer said. 'If they broke this Party guy's daughter, how come she's back to work?'

'Politics?' Moore mused. 'You suppose the KGB's unable to hurt this guy's family?'

'Right!' the DDO snorted. 'Gerasimov's in the opposing faction, and he'd pass the opportunity to deny a Politburo seat to Narmonov's man? It smells like politics, all right, but not that kind. More likely our friend Alexandrov has the new boy in his back pocket and Narmonov doesn't know about it.'

'So, you think they've broken her, but let her go and are using her as leverage on the old man?' Moore asked. 'It does make sense. But there's no evidence.'

'Alexandrov's too old to go after the post himself, and anyway the ideologue never seems to get the top spot – more fun to play kingmaker. Gerasimov's his fair-haired boy, though, and we know that he's got enough ambition to have himself crowned Nicholas the Third.'

'Bob, you've just come up with another reason not to rock the boat right now.' Greer sipped at his coffee for a moment. 'I don't like the idea of leaving Filitov in place either. What are the chances that he can just lay low? I mean, the way things are set up, he might just talk his way out of anything they can bring against him.'

'No, James.' Ritter shook his head emphatically. 'We can't have him lay low, because we need the rest of this report, don't we? If he runs the risk of getting it out despite the attention he's getting, we can't then leave him to fate. It's not right. Remember what this man's done for us over the years.' Ritter argued on for several minutes, demonstrating the ferocious loyalty to his people that he'd learned as a young case officer. Though agents often had to be treated like children, encouraged, supported, and often disciplined, they became like your own children, and danger to them was something to be fought.

Judge Moore ended the discussion. 'Your points are well taken, Bob, but I still have to go to the President. This isn't just a field operation anymore.'

Ritter stood his ground. 'We put all the assets in place.'

'Agreed, but it won't be carried out until we get approval.'

The weather at Faslane was miserable, but at this time of year it usually was. A thirty-knot wind was lashing the Scottish coast with snow and sleet when *Dallas* surfaced. Mancuso took his station atop the sail and surveyed the rocky hills on the horizon. He'd just completed a speed run, zipping across the Atlantic at an average of thirty-one knots, about as hard as he cared to push his boat for any extended period of time, not to mention his running submerged far closer to the coast than he would have preferred. Well, he was paid to follow orders, not to love them.

The seas were rolling about fifteen feet, and his submarine rolled with them, wallowing her way forward at twelve knots. The seas came right over the spherical bow and splashed high on meeting the blunt face of the sail. Even the foul-weather gear didn't help much. Within a few minutes he was soaked and shivering. A Royal Navy tug approached and took station off *Dallas'* port bow, leading her in to the loch while Mancuso came to terms with the rolling. One of his best-kept professional secrets was an occasional touch of seasickness. Being on the sail helped, but those inside the submarine's cylindrical hull were now regretting the heavy lunch served a few hours earlier.

Within an hour they were in sheltered waters, taking the S-turns into the base that supported British and American nuclear submarines. Once there, the wind helped, easing the slate-gray bulk of the submarine up to the pier. People were already waiting there, sheltered in a few cars as the lines were passed and secured by the submarine's deck crew. As soon as the brow was passed, Mancuso went below to his cabin.

His first visitor was a commander. He'd expected a submarine officer, but this one had no service badges at all. That made him an intelligence type.

'How was the crossing, Captain?' the man asked.

'Quiet.' *Well, get on with it!*

'You sail in three hours. Here are your mission orders.' He handed over a manila envelope with wax seals, and a note on the front that told Mancuso when he could open it. Though often a feature in movies, it was the first time this had happened to him as a CO. You were supposed to be able to discuss your mission with the people who gave it to you. But not this time. Mancuso signed for them, locked them in his safe under the watchful eyes of the spook, and sent him back on his way.

'Shit,' the Captain observed to himself. Now his guests could come aboard.

There were two of them, both in civilian clothes. The first came down the torpedo-loading hatch with the aplomb of a real sailor. Mancuso soon saw why.

'Howdy, skipper!'

'Jonesy, what the hell are you doing here?'

'Admiral Williamson gave me a choice: either be recalled to temporary active duty or come aboard as a civilian tech-rep. I'd rather be a tech-rep. Pay's better.' Jones lowered his voice. 'This here's Mr Clark. He doesn't talk much.'

And he didn't. Mancuso assigned him to the spare bunk in the engineer's stateroom. After his gear came down the hatch, Mr Clark walked into the room, closed the door behind him, and that was that.

'Where do you want me to stash my stuff?' Jones asked.

'There's a spare bunk in the goat locker,' Mancuso replied.

'Fine. The chiefs eat better anyway.'

'How's school?'

'One more semester till my masters. I'm already getting nibbles from some contractors. And I'm engaged.' Jones pulled out his wallet and showed the Captain a photo. 'Her name's Kim, and she works in the library.'

'Congratulations, Mr Jones.'

'Thanks, skipper. The Admiral said you really needed me. Kim understands. Her dad's Army. So, what's up? Some kind of spec-op, and you couldn't make it without me, right?' 'Special Operations' was a euphemism that covered all sorts of things, most of which were dangerous.

'I don't know. They haven't told me yet.'

'Well, one more trip "up north" wouldn't be too bad,' Jones observed. 'To be honest, I kind of missed it.'

Mancuso didn't think they were going there, but refrained from saying so. Jones went aft to get settled. Mancuso went into the engineer's stateroom.

'Mr Clark?'

'Yes, sir.' He'd hung up his jacket, revealing that he wore a short-sleeved shirt. The man was a little over forty, Mancuso judged. On first inspection, he didn't look all that special, perhaps six-one, and slim, but then Mancuso noted that the man didn't have the normal middle roll at the waist, and his shoulders were broader than they looked on the tall frame. It was the second glance at an arm that added a piece to the jigsaw. Half hidden under the black hair on his forearm was a tattoo, a red seal, it seemed to be, with a wide, impudent grin.

'I knew a guy with a tattoo like that. Officer – he's with Team-Six now.'

'Once upon a time, Captain. I'm not supposed to talk about that, sir.'

'What's this all about?'

'Sir, your mission orders will —'

'Humor me.' Mancuso smiled out the order. 'They just took in the brow.'

'It involves making a pickup.'

My God. Mancuso nodded impassively. 'Will you need any additional support?'

'No, sir. Solo shot. Just me and my gear.'

'Okay. We can go over it in detail after we sail. You'll eat in the wardroom. Right down the ladder outside, then a few feet aft, on the starboard side. One other thing: is time a problem?'

'Shouldn't be, unless you mind waiting. Part of this is still up in the air — and that's all I can say for now, Captain. Sorry, but I have my orders, too.'

'Fair enough. You take the top bunk. Get some sleep if you need it.'

'Thank you, sir.' Clark watched the Captain leave, but didn't smile until the door closed. He'd never been on a Los Angeles-class submarine before. Most intelligence missions were conducted by the smaller, more maneuverable Sturgeons. He always slept in the same place, though always in the upper bunk in the engineer's stateroom, the only spare bed on the ship. There was the usual problem stowing his gear, but 'Clark' had done it enough to know all the tricks. When he'd finished that, he climbed up into the bunk. He was tired from the flight and needed a few hours to relax. The bunk was always the same, hard against the curved hull of the submarine. It was like being in a coffin with the lid half-open.

'One must admire the Americans for their cleverness,' Morozov said. It had been a busy several weeks at Dushanbe. Immediately after the test — more precisely, immediately after their visitor from Moscow had left — two of the six lasers had been defrosted and disassembled for service, and it was found that their optics had been badly scorched. So there was still a problem with the optical coating, after all. More likely quality-control, his section chief had observed, dismissing the problem to another team of engineers. What they had now was far more exciting. Here was the American mirror design that they'd heard about for years.

'The idea came from an astronomer. He wanted a way to make stellar photographs that didn't suffer from "twinkling". Nobody bothered to tell him that it was impossible, so he went ahead and did it. I knew the rough idea, but not the details. You were right, young man. This is very clever. Too clever for us,' the man growled briefly as he flipped to the page on computer specifications. 'We don't have anything that can duplicate this performance. Just building the actuators – I don't know if we can even do that.'

'The Americans are building the telescope –'

'Yes, at Hawaii. I know. But the one at Hawaii is far behind this one, technically speaking. The Americans have made a breakthrough that has not yet found its way into the general scientific community. Note the date on the diagram. They may actually have this one operating now.' He shook his head. 'They're ahead of us.'

'You have to leave.'

'Yes. Thank you for protecting me this long.' Eduard Vassilyevich Altunin's gratitude was genuine. He'd had a floor on which to sleep, and several warm meals to sustain him while he made his plans.

Or attempted to. He couldn't even appreciate the disadvantages under which he labored. In the West he could easily have obtained new clothing, a wig to disguise his hair, even a theatrical makeup kit that came with instructions on how to alter his features. In the West he could hide in the back seat of a car, and be driven two hundred miles in under four hours. In Moscow he had none of those options. The KGB would have searched his flat by now, and determined what clothing he wore. They'd know his face and his hair color. The only thing they evidently did not know was his small circle of friends from military service in Afghanistan. He'd never talked to anyone about them.

They offered him a different sort of coat, but it didn't fit, and he had no wish to endanger these people further. He already had his cover story down: he'd hidden out with a criminal group a few blocks away. One fact about Moscow little known in the West was its crime situation, which was bad and getting worse. Though Moscow had not yet caught up with American cities of comparable size, there were districts where the prudent did not walk alone at night. But since foreigners didn't often visit such areas, and since the street criminals rarely troubled foreigners – doing so guaranteed a vigorous response from the Moscow Militia – the story was slow getting out.

He walked out onto Trofimovo, a dingy thoroughfare near the river. Altunin marveled at his stupidity. He'd always told himself that if he needed to escape from the city, he'd do so on a cargo barge. His father had worked on them all his life, and Eduard knew hiding places that no one could find – but the river was frozen, and barge traffic was at a stop, and he hadn't thought of it! Altunin raged at himself.

There was no sense worrying about that now, he told himself. There had to be another way. He knew that the Moskvich auto plant was only a kilometer away, and the trains ran year round. He'd try to catch one going south, perhaps hide in a freight car filled with auto parts. With luck he'd make it to Soviet Georgia, where no one would inspect his new papers all that closely. People could disappear in the Soviet Union. After all, it was a country of 280,000,000, he told himself. People were always losing or damaging their papers. He wondered how many of these thoughts were realistic and how many were simply an attempt to cheer himself up.

But he couldn't stop now. It had started in Afghanistan and he wondered if it would ever stop.

He'd been able to shut it out at first. A corporal in an ordnance company, he worked with what the Soviet military euphemistically referred to as 'counterterrorist devices.' These were distributed by air, or most often by Soviet soldiers completing a sweep through a village. Some were the prototypical Russian *matryoshka* dolls, a bandanaed figure with a roly-poly bottom; or a truck; or a fountain pen. Adults learned fast, but children were cursed both with curiosity and the inability to learn from the mistakes of others. Soon it was learned that children would pick up anything, and the number of doll-bombs distributed was reduced. But one thing remained constant: when picked up, a hundred grams of explosive would go off. His job had been assembling the bombs and teaching the soldiers how to use them properly.

Altunin hadn't thought about it much at first. It had been his job, the orders for which came from on high; Russians are neither inclined by temperament nor conditioned by education to question orders from on high. Besides, it had been a safe, easy job. He hadn't had to carry a rifle and go walking in the bandit country. The only dangers to him had been in the bazaars of Kabul, and he'd always been careful to walk about in groups of five or more. But on one such trip he'd seen a young child – boy or girl, he didn't know – whose right hand was now a claw, and whose mother stared at him and his comrades in a way he would never forget. He'd known the stories, how the Afghan bandits took particular delight in flaying captured Soviet pilots alive, how their women often handled the matter entirely. He'd thought it clear evidence of the barbarism of these primitive people – but a child wasn't primitive. Marxism said that. Take any child, give it proper schooling and leadership, and you'd have a communist for life. Not that child. He remembered it, that cold November day two years ago. The wound was fully healed, and the child had actually been smiling, too young to understand that its disfigurement would last forever. But the mother knew, and knew how and why her child had been punished for being ... born.

And after that, the safe, easy job hadn't been quite the same. Every time he screwed the explosives section onto the mechanism, he saw a small, pudgy child's hand. He started seeing them in his sleep. Drink, and even an experiment with hashish hadn't driven the images away. Speaking with his fellow technicians hadn't helped – though it had earned him the wrathful attention of his company *zampolit*. It was a hard thing he had to do, the political officer had explained, but necessary to prevent greater loss of life, you see. Complaining about it would not change matters, unless Corporal Altunin wanted transfer to a rifle company, where he might see for himself why such harsh measures were necessary.

He knew now that he should have taken that offer, and hated himself for the cowardice that had prevented the impulse. Service in a line company might have restored his self-image, might have – might have done a lot of things, Altunin told himself, but he hadn't made the choice and it hadn't made the difference. In the end, all he'd earned for himself was a letter from the *zampolit* that would travel with him for the rest of his life.

So now he tried to expiate that wrong. He told himself that perhaps he already had – and now, if he were very lucky, he could disappear, and perhaps he could forget the toys that he'd prepared for their evil mission. That was the only positive thought that his mind had room for, this cold, cloudy night.

He walked north, keeping off the dirt sidewalks, staying in shadows, away from the streetlamps. Shift workers coming home from the Moskvich plant made the streets agreeably crowded, but when he arrived at the railyard outside the plant, all the commuting was over. Snow started to fall heavily, reducing visibility to a hundred meters or so, with small globes of flakes around each of the lights over the stationary freight cars. A train seemed to be forming up, probably heading south, he told himself. Switching locomotives were moving back and forth, shunting boxcars from one siding to another. He spent a few minutes huddled by a car to make sure that he knew what was happening. The wind picked up as he watched, and Altunin looked for a better vantage point. There were some boxcars fifty or so meters away, from which he could observe better. One of them had an opened door, and he'd need to inspect the locking mechanism if he wanted to break inside one. He walked over with his head down to shield his face from the wind. The only thing he could hear, other than the crunch of snow under his boots, was the signal whistles of the switch engines. It was a friendly sound, he told himself, the sound that would change his life, perhaps lead the way to something like freedom.

He was surprised to see that there were people in the boxcar. Three of them. Two held cartons of auto parts. The third's hands were empty, until he reached into his pocket and came out with a knife.

Altunin started to say something. He didn't care if they were stealing parts for sale on the black market. He wasn't concerned at all, but before he could speak, the third one leaped down on him. Altunin was stunned when his head struck a steel rail. He was conscious, but couldn't move for a second, too surprised even to be afraid. The third one turned and said something. Altunin couldn't make out the reply, but knew it was sharp and quick. He was still trying to understand what was happening when his assailant turned back and slashed his throat. There wasn't even any pain. He wanted to explain that he wasn't . . . concerned . . . didn't care . . . just wanted to . . . one of them stood over him, two cartons in his arms, and clearly he was afraid, and Altunin thought this very odd, since he was the one who was dying . . .

Two hours later, a switch engine couldn't stop in time when its engineer noted an odd, snow-covered shape on the rails. On seeing what he'd run over, he called for the yardmaster.

13

Councils

'Beautiful job,' Vatutin commented. 'The bastards.'
They've broken the rule, he said to himself. The rule was
unwritten but nevertheless very real: CIA does not kill
Soviets in the Soviet Union; KGB does not kill Americans,
or even Soviet defectors, in the United States. So far as
Vatutin knew, the rule had never been broken by either
side – at least not obviously so. The rule made sense: the
job of intelligence agencies was to gather intelligence; if
KGB and CIA officers spent their time killing people – with
the inevitable retaliation and counter-retaliation – the
primary job would not get done. And so the business of
intelligence was a civilized, *predictable* business. In
third-world countries, different rules applied, of course,
but in America and the Soviet Union, the rules were
assiduously followed.

*Until now, that is – unless I'm supposed to believe that this
poor, sad bastard was murdered by auto-parts thieves!*
Vatutin wondered if CIA might have contracted the job out
to a criminal gang – he suspected that the Americans used
Soviet criminals for some things too sensitive for their own
lily-white hands. *That would not be a* technical *violation of
the rules, would it?* He wondered if the First Directorate
men ever used a similar dodge. . . .

All he knew right now was that the next step in the
courier chain was dead at his feet, and with it his only hope
of linking the microfilm to the American spy in the Defense
Ministry. Vatutin corrected himself: He also knew that
he'd have to report this to the Chairman in about six hours.
He needed a drink. Vatutin shook his head and looked

down at what was left of his suspect. The snow was falling so rapidly that you couldn't see the blood anymore.

'You know, if they'd only been a little bit more clever putting his body on the tracks, we might have written it off to an accident,' another KGB officer observed. Despite the horrendous work done to the body by the wheels of the locomotive, it was clear that Altunin's throat had been expertly sliced by a narrow-bladed knife. Death, the responding physician reported, could not have taken longer than a minute. There were no signs of a struggle. The victim's – the traitor's! – hands were not bruised or cut. He hadn't fought back against whoever had killed him. Conclusion: his killer was probably known to him. Might it have been an American?

'First thing,' Vatutin said. 'I want to know if any Americans were away from their flats between eighteen and twenty-three hours.' He turned. 'Doctor!'

'Yes, Colonel?'

'Time of death again?'

'Judging by the temperature of the larger pieces, between twenty-one and midnight. Earlier rather than later, I think, but the cold and snow cover complicate matters.' *Not to mention the state of the remains*, he didn't add.

Vatutin turned back to his principal assistant. 'Any who were away from quarters, I want to know who, where, when, and why.'

'Step up surveillance of all the foreigners?' the man wondered aloud.

'I'll have to go to the Chairman for that, but I'm thinking about it. I want you to speak to the chief Militia investigator. This is to be classified most-secret. We don't need a mob of fumbling policemen messing this affair up.'

'Understood, Comrade Colonel. They'd only be interested in recovering the auto parts anyway,' the man noted sourly. *This* perestroika *business is turning everyone into a capitalist!*

Vatutin walked over to the locomotive driver. 'It's cold, isn't it?'

The message was received. 'Yes, Comrade. Perhaps you'd like something to take away the chill?'

'That would be very kind of you, Comrade Engineer.'

'My pleasure, Comrade Colonel.' The engine driver produced a small bottle. As soon as he'd seen that the man was a colonel of the KGB, he'd thought himself doomed. But the man seemed decent enough. His colleagues were businesslike, their questions had been reasonable ones, and the man was almost at ease – until he realized that he could be punished for having a bottle on the job. He watched the man take a long pull, then hand the bottle back.

'*Spasibo*,' the KGB man said, and walked off into the snow.

Vatutin was waiting in the Chairman's anteroom when he arrived. He'd heard that Gerasimov was a serious worker, always at his desk by seven-thirty. The stories were right. He came through the door at seven twenty-five and waved for the 'Two' man to follow him into his office.

'Well?'

'Altunin was killed late last night in the railyards outside the Moskvich Auto Factory. His throat was cut and his body left on the tracks, where a switch engine ran over it.'

'You're sure it's him?' Gerasimov asked with a frown.

'Yes, he was positively identified. I recognized the face myself. He was found next to a railcar that had ostensibly been broken into, and some auto parts were missing.'

'Oh, so he stumbled upon a gang of black marketeers and they conveniently killed him?'

'So it is meant to appear, Comrade Chairman.' Colonel Vatutin nodded. 'I find the coincidence unconvincing, but there is no physical evidence to contradict it. Our investigations are continuing. We are now checking to see if any of Altunin's comrades from his military service live in the area, but I am not hopeful along these lines.'

Gerasimov rang for tea. His secretary appeared in an instant, and Vatutin realized that this had to be part of the regular morning routine. The Chairman was taking things more easily than the Colonel had feared. Party man or not, he acted like a professional:

'So, to this point, we have three confessed document couriers, and one more positively identified, but unfortunately dead. The dead one was seen in close physical proximity to the senior aide of the Defense Minister, and one of the live ones has identified his contact as a foreigner, but cannot positively identify his face. In short, we have the middle of this line, but neither end.'

'That is correct, Comrade Chairman. Surveillance of the two Ministry colonels continues. I propose that we step up surveillance of the American Embassy community.'

Gerasimov nodded. 'Approved. It's time for my morning brief. Keep pushing for a break in the case. You look better now that you've cut back on your drinking, Vatutin.'

'I feel better, Comrade Chairman,' he admitted.

'Good.' Gerasimov rose, and his visitor did the same. 'Do you really think that our CIA colleagues killed their own man?'

'Altunin's death was most convenient for them. I realize that this would be a violation of our – our agreement along these lines, but –'

'But we are probably dealing with a highly placed spy, and they are undoubtedly most interested in protecting him. Yes, I understand that. Keep pushing, Vatutin,' Gerasimov said again.

Foley was already at his office also. On his desk were three film cassettes for CARDINAL. The next problem was delivering the damned things. The business of espionage was a mass of interlocking contradictions. Some parts of it were devilishly hard. Some carried the sort of danger that made him wish he'd stayed with the *New York Times*. But others were so simple that he could have had one of his kids handle it. That very thought had occurred to him several times – not that he'd ever entertain it seriously, but in moments when his mind was affected by a few stiff drinks, he'd muse that Eddie could take a piece of chalk and make a certain mark in a certain place. From time to time, embassy personnel would walk about Moscow doing things that were just slightly out of the ordinary. In summer, they'd wear flowers in buttonholes, and remove them for no apparent reason – and the KGB officers watching them would anxiously scan the sidewalks for the person at whom the 'signal' was aimed. Year round, some would wander about, taking photographs of ordinary street scenes. In fact, they scarcely needed to be told. Some of the embassy people merely had to act like their eccentric American selves to drive the Russians nuts. To a counterespionage officer, *anything* could be a secret sign: a turned-down sun visor in a parked car, a package left on its front seat, the way the wheels were pointed. The net effect of all these measures, some deliberate, some merely random, had 'Two' men scurrying all over the city running down things that simply didn't exist. It was something Americans did better than Russians, who were too regimented to act in a truly random fashion, and it was something that made life thoroughly miserable for the counterspies of the Second Chief Directorate.

But there were thousands of them, and only seven hundred Americans (counting dependents) assigned to the embassy.

And Foley still had the film to deliver. He wondered why it was that CARDINAL had always refused to use dead-drops. It was the perfect expedient for this. A dead-drop was typically an object that looked like an ordinary stone, or anything else common and harmless, hollowed out to hold the thing to be transferred. Bricks were especially favored in Moscow, as the city was mainly one of brick, many of which were loose due to the uniformly poor workmanship found here, but the variety of such devices was endless.

On the other hand, the variety of ways to make a brush-pass was limited, and depended upon the sort of timing to be found in a wishbone backfield. Well, the Agency hadn't given him this job because it was easy. He couldn't risk it again himself. Perhaps his wife could make the transfer . . .

'So, where's the leak?' Parks asked his security chief.

'It could be any one of a hundred or so people,' the man answered.

'That's good news,' Pete Wexton observed dryly. He was an inspector in the FBI's counterintelligence office. 'Only a hundred.'

'Could be one of the scientific people, or somebody's secretary, or someone in the budget department – that's just in the program itself. There are another twenty or so here in the D.C. area who're into Tea Clipper deep enough to have seen this stuff, but they're all very senior folks.' SDIO's security chief was a Navy captain who customarily wore civilian clothes. 'More likely, the person we're looking for is out West.'

'And they're mostly scientific types, mostly under forty.' Wexton closed his eyes. *Who live inside computers and think the world's just one big videogame.* The problem with scientists, especially the young ones, was simply that they lived in a world very different from that understood and appreciated by the security community. To them, progress depended on the free transfer of information and ideas. They were people who got excited about new things, and talked about them among themselves, unconsciously seeking the synergism that made ideas sprout like weeds in the disordered garden of the laboratory. To a security officer the ideal world was one where nobody talked to anyone else. The problem with that, of course, was that such a world rarely did anything worth securing in the first place. The balance was almost impossible to strike, and the security people were always caught exactly in the middle, hated by everyone.

'What about internal security on the project documents?' Wexton asked.

'You mean canary traps?'

'What the hell is that?' General Parks asked.

'All these papers are done on word processors. You use the machine to make subtle alterations in each copy of the important papers. That way you can track every one, and identify the precise one that's being leaked to the other side,' the Captain explained. 'We haven't done much of that. It's too time-intensive.'

'CIA has a computer subroutine that does it automatically. They call it Spookscribe, or something like that. It's closely held, but you should be able to get it if you ask.'

'Nice of 'em to tell us about it,' Parks groused. 'Would it matter in this case?'

'Not at the moment, but you play all the cards you got,' the Captain observed to his boss. 'I've heard about the program. It can't be used on scientific documents. The way they use language is too precise. Anything more than inserting a comma – well, it can screw up what they're trying to say.'

'Assuming anyone can understand it in the first place,' Wexton said with a rueful shake of the head. 'Well, it's for damned sure that the Russians can.' He was already thinking about the resources that this case would require – possibly hundreds of agents. They'd be conspicuous. The community in question might be too small to absorb a large influx of people without someone's notice.

The other obvious thing to do was restrict access to information on the mirror experiments, but then you ran the risk of alerting the spy. Wexton wondered why he hadn't stuck to simple things like kidnappings and Mafia racketeering. But he'd gotten his brief on Tea Clipper from Parks himself. It was an important job, and he was the best man for it. Wexton was sure of this: Director Jacobs had said so himself.

Bondarenko noticed it first. He'd had an odd feeling a few days previously while doing his morning run. It was something he'd always had, but those three months in

280

Afghanistan had taken a latent sixth sense and made it blossom fully. There were eyes on him. *Whose?* he wondered.

They were good. He was sure of that. He also suspected that there were five or more of them. That made them Russian . . . probably. Not certainly. Colonel Bondarenko was one kilometer into his run, and decided to perform a small experiment. He altered his route, taking a right where he normally took a left. That would take him past a new apartment block whose first-floor windows were still polished. He grinned to himself, but his right hand unconsciously slapped down on his hip, searching for his service automatic. The grin ended when he realized what his hand had done, and felt the gnawing disappointment that he did not have the wherewithal to defend himself with anything other than bare hands. Bondarenko knew how to do that quite well, but a pistol has longer reach than a hand or foot. It wasn't fear, not even close to it, but Bondarenko was a soldier, accustomed to knowing the limits and rules of his own world.

His head swiveled, looking at the reflection of the windows. There was a man a hundred meters behind him, holding a hand to his face, as though speaking on a small radio. Interesting. Bondarenko turned and ran back for a few meters, but by the time his head had come around, the man's hand was at his side, and he was walking normally, seemingly uninterested in the jogging officer. Colonel Bondarenko turned and resumed his normal pace. His smile was now thin and tight. He'd confirmed it. But what had he confirmed? Bondarenko promised himself that he'd know that an hour after getting to his office.

Thirty minutes later, home, showered, and dressed, he read his morning paper – for him it was *Krasnaya Zvesda*, 'Red Star,' the Soviet military daily – while he drank a mug of tea. The radio was playing while his wife prepared the children for school. Bondarenko didn't hear either, and his eyes merely scanned the paper while his mind churned.

Who are they? Why are they watching me? Am I under suspicion? If so, suspicion of what?

'Good morning, Gennady Iosifovich,' Misha said on entering his office.

'Good morning, Comrade Colonel,' Bondarenko answered.

Filitov smiled. 'Call me Misha. The way you're going, you will soon outrank this old carcass. What is it?'

'I'm being watched. I had people following me this morning when I did my run.'

'Oh?' Misha turned. 'Are you sure?'

'You know how it is when you know you're being watched – I'm certain *you* know, Misha!' the young Colonel observed.

But he was wrong. Filitov had noticed nothing unusual, nothing to arouse his instincts until this moment. Then it hit him that the bath attendant wasn't back yet. What if the signal was about something more than a routine security check? Filitov's face changed for an instant before he got it back under control.

'You've noticed something, too, then?' Bondarenko asked.

'Ah!' A wave of the hand, and an ironic look. 'Let them look; they will find this old man more boring than Alexandrov's sex life.' The reference to the Politburo's chief ideologue was becoming a popular one in the Defense Ministry. A sign, Misha wondered, that General Secretary Narmonov was planning to ease him out?

They ate in the Afghan way, everyone taking food barehanded from a common plate. Ortiz had a virtual banquet laid out for lunch. The Archer had the place of honor, with Ortiz at his right hand to act as translator. Four very senior CIA people were there, too. He thought they were overdoing things, but then, the place that put the light in the sky must have been important. Ortiz opened the talking with the usual ceremonial phrases.

'You do me too much honor,' the Archer replied.

'Not so,' the senior CIA visitor said through Ortiz. 'Your skill and courage are well known to us, and even among our soldiers. We are ashamed that we can give you no more than the poor help that our government allows.'

'It is our land to win back,' the Archer said with dignity. 'With Allah's help it will be ours again. It is well that Believers should strive together against the godless ones, but the task is that of my people, not yours.'

He doesn't know, Ortiz thought. *He doesn't know that he's being used.*

'So,' the Archer went on. 'Why have you traveled around the world to speak with this humble warrior?'

'We wish to talk with you about the light you saw in the sky.'

The Archer's face changed. He was surprised at that. He'd expected to be asked about how well his missiles worked.

'It was a light – a strange light, yes. Like a meteor, but it seemed to go up instead of down.' He described what he had seen in detail, giving the time, where he'd been, the direction of the light, and the way it had sliced across the sky.

'Did you see what it hit? Did you see anything else in the sky?'

'Hit? I don't understand. It was a light.'

Another of the visitors spoke. 'I am told that you were a teacher of mathematics. Do you know what a laser is?'

His face changed at the new thought. 'Yes, I read of them when I was in university. I –' The Archer sipped at a glass of juice. 'I know little of lasers. They project a beam of light, and are used mainly for measuring and surveying. I have never seen one, only read of them.'

'What you saw was a test of a laser weapon.'

'What is its purpose?'

'We do not know. The test you saw used the laser system to destroy a satellite in orbit. That means –'

'I know of satellites. A laser can be used for this purpose?'

'Our country is working on similar things, but it would seem that the Russians are ahead of us.'

The Archer was surprised by that. Was not America the world's leader in technical things? Was not the Stinger proof of that? Why had these men flown twelve thousand miles – merely because he'd seen a light in the sky?

'You are fearful of this laser?'

'We have great interest,' the senior man replied. 'Some of the documents you found gave us information about the site which we did not have, and for this we are doubly in your debt.'

'I, too, have interest now. Do you have the documents?'

'Emilio?' The senior visitor gestured at Ortiz, who produced a map and a diagram.

'This site has been under construction since 1983. We were surprised that the Russians would build so important a facility so near to the borders of Afghanistan.'

'In 1983, they still thought they would win,' the Archer observed darkly. The idea that they'd felt that way was taken as an insult. He noted the position on the map, the mountaintop nearly surrounded by a sweeping loop of the Vakhsh River. He saw immediately why it was there. The power dam at Nurek was only a few kilometers away. The Archer knew more than he let on. He knew what lasers were, and a little of how they operated. He knew that their light was dangerous, that it could blind. . . .

It destroyed a satellite? Hundreds of kilometers up in space, higher than airplanes could fly . . . what could it do to people on the ground . . . perhaps they'd built so close to his country for another reason. . . .

'So you merely saw the light? You have heard no stories about such a place, no stories of strange lights in the sky?'

The Archer shook his head. 'No, only the one time.' He saw the visitors exchange looks of disappointment.

'Well, that does not matter. I am permitted to offer you the thanks of my government. Three truckloads of weapons are coming to your band. If there is anything else you need, we will try to get it for you.'

284

The Archer nodded soberly. He'd expected a great reward for the delivery of the Soviet officer, then been disappointed at his death. But these men had not visited him about that. It was all about the documents and the light – was this place so important that the death of the Russian was considered trivial? Were the Americans actually afraid of it?

And if they were fearful, how should he feel?

'No, Arthur, I don't like it,' the President said tentatively. Judge Moore pressed the attack.

'Mr President, we are aware of Narmonov's political difficulties. The disappearance of our agent will not have any more of an effect than his arrest by the KGB, possibly less. After all, the KGB can't very well raise too much of a ruckus if they let him slip away,' the DCI pointed out.

'It's still too great a risk,' Jeffrey Pelt said. 'We have an historic opportunity with Narmonov. He really wants to make fundamental changes in their system – hell, your people are the ones who made the assessment.'

We had this chance before and blew it, during the Kennedy Administration, Moore thought. *But Khrushchev fell, and we had twenty years of Party hacks. Now there may be another chance. You're afraid we might never get another opportunity as good as this one. Well, that's one way to look at it,* he admitted to himself.

'Jeff, his position will not be affected any more by extracting our man than by his capture –'

'If they're on to him, why haven't they grabbed him already?' Pelt demanded. 'What if you're overreacting?'

'This man has been working for us over thirty years – thirty years! Do you know the risks he's run for us, the information we've gotten from him? Can you appreciate the frustration he's felt the times we ignored his advice? Can you imagine what it's like to live with a death sentence for thirty years? If we abandon the man, what's this country all about?' Moore said with quiet determination. The

President was a man who could always be swayed by arguments based on principle.

'And if we topple Narmonov in the process?' Pelt demanded. 'What if Alexandrov's clique does take over, and it's back to the bad old days all over again – more tension, more arms races? How do we explain to the American people that we sacrificed this opportunity for the life of one man?'

'For one thing, they'd never know unless somebody leaked it,' the DCI replied coldly. 'The Russians wouldn't make it all public, and you know that. For another, how would we explain throwing this man away like a used Kleenex?'

'They wouldn't know that either, unless somebody leaked it,' Pelt answered in an equally cold voice.

The President stirred. His first instinct had been to put the extraction operation on hold. How could he explain any of this? Either by an act of commission or omission, they were discussing the best way to prevent something unfavorable from happening to America's principal enemy. *But you can't even say that in public*, the President reflected. *If you said out loud that the Russians are our enemy, the papers would throw a fit. The Soviets have thousands of nuclear warheads aimed at us, but we can't risk offending their sensibilities* . . .

He remembered his two face-to-face meetings with the man, Andrey Il'ych Narmonov, General Secretary of the Communist Party of the Soviet Union. Younger than he was, the President reflected. Their initial conversations had been cautious, each man feeling out the other, looking both for weaknesses and common ground, for advantage and compromise. A man with a mission, a man who probably did wish to change things, the President thought –

But is that a good thing? What if he did decentralize their economy, introduce market forces, give them a little freedom – not much, of course, but enough to get things moving? Quite a few people were warning him about that possibility: Imagine a country with the Soviets' political will, backed up by an economy that could deliver quality goods both in the civilian and military sectors. Would it make the Russian people believe again in their system; would it revive the sense of mission that they'd had in the 1930s? *We might be faced with a more dangerous enemy than ever before.*

On the other side, he was told that there is no such thing as a little freedom – one could ask Duvalier of Haiti, Marcos of the Philippines, or the ghost of Shah Mohammed Reza Pahlavi. The momentum of events could bring the Soviet Union out of the dark ages and into the 20th-century era of political thought. It might take a generation, perhaps two, but what if the country did start to evolve into something approaching a liberal state? There was another lesson of history: Liberal democracies don't make war on one another.

Some choice I have, the President thought. *I can be remembered as the regressive idiot who reinstated the Cold War in all its grim majesty – or the Pollyanna who expected the leopard to change its spots, only to find that it had grown bigger, sharper fangs. Jesus,* he told himself as he stared at his two interlocutors, *I'm not thinking about success at all, only the consequences of failure.*

That's one area in which America and Russia have paralleled their history – our postwar governments have never lived up to the expectations of our people, have they? I'm the President, *I'm supposed to* know *what the Right Thing is. That's why the people elected me. That's what they're paying me for. God, if they only knew what frauds we all are. We're not talking about how to succeed. We're talking about who'll leak the reason for the failure of policy. Right here in the Oval Office, we're discussing who'll get the blame if something we haven't yet decided upon doesn't work.*

'Who knows about this?'

Judge Moore held his hands out. 'Admiral Greer, Bob Ritter, and me at CIA. A few field personnel know about the proposed operation – we had to send out the heads-up signal – but they do not know the political issues, and never will. They don't need to know. Aside from that, only we three at the Agency have the entire picture. Add you, sir, and Dr Pelt, and that makes five.'

'And already we're talking about leaks! Goddamn it!' the President swore with surprising passion. 'How did we ever get so screwed up as this!'

Everyone sobered up. There was nothing like a presidential curse to settle people down. He looked at Moore and Pelt, his chief intelligence advisor, and his national-security advisor. One was pleading for the life of a man who had served America faithfully and well, at peril of his life; the other took the long, cold look at the *realpolitik* and saw an historic opportunity more important than any single human life.

'Arthur, you're saying that this agent – and I don't even want to know his name – has been giving us critically important data for thirty years, up to and including this laser project that the Russians have operating; you say that he is probably in danger, and it's time to run the risk of getting him out of there, that we have a moral obligation to do so.'

'Yes, Mr President.'

'And you, Jeff, you say that the timing's bad, that the revelation of a leak so high up in their government could endanger Narmonov politically, could topple him from his leadership position and replace him with a government less attractive to us.'

'Yes, Mr President.'

'And if this man dies because we haven't helped him?'

'We would lose important information,' Moore said. 'And it might have no tangible difference in its effect on Narmonov. And we'd be betraying a trust to a man who has served us faithfully and well for thirty years.'

'Jeff, can you live with that?' the President asked his national-security advisor.

'Yes, sir, I can live with that. I don't like it but I can live with it. With Narmonov we have already gotten an agreement on intermediate nuclear arms, and we have a chance at one on strategic forces.'

It's like being a judge. I have two advocates who believe fully in their positions. I wonder if their principles would be quite so firm if they were in my chair, if they had to make the decision?

But they didn't run for President.

This agent's been serving the United States since I was a junior prosecutor handling whores in night court.

Narmonov may be the best chance we've had for world peace since God knows when.

The President stood and walked to the windows behind his desk. They were very thick, to protect him from people with guns. They could not protect him against the duties of his office. He looked at the south lawn, but found no answers. He turned back.

'I don't know. Arthur, you can get your assets in place, but I want your word that nothing will happen without my authorization. No mistakes, no initiative, no action at all without my say-so. I'm going to need time on this one. We have time, don't we?'

'Yes, sir. It will take several more days before we have the pieces in place.'

'I'll let you know when I make my decision.' He shook hands with both men and watched them leave. The President had five more minutes before his next appointment, and used the time to visit the bathroom that adjoins the office. He wondered if there were any underlying symbolism in the act of washing his hands, or did he just want the excuse to look at himself in the mirror? *And you're supposed to be the man with all the fucking answers!* the image told him. *You don't even know why you went to the bathroom!* The President smiled at that. It was funny, funny in a way that few other men would ever understand.

'So what the hell do I tell Foley?' Ritter snapped twenty minutes later.

'Back off, Bob,' Moore warned. 'He's thinking about it.

We don't need an immediate decision, and a "maybe" beats hell out of a "no".'

'Sorry, Arthur. It's just that – damn it, I've tried to get him to come out before. We can't let this man go down.'

'I'm sure he won't make a final decision until I've had a chance to talk with him again. For the moment, tell Foley to continue the mission. And I want a fresh look at Narmonov's political vulnerability. I get the impression that Alexandrov may be on the way out – he's too old to take over from the current man; the Politburo wouldn't stand for replacing a relatively young man with an old one, not after the death parade they had a few years back. Who does that leave?'

'Gerasimov,' Ritter said at once. 'Two others may be in the running, but he's the ambitious one. Ruthless, but very, very smooth. The Party bureaucracy likes him because he did such a nice job on the dissidents. And if he wants to make a move, it'll have to be pretty soon. If the arms agreement goes through, Narmonov gains a lot of prestige, and the political clout that goes with it. If Alexandrov isn't careful, he'll miss the boat entirely, get moved out himself, and Narmonov will have his seat nice and safe for years.'

'That'll take at least five years to accomplish,' Admiral Greer noted, speaking for the first time. 'He may not have five years. We do have those indications that Alexandrov may be on his way out. If that's more than a rumor, it might force his hand.'

Judge Moore looked up at the ceiling. 'It sure would be easier to deal with the bastards if they had predictable ways of running things.' *Of course, we have it, and they can't predict us.*

'Cheer up, Arthur,' Greer said. 'If the world made sense, we'd all have to find honest work.'

14

Changes

Passage through the Kattegat is a tricky affair for a submarine, doubly so when it is necessary to be covert. The water is shallow there, too shallow to run submerged. The channels can be tricky in daylight. They are worse at night, and worse still without a pilot. Since *Dallas*' passage was supposedly a secret one, a pilot was out of the question.

Mancuso rode the bridge. Below, his navigator sweated at the chart table while a chief quartermaster manned the periscope and called out bearings to various landmarks. They couldn't even use radar to help with navigation, but the periscope had a low-light amplifier, which didn't quite turn night to day, but at least made the starless darkness look like twilight. The weather was a gift, with low clouds and sleet that restricted visibility just enough that the low, dark shape of the 688-class submarine would be difficult to spot from land. The Danish Navy knew of the submarine's transit, and had a few small craft out to ward off any possible snoopers – there were none – but aside from that, *Dallas* was on her own.

'Ship on the port bow,' a lookout called.

'I got him,' Mancuso answered at once. He held a pistol-like light-amplifying scope and saw the medium-sized container ship. The odds, he thought, made it an East Bloc vessel. Within a minute, the course and speed of the inbound ship were plotted, with a CPA – Closest Point of Approach – of seven hundred yards. The Captain swore and gave his orders.

Dallas had her running lights on – the Danes had insisted on it. The rotating amber one above the masthead light marked her positively as a submarine. Aft, a seaman struck down the American flag and replaced it with a Danish one.

'Everybody look Scandinavian,' Mancuso noted wryly.

'Ja-ja, Kept'n,' a junior officer chuckled in the darkness. It would be hard for him. He was black. 'Slow bearing change on our friend. He isn't altering course that I can tell, sir. Look –'

'Yeah, I see 'em.' Two of the Danish craft were racing forward to interpose themselves between the container ship and *Dallas*. Mancuso thought that would help. All cats are gray at night, and a submarine on the surface looks like . . . a submarine on the surface, a black shape with a vertical sail.

'I think she's Polish,' the Lieutenant observed. 'Yeah, I got the funnel now. Maersk Line.'

The two ships closed at a rate of a half a mile per minute. Mancuso turned to watch, keeping his scope on the ship's bridge. He saw no special activity. Well, it was three in the morning. The bridge crew had a tough navigating job to do, and probably their interest in his submarine was the same as his main interest in their merchantman – *please don't hit me, you idiot*. It was over surprisingly fast, and then he was staring at her stern light. It occurred to Mancuso that having the lights on was probably a good idea. If they'd been blacked out and then spotted, greater notice might have been taken.

They were in the Baltic Sea proper an hour later, on a course of zero-six-five, using the deepest water they could find as *Dallas* picked her way east. Mancuso took the navigator into his stateroom and together they plotted the best approach to, and the safest place on, the Soviet coast. When they'd selected it, Mr Clark joined them, and together the three discussed the delicate part of the mission.

In an ideal world, Vatutin thought wryly, they would take their worries to the Defense Minister, and he would cooperate fully with the KGB investigation. But the world

292

was not ideal. In addition to the expected institutional rivalries, Yazov was in the pocket of the General Secretary and knew of the differences of opinion between Gerasimov and Narmonov. No, the Defense Minister would either take over the entire investigation through his own security arm, or use his political power to close the case entirely, lest KGB disgrace Yazov himself for having a traitor for an aide, and so endanger Narmonov.

If Narmonov fell, at best the Defense Minister would go back to being the Soviet Army's chief of personnel; more likely, he'd be retired in quiet humiliation after the removal of his patron. Even if the General Secretary managed to survive the crisis, Yazov would be the sacrificial goat, just as Sokolov had been so recently. What choice did Yazov have?

The Defense Minister was also a man with a mission. Under the cover of the 'restructuring' initiative of the General Secretary, Yazov hoped to use his knowledge of the officer corps to remake the Soviet Army – in the hope, supposedly, of professionalizing the entire military community. Narmonov said that he wanted to save the Soviet economy, but no less an authority than Alexandrov, the high priest of Marxism-Leninism, said that he was destroying the purity of the Party itself. Yazov wanted to rebuild the military from the ground up. It would also have the effect, Vatutin thought, of making the Army personally loyal to Narmonov.

That worried Vatutin. Historically, the Party had used the KGB to keep the military under control. After all, the military had all the guns, and if it ever awoke to its power and felt the loosening of Party control . . . it was too painful a concept on which to dwell. An army loyal exclusively to the General Secretary rather than the Party itself was even more painful to Vatutin, since it would change the relationship the KGB had to Soviet society as a whole. There could then be no check on the General Secretary. With the military behind him, he could break KGB to his will and use it to 'restructure' the entire Party. He would have the power of another Stalin.

How did I ever start along this line? Vatutin asked himself. *I'm a counterintelligence officer, not a Party theorist.* For all his life, Colonel Vatutin had never dwelt on the Big Issues of his country. He'd trusted his superiors to handle the major decisions and allow him to handle the small details. No longer. By being taken into Chairman Gerasimov's confidence he was now inextricably allied with the man. It had happened too easily! Virtually overnight – *you have to be noticed to get general's stars*, he thought with a sardonic smile. *You always wanted to get noticed. So, Klementi Vladimirovich, you got yourself noticed all right. Now look where you are!*

Right in the middle of a power play between the KGB Chairman and the General Secretary himself.

It was actually quite funny, he told himself. He knew it would be less so if Gerasimov miscalculated – but the crowning irony of all was that if the KGB Chairman fell, then the liberal influences already put in place by Narmonov would protect Vatutin, who was, after all, merely doing the job assigned him by his duly appointed superiors. He didn't think that he'd be imprisoned, much less shot, as had once been the case. His advancement would be at an end. He'd find himself demoted, running the KGB regional office at Omsk, or the least pleasant opening they could find, never again to return to Moscow Center.

That wouldn't be so bad, he thought. On the other hand, if Gerasimov succeeded . . . head of 'Two' perhaps? And that wouldn't be very bad at all.

And you actually believed that you could advance your career without becoming 'political'. But that was no longer an option. If he tried to get out, he'd be disgraced. Vatutin was trapped, and knew it. The only way out was to do his job to the best of his ability.

The reverie ended as he turned back to his reports. Colonel Bondarenko was totally clean, he thought. His record had been examined and re-examined, and there was nothing to indicate that he was anything less than a patriot and an above-average officer. Filitov is the one, Vatutin thought. As insane as it seemed on the surface, this decorated hero was a traitor.

But how the hell do we prove that? How do we even investigate it properly without the cooperation of the Defense Minister? That was the other rub. If he failed in his investigation, then Gerasimov would not look kindly upon his career; but the investigation was hindered by political constraints imposed by the Chairman. Vatutin remembered the time he'd almost been passed over for promotion to major and realized how unlucky he'd been when the promotion board had changed its mind.

Oddly, it did not occur to him that all his problems resulted from having a KGB Chairman with political ambition. Vatutin summoned his senior officers. They arrived in a few minutes.

'Progress on Filitov?' he asked.

'Our best people are shadowing him,' a middle-level officer answered. 'Six of them round the clock. We're rotating schedules so that he doesn't see the same faces very often, if at all. We now have continuous television surveillance all around his apartment block, and half a dozen people check the tapes every night. We've stepped up coverage of suspected American and British spies, and of their diplomatic communities in general. We're straining our manpower and risking counterdetection, but there's no avoiding that. About the only new thing I have to report is that Filitov talks in his sleep occasionally – he's talking to somebody named Romanov, it sounds like. The words are too distorted to understand, but I have a speech pathologist working on it, and we may get something. In any case, Filitov can't fart without our knowing it. The only thing we can't do is maintain continuous visual contact without getting our people in too close. Every day, turning a corner or entering a shop, he's out of sight for five to fifteen seconds – long enough to make a brush-pass or a dead-drop. Nothing I can do about that unless you want us to risk alerting him.'

Vatutin nodded. Even the best surveillance had its limitations.

'Oh, there is one odd thing,' the Major said. 'Just learned about it yesterday. About once a week or so, Filitov takes the burn-bag down to the incinerator chute himself. It's so routine that the man in the destruct room forgot to tell us until last evening. He's a youngster, and came in himself to report it – after hours, and in civilian clothes. Bright boy. It turns out that Filitov looked after the installation of the system, years back. I checked the plans myself, nothing out of the way. Completely normal installation, just like what we have here. And that's all. For all practical purposes the only unusual thing about the subject is that he ought to be retired by now.'

'What of the Altunin investigation?' Vatutin asked next.

Another officer opened his notebook. 'We've no idea where he was before being killed. Perhaps he was hiding out alone somewhere, perhaps he was protected by friends whom we have been unable to identify. We've established no correlation between his death and the movement of foreigners. He was carrying nothing incriminating except some false papers that looked amateurishly done, but probably good enough for the outlying republics. If he was murdered by CIA, it was a remarkably complete job. No loose ends. None.'

'Your opinions?'

'The Altunin case is a dead end,' the Major answered. 'There are still a half-dozen things that we have to check out, but none has the least promise of an important break.' He paused for a moment. 'Comrade. . . .'

'Go on.'

'I believe this was a coincidence. I think Altunin was the victim of a simple murder, that he tried to get aboard the wrong railcar at the wrong time. I have no evidence to point to, but that is how it feels to me.'

Vatutin considered that. It took no small amount of moral courage for an officer of the Second Chief Director-ate to say that he was *not* on a counterespionage case.

'How sure are you?'

'We'll never be sure, Comrade Colonel, but if CIA had done the murder, would they not have disposed of the body – or, if they were trying to use his death to protect a highly placed spy, why not leave evidence to implicate him as a totally separate case? There were no false flags left behind, even though this would seem the place to do so.'

'Yes, we would have done that. A good point. Run down all your leads anyway.'

'Of course, Comrade General. Four to six days, I think.'

'Anything else?' Vatutin asked. Heads shook negatively. 'Very well, return to your sections, Comrades.'

She'd do it at the hockey game, Mary Pat Foley thought. CARDINAL would be there, alerted by a wrong-number telephone call from a pay phone. She'd make the pass herself. She had three film cassettes in her purse, and a simple handshake would do it. Her son played on this junior-league team, as did Filitov's grand-nephew, and she went to every game. It would be unusual if she didn't go, and the Russians depended on people to stick to their routines. She was being followed. She knew it. Evidently the Russians had stepped up surveillance, but the shadow she rated wasn't all that good – or at least they were using the same one on her, and Mary Pat knew when she saw a face more than once in a day.

Mary Patricia Kaminskiy Foley had typically muddled American ancestry, though some aspects of it had been left off her passport documents. Her grandfather had been an equerry to the House of Romanov, had taught the Crown Prince Aleksey to ride – no small feat since the youngster was tragically stricken with hemophilia, and the utmost caution had needed to be exercised. That had been the crowning achievement of an otherwise undistinguished life. He'd been a failure as an Army officer, though friends at court had ensured his advancement to colonel. All that he had accomplished was the utter destruction of his regiment in the Tannenberg Forests, and his capture by the

Germans – and his survival past 1920. Upon learning that his wife had died in the revolutionary turmoil that followed the First World War, he'd never returned to Russia – he always called it *Russia* – and eventually drifted to the United States, where he'd settled in the suburbs of New York and remarried after establishing a small business. He'd lived to the ripe old age of ninety-seven, outliving even a second wife twenty years his junior, and Mary Pat never forgot his rambling stories. On entering college and majoring in history, she learned better, of course. She learned that the Romanovs were hopelessly inept, their court irredeemably corrupt. But one thing she'd never forget was the way her grandfather wept when he got to the part about how Aleksey, a brave, determined young man, and his entire family had been shot like dogs by the Bolsheviks. That one story, repeated to her a hundred times, gave Mary Pat a view of the Soviet Union which no amount of time or academic instruction or political realism could ever erase. Her feelings for the government which ruled her grandfather's land were completely framed by the murder of Nicholas II, his wife, and his five children. Intellect, she told herself in reflective moments, had very little to do with the way people feel.

Working in Moscow, working against that same government, was the greatest thrill of her life. She liked it even more than her husband, whom she'd met while a student at Columbia. Ed had joined CIA because *she* had decided very early in life to join CIA. Her husband was good at it, Mary Pat knew, with brilliant instincts and administrative skills – but he lacked the passion she gave to the job. He also lacked the genes. She had learned the Russian language at her grandfather's knee – the richer, more elegant Russian that the Soviets had debased into the current patois – but more importantly she understood the people in a way that no number of books could relate. She understood the racial sadness that permeates the Russian character, and the oxymoronic private openness, the total exposure of self and soul displayed only to the closest friends and denied by a Moscovite's public demeanor. As a result of this talent, Mary Pat had recruited five well-placed agents, only one shy of the all-time record. In the CIA's Directorate of Operations, she was occasionally known as Supergirl, a term she didn't care for. After all, Mary Pat was the mother of two, with the stretchmarks to prove it. She smiled at herself in the mirror. *You've done it all, kid.* Her grandfather would be proud.

And the best part of all: nobody had the least suspicion of what she really was. She made a final adjustment in her clothing. Western women in Moscow were supposed to be more conscious of their dress than Western men. Hers were always just a touch overdone. The image she projected to the public was carefully conceived and exquisitely executed. Educated but shallow, pretty but superficial, a good mother but little more, quick with her Western display of emotions but not to be taken very seriously. Scurrying about as she did, substitute-teaching occasionally at the kids' school, attending various social functions, and endlessly wandering about like a perpetual tourist, she fitted perfectly the preconceived Soviet notion of an American female bubblehead. One more smile in the mirror: *If the bastards only knew.*

Eddie was already waiting impatiently, his hockey stick jerking up and down at the drab carpet in the living room. Ed had the TV on. He kissed his wife goodbye, and told Eddie to kick ass – the senior Foley had been a Rangers fan before he learned to read.

It was a little sad, Mary Pat thought on the elevator. Eddie had made some real friends here, but it was a mistake to get too friendly with people in Moscow. You might forget that they were the enemy. She worried that Eddie was getting the same sort of indoctrination that she'd gotten, but from the wrong direction. Well, that was easily remedied, she told herself. In storage at home she had a photograph of the Czarevich Aleksey, autographed to his favorite teacher. All she really had to do was explain how he'd died.

The drive to the arena was the routine one, with Eddie getting ever more hyper as game time approached. He was tied as the league's third leading scorer, only six points behind the lead center for the team they were playing tonight, and Eddie wanted to show Ivan Whoeverhewas that Americans could beat Russians at their own game.

It was surprising how crowded the parking lot was, but then it wasn't a very large parking lot and ice hockey is the closest thing to religion permitted in the Soviet Union. This game would decide the playoff standings for the league championship, and quite a few people had come to see it. That was fine with Mary Pat. She'd barely set the parking brake when Eddie tore open the door, lifted his dufflebag, and waited impatiently for his mother to lock the car. He managed to walk slowly enough for his mother to keep up, then raced into the locker room as she went up to the rink.

Her place was predetermined, of course. Though reluctant to be overly close to foreigners in public, at a hockey game the rules were different. A few parents greeted her, and she waved back, her smile just a little too broad. She checked her watch.

'I haven't seen a junior-league game in two years,' Yazov said as they got out of the staff car.

'I don't go much either, but my sister-in-law said that this one is important, and little Misha demanded my presence.' Filitov grinned. 'They think I am good luck – perhaps you will be too, Comrade Marshal.'

'It is good to do something a little different,' Yazov conceded with mock gravity. 'The damned office will still be there tomorrow. I played this game as a boy, you know.'

'No, I didn't. Were you any good?'

'I was a defenseman, and the other children complained that I checked too hard.' The Defense Minister chuckled, then waved for his security people to go ahead.

'We never had a rink out where I grew up – and the truth is I was too clumsy as a child. Tanks were perfect for me –

you're expected to destroy things with them.' Misha laughed.

'So how good is this team?'

'I like the junior league better than the real ones,' Colonel Filitov answered. 'More – more exuberant. I suppose I just like to see children having a good time.'

'Indeed.'

There weren't many seats around the rink – and besides, what real hockey fan wanted to sit? Colonel Filitov and Marshal Yazov found a convenient place near some of the parents. Their Soviet Army greatcoats and glistening shoulder boards guaranteed them both a good view and breathing space. The four security people hovered about, trying not to look too obviously at the game. They were not terribly concerned, since the trip to the game had been a spur-of-the-moment decision on the Minister's part.

The game was an exciting one from the first moment. The center for the other team's first line moved like a weasel, handling the puck with skilful passes and adroit skating. The home team – the one with the American and Misha's grand-nephew – was pressed back into its own zone for most of the first period, but little Misha was an aggressive defenseman, and the American boy stole a pass, taking it the length of the rink only to be foiled by a dazzling save that evoked cheers of admiration from supporters of both sides. Though as contentious a people as any on earth, the Russians have always been imbued with generous sportsmanship. The first period ended zero-zero.

'Too bad,' Misha observed while people hustled off to the rest rooms.

'That was a beautiful breakaway, but the save was marvelous,' Yazov said. 'I'll have to get them this child's name for Central Army. Misha, thanks for inviting me to this. I'd forgotten how exciting a school game could be.'

'What do you suppose they're talking about?' the senior KGB officer asked. He and two other men were up in the rafters, hidden by the lights that illuminated the rink.

'Maybe they're just hockey fans,' the man with the camera replied. 'Shit, it sounds like quite a game we're missing. Look at those security guards – fucking idiots are watching the ice. If I wanted to kill Yazov . . .'

'Not a terribly bad idea, I hear,' observed the third man. 'The Chairman –'

'That is not our concern,' the senior man snapped, ending the conversation.

'Come on, Eddieeee!' Mary Pat screamed as the second period began. Her son looked up in embarrassment. His mom always got too excited at these things, he thought.

'Who was that?' Misha asked, five meters away.

'Over there, the skinny one – we met her, remember?' Yazov said.

'Well, she's a fan,' Filitov noted as he watched the action swing to the other end. *Please, Comrade Minister, you do it . . .* He got his wish.

'Let's go over and say hello.' The crowd parted before them, and Yazov sidled up on her left.

'Mrs Foley, I believe?'

He got a quick turn and a quicker smile before she turned back to the action. 'Hello, General –'

'Actually, my rank is Marshal. Your son is number twelve?'

'Yes, and did you see how the goalie robbed him!'

'It was a fine save,' Yazov said.

'Then let him do it to somebody else!' she said as the other team started moving into Eddie's end.

'Are all American fans like you?' Misha asked.

She turned again, and her voice showed a little embarrassment. 'It's terrible, isn't it? Parents are supposed to act –'

'Like parents?' Yazov laughed.

'I'm turning into a little-league mom,' Mary Pat admitted. Then she had to explain what that was.

'It is enough that we've taught your son to be a proper hockey wingman.'

'Yes, perhaps he'll be on the Olympic team in a few years,' she replied with a wicked, though playful smile. Yazov laughed. That surprised her. Yazov was supposed to be a tight, serious son of a bitch.

'Who's the woman?'

'American. Her husband's the press attaché. Her son's on this team. We have a file on both of them. Nothing special.'

'Pretty enough. I didn't know Yazov was a lady's man.'

'Do you suppose he wants to recruit her?' the photographer suggested, snapping away.

'I wouldn't mind.'

The game had unexpectedly settled down into a defense struggle that hovered around center ice. The children lacked the finesse necessary for the precise passing that marked Soviet hockey, and both teams were coached not to play an overly physical game. Even with their protective equipment, they were still children whose growing bones didn't need abuse. That was a lesson the Russians could teach Americans, Mary Pat thought. Russians had always been highly protective of their young. Life for adults was difficult enough that they always tried to shield their children from it.

Finally, in the third period, things broke loose. A shot on goal was stopped, and the puck rebounded out from the goalie. The center took it and turned, racing directly for the opposite goal, with Eddie twenty feet to his right. The center passed an instant before being poke-checked, and Eddie swept around to the corner, unable to take a shot at the goal and blocked from approaching it himself by a charging defenseman.

'*Center it!*' his mother screamed. He didn't hear her, but didn't need to. The center was now in place, and Eddie fired the puck to him. The youthful center stopped it with his skate, stepped back, and sent a blazing shot between the legs of the opposing goalie. The light behind the cage flashed, and sticks went soaring into the air.

'Fine centering pass,' Yazov noted with genuine admiration. He continued on in a chiding tone. 'You realize that your son now possesses State secrets, and we cannot allow him to leave the country.'

Mary Pat's eyes widened in momentary alarm, persuading Yazov that she was indeed a typical bubbleheaded Western female, though she was probably quite a handful in bed. *Too bad that I'll never find out.*

'You're joking?' she asked quietly. Both the soldiers broke out into laughter.

'The Comrade Minister is most certainly joking,' Misha said after a moment.

'I thought so!' she said rather unconvincingly before she turned back to the game. '*Okay, let's get another one!*'

Heads turned briefly, mainly in amusement. Having this American at the game was always good for a laugh. Russians find the exuberance of Americans immensely entertaining.

'Well, if she's a spy, I'll eat this camera.'

'Think on what you just said, Comrade,' the officer in charge whispered. The amusement in his voice died in an instant. *Think on what he just said*, the man told himself. *Her husband, Edward Foley, is regarded by the American press as a dolt, not smart enough to be a proper reporter, certainly not good enough to be on the staff of the* New York Times. The problem was, while that was the sort of cover that every real intelligence officer dreamed of, it was one naturally shared by all the government-service dolts serving every nation in the world. He himself knew that his cousin was a cretin, and *he* worked for the Foreign Ministry.

'Are you sure you have enough film?'

Eddie got his chance with forty seconds left. A defenseman fanned on a shot from the point, and the puck skittered back to center ice. The center flipped it to the right as the flow of the game changed. The other team had been on the verge of pulling its goalie, and the youngster was out of position when Eddie took the pass and streaked in from his left. Edward Foley II turned sharply and fired behind the goalie's back. The puck *clanged* on the post, but fell right on the goal line and dribbled across.

'*Score!*' Mary Pat howled, jumping up and down like a cheerleader. She threw her arms around Yazov, much to the consternation of his security guards. The Defense Minister's amusement was tempered by the realization that he'd have to write up a contact report on this tomorrow. Well, he had Misha as a witness that they'd discussed nothing untoward. She grabbed Filitov next.

'I *told* you you were good luck!'

'My God, are all American hockey fans like this?' Misha asked, disengaging himself. Her hand had touched his for a half-imaginary fraction of a second, and the three film cassettes were inside the glove. He felt them there and was amazed that it had been done so skillfully. Was she a professional magician?

'Why are you Russians so grim all the time – don't you know how to have a good time?'

'Maybe we should have more Americans around,' Yazov conceded. *Hell, I wish my wife were as lively as this one!* 'You have a fine son, and if he plays against us in the Olympics, I will forgive him.' He was rewarded with a beaming smile.

'That's such a nice thing to say.' *I hope he kicks your commie asses all the way back to Moskva.* If there was anything she couldn't stand, it was being patronized. 'Eddie got two more points tonight, and that Ivan Somebody didn't get any!'

'Are you really that competitive, even with children's games?' Yazov asked.

Mary Pat slipped, just a little, so fast that her brain couldn't keep up with the automatic reply: 'Show me a good loser, and I'll show you a loser.' She paused, then covered the mistake. 'Vince Lombardi, a famous American coach, said that. Excuse me, you must think me *nekulturny*. You're right, this is just a game for children.' She smiled broadly. *In your face!*

'Did you see anything?'

'A foolish woman who gets overly excited,' the photographer replied.

'How quickly will you have the film developed?'

'Two hours.'

'Get moving,' the senior man said.

'Did *you* see anything?' the remaining officer asked his boss.

'No, I don't think so. We've watched her for nearly two hours, and she acts like a typical American parent who gets too worked up at an athletic match, but just happens to attract the attention of the Defense Minister and the main suspect of a treason case. I think that's enough, Comrade, don't you?' *What a grand game this is. . . .*

Two hours later, over a thousand black-and-white photographs were laid on the officer's desk. The camera was a Japanese one that put a time reference on the lower edge, and the KGB photographer was as good as any newspaper professional. He'd shot almost continuously, stopping only long enough to replace the oversized film magazines on the autodriven camera. At first he'd wished to use a portable TV camera, but the photographer had talked him out of it. The resolution wasn't as good, nor was the speed. A still camera was still the best for catching something quick and small, though you couldn't read lips from its record as you could with a videotape.

Each frame required a few seconds as the officer used a magnifying glass to examine the subjects of his interest. When Mrs Foley entered the sequence of photos, he needed a few more seconds. He examined her clothing and jewelry at some length, and her face. Her smile was particularly mindless, like something in a Western television commercial, and he remembered hearing her screams over the crowd. Why were Americans so damned noisy?

Good dresser, though, he admitted to himself. *Like most American women in a Moscow scene, she stood out like a pheasant in a barnyard* – he snorted annoyance at the thought. So what that the Americans spend more money on clothing? What did clothing matter to anyone? *Through my binoculars, she looked like she had the brains of a bird . . . but not in these photos – why?*

It was the eyes, he thought. In the still photos her eyes sparkled with something different from what he'd watched in person. Why was that?

In the photographs, her eyes – they were blue, he remembered – were always focused on something. The face, he noticed, had vaguely Slavic cheekbones. He knew that Foley was an Irish name, and assumed that her ancestry was Irish, too. That America was a country of immigrants, and that immigrants cross ethnic lines in marriage, were foreign concepts to the Russians. Add a few kilograms, change her hair and clothing, and she could be any face encountered on a street in Moscow . . . or Leningrad. The latter was more likely, he thought. She looked more like a Leningrader. Her face proclaimed the slight arrogance affected by people from that city. *I wonder what her ancestry really is.*

He kept flipping through the photos, and remembered that the Foleys had never been given this sort of scrutiny. The file on both was a relatively thin one. They were regarded by 'Two' as nonentities. Something told him that this was a mistake, but the voice in the back of his head wasn't yet loud enough. He approached the last of the photographs, checking his watch. Three in the damned morning! he grumbled to himself and reached for another cup of tea.

Well, that must have been the second score. She was jumping like a gazelle. Nice legs, he saw for the first time. As his colleagues had noted up in the rafters, she was probably very entertaining in bed. Only a few more frames till the end of the game and . . . yes, there she was, embracing Yazov – that randy old goat! – then hugging Colonel Filitov –

He stopped dead. The photograph caught something that he hadn't seen through the binoculars. While giving Filitov a hug, her eyes were locked on one of the four security guards, the only one not watching the game. Her hand, her left hand, was not wrapped around Filitov at all, but rather down by his right one, hidden from view. He flipped back a few frames. Right before the embraces her hand had been in her coat pocket. Around the Defense Minister, it was balled into a fist. After Filitov, it was open again, and still her eyes were on the security guard, a smile on her face that was very Russian indeed, one that stopped at the lips – but in the next frame, she was back to her normal, flighty self. In that moment he was sure.

'Son of a bitch,' he whispered to himself.

How long have the Foleys been here? He searched his weary memory but couldn't dredge it up. *Over two years at least – and we didn't know, we didn't even suspect . . . what if it's only her?* That was a thought – what if she were a spy and her husband were not? He rejected the idea out of hand, and was correct, but for the wrong reason. He reached for the phone and called Vatutin's home.

'Yes,' the voice answered after only half a ring.

'I have something of interest,' the officer said simply.

'Send a car.'

Vatutin was there twenty-five minutes later, unshaven and irritable. The Major merely set out the crucial series of photographs.

'We never suspected her,' he said while the Colonel examined the pictures through a magnifying glass.

'A fine disguise,' Vatutin observed sourly. He'd been asleep only for an hour when the phone rang. He was still learning how to sleep without a few stiff drinks beforehand – trying to learn, he corrected himself. The Colonel looked up.

'Can you believe it? Right in front of the Defense

Minister and four security guards! The *balls* of this woman! Who's her regular shadow?'

The Major merely handed over the file. Vatutin leafed through it and found the proper sheet.

'That old fart! He couldn't follow a child to school without being arrested as a pervert. Look at this – a lieutenant for twenty-three years!'

'There are seven hundred Americans attached to the embassy, Comrade Colonel,' the Major observed. 'We have only so many really good officers –'

'All watching the wrong people.' Vatutin walked to the window. 'No more! Her husband, too,' he added.

'That will be my recommendation, Comrade Colonel. It would seem likely that they both work for CIA.'

'She passed something to him.'

'Probably – a message, perhaps something else.'

Vatutin sat down and rubbed his eyes. 'Good work, Comrade Major.'

It was already dawn at the Pakistan-Afghanistan border. The Archer was preparing to return to his war. His men had packed their new weapons while their leader – now that was a new thought, the Archer told himself – reviewed his plans for the coming weeks. Among the things he'd received from Ortiz was a complete set of tactical maps. These were made from satellite photographs, and were updated to show current Soviet strongpoints and areas of heavy patrol activity. He had a long-range radio now on which he could tune to weather forecasts – including Russian ones. Their journey wouldn't start until nightfall.

He looked around. Some of his men had sent their families to this place of safety. The refugee camp was crowded and noisy, but a far happier place than the deserted villages and towns bombed flat by the Russians. There were children here, the Archer saw, and children were happy anywhere they had their parents, and food, and friends. The boys were already playing with toy guns – and with the older ones, they were not toys. He accepted that with a degree of regret that diminished on every trip. The losses among the *mudjaheddin* demanded replacements, and the youngest were the bravest. If freedom required their deaths – well, their deaths came in a holy cause and Allah was beneficent to those who died for Him. The world was indeed a sad place, but at least here a man could find a time for amusement and rest. He watched one of his riflemen helping his firstborn son to walk. The baby could not do it alone, but with each tottering step he looked up at the smiling, bearded face of a father he'd seen only twice since birth. The new chief of the band remembered doing the same for his son . . . now being taught to walk a very different path. . . .

The Archer returned to his own work. He couldn't be a missileer anymore, but he'd trained Abdul well. Now the Archer would lead his men. It was a right that he'd earned, and, better still, his men thought him lucky. It would be good for morale. Though he had never in his life read books on military theory, the Archer felt that he knew their lessons well enough.

There was no warning – none at all. The Archer's head snapped around as he heard the cracking sound of exploding cannon shells, then he saw the dart-shapes of the Fencers, barely a hundred meters high. He hadn't yet reached for his rifle when he watched the bombs falling free of the ejector racks. The black shapes wobbled slightly before the fins stabilized them, their noses tipping down in slow motion. The engine noise of the Soviet Su-24 attack-bombers came next, and he turned to follow them as his rifle came up to his shoulder, but they were too fast. There was nothing left to do but dive to the ground, and it seemed that everything was happening very, very slowly. He was almost hovering in the air, the earth reluctant to come to meet him. His back was turned to the bombs, but he knew they were there, heading down. His eyes snapped up to see people running, his rifleman trying to cover the infant son with his body. The Archer turned to look up and was horrified to see that one bomb seemed to come straight at him, a black circle against the clear morning sky. There was no time even to say Allah's name as it passed over his head, and the earth shook.

He was stunned and deafened by the blast, and felt wobbly when he stood. It seemed strange to see and feel noise, but not to hear it. Instinct alone flipped the safety off his rifle as he looked around for the next plane. There it was! The rifle came up and fired of its own accord, but made no difference. The next Fencer dropped its load a hundred meters farther on and raced away before a trail of black smoke. There were no more.

The sounds came back slowly, and seemed distant, like the noises of a dream. But this was no dream. The place where his man and the baby had been was now a hole in the ground. There was no trace of the freedom fighter or his son, and even the certainty that both now stood righteously before their God could not mask the bloodchilling rage that coursed through his body. He remembered showing mercy to the Russian, feeling some regret at his death. No more. He'd never show mercy to an infidel again. His hands were chalkwhite around the rifle.

Too late, a Pakistani F-16 fighter streaked across the sky, but the Russians were already across the border, and a minute later, the F-16 circled over the camp twice before heading back to its base.

'Are you all right?' It was Ortiz. His face had been cut by something or other, and his voice was far away.

There was no verbal answer. The Archer gestured with his rifle as he watched a newly made widow scream for her family. Together the two men looked for wounded who might be saved. Luckily, the medical section of the camp was unhurt. The Archer and the CIA officer carried a half-dozen people there, to see a French doctor cursing with the fluency of a man accustomed to such things, his hands already bloody from his work.

They found Abdul on their next trip. The young man had a Stinger up and armed. He wept as he confessed that he'd been asleep. The Archer patted his shoulder and said it

311

wasn't his fault. There was supposed to be an agreement between the Soviets and the Pakistanis that prohibited cross-border raids. So much for agreements. A television news crew – French – appeared, and Ortiz took the Archer to a place where neither could be seen.

'Six,' the Archer said. He didn't mention the non-combatant casualties.

'It is a sign of weakness that they do this, my friend,' Ortiz replied.

'To attack a place of women and children is an abomination before God!'

'Have you lost any supplies?' To the Russians this was a guerrilla camp, of course, but Ortiz didn't bother voicing their view of things. He'd been here too long to be objective about such matters.

'Only a few rifles. The rest is outside the camp already.'

Ortiz had no more to say. He'd run out of comforting observations. His nightmare was that his operation to support the Afghans was having the same effect as earlier attempts to aid the Hmong people of Laos. They'd fought bravely against their Vietnamese enemies, only to be virtually exterminated despite all their Western assistance. The CIA officer told himself that this situation was different, and objectively, he thought that this was true. But it tore at what was left of his soul to watch these people leave the camp, armed to the teeth, and then to count the number that returned. Was America really helping the Afghans to redeem their own land, or were we merely encouraging them to kill as many Russians as possible before they, too, were wiped out?

What is the right policy? he asked himself. Ortiz admitted that he didn't know.

Nor did he know that the Archer had just made a policy decision of his own. The old-young face turned west, then north, and told himself that Allah's will was no more restricted by borders than was the will of His enemies.

15

Culmination

'All we need to do now is spring the trap,' Vatutin told his Chairman. His voice was matter-of-fact, his face impassive as he gestured to the evidence laid out on Gerasimov's desk.

'Excellent work, Colonel!' The Chairman of the KGB allowed himself a smile. Vatutin saw that there was more in it than the satisfaction of closing a difficult and sensitive case. 'Your next move?'

'Given the unusual status of the subject, I believe we should attempt to compromise him at the time of document transfer. It would seem that the CIA knows that we have broken the courier chain from Filitov to them. They took the unusual step of using one of their own officers to make this transfer – and make no mistake, this was an act of desperation despite the skill with which it was done. I would like to expose the Foleys at the same time. They must be a proud pair for having deceived us this long. To catch them in the act will destroy that pride and be a major psychological blow to CIA as a whole.'

'Approved.' Gerasimov nodded. 'It is your case to run, Colonel. Take all the time you want.' Both men knew that he meant less than a week.

'Thank you, Comrade Chairman.' Vatutin returned at once to his office, where he briefed his section chiefs.

The microphones were very sensitive. Like most sleepers, Filitov tossed and turned quite a bit in his sleep, except when dreaming, and the reel-to-reel tape recorders kept a record of the rustle of linen and the barely intelligible murmurs. Finally a new sound came through and the man with the headphones gestured to his comrades. It sounded like a sail filling with wind, and it meant that the subject was tossing the covers off the bed.

Next came the coughing. The old man had lung problems, his medical file said. He was particularly vulnerable to colds and respiratory infections. Evidently he was coming down with something. Next he blew his nose, and the KGB men smiled at one another. It sounded like a locomotive whistle.

'Got him,' the man on the TV camera said. 'Heading toward the bathroom.' The next set of sounds was predictable. There were two television cameras whose powerful lenses were framed on the apartment's two windows. Special settings allowed them to see into the apartment despite the glare of morning light.

'You know, doing this to someone is enough,' a technician observed. 'If you showed anyone a tape of one of us right after waking, we'd die of simple embarrassment.'

'This one's death will be of another cause,' the senior officer noted coldly. That was one problem with these investigations. You started identifying too closely with the subject, and had to remind yourself periodically just how loathsome traitors were. *Where did you go wrong?* the Major wondered. *A man with your war record!* He was already wondering how the case would be handled. A public trial? Could they dare to go public with so famous a war hero? That, he told himself, was a political question.

The door opened and closed, indicating that Filitov had gotten the copy of *Red Star* dropped off daily by a Defense Ministry messenger. They heard the gurgling of his coffee machine, and shared a look – this bastard traitor drinks good coffee every morning.

He was visible now, sitting at the small kitchen table and reading his paper. He was a note-taker, they saw, scratching on a pad or marking the paper itself. When the coffee was ready he rose to get milk from the small refrigerator. He sniffed at it before adding it to the cup to be sure it hadn't gone bad. He had enough butter to spread it lavishly on his black bread, which they knew was his usual breakfast.

'Still eats like a soldier,' the cameraman said.

'He was a good one once,' another officer observed. 'You foolish old man, how could you do it?'

Breakfast was over soon thereafter, and they watched Filitov walk toward the bathroom, where he washed and shaved. He returned to view to dress. On the videoscreen, they saw him take out a brush to polish his boots. He always wore his boots, they knew, which was unusual for Ministry officers. But so were the three gold stars on his uniform blouse. He stood before the bureau mirror, inspecting himself. The paper went into his briefcase, and Filitov walked out the door. The last noise they heard was the key setting the lock on the apartment door. The Major got on the phone.

'Subject is moving. Nothing unusual this morning. Shadow team is in place.'

'Very well,' Vatutin replied and hung up.

One of the cameramen adjusted his instrument to record Filitov's emergence from the building. He took the salute from the driver, got into the car, and disappeared down the street. A completely unremarkable morning, they all agreed. They could afford to be patient now.

The mountains to the west were sheathed in clouds, and a fine drizzle was falling. The Archer hadn't left yet. There were prayers to be said, people to console. Ortiz was off having his face attended to by one of the French doctors, while his friend was riffling through the CIA officer's papers.

It made him feel guilty, but the Archer told himself that he was merely looking for records that he himself had delivered to the CIA officer. Ortiz was a compulsive note-taker, and, the Archer knew, a map fancier. The map he wanted to see was in its expected place, and clipped to it were several diagrams. These he copied by hand, quickly and accurately, before replacing all as it had been.

'You guys are so square,' Bea Taussig laughed.

'It would be a shame to spoil the image,' Al replied, a smile masking his distaste for their guest. He never understood why Candi liked this . . . whatever the hell she was. Gregory didn't know why she rang bells in the back of his head. It wasn't the fact that she didn't like him – Al didn't give a damn one way or the other about that. His family and his fiancée loved him, and all his co-workers respected him. That was enough. If he didn't fit into somebody's notion of what an Army officer was supposed to be, screw 'em. But there was *something* about Bea that –

'Okay, we'll talk business,' their guest said with amusement. 'I have people from Washington asking me how soon –'

'Somebody ought to tell those bureaucrats that you don't just turn things like this on and off,' Candi growled.

'Six weeks, tops.' Al grinned. 'Maybe less.'

'When?' Candi asked.

'Soon. We haven't had a chance to run it on the simulator yet, but it feels right. It was Bob's idea. He was about due, and it streamlined the software package even better than what I was trying. We don't have to use as much AI as I thought.'

'Oh?' The use of AI – artificial intelligence – was supposed to be crucial to mirror performance and target discrimination.

'Yeah, we were overengineering the problem, trying to use reason instead of instinct. We don't have to tell the computer how to think everything out. We can reduce the command load twenty percent by putting pre-set options in the program. It turns out to be quicker and easier than making the computer make most judgments off a menu.'

'What about the anomalies?' Taussig asked.

'That's the whole point. The AI routines were actually slowing things down more than we thought. We were trying

316

to make the thing so flexible that it had trouble doing anything. The expected laser performance is good enough that it can take the fire-option faster than the AI program can decide whether to aim it – so why not take the shot? If it doesn't fit the profile, we pop it anyway.'

'Your laser specs have changed,' Bea observed.

'Well, I can't talk about that.'

Another grin from the little geek. Taussig managed to smile back. *I know something you don't know!* is it? Just looking at him made her skin crawl, but what was worse was the way Candi looked at him, like he was Paul Newman or something! Sallow complexion, even zits, and she loved this thing. Bea didn't know whether to laugh or cry. . . .

'Even us admin pukes have to be able to plan ahead,' Taussig said.

'Sorry, Bea. You know the security rules.'

'Makes you wonder how we get anything done.' Candi shook her head. 'If it gets any worse, Al and I won't be able to talk to each other between . . .' She smiled lecherously at her lover.

Al laughed. 'I have a headache.'

'Bea, do you believe this guy?' Candi asked.

Taussig leaned back. 'I never have.'

'When are you going to let Dr Rabb take you out? You know he's been mooning over you for six months.'

'The only mooning I expect out of him is from a car. God, that's a ghastly thought.' Her look at Candi masked her feelings exquisitely well. She also realized that' the programming information that she'd gotten out was now invalid. Damn the little geek for changing it!

'That's something. Question is, what?' Jones keyed his microphone. 'Conn, Sonar, we have a contact bearing zero-nine-eight. Designate this contact Sierra-Four.'

'You sure it's a contact?' the young petty officer asked.

'See this?' Jones ran his finger along the screen. The 'waterfall display' was cluttered with ambient noise. 'Remember that you're looking for nonrandom data. This line ain't random.' He typed in a command to alter the display. The computer began processing a series of discrete frequency bands. Within a minute the picture was clear. At least Mr Jones thought so, the young sonarman noted. The stroke of light on the screen was irregularly shaped, bowing out and narrowing down, covering about five degrees of bearing. The 'techrep' stared at the screen for several more seconds, then spoke again.

'Conn, Sonar, classify target Sierra-Four as a Krivak-class frigate, bearing zero-nine-six. Looks like he's doing turns for fifteen or so knots.' Jones turned to the youngster. He remembered his own first cruise. This nineteen-year-old didn't even have his dolphins yet. 'See this? That's the high-frequency signature from his turbine engines, it's a dead giveaway and you can hear it a good ways off, usually, 'cause the Krivak doesn't have good sound-isolation.'

Mancuso came into the compartment. *Dallas* was a 'first-flight' 688, and didn't have direct access from the control room to sonar as the later ones did. Instead, you had to come forward and step around a hole in the deck that led below. Probably the overhaul would change that. The Captain waved his coffee mug at the screen.

'Where's the Krivak?'

'Right here, bearing still constant. We have good water around us. He's probably a good ways off.'

The skipper smiled. Jones was always trying to guess range. The hell of it was that in the two years that Mancuso had had him aboard as a member of the crew he'd been right more often than not. Aft in the control room, the fire-control tracking party was plotting the position of the target against *Dallas'* known track to determine range and course of the Soviet frigate.

There wasn't much activity on the surface. The other three sonar contacts plotted were all single-screw merchantmen. Though the weather was decent today, the Baltic Sea – an oversized lake to Mancuso's way of thinking – was rarely a nice place in the winter. Intelligence reports said that most of the opposition's ships were tied alongside for repairs. That was good news. Better still, there wasn't much in the way of ice. A really cold season could freeze things solid, and that would put a crimp in their mission, the Captain thought.

Thus far only their other visitor, Clark, knew what that mission was.

'Captain, we have a posit on Sierra-Four,' a lieutenant called from control.

Jones folded a slip of paper and handed it to Mancuso.

'I'm waiting.'

'Range thirty-six thousand, course roughly two-nine-zero.'

Mancuso unfolded the note and laughed. 'Jones, you're still a fucking witch!' He handed it back, then went aft to alter the submarine's course to avoid the Krivak.

The sonarman at Jones's side grabbed the note and read it aloud. 'How did you know? You aren't supposed to be able to do that.'

'Practice, m'boy, practice,' Jones replied in his best W. C. Fields accent. He noted the submarine's course change. It wasn't like the Mancuso he remembered. In the old days, the skipper would close to get photos through the periscope, run a few torpedo solutions, and generally treat the Soviet ship like a real target in a real war. This time they were opening the range to the Russian frigate, creeping away. Jones didn't think Mancuso had changed all that much, and started wondering what the hell this new mission was all about.

He hadn't seen much of Mr Clark. He spent a lot of time aft in the engine room, where the ship's fitness center was – a treadmill jammed between two machine tools. The crew was already murmuring that he didn't talk very much. He just smiled and nodded and went on his way. One of the chiefs noted the tattoo on Clark's forearm and was whispering some stuff about the meaning of the red seal, specifically that it stood for the real SEALs. *Dallas* had never had one of those aboard, though other boats had, and the stories, told quietly except for the occasional 'no shit!' interruptions, had circulated throughout the submarine community but nowhere else. If there was anything submariners knew how to do, it was keeping secrets.

Jones stood and walked aft. He figured he'd taught enough lessons for one day, and his status as a civilian technical representative allowed him to wander about at will. He noted that *Dallas* was taking her own sweet time, heading east at nine knots. A look at the chart told him where they were, and the way the navigator was tapping his pencil on it told him how much farther they'd be going. Jones started to do some serious thinking as he went below for a Coke. He'd come back for a really tense one after all.

'Yes, Mr President?' Judge Moore answered the phone with his own tense look. *Decision time?*

'That thing we talked about in here the other day . . .'

'Yes, sir.' Moore looked at the phone. Aside from the handset that he held, the 'secure' phone system was a three-foot cube, cunningly hidden in his desk. It took words, broke them into digital bits, scrambled them beyond recognition, and sent them out to another similar box which put them back together. One interesting sidelight of this was that it made for very clear conversations, since the encoding system eliminated all the random noise on the line.

'You may go ahead. We can't – well, I decided last night that we can't just leave him.' This had to be his first call of the morning, and the emotional content came through, too. Moore wondered if he'd lost sleep over the life of the faceless agent. Probably he had. The President was that sort of man. He was also the sort, Moore knew, to stick with a decision once made. Pelt would try to change it all day, but the President was getting it out at eight in the morning and would have to stick with it.

'Thank you, Mr. President. I'll set things in motion.' Moore had Bob Ritter in his office two minutes later:

'The CARDINAL extraction is a "go"!'

'Makes me glad I voted for the man,' Ritter said as he smacked one hand into the other. 'Ten days from now we'll have him in a nice safehouse. Jesus, the debrief'll take *years!*' Then came the sober pause. "It's a shame to lose his services, but we owe it to him. Besides, Mary Pat has recruited a couple of real live ones for us. She made the film pass last night. No details, but I gather that it was a hairy one.'

'She always was a little too –'

'More than a little, Arthur, but all field officers have some cowboy in them.' The two Texas natives shared a look. 'Even the ones from New York.'

'Some team. With those genes, you gotta wonder what their kids'll be like,' Moore observed with a chuckle. 'Bob, you got your wish. Run with it.'

'Yes, sir.' Ritter went off to send his message, then informed Admiral Greer.

The telex went via satellite and arrived in Moscow only fifteen minutes later: TRAVEL ORDERS APPROVED. KEEP ALL RECEIPTS FOR ROUTINE REIMBURSEMENT.

Ed Foley took the decrypted message into his office. *So, whatever desk-sitter got cold feet on us found his socks after all*, he thought. *Thank God.*

Only one more transfer to go! We'll pass the message at the same time, and Misha'll catch a flight to Leningrad, then just follow the plan. One good thing about CARDINAL was that he'd practiced his escape routine at least once a year. His old tank outfit was now assigned to the Leningrad Military District, and the Russians understood that kind of sentiment. Misha had also seen to it over the years that his regiment was the first to get new equipment and to train in new tactics. After his death, it would be designated the Filitov Guards – or at least that's what the Soviet Army was planning to do. It was too bad, Foley thought, that they'd have to change that plan. On the other hand, maybe CIA would make some other sort of memorial to the man. . . .

But there was still that one more transfer to make, and it

would not be an easy one. One step at a time, he told himself. First we have to alert him.

Half an hour later, a nondescript embassy staffer left the building. At a certain time he'd be standing at a certain place. The 'signal' was picked up by someone else who was not likely to be shadowed by 'Two'. This person did something else. He didn't know the reason, only where and how the mark was to be made. He found that very frustrating. Spy work was supposed to be exciting, wasn't it?

'There's our friend.' Vatutin was riding in the car, wanting to see for himself that things were going properly. Filitov entered his car, and the driver took him off. Vatutin's car followed for half a kilometer, then turned off as a second car took over, racing over to a parallel street to keep pace.

He kept track of events by radio. The transmissions were crisp and businesslike as the six cars rotated on and off surveillance, generally with one ahead of the target vehicle and one behind. Filitov's car stopped at a grocery store that catered to senior Defense Ministry officials. Vatutin had a man inside – Filitov was known to stop there two or three times per week – to see what he bought and whom he talked to.

He could tell that things were going perfectly, as was not unexpected once he'd explained to everybody on the case that the Chairman had personal interest in this one. Vatutin's driver raced ahead of their quarry, depositing the Colonel across the street from Filitov's apartment building. Vatutin walked inside and went up to the apartment that they had taken over.

'Good timing,' the senior officer said as Vatutin came in the door.

The 'Two' man looked discreetly out the window and saw Filitov's car come to a halt. The trailing car motored past without a pause as the Army Colonel walked into the building.

'Subject just entered the building,' a communications specialist said. Inside, a woman with a string-bag full of apples would get on the elevator with Filitov. Up on Filitov's floor, two people who looked young enough to be teenagers would stroll past the elevator as he got out, continuing down the corridor with overly loud whispers of undying love. The surveillance   .es caught the end of that as Filitov opened the door.

'Got him,' the cameraman said.

'Let's keep away from the windows,' Vatutin said unnecessarily. The men with binoculars stood well back from them, and so long as the lights in the apartment were left off – the bulbs had been removed from the fixtures – no one could tell that the rooms were occupied.

One thing they liked about the man was his aversion to pulling down the shades. They followed him into the bedroom, where they watched him change into casual clothes and slippers. He returned to the kitchen and fixed himself a simple meal. They watched him tear the foil top off a half-liter bottle of vodka. The man was sitting and staring out the window.

'An old, lonely man,' one officer observed. 'Do you suppose that's what did it?'

'One way or another, we'll find out.'

Why is it that the State can betray us? Misha asked Corporal Romanov two hours later.

Because we are soldiers, I suppose. Misha noted that the corporal was avoiding the question, and the issue. Did he know what his Captain was trying to ask?

But if we betray the State . . .?

Then we die, Comrade Captain. That is simple enough. We earn the hatred and contempt of the peasants and workers, and we die. Romanov stared across time into his officer's eyes. The corporal now had his own question. He lacked the will to ask it, but his eyes seemed to proclaim: *What have you done, my Captain?*

Across the street, the man on the recording equipment noted sobbing, and wondered what caused it.

*

323

'What're you doing, honey?' Ed Foley asked, and the microphones heard.

'Starting to make lists for when we leave. So many things to remember, I'd better start now.'

Foley bent over her shoulder. She had a pad and a pencil, but she was writing on a plastic sheet with a marker pen. It was the sort of arrangement that hung on many refrigerators, and could be wiped clean with a swipe of a damp cloth.

I'LL DO IT, she'd written. I HAVE A PERFECT DODGE. Mary Pat smiled and held up a team photo of Eddie's hockey squad. Each player had signed it, and at the top in scrawling Russian, Eddie had put, with his mother's coaching: 'To the man who brings us luck. Thanks, Eddie Foley.'

Her husband frowned. It was typical of his wife to use the bold approach, and he knew that she'd used her cover with consummate skill. But . . . he shook his head. But what? The only man in the CARDINAL chain who could identify him had never seen his face. Ed may have lacked her *panache*, but he was more circumspect. He felt that he was better than his wife at countersurveillance. He acknowledged Mary Pat's passion for the work, and her acting skill, but – damn it, she was just too bold sometimes. *Fine – why don't you tell her?* he asked himself.

He knew what would happen – she'd go practical on him. There wasn't time to establish another series of cutouts. They both knew that her cover was a solid one, that she hadn't even come close to suspicion yet.

But – Goddamn it, this business is one continuous series of fucking BUTs!

OK BUT COVER YOUR CUTE LITTLE ASS!!!! he wrote on the plastic pad. Her eyes sparkled as she wiped it clean. Then she wrote her own message:

LET'S GIVE THE MICROPHONES A HARD-ON!

Ed nearly strangled trying not to laugh. *Every time before a job*, he thought. It wasn't that he minded. He did find it a little odd, though.

Ten minutes later, in a room in the basement of the apartment building, a pair of Russian wiretap technicians listened with rapt attention to the sounds generated in the Foley bedroom.

Mary Pat Foley woke up at her customary six-fifteen. It was still dark outside, and she wondered how much of her grandfather's character had been formed by the cold and the dark of the Russian winters . . . and how much of hers. Like most Americans assigned to Moscow, she thoroughly hated the idea of listening devices in her walls. She occasionally took perverse pleasure in them, as she had the previous night, but then there was also the thought that the Soviets had placed them in the bathroom, too. That seemed like something they'd do, she thought, looking at herself in the mirror. The first order of business was to take her temperature. They both wanted another child, and had been working on it for a few months – which beat watching Russian TV. Professionally, of course, pregnancy made one hell of a cover. After three minutes she noted the temperature on a card she kept in the medicine cabinet. *Probably not yet*, she thought. *Maybe in a few more days*. She dropped the remains of an Early Pregnancy Test kit in the waste can anyway.

Next, there were the children to rouse. She got breakfast going, and shook everyone loose. Living in an apartment with but a single bathroom imposed a rigid schedule on them. There came the usual grumbles from Ed, and the customary whines and groans from the kids.

God, it'll be nice to get home, she told herself. As much as she loved the challenge of working in the mouth of the dragon, living here wasn't exactly fun for the kids. Eddie loved his hockey, but he was missing a normal childhood in this cold, barren place. Well, that would change soon enough. They'd load everyone aboard the Pan Am clipper and wing home, leaving Moscow behind – if not forever, at least for five years. Life in Virginia's tidewater country. Sailing on the Chesapeake Bay. *Mild winters! You had to bundle kids up here like Nanook of the fucking North*, she thought. *I'm always fighting off colds*.

She got breakfast on the table just as Ed vacated the bathroom, allowing her to wash and dress. The routine was that he managed breakfast, then dressed while his wife got the kids going.

In the bathroom, she heard the TV go on, and laughed into the mirror. Eddie loved the morning exercise show – the woman who appeared on it looked like a longshoreman, and he called her Workerwom*mannn!* Her son yearned for mornings of the Transformers – 'More than meets the eye!' he still remembered the opening song. Eddie would miss his Russian friends some, she thought, but the kid was an American and nothing would ever change that. By seven-fifteen everyone was dressed and ready to go. Mary Pat tucked a wrapped parcel under her arm.

'Cleaning day, isn't it?' Ed asked his wife.

'I'll be back in time to let her in,' Mary Pat assured him.

'Okay.' Ed opened the door and led the procession to the elevator. As usual, his family was the first one to get moving in the morning. Eddie raced forward and punched the elevator button. It arrived just as the rest of the family reached the door. Eddie jumped onto it, enjoying the usual springiness of Soviet elevator cables. To his mother, it always seemed as though the damned thing was going to fall all the way to the basement, but her son thought it entertaining when the car dropped a few inches. Three minutes later they got into the car. Ed took the wheel this morning. On the drive out, the kids waved at the militiaman, who was really KGB, and who waved back with a smile. As soon as the car had turned onto the street, he lifted the phone in his booth.

Ed kept his eye on the rearview mirror, and his wife had already adjusted the outside one so that she could see aft also. The kids got into a dispute in the back, which both parents ignored.

'Looks like a nice day,' he said quietly. *Nothing following us*.

'Uh huh.' *Agreed.* They had to be careful what they said around the kids, of course. Eddie could repeat anything they said as easily as the opening ditty of the Transformers cartoon. There was always the chance of a radio bug in the car, too.

Ed drove to the school first, allowing his wife to take the kids in. Eddie and Katie looked like teddy bears in their cold-weather clothing. His wife looked unhappy when she came out.

'Nikki Wagner called in sick. They want me to take over her class this afternoon,' she told him on reentering the car. Her husband grunted. Actually, it was perfect. He dropped the Volkswagen into gear and pulled back onto Leninskiy Prospekt. *Game time.*

Now their checks of the mirrors were serious.

Vatutin hoped that they'd never thought of this before. Moscow streets are always full of dumptrucks, scurrying from one construction site to another. The high cabs of the vehicles made for excellent visibility, and the meanderings of the look-alike vehicles appeared far less sinister than would those of unmarked sedans. He had nine of them working for him today, and the officers driving them communicated via encrypted military radios.

Colonel Vatutin himself was in the apartment next door to Filitov's. The family who lived there had moved into the Hotel Moscow two days before. He'd watched the video-tapes of his subject, drinking himself to insensibility, and used the opportunity to get three other 'Two' officers in. They had their own spike-microphones driven into the party wall between the two flats, and listened intently to the Colonel's staggering through his morning routine. Something told him that this was the day.

It's the drinking, he told himself while he sipped tea. That drew an amused grimace. Perhaps it takes one drinker to understand another. He was sure that Filitov had been working himself up to something, and he also remembered that the time he'd seen the Colonel with the traitorous bath attendant, he'd come into the steam room with a hangover . . . *just as I had*. It fitted, he decided. Filitov was a hero who'd gone bad – but a hero still. It could not have been easy for him to commit treason, and he probably needed the drink to sleep in the face of a troubled conscience. It pleased Vatutin that people felt that way, that treason was still a hard thing to do.

'They're heading this way,' a communications man reported over the radio.

'Right here,' Vatutin told his subordinates. 'It will happen within a hundred meters of where we stand.'

Mary Pat ran over what she had to do. Handing over the wrapped photo would allow her to recover the film that she would slip inside her glove. Then there was the signal. She'd rub the back of her gloved hand across her forehead as though wiping off sweat, then scratch her eyebrow. That was the danger-breakout signal. She hoped he'd pay attention. Though she'd never done the signal herself, Ed had once offered a breakout, only to be rejected. It was something she understood better than her husband had – after all, her work with CIA was based more on passion than reason – but enough was enough. This man had been sending data West when she'd learned to play with dolls.

There was the building. Ed headed for the curb, jostling over the potholes as her hand gripped the parcel. As she grabbed the door handle, her husband patted her on the leg. *Good luck, kid.*

'Foleyeva just got out of the car and is headed to the side entrance,' the radio squawked. Vatutin smiled at the Russification of the foreign name. He debated drawing the service automatic in his belt, but decided against it. Better to have his hands free, and a gun might go off accidentally. This was no time for accidents.

'Any ideas?' he asked.

'If it was me, I'd try a brush-pass,' one of his men offered.

Vatutin nodded agreement. It worried him that they'd been unable to establish camera surveillance of the corridor itself, but technical factors had militated against it. That was the problem with the really sensitive cases. The smart ones were the wary ones. You couldn't risk alerting them, and he was sure that the Americans were alerted already. Alerted enough, he thought, to have killed one of their own agents in that railyard.

Fortunately, most Moscow apartments had peepholes installed in them now. Vatutin found himself grateful for the increase in burglaries, because his technicians had been able to replace the regular lens with one that allowed them to see most of the corridor. He took this post himself.

We should have put microphones on the stairwells, he told himself. *Make a note of that for the next time. Not all enemy spies use elevators.*

Mary Pat was not quite the athlete her husband was. She paused on the landing, looking up and down the stairwell and listening for any sound at all as her heart rate slowed somewhat. She checked her digital watch. Time.

She opened the firedoor and walked straight down the middle of the corridor.

Okay, Misha. I hope you remembered to set your watch last night.

Last time, Colonel. Will you for Christ's sake take the breakout signal this time, and maybe they'll do the debrief on the Farm, and my son can meet a real Russian hero . . . ?

God, I wish my grandfather could see me now. . . .

She'd never been here before, never done a pass in this building. But she knew it by heart, having spent twenty minutes going over the diagram. The CARDINAL's door was . . . that one!

Time! Her heart skipped a beat as she saw the door open, thirty feet away.

What a pro! But what came next was as cold as a dagger made of ice.

*

Vatutin's eyes widened in horror at the noise. The deadbolt on the apartment door had been installed with typical Russian workmanship, about half a millimeter out of line. As he slipped it in preparation to leap from the room, it made an audible *click*.

Mary Pat Foley scarcely broke stride. Her training took over her body like a computer program. There was a peephole on the door that went from dark to light:

– there was somebody there
– that somebody just moved
– that somebody just slipped the door lock.

She took half a step to her right and rubbed the back of her gloved hand across her forehead. She wasn't pretending to wipe sweat away.

Misha saw the signal and stopped cold, a curious look on his face that began to change to amusement until he heard the door wrenched open. He knew in an instant that the man who emerged was not his neighbor.

'You are under arrest!' Vatutin shouted, then saw that the American woman and the Russian man were standing a meter apart, and both had their hands at their sides. It was just as well that the 'Two' officers behind him couldn't see the look on his face.

'Excuse me?' the woman said in excellent Russian.

'*What!*' Filitov thundered with the rage only possible to a hungover professional soldier.

'You' – he pointed to Mrs Foley – 'up against the wall.'

'I'm an American citizen, and you can't –'

'You're an American spy,' a captain said, pushing her against the wall.

'What?' Her voice contained panic and alarm, not the least amount of professionalism here, the Captain thought, but then his mind nearly choked on the observation. 'What are you talking about? What is this? Who are you?' Next she started screaming: '*Police – somebody call the police. I'm being attacked! Somebody help me, please!*'

Vatutin ignored her. He had already grabbed Filitov's

hand, and as another officer pushed the Colonel against the wall, he took a film cassette. For a flicker of time that seemed to stretch into hours, he'd been struck with the horrible thought that he'd blown it, that she really wasn't CIA. With the film in his hand, he swallowed and looked into Filitov's eyes.

'You are under arrest for treason, *Comrade Colonel.*' His voice hissed out the end of the statement. 'Take him away.'

He turned to look at the woman. Her eyes were wide with fear and outrage. Four people now had their heads out of doors, staring into the hall.

'I am Colonel Vatutin of the Committee for State Security. We have just made an arrest. Close your doors and go about your business.' He noted that compliance with his order took under five seconds. Russia was still Russia.

'Good morning, Mrs Foley,' he said next. He saw her struggle to gain control of herself.

'Who are you – and what is this all about?'

'The Soviet Union does not look kindly upon its guests stealing State secrets. Surely they told you that in Washington – excuse me, Langley.'

Her voice trembled as she spoke. 'My husband is an accredited member of the US diplomatic mission to your country. I wish to be put in contact with my embassy at once. I don't know what you're jabbering about, but I do know that if you make the pregnant wife of a diplomat lose her baby, you'll have a diplomatic incident big enough to make the TV news! I didn't talk to that man. I didn't touch him, and he didn't touch me – and you know it, mister. What they warned me about in Washington is that you clowns love to embarrass Americans with your damned-fool little spy games.'

Vatutin took all of the speech impassively, though the word 'pregnant' did get his attention. He knew from the reports of the maid who cleaned their apartment twice a week that Foleyeva had been testing herself. And if – there would be a larger incident over this than he wanted. Again the political dragon raised its head. Chairman Gerasimov would have to rule on this.

'My husband is waiting for me.'

'We'll tell him that you are being detained. You will be asked to answer some questions. You will not be mistreated.'

Mary Pat already knew that. Her horror at what had just happened was muted by her pride. She'd performed beautifully and knew it. As part of the diplomatic community, she was fundamentally safe. They might hold on to her for a day, even two, but any serious mistreatment would result in having a half-dozen Russians shipped home from Washington. Besides, she wasn't really pregnant.

All that was beside the point. She didn't shed any tears, showed no emotion other than what was expected, what she'd been briefed and trained to show. What mattered was that her most important agent was blown, and with him, information of the highest importance. She wanted to cry, needed to cry, but she wouldn't give the fuckers the satisfaction. The crying would come on the plane ride home.

16

Damage Assessment

'It says a lot about the man that the first thing he did was to get to the embassy and send the telex,' Ritter said at last. 'The Ambassador delivered his protest note to their Foreign Ministry before they went public on the arrest "for conduct incompatible with diplomatic status".'

'Some consolation,' Greer noted gloomily.

'We ought to have her back in a day or less,' Ritter went on. 'They're already PNG'd, and they're going on the next Pan Am flight out.'

Ryan squirmed in his chair. *What about CARDINAL?* he wondered. *Jesus, they tell me about this superagent, and a week later . . . They sure as hell don't have a Supreme Court over there that makes it hard to execute people.*

'Any chance we can do a trade for him?' Jack asked.

'You are kidding, boy.' Ritter rose and walked to the window. At three in the morning, the CIA parking lot was nearly empty, only a loose handful of cars sitting among the piles of plowed snow. 'We don't even have anybody big enough to trade for a mitigation of sentence. No way in hell they'll let him out, even for a chief of station, which we don't have.'

'So he's dead and the data is lost with him.'

'That's what the man's saying,' Judge Moore agreed.

'Help from the allies?' Ryan asked. 'Sir Basil might have something hopping that can help us.'

'Ryan, there is nothing we can do to save the man.' Ritter turned to take out his anger on the nearest target of opportunity. 'He's dead – sure, he's still breathing, but he's dead all the same. A month, or two, or three from now, the announcement will be made, and we'll confirm it through other assets, and then we'll pry open a bottle and have a few to his memory.'

'What about *Dallas?*' Greer asked.

'Huh?' Ryan turned.

'You don't need to know about that,' Ritter said, now grateful to have a target. 'Give her back to the Navy.'

'Okay.' Greer nodded. 'This is likely to have some serious consequences.' That earned the Admiral a baleful look from Judge Moore. He now had to go to the President.

'What about it, Ryan?'

'On the arms-control talks?' Jack shrugged. 'Depends on how they handle it. They have a wide range of options, and anybody who tells you he can predict which one they'll choose is a liar.'

'Nothing like an expert opinion,' Ritter observed.

'Sir Basil thinks Gerasimov wants to make a move on the top spot. He could conceivably use this toward that end,' Ryan said coolly, 'but I think Narmonov has too much political clout now that he has that fourth man on the Politburo. He can, therefore, choose to go forward toward the agreement and show the Party how strong he is by moving forward for peace, or if he senses more political vulnerability than I see in the picture, he can consolidate his hold on the Party by trashing us as the incorrigible enemies of Socialism. If there's a way to put a probability assessment on that choice that's anything more than a wild-ass guess, I haven't seen it yet.'

'Get to work on it,' Judge Moore ordered. 'The President'll want something hard enough to grab hold of before Ernie Allen starts talking about putting SDI on the table again.'

'Yes, sir.' Jack stood. 'Judge, do we expect the Sovs to go public on CARDINAL's arrest?'

'There's a question,' Ritter said.

Ryan headed for the door and stopped again. 'Wait a minute.'

'What is it?' Ritter asked.

'You said that the Ambassador delivered his protest before their Foreign Ministry said anything, right?'

'Yeah, Foley worked real fast to beat them to the punch.'

'With all due respect to Mr Foley, nobody's that fast,' Ryan said. 'They should have had their press release already printed before they made the pickup.'

'So?' Admiral Greer asked.

Jack walked back toward the other three. 'So the Foreign Minister is Narmonov's man, isn't he? So's Yazov at the Defense Ministry. They didn't know,' Ryan said. 'They were as surprised as we were.'

'No chance,' Ritter snorted. 'They don't do things like that.'

'Assumption on your part, sir.' Jack stood his ground. 'What evidence backs up that statement?'

Greer smiled. 'None that we know of right now.'

'Damn it, James, I know he's –'

'Keep going, Dr Ryan,' Judge Moore said.

'If those two ministers didn't know what was going down, it puts a different spin on this case, doesn't it?' Jack sat on the back of a chair. 'Okay, I can see cutting Yazov out – CARDINAL was his senior aide – but why cut out the Foreign Minister? This sort of thing, you want to move fast, catch the newsies with the breaking story – for damned sure you don't want the other side to get the word out first.'

'Bob?' the DCI asked.

The Deputy Director for Operations never had liked Ryan very much – he thought that he'd come too far too fast – but, for all that, Bob Ritter was an honest man. The DDO sat back down and sipped at his coffee for a moment. 'Boy may have a point. We'll have to confirm a few details, but if they check out . . . it's as much a political operation as a simple "Two" case.'

'James?'

The Deputy Director for Intelligence nodded agreement. 'Scary.'

'We may not be talking about just losing a good source,' Ryan went on, speculating as he spoke. 'KGB might be using this for political ends. What I don't see is his power base. The Alexandrov faction has three solid members. Narmonov now has four, counting the new guy, Vaneyev –'

'Shit!' This was Ritter. 'We assumed that when his daughter was picked up and let go that they either didn't break her – hell, they say she looks okay – or her father was too important for them to –'

'Blackmail.' Now it was Judge Moore's turn. 'You were right, Bob. And Narmonov doesn't know. You have to hand it to Gerasimov, the bastard has some beautiful moves . . . If all this is true, Narmonov is outnumbered and doesn't know it.' He paused for a frown. 'We're speculating like a bunch of amateurs.'

'Well, it makes for one hell of a scenario.' Ryan almost smiled until he reached the logical conclusion. 'We may have brought down the first Soviet government in thirty years that wanted to liberalize their own country.' *What will the papers make of that?* Jack asked himself. *And you know that it'll get out. Something like this is too juicy to stay secret long. . . .*

'We know what you've been doing, and we know how long you've been doing it. Here is the evidence.' He tossed the photographs onto the table.

'Nice pictures,' Mary Pat said. 'Where's the man from my embassy?'

'We don't have to let anyone talk with you. We can keep you here as long as we wish. Years, if necessary,' he added ominously.

'Look, mister, I'm an American, okay? My husband is a diplomat. He has diplomatic immunity and so do I. Just because you think I'm a dumb American housewife, you think you can push me around and scare me into signing that damned-fool confession that I'm some kind of idiot spy. Well, I'm not, and I won't, and my government will protect me. So as far as I'm concerned you can take that confession and spread mustard on it and eat it. God knows the food over here is so bad you could use the fiber in your diet,' she observed. 'And you're saying that that nice old man I was taking the picture to was arrested too, eh? Well, I think you're just crazy.'

'We know that you have met him many times.'

'Twice. I saw him at a game last year, too – no, excuse me, I met him at a diplomatic reception a few weeks ago. That's three times, but only the hockey matters. That's why I brought the picture. The boys on the team think he's good luck for them – ask them, they all signed the picture, didn't they? Both times he came, we won big games and my son scored a couple of goals. And you think he's a spy just because he went to a junior-league hockey game? My God, you guys must think American spies are under every bed.'

She was actually enjoying herself. They treated her carefully. Nothing like a threatened pregnancy, Mary Pat told herself, as she broke yet another time-honored rule in the spy business: *Don't say anything*. She jabbered on, as would any outraged private citizen – with the shield of diplomatic immunity, of course – at the rank stupidity of the Russians. She watched her interrogator closely for a reaction. If there was anything Russians hated, it was to be looked down on, and most of all by the Americans, to whom they had a terminal inferiority complex.

'I used to think that the security people at the embassy were a pain,' she huffed after a moment. 'Don't do this, don't do that, be careful taking pictures of things. I wasn't taking a picture, I was *giving* him a picture! And the kids in it are Russian kids – except for Eddie.' She turned away, looking into the mirror. Mary Pat wondered if the Russians had thought that touch up themselves or if they had gotten the idea from American cop shows.

'Whoever trained that one knew his business,' Vatutin observed, looking through the mirror from the next room.

'She knows we're here but doesn't let on. When are we turning her loose?'

'Late this afternoon,' the head of the Second Chief Directorate answered. 'Holding her isn't worth the effort. Her husband is already packing up the apartment. You should have waited a few more seconds,' the General added.

'I know.' There was no point in explaining the faulty door lock. The KGB didn't accept excuses, even from colonels. That was beside the point in any case, Vatutin and his boss knew. They'd caught Filitov – not quite in the act, but he was still caught. That was the objective of the case, at least so far as they were concerned. Both men knew the other parts of it, but treated them as though they didn't exist. It was the smartest course for both.

'Where is my man!' Yazov demanded.

'He is in Lefortovo Prison, of course,' Gerasimov answered.

'I want to see him. At once.' The Defense Minister hadn't even paused to take off his cap, standing there in his calf-length greatcoat, his cheeks still pink from the chilly February air – or perhaps with anger, Gerasimov thought. Maybe even with fear . . .

'This is not a place to make demands, Dmitri Timofeye-vich. I, too, am a Politburo member. I, too, sit on the Defense Council. And it may be that you are implicated in this investigation.' Gerasimov's fingers played with a file on the desktop.

That changed Yazov's complexion. He went pale, definitely not from fear. Gerasimov was surprised that the soldier didn't lose control, but the Marshal made a supreme effort and spoke as though to a new draftee:

'Show me your evidence here and now if you have the balls for it!'

'Very well.' The KGB Chairman flipped open the folder and removed a series of photographs, handing them over.

'You had *me* under surveillance?'

'No, we've been watching Filitov. You just happened to be there.'

Yazov tossed the prints back with contempt. 'So what? Misha was invited to a hockey game. I accompanied him. It was a good game. There is an American boy on the team – I met the mother at some reception or other – oh, yes, it was in George Hall when the American negotiators were last over. She was at this game, and we said hello. She is an amusing woman, in an empty-headed sort of way. The next morning I filled out a contact report. So did Misha.'

'If she is so empty-headed, why did you bother?' Gerasimov inquired.

'Because she is an American, and her husband is a diplomat of some kind or other, and I was foolish enough to allow her to touch me, as you see. The contact report is on file. I will send you a copy of mine, and Colonel Filitov's.' Yazov was speaking with more confidence now. Gerasimov had miscalculated somewhat.

'She is an agent of the American CIA.'

'Then I am confident that Socialism will prevail, Nikolay Borissovich. I didn't think that you employed such fools – not until today, that is.'

Defense Minister Yazov allowed himself to calm down. Though new to the Moscow scene – until very recently he'd been commander of the Far East Military District, where Narmonov had spotted him – he knew what the real struggle here was all about. He did not, could not believe that Filitov was a traitor – did not believe because of the man's record; could not believe because the scandal would destroy one of the most carefully planned careers in the Soviet Army. His.

'If you have real evidence against my man, I want my own security people to review it. You, Nikolay Borissovich, are playing a political game with my Ministry. I will not have KGB interference in the way I run my Army. Someone from GRU will be here this afternoon. You will cooperate with him or I will take this to the Politburo myself.'

Gerasimov showed no reaction at all as the Defense Minister left the room, but realized that he'd made an error of his own. He'd overplayed his hand – no, he told himself, you played it a day too soon. You expected Yazov to collapse, to bend to the pressure, to accept a proposal not yet made.

And all because that fool Vatutin hadn't gotten positive evidence. Why couldn't he have waited one more second!

Well, the only thing to do is to get a full confession from Filitov.

Colin McClintock's official job was in the commercial office at Her Britannic Majesty's Embassy, just across the Moscow River from the Kremlin, a location that predated the revolution and had annoyed the Soviet leadership since Stalin's time. But he, too, was a player in the Great Game. He was, in fact, the case officer who 'ran' Svetlana Vaneyeva and had seconded her to the CIA for a purpose which had never been explained, but the orders for which had come direct from London's Century House, the headquarters of the SIS. At the moment, he was taking a group of British businessmen through GOSPLAN, introducing them to some of the bureaucrats with whom they'd have to negotiate the contracts for whatever they hoped to sell to the local barbarians, McClintock thought. An 'Islander' from Whalsay off the Scottish coast, he regarded anyone from south of Aberdeen as a barbarian, but worked for the Secret Intelligence Service anyway. When he spoke in English, he used a lilting accent laced with words spoken only in Northern Scotland, and his Russian was barely comprehensible, but he was a man who could turn accents on and off as though with a switch. And his ears had no accent at all. People invariably think that a person who has trouble speaking a language also has trouble hearing it. It was an impression that McClintock assiduously cultivated.

He'd met Svetlana this way, had reported her to London as a possible target for recruitment, and a senior SIS officer had done just that in the second-floor dining room of

Langan's Brasserie on Stratton Street. Since then McClintock had seen her only on business, only with other British subjects and Russians around. Other SIS officers in Moscow handled her dead-drops, though he was actually responsible for her operations. The data that she'd gotten out was disappointing but occasionally useful in a commercial sense. With intelligence agents you tended to take what you got, and she did forward insider gossip that she picked up from her father.

But something had gone wrong with Svetlana Vaneyeva. She'd disappeared from her desk, then returned, probably after interrogation at Lefortovo, the CIA had said. That made little sense to McClintock. Once they got you into Lefortovo, they had you for more than a day or two. Something very strange had happened, and he'd waited for a week to figure a way to find out exactly what it might have been. Her drops were untouched now, of course. Nobody from SIS would ever go near them except to see if they'd been disturbed, from a discreet distance.

Now, however, he had his chance, taking his trade delegation across the room that held the textile section of the planning agency. She looked up and saw the foreigners walking by. McClintock gave the routine interrogation signal. He didn't know which reply he'd get, nor what the reply would really mean. He had to assume that she'd been broken, totally compromised, but she had to react some way. He gave the signal, a brush of his hands against his hair as natural as breathing, as all such signals were. Her reply was to open a desk drawer and extract a pencil or a pen. The former was the 'all clear' signal, the latter a warning. She did neither, and merely returned to the document she was reading. It almost surprised the young intelligence officer enough to stare, but he remembered who and where he was, and turned away, scanning other faces in the room as his hands fluttered nervously about, doing various things that could have meant anything to whoever was watching.

What stuck in his mind was the look on her face. What had once been animated was now blank. What had once been lively was now as emotionless as any face on a Moscow street. The person who'd once been the privileged daughter of a very senior Party man was different now. It wasn't an act. He was sure of it; she didn't have the skill for that.

They got to her, McClintock told himself. *They got to her and let her go*. He didn't have a clue why they'd let her go, but that wasn't his concern. An hour later he drove the businessmen back to their hotel and returned to his office. The report he dashed off to London was only three pages long. He had no idea of the firestorm it would ignite. Nor did he know that another SIS officer had sent another report the same day, in the same pouch.

'Hello, Arthur,' the voice on the phone said.

''Morning – excuse me, good afternoon, Basil. How's the weather in London?'

'Cold, wet, and miserable. Thought I might come over to your side of the pond and get some sun.'

'Be sure to stop over to the shop.'

'I planned to do that. First thing in the morning?'

'I always have room on the calendar for you.'

'See you tomorrow, then.'

'Great. See ya.' Judge Moore hung up.

That was some day, the Director of Central Intelligence thought. *First we lose CARDINAL, now Sir Basil Charleston wants to come over here with something he can't talk about over the most secure phone system NSA and GCHQ ever came up with!* It was still before noon and he'd already been in his office for nine hours. *What the hell is going wrong?*

'You call this evidence?' General Yevgeniy Ignat'yev was in charge of the counterespionage office of the GRU, the Soviet military's own intelligence arm. 'To these tired old eyes it looks as though your people have jumped onto thin ice looking for a fish.'

Vatutin was amazed – and furious – that the KGB Chairman had sent this man into *his* office to review *his* case.

'If you can find a plausible explanation for the film, the camera, and the diary, perhaps you would be so kind as to share it with me, Comrade.'

'You say you took it from his hand, not the woman's.' A statement, not a question.

'A mistake on my part for which I make no excuses,' Vatutin said with dignity, which struck both men as slightly odd.

'And the camera?'

'It was found attached magnetically to the inside of the service panel on his refrigerator.'

'You didn't find it the first time you searched the apartment, I see. And it had no fingerprints on it. And your visual record of Filitov does not show him using it. So if he tells me that you planted both the film and the camera on him, how am I supposed to convince the Minister that he's the one doing the lying?'

Vatutin was surprised by the tone of the question. 'You believe that he is a spy after all?'

'What I believe is of no importance. I find the existence of the diary troubling, but you would not believe the breaches of security I have to deal with, especially at the higher levels. The more important people become, the less important they think the rules are. You know who Filitov is. He's more than just a hero, Comrade. He is famous throughout the Soviet Union – Old Misha, the Hero of Stalingrad. He fought at Minsk, at Vyasma, outside Moscow when we stopped the fascists, the Kharkov disaster, then the fighting retreat to Stalingrad, then the counterattack –'

'I have read his file,' Vatutin said neutrally.

'He is a symbol to the entire Army. You cannot execute a symbol on evidence as equivocal as this, Vatutin. All you

343

have are these photographic frames, with no objective evidence that he shot them.'

'We have not yet interrogated him.'

'And you think that will be easy?' Ignat'yev rolled his eyes. His laugh was a harsh bark. 'Do you know how tough this man is? This man killed Germans while he was on fire! This man looked at death a thousand times and pissed on it!'

'I can get what I want out of him,' Vatutin insisted quietly.

'Torture, is it? Are you mad? Keep in mind that the Taman Guards Motor-Rifle Division is based a few kilometers from here. You think the Red Army will sit still while you torture one of its heroes? Stalin is dead, Comrade Colonel, and so is Beriya.'

'We can extract the information without doing physical harm,' Vatutin said. That was one of KGB's most closely guarded secrets.

'Rubbish!'

'In that case, General, what do you recommend?' Vatutin asked, knowing the answer.

'Let me take over the case. We'll see to it that he never betrays the *Rodina* again, you can be sure of that,' Ignat'yev promised.

'And save the Army the embarrassment, of course.'

'We would save embarrassment for everyone, not the least you, Comrade Colonel, for fucking up this so-called investigation.'

Well, that's about what I expected. A little bluster and a few threats, mixed with a little sympathy and comradeliness. Vatutin saw that he had a way out, but that the safety it promised also promised to end his advancement. The handwritten message from the Chairman had made that clear enough. He was trapped between two enemies, and though he could still win the approval of one, the largest goal involved the largest risk. He could retreat from the true objective of the investigation, and stay a colonel the rest of his life, or he could do what he'd hoped to do when he began – without any political motives, Vatutin remembered bleakly – and risk disgrace. The decision was paradoxically an easy one. Vatutin was a 'Two' man –

'It is my case. The Chairman has given it to me to run, and I will run it in my way. Thank you for your advice, Comrade General.'

Ignat'yev appraised the man and the statement. It wasn't often that he encountered integrity, and it saddened him in a vague, distant way that he could not congratulate the man who demonstrated this rarest of qualities. But loyalty to the Soviet Army came first.

'As you wish. I expect to be kept informed of all your activities.' Ignat'yev left without another word.

Vatutin sat at his desk for a few minutes, appraising his own position. Then he called for his car. Twenty minutes later he was at Lefortovo.

'Impossible,' the doctor told him before he had even asked the question.

'What?'

'You want to put this man into the sensory-deprivation tank, don't you?'

'Of course.'

'It would probably kill him. I don't think you want to do that, and I am sure that I will not risk my project on something like this.'

'It's my case, and I'll run it –'

'Comrade Colonel, the man in question is over seventy years old. I have his medical file here. He has all the symptoms of moderate cardiovascular disease – normal at this age, of course – and a history of respiratory problems. The onset of the first anxiety period would explode his heart like a balloon. I can almost guarantee it.'

'What do you mean – explode his heart –'

'Excuse me – it's difficult to explain medical terms to the layman. His coronary arteries are coated with moderate amounts of plaque. It happens to all of us; it comes from the food we eat. His arteries are more blocked than yours or mine because of his age, and also, because of his age, the

345

arteries are less flexible than those of a younger person. If his heart rate goes too high, the plaque deposits will dislodge and cause a blockage. That's what a heart attack is, Colonel, a blockage of a coronary artery. Part of the heart muscle dies, the heart stops entirely or becomes arrhythmic; in either case it ceases to pump blood, and the whole patient dies. Is that clear? Use of the tank will almost certainly induce a heart attack in the subject, and that attack will almost certainly be fatal. If not a heart attack, there is the somewhat lesser probability of a massive stroke – or both could happen. No, Comrade Colonel, we cannot use the tank for this man. I do not think that you wish to kill him before you get your information.'

'What about other physical measures?' Vatutin asked quietly. *My God, what if I can't . . .?*

'If you're certain that he's guilty, you can shoot him at once and be done with it,' the physician observed. 'But any gross physical abuse is likely to kill the patient.'

And all because of a goddamned door lock, Colonel Vatutin told himself.

It was an ugly rocket, the sort of thing that a child might draw or a fireworks company might build, though either would know better than to put it on top of an airplane instead of its proper place, underneath. But it was atop the airplane, as the runway's perimeter lights showed in the darkness.

The airplane was the famous SR-71 Blackbird, Lockheed's Mach-three reconnaissance aircraft. This one had been flown in from Kadena Air Force Base on the western rim of the Pacific two days before. It rolled down the runway at Nellis Air Force Base, Nevada, before the twin flames of its afterburning engines. Fuel that leaked from the SR-71's tanks – the Blackbird leaked a lot – was ignited by the heat, much to the entertainment of the tower crew. The pilot pulled back on the stick at the appropriate time, and the Blackbird's nose came up. He held the stick back for longer than usual, pointing the bird into a steep forty-

346

five-degree climb on full burner, and in a moment all that was left on the ground was a thundering memory. The last view the people had was of the twin angry dots of the engines, and soon these disappeared through the clouds that wafted by at ten thousand feet.

The Blackbird kept going up. The air-traffic controllers at Las Vegas noted the blip on their screens, saw that it was barely moving laterally, though its altitude readout was changing as rapidly as the wheels of the slot machines on the airport concourse. They shared a look – another Air Force hot dog – then they went back to work.

The Blackbird was now passing through sixty thousand feet, and leveled off to head southeast toward the White Sands Missile Range. The pilot checked his fuel – there was plenty – and relaxed after the exhilarating climb. The engineers had been right. The missile sitting on the aircraft's back hadn't mattered at all. By the time he'd gotten to fly the Blackbird, the purpose of the back mount had been overtaken by events. Designed to hold a single-engine photoreconnaissance drone, the fittings had been removed from nearly all the SR-71s, but not this one, for reasons that were not clear from the aircraft's maintenance book. The drone had originally been designed to go places the Blackbird could not, but it had become redundant on discovery of the fact that there was nowhere the SR-71 could not go in safety, as the pilot regularly proved on flights from Kadena. The only limit on the aircraft was fuel, and that didn't play today.

'Juliet Whiskey, this is Control. Do you read, over,' the sergeant said into the headset.

'Control, this is Juliet Whiskey. All systems go. We are nominal to profile.'

'Roger. Commence launch sequence on my mark. Five, four, three, two, one: *mark!*'

A hundred miles away, the pilot punched burners again and hauled back on the stick. The Blackbird performed as beautifully as always, standing on her tail and rocketing into the sky before nearly a hundred thousand pounds of thrust. The pilot's eyes were locked on his instruments as the altimeter spun around like a maddened clock. His speed was now thirteen hundred miles per hour and increasing, while the SR-71 showed her contempt for gravity.

'Separation in twenty seconds,' the systems operator in the back seat told the pilot. The Blackbird was now passing through a hundred thousand feet. The target was one-twenty. The controls were already mushy. There wasn't enough air up here to control the aircraft properly, and the pilot was being even more careful than usual. He watched his speed hit nineteen hundred several seconds early, then:

'Standby for separation . . . breakaway, breakaway!' the man in back called. The pilot dropped the nose and started a gentle turn to the left that would take him right across New Mexico before heading back to Nellis. This was much easier than flying along the Soviet border – and, occasionally, across it. . . . The pilot wondered if he could drive down to Vegas to catch a show after he landed.

The target kept going up for a few more seconds, but surprisingly did not ignite its rocket motor. It was now a ballistic object, traveling in obedience to the laws of physics. Its oversized fins provided enough aerodynamic drag to keep it pointed in the proper direction as gravity began to reclaim the object for its own. The rocket tipped over at one hundred thirty thousand feet, reluctantly pointing its nose at the earth.

Then its motor fired. The solid-fuel engine burned for only four seconds, but that was enough to accelerate its conical nose to a speed that would have terrified the Blackbird's pilot.

'Okay,' an Army officer said. The point-defense radar went from standby to active. It immediately saw the inbound. The target rocket was pushing itself down through the atmosphere at roughly the same speed as an ICBM warhead. He didn't have to give a command. The system was fully automated. Two hundred yards away a fiberglass cover exploded off a concrete hole drilled in the gypsum flats, and a FLAGE erupted skyward. The Flexible Light-weight Agile Guided Experiment looked more like a lance than a rocket, and was nearly that simple. Millimeter-wave radar tracked the inbound, and the data was processed through an onboard microcomputer. The remarkable part of this was that all the parts had been taken off the shelf from existing high-tech weaponry.

Outside, men watched from behind a protective earthen berm. They saw the upward streak of yellow light and heard the roar of the solid rocket motor, then nothing for several seconds.

The FLAGE homed in on its target, maneuvering a few fractions of degrees with tiny attitude-control rockets. The nosecap blew off, and what unfolded would have looked to an outsider like a collapsing umbrella's framework, per-haps ten yards across. . . .

It looked just like a Fourth of July rocket, but without the noise. A few people cheered. Though both the target and the FLAGE 'warhead' were totally inert, the energy of the collision converted metal and ceramic to incandescent vapor.

'Four for four,' Gregory said. He tried not to yawn. He'd seen fireworks before.

'You're not going to get all the boosters, Major,' General Parks chided the younger man. 'We still need the midcourse systems, and the terminal-defense ones.'

'Yes, sir, but you don't need me here. It works.'

For the first three tests, the target rocket had been fired from a Phantom fighter, and people in Washington had claimed that the test series had underestimated the difficulty of intercepting the inbound warheads. Using the SR-71 as the launch platform had been Parks's idea. Launching the drone from higher altitude, and with a higher initial speed, had made for a much faster reentry target. This test had actually made things slightly harder than was expected, and the FLAGE hadn't cared a bit.

Parks had been a little worried about the missile-guidance software, but, as Gregory had noted, it worked.

'Al,' Parks said, 'I'm starting to think that this whole program is going to work.'

'Sure. Why not?' *If those Agency pukes can get us the plans for the Russian laser.* . . .

CARDINAL sat alone in a bare cell, one and a half meters wide, two and a half meters long. There was a bare light bulb overhead, a wooden cot with a bucket underneath, but not a window except the spy hole in the rusted iron door. The walls were solid concrete, and there was no sound at all. He couldn't hear the pacing of the corridor guard, nor even the rumble of traffic on the street outside the prison, They'd taken his uniform blouse, and belt, and his polished boots, replacing the last with cheap slippers. The cell was in the basement. That was all he knew, and he could tell from the damp air. It was cold.

But not so cold as his heart. The enormity of his crime came to him as it never had. Colonel Mikhail Semyonovich Filitov, three times Hero of the Soviet Union, was alone with his treason. He thought of the magnificent, broad land in which he lived, whose distant horizons and endless vistas were peopled with his fellow Russians. He'd served them all his life with pride and honor, and with his own blood, as the scars on his body proclaimed. He remembered the men with whom he'd served, so many of whom had died under his command. And how they had died, defiantly cursing the German tanks and guns as they burned alive in T-34s, retreating only when forced to, preferring to attack even when they knew it to be doomed. He remembered leading his troops in a hundred engagements, the frantic exhilaration that accompanied the roar of the diesel engines, the reeking clouds of smoke, the determination even unto the death that he had cheated so many times.

And he'd betrayed it all.

What would my men say of me now? He stared at the blank concrete wall opposite his cot.

What would Romanov say?

I think we both need a drink, my Captain, the voice chimed in. Only Romanov could be both serious and amused at the same time. *Such thoughts are more easily considered with vodka or Samogan.*

Do you know why? Misha asked.

You've never told us why, my Captain. And so Misha did. It took but a brief flicker of time.

Both your sons, and your wife. Tell me, Comrade Captain, for what did we die?

Misha didn't know that. Even during the shooting he hadn't known. He'd been a soldier, and when a soldier's country is invaded, the soldier fights to repel the enemy. So much the easier when the enemy is as brutal as the Germans were. . . .

We fought for the Soviet Union, Corporal.

Did we, now? I seem to remember fighting for Mother Russia, but mainly I remember fighting for you, Comrade Captain.

But –

A soldier fights for his comrades, my Captain. I fought for my family. You and our troop, they were my only family. I suppose you also fought for your family, the big one and the little one. I always envied you that, my Captain, and I was proud that you made me part of both in the way that you did.

But I killed you, I shouldn't have –

We all have our destiny, Comrade Captain. Mine was to die young at Vyasma without a wife, without children, but even so I did not die without a family.

I avenged you, Romanov. I got the Mark-IV that killed you.

I know. You avenged all the dead of your family. Why do you think we loved you? Why do you think we died for you?

You understand? Misha asked in surprise.

The workers and peasants may not, but your men will. We understand destiny now, as you cannot.

But what shall I do?

Captains do not ask such questions of corporals.

351

Romanov laughed. *You had all the answers to* our *questions*.

Filitov's head jerked up as the latch slipped on the door of his cell.

Vatutin expected to find a broken man. The isolation of the cell, the prisoner stripped of identity and alone with his fears and his crimes, always had the proper effect. But while he looked at a tired, crippled old man, he saw the eyes and mouth change.

Thank you, Romanov.

'Good morning, Sir Basil,' Ryan said as he reached for the man's bags.

'Hello, Jack! I didn't know they were using you as a gofer.'

'Depends on who I'm going-fer, as they say. The car's over this way.' He waved. It was parked fifty yards away.

'Constance sends her love. How is the family?' Sir Basil Charleston asked.

'Fine, thanks. How's London?'

'Surely you haven't forgotten our winters already.'

'No.' Jack laughed as he wrenched open the door. 'I remember the beer, too.' A moment later both doors were closed and locked.

'They sweep the wheels every week,' Jack said. 'How bad is it?'

'How bad? That's what I came over here to find out. Something very odd is happening. Your chaps had an op go wrong, didn't you?'

'I can say yes to that, but the rest'll have to come from the Judge. Sorry, but I was just cleared for part of it.'

'Recently, I'll wager.'

'Yep.' Ryan shifted up as he took the turn off the airport road.

'Then let's see if you can still put two and two together, Sir John.'

Jack smiled as he changed lanes to pass a truck. 'I was doing the intelligence estimate on the arms talks when I broke into it. Now I'm supposed to be looking at

Narmonov's political vulnerability. Unless I'm wrong, that's why you've flown over.'

'And unless I'm very far off the mark, your op has triggered something very serious indeed.'

'Vaneyev?'

'Correct.'

'Jesus.' Ryan turned briefly. 'I hope you have some ideas, 'cause we sure as hell don't.' He took the car to seventy-five. Fifteen minutes later he pulled into Langley. They parked in the underground garage and took the VIP elevator to the seventh floor.

'Hello, Arthur. It's not often I have a knight chauffeur me about, even in London.' The head of SIS took a chair while Ryan summoned Moore's department chiefs.

'Hi, Bas',' Greer said on entering. Ritter just waved. It was his operation that had triggered this crisis. Ryan took the least comfortable chair available.

'I'd like to know exactly what went wrong,' Charleston said simply, not even waiting for the coffee to be passed around.

'An agent got arrested. A very well placed agent.'

'Is that why the Foleys are flying out today?' Charleston smiled. 'I didn't know who they were, but when two people get ejected from that delightful country, we generally assume –'

'We don't know what went wrong yet,' Ritter said. 'They should be landing at Frankfurt right about now, then ten more hours till we have them here for the debrief. They were working an agent who –'

'Who was an aide to Yazov – Colonel M. S. Filitov. We've deduced that much. How long have you had him?'

'It was one of your folks who recruited him for us,' Moore replied. 'He was a colonel, too.'

'You don't mean . . . Oleg Penkovskiy . . . ? Bloody hell!' Charleston was amazed for once, Ryan saw. It didn't happen often. '*That* long?'

'That long,' Ritter said. 'But the numbers caught up with us.'

'And the Vaneyeva woman we seconded to you for courier service was part of that –'

'Correct. She never came close to either end of the chain, by the way. We know that she was probably picked up, but she's back at work. We haven't checked her out yet, but –'

'We have, Bob. Our chap reported that she'd – changed somehow. He said it was hard to describe but impossible to miss. Like the hoary tales of brainwashing, Orwell and all that. He noted that she was free – or what passes for it over there – and related that to her father. Then we learned of something big in the Defense Ministry – that a senior aide to Yazov had been arrested.' Charleston paused to stir his coffee. 'We have a source inside the Kremlin that we guard rather closely. We have learned that Chairman Gerasimov spent several hours with Alexandrov last week and under fairly unusual circumstances. This same source has warned us that Alexandrov has a considerable urge to sidetrack this *perestroika* business.

'Well, it's clear, isn't it?' Charleston asked rhetorically. It was quite clear to everyone. 'Gerasimov has suborned a Politburo member thought to be loyal to Narmonov, at the very least compromised the support of the Defense Minister, *and* been spending a good deal of time with the man who wants Narmonov out. I'm afraid that your operation may have triggered something with the most unpleasant consequences.'

'There's more,' the DCI said. 'Our agent was getting us material on Soviet SDI research. Ivan may have made a breakthrough.'

'Marvelous,' Charleston observed. 'A return to the bad old days, but this time the new version of the "missile gap" is potentially quite real, I take it? I am awfully old to change my politics. Too bad. You know, of course, that there is a leak in your program?'

'Oh?' Moore asked with a poker face.

'Gerasimov told Alexandrov that. No details, unfortunately, except that KGB think it highly important.'

'We've had some warnings. It's being looked at,' Moore said.

'Well, the technical matters can sort themselves out. They generally do. The political question, on the other hand, has created a bit of a bother with the PM. There's trouble enough when we bring down a government that we wish to bring down, but to do so by accident. . . .'

'We don't like the consequences any more than you do, Basil,' Greer noted. 'But there's not a hell of a lot we can do about it from this end.'

'You can accept their treaty terms,' Charleston suggested. 'Then our friend Narmonov would have his position sufficiently strengthened that he might be able to tell Alexandrov to bugger off. That, in any case, is the unofficial position of Her Majesty's government.'

And that's the real purpose of your visit to us, Sir Basil, Ryan thought. It was time to say something:

'That means putting unreasonable restrictions on our SDI research and reducing our warhead inventory in the knowledge that the Russians are racing forward with their own program. I don't think that's a very good deal.'

'And a Soviet government headed by Gerasimov is?'

'And what if we end up with that anyway?' Ryan asked. 'My estimate is already written. I recommend against additional concessions.'

'One can always change a written document,' Charleston pointed out.

'Sir, I have a rule. If something goes out with my name on the front, it says what I think, not what somebody else tells me to think,' Ryan said.

'Do remember, gentlemen, that I am a friend. What is likely to happen to the Soviet government would be a greater setback to the West than a temporary restriction on one of your defense programs.'

'The President won't spring for it,' Greer said.

'He might have to,' Moore replied.

'There has to be another way,' Ryan observed.

'Not unless you can bring Gerasimov down.' It was

Ritter this time. 'We can't offer any direct help to Narmonov. Even if we assume that he'd take a warning from us, which he probably wouldn't, we'd be running an even greater risk by involving ourselves in their internal politics. If the rest of the Politburo got one whiff of that . . . I suppose it might start a little war.'

'But what if we can?' Ryan asked.

'What if we can *what?*' Ritter demanded.

17
Conspiracy

'Ann' came back to Eve's Leaves earlier than expected, the owner noted. With her usual smile, she selected a dress off the rack and took it to the dressing room. She was out by the full-length mirrors only a minute later, and accepted the customary compliments on how it looked rather more perfunctorily than usual. Again she paid cash, leaving with yet another engaging smile.

Out in the parking lot, things were a little different. Captain Bisyarina broke tradecraft by opening the capsule and reading the contents. That evoked a brief but nasty curse. The message was but a single sheet of notepaper. Bisyarina lit a cigarette with a butane lighter, then burned the paper in her car's ashtray.

All that work wasted! And it was already in Moscow, was already being analyzed. She felt like a fool. It was doubly annoying that her agent had been completely honest, had forwarded what she'd thought was highly classified material, and on learning that it had been rendered invalid, had gotten that word out quickly. She would not even have the satisfaction of forwarding a small portion of the reprimand that she would surely get for wasting Moscow Center's time.

Well, they warned me about this. It may be the first time, but it will not be the last. She drove home and dashed off her message.

The Ryans weren't known for their attendance on the Washington cocktail circuit, but there were a few that they couldn't avoid. The reception was intended to raise money for D.C. Children's Hospital, and Jack's wife was a friend of the chief of surgery. The evening's entertainment was the big draw. A prominent jazz musician owed his granddaughter's life to the hospital, and he was paying off that debt with a major benefit performance at the Kennedy Center. The reception was intended to give the D.C. elite a chance to meet him 'up close and personal' and hear his sax in greater privacy. Actually, as with most 'power' parties, it was really for the elite to see and be seen by one another, confirming their importance. As was true in most parts of the world, the elite felt the need to pay for the privilege. Jack understood the phenomenon, but felt that it made little sense. By eleven o'clock the elite of Washington had proved that they could talk just as inanely about just as little, and get just as drunk, as anyone else in the world. Cathy had held herself to one glass of white wine, however; Jack had won the toss tonight: he could drink and she had to drive. He'd indulged himself tonight, despite a few warning looks from his wife, and was basking in a mellow, philosophical glow that made him think he'd overdone the act a little bit – but then it wasn't supposed to look like an act. He just hoped to God everything went as planned tonight.

The amusing part was the way in which Ryan was treated. His position at the Agency had always been a sketchy one. The opening comments went something like, 'How are things at Langley?', usually in an affected conspiratorial tone, and Jack's reply that CIA was just another government bureaucracy, a large building that contained lots of moving paper, surprised most questioners. The CIA was thought to have thousands of active field spooks. The actual figure was classified, of course, but far lower.

'We work normal business hours,' Jack explained to a well-dressed woman whose eyes were slightly dilated. 'I even have tomorrow off.'

'Really?'

'Yes, I killed a Chinese agent on Tuesday and you always

get a day off with pay for that sort of thing,' he said seriously, then grinned.

'You're kidding!'

'That's right, I'm kidding. Please forget that I ever said it.' *Who is this overaged bimbo?* he wondered.

'What about the reports that you're under investigation?' another person asked.

Jack turned in surprise. 'And who might you be?'

'Scott Browning, *Chicago Tribune*.' He didn't offer to shake hands. The game had just begun. The reporter didn't know that he was a player, but Ryan did.

'Could you run that one by me again?' Jack said politely.

'My sources tell me that you're being investigated for illegal stock transactions.'

'It's news to me,' Jack replied.

'I know that you've met with investigators from the SEC,' the reporter announced.

'If you know that, then you also know that I gave them the information they wanted, and they left happy.'

'You're sure of that?'

'Of course I am. I didn't do anything wrong and I have the records to prove it,' Ryan insisted, perhaps a little too forcefully, the reporter thought. He loved it when people drank too much. *In vino veritas*.

'That's not what my sources tell me,' Browning persisted.

'Well, I can't help that!' Ryan said. There was emotion in his voice now, and a few heads turned.

'Maybe if it wasn't for people like you, we might have an intelligence agency that worked,' observed a newcomer.

'And who the fuck are you!' Ryan said before he turned. *Act 1, Scene 2*.

'Congressman Trent,' the reporter said. Trent was on the House Select Committee.

'I think an apology is owed,' Trent said. He looked drunk.

'What for?' Ryan asked.

'How about for all the screw-ups across the river?'

'As opposed to the ones on this side?' Jack inquired. People were drifting over. Entertainment is where you find it.

'I know what you people just tried to pull off, and you fell right on your ass. You didn't let us know, as the law requires. You went ahead anyway, and I'm telling you, you're going to pay, you're going to pay big.'

'If we have to pay your bar bill, we'll have to pay big.' Ryan turned, dismissing the man.

'Big man,' Trent said behind his back. 'You're heading for a fall, too.'

Perhaps twenty people were watching and listening now. They saw Jack take a glass of wine off a passing tray. They saw a look that could kill, and a few people remembered that Jack Ryan was a man who had killed. It was a fact and a reputation that gave him a sort of mystery. He took a measured sip of the chablis before turning back around.

'What sort of fall might that be, Mr Trent?'

'You might be surprised.'

'Nothing you do would surprise me, pal.'

'That may be, but you've surprised us, Dr Ryan. We didn't think you were a crook, and we didn't think you were dumb enough to be involved in that disaster. I guess we were wrong.'

'You're wrong about a lot of things,' Jack hissed.

'You know something, Ryan? For the life of me I can't figure just what the hell kind of a man you are.'

'That's no surprise.'

'So, what kind of man are you, Ryan?' Trent inquired.

'You know, Congressman, this is a unique experience for me,' Jack observed lightheartedly.

'How's that?'

Ryan's manner changed abruptly. His voice boomed across the room. 'I've never had my manhood questioned by a *queer* before!' *Sorry pal. . . .*

The room went very quiet. Trent made no secret of his orientation, had gone public six years before. That didn't prevent him from turning pale. The glass in his hand shook enough to spill some of its contents onto the marble floor, but the Congressman regained his control and spoke almost gently.

'I'll break you for that.'

'Take your best shot, sweetie.' Ryan turned and walked out of the room, the eyes heavy on his back. He kept going until he stared at the traffic on Massachusetts Avenue. He knew that he'd drunk too much, but the cold air started to clear his head.

'Jack?' His wife's voice.

'Yeah, babe?'

'What was that all about?'

'Can't say.'

'I think it's time for you to go home.'

'I think you're right. I'll get the coats.' Ryan walked back inside and handed over the claim check. He heard the silence happen when he returned. He could feel the looks at his back. Jack shrugged into his overcoat and slung his wife's fur over his arm, before turning to see the eyes on him. Only one pair held any interest for him. They were there.

Misha was not an easy man to surprise, but the KGB succeeded. He'd steeled himself for torture, for the worse sort of abuse, only to be . . . disappointed? he asked himself. That certainly wasn't the right word.

He was kept in the same cell, and so far as he could determine he was alone on this cellblock. That was probably wrong, he thought, but there was no evidence that anyone else was near him, no sounds at all, not even taps on the concrete walls. Perhaps they were too thick for that. The only 'company' he had was the occasional metallic rasp of the spy hole in his cell's door. He thought that the solitude was supposed to do something to him. Filitov smiled at that. *They think I'm alone. They don't know about my comrades.*

There was only one possible answer: this Vatutin fellow was afraid that he might actually be innocent – but that *wasn't* possible, Misha told himself. That *chekist* bastard had taken the film from his hand.

He was still trying to figure that one out, staring at the blank concrete wall. None of it made any sense.

But if they expected him to be afraid, they would have to live with their disappointment. Filitov had cheated death too many times. Part of him even yearned for it. Perhaps he would be reunited with his comrades. He talked to them, didn't he? Might they still be . . . well, not exactly alive, but not exactly gone either? What *was* death? He'd reached the point in life where the question was an intellectual one. Sooner or later he'd find out, of course. The answer to that question had brushed past him many times, but his grasp – and its – had never quite been firm enough . . . .

The key rattled in the door, and the hinges creaked.

'You should oil that. Machinery lasts longer if you maintain it properly,' he said as he stood.

The jailer didn't reply, merely waving him out of the cell. Two young guards stood with the turnkey, beardless boys of twenty or so, Misha thought, their heads tilted up with the arrogance common to the KGB. Forty years earlier and he might have done something about that, Filitov told himself. They were unarmed, after all, and he was a combat soldier for whom the taking of life was as natural as breathing. They were not effective soldiers. One look confirmed it. It was fine to be proud, but a soldier should also be wary . . . .

Was that it? he thought suddenly. *Vatutin treats me with wariness despite the fact that he knows* . . . .

But why?

'What does this mean?' Mancuso asked.

'Kinda hard for me to tell,' Clark answered. 'Probably some candyass in D.C. can't make up his mind. Happens all the time.'

The two signals had arrived within twelve hours of one another. The first had aborted the mission and ordered the submarine back to open waters, but the second told *Dallas* to remain in the western Baltic and await further orders.

'I don't like being put on hold.'

'Nobody does, Captain.'

'How does it affect you?' Mancuso asked.

Clark shrugged eloquently. 'A lot of this is mental. Like you work up to play a ball game. Don't sweat it, Cap'n. I teach this sort of thing – when I'm not actually doing it.'

'How many?'

'Can't say, but most of them went pretty well.'

'Most – not all? But when they don't –'

'It gets real exciting for everybody.' Clark smiled. 'Especially me. I have some great stories, but I can't tell 'em. Well, I expect you do, too.'

'One or two. Does take some of the fun out of life, doesn't it?' The two men traded an insider's look.

Ryan was shopping alone. His wife's birthday was coming up – it would happen during his next Moscow trip – and he had to get everything out of the way early. The jewelry stores were always a good place to start. Cathy still wore the heavy gold necklace he'd given her a few years before, and he was looking for earrings that would go with it. The problem was that he had trouble remembering the exact pattern . . . His hangover didn't help, nor did his nervousness. What if they didn't bite?

'Hello, Dr Ryan,' a familiar voice said. Jack turned with some surprise.

'I didn't know they let you guys come out this far.' *Act II, Scene 1*. Jack didn't let his relief show. In that respect the hangover helped.

'The travel radius cuts right through Garfinckels, if you examine the map carefully,' Sergey Platonov pointed out. 'Shopping for your wife?'

'I'm sure my file gave you all the necessary clues.'

'Yes, her birthday.' He looked down at the display case. 'A pity that I cannot afford such things for mine . . .'

'If you were to make the appropriate overtures, the Agency could probably arrange something, Sergey Nikolay'ch.'

'But the *Rodina* might not understand,' Platonov said.

'A problem with which you are becoming familiar, are you not?'

'You're remarkably well informed,' Jack muttered.

'That is my function. I am also hungry. Perhaps you might use some of your fortune to buy me a sandwich?'

Ryan looked up and down the mall with professional interest.

'Not today.' Platonov chuckled. 'A few of my fellow . . . a few of my comrades are busy today, more than usual, and I fear your FBI is undermanned for its surveillance task.'

'A problem the KGB does not have,' Jack observed as they moved away from the store.

'You might be surprised. Why do Americans assume that our intelligence organs are any different from yours?'

'If by that you mean screwed up, I suppose it's a comforting thought. How does a hot dog grab you?'

'If it's kosher,' Platonov answered, then explained. 'I'm not Jewish, as you know, but I prefer the taste.'

'You've been here too long,' Jack said with a grin.

'But the Washington area is such a nice place.'

Jack walked into a fast-food shop that specialized in bagels and corned beef, but also served other fare. Service was quick, and the men took a white plastic table that sat by itself in the center of the mall's corridor. Cleverly done, Jack thought. People could walk past and not hear more than a few random words. But he knew Platonov was a pro.

'I have heard that you face some rather unfortunate legal difficulties.' With every word, Platonov smiled. It was supposed to appear that they were discussing ordinary pleasantries, Jack supposed, with the added dimension that his Russian colleague was enjoying himself.

'Do you believe that little prick last night? You know, one thing I actually admire about Russia is the way you handle –'

'Antisocial behavior? Yes – five years in a camp of strict regime. Our new openness does not extend to condoning sexual perversion. Your friend Trent made an acquaintance on his last trip to the Soviet Union. The young . . .

man in question is now in such a camp.' Platonov didn't say that he had refused to cooperate with the KGB, and so earned his sentence. Why confuse the issue? he thought.

'You can have him with my blessings. We have enough of them over here,' Jack growled. He felt thoroughly awful; his eyes were pounding to escape from his head as a result of all the wine and insufficient sleep.

'So I have noticed. And may we have the SEC also?' Platonov asked.

'You know, I didn't do anything wrong. Not a damned thing! I got a tip from a friend and I followed up on it. I didn't go looking for it, it just happened. So I made a few bucks – so what? I write intelligence briefs for the President! I'm good at it – and they're coming after *me!* After all the –' Ryan stopped and stared painfully into Platonov's eyes. 'So what the hell do you care?'

'Ever since we first met at Georgetown some years ago, frankly I have admired you. That business with the terrorists. I do not agree with your political views, as you plainly do not agree with mine. But as one man to another, you took some vermin off the street. You may choose to believe this or not, but I have argued against State support for such animals. True Marxists who want to free their peoples – yes, we should support them in any way we can – but bandits are murderers, they are mere scum who view us as a source of arms, nothing more. My country gains nothing by it. Politics aside, you are a man of courage and honor. Of course I respect that. It is a pity that your country does not. America only places its best men on pedestals so that lesser ones can use them as targets.'

Ryan's wary look was replaced briefly with one of measurement. 'You have that one right.'

'So, my friend – what will they do to you?'

Jack let out a long breath as he focused his eyes down the corridor. 'I have to get a lawyer this week. I suppose he'll know. I'd hoped to avoid that. I thought I could talk my way out of it, but – but this new bastard in SEC, a pansy that Trent –' Another breath. 'Trent used his influence to get the job for him. How much you want to bet that the two of them . . . I find myself in agreement with you. If one must have enemies, they should at least be enemies you can respect.'

'And CIA cannot help you?'

'I don't have many friends there – well, you know that. Moved up too fast, richest kid on the block, Greer's fairhaired boy, my connections with the Brits. You make enemies that way, too. Sometimes I wonder if one of them might have . . . I can't prove it, but you wouldn't believe that computer network we have at Langley, and all my stock transactions are stored in computer systems . . . and you know what? Computer records can be changed by someone who knows how . . . But try to prove that one, pal.' Jack took two aspirins from a small tin and swallowed them.

'Ritter doesn't like me at all, never has. I made him look bad on something a few years back, and he isn't the sort of man to forget that sort of thing. Maybe one of his people . . . he has some good ones. The Admiral wants to help, but he's old. The Judge is on his way out, supposed to have left a year ago, but he's hanging on somehow – he couldn't help me if he wanted to.'

'The President likes your work. We know that.'

'The President's a lawyer, a prosecutor. He gets even a whiff that you might have bent a law, and – it's amazing how quick you can get lonely. There's a bunch in the State Department who're after my ass, too. I don't see things quite their way. This is a bitch of a town to be honest in.'

It's correct, then, Platonov thought. They'd gotten the report first from Peter Henderson, code-named Cassius, who'd been feeding data to the KGB for over ten years, first as special assistant to the retired Senator Donaldson of the Senate's intelligence committee, now an intelligence analyst for the General Accounting Office. KGB knew Ryan to be the bright, rising star of the CIA's Intelligence Directorate. His evaluation at Moscow Center had at first called him a wealthy dilettante. That had changed a few years ago. He'd done something to earn him presidential attention, and now wrote nearly half of the special intelligence briefing papers that went to the White House. It was known from Henderson that he had assembled a massive report on the strategic-arms situation, one that had raised hackles at Foggy Bottom. Platonov had long since formed his own impression. A good judge of character, from their first meeting at Georgetown's Galleria he'd deemed Ryan a bright opponent, and a brave one – but a man too accustomed to privilege, too easily outraged at personal attack. Sophisticated, but strangely naive. What he saw over lunch confirmed it. Fundamentally, Ryan was too American. He saw things in blacks and whites, goods and bads. But what mattered today was that Ryan had felt himself invincible, and was only now learning that this was not the case. Because of that, Ryan was an angry man.

'All that work wasted,' Jack said after a few seconds. 'They're going to trash my recommendations.'

'What do you mean?'

'I mean that Ernest *Fucking* Allen has talked the President into putting SDI on the table.' It required all of Platonov's professionalism not to react visibly to that statement. Ryan went on: 'It's all been for nothing. They've discredited my analysis because of this idiot stock thing. The Agency isn't backing me up like they should. They're throwing me to the fucking dogs. Not a damned thing I can do about it, either.' Jack finished off the hot dog.

'One can always take action,' Platonov suggested.

'Revenge? I've thought of that. I could go to the papers, but the *Post* is going to run a story about the SEC thing. Somebody on the Hill is orchestrating the hanging party. Trent, I suppose. I bet he put that reporter on me last night, too, the bastard. If I try to get the real word out, well, who'll listen? Christ, I'm putting my tight little ass on the line just sitting here with you, Sergey.'

'Why do you say that?'

'Why don't you guess?' Ryan allowed himself a smile that ended abruptly. 'I'm not going to go to jail. I'd rather die than have to disgrace myself like that. God damn it, I've risked my life – I've put it all on the line. Some things you know about, and one that you don't. I have risked my life for this country, and they want to send me to prison!'

'Perhaps we can help.' The offer finally came across.

'Defect? You have to be joking. You don't really expect me to live in your workers' paradise, do you?'

'No, but for the proper incentive, perhaps we could change your situation. There will be witnesses against you. They could have accidents . . . .'

'Don't give me that shit!' Jack leaned forward. 'You don't do jobs like that in our country and we don't do them in yours.'

'Everything has a price. Surely you understand that better than I.' Platonov smiled. 'For example, the "disaster" Mr Trent referred to last night. What might that have been?'

'And how do I know who you're really working for?' Jack asked.

'What?' That surprised him, Ryan saw past the pain in his sinuses.

'You want an incentive? Sergey, I am about to put my life on the line. Just because I've done it before, don't you think that it's easy. We have somebody inside Moscow Center. Somebody big. You tell me now what that name would buy me.'

'Your freedom,' Platonov said at once. 'If he's as high as you say, we would do very much indeed.' Ryan didn't say a word for over a minute. The two men stared at each other as though over cards, as though they were gambling for everything each man owned – and as though Ryan knew that he held the lesser hand. Platonov matched the power of the American's stare, and was gratified to see that it was his power that prevailed.

'I'm flying to Moscow the end of the week, unless the story breaks before then, in which case I'm fucked. What I just told you, pal, it doesn't go through channels. The only person I'm sure it *isn't* is Gerasimov. It goes to the Chairman himself, direct to him, no intermediaries, or you risk losing the name.'

'And why am I supposed to believe you know it?' The Russian pressed his advantage, but carefully.

It was Jack's turn to smile. His hole card had turned out to be a good one. 'I don't know the *name*, but I know the data. With the four things that I know from CONDUCTOR – that's the code name – your troops can handle the rest. If your letter goes through channels, probably I don't get on the airplane. That's how far up the chain he is – if it's a he, but it probably is. How do I know you'll keep your word?'

'In the intelligence business one must keep one's promises,' Platonov assured him.

'Then tell your Chairman that I want to meet him if he can arrange it. Man to man. No bullshit.'

'The Chairman? The Chairman doesn't –'

'Then I'll make my own legal arrangements and take my chances. I'm not going to jail for treason either, if I can help it. That's the deal, Comrade Platonov,' Jack concluded. 'Have a nice drive home.'

Jack rose and walked away. Platonov did not follow. He looked around and found his own security man, who signaled that they had not been observed.

And he had his own decision to make. Was Ryan genuine? Cassius said so.

He had run Agent Cassius for three years. Peter Henderson's data had always checked out. They'd used him to track down and arrest a colonel in Strategic Rocket Forces who'd been working for CIA, had gotten priceless strategic and political intelligence, and even inside American analysis of that *Red October* business of the previous – no, it was two years now, wasn't it, right before Senator Donaldson had retired – and now that he worked in the GAO, he had the best of all possible worlds: direct access to classified defense data and all his political contacts on the Hill. Cassius had told them some time before that Ryan was

369

under investigation. At the time it had been merely a tidbit, no one had taken it seriously. The Americans were always investigating one another. It was their national sport. Then a second time he'd heard the same story, then the scene with Trent. Was it really possible . . .?

A leak high up in KGB, Platonov thought. There was a protocol, of course, for getting important data directly to the Chairman. The KGB allowed for any possibility. Once that message was sent, it would have to be followed up. Just the hint that CIA had an agent high in the KGB hierarchy . . . .

But that was only one consideration.

Once we set the hook, we will own Dr Ryan. Perhaps he is foolish enough to think that a one-time exchange of information for services is possible, that he will never again . . . more likely that he is so desperate that he does not care at the moment. What kind of information might we get from him?

Special assistant to the Deputy Director for Intelligence! Ryan must see nearly everything! To recruit so valuable an agent – that hadn't been done since Philby, and *that* was over fifty years ago!

But is it important enough to break the rules? Platonov asked himself as he finished off his drink. Not in living memory had the KGB committed an act of violence in the United States – there *was* a gentlemen's agreement on that. But what were rules against this sort of advantage? Perhaps an American or two might have an auto accident, or an unexpected heart attack. That would also have to be approved by the Chairman. Platonov would give his recommendation. It would be followed. He was sure of that.

The diplomat was a fastidious man. He wiped his face with the paper napkin, put all the trash in the paper drink cup, and deposited it in the nearest receptacle. He left nothing behind to suggest that he'd ever been there.

The Archer was sure that they were winning. On announcing his mission to his subordinates, the reaction could not have been better. Grim, amused smiles, sideways looks, nods. The most enthusiastic of all had been their new member, the former Major of the Afghan Army. In their tent, twenty kilometers inside Afghanistan, the plans had been put together in five tense hours.

The Archer looked down at phase one, already complete. Six trucks and three BTR-60 infantry carriers were in their hands. Some were damaged, but that was not unexpected. The dead soldiers of the puppet army were being stripped of their uniforms. Eleven survivors were being questioned. They would not join in this mission, of course, but if they proved to be reliable, they would be allowed to join allied guerrilla bands. For the others . . . .

The former Army officer recovered maps and radio codes. He knew all the procedures that the Russians had so assiduously taught to their Afghan 'brothers'.

There was a battalion base camp ten kilometers away, due north on the Shékábád road. The former Major contacted it on the radio, indicating that 'Sunflower' had repulsed the ambush with moderate losses and was heading in. This was approved by the battalion commander.

They loaded a few of the bodies aboard, still in their bloody uniforms. Trained former members of the Afghan Army manned the heavy machine guns on the BTR carriers as the column moved out, keeping proper tactical formation on the gravel road. The base camp was just on the far side of the river. Twenty minutes later they could see it. The bridge had long since been wrecked, but Russian engineers had dumped enough gravel to make a ford. The column halted at the guard post on the east side.

This was the tense part. The Major made the proper signal, and the guard post waved them through. One by one the vehicles moved across the river. The surface was frozen and the drivers had to follow a line of sticks across to keep from becoming trapped in the deep water that lay under the crackling ice. Another five hundred meters.

The base camp was on a small rise. It was surrounded by low-lying bunkers made of sandbags and logs. None were fully manned. The camp was well sited, with wide fields of fire in all directions, but they'd only man their weapons pits fully at night. Only a single company of troops was actually in the post, while the remainder were out patrolling the hills around the camp. Besides, the column was coming in at mealtime. The battalion motor pool was in sight.

The Archer was in the front of the lead truck. He wondered to himself why he trusted the defected Major so fully, but decided that this was not a good time for that particular worry.

The battalion commander came out of his bunker, his mouth working on some food as he watched the soldiers jump out of the trucks. He was waiting for the unit commander, and showed some annoyance as the side door on the BMP opened slowly, and a man in an officer's uniform appeared.

'Who the devil are you?'

'*Allahu akhbar!*' the Major screamed. His rifle cut down the questioner. The heavy machine guns on the infantry carriers ripped into the mass of men eating their noon meal while the Archer's men raced to the half-manned bunkers. It took ten minutes before all resistance ceased, but there was never a chance for the defenders, not with nearly a hundred armed men inside the camp. Twenty prisoners were taken. The only Russians in the post – two lieutenants and a communications sergeant – were killed out of hand and the rest were placed under guard as the Major's men ran to the motor pool.

They got two more BTRs there and four trucks. That would have to be enough. The rest they burned. They burned everything they couldn't carry. They took four mortars, half a dozen machine guns, and every spare uniform they could find. The rest of the camp was totally destroyed – especially the radios, which were first smashed with rifle butts, then burned. A small guard force was left behind with the prisoners, who would also be given the chance to join the *mudjaheddin* – or die for their loyalty to the infidel.

372

It was fifty kilometers to Kabul. The new, larger vehicle column ran north. More of the Archer's men linked up with it, hopping aboard the vehicles. His force now numbered two hundred men, dressed and equipped like regular soldiers of the Afghan Army, rolling north in Russian-built army vehicles.

Time was their most dangerous enemy. They reached the outskirts of Kabul ninety minutes later, and encountered the first of several checkpoints.

The Archer's skin crawled to be near so many Russian soldiers. When dusk came, the Russians returned to their laagers and bunkers, he knew, leaving the streets to the Afghans, but even the setting sun did not make him feel secure. The checks were more perfunctory than he expected, and the Major talked his way through all of them, using travel documents and code words from the base camp so recently extinguished. More to the point, their route of travel kept them away from the most secure parts of the city. In less than two hours the city was behind them, and they rolled forward under the friendly darkness.

They went until they began to run out of fuel. At this point the vehicles were rolled off the roads. A Westerner would have been surprised that the *mudjaheddin* were happy to leave their vehicles behind, even though it meant carrying weapons on their backs. Well rested, the guerrillas moved at once into the hills, heading north.

The day had held nothing but bad news, Gerasimov noted, as he stared at Colonel Vatutin. 'What do you mean, you cannot break him?'

'Comrade Chairman, our medical people advise me that both the sensory-deprivation procedure, or any form of physical abuse' – *torture* was no longer a word used at KGB headquarters – 'might kill the man. In view of your insistence on a confession, we must use . . . primitive interrogation methods. The subject is a difficult man. Mentally, he is far tougher than any of us expected,' Vatutin said as evenly as he could. He would have killed for a drink at the moment.

'All because you bungled the arrest!' Gerasimov observed coldly. 'I had high hopes for you, *Colonel*. I thought you were a man with a future. I thought you were ready for advancement. Was I mistaken, Comrade Colonel?' he inquired.

'My concern with this case is limited to exposing a traitor to the Motherland.' It required all of Vatutin's discipline not to flinch. 'I feel that I have already done this. We know that he has committed treason. We have the evidence –'

'Yazov will not accept it.'

'Counterintelligence is a KGB matter, not one for the Defense Ministry.'

'Perhaps you would be so kind as to explain that to the Party General Secretary,' Gerasimov said, letting his anger out a bit too far. 'Colonel Vatutin, I must have this confession.'

Gerasimov had hoped to score another intelligence coup today, but the FLASH report from America had invalidated it – worse still, Gerasimov had delivered the information a day before he'd learned that it was valueless. Agent Livia was apologetic, the report said, but the computer-program data so recently transmitted through Lieutenant Bisyarina was, unfortunately, obsolete. Something that might have helped to smooth the water between KGB and the Defense Ministry's darling new project was now gone.

He had to have a confession, and it had to be a confession that was not extracted by torture. Everyone knew that torture could yield anything that the questioners wanted, that most subjects would have enough incentive in their pain to say whatever was required of them. He needed something good enough to take to the Politburo itself, and the Politburo members no longer held KGB in so much fear they they would take Gerasimov's words at face value.

'Vatutin, I need it, and I need it soon. When can you deliver?'

'Using the methods to which we are now limited, no more than two weeks. We can deprive him of sleep. That takes time, more so since the elderly need less sleep than the young. He will gradually become disoriented and crack. Given what we have learned of this man, he will fight us with all of his courage – this is a brave man. But he is only a man. Two weeks,' Vatutin said, knowing that ten more days ought to be sufficient. Better to deliver early.

'Very well.' Gerasimov paused. It was time for encouragement. 'Comrade Colonel, objectively speaking you have handled the investigation well, despite the disappointment at the final phase. It is unreasonable to expect perfection in all things, and the political complications are not of your making. If you provide what is required, you will be properly rewarded. Carry on.'

'Thank you, Comrade Chairman.' Gerasimov watched him leave, then called for his car.

The Chairman of the KGB did not travel alone. His personal Zil – a handmade limousine that looked like an oversized American car of thirty years before – was followed by an even uglier Volga, full of bodyguards selected for their combat skills and absolute loyalty to the office of chairman. Gerasimov sat alone in the back, watching the buildings of Moscow flash by as the car was routed down the center lane of the wide avenues. Soon he was out of the city, heading into the forests where the Germans had been stopped in 1941.

Many of those captured – those who had survived typhus and poor food – had built the dachas. As much as the Russians still hated the Germans, the *nomenklatura* – the ruling class of this classless society – was addicted to German workmanship. Siemens electronics and Blaupunkt appliances were as much a part of their homes as the copies of *Pravda* and the uncensored 'White TASS' news. The frame dwellings in the pine forests west of Moscow were as well built as anything left behind by the czars. Gerasimov often wondered what had happened to the German soldiers who had labored to make them. Not that it mattered.

The official dacha of Academician Mikhail Petrovich Alexandrov was no different from the rest, two stories, its wood siding painted cream, and a steeply pitched roof that might have been equally at home in the Black Forest. The driveway was a twisty gravel path through the trees. Only one car was parked there. Alexandrov was a widower, and past the age when he might crave young female company. Gerasimov opened his own door, checking briefly to see that his security entourage was dispersing as usual into the trees. They paused only to pull cold-weather gear from the trunk of their car, thickly insulated white anoraks and heavy boots to keep their feet warm in the snow.

'Nikolay Borissovich!' Alexandrov got the door himself. The dacha had a couple who did the cooking and cleaning, but they knew when to stay out of the way. This was such a time. The academician took Gerasimov's coat and draped it on a peg by the door.

'Thank you, Mikhail Petrovich.'

'Tea?' Alexandrov gestured toward the table in the sitting room.

'It is cold out there,' Gerasimov admitted.

The two men sat on opposite sides of the table in old overstuffed chairs. Alexandrov enjoyed being a host – at least to his associates. He poured the tea, then dished out a small amount of white-cherry preserves. They drank their tea in the traditional way, first putting some of the sweetened cherries into their mouths, then letting the tea wash around them. It made conversation awkward, but it was Russian. More to the point, Alexandrov liked the old ways. As much as he was married to the ideals of Marxism, the Politburo's chief ideologue kept to the ways of his youth in the small things.

'What news?'

Gerasimov gestured annoyance. 'The spy Filitov is a tough old bird. It will take another week or two to get the confession.'

'You should shoot that Colonel of yours who –'

The KGB Chairman shook his head. 'No, no. One must be objective. Colonel Vatutin has done very well. He ought to have left the actual arrest to a younger man, but I told him that it was his case, and he doubtless took my instructions too literally. His handling of the rest of the case was nearly perfect.'

'You grow generous too soon, Kolya,' Alexandrov observed. 'How hard is it to surprise a seventy-year-old man?'

'Not him. The American spy was a good one – as one might expect. Good field officers have sharp instincts. If they were not so skilled, World Socialism would have been realized by now,' he added offhandedly. Alexandrov lived within his academic world, the Chairman knew, and had little understanding of how things worked in the real one. It was hard to respect a man like that, but not so hard to fear him.

The older man grunted. 'I suppose we can wait a week or two. It troubles me to do this while the American delegation is here –'

'It will be after they leave. If agreement is reached, we lose nothing.'

'It is madness to reduce our arms!' Alexandrov insisted. Mikhail Petrovich still thought nuclear weapons were like tanks and guns: the more, the better. Like most political theorists, he didn't bother learning facts.

'We will retain the newest and the best of our rockets,' Gerasimov explained patiently. 'More importantly, our Project Bright Star is progressing well. With what our own scientists have already accomplished, and what we are learning about the American program, in less than ten years we will have the ability to protect the *Rodina* against foreign attack.'

'You have good sources within the American effort?'

'Too good,' Gerasimov said, setting down his tea. 'It seems that some data we just received was sent out too soon. Part of the American computer instructions were sent to us before they were certified, and turned out to be faulty. An embarrassment, but if one must be embarrassed, better that it should result from being too effective than not effective enough.'

Alexandrov dismissed the subject with a wave of the hand. 'I spoke to Vaneyev last night.'

'And?'

377

'He is ours. He cannot bear the thought of that darling slut of a daughter in a labor camp – or worse. I explained what is required of him. It was very easy. Once you have the confession from the Filitov bastard, we will do everything at the same time. Better to accomplish everything at once.' The academician nodded to reinforce his words. He was the expert on political maneuvering.

'I am troubled by possible reactions from the West . . .' Gerasimov noted cautiously.

The old fox smiled into his tea. 'Narmonov will have a heart attack. He is of the proper age. Not a fatal one, of course, but enough to make him step aside. We will assure the West that his policies will continue – I can even live with the arms agreement if you insist.' Alexandrov paused. 'It does make sense to avoid alarming them unduly. All that concerns me is the primacy of the Party.'

'Naturally.' Gerasimov knew what was to follow, and leaned back to hear it yet again.

'If we don't stop Narmonov, the Party is doomed! The fool, casting away all we have worked for. Without the leadership of the Party, a *German* would be living in this house! Without Stalin to put steel in the people's backbone, where would we be, and Narmonov condemns our greatest hero – after Lenin,' the academician added quickly. 'This country needs a strong hand, *one* strong hand, not a thousand little ones! Our people understand that. Our people *want* that.'

Gerasimov nodded agreement, wondering why this doddering old fool always had to say the same thing. The Party didn't want one strong hand, much as Alexandrov denied the fact. The Party itself was composed of a thousand little, grabbing, grasping hands: the Central Committee members, the local *apparatchiki* who had paid their dues, mouthed their slogans, attended the weekly meetings until they were sick to death of everything the Party said, but still stayed on because that was the path to advancement, and advancement meant privilege. Advancement meant a car, and trips to Sochi . . . and Blaupunkt appliances.

All men had their blind spots, Gerasimov knew. Alexandrov's was that so few people really believed in the Party anymore. Gerasimov did not. The Party was what ran the country, however. The Party was what nurtured ambitions. Power had its own justification, and for him, the Party was the path to power. He'd spent all of his working life protecting the Party from those who wished to change the power equation. Now, as Chairman of the Party's own 'sword and shield', he was in the best possible position to take the Party's reins. Alexandrov would have been surprised, scandalized to learn that his young student saw power as his only goal, and had no plan other than *status quo ante*. The Soviet Union would plod along as before, secure behind its borders, seeking to spread its own form of government into whatever country offered the opportunity. There would be progress, partly from internal changes, partly from what could be obtained from the West, but not enough to raise expectations too much, or too rapidly, as Narmonov threatened to do. But best of all, Gerasimov would be the man with the reins. With the power of the KGB behind him, he need not fear for his security – certainly not after breaking the Defense Ministry. So he listened to Alexandrov's ranting about Party theory, nodding when appropriate. To an outsider it would look like the thousands of old pictures – nearly all of them fakes – of Stalin listening with rapt attention to the words of Lenin, and like Stalin, he would use the words to his own advantage. Gerasimov believed in Gerasimov.

18

Advantages

'But I just finished eating!' Misha said.

'Rubbish,' the jailor responded. He held out his watch. 'Look at the time, you foolish old man. Eat up, it'll be time for your interrogation soon.' The man bent forward. 'Why don't you tell them what they want to hear, Comrade?'

'I am not a traitor! I'm not!'

'As you wish. Eat hearty.' The cell door hit its frame with a metallic rattle.

'I am not a traitor,' Filitov said after the door closed. 'I'm not,' the microphone heard. 'I'm not.'

'We're getting there,' Vatutin said.

What was happening to Filitov was little different in net effect from what the doctor was trying to achieve in the sensory-deprivation tank. The prisoner was losing touch with reality, though much more slowly than the Vaneyeva woman had. His cell was in the interior of the building, denying the prisoner the march of day and night. The single bare light bulb never went off. After a few days Filitov lost all track of what time was. Next his bodily functions began to show some irregularity. Then they started altering the interval between meals. His body knew that something was wrong, but it sensed that so many things were wrong, and was so unsuccessful in dealing with the disorientation, that what happened to the prisoner was actually akin to mental illness. It was a classic technique, and it was a rare individual indeed who could withstand it for more than two weeks, and then it was generally discovered that the successful resister had depended on some outside register unknown to his interrogators, such as traffic or plumbing sounds, sounds that followed regular patterns. Gradually 'Two' had learned to isolate out all of these. The new block of special cells was sound-isolated from the rest of the world. Cooking was done on a floor above to eliminate smells. This part of Lefortovo reflected generations of clinical experience in the business of breaking the human spirit.

It was better than torture, Vatutin thought. Torture invariably affected the interrogators, too. That was the problem. Once a man – and in rare cases, a woman – became too good at it, that person's mind changed. The torturer would gradually go mad, resulting in unreliable interrogation results and a useless KGB officer who would then have to be replaced, and, occasionally, hospitalized. In the 1930s such officers had often been shot when their political masters realized what they had created, only to be replaced with new ones until interrogators looked for more creative, more intelligent methods. Better for everyone, Colonel Vatutin knew. The new techniques, even the abusive ones, inflicted no permanent physical harm. Now it almost seemed that they were treating the mental illnesses that they inflicted, and the physicians who managed the affair for the KGB could now confidently observe that treason against the Motherland was itself a symptom of a grave personality disorder, something that demanded decisive treatment. It made everyone feel better about the job. While one could feel guilty inflicting pain on a brave enemy, one need only feel good about helping to cure a sick mind.

This one is sicker than most, Vatutin thought wryly. He was a touch too cynical to believe all the folderol that the new crop of 'Two' people got today in Training-and-Orientation. He remembered the nostalgic stories of the men who'd trained him almost thirty years before – the good old days under Beriya . . . Though his skin had crawled to hear those madmen speak, at least they were honest about what they did. Though he was grateful that he had not become like them, he didn't delude himself by believing that Filitov was mentally ill. He was, in fact, a courageous man who had chosen of his own free will to betray his country. An evil man, to be sure, because he had violated the rules of his parent society, he was a worthy adversary for all that. Vatutin looked into the fiber-optic tube that ran into the ceiling of Filitov's cell, watching him as he listened to the sound pickup from the microphone.

How long have you been working for the Americans? Since your family died? That long? Nearly thirty years . . . is it possible? the Colonel of the Second Chief Directorate wondered. It was an awesome amount of time. Kim Philby hadn't lasted nearly so long. Richard Sorge's career, though brilliant, had been a brief one.

But it made sense. There was also homage to pay to Oleg Penkovskiy, the treasonous GRU Colonel whose capture was one of Two's greatest cases – but now poisoned by the thought that Penkovskiy had used his own death to elevate the career of an even greater spy . . . whom he himself had probably recruited. That was courage, Vatutin told himself. *Why must such virtue be invested in treason!* he raged at himself. *Why can they not love their Motherland as I do?* The Colonel shook his head. Marxism demanded objectivity of its adherents, but this was too much. There was always the danger of identifying too closely with one's subject. He rarely had the problem, but then he had never handled a case like this one. Three times Hero of the Soviet Union! A genuine national icon whose face had been on the covers of magazines and books. Could we ever let it be known what he had done? How would the Soviet people react to the knowledge that Old Misha, Hero of Stalingrad, one of the most courageous warriors of the Red Army . . . had turned traitor to the *Rodina*? The effect on national morale was something to be considered.

Not my problem, he told himself. He watched the old man through the hi-tech peephole. Filitov was trying to eat his food, not quite believing that it was time to eat, but not knowing that his breakfast – all meals were the same, for obvious reasons – had been only ninety minutes before.

Vatutin stood and stretched to ease the ache in his back. A side effect of this technique was the way it disrupted the lives of the interrogators themselves. His own schedule was wrecked. It was just past midnight, and he'd gotten a bare seven hours of sleep in the past thirty-six. But at least he knew the time, and the day, and the season. Filitov, he was sure, did not. He bent back down to see his subject finishing off his bowl of kasha.

'Get him,' Colonel Klementi Vladimirovich Vatutin ordered. He walked into the washroom to splash some cold water on his face. He peered into the mirror and decided that he didn't need to shave. Next he made sure that his uniform was perfectly turned out. The one constant factor in the prisoner's disrupted world had to be the face and image of his interrogator. Vatutin even practiced his look in the mirror: proud, arrogant, but also compassionate. He was not ashamed of what he saw. That is a professional, he told himself of the reflection in the mirror. Not a barbarian, not a degenerate, but only a skilled man doing a difficult, necessary job.

Vatutin was seated in the interrogation room, as always, when the prisoner came in. He invariably appeared to be doing something when the door opened, and his head always had to come up in semisurprise as though to say, *Oh, is it time for you again?* He closed the folder before him and placed it in his briefcase as Filitov sat in the chair opposite his. That was good, Vatutin noted without looking. The subject doesn't have to be told what he must do. His mind was fixing upon the only reality he had: Vatutin.

'I hope you slept well,' he told Filitov.

'Well enough,' was the answer. The old man's eyes were clouded. The blue no longer had the luster that Vatutin had admired in their first session.

'You are being properly fed, I trust?'

'I have eaten better.' A weary smile, still some defiance and pride behind it, but not as much as its wearer thought. 'But I have also eaten worse.'

Vatutin dispassionately gauged the strength in his prisoner; it had diminished. *You know*, the Colonel thought, *you know that you must lose. You know that it is only a matter of time. I can see it,* he said with his eyes, looking for and finding weakness under his stare. Filitov was trying not to wilt under the strain, but the edges were frayed, and something else was coming loose as Vatutin watched. *You know you're losing, Filitov.*

What is the point, Misha? part of him asked. *He has time – he* controls *time. He'll use all he needs to break you. He's winning. You know that,* despair told him.

Tell me, Comrade Captain, why do you ask yourself such foolish things? Why do you need to explain to yourself why you are a man? asked a familiar voice. *All the way from Brest-Litovsk to Vyasma we knew we were losing, but I never quit, and neither did you. If you can defy the German Army, certainly you can defy this city-soft slug of a chekist!*

Thank you, Romanov.

How did you ever get on without me, my Captain? the voice chuckled. *For all your intelligence, you can be a most foolish man.*

Vatutin saw that something had changed. The eyes blinked clear, and the weary old back straightened.

What is sustaining you? Hate? Do you so detest the State for what happened to your family . . . or is it something else entirely . . .?

'Tell me,' Vatutin said. 'Tell me why you hate the Motherland.'

'I do not,' Filitov replied. 'I have killed for the Motherland. I have bled for the Motherland. I have *burned* for the Motherland. But I did not do these things for the likes of you.' For all his weakness, the defiance blazed in his eyes like a flame. Vatutin was unmoved.

I was close, but something changed. If I can find what that is, Filitov, I will have you! Something told Vatutin that he already had what he needed. The trick was to identify it.

The interrogation continued. Though Filitov would successfully resist this time, and the next time, and even the time after that, Vatutin was drawing down on the man's physical and emotional energy. Both knew it. It was just a matter of time. But on one issue both men were wrong. Both thought that Vatutin controlled time, even though time is man's final master.

Gerasimov was surprised by the new FLASH dispatch from America, this one from Platonov. It arrived by cable, alerting him to an Eyes-Only-Chairman message en route in the diplomatic pouch. That was truly unusual. The KGB, more than other foreign-intelligence agencies, still depended on one-time-pad cipher systems. These were unbreakable, even in a theoretical sense, unless the code sequence itself were compromised. It was slow, but it was sure, and the KGB wanted 'sure'. Beyond that level of transmission, however, was another protocol. For each major station, there was a special cipher. It didn't even have a name, but ran directly from the *rezident* to the Chairman. Platonov was more important than even CIA suspected. He was the *rezident* for Washington, the chief of station.

When the dispatch arrived, it was brought directly to Gerasimov's office. His personal code clerk, a captain with impeccable credentials, was not called. The Chairman deciphered the first sentence himself, to learn that this was a mole warning. The KGB did not have a stock term for a traitor within its own ranks, but the higher ranks knew the Western word.

The dispatch was a lengthy one and took Gerasimov fully an hour to decode, cursing all the while at his clumsiness as he deciphered the random transpositions in the thirty-three-letter Russian alphabet.

An agent-in-place inside KGB? Gerasimov wondered. *How high?* He summoned his personal secretary and ordered the files on Agent Cassius, and Ryan, I. P., of CIA. As with all such orders, it didn't take long. He set Cassius aside for the moment and opened the file on Ryan.

There was a six-page biographical sketch, updated only six months previously, plus original newspaper clippings and translations. He didn't need the latter. Gerasimov spoke acceptable though accented English. Age thirty-five, he saw, with credentials in the business world, academia, and the intelligence community. He'd advanced rapidly within CIA. Special liaison officer to London. His first shortform evaluation at Dzerzhinskiy Square had been colored by some analyst's political views, Gerasimov saw. A rich, soft dilettante. No, that was not right. He'd advanced too rapidly for that, unless he had political influence that appeared absent from the profile. Probably a bright man – an author, Gerasimov saw, noting that there were copies of two of his books in Moscow. Certainly a proud one, accustomed to comfort and privilege.

So you broke American money-exchange laws, did you? The thought came easily to the KGB Chairman. Corruption was the way to wealth and power in any society. Ryan had his flaw, as did all men. Gerasimov knew that his own flaw was a lust for power, but he deemed the desire for anything less the mark of a fool. He turned back to Platonov's dispatch.

'Evaluation,' the message concluded. 'The subject is motivated neither by ideological nor by monetary consider-ations, but by anger and ego. He has a genuine fear of prison, but more of the personal disgrace. I. P. Ryan probably has the information which he claims. If CIA does have a highly placed mole in Moscow Center, it is likely that Ryan has seen data from him, though not the name or face. The data should be sufficient to identify the leak.

'Recommendation: The offer should be accepted for two reasons. First, to identify the American spy. Second, to make use of Ryan in the future. The unique opportunity offered has two faces. If we eliminate witnesses against the subject, he is in our debt. If this action is discovered, it can be blamed on CIA, and the resulting inquiries will damage the American intelligence service severely.'

'Hmm,' Gerasimov murmured to himself as he set the file aside.

Agent Cassius's file was far thicker. He was on his way to becoming one of KGB's best sources in Washington. Gerasimov had already read this one several times, and merely skimmed until he reached the most recent information. Two months earlier, Ryan had been investigated, details unknown – Cassius had reported it as unsubstantiated gossip. That was a point in its favor, the Chairman thought. It also disconnected Ryan's overtures from anything else that had developed recently . . . .

Filitov?

What if the highly placed agent whom Ryan could identify was the one we just arrested? Gerasimov wondered.

No. Ryan was himself sufficently high in CIA that he would not confuse one ministry with another. The only bad news was that a leak high in KGB wasn't something Gerasimov needed at the moment. Bad enough that it existed at all, but to let the word get outside the building . . . That could be a disaster. *If we launched a real investigation, word will get out. If we don't find the spy in our own midst . . . and if he's placed as highly as this Ryan says . . . what if CIA discovered what Alexandrov and I . . .?*

What would they do?

What if this . . .?

Gerasimov smiled and looked out the window. He'd miss this place. He'd miss the game. Every fact had at least three sides, and every thought had six. No, if he were to believe that, then he had to believe that Cassius was under CIA control, and that this had all been planned before Filitov had been arrested. That was plainly impossible.

The Chairman of the Committee for State Security checked his calendar to see when the Americans were coming over. There would be more social affairs this time. If the Americans had really decided to put their Star Wars systems on the table – it would make General Secretary Narmonov look good, but how many Politburo votes would that sway? *Not many, so long as I can keep Alexandrov's obstinacy in control. And if I can show that I've recruited an agent of our own that high in CIA . . . if I can predict that the Americans will trade away their defense programs, then I can steal a march on Narmonov's peace initiative myself . . . .*

The decision was made.

But Gerasimov was not an impulsive man. He sent a signal to Platonov to verify some details through Agent Cassius. This signal he could send via satellite.

That signal arrived in Washington an hour later. It was duly copied from the Soviet Raduga-19 communications bird both by the Soviet Embassy and by the American National Security Agency, which put it on a computer tape along with thousands of other Russian signals that the Agency worked round the clock to decipher.

It was easier for the Soviets. The signal was taken to a secure section of the embassy, where a KGB lieutenant converted the scrambled letters into clear text. Then it was locked up in a guarded safe until Platonov arrived in the morning.

That happened at 6:30. The usual newspapers were on his desk. The American press was very useful to the KGB, he thought. The idea of a free press was so alien to him that he never even considered its true function. But other things came first. The night-watch officer came in at 6:45 and briefed him on the events of the previous night, and also delivered messages from Moscow, where it was already after lunch. At the top of the message list was a notice of an eyes-only-*rezident*. Platonov knew what that had to be, and walked to the safe at once. The young KGB officer who guarded this part of the embassy checked Platonov's ID scrupulously – his predecessor had lost his job by being so bold as to assume that he knew Platonov by sight after a mere nine months. The message, properly labeled in a sealed envelope, was in its proper cubbyhole, and Platonov tucked it in his pocket before closing and locking the door.

The KGB's Washington station was larger than that of CIA in Moscow, though not large enough to suit Platonov, since the number of people in the mission had been reduced to numerical equivalence with the American Embassy staff in the Soviet Union, something the Americans had taken years to do. He usually summoned his section chiefs at 7:30 for their morning conference, but today he called one of his officers early.

'Good morning, Comrade Colonel,' the man said correctly. The KGB is not known for its pleasantries.

'I need you to get some information from Cassius on this Ryan business. It is imperative that we confirm his current legal difficulties as quickly as possible. That means today if you can manage it.'

'Today?' the man asked in some discomfort as he took the written instructions. 'There is risk in moving so rapidly.'

'The Chairman is aware of that,' Platonov observed dryly.

'Today,' the man nodded.

The *rezident* smiled inwardly as his man left. That was as much emotion as he'd shown in a month. This one had a real future.

'There's Butch,' an FBI agent observed as the man came out of the embassy compound. They knew his real name, of course, but the first agent who'd shadowed him had noted that he looked like a Butch, and the name had stuck. His normal morning routine was ostensibly to unlock a few embassy offices, then to run errands before the senior diplomatic personnel appeared at nine. That involved catching breakfast at a nearby coffee shop, buying several newspapers and magazines . . . and frequently leaving a mark or two in one of several places. As with most counterintelligence operations, the really hard part was getting the first break. After that it was straight police work. They'd gotten the first break on Butch eighteen months before.

He walked the four blocks to the shop, well dressed for the cold – he probably found Washington winters pretty mild, they all agreed – and turned into the place right on schedule. As with most coffee shops, this one had a regular trade. Three of them were FBI agents. One was dressed like a businesswoman, always reading her *Wall Street Journal* by herself in a corner booth. Two wore the toolbelts of carpenters, and swaggered to the counter either before or after Butch entered. Today they were waiting for him. They were not always there, of course. The woman, Special Agent Hazel Loomis, coordinated her schedule with a real business, careful to miss work holidays. It was a risk, but a close surveillance, no matter how carefully planned, could not be too regular. Similarly, they appeared at the café on days when they knew Butch was away, never altering their routine to show that their interest was in their subject.

Agent Loomis noted his arrival time on the margin of an article – she was always scribbling on the paper – and the carpenters watched him in the mirrored wall behind the counter as they savaged their way through their hash-browns and traded a few boisterous jokes. As usual, Butch had gotten four different papers from a newsstand right outside the coffee shop. The magazines he got all hit the stands on Tuesdays. The waitress poured his coffee without being asked. Butch lit his customary cigarette – an American Marlboro, the favorite of the Russians – and drank his first cup of coffee as he scanned the first page of the *Washington Post*, which was *his* usual paper.

Refills were free here, and his arrived on schedule. He took a scant six minutes, which was about right, everyone noted. Finished, he picked up his papers and left some money on the table. When he moved away from the plate, they could all see that he'd crumpled his paper napkin to a ball and set it in the saucer next to the empty coffee cup.

Business, Loomis noted at once. Butch took his bill to the register at the end of the counter, paid it, and left. He was good, Loomis noted yet again. She knew where and how he made the drop, but still she rarely caught him planting it.

Another regular came in. He was a cabdriver who usually got a cup of coffee before beginning his day, and sat alone at the end of the counter. He opened his paper to the sports page, looking around the café as he usually did. He could see the napkin on the saucer. He wasn't quite as good as Butch. Setting the paper in his lap, he reached under the counter and retrieved the message, tucking it in the Style section.

After that, it was pretty easy. Loomis paid her bill and left, hopping into her Ford Escort and driving to the Watergate apartments. She had a key to Henderson's apartment.

'You're getting a message today from Butch,' she told Agent Cassius.

'Okay.' Henderson looked up from his breakfast. He didn't at all enjoy having this girl 'running' him as a double agent. He especially didn't like the fact that she was on the case because of her looks, that the 'cover' for their association was a supposed affair which, of course, was pure fiction. For all her sweetness, her syrupy Southern accent – and her stunning good looks! he grumped – Henderson knew all too well that Loomis viewed him as half a step above a microbe. 'Just remember,' she'd told him once, 'there's a room waiting for you.' She was referring to the United States Penitentiary – not 'correctional facility' – at Marion, Illinois, the one that had replaced Alcatraz as the home of the worst offenders. No place for a Harvard man. But she'd only done that once, and otherwise treated him politely, even occasionally grabbing his arm in public. That only made it worse.

'You want some good news?' Loomis asked.

'Sure.'

'If this one goes through the way we hope, you might be clear. All the way out.' She'd never said that before.

'What gives?' Agent Cassius asked with interest.

'There's a CIA officer named Ryan –'

'Yeah, I heard the SEC's checking him out – well, they did, a few months back. You let me tell the Russians about that . . . .'

'He's dirty. Broke the rules, made half a million dollars on insider information, and there's a grand jury meeting in two weeks that's going to burn his ass, big-time.' Her profanity was all the more vivid from the sweet, Southern-Belle smile. 'The Agency's going to hang him out to dry. No help from anybody. Ritter hates his guts. You don't know why, but you heard it from Senator Fredenburg's aide. You get the impression that he's a sacrificial goat for something that went wrong, but you don't know what. Something a few months back in Central Europe, maybe, but that's all you heard. Some of it you tell right off. Some you make them wait till this afternoon. One more thing – you've heard a rumor that SDI may actually be on the table. You think it's bad information, but you heard a senator say something about it. Got it?'

'Yeah.' Henderson nodded.

'Okay.' Loomis walked off to the bathroom. Butch's favorite coffee shop was too greasy for her system.

Henderson went to his bedroom and selected a tie. *Out?* he wondered as he knotted it partway, then changed his mind. If that were true – he had to admit that she'd never lied to him. *Treated me like scum, but never lied to me*, he thought. *Then I can get out . . .?* Then what? he asked himself. *Does it matter?*

It mattered, but it mattered more that he'd get out.

'I like the red one better,' Loomis observed from the door. She smiled sweetly. 'A "power" tie for today, I think.'

Henderson dutifully reached for the red one. It never occurred to him to object. 'Can you tell me . . .?'

'I don't know – and you know better. But they wouldn't let me say this unless everybody figured that you paid some back, Mr Henderson.'

'Can't you call me Peter, just once?' he asked.

'My father was the twenty-ninth pilot shot down over

North Vietnam. They got him alive – there were pictures of him, alive – but he never came out.'

'I didn't know.'

She spoke as evenly as though discussing the weather. 'You didn't know a lot of things, Mr Henderson. They won't let me fly airplanes like Daddy did, but in the Bureau I make life as hard on the bastards as I can. They let me do that. I just hope that it hurts 'em like they've hurt me.' She smiled again. 'That's not very professional, is it?'

'I'm sorry. I'm afraid I don't know what else to say.'

'Sure you do. You'll tell your contact what I told you to say.' She tossed him a miniature tape recorder. It had a special computerized timer and an antitamper device. While in the taxicab, he'd be under intermittent surveillance. If he tried to warn his contact in any way, there was a chance – how great or small he did not know – that he'd be detected. They didn't like him and they didn't trust him. He knew that he'd never earn affection or trust, but Henderson would settle for getting out.

He left his apartment a few minutes later and walked downstairs. There was the usual number of cabs circulating about. He didn't gesture, but waited for one to come to him. They didn't start talking until it pulled into the traffic on Virginia Avenue.

The cab took him to the General Accounting Office headquarters on G Street, Northwest. Inside the building, he handed the tape recorder over to another FBI agent. Henderson suspected that it was a radio as well, though actually it was not. The recorder went to the Hoover Building. Loomis was waiting when it got there. The tape was rewound and played.

'CIA got it right for once,' she observed to her supervisor. Someone even more senior was here. This was more important than she'd thought, Loomis knew at once.

'It figures. A source like Ryan doesn't come along real often. Henderson got his lines down pretty good.'

'I told him that this may be his ticket out.' Her voice said more than that.

'You don't approve?' the Assistant Director asked. He ran all of the FBI's counterintel operations.

'He hasn't paid enough, not for what he did.'

'Miss Loomis, after this is all over, I'll explain to you why you're wrong. Put that aside, okay? You've done a beautiful job handling this case. Don't blow it now.'

'What'll happen to him?' she asked.

'The usual, into the witness-protection program. He may end up running the Wendy's in Billings, Montana, for all I know.' The AD shrugged. 'You're getting promoted and sent to the New York Field Office. We have another one we think you're ready for. There's a diplomat attached to the UN who needs a good handler.'

'Okay.' The smile this time was not forced.

'They bit. They bit hard,' Ritter told Ryan. 'I just hope you're up to it, sonny boy.'

'No danger involved.' Jack spread his hands. 'This ought to be real civilized.'

Only the parts you know about. 'Ryan, you are still an amateur so far as field ops are concerned. Remember that.'

'I have to be for this to work,' Jack pointed out.

'Those whom the gods would destroy, they first make proud,' the DDO said.

'That's not the way Sophocles said it,' Jack grinned.

'My way's better. I even had a sign put up at the Farm that quotes me.'

Ryan's idea for the mission had been a simple one – too simple, and Ritter's people had refined it over a period of ten hours into a real operation. Simple in concept, it would have its complications. They all did, but Ritter didn't like that fact.

Bart Mancuso had long since gotten used to the idea that sleeping wasn't included in the list of things that submarine skippers were expected to do, but what he especially hated was a knock on the door fifteen minutes after he *was* able to lie down.

'Come!' *And die!* he didn't say.

'FLASH traffic, eyes-only-captain,' the Lieutenant said apologetically.

'It better be good!' Mancuso snarled, snapping the covers off the bunk. He walked aft in his skivvies to the communications room, to port and just aft of the attack center. Ten minutes later he emerged and handed a slip of paper to the navigator.

'I want to be there in ten hours.'

'No sweat, Cap'n.'

'The next person who bothers me, it better be a grave national emergency!' He walked forward, barefoot on the tile deck.

'Message delivered,' Henderson told Loomis over dinner.

'Anything else?' *Candlelight and all*, she thought.

'Just wanted to confirm. They didn't want new info, just to back up what they already had from some different sources. At least, that's the way I read it. I have another delivery for them.'

'Which one's that?'

'The new battlefield air-defense report. I never could understand why they bother. They can read it in *Aviation Week* before the end of the month anyway.'

'Let's not blow the routine now, Mr Henderson.'

This time the message could be handled as routine intelligence traffic. It would be flagged to the Chairman's attention because it was 'personal' information on a senior enemy intelligence official. Gerasimov was known in the higher echelons of KGB to be a man interested as much in Western gossip as Russian.

It was waiting when he arrived the next morning. The KGB Chairman hated the eight-hour time differential between Moscow and Washington – it made things so damned inconvenient! For Moscow Center to order any immediate action automatically risked having his field officers cue the Americans as to who they were. As a result, few real 'immediate-action' signals were ever sent out, and it offended the KGB Chairman that his personal power could be undone by something as prosaic as longitudinal lines.

'Subject P,' the dispatch began, the English 'R' being a 'P' in the Cyrillic alphabet, 'is now the target of a secret criminal investigation as part of a nonintelligence matter. It is suspected, however, that interest in P is politically based, probably an effort on the part of progressive congressional elements to damage CIA because of an unknown operational failure – possibly involving Central Europe, but this is not RPT not confirmed. P's criminal disgrace will be damaging to higher CIA officials due to his placement. This station grades the intelligence reliability of the case as A. Three independent sources now confirm the allegations dispatched in my 88(B)531-C/EOC. Full details to follow via pouch. Station recommends pursuing. *Rezident* Washington. Ends.'

Gerasimov tucked the report away in his desk.

'Well,' the Chairman murmured to himself. He checked his watch. He had to be at the regular Thursday-morning Politburo meeting in two hours. How would it go? One thing he knew: it would be an interesting one. He planned to introduce a new variant on his game – the Power Game.

His daily operational briefing was always a little longer on Thursdays. It never hurt to drop a few harmless tidbits at the meetings. His fellow Politburo members were all men to whom conspiracy came as easily as breathing, and there hadn't been a government anywhere in the last century whose senior members did not enjoy hearing about covert operations. Gerasimov made a few notes, careful to choose only things that he could discuss without compromising important cases. His car came around at the appointed time, as always accompanied by a lead car of bodyguards, and sped off to the Kremlin.

Gerasimov was never the first to arrive, and never the last. This time he walked in just behind the Defense Minister.

'Good morning, Dmitri Timofeyevich,' the Chairman said without a smile, but cordially enough for all that.

'And to you, Comrade Chairman,' Yazov said warily. Both men took their seats. Yazov had more than one reason to be wary. In addition to the fact that Filitov was hanging over his head like a sword out of myth, he was not a full voting member of the Supreme Soviet Council. Gerasimov was. That gave KGB more political power than Defense, but the only times in recent history that the Defense Minister had had a vote in this room, he'd been a Party man first – like Ustinov had been. Yazov was a soldier first. A loyal Party member for all that, his uniform was not the costume it had been for Ustinov. Yazov would never have a vote at this table.

Andrey Il'ych Narmonov came into the room with his usual vigor. Of all the Politburo members, only the KGB Chairman was younger than he, and Narmonov felt the need to show bustling energy whenever he appeared before the older men who were arrayed around 'his' conference table. The strain and stress of his job were telling on him. Everyone could see it. The black bush of hair was beginning to gray rapidly, and it also seemed that his hairline was receding. But that was hardly unusual for a man in his fifties. He gestured for everyone to sit.

'Good morning, Comrades,' Narmonov said in a businesslike voice. 'The initial discussion will concern the arrival of the American arms-negotiations team.'

'I have good news to report,' Gerasimov said at once.

'Indeed?' Alexandrov asked before the General Secretary could, staking out his own position.

'We have information that suggests that the Americans are willing in principle to place their strategic-defense program on the table,' the KGB Chairman reported. 'We do not know what concessions they will demand for this, nor the extent of the concessions in their program that they are willing to make, but this is nevertheless a change in the American posture.'

'I find that difficult to believe,' Yazov spoke up. 'Their

program is well along – as you yourself told me last week, Nikolay Borissovich.'

'There are some political dissenters within the American government, and possibly a power struggle under way within CIA itself at the moment, we have just learned. In any case, that is our information, and we regard it to be fairly reliable.'

'That is quite a surprise.' Heads turned to where the Foreign Minister was sitting. He looked skeptical. 'The Americans have been totally adamant on this point. You say "fairly reliable", but not totally so?'

'The source is highly placed, but the information has not been adequately confirmed as yet. We will know more by the weekend.'

Heads nodded around the table. The American delegation would arrive noon Saturday, and negotiations would not begin until Monday. The Americans would be given thirty-six hours to overcome their jet lag, during which there would be a welcoming dinner at the Academy of Sciences Hotel, and little else.

'Such information is obviously a matter of great interest to my negotiating team, but I find it most surprising, particularly in view of the briefings we've been given here on our Bright Star program, and their counterpart to it.'

'There is reason to believe that the Americans have learned of Bright Star,' Gerasimov replied smoothly. 'Perhaps they have found our progress sobering.'

'Bright Star penetrated?' another member asked. 'How?'

'We're not sure. We're working on it,' Gerasimov replied, careful not to look in Yazov's direction. *Your move, Comrade Defense Minister.*

'So the Americans might really be more interested in shutting our program down than in curtailing theirs,' Alexandrov observed.

'And they think that our efforts have been the reverse of that.' The Foreign Minister grunted. 'It would be nice for me to be able to tell my people what the real issues are!'

'Marshal Yazov?' Narmonov said. He didn't know that he was putting his own man on the spot.

Until now, Gerasimov hadn't been sure about Yazov, about whether he might not feel safe taking his political vulnerability over the Filitov matter to his master. This would give him the answer. *Yazov was afraid of the possibility – CERTAINTY, he corrected himself, Yazov has to know that by now – that we can disgrace him. He's also afraid that Narmonov won't risk his own position to save him. So have I co-opted both Yazov and Vaneyev? If so, I wonder if it might be worth keeping Yazov on after I replace the General Secretary . . . Your decision, Yazov . . . .*

'We have overcome the problem of laser power output. The remaining problem is in computer control. Here we are far behind American techniques due to the superiority of their computer industry. Only last week, Comrade Gerasimov furnished us with some of the American control program, but we had not even begun to examine it when we learned that the program was itself overtaken by events.

'I do not mean this to be criticism of the KGB, of course –'

Yes! In that moment Gerasimov was sure. *He's making his own overture to me. And the best part – no other man in the room, not even Alexandrov, understands what just happened.*

'– actually, it illustrates the technical problem rather clearly. But it is only a technical problem, Comrades. This one, too, can be overcome. My opinion is that we are ahead of the Americans. If they know this, they will be fearful of it. Our negotiating position to this point has been to object to space-based programs only, never ground-based, since we have known all along that our ground-based systems have greater promise than their American counterparts. Possibly the change in the American position confirms this. If so, I would recommend against trading Bright Star for anything.'

'That is a defensible opinion,' Gerasimov commented after a moment. 'Dmitri Timofeyevich has raised a thoughtful issue here.' Heads nodded around the table – knowingly, they all thought, but more wrongly than any would dare guess – as the Chairman of the Committee for State Security and the Minister of Defense consummated their bargain with nothing more than a glance and a raised eyebrow.

Gerasimov turned back to the head of the table as the discussion went on around him. General Secretary Narmonov watched the debate with interest, making a few notes, not noticing the gaze of his KGB Chairman.

I wonder if that chair is more comfortable than mine.

19

Travelers

Even the 89th Military Airlift Wing worried about security, Ryan was glad to see. The sentries who guarded the 'President's Wing' at Andrews Air Force Base carried loaded rifles and wore serious looks to impress the 'Distinguished Visitors' – the US Air Force eschews the term Very Important Persons. The combination of armed troops and the usual airport rigamarole made it certain that no one would hijack the airplane and take it to . . . Moscow. They had a flight crew to accomplish that.

Ryan always had the same thought before flying. As he waited to pass through the doorway-shaped magneto-meter, he imagined that someone had engraved on the lintel: ABANDON ALL HOPE YE WHO ENTER HERE. He'd just about overcome his terror of flying; his anxiety now was of something else entirely, he told himself. It didn't work. Fears are additive, not parallel, he discovered as he walked out of the building.

They were taking the same plane as the last time. The tail number was 86971. It was a 707 that had rolled out of Boeing's Seattle plant in 1958 and had been converted to the VC-137 configuration. More comfortable than the VC-135, it also had windows. If there was anything Ryan hated, it was being aboard a windowless aircraft. There was no level jetway to traverse into the bird. Everyone climbed up an old-fashioned wheeled stairway. Once inside, the plane was a curious mix of the commonplace and the unique. The forward washroom was in the usual place, just across from the front door, but aft of that was the communications console that gave the plane instantaneous, secure satellite-radio links with anyplace in the world. Next came the relatively comfortable crew accommodations, and then the galley. Food aboard the airplane was pretty good. Ryan's seat was in the almost-DV area, on one of the two couches set on either side of the fuselage, just forward of the six-seat space for the really important folks. Aft of that was the five-across seating for reporters, Secret Service, and other people considered less distinguished by whoever made such decisions. It was mainly empty for this trip, though some junior members of the delegation would be back there, able to stretch out a bit for a change.

The only really bad thing about the VC-137 was its limited range. It couldn't one-hop all the way to Moscow, and usually stopped off for refueling at Shannon before making the final leg. The President's aircraft – actually there were *two* Air Force Ones – were based on the longer-range 707-320, and would soon be replaced with ultramodern 747s. The Air Force was looking forward to having a presidential aircraft that was younger than most of its flight crew. So was Ryan. This one had rolled out of the factory door when he'd been in second grade, and it struck him as odd that it should be so. But what should have happened? he wondered. Should his father have taken him to Seattle, pointed to that airplane and said, *See, you'll fly to Russia on that one someday . . .?*

I wonder how you predict fate? I wonder how you predict the future . . . At first playful, in a moment the thought chilled him.

Your business is *predicting the future, but what makes you think that you can really do it? What have you guessed wrong on this time, Jack?*

Goddamn it! he raged at himself. *Every time I get on a fucking airplane . . .* He strapped himself in, facing across the airplane some State Department technical expert who loved to fly.

The engines started a minute later, and presently the airplane started to roll. The announcements over the intercom weren't very different from that on an airliner, just enough to let you know that the ownership of the plane was not corporate. Jack had already deduced that. The stewardess had a mustache. It was something to chuckle about as the aircraft taxied to the end of runway One-Left.

The winds were northerly, and the VC-137 took off into them, turning right a minute after it lifted off. Jack turned, too, looking down at US Route 50. It was the road that led to his home in Annapolis. He lost sight of it as the aircraft entered the clouds. The impersonal white veil had often seemed a beautiful curtain, but now . . . but now it just meant that he couldn't see the way home. Well, there wasn't much he could do about that. Ryan had the couch to himself, and decided to take advantage of the fact. He kicked off his shoes and stretched out for a nap. One thing he'd need would be rest. He was sure of that.

Dallas had surfaced at the appointed time and place, then been told of a hitch in the plans. Now she surfaced again. Mancuso was the first one up the ladder to the control station atop the sail, followed by a junior officer and a pair of lookouts. Already the periscope was up, scanning the surface for traffic, of course. The night was calm and clear, the sort of sky you get only at sea, ablaze with stars, like gemstones on a velvet sheet.

'Bridge, conn.'

Mancuso pressed the button. 'Bridge, aye.'

'ESM reports an airborne radar transmitter bearing one-four-zero, bearing appears steady.'

'Very well.' The Captain turned. 'You can flip on the running lights.'

'All clear starboard,' one lookout said.

'All clear port,' echoed the other.

'ESM reports contact is still steady on one-four-zero. Signal strength is increasing.'

'Possible aircraft fine on the port bow!' a lookout called.

Mancuso raised his binoculars to his eyes and started searching the blackness. If it was here already, it didn't have his running lights on . . . but then he saw a handful of stars disappear, occulted by something . . . .

'I got him. Good eye, Everly! Oh, there go his flying lights.'

'Bridge, conn, we have a radio message coming in.'

'Patch it,' Mancuso replied at once.

'Done, sir.'

'Echo-Golf-Nine, this is Alfa-Whiskey-Five, over.'

'Alfa-Whiskey-Five, this is Echo-Golf-Nine. I read you loud and clear. Authenticate, over.'

'Bravo-Delta-Hotel, over.'

'Roger, thank you. We are standing by. Wind is calm. Sea is flat.' Mancuso reached down and flipped on the lights for the control station instruments. Not actually needed at the moment – the Attack Center still had the conn – they'd give the approaching helicopter a target.

They heard it a moment later, first the flutter of the rotor blades, then the whine of the turboshaft engines. Less than a minute later they could feel the downdraft as the helicopter circled twice overhead for the pilot to orient himself. Mancuso wondered if he'd turn on his landing lights . . . or hot-dog it.

He hot-dogged it, or more properly, he treated it as what it was, a covert personnel transfer: a 'combat' mission. The pilot fixed on the submarine's cockpit lights and brought the aircraft to a hover fifty yards to port. Next he reduced altitude and sideslipped the helo toward the submarine. Aft, they saw the cargo door slide open. A hand reached out and grabbed the hook-end of the winch cable.

'Standby, everybody,' Mancuso told his people. 'We've done it before. Check your safety lines. Everybody just be careful.'

The prop wash from the helicopter threatened to blow them all down the ladder into the Attack Center as it hovered almost directly overhead. As Mancuso watched, a man-shape emerged from the cargo door and was lowered straight down. The thirty feet seemed to last forever as the shape came down, twirling slightly from the torsion of the steel winch cable. One of his seamen reached and grabbed a foot, pulling the man toward them. The Captain got his hand and both men pulled him inboard.

'Okay, we got ya,' Mancuso said. The man slipped from the collar and turned as the cable went back up.

'Mancuso!'

'Son of a bitch!' the Captain exclaimed.

'Is this the way to greet a comrade?'

'Damn!' But business came first. Mancuso looked up. The helicopter was already two hundred feet overhead. He reached down and blinked the sub's running lights on and off three times: TRANSFER COMPLETE. The helicopter immediately dropped its nose and headed back toward the German coast.

'Get on below,' Bart laughed. 'Lookouts below. Clear the bridge. Son of a bitch,' he said to himself. The Captain watched his men go down the ladder, switched off the cockpit lights, and made a final safety check before heading down behind them. A minute later he was in the Attack Center.

'Now do I request permission to come aboard?' Marko Ramius asked.

''Gator?'

'All systems aligned and checked for dive. We are rigged for dive,' the navigator reported. Mancuso turned automatically to check the status boards.

'Very well. Dive. Make your depth one hundred feet, course zero-seven-one, one-third.' He turned. 'Welcome aboard, Captain.'

'Thank you, Captain.' Ramius wrapped Mancuso in a ferocious bear-hug and kissed him on the cheek. Next he slipped off the backpack he was wearing. 'Can we talk?'

'Come on forward.'

'First time I come aboard your submarine,' Ramius observed. A moment later a head poked out of the sonar room.

'Captain Ramius! I thought I recognized your voice!' Jones looked at Mancuso. 'Beg pardon, sir. We just got a contact, bearing zero-eight-one. Sounds like a merchant.

Single screw, slow-speed diesels driving it. Probably a ways off. Being reported to the ODD now, sir.'

'Thanks, Jonesy.' Mancuso took Ramius into his stateroom and closed the door.

'What the hell was that?' a young sonarman asked Jones a moment later.

'We just got some company.'

'Didn't he have an accent, sort of?'

'Something like that.' Jones pointed to the sonar display. 'That contact has an accent, too. Let's see how fast you can decide what kinda merchie he is.'

It was dangerous, but all life was dangerous, the Archer thought. The Soviet-Afghan border here was a snow-fed river that snaked through gorges it had carved through the mountains. The border was also heavily guarded. It helped that his men were all dressed in Soviet-style uniforms. The Russians have long put their soldiers in simple but warm winter gear. Those they had on were mainly white to suit the snowy background, with just enough stripes and spots to break up their outline. Here they had to be patient. The Archer lay athwart a ridge, using Russian-issue binoculars to sweep the terrain while his men rested a few meters behind and below him. He might have gotten a local guerilla band to provide help, but he'd come too far to risk that. Some of the northern tribes had been co-opted by the Russians, or at least that was what he'd been told. True or not, he was running enough risks.

There was a Russian guard post atop the mountain to his left, six kilometers away. A large one, perhaps a full platoon lived there, and those KGB soldiers were responsible for patrolling this sector. The border itself was covered with a fence and minefields. The Russians loved their minefields . . . but the ground was frozen solid, and Soviet mines often didn't work well in frozen ground, although occasionally they'd set themselves off when the frost heaved around them.

He'd chosen the spot with care. The border here looked

virtually impassable – on a map. Smugglers had used it for centuries, however. Once across the river, there was a snaky path formed by centuries of snowmelt. Steep, and slippery, it was also a mini-canyon hidden from any view except direct overhead. If Russians guarded it, of course, it would be a deathtrap. That would be Allah's will, he told himself, and consigned himself to destiny. It was time.

He saw the flashes first. Ten men with a heavy machine gun and one of his precious mortars. A few yellow tracer streaks cut across the border into the Russian base camp. As he watched, a few of the bullets caromed off the rocks, tracing erratic paths in the velvet sky. Then the Russians started returning fire. The sound reached them soon after that. He hoped that his men would get away as he turned and waved his group forward.

They ran down the forward slope of the mountain, heedless of safety. The only good news was that winds had swept the snow off the rocks, making for decent footing. The Archer led them down toward the river. Amazingly enough, it was not frozen, its path too steep for the water to stop, even in subzero temperatures. There was the wire!

A young man with a two-handed pair of cutters made a path, and again the Archer led them through. His eyes were accustomed to the darkness, and he went more slowly now, looking at the ground for the telltale humps that indicated mines in the frozen ground. He didn't need to tell those behind him to stay in single file and walk on rocks wherever possible. Off to the left flares now decorated the sky, but the firing had died down somewhat.

It took over an hour, but he got all of his men across and into the smugglers' trail. Two men would stay behind, each on a hilltop overlooking the wire. They watched the amateur sapper who'd cut the wire make repairs to conceal their entry. Then he, too, faded into the darkness.

The Archer didn't stop until dawn. They were on schedule as they all paused a few hours for rest and food. All had gone well, his officers told him, better than they had hoped.

*

The stopover in Shannon was a brief one, just long enough to refuel and take aboard a Soviet pilot whose job it was to talk them through the Russian air-traffic-control system. Jack awoke on landing and thought about stretching his legs, but decided that the duty-free shops could wait until the return leg. The Russian took his place in the cockpit jump seat, and 86971 started rolling again.

It was night now. The pilot was in a loquacious mood tonight, announcing their next landfall at Wallasey. All of Europe, he said, was enjoying clear, cold weather, and Jack watched the orange-yellow city lights of England slide beneath them. Tension on the aircraft increased – or perhaps anticipation was a better word, he thought, as he listened to the pitch of the voices around him increase somewhat, though their volume dropped. You couldn't fly toward the Soviet Union without becoming a little conspiratorial. Soon all the conversations were in raspy whispers. Jack smiled thinly at the plastic windows, and his reflection asked what was so damned funny. Water appeared below them again as they flew across the North Sea toward Denmark.

The Baltic came next. You could tell where East and West met. To the south, the West German cities were all gaily lit, each surrounded by a warm glow of light. Not so on the eastern side of the wire-minefield barrier. Everyone aboard noticed the difference, and conversations grew quieter still.

The aircraft was following air route G-24; the navigator in front had the Jeppesen chart partially unfolded on his table. Another difference between East and West was the dearth of flight routes in the former. Well, he told himself, not many Pipers and Cessnas here – of course, there was that *one* Cessna . . . .

'Coming up on a turn. We'll be coming to new heading zero-seven-eight, and entering Soviet control.'

'Right,' the pilot – 'aircraft commander' – responded after a moment. He was tired. It had been a long day's flying. They were already at Flight Level 381 – 38,100 feet, or 11,600 meters as the Soviets preferred to call it. The pilot didn't like meters, even though his instruments were calibrated both ways. After executing the turn, they flew for another sixty miles before crossing the Soviet border at Ventspils.

'We're heeere,' somebody said a few feet from Ryan. From the air, at night, Soviet territory made East Germany look like New Orleans at Mardi Gras. He remembered night satellite shots. It was so easy to pick out the camps of the GULAG. They were the only lighted squares in the whole country . . . what a dreary place that only the prisons were well lighted . . . .

The pilot marked the entry only as another benchmark. Eighty-five more minutes, given the wind conditions. The Soviet air-traffic-control system along this routing – called G-3 now – was the only one in the country that spoke English. They didn't really need the Soviet officer to complete the mission – he was an air-force intelligence officer, of course – but if something went wrong, things might be different. The Russians liked the idea of positive control. The orders he got now for course and altitude were far more exact than those given in American air space, as though he didn't know what to do unless some jerk-off on the ground told him. Of course there was an element of humor to it. The pilot was Colonel Paul von Eich. His family had come to America from Prussia a hundred years before, but none of them had been able to part with the 'von' that had once been so important to family status. Some of his ancestors had fought down there, he reflected, on the flat, snow-covered Russian ground. Certainly a few more recent relatives had. Probably a few lay buried there while he whizzed overhead at six hundred miles per hour. He wondered vaguely what they'd think of his job while his pale blue eyes scanned the sky for the lights of other aircraft.

Like most passengers, Ryan judged his height above the ground by what he could see, but the dark Soviet countryside denied him that. He knew they were close when the aircraft commenced a wide turn to the left. He heard the mechanical whine as the flaps went down and noted the reduced engine noise. Soon he could just pick out individual trees, racing by. The pilot's voice came on, telling smokers to put them out, and that it was time for seat belts again. Five minutes later they returned to ground level again at Sheremetyevo Airport. Despite the fact that airports all over the world look exactly alike, Ryan could be sure of this one – the taxiways were the bumpiest anywhere.

The cabin talk was more lively now. The excitement was beginning as the airplane's crew started moving about. What followed went in a blur. Ernie Allen was met by a welcoming committee of the appropriate level and whisked off in an embassy limousine. Everyone else was relegated to a bus. Ryan sat by himself, still watching the countryside outside the German-made vehicle.

Will Gerasimov bite – really bite?

What if he doesn't?

What if he does? Ryan asked himself with a smile.

It had all seemed pretty straighforward in Washington, but here, five thousand miles away . . . well. First he'd get some sleep, aided by a single government-issue red capsule. Then he'd talk to a few people at the embassy. The rest would have to take care of itself.

20

The Key of Destiny

It was bitterly cold when Ryan awoke to the beeping sound of his watch alarm. There was frost on the windows even at ten in the morning, and he realized that he hadn't made sure the heat in his room was operating. His first considered action of the day was to pull on some socks. His seventh-floor room – it was called an 'efficiency apartment' – overlooked the compound. Clouds had moved in, and the day was leaden gray with the threat of snow.

'Perfect,' Jack observed to himself on the way to the bathroom. He knew that it could have been worse. The only reason he had this room was that the officer who ordinarily lived here was on honeymoon leave. At least the plumbing worked, but he found a note taped to the medicine cabinet mirror admonishing him not to mess the place up the way the last transient had. Next he checked the small refrigerator. Nothing: *Welcome to Moscow*. Back in the bathroom, he washed and shaved. One other oddity of the embassy was that to get down from the seventh floor, you first had to take an elevator up to the ninth floor and another one down from there to the lobby. Jack was still shaking his head over that one when he got into the canteen.

'Don't you just love jet lag?' a member of the delegation greeted him. 'Coffee's over there.'

'I call it travel shock.' Ryan got himself a mug and came back. 'Well, the coffee's decent. Where's everybody else?'

'Probably still sacked out, even Uncle Ernie. I caught a few hours on the flight, and thank God for the pill they gave us.'

411

Ryan laughed. 'Yeah, me too. Might even feel human in time for dinner tonight.'

'Feel like exploring? I'd like to take a walk, but –'

'Travel in pairs.' Ryan nodded. The rule applied only to the arms negotiators. This phase of negotiations would be sensitive, and the rules for the team were much tighter than usual. 'Maybe later. I have some work to do.'

'Today and tomorrow's our only chance,' the diplomat pointed out.

'I know,' Ryan assured him. He checked his watch and decided that he'd wait to eat until lunchtime. His sleep cycle was almost in synch with Moscow, but his stomach wasn't quite sure yet. Jack walked back to the chancery.

The corridors were mainly empty. Marines patrolled them, looking very serious indeed after the problems that had occurred earlier, but there was little evidence of activity on this Saturday morning. Jack walked to the proper door and knocked. He knew it was locked.

'You're Ryan?'

'That's right.' The door opened to admit him, then was closed and relocked.

'Grab a seat.' His name was Tony Candela. 'What gives?'

'We have an op laid on.'

'News to me – you're not operations, you're intelligence,' Candela objected.

'Yeah, well, Ivan knows that, too. This one's going to be a little strange'. Ryan explained for five minutes.

'"A little strange," you say?' Candela rolled his eyes.

'I need a keeper for part of it. I need some phone numbers I can call, and I may need wheels that'll be there when required.'

'This could cost me some assets.'

'We know that.'

'Of course, if it works . . .'

'Right. We can put some real muscle on this one.'

'The Foleys know about this?'

''Fraid not.'

412

'Too bad, Mary Pat would have loved it. She's the cowboy. Ed's more the button-down-collar type. So, you expect him to bite Monday or Tuesday night?'

'That's the plan.'

'Let me tell you something about plans,' Candela said.

They were letting him sleep. The doctors had warned him again, Vatutin growled. How was he supposed to accomplish anything when they kept –

'There's that name again,' the man with the headphones said tiredly. 'Romanov. If he must talk in his sleep, why can't he confess . . . ?'

'Perhaps he's talking with the Czar's ghost,' another officer joked. Vatutin's head came up.

'Or perhaps someone else's.' The Colonel shook his head. He'd been at the point of dozing himself. Romanov, though the name of the defunct royal family of the Russian Empire, was not an uncommon one – even a Politburo member had had it. 'Where's his file?'

'Here.' The joker pulled open a drawer and handed it over. The file weighed six kilograms, and came in several different sections. Vatutin had committed most of it to memory, but had concentrated on the last two parts. This time he opened the first section.

'Romanov,' he breathed to himself. 'Where have I seen that . . . ?' It took him fifteen minutes, flipping through the frayed pages as speedily as he dared.

'I have it!' It was a citation, scrawled in pencil. 'Corporal A. I. Romanov, killed in action 6 October 1941, " . . . defiantly placed his tank between the enemy and his disabled troop commander's, allowing the commander to withdraw his wounded crew . . ." Yes! This one's in a book I read as a child. Misha got his crew on the back deck of a different tank, jumped inside, and personally killed the tank that got Romanov's. He'd saved Misha's life and was posthumously awarded the Red Banner –' Vatutin stopped. He was calling the subject *Misha*, he realized.

413

'Almost fifty years ago?'

'They were comrades. This Romanov fellow had been part of Filitov's own tank crew through the first few months. Well, he was a hero. He died for the Motherland, saving the life of his officer,' Vatutin observed. *And Misha still talks to him . . .*

I have you now, Filitov.

'Shall we wake him up and –'

'Where's the doctor?' Vatutin asked.

It turned out that he was about to leave for home and was not overly pleased to be recalled. But he didn't have the rank to play power games with Colonel Vatutin.

'How should we handle it?' Vatutin asked after outlining his thoughts.

'He should be weary but wide awake. That is easily done.'

'So we should wake him up now and –'

'No.' The doctor shook his head. 'Not in REM sleep –'

'What?'

'Rapid Eye Movement sleep – that's what it's called when the patient is dreaming. You can always tell if the subject is in a dream by the eye movement, whether he talks or not.'

'But we can't see that from here,' another officer objected.

'Yes, perhaps we should redesign the observation system,' the doctor mused. 'But that doesn't matter too much. During REM sleep the body is effectively paralyzed. You'll notice that he's not moving now, correct? The mind does that to prevent injury to the body. When he starts moving again, the dream is over.'

'How long?' Vatutin asked. 'We don't want him to get too rested.'

'Depends on the subject, but I would not be overly concerned. Have the turnkey get a breakfast ready for him, and as soon as he starts moving, wake him up and feed him.'

'Of course.' Vatutin smiled.

'Then we just keep him awake . . . oh, eight hours or so more. Yes, that should do it. Is it enough time for you?'

'Easily,' Vatutin said with more confidence than he should have. He stood and checked his watch. The Colonel of 'Two' called the Center and gave a few orders. His system, too, cried out for sleep. But for him there was a comfortable bed. He wanted to have all of his cleverness when the time came. The Colonel undressed fastidiously, calling for an orderly to polish his boots and press his uniform while he slept. He was tired enough that he didn't even feel the need for a drink. 'I have you now,' he murmured as he faded into sleep.

'G'night, Bea,' Candi called from the door as her friend opened up her car. Taussig turned one last time and waved before getting in. Candi and the Geek couldn't have seen the way she stabbed the key into the ignition. She drove only half a block, turning a corner before pulling to the curb and staring at the night.

They're doing it already, she thought. *All the way through dinner, the way he looked at her – the way she looked at him! Already those wimpy little hands are fumbling with the buttons on her blouse . . .*

She lit a cigarette and leaned back, picturing it while her stomach tightened into a rigid, acid-filled ball. Zit-face and Candi. She'd endured three hours of it. Candi's usual beautifully prepared dinner. For twenty minutes while the finishing touches had been under way, she'd been stuck in the living room with *him*, listening to his idiot jokes, having to smile back at him. It was clear enough that Alan didn't like her either, but because she was Candi's friend he'd felt obligated to be nice to her, nice to poor Bea, who was heading towards old-maidhood, or whatever they called it now – she'd seen it in his stupid eyes. To be patronized by him was bad enough, but to be pitied . . .

And now he was touching her, kissing her, listening to her murmurs, whispering his stupid, disgusting endearments – and Candi liked it! How was that *possible?*

415

Candace was more than just pretty, Taussig knew. She was a free spirit. She had a discoverer's mind mated to a warm, sensitive soul. She had real feelings. She was so wonderfully feminine, with the kind of beauty that begins at the heart and radiates out through a perfect smile.

But now she's giving herself to that thing! He's probably doing it already. That geek doesn't have the first idea of taking his time and showing real love and sensitivity. I bet he just does it, drooling and giggling like some punk fifteen-year-old football jock. How can she!

'Oh, Candace.' Bea's voice broke. She was swept with nausea, and had to fight to control herself. She succeeded, and sat alone in her car for twenty minutes of silent tears before she managed to drive on.

'What do you make of that?'

'I think she's a lesbian,' Agent Jennings said after a moment.

'Nothing like that in her file, Peggy,' Will Perkins observed.

'The way she looks at Dr Long, the way she acts around Gregory . . . that's my gut feeling.'

'But –'

'Yeah, but what the hell can we do about that?' Margaret Jennings noted as she drove away. She toyed briefly with the idea of going after Taussig, but the day had been long enough already. 'No evidence, and if we got it, and acted on it, there'd be hell to pay.'

'You suppose the three of them . . . ?'

'Will, you've been reading those magazines again.' Jennings laughed, breaking the spell for a moment. Perkins was a Mormon, and had never been seen to touch pornographic material. 'Those two are so much in love they don't have the first idea of what's going on around them – except work. I bet their pillow talk is classified. What's happening, Will, is that Taussig is being cut out of her friend's life and she's unhappy about it. Tough.'

'So how do we write this one up?'

'Zip. A whole lot of nothing.' Their assignment for the evening had been to follow up a report that strange cars were occasionally seen at the Gregory-Long residence. It had probably originated, Agent Jennings thought, from a local prude who didn't like the idea of the two young people living together without the appropriate paperwork. She was a little old-fashioned about that herself, but it didn't make either one of them a security risk. On the other hand –

'I think we ought to check out Taussig next.'

'She lives alone.'

'I'm sure.' It would take time to look at every senior staffer at Tea Clipper, but you couldn't rush this kind of investigation.

'You shouldn't have come here,' Tania observed at once. Bisyarina's face didn't show her rage. She took Taussig's hand and brought her inside.

'Ann, it's just so awful!'

'Come sit down. Were you followed?' *Idiot! Pervert!* She'd just gotten out of the shower, and was dressed in a bathrobe, with a towel over her hair.

'No, I watched all the way.'

Sure, Bisyarina thought. She would have been surprised to learn that it was true. Despite the lax security at Tea Clipper – it allowed someone like this inside! – her agent had broken every rule there was in coming here.

'You cannot stay long.'

'I know.' She blew her nose. 'They've about finished the first draft of the new program. The Geek has cut it down by eighty thousand lines of code – taking out all that AI stuff really made a difference. You know, I think he has the new stuff memorized – I know, I know, that's impossible, even for *that*.'

'When will you be able –'

'I don't know.' Taussig smiled for a second. 'You ought to have him working for you. I think he's the only one who really understands the whole program – I mean, the whole project.'

Unfortunately all we have is you, Bisyarina didn't say. What she did was very hard. She reached out and took Taussig's hand.

The tears started again. Beatrice nearly leaped into Tania's arms. The Russian officer held her close, trying to feel sympathy for her agent. There had been many lessons at the KGB school, all of them intended to help her in handling agents. You had to have a mixture of sympathy and discipline. You had to treat them like spoiled children, mixing favors and scoldings to make them perform. And Agent Livia was more important than most.

It was still hard to turn her face toward the head on her shoulder and kiss the cheek that was salty with tears both old and new. Bisyarina breathed easier at the realization that she needed go no further than this. She'd never yet needed to go further, but lived in fear that 'Livia' would one day demand it of her – certainly it would happen if she ever realized that her intended lover had not the slightest interest in her advances. Bisyarina marveled at that. Beatrice Taussig was brilliant in her way, certainly brighter than the KGB officer who 'ran' her, but she knew so little about people. The crowning irony was that she was very much like that Alan Gregory man she so detested. Prettier, more sophisticated though Taussig was, she lacked the capacity to reach out when she needed to. Gregory had probably done it only once in his life, and that was the difference between him and her. He had gotten there first because Beatrice had lacked the courage. It was just as well, Bisyarina knew. The rejection would have destroyed her.

Bisyarina wondered what Gregory was really like. Probably another academic – what was it the English called them? Boffins. A brilliant boffin – well, everyone attached to Tea Clipper was brilliant in one way or another. That frightened her. In her way, Beatrice was proud of the program, though she deemed it a threat to world peace, a point on which Bisyarina agreed. Gregory was a boffin who wanted to change the world. Bisyarina understood the motivation. She wanted to change it, too. Just in a different way. Gregory and Tea Clipper were a threat to that. She didn't hate the man. If anything, she thought, she'd probably like him. But personal likes and dislikes had absolutely nothing to do with the business of intelligence.

'Feel better?' she asked when the tears stopped.

'I have to leave.'

'Are you sure you're all right?'

'Yes. I don't know when I'll be able to –'

'I understand.' Tania walked her to the door. At least she'd had the good sense to park her car on a different block, 'Ann' noticed. She waited, holding the door cracked open, to hear the distinctive sound of the sports car. After closing the door, she looked at her hands and went back to the bathroom to wash them.

Night came early in Moscow, the sun hidden by clouds that were starting to shed their load of snow. The delegation assembled in the embassy's foyer and filed off into their assigned cars for the arrival dinner. Ryan was in car number three – a slight promotion from the last trip, he noted wryly. Once the procession started moving, he remembered a driver's remark from the last time, that Moscow had street names mainly to identify the pothole collections. The car jolted its way east through the city's largely empty streets. They crossed the river right at the Kremlin, and motored past Gorkiy Park. He could see that the place was gaily lit, with people ice-skating in the falling snow. It was nice to see real people having real fun. Even Moscow was a city, he reminded himself, full of ordinary people living fairly ordinary lives. It was a fact too easy to forget when your job forced you to concentrate on a narrow group of enemies.

The car turned off October Square, and after an intricate maneuver, pulled up to the Academy of Sciences Hotel. It was a quasi-modern building that in America might have been taken for an office block. A forlorn string of birch trees sat between the gray concrete wall and the street, their bare, lifeless branches reaching into the speckled sky. Ryan shook his head. Given a few hours of snowfall, and it might actually be a beautiful scene. The temperature was zero or so – Ryan thought in Fahrenheit, not Celsius – and the wind almost calm. Perfect conditions for snow. He could feel the air heavy and cold around him as he walked into the hotel's main entrance.

Like most Russian buildings, it was overheated. Jack removed his overcoat and handed it over to an attendant. The Soviet delegation was already lined up to greet their American counterparts, and the Americans shuffled down the rank of Soviets, ending at a table of drinks of which everyone partook. There would be ninety minutes of drinking and socializing before the actual dinner. Welcome to Moscow. Ryan approved of the plan. Enough alcohol could make any meal seem a feast, and he'd yet to experience a Russian meal that rose above the ordinary. The room was barely lit, allowing everyone to watch the falling snow through the large plate-glass windows.

'Hello again, Dr Ryan,' a familiar voice said.

'Sergey Nikolayevich, I hope you are not driving tonight,' Jack said, gesturing with his wineglass to Golovko's vodka. His cheeks were already florid, his blue eyes sparkling with alcoholic mirth.

'Did you enjoy the flight in last night?' the GRU Colonel asked. He laughed merrily before Ryan could reply. 'You still fear flying?'

'No, it's hitting the ground that worries me.' Jack grinned. He had always been able to laugh at his own pet fear.

'Ah, yes, your back injury from the helicopter crash. One can sympathize.'

Ryan waved at the window. 'How much snow are we supposed to get tonight?'

'Perhaps half a meter, perhaps more. Not a very large storm, but tomorrow the air will be fresh and clear, and the city will sparkle with a clean blanket of white.' Golovko was almost poetic in his description.

Already he's drunk, Ryan told himself. Well, tonight was supposed to be a social occasion, nothing more, and the Russians could be hospitable as hell when they wanted to be. Though one man was experiencing something very different, Jack reminded himself.

'Your family is well?' Golovko asked within earshot of another American delegate.

'Yes, thank you. Yours?'

Golovko gestured for Ryan to follow him over to the drink table. The waiters hadn't come out yet. The intelligence officer selected another glass of clear liquor. 'Yes, they are all well.' He smiled broadly. Sergey was the very image of Russian good fellowship. His face didn't change a whit as he spoke his next sentence: 'I understand that you want to meet Chairman Gerasimov.'

Jesus! Jack's expression froze in place; his heart skipped a beat or two. 'Really? How did you ever get that idea?'

'I'm not GRU, Ryan, not really. My original assignment was in Third Directorate, but I have since moved on to other things,' he explained before laughing again. This laugh was genuine. He'd just invalidated CIA's file on himself – and, he could see, Ryan's own observation. His hand reached out to pat Ryan on the upper arm. 'I will leave you now. In five minutes you will walk through the door behind you and to the left as though looking for the men's room. After that, you will follow instructions. Understood?' He patted Ryan's arm again.

'Yes.'

'I will not see you again tonight.' They shook hands and Golovko moved off.

'Oh, shit,' Ryan whispered to himself. A troupe of violins came into the reception room. There must have been ten or fifteen of them, playing gypsy airs as they circulated about. They must have practiced hard, Jack thought, to play in perfect synchronization despite the dark room and their own random meanderings. Their movement and the relative darkness would make it hard to pick out individuals during the reception. It was a clever, professional touch aimed at making it easier for Jack to slip away.

'Hello, Dr Ryan,' another voice said. He was a young Soviet diplomat, a gofer who kept notes and ran errands for the senior people. Now Jack knew that he was also KGB. Gerasimov was not content with a single surprise for the evening, he realized. He wanted to dazzle Ryan with KGB's prowess. *We'll see about that*, Jack thought, but the bravado seemed hollow even to himself. Too soon. Too soon.

'Good evening – we've never met.' Jack reached into his pants pocket and felt for his keychain. He hadn't forgotten it.

'My name is Vitaliy. Your absence will not be noticed. The men's room is that way.' He pointed. Jack handed over his glass and walked toward the door. He nearly stopped dead on leaving the room. No one inside could have known it, but the corridor had been cleared. Except for one man at the far end, who gestured once. Ryan walked toward him.

Oh, shit. Here we go . . .

He was a youngish man, on the short side of thirty. He looked like the physical type. Though his build was concealed by an overcoat, he moved in the brisk, efficient way of an athlete. His facial expression and penetrating eyes made him a bodyguard. The best thought that came to Ryan was that he was supposed to appear nervous. It didn't require much in the way of talent to do so. The man took him around the corner and handed him a Russian-made overcoat and fur hat, then spoke a single word:

'Come.'

He led Ryan down a service corridor and out into the cold air of an alley. Another man was waiting outside, watching. He nodded curtly to Ryan's escort, who turned once and waved for Jack to hurry. The alley ended on Shabolovka Street, and both men turned right. This part of town was old, Jack saw at once. The buildings were mostly pre-revolution. The center of the street had trolley tracks embedded in cobblestones, and overhead were the catenary wires that supplied power to the streetcars. He watched as one rumbled past – actually it was two trams linked together, the colors white over red. Both men sprinted across the slippery street toward a red brick building with what looked like a metal roof. Ryan wasn't sure what it was until they turned the corner.

The car barn, he realized, remembering similar places from his boyhood in Baltimore. The tracks curved in here, then diverged to the various bays in the barn. He paused for a moment, but his escort waved him forward urgently, moving to the left-most service bay. Inside it, of course, were streetcars, lined up like sleeping cattle in the darkness. It was totally still in there, he realized with surprise. There should have been people working, the sound of hammers and machine tools, but there was none of that. Ryan's heart pounded as he walked past two motionless trams. His escort stopped at the third. Its doors were open, and a third bodyguard-type stepped down and looked at Ryan. He immediately patted Jack down, seeking weapons but finding none in a quick but thorough search. A jerk of the thumb directed him up and into the tram.

It had evidently just come in, and there was snow on the first step. Ryan slipped and would have fallen had not one of the KGB men caught his arm. He gave Jack a look that in the West would have been accompanied by a smile, but the Russians are not a smiling people except when they want to be. He went up again, his hands firm on the safety rails. *All you have to do . . .*

'Good evening,' a voice called. Not very loudly, but it didn't have to be. Ryan squinted in the darkness and saw the glowing orange light of a cigarette. He took a deep breath and walked toward it.

'Chairman Gerasimov, I presume?'

'You do not recognize me?' A trace of amusement. The man flicked his Western-made butane lighter to illuminate

423

his face. It was Nikolay Borissovich Gerasimov. The flame gave his face exactly the right sort of look. The Prince of Darkness himself . . .

'I do now,' Jack said, struggling to control his voice.

'I understand that you wish to speak with me. How may I be of service?' he asked in a courtly voice that belied the setting.

Jack turned and gestured to the two bodyguards who were standing at the front of the car. He turned back but didn't have to say anything. Gerasimov spoke a single word in Russian, and both men left.

'Please excuse them, but their duty is to protect the Chairman, and my people take their duties seriously.' He waved to the seat opposite his. Ryan took it.

'I didn't know your English was so good.'

'Thank you.' A courteous nod followed by a businesslike observation: 'I caution you that time is short. You have information for me?'

'Yes, I do.' Jack reached inside his coat. Gerasimov tensed for a moment, then relaxed. Only a madman would try to kill the chief of the KGB, and he knew from Ryan's dossier that he was not mad. 'I have something for you,' said Ryan.

'Oh?' Impatience. Gerasimov was not a man who liked to be kept waiting. He watched Ryan's hands fumble with something, and was puzzled to hear the rasp of metal scraping against metal. Jack's clumsiness disappeared when the key came off the ring, and when he spoke, he was a man claiming another's pot.

'Here.' Ryan handed it over.

'What is this?' Suspicion now. Something was very badly wrong, wrong enough that his voice betrayed him.

Jack didn't make him wait. He spoke in a voice he'd been rehearsing for a week. Without knowing it, he spoke faster than he'd planned. 'That, Chairman Gerasimov, is the warhead-control key from the Soviet ballistic-missile submarine *Krazny Oktyabr*. It was given to me by Captain Marko Aleksandrovich Ramius when he defected. You will be pleased to know that he likes his new life in America, as do all of his officers.'

'The submarine was –'

Ryan cut him off. There was scarcely enough light to see the outline of his face, but that was enough to see the change in the man's expression.

'Destroyed by her own scuttling charges? No. The spook aboard whose cover was ship's cook, Sudets, I think his name was – well, no sense in hiding it. I killed him. I'm not especially proud of that, but it was either him or me. For what it's worth, he was a very courageous young man,' Jack said, remembering the ten horrible minutes in the submarine's missile room. 'Your file on me doesn't say anything about operations, does it?'

'But –'

Jack cut him off again. It was not yet the time for finesse. They had to jolt him, had to jolt him hard.

'Mr Gerasimov, there are some things we want from you.'

'Rubbish. Our conversation is ended.' But Gerasimov didn't rise, and this time Ryan made him wait for a few beats.

'We want Colonel Filitov back. Your official report to the Politburo on *Red October* stated that the submarine was positively destroyed, and that a defection had probably never been planned, but rather that GRU security had been penetrated and that the submarine had been issued bogus orders after her engines had been sabotaged. That information came to you through Agent Cassius. He works for us,' Jack explained. 'You used it to disgrace Admiral Gorshkov and to reinforce your control over the military's internal security. They're still angry about that, aren't they? So, if we do not get Colonel Filitov back, this coming week in Washington a story will be leaked to the press for the Sunday editions. It will have some of the details of the operation, and a photograph of the submarine sitting in a covered drydock in Norfolk, Virginia. After that we will produce Captain Ramius. He'll say that the ship's political officer – one of your Department Three men, I believe – was part of the conspiracy. Unfortunately, Putin died after arriving, of a heart attack. That's a lie, but try proving it.'

'You cannot blackmail me, Ryan!' There was no emotion at all now.

'One more thing. SDI is not on the bargaining table. Did you tell the Politburo that it was?' Jack asked. 'You're finished, Mr Gerasimov. We have the ability to disgrace you, and you're just too good a target to pass up. If we don't get Filitov back, we can leak all sorts of things. Some will be confirmed, but the real good ones will be denied, of course, while the FBI launches an urgent investigation to identify the leakers.'

'You did not do all this for Filitov,' Gerasimov said, his voice measured now.

'Not exactly.' Again he made him wait for it: 'We want you to come out, too.'

Jack walked out of the tram five minutes later. His escort walked him back to the hotel. The attention to detail was impressive. Before rejoining the reception, Jack's shoes were wiped dry. On re-entering the room he walked at once to the drink table, but found it empty. He spotted a waiter with a tray, and took the first thing he could reach. It turned out to be vodka, but Ryan gunned it down in a single gulp before reaching for another. When he finished that one, he started wondering where the men's room really was. It turned out to be exactly where he'd been told. Jack got there just in time.

It was as worked up as anyone had ever been with a computer simulation. They'd never run one quite this way before, of course, and that was the purpose of the test. The ground-control computer didn't know what it was doing, nor did any of the others. One machine was programmed to report a series of distant radar contacts. All it did was to receive a collection of signals like those generated by an orbiting Flying Cloud satellite, cued in turn by one of the DSPS birds at geosynchronous height. The computer relayed this information to the ground-control computer, which examined its criteria for weapons-free authority and decided that they had been met. It took a few seconds for the lasers to power up, but they reported being ready a few seconds later. The fact that the lasers in question did not exist was not pertinent to the test. The ground mirror did, and it responded to instructions from the computer, sending the imaginary laser beam to the relay mirror eight hundred kilometers overhead. This mirror, so recently carried by the space shuttle and actually in California, received its own instructions and altered its configuration accordingly, relaying the laser beam to the battle mirror. This mirror was at the Lockheed factory rather than in orbit, and received its instructions via landline. At all three mirrors a precise record was kept of the ever-changing focal-length and azimuth settings. This information was sent to the score-keeping computer at Tea Clipper Control.

There had been several purposes to the test that Ryan had observed a few weeks before. In validating the system architecture, they had also received priceless empirical data on the actual functioning characteristics of the hardware. As a result they could simulate real exercises on the ground with near-absolute confidence in the theoretical results.

Gregory was rolling a ballpoint pen between his hands as the data came up on the video-display terminal. He'd just stopped chewing on it for fear of getting a mouth full of ink.

'Okay, there's the last shot,' an engineer observed. 'Here comes the score . . .'

'Wow!' Gregory exclaimed. 'Ninety-six out of a hundred! What's the cycle time?'

'Point zero-one-six,' a software expert replied. 'That's point zero-zero-four *under* nominal – we can double-check every aim-command while the laser cycles –'

'And that increases the Pk thirty percent all by itself,' Gregory said. 'We can even try doing shoot-look-shoot instead of shoot-shoot-look and still save time on the back end. *People!*' – he jumped to his feet – '*we have done it!* The software is in the fuckin' can!' *Four months sooner than promised!*

The room erupted with cheering that no one outside the team of thirty people could possibly have understood.

'Okay, you laser pukes!' someone called. 'Get your act together and build us a death ray! The gunsight is *finished!*'

'Be nice to the laser pukes.' Gregory laughed. 'I work with them too.'

Outside the room, Beatrice Taussig was merely walking past the door on her way to an admin meeting when she heard the cheering. She couldn't enter the lab – it had a cipher lock, and she didn't have the combination – but didn't have to. The experiment that they'd hinted at over dinner the night before had just been run. The result was obvious enough. Candi was in there, probably standing right next to the Geek, Bea thought. She kept walking.

'Thank God there's not much ice,' Mancuso observed, looking through the periscope. 'Call it two feet, maybe three.'

'There will be a clear channel here. The coastal ice-breakers keep all the coastal ports open,' Ramius said.

'Down 'scope,' the Captain said next. He walked over to the chart table. 'I want you to move us two thousand yards south, then bottom us out. That'll put us under a hard roof and ought to keep the Grishas and Mirkas away.'

'Aye, Captain,' the XO replied.

'Let's go get some coffee,' Mancuso said to Ramius and Clark. He led them down one deck and to starboard into the wardroom. For all the times he'd done things like this in the past four years, Mancuso was nervous. They were in less than two hundred feet of water, within sight of the Soviet coast. If detected and then localized by a Soviet ship, they would be attacked. It had happened before. Though no Western submarine had ever suffered actual damage, there was a first time for everything, especially if you started taking things for granted, the Captain of USS *Dallas* told himself. Two feet of ice was too much for the thin-hulled Grisha-class patrol boats to plow through, and their main antisubmarine weapon, a multiple rocket launcher called a RBU-6000, was useless over ice, but a Grisha could call in a submarine. There were Russian subs about. They'd heard two the previous day.

'Coffee, sir?' the wardroom attendant asked. He got a nod and brought out a pot and cups.

'You sure this is close enough?' Mancuso asked Clark.

'Yeah, I can get in and out.'

'It won't be much fun,' the Captain observed.

Clark smirked. 'That's why they pay me so much. I –'

Conversation stopped for a moment. The submarine's hull creaked as it settled on the bottom, and the boat took on a slight list. Mancuso looked at the coffee in his cup and figured it for six or seven degrees. Submariner machismo prevented him from showing any reaction, but he'd never done this, at least not with *Dallas*. A handful of submarines in the US Navy were specially designed for these missions. Insiders could identify them at a glance from the arrangement of a few hull fittings, but *Dallas* wasn't one of them.

'I wonder how long this is going to take?' Mancuso asked the overhead.

'May not happen at all,' Clark observed. 'Almost half of them don't. The longest I've ever had to sit like this was . . . twelve days, I think. Seemed like an awfully long time. That one didn't come off.'

'Can you say how many?' Ramius asked.

'Sorry, sir.' Clark shook his head.

Ramius spoke wistfully. 'You know, when I was a boy, I fished here – right here many times. We never knew that you Americans came here to fish also.'

'It's a crazy world,' Clark agreed. 'How's the fishing?'

'In the summer, very good. Old Sasha took me out on his boat. This is where I learned the sea, where I learned to be a sailor.'

'What about the local patrols?' Mancuso asked, getting everyone back to business.

'There will be a low state of readiness. You have diplomats in Moscow, so the chance of war is slight. The surface patrol ships are mainly KGB. They guard against smugglers – and spies.' He pointed to Clark. 'Not so good against submarines, but this was changing when I left. They were increasing their ASW practice in Northern Fleet, and, I hear, in Baltic Fleet also. But this is bad place for submarine detection. There is much fresh water from the rivers, and the ice overhead – all makes for difficult sonar conditions.'

That's good to hear, Mancuso thought. His ship was in an increased state of readiness. The sonar equipment was fully manned and would remain so indefinitely. He could get *Dallas* moving in a matter of two minutes, and that should be ample, he thought.

Gerasimov was thinking, too. He was alone in his office. A man who controlled his emotions even more than most Russians, his face displayed nothing out of the way, even though there was no one else in the room to notice. In most people that would have been remarkable, for few can contemplate their own destruction with objectivity.

The Chairman of the Committee for State Security assessed his position as thoroughly and dispassionately as he examined any aspect of his official duties. *Red October*. It all flowed out from that. He had used the *Red October* incident to his advantage, first suborning Gorshkov, then disposing of him; he'd also used it to strengthen the position of his Third Directorate arm. The military had begun to manage its own internal security – but Gerasimov had seized upon his report from Agent Cassius to convince the Politburo that the KGB alone could ensure the loyalty and security of the Soviet military. That had earned him resentment. He'd reported, again via Cassius, that *Red October* had been destroyed. Cassius had told KGB that Ryan was under criminal suspicion, and –

And we – I! – walked into the trap.

How could he explain that to the Politburo? One of his

best agents had been doubled – but when? They'd ask that, and he didn't know the answer; therefore all the reports received from Cassius would become suspect. Despite the fact that much good data had come from the agent, knowledge that he'd been doubled at an unknown time tainted all of it. And that wrecked his vaunted insights in Western political thought.

He'd wrongly reported that the submarine hadn't defected, and not discovered the error. The Americans had gotten an intelligence windfall, but KGB didn't know of it. Neither did GRU, but that was little comfort.

And he'd reported that the Americans had made a major change in their arms-negotiation strategy, and that, too, was wrong.

Could he survive all three disclosures at once? Gerasimov asked himself.

Probably not.

In another age he would have faced death, and that would have made the decision all the easier. No man chooses death, at least not a sane one, and Gerasimov was coldly sane in everything he did. But that sort of thing didn't happen now. He'd end up with a subministerial job somewhere or other, shuffling papers. His KGB contacts would be useless to him beyond such meaningless favors as access to decent groceries. People would watch him walking on the street – no longer afraid to look him in the face, no longer fearful of his power, they'd point and laugh behind his back. People in his office would gradually lose their deference, and talk back, even shout at him once they knew that his power was well and truly gone. No, he said to himself, I will not endure that.

To defect, then? To go from being one of the world's most powerful men to becoming a hireling, a mendicant who traded what he knew for money and a comfortable life? Gerasimov accepted the fact that his life would become more comfortable in physical terms – but to lose his *power!*

That was the issue, after all. Whether he left or stayed, to

431

become just another man . . . *that would be like death, wouldn't it?*

Well, what do you do now?

He had to change his position, had to change the rules of the game, had to do something so dramatic . . . but what?

The choice was between disgrace and defection? To lose everything he'd worked for – within sight of his goal – and face a choice like this?

The Soviet Union is not a nation of gamblers. Its national strategy has always been more reflective of the Russians' national passion for chess, a series of careful, pre-planned moves, never risking much, always protecting its position by seeking small, progressive advantages wherever possible. The Politburo had almost always moved in that way. The Politburo itself was largely composed of similar men. More than half were *apparatchiks* who had spoken the appropriate words, filled the necessary quotas, taking what advantages they could, and who had won advancement through a stolidity whose perfection they could display around the table in the Kremlin. But the function of those men was to provide a moderating influence on those who aspired to rule, and these men were the gamblers. Narmonov was a gambler. So was Gerasimov. He'd play his own game, allying himself with Alexandrov to establish his ideological constituency, blackmailing Vaneyev and Yazov to betray their master.

And it was too fine a game to quit so easily. He had to change the rules again, but the game did not really have any rules – except for the one: Win.

If he won – the disgraces would not matter, would they?

Gerasimov took the key from his pocket and examined it for the first time in the light of his desk lamp. It looked ordinary enough. Used in the designed manner, it would make possible the deaths of – fifty million? A hundred? More? The Directorate Three men on the submarines and in the land-based rocket regiments held that power – the *zampolit*, the political officer alone had the authority to activate the warheads without which the rockets were mere

432

fireworks. Turn this key in the proper way at the proper time, he knew, and the rockets were transformed into the most frightening instruments of death yet devised by the mind of man. Once launched, nothing could stop them . . .

But that rule was going to be changed, too, wasn't it?

What was it worth to be the man who could do that?

'Ah.' Gerasimov smiled. It was worth more than all the other rules combined, and he remembered that the Americans had broken a rule, too, in killing their courier in the Moskvich railyard. He lifted his phone and called for a communications officer. For once the longitudinal lines worked in his favor.

Dr Taussig was surprised when she saw the signal. One thing about 'Ann' was that she never altered her routine. Despite the fact that she'd impulsively visited her contact, heading to the shopping center was her normal Saturday routine. She parked her Datsun fairly far out, lest some klutz in a Chevy Malibu smash his door against hers. On the way in, she saw Ann's Volvo, and the driver's side visor was down. Taussig checked her watch and increased her pace to the entrance. On going in, she turned left.

Peggy Jennings was working alone today. They were spread too thin to get the job done as fast as Washington wanted, but that wasn't exactly a new story, was it? The setting was both good and bad. Following her subject to the shopping mall was fairly easy, but once inside it was damned near impossible to trail a subject properly, unless you had a real team of agents operating. She got to the door only a minute behind Taussig, already knowing that she'd lost her. Well, this was only a preliminary look at her. Routine, Jennings told herself on opening the door.

Jennings looked up and down the mall and failed to see her subject. Frowning for a moment, she commenced a leisurely stroll from shop to shop, gazing in the windows and wondering if Taussig had gone to a movie.

*

433

'Hello, Ann!'

'Bea!' Bisyarina said inside Eve's Leaves. 'How are you?'

'Keeping busy,' Dr Taussig replied. 'That looks wonderful on you.'

'She's so easy to fit,' the shop owner observed.

'Easier than me,' Taussig agreed glumly. She lifted a suit from the nearest rack and walked to a mirror. Severely cut, it suited her present mood. 'Can I try this one on?'

'Surely,' the owner said at once. It was a three-hundred-dollar outfit.

'Need a hand?' 'Ann' asked.

'Sure – you can tell me what you're up to.' Both women walked back to the dressing rooms.

Within the booth, both women chatted away, discussing the everyday things that differ little between women and men. Bisyarina handed over a slip of paper, which Taussig read. The latter's conversation stuttered for a moment before she nodded agreement. Her face switched from shock to acceptance, then switched again to something that Bisyarina did not like at all – but the KGB didn't pay her to like her job.

The suit fitted rather nicely, the owner saw when they came out. Taussig paid the way most people did, with a credit card. Ann waved and left, turning to walk past the gun shop on her way out the mall.

Jennings saw her subject come out of the shop a few minutes later, carrying a clear plastic garment bag. *Well, that's what it was*, she told herself. *Whatever was bothering her the other night, she went shopping to make herself feel better and got another one of those suits*. Jennings followed her for another hour before breaking off the surveillance. Nothing there.

'He's one cool dude,' Ryan told Candela. 'I didn't expect him to jump into my lap and thank me for the offer, but I expected *some* reaction!'

'Well, if he bites, he'll get word to you easy enough.'

'Yeah.'

21

Knave's Gambit

The Archer tried to tell himself that the weather was no man's ally, but surely this was not true. The skies were clear, the winds cold and from the northeast, sweeping down from the frigid center of Siberia. He wanted clouds. They could move only in darkness now. That made progress slow, and the longer they were here in Soviet territory, the greater the chance that someone would notice them, and if they were noticed . . .

There was little need to speculate about that. All he had to do was raise his head to watch the armored vehicles motoring along the Dangara road. There was at least a battalion stationed around here, possibly a whole regiment of motor-rifle troops who constantly patrolled the roads and tracks. His force was large and formidable by *mud-jaheddin* standards, but against Russians in regimental force on their own land, only Allah Himself could save them. *And perhaps not even Him?* the Archer wondered, then chastised himself for the unspoken blasphemy.

His son was not far away, probably less than the distance they'd traveled to be here – but where? A place he would never find. The Archer was certain of that. He'd given up hope long ago. His son would be raised in the alien, infidel ways of the Russians, and all he could do was pray that Allah would come to his son before it was too late. To steal children, surely that was the most heinous of all crimes. To rob them of their parents and their faith . . . well, there was no need to dwell on that.

Every one of his men had reason enough to hate the Russians. Families killed or scattered, homes bombed. His men did not know that this was the usual business of modern war. As 'primitives', they felt that battles were affairs for warriors alone. Their leader knew that this had stopped being true long before any of them was born. He didn't understand why the 'civilized' nations of the world had changed this sensible rule, but he only needed to know that it was. With this knowledge had come the awareness that his destiny was not the one he'd selected for himself. The Archer wondered if any man truly chose his fate, or was it not all in greater hands than those which held book or rifle? But that was another complex, useless thought, since for the Archer and his men, the world had distilled itself to a few simple truths and a few deep hates. Perhaps that would someday change, but for the *mudjaheddin* the world was limited to what they could see and feel now. To search further was to lose sight of what mattered, and that meant death. The only great thought held by his men was their faith, and for the moment that was enough.

The last vehicle in the column disappeared around the bend in the road. The Archer shook his head. He'd had enough of thinking for the present. The Russians he'd just watched had all been inside their tracked BMP infantry carriers, inside where they could be kept warm by the fighting vehicle's heater; inside where they could not see out very well. That was what mattered. He raised his head to see his men, well camouflaged by their Russian-issue clothing and hidden behind rocks, lying in crevices, paired off, which allowed one to sleep while the other, like their leader, watched and kept guard.

The Archer looked up to see the sun now in decline. Soon it would slide behind the mountain ridge, and his men could resume their march north. He saw the sun glint off the aluminium skin of an aircraft as it turned in the air high overhead.

Colonel Bondarenko had a window seat and was staring down at the forbidding mountains. He remembered his brief tour of duty in Afghanistan, the endless, leg-killing mountains where one could travel in a perfect circle and seem to go uphill all the way. Bondarenko shook his head. That, at least, was behind him. He'd served his time, tasted combat, and now he could go back to applied engineering science which was, after all, his first love. Combat operations were a young man's game, and Gennady Iosifovich was over forty now. Having once proven that he could climb the rocks with the young bucks, he was resolved never to do so again. Besides, there was something else on his mind.

What's happening with Misha? he asked himself. When the man had disappeared from the Ministry, he'd naturally assumed that the older man was ill. When the absence had lasted several days, he took it to be serious and asked the Minister if Colonel Filitov had been hospitalized. The reply at the time had been reassuring – but now he wondered. Minister Yazov had been a little too glib – then Bondarenko had gotten orders to return to Bright Star for an extended evaluation of the site. The Colonel felt that he was being shuffled out of the way – but why? Something about the way Yazov had reacted to his innocent inquiry? Then there was the matter of the surveillance he'd spotted. Could the two things be connected? The connection was so obvious that Bondarenko ignored it without conscious consideration. It was simply impossible that Misha could have been the target of a security investigation, and even less possible that the investigation should develop substantive evidence of misdeeds. The most likely thing, he concluded, was that Misha was off on a top-secret job for Yazov. Surely he did a lot of that. Bondarenko looked down at the massive earthwork of the Nurek power dam. The second string of power lines was almost done, he noted, as the airliner dropped flaps and wheels for a landing at Dushanbe-East. He was the first man to leave the aircraft after landing.

'Gennady Iosifovich!'

'Good morning, Comrade General,' Bondarenko said in some surprise.

'Come with me,' Pokryshkin said, after returning the Colonel's salute. 'You don't want to ride that damned bus.' He waved to his sergeant, who wrested away Bondarenko's bag.

'You didn't need to come yourself.'

'Rubbish.' Pokryshkin led the parade to his personal helicopter, whose rotor was already turning. 'One day I must read that report you drafted. I just had three *ministers* here yesterday. Now everyone understands how important we are. Our funding is being increased twenty-five percent – I wish *I* could write that kind of report!'

'But I –'

'Colonel, I don't want to hear it. You have seen the truth and communicated it to others. You are now part of the Bright Star family. I want you to think about coming to us full time after your Moscow tour is finished. According to your file, you have excellent engineering and administrative credentials, and I need a good second-in-command.' He turned with a conspiratorial look. 'I don't suppose I could talk you into an air-force uniform?'

'Comrade General, I –'

'I know, once a soldier of the Red Army, always a soldier of the Red Army. We will not hold it against you. Besides, you can help me with those KGB boneheads on perimeter guard. They can bluster their expertise at a broken-down fighter pilot, but not against a man with the Red Banner for close combat.' The General waved for the pilot to take off. Bondarenko was surprised that the commander wasn't flying the aircraft himself. 'I tell you, Gennady, in a few years this will be a whole new service branch. "Cosmic Defense Troops", perhaps. There will be room for you to create a whole new career, and plenty of room for advancement. I want you to give that some serious thought. You will probably be a general in three or four years anyway, but I can guarantee you more stars than the Army can.'

'For the moment, however . . . ?' He'd think about that, but not in a helicopter.

'We're looking at the mirror and computer plans the Americans are using. The chief of our mirror group thinks he can adapt their designs to our hardware. It will take about a year to come up with the plans, he says, but he doesn't know about the actual engineering. Meanwhile we're assembling some reserve lasers and trying to simplify the design to make maintenance easier.'

'That's another two years' work,' Bondarenko observed.

'At least,' General Pokryshkin agreed. 'This program will not come to fruition before I leave. That's inevitable. If we have one more major test success, I will be recalled to Moscow to head the Ministry office, and at best the system will not be deployed before I retire.' He shook his head sadly. 'It's a hard thing to accept, how long these projects take now. That's why I want you here. I need a young man who will carry this project all the way through. I've looked at a score of officers. You're the best of them, Gennady Iosifovich. I want you here to take over from me when the time comes.'

Bondarenko was stunned. Pokryshkin had selected him, doubtless in preference to men from his own service branch. 'But you hardly know me –'

'I did not get to be a general officer by being ignorant of people. You have the qualities that I look for, and you are at just the right part of your career – ready for an independent command. Your uniform is less important than the type of man you are. I've already telexed the Minister to this effect.'

Well. Bondarenko was still too surprised to be pleased. *And all because Old Misha decided that I was the best man to make an inspection tour. I hope he's not too ill.*

'He's been going over nine hours now,' one of the officers said almost accusingly to Vatutin. The Colonel bent to look in the fiber-optic tube and watched the man for several minutes. He was lying down at first, tossing and turning fitfully as he tried willing himself to sleep, but that effort was doomed to failure. After that came the nausea and diarrhea from the caffeine that denied him sleep. Next he rose and resumed the pacing he'd been doing for hours, trying to tire himself into the sleep that part of his body demanded while the remainder objected.

'Get him up here in twenty minutes.' The KGB Colonel looked at his subordinate with amusement. He'd slept only seven hours and spent the last two making sure that the orders he'd given before turning in had been carried out in full. Then he'd showered and shaved. A messenger had fetched a fresh uniform from his apartment while an orderly had polished his boots to a mirrorlike luster. Vatutin finished off his own breakfast and treated himself to an extra cup of coffee brought down from the senior-officers' mess. He ignored the looks he was getting from the other members of his interrogation team, not even giving them a cryptic smile to indicate that he knew what he was doing. If they didn't know that by now, then the hell with them. Finished, he wiped his mouth with the napkin and walked to the interrogation room.

Like most such rooms, the bare table it held was more than it appeared to be. Under the lip where the tabletop overlapped the supporting frame were several buttons that he could press without anyone's noticing. Several microphones were set in the apparently blank walls, and the single adornment on them, a mirror, was actually two-way, so that the subject could be observed and photographed from the next room.

Vatutin sat down and got out the folder that he'd be putting away when Filitov arrived. His mind went over what he'd do. He already had it fully planned, of course, including the wording of his verbal report to Chairman Gerasimov. He checked his watch, nodded to the mirror, and spent the next several minutes composing himself for what was to come. Filitov arrived right on time.

He looked strong, Vatutin saw. Strong but haggard. That was the caffeine with which his last meal had been laced. The façade he projected was hard, but brittle and thin. Filitov showed irritation now. Before, he'd shown only resolve.

'Good morning, Filitov,' Vatutin said, hardly looking up.

'*Colonel* Filitov to you. Tell me, when will this charade be over?'

He probably believes that, too, Vatutin told himself. The subject had so often repeated the story of how Vatutin had placed the film cassette in his hand that he might have halfway believed it now. That was not unusual. He took his chair without asking permission, and Vatutin waved the turnkey out of the room.

'When did you decide to betray the Motherland?' Vatutin asked.

'When did you decide to stop buggering little boys?' the old man replied angrily.

'Filitov – excuse me, *Colonel* Filitov – you know that you were arrested with a microfilm cassette in your hand, only two meters from an American intelligence officer. On that microfilm cassette was information about a highly secret State defense-research installation, which information you have been giving for years to the Americans. There is no question of this, in case you have forgotten,' Vatutin explained patiently. 'What I am asking is, how long you have been doing this?'

'Go bugger yourself,' Misha suggested. Vatutin noticed a slight tremor in his hands. 'I am three times Hero of the Soviet Union. I was killing the enemies of this country while you were an ache in your father's crotch, and you have the balls to call me traitor?'

'You know, when I was in grammar school, I read books about you. Misha, driving the *fascisti* back from the gates of Moscow. Misha, the demon tankist. Misha, the Hero of Stalingrad. Misha, killer of Germans. Misha, leading the counterattack at the Kursk Bulge. Misha,' Vatutin said finally, 'traitor to the Motherland.'

Misha waved his hand, looking in annoyance at the way it shook. 'I have never had much respect for the *chekisti*. When I was leading my men, they were there – behind us. They were very efficient at shooting prisoners – prisoners

441

that real soldiers had taken. They were also rather good at murdering people who'd been forced to retreat. I even remember one case where a *chekist* lieutenant took command of a tank troop and led it into a fucking swamp. At least the Germans I killed were men, fighting men. I hated them, but I could respect them for the soldiers they were. Your kind, on the other hand . . . perhaps we simple soldiers never really understood who the enemy was. Sometimes I wonder who has killed more Russians, the Germans – or people like you?'

Vatutin was unmoved. 'The traitor Penkovskiy recruited you, didn't he?'

'Rubbish! I reported Penkovskiy myself.' Filitov shrugged. He was surprised at the way he felt, but was unable to control it. 'I suppose your kind does have its use. Oleg Penkovskiy was a sad, confused man who paid the price that such men have to pay.'

'As will you,' Vatutin said.

'I cannot prevent you from killing me, but I have seen death too many times. Death has taken my wife and my sons. Death has taken so many of my comrades – and death has tried to take me often enough. Sooner or later death will win, whether from you or someone else. I have forgotten how to fear that.'

'Tell me, what do you fear?'

'Not you.' This was delivered not with a smile, but with a cold, challenging glare.

'But all men fear something,' Vatutin observed. 'Did you fear combat?' *Ah, Misha, you're talking too much now. Do you even know that?*

'Yes, at first. The first time a shell hit my T-34, I wet my pants. But only that first time. After that I knew that the armor would stop most hits. A man can get accustomed to physical danger, and as an officer you are often too busy to realize that you're supposed to be afraid. You fear for the men under your command. You fear failure in a combat assignment, because others depend on you. You always fear pain – not death, but pain.' Filitov surprised himself by

442

talking this much, but he'd had enough of this KGB slug. It was almost like the frenetic excitement of combat, sitting here and dueling with this man.

'I have read that all men fear combat, but that what sustains them is their self-image. They know that they cannot let their comrades perceive them to be less than what they are supposed to be. Men, therefore, fear cowardice more than danger. They fear betraying their manhood, and their fellow soldiers.' Misha nodded slightly. Vatutin pressed one of the buttons under the table. 'Filitov, you have betrayed your men. Can't you see that? Don't you understand that in giving defense secrets to the enemy, you have betrayed all the men who served with you?'

'It will take more than your words to –'

The door opened quietly. The young man who entered wore dirty, greasy coveralls, and wore the ribbed helmet of a tank crewman. All the details were right: there was a trailing wire for the tank's interphones, and the powerful smell of powder came into the room with the young man. The coverall was torn and singed. His face and hands were bandaged. Blood dripped down from the covered eye, clearing a trail through the grime. And he was the living image of Aleksey Il'ych Romanov, Corporal of the Red Army, or as close to is as the KGB could manage in one frantic night's effort.

Filitov didn't hear him enter, but turned as soon as he noticed the smell. His mouth dropped open in shock.

'Tell me, Filitov,' Vatutin said. 'How do you think your men would react if they learned what you have done?'

The young man – he was in fact a corporal who worked for a minor functionary in the Third Directorate – did not say a word. The chemical irritant in his right eye was making it water, and while the youngster struggled not to grimace at the pain it caused him, the tears ran down his cheeks. Filitov didn't know that his meal had been drugged – so disoriented was he by his stay in Lefortovo that he no longer had the ability to register the things that were being done to him. The caffeine had induced the exact opposite of a drunken state. His mind was as wide awake as it had been in combat, all his senses sought input, noticed everything that was happening around him – but all through the night there had been nothing to report. Without data to pass on, his senses had begun making thing up, and Filitov had been hallucinating when the guards had come to fetch him. In Vatutin he had a target on which to fix his psyche. But Misha was also tired, exhausted by the routine to which he had been subjected, and the combination of wakefulness and bone-crushing fatigue had placed him in a dreamlike state where he no longer had the ability to distinguish the real from the imaginary.

'Turn *around*, Filitov!' Vatutin boomed. 'Look at me when I address you! I asked you a question: *What of all the men who served you?*'

'Who –'

'Who? The men you led, you old fool!'

'But –' He turned again, and the figure was gone.

'I've been looking through your file, all those citations you wrote for your men – more than most commanders. Ivanenko here, and Pukhov, and this Corporal Romanov. All the men who died for you, what would they think now?'

'They would understand!' Misha insisted as the anger took over completely.

'What would they understand? Tell me now, what is it that they would understand?'

'Men like you killed them – not I, not the Germans, but men like you!'

'And your sons, too, eh?'

'Yes! My two handsome sons, my two strong, brave boys, they went to follow in my footsteps and –'

'Your wife, too?'

'That above all!' Filitov snarled back. He leaned forward across the table. 'You have taken everything from me, you *chekist* bastard – and you wonder that I needed to fight back at you? No man has served the State better than I, and look at my reward, look at the gratitude of the Party. All that was my world you have taken away, and you say that I have betrayed the *Rodina*, do you? *You* have betrayed her, and you have betrayed me!'

'And because of that, Penkovskiy approached you, and because of that you have been feeding information to the West – you've fooled us all these years!'

'It is no great thing to fool the likes of you!' He pounded his fist on the table. 'Thirty years, Vatutin, thirty years I have – I have –' He stopped, a curious look on his face, wondering what he had just said.

Vatutin took his time before speaking, and when he did so, his voice was gentle. 'Thank you, Comrade Colonel. That is quite enough for now. Later we will talk about exactly what you have given the West. I despise you for what you have done, Misha. I cannot forgive or understand treason, but you're the bravest man I have ever met. I hope that you can face what remains of your life with equal bravery. It is important now that you face yourself and your crimes as courageously as you faced the *fascisti*, so that your life can end as honorably as you lived it.' Vatutin pressed a button and the door opened. The guards took Filitov away, still looking back at the interrogator, more surprised than anything else. Surprised that he'd been tricked. He'd never understand how it had been done, but then they rarely did, the Colonel of the Second Chief Directorate told himself. He rose, too, after a minute, collecting his files in a businesslike way before he walked out of the room and upstairs.

'You would have been a fine psychiatrist,' the doctor observed first of all.

'I hope the tape machines got all of that,' Vatutin said to his technicians.

'All three, plus the television record.'

'That was the hardest one I've ever come across,' a major said.

'Yes, he was a hard one. A brave one. Not an adventurer, not a dissident. That one was a patriot – or that's what the poor bastard thought he was. He wanted to save

445

the country from the Party.' Vatutin shook his head in wonderment. 'Where do they get such ideas?'

Your Chairman, he reminded himself, *wants to do much the same thing – or more accurately to save the country* for *the Party.* Vatutin leaned against the wall for a moment while he tried to decide how similar or how different the motivation was. He concluded quickly that this was not a proper thought for a simple counterintelligence officer. At least not yet. *Filitov got his ideas from the clumsy way the Party treated his family. Well, even though the Party says it never makes mistakes, we all know differently. What a pity that Misha couldn't make that allowance. After all, the Party is all we have.*

'Doctor, make sure he gets some rest,' he said on the way out. There was a car waiting for him.

Vatutin was surprised to see that it was morning. He'd allowed himself to focus too fully these last two days, and he'd thought that it would be night-time. So much the better, though: he could see the Chairman right now. The really amazing part was that he was actually on a fairly normal schedule. He could go home tonight and get a normal night's sleep, reacquaint himself with wife and family, watch some television. Vatutin smiled to himself. He could also look forward to a promotion, he told himself. After all, he'd broken the man earlier than promised. That ought to make the Chairman happy.

Vatutin caught him between meetings. He found Gerasimov in a pensive mood, staring out his window at the traffic on Dzerzhinskiy Square.

'Comrade Chairman, I have the confession,' Vatutin announced. Gerasimov turned.

'Filitov?'

'Why, yes, Comrade Chairman.' Vatutin allowed his surprise to show.

Gerasimov smiled after a moment. 'Excuse me, Colonel. There is an operational matter on my mind at the moment. You do have his confession?'

'Nothing detailed yet, of course, but he did admit that he

was sending secrets to the West, and that he has been doing so for thirty years.'

'Thirty years – and all that time we didn't detect it . . .' Gerasimov noted quietly.

'That is correct,' Vatutin admitted. 'But we have caught him, and we will spend weeks learning all that he has compromised. I think we will find that his placement and operational methods made detection difficult, but we will learn from this, as we have learned from all such cases. In any event, you required the confession and now we have it,' the Colonel pointed out.

'Excellent,' the Chairman replied. 'When will your written report be ready?'

'Tomorrow?' Vatutin asked without thinking. He nearly cringed awaiting the reply. He expected to have his head snapped off, but Gerasimov thought for an infinity of seconds before nodding.

'That is sufficient. Thank you, Comrade Colonel. That will be all.'

Vatutin drew himself to attention and saluted before leaving.

Tomorrow? he asked himself in the corridor. *After all that, he's willing to wait until tomorrow?*

What the hell? It didn't make any sense. But Vatutin had no immediate explanation, either, and he did have a report to file. The Colonel walked to his office, pulled out a lined pad, and started drafting his interrogation report.

'So that's the place?' Ryan asked.

'That's it. Used to be they had a toy store right across from it, over there. Called Children's World, would you believe? I suppose somebody finally noticed how crazy that was, and they just moved it. The statue in the middle is Feliks Dzerzhinskiy. That was a cold bloody piece of work – next to him Heinrich Himmler was a boy scout.'

'Himmler wasn't as smart,' Jack observed.

'True enough. Feliks broke at least three attempts to bring Lenin down, and one of them was pretty serious. The full story on that never has gotten out, but you can bet the records are right in there,' the driver said. He was an Australian, part of the company contracted to handle perimeter security for the embassy, and a former commando of the Aussie SAS. He never performed any actual espionage activities – at least not for America – but he often played the part, doing strange things. He'd learned to spot and shake tails along the way, and that made the Russians certain that he was CIA or some sort of spook. He made an excellent tour guide, too.

He checked the mirror. 'Our friends are still there. You don't expect anything, do you?'

'We'll see.' Jack turned. They weren't being very subtle, but he hadn't expected that they would. 'Where's Frunze?'

'South of the embassy, mate. You should have told me that you wanted to go there, we'd have hit it first.' He made a legal U-turn while Ryan kept looking back. Sure enough, the Zhiguli – it looked like an old Fiat – did the same, following them like a faithful dog. They went past the American compound again on the way, past the former Greek Orthodox church known to embassy wags as Our Lady of the Microchips for all the surveillance devices it surely contained.

'What exactly are we doing?' the driver asked.

'We're just driving around. The last time I was here, all I saw was the way to and from the Foreign Ministry and the inside of a palace.'

'And if our friends get any closer?'

'Well, if they want to talk with me, I suppose I might oblige,' Ryan answered.

'Are you serious?' He knew Ryan was CIA.

'You bet.' Jack chuckled.

'You know I have to do a written report on things like that?'

'You have your job, I have mine.' They drove around for another hour, but nothing happened. That was to Ryan's disappointment, and the driver's relief.

*

They arrived the usual way. Though the crossing points were shuffled at random, the car – it was a Plymouth Reliant, about four years old, with Oklahoma tags – stopped at the Border Patrol control booth. There were three men inside, one of whom appeared to be asleep and had to be roused.

'Good evening,' the Border Patrolman said. 'Could I see some identification, please?' All three men handed over driver's licenses, and the photographs matched. 'Anything to declare?'

'Some booze. Two quarts – I mean liters – for each of us.' He watched with interest as a dog sniffed around the car. 'You want us to pull over and pop the trunk?'

'Why were you in Mexico?'

'We represent Cummings-Oklahoma Tool and Die. Pipeline and refinery equipment,' the driver explained. 'Mainly large-diameter control valves and like that. We're trying to sell some to Pemex. The sales stuff is in the trunk, too.'

'Any luck?' the Border Patrolman asked.

'First try. It'll take a few more. They usually do.'

The dog handler shook his head negatively. His Labrador wasn't interested in the car. No smell of drugs. No smell of nitrates. The men in the car didn't fit the profile. They looked fairly clean-cut, but not overly so, and had not chosen a busy time to make the crossing.

'Welcome back,' the patrolman said. 'Safe trip home.'

'Thank you, sir.' The driver nodded and dropped the car into drive. 'See ya.'

'I don't believe it,' the man in the back said, once they were a hundred meters away from the control point. He spoke in English. 'They don't have the first idea of security.'

'My brother's a major in the Border Guards. I think he'd have a heart attack if he saw how easy that was,' the driver observed. He didn't laugh. The hard part would be getting out, and as of now they were in enemy territory. He drove

449

right at the posted speed limit while local drivers whizzed by him. He liked the American car. Though it lacked power, he'd never driven a car with more than four cylinders and didn't really know the difference. He'd been in the United States four times before, but never for a job like this, and never with so little preparation.

All three spoke perfect American English, with a prairie twang to coincide with their identification papers – that's how they all thought of their driver's licenses and Social Security cards, even though they could hardly be called proper 'papers'. The odd thing was that he liked America, especially the easy availability of inexpensive, wholesome food. He'd stop at a fast-food place on the way to Santa Fe, preferably a Burger King, where he'd indulge his love for a charcoal-cooked hamburger served with lettuce, tomatoes, and mayonnaise. That was one of the things Soviets found most amazing about America, the way anyone could get food without standing in a block-long line. And it was usually good food. How could Americans be so good at difficult tasks like food production and distribution, he wondered, and be so stupid about simple things like proper security? They just didn't make any sense at all, but it was wrong – dangerous – to be contemptuous of them. He understood that. The Americans played by a set of rules so different as to be incomprehensible . . . and there was so much *randomness* here. That frightened the KGB officer in a fundamental way. You couldn't tell which way they'd jump any more than you could predict the behavior of a driver on a highway. More than anything else, it was that unpredictability that reminded him that he was on the enemy's ground. He and his men had to be careful, had to keep to their training. Being at ease in an alien environment was the surest route to disaster – that lesson had been pounded home all the way through the academy. There were just too many things that training could not do. The KGB could scarcely predict what the American government would do. There was no way they could be prepared for the individual actions of two hundred-plus million people who bounced from decision to decision.

That was it, he thought. They have to make so many *decisions* every day. Which food to buy, which road to take, which car to drive. He wondered how his countrymen would handle such a huge load of decisions, forced upon you every day. Chaos, he knew. It would result in anarchy, and that was historically the greatest fear of Russians.

'I wish we had roads like this at home,' the man next to him said. The one in the back was asleep, for real this time. For both of them it was the first time in America. The operation had been laid on too fast. Oleg had done several jobs in South America, always covered as an American businessman. A Moscovite, he remembered that there, once you were twenty kilometers beyond the outer ring road, all the roads were gravel, or simply dirt. The Soviet Union did not have a single paved road that led from one border to another.

The driver – his name was Leonid – thought about that. 'Where would the money come from?'

'True,' Oleg agreed tiredly. They'd been driving for ten hours. 'But you'd think we could have roads as good as Mexico.'

'Hmph.' *But then people would have to choose where they wanted to go, and no one had ever bothered to train them how.* He looked at the clock on the dashboard. Six more hours, maybe seven.

Captain Tania Bisyarina came to much the same conclusion as she checked the dashboard clock in her Volvo. The safe house in this case wasn't a house at all, but an old house-trailer that looked more like the sort used as mobile offices by contractors and engineers. It had started life as the former, but ended as the latter when an engineering firm had abandoned it a few years before after half-completing their project in the hills south of Santa Fe. The drainage lines and sewers they'd been installing for a new housing development had never been finished. The developer had lost his financing, and the property was still tied up in court battles. The location was perfect, close to the interstate, close to the city, but hidden away behind a ridge and marked only by a dirt access road that even the local teenagers hadn't discovered yet for their post-dance parking. The visibility question was both good and bad news. Scrub pines hid the trailer from view, but also allowed clandestine approach. They'd have to post an outside guard. Well, you couldn't have everything. She'd driven in without lights, having carefully timed her arrival for a time when the nearest road was effectively deserted. From the back of her Volvo, she unloaded two bags of groceries. The trailer had no electricity, and all the food had to be nonperishable. That meant the meat was plastic-wrapped sausage, and she had a dozen cans of sardines. Russians love them. Once the groceries were in, she got a small suitcase from her car and set it next to the two jerricans of water in the nonfunctional bathroom.

She would have preferred curtains on the windows, but it was not a good idea to alter the appearance of the trailer too much. Nor was it a very good idea to have a car there. After the team arrived, they'd find a heavily wooded spot a hundred meters up the dirt road to leave it. That was also a minor annoyance, but one for which they had to prepare. Setting up safe houses was never as easy as people thought, certainly not the covert kind, even in places as open as America. It would have been somewhat easier if she'd had decent warning, but this operation had been laid on virtually overnight, and the only place she had was the rough-and-ready spot she'd picked out soon after arriving. It wasn't intended for anything other than a place for her to hole up, or perhaps safeguard her agent should it ever become necessary. It had never been intended for the mission at hand, but there wasn't time to make any other arrangements. The only other alternative was her own home, and that was definitely out. Bisyarina wondered if she'd be disciplined for not having scouted out a better location, but knew that she'd followed her instructions to the letter in all of her field activities.

The furniture was functional, though dirty. With nothing better to do, she wiped it off. The team leader coming in was a senior officer. She didn't know his name or face, but he had to have more rank than she did for this kind of job. When the trailer's single couch was reasonably presentable, she stretched out for a nap, having first set a small alarm clock to wake her in several hours. It seemed that she'd just lain down when the bell startled her off the vinyl cushions.

They arrived an hour before dawn. The road signs made it easy, and Leonid had the route completely memorized. Five miles – he had to think in miles now – off the interstate, he turned right onto a side road. Just past a road sign advertising a cigarette, he saw the dirt road that seemingly led nowhere. He switched off the car's lights and coasted up to it, careful to keep his foot off the brake lest his tail-lights betray him in the trees. Over the first small ridge, the road dropped and curved to the right. There was the Volvo. Next to it was a figure.

This was always the tense part. He was making contact with a fellow KGB officer, but he knew of cases where things hadn't gone quite right. He set the parking brake and got out.

'Lost?' the woman's voice asked.

'I'm looking for Mountain View,' he replied.

'That's on the other side of town,' she said.

'Oh, I must have taken the wronge exit.' He could see her relax when he completed the sequence.

'Tania Bisyarina. Call me Ann.'

'I'm Bob,' Leonid said. 'In the car are Bill and Lenny.'

'Tired?'

'We've been driving since dawn yesterday,' Leonid/Bob answered.

'You can sleep inside. There's food and drink. No electricity, no running water. There are two flashlights and a gasoline lantern – you can use that to boil water for coffee.'

453

'When?'

'Tonight. Get your people inside and I'll show you where to move the car.'

'How about getting out?'

'I don't know yet. What we have to do later today is complex enough.' That launched her into a description of the operation. What surprised her, though it shouldn't have, was the professionalism of the three. Each of them had to be wondering what Moscow Center had in its head when it ordered this operation. What they were doing was insane enough, much less the timing. But none of the four allowed their personal feelings to interfere with business. The operation was ordered by Moscow Center, and Moscow knew what it was doing. The manuals all said so, and the field officers believed it, even when they knew they shouldn't.

Beatrice Taussig awoke an hour later. The days were getting longer, and now the sun didn't shine in her face when she drove to work. Instead it stared right through her bedroom window like an accusing eye. Today, she told herself, the dawn marked what was supposed to be a really new day, and she prepared herself to meet it. She started off with a shower and blow-dried her hair. Her coffee machine had already switched on, and she drank her first cup while she decided what she'd wear today. She told herself that it was an important decision, and found that it required more of a breakfast than a cup of coffee and a muffin. Such things require energy, she told herself gravely, and fixed eggs to go along with the rest. She'd have to remind herself to go light on lunch as a result. Taussig had kept to a constant weight for the past four years, and was very careful of her figure.

Something frilly, she decided. She didn't have many outfits like that, but maybe the blue one . . . She switched on the TV as she ate her breakfast, catching the CNN Headline News blurb about the arms negotiations in Moscow. Maybe the world would become a safer place. It

454

was good to think that she was working for something. A fastidious person, she put all her dishes in the dishwasher rack before returning to her bedroom. The blue outfit with the frills was a year out of date, but few at the project would notice – the secretaries would, but who cared about them? She added a paisley scarf around her neck to show that Bea was still Bea.

Taussig pulled into her reserved parking place at the normal time. Her security pass came out of her purse and went around her neck, suspended by a gold chain, and she breezed in the door, past the security checkpoints.

''Mornin', doc,' said one of the guards. It had to be the outfit, Bea thought. She gave him a smile anyway, which made it an unusual morning for both of them, but didn't say anything, not to some high-school dropout.

She was the first one in her office, as usual. That meant that she fixed the coffee machine the way she liked, very strong. While it was perking, she opened her secure file cabinet and took out the package that she'd been working on the previous day.

Surprisingly, the morning went much more quickly than she had expected. The work helped. She had to deliver a cost-projection analysis by the end of the month, and to do that she had to shuffle through reams of documents, most of which she'd already photographed and forwarded to Ann. It was so convenient to have a private office with a door, and a secretary who always knocked before entering. Her secretary didn't like her, but Taussig didn't much care for her, either, a born-again jerk whose idea of a good time was practicing hymns. Well, a lot of things would change, she told herself. This *was* the day. She'd seen the Volvo on the drive in, parked in the appropriate place.

'Eight-point-one on the dyke-meter,' Peggy Jennings said. 'You ought to see the clothes she buys.'

'So she's eccentric,' Will Perkins observed tolerantly. 'You see something I don't, Peg. Besides, I saw her coming

455

in this morning, and she looked fairly decent, except for the scarf.'

'Anything unusual?' Jennings asked. She put her personal feelings aside.

'No. She gets up awfully early, but maybe she takes time to get untracked in the morning. I don't see any special reason to extend the surveillance.' The list was long, and manpower was short. 'I know you don't like gays, Peg, but you haven't even got a confirmation on that yet. Maybe you just don't like the gal,' he suggested.

'The subject is flamboyant in mannerisms but conservative in dress. Outspoken on most things, but she doesn't talk at all about work. She's a collection of contradictions.' *And that fits the profile*, she didn't have to add.

'So maybe she doesn't talk about work because she's not supposed to, like the security weenies tell them. She drives like an Easterner, always in a hurry, but she dresses in conservative clothes – maybe she likes the way she looks in clothes like that? Peg, you can't be suspicious about everything.'

'I thought that was our job,' Jennings snorted. 'Explain what we watched the other night.'

'I can't explain it, but you're putting your own spin on it. There's no evidence, Peg, not even enough to intensify the surveillance. Look, after we get through the people on the list, we'll take another look at her.'

'This is crazy, Will. We have a supposed leak in a top-security project, and we have to pussyfoot around like we're afraid we might offend somebody.' Agent Jennings stood and walked over to her desk for a moment. It wasn't much of a walk. The local FBI office was crowded with arrivals from the Bureau's counterintel office, and the headquarters people had usurped the lunchroom. Their 'desks' were actually lunch tables.

'Tell you what – we can take the people who have access to the leaked material and put 'em all on the box.' *On the box* meant subjecting everyone to a lie-detector test. The last time that had been done here, it had nearly started a revolution at Tea Clipper. The scientists and engineers were not intelligence types who understood that such things were necessary, but academics who considered the whole process an insult to their patriotism. Or a game: one of the software engineers had even tried using biofeedback techniques to screw up the test results. The main result from this effort, eighteen months before, had been to show that the scientific staff had a great deal of hostility to the security weenies, which was not much of a surprise. What had finally stopped the testing was a wrathful paper from a senior scientist who'd shown that a few deliberate lies he'd told went undetected. That, and the disruption it had caused within the various sections, had ended things before the program had been completed.

'Taussig didn't go on the box the last time,' Jennings noted. She'd checked. 'None of the admin people did. The revolt stopped things before they got that far. She was one of the people who –'

'Because the software bunch brought their protests to her. She's admin, remember, she's *supposed* to keep all the scientific people happy.' Perkins had checked, too. 'Look, if you feel this strongly about it, we can come back to her later. I don't see anything myself, but I'll trust your instincts – *but* for now, we have all these others to check out.'

Margaret Jennings nodded her surrender. Perkins was right, after all. They had nothing solid to point to. It was just her – *what?* Jennings wondered. She thought Taussig was gay, but that wasn't such a big thing anymore – the courts had said so in enough cases – and there was no proof to support her suspicion anyway. That's what it was, she knew. Three years earlier, right before she'd joined the counterintelligence office, she'd handled a kidnapping involving a couple of . . .

She also knew that Perkins was being more professional about it. Even though a Mormon, and straighter than most arrows, he didn't let his personal feelings interfere with business. What she couldn't shake was the gut feeling that

457

despite everything logic and experience told her, she was still right. Right or wrong, she and Will had six reports to fill out before they went back into the field. You couldn't spend more than half your time in the field anymore. The rest was always stuck at a desk – or a converted lunch table – explaining to people what it was that you did when you weren't stuck at a desk.

'Al, this is Bea. Could you come over to my office?'

'Sure. Be over in five minutes.'

'Great. Thanks.' Taussig hung up. Even Bea admired Gregory for his punctuality. He came through the door exactly on time.

'I didn't interrupt anything, did I?'

'No. They're running another target-geometry simulation, but they don't need me for that. What's up?' Major Gregory asked, then said, 'I like the outfit, Bea.'

'Thanks, Al. I need you to help me with something.'

'What?'

'It's a birthday present for Candi. I'm picking it up this afternoon and I need somebody to help me with it.'

'Eek, you're right. It is in three weeks, isn't it?'

Taussig smiled at Al. He even made geeky noises. 'You're going to have to start remembering those things.'

'So what are you getting her?' He grinned like a little boy.

'It's a *surprise*, Al.' She paused. 'It's something Candi needs. You'll see. Candi drove herself in today, didn't she?'

'Yeah, she has to see the dentist after work.'

'And don't tell her anything, please? It's a big surprise,' Bea explained.

He could see that it was all she could do to keep her face straight. It must be some surprise, he smiled. 'Okay, Bea. I'll see you at five.'

They woke after noon. 'Bob' trudged to the bathroom first before he remembered that there was no running water. He checked the windows for signs of activity before he went outside. By the time he was back, the others had water boiling. They only had instant coffee, but Bisyarina had gotten them a decent brand, and the breakfast food was all typically American, loaded with sugar. They knew that they'd need it. When each had finished his 'morning' routine, they got out their maps and their tools and went over the operation's details. Over a period of three hours, they walked through them mentally until each man knew exactly what had to happen.

And there it was, the Archer told himself. Mountains made for long views. In this case, the objective was still two nights' march away, despite the fact that they could see it now. While his subordinates tucked their men into hiding places, he rested his binoculars on a rock and examined the site, still . . . twenty-five kilometers away? he wondered, then checked his map. Yes. He'd have to take his men downhill, cross a small stream, then up the slopes on a man-killing climb, and they would make their last camp . . . there. He concentrated his viewing on that spot. Five kilometers from the objective itself, shielded from view by the mountain's contours . . . the final climb would be a hard one. But what choice was there? He might give his people an hour's rest before the actual assault. That would help, and he'd also be able to brief his men on their individual missions, and give them all time to pray. His eyes went back to the objective.

Clearly, construction was still under way, but on this sort of place, they'd never stop building. It was well that they were here now. In a few more years it would be impregnable. As it was . . .

His eyes strained to make out the details. Even with binoculars he couldn't make out anything smaller than the guard towers. In the first light of dawn he could see the individual bumps that marked buildings. He'd have to be closer to make out items on which the last-minute details of his plan would depend, but for the moment his interest was in the lay of the land. How best to approach the place? How to use the mountain to their advantage? If this place were guarded by KGB troops, as the CIA documents he'd inspected had said, he knew that they were as lazy as they were cruel.

Guard towers, three, north side. There will be a fence there. Mines? he wondered. Mines or not, those guard towers would have to go fast. They'd hold heavy machine guns, and the view from them commanded the terrain. How to do that?

'So that is the place?' The former Army Major came down beside him.

'The men?'

'All hidden,' the Major answered. He spent a minute examining the place in silence. 'Remember the stories about the Assassins' stronghold in Syria?'

'Oh.' The Archer turned sharply. That's what it reminded him of! 'And how was that fortress taken?'

The Major smiled, keeping his eyes to the objective. 'With more resources than we have, my friend . . . if they ever fortify the whole hilltop, it would take a regiment with helicopter support even to get inside the perimeter. So how do you plan to do it?'

'Two groups.'

'Agreed.' The Major didn't agree with any of this. His training – all of it supplied by the Russians – told him that this mission was madness for so small a force, but before he could contradict a man like the Archer he would have to show his combat skills. That meant running mad risks. In the meantime, the Major would try to nudge his tactics in the right direction.

'The machines are on the slopes to the north. The people are on the knoll to the south.' As they watched, the headlights of buses were moving from one place to the other. It was shift-change. The Archer considered that, but he had to make his attack in darkness and leave in darkness, else they'd never get away.

'If we can get in close without being detected . . . may I make a suggestion?' the Major asked quietly.

'Go on.'

'Take everything in together to the high ground in the center, then attack downhill against both places.'

'It's dangerous,' the Archer noted at once. 'There is much open ground to be covered on both sides.'

'It's also easier to reach the jump-off point unobserved. An approach by one group is less likely to be spotted than one by two groups. Place our heavy weapons there, and they can observe and support both assault teams . . .'

Here was the difference between an instinctive warrior and a trained soldier, the Archer admitted to himself. The Major knew better than he how to measure hazards one against the other. 'I don't know about the guard towers, though. What do you think?'

'I'm not sure. I –' The Major pushed his commander's head down. A moment later an airplane streaked down the valley.

'That was an MiG-21, reconnaissance version. We are not dealing with fools.' He looked to make sure that all his men were under cover. 'We may just have had our pictures taken.'

'Did they –'

'I don't know. We'll have to trust in God for that, my friend. He has not let us come this far to fail,' the Major said, wondering if that were true or not.

'So where are we going?' Gregory asked in the parking lot.

'Meet me at the mall, south side of the lot, okay? I just hope it'll fit in the car.'

'See you there.' Gregory walked to his car and drove off.

Bea waited a few minutes before following. There was no sense in having anyone notice that they left at the same time. She was excited now. To combat this, she tried driving slowly, but it was so out of character that it merely fed her excitement, and as though by its own accord the Datsun seemed to work its way up through the gears and change lanes. She arrived in the mall parking lot twenty minutes later.

Al was waiting. He'd parked his car two spaces away from a station wagon, well out from the nearest store. He'd even picked more or less the right place, Bea Taussig noticed as she pulled in alongside his car and got out.

'What kept you?' he asked.

'No real hurry.'

'So now what?'

Bea didn't really know. She knew what was to happen, but not how they planned to do it – in fact, she didn't even know for sure that it was a *they* doing it. Perhaps Ann was going to handle the thing all by herself. She laughed to cover her nervousness.

'Come on,' she said, waving for him to follow.

'This must be some birthday present,' Gregory noted. Off to his right, he noted a car backing out of its place.

Bea noted that the lot was crowded with cars but not people. The afternoon shoppers had gone home for dinner, the new arrivals were just beginning their activity, and the movie crowd wouldn't come for another hour or so. Even so, she was tense as her eyes scanned left and right. She was to be one lane over from the movie entrance. The time was right. If anything went wrong, she almost giggled to herself, she'd have to pick out a large, bulky present. But she didn't have to. Ann was walking toward her. She carried nothing but a large purse.

'Hi, Ann!' Taussig called.

'Hello, Bea – oh, it's Major Gregory.'

'Hi,' Al said, while he tried to remember if he knew this woman or not. Al didn't have much of a memory for faces, so occupied was his brain with numbers.

'We met last summer,' Ann said, confusing him all the more.

'What are you doing here?' Taussig asked her controller.

'Just some quick shopping. I have a date tonight, and I needed – well, I'll show you.'

She reached into her purse and pulled out what to Gregory looked like a perfume dispenser – or whatever they called those little spray gadgets, he thought while he waited. He was glad Candi wasn't like this. Ann seemed to spray some of the stuff on her wrist and held it up to Bea's nose as a car came down the lane.

'Candi would love it – what do you think, Al?' Bea asked as the dispenser came up towards his face.

'Huh?' At that moment he got a face full of chemical Mace.

Ann had timed it perfectly, spraying Gregory just as he was taking a breath, and aimed it to get under the glasses into his eyes. It seemed that his face had been set afire, and the searing pain went down into his lungs. In a moment he was on his knees, hands to his face. He couldn't make a sound, and couldn't see the car stop right beside him. The door opened, and the driver only had to take half a step before chopping him on the side of the neck.

Bea watched him go limp – so perfect, she thought. The car's rear door opened and hands came out to grab his shoulders. Bea and Ann helped with the legs as the driver got back in. Just as the rear door closed. Gregory's car keys flew out the window to them, and the Plymouth rolled away, having hardly stopped at all.

Instantly, Ann looked around. No one had seen them. She was sure of it as she and Bea walked back away from the stores to where the cars were.

'What are you going to do with him?' Bea asked.

'What do you care?' Bisyarina replied quickly.

'You're not going –'

'No, we're not going to kill him.' Ann wondered if that were true or not. She didn't know, but suspected that a murder was not in the cards. They'd broken one inviolable rule. That was enough for one day.

22

Active Measures

Leonid, whose current cover required him to say, 'Call me Bob,' headed for the far end of the parking lot. For an operation with virtually no planning, its most dangerous phase had gone smoothly enough. Lenny, in back, had the job of controlling the American officer they'd just kidnapped. A physical type, he'd once been part of the Soviet 'special-purpose' forces, known by the abbreviation *Spetznaz*. Bill, next to him, had been assigned to the mission because he was a scientific intelligence specialist; the fact that his area of expertise was chemical engineering hadn't mattered to Moscow. The case called for a scientific specialist, and he was the closest.

In the back, Major Gregory started to moan and move. The chop on his neck had been enough to stun, but not enough to produce any injury more serious than a blinding headache. They hadn't gone to all this trouble to kill the man by accident, something that had happened before. For the same reason, he hadn't been drugged. An exercise much more dangerous than most people might think, it had once accidentally killed a Soviet defector whose mind, as a result, had never been picked by the people of the Second Chief Directorate. To Lenny he seemed much like an infant coming out of a long sleep. The smell of chemical Mace was thick enough in the car that all of the windows were down a few inches to keep it from overpowering the KGB officers. They wanted to use physical restraints on their prisoner, but those might be troublesome if spotted. Lenny was able to control the American, of course. It was just that caution, the distillation of experience, taught them to take nothing for granted. For all they knew, Gregory's hobby might have been unarmed combat – stranger things had happened. When he became vaguely conscious, the first thing he saw was an automatic pistol's silencer pressed against his nose.

'Major *Gregoriy*,' Lenny said, using the Russian pronunciation for a purpose, 'we know that you are a bright young man, and perhaps a courageous one also. If you resist, you will be killed,' he lied. 'I am very skilled in this. You will say nothing at all, and you will be still. If you do these things, no harm will come to you. Do you understand – just nod if you do.'

Gregory was fully conscious. He'd never quite been out, merely stunned by the blow that still made his head as taut as a swollen balloon. His eyes were shedding tears as though from a leaky faucet, and every breath seemed to light a fire in his chest. He'd commanded himself to move as they pulled him into the car, but his limbs had ignored his frantic wishes while his mind raged at them. It had come to him in an instant: *That's why I hate Bea!* It wasn't her snotty manner and her weird way of dressing at all. But he set that one far aside. There were more important things to worry about, and his mind was racing as it had never raced before. He nodded.

'Very good,' the voice said, and strong arms lifted him off the floor and onto the rear seat. The metallic prod of the pistol was against his chest, hidden under the other man's left arm.

'The effect of the chemical irritant will pass in about an hour,' Bill told him. 'There will be no permanent effect.'

'Who are you?' Al asked. His voice was a mere whisper, as raspy as sandpaper.

'Lenny told you to be still,' the driver replied. 'Besides, someone as bright as you must already know who we are. Am I correct?' Bob looked in the mirror and was rewarded with a nod.

Russians! Al told himself in a combination of amazement and certainty. *Russians here, doing this . . . why do they want me? Will they kill me?* He knew that he could not believe a thing they said. They'd say anything to keep him under control. He felt like a fool. He was supposed to be a man, an officer, and he was as helpless as a four-year-old girl – and crying like one, he realized, hating every tear that dripped from his eyes. Never in his life had Gregory felt such a killing rage. He looked to his right and realized that he didn't have the smallest chance. The man with the gun was almost twice his weight, and besides, he did have the gun pressed right against his chest. Gregory's eyes were blinking now almost like the windshield wipers of a car. He couldn't see well, but he could tell that the man with the gun was watching him with clinical interest, no emotion at all in his eyes. The man was a professional in the application of violence. *Spetznaz*, Gregory thought at once. Al took a deep breath, or tried to. He nearly exploded in a convulsion of coughs.

'You don't want to do that,' the man in the right-front seat cautioned. 'Take shallow breaths. The effect will pass in time.' Wonderful stuff, this chemical Mace, Bill thought. And anyone could buy it in America. Amazing.

Bob was now out of the enormous parking lot and driving back to the safe house. He had the route memorized, of course, though he was not entirely at ease. He hadn't had the chance to drive it beforehand, to practice travel times and plot out alternative routes, but he had spent enough time in America that he knew how to drive lawfully and carefully. Driving habits here were better than in the Northeast – except on the interstates, where every Westerner felt the God-given right to race like a maniac. But he wasn't on the interstate, and on this four-lane highway the late rush-hour traffic moved placidly from light to light. He realized that his time estimate had been overly optimistic, but that didn't matter. Lenny would have no problem controlling their guest. It was quite dark, there were few street-lights, and theirs was just one more car driving home from work.

*

Bisyarina was already five miles away, heading in the opposite direction. The inside of the car was worse than she'd expected. A neat person, she was appalled to see that the young man had virtually covered the floor with plastic wrappers of some sort, and she wondered why the Chevy wasn't full of ants. The very thought made her skin crawl. She checked her mirror to make sure that Taussig was there. Ten minutes later she pulled into a working-class neighborhood. All of the houses had driveways, but even here most families had more than one car, and the extra ones were parked on the street. She found a vacant spot by a corner and pulled over to it. Taussig's Datsun appeared beside the Chevy, and she left it there, just another car parked at the curb. When Taussig halted at the next stop sign, Bisyarina rolled down her window and tossed Gregory's keys into a sewer. With that ended what was the most dangerous part of the mission for her. Without being told, Taussig drove back toward the shopping mall, where Bisyarina would retrieve her Volvo.

'You're sure you won't kill him,' Bea said again after another minute.

'Quite positive, Bea,' Ann replied. She wondered why Taussig had suddenly acquired a conscience. 'If I guess correctly, he might even be given the chance to continue his work . . . elsewhere. If he cooperates, then he will be treated very well.'

'You'll even assign him a girlfriend, won't you?'

'It's one way of keeping men happy,' Bisyarina admitted. 'Happy people work better.'

'Good,' Taussig said, surprising her controller quite a bit. Taussig explained after a moment: 'I don't want him hurt. What he knows will help both sides make the world safer.' *And I just want him out of my way!* she didn't say.

'He's too valuable to hurt,' Ann observed. *Unless things go wrong, in which case other orders might apply . . . ?*

Bob was surprised when the traffic backed up. He was right behind a mini-van. Like many American drivers, he hated the things because he couldn't see around them. He opened the ashtray and pushed in the cigarette lighter while he frowned in frustration. Bill, next to him, fished out a smoke also. If nothing else, it helped to mask the acrid stink of the Mace which permeated the cloth upholstery of the car. Bob decided that he'd leave all the windows open when he parked tonight, just to get rid of the smell. His own eyes were watering, now that there was no blowing air to carry the chemical vapors out of the car. It almost made him feel sorry about the straight dose they'd given their prisoner, but at least it was preferable to a drug that might kill, or a blow that could break his scrawny little neck. At least he was behaving himself. If all went according to plan, by the end of the week he'd be in Moscow. They'd wait a day or so before heading into Mexico. A different crossing point would be used, and a diversion, not yet set up, would probably be used to ensure their speedy crossing into that convenient country, where one could catch a plane to Cuba, and from there a direct flight to Moscow. After that, this team of the First Chief Directorate would have a month's rest. It would be good, Bob told himself, to see his family again. It was always lonely abroad. So lonely that once or twice he'd been unfaithful to his wife, which was also a violation of standing orders. Though not a violation that many officers took seriously, it was something of which he wasn't proud. Perhaps he could get a new posting at the KGB Academy. He had the seniority now, and with a mission like this under his belt . . .

Traffic started moving again. He was surprised to see the mini-van's blinkers go on. Two minutes later he was horrified to see why. A jack-knifed tractor-trailer blocked the entire road, with the remains of a small car crushed beneath its front wheels. What looked like a score of rotating ambulance lights illuminated the efforts of police officers and firemen to extricate whatever fool had been driving the small import. Bob couldn't even tell what sort of car it had been, but like the majority of the other drivers, he stared at the wreckage with fascination for a few seconds, until he reminded himself who and where he was. A black-clad police officer was replacing flares on the pavement and waving all southbound traffic onto a side road. Bob reverted to intelligence officer in a moment. He waited until there was a clear path around the cop, and shot past. That earned him an angry look, but nothing more. Most important, the policeman hadn't gotten much of a look at the car. Bob raced up a hill before he realized that another effect of his hesitation was that he couldn't see where the detoured traffic was heading.

I didn't bring the map, he thought next. He'd destroyed it because of all the markings on it. In fact, the car held no maps at all. Maps were dangerous things to have, and besides, he knew how to memorize all the information he needed for his missions. But he hadn't been here long enough to learn the area, and knew only one route back to the safe house.

Goddamn these 'immediate-priority' operations!

He took a left at the first crossroads, onto a curving street into a residential development. It took several minutes for him to realize that the land here was so hilly that all the roads curved back and forth upon themselves to the point where he didn't know which direction he was heading. For the first time, he began to lose his composure, but only for an instant. One mental curse in his native language reminded him that he couldn't even think in Russian. Bob lit another cigarette and drove slowly as he tried to orient himself. The tears in his eyes didn't help.

He's lost, Gregory realized after a moment. He'd read enough spy novels to know that they were taking him to a safe house – or a clandestine airfield? – or another vehicle that would carry him . . . where? – but as soon as he recognized the same car that they'd passed a few minutes before, he had to stop himself from smiling. They'd actually done something wrong. The next turn they took went downhill, and Gregory confirmed his suspicion when he again saw the rotating lights at the car wreck. He noted the curses as the driver pulled into a driveway and had to back up before they could climb the hill again.

Everything Russians hated about America flooded back into Bob's consciousness. Too many roads, too many cars – some damned fool of an American had run a stop sign and – *I hope he's dead!* the driver raged at the parked cars on the residential street. *I hope he died screaming in agony*. It felt better to get that thought out from the back of his mind.

Now what?

He continued on a different route, taking the road over the crest of the hill, where he was able to look down and see another highway. Perhaps if he went south on this one, it might connect with the road he'd been on . . . It was worth a try, he thought. To his right, Bill gave him a questioning look, but Lenny in the back was too busy with the prisoner to know that anything was badly wrong. As they picked up speed, at least the air through the windows allowed his eyes to clear. There was a traffic light at the bottom of the hill – but there was also a sign that said NO LEFT TURN.

Govno! Bob thought to himself as he turned right. This four-lane road was divided by a concrete barrier.

You should have spent more time studying the map. You should have taken a few hours to drive around the area. But it was too late for that now, and he knew that he hadn't had the time. That left them heading back north. Bob checked his watch, forgetting that there was a clock on the dashboard. He'd already lost fifteen minutes. He was out in the open and vulnerable, on enemy ground. What if someone had seen them in the parking lot? What if the policeman at the wreck had taken down their number?

Bob didn't panic. He was too well trained for that. He commanded himself to take a deep breath and mentally examined all the maps he'd seen of the area. He was west of the interstate highway. If he could find that, he still remembered the exit he'd used earlier in the day – was it still the same day? – and could get to the safe house blindfolded. If he were west of the interstate, all he had to do was find a road that went east. Which way was east – right. Another deep breath. He'd head north until he saw what looked like a major east-west road, and he'd turn right. Okay.

It took nearly five minutes, but he found an east-west highway – he didn't bother to look for the name. Five minutes after that he was grateful to see the red, white, and blue shield that informed him the interstate was half a mile ahead. Now he breathed easier.

'What's the trouble?' Lenny finally asked from the back. Bob replied in Russian.

'Had to change routes,' he said in a tone far more relaxed than he'd felt only a few minutes earlier. In turning to reply, he missed a sign.

There was the overpass. The green signs announced that he could go north or south. He wanted to go south, and the exit ramp would be –

In the wrong place. He was in the right lane, but the exit went to the left, and was only fifty meters ahead. He swerved across the highway without looking. Immediately behind him, an Audi driver stood on his brakes and jammed his hand on the horn. Bob ignored the irrelevancy as he took the left turn onto the ramp. He was on the upward, sweeping curve and was looking at the traffic on the interstate when he saw lights flashing in the grille of the black car behind him. The headlights blinked at him, and he knew what would come next.

Don't panic, he told himself. He didn't have to say anything to his comrades. Bob didn't even consider making a run for it. They'd been briefed on this, too. American police are courteous and professional. They didn't demand payment on the spot, as the Moscow traffic police did. He also knew that American cops were armed with Magnum revolvers.

Bob pulled his Plymouth over just beyond the overpass and waited. As he watched his mirror, the police car stopped behind his, slightly more to the left. He could see the officer getting out, carrying a clipboard in his left hand. That left the right one free, Bob knew, and that was the gun hand. In the back, Lenny told the prisoner what would happen if he made a noise.

'Good evening, sir,' the police officer said. 'I don't know what the rules are in Oklahoma, but here we prefer that you don't change lanes like that. Could I have your driver's license and registration, please?' His black uniform and silver trim made Leonid think of the SS, but this wasn't the time for such thoughts. *Just be polite*, he told himself calmly, *take the ticket and move on*. He handed over the proper cards and waited as the police officer started filling out the ticket blank. Perhaps an apology was due now . . . ?

'Sorry, officer, I thought the exit was on the right side, and –'

'That's why we spend all that money on signs, Mr Taylor. Is this your correct address?'

'Yes, sir. Like I said, I'm sorry. If you have to give me a ticket, I guess I deserve it.'

'I wish everybody was that cooperative,' the officer observed. Not everyone was, and he decided to see what this polite fellow looked like. He looked at the photograph on the license and bent down to make sure it was the right person. He shined the light in Bob's face. It was the same face, but . . . 'What the hell is that smell?'

Mace, the officer knew an instant later. The light swiveled. The people in the car looked normal enough, two in the front, two in the back, and . . . one of the people in the back was wearing what looked like a uniform jacket . . .

Gregory wondered if his life was really on the line. He decided that he'd find out, and prayed the policeman was alert.

In back, the one on the left side – the one in the jacket – mouthed a single word: *Help*. That merely made the policeman more curious, but the one in the right-front seat saw him do it and stirred. The cop's instincts all lit off at once. His right hand slid down to his service revolver, flipping the safety strap off the hammer.

'Out of the car, one at a time, and *right now!*'

He was horrified to see a gun. It appeared as though by magic from the guy in the right-rear, and before he could get his own revolver out –

Gregory's right hand didn't get there in time, but his elbow did, spoiling Lenny's aim.

The officer was surprised that he didn't hear anything except a shout in a language he couldn't understand, but by the time that occurred to him, his jaw had already exploded in a puff of white more heard than felt. He fell backward, his gun out now and shooting of its own accord.

Bob cringed and dropped the car into gear. The front wheels spun on the loose gravel, but caught, hauling the Plymouth all too slowly away from the noise of the gun. In the back, Lenny, who'd gotten off the one shot, slammed the butt of his automatic on Gregory's head. His perfectly aimed shot should have gone straight through the policeman's heart, but he'd gotten the face instead, and he didn't know how good the shot had been. He shouted something that Bob didn't bother listening to.

Three minutes later the Plymouth went off the interstate. Below the accident that still blocked the highway, the road was nearly clear. Bob took the dirt road off it, lights out, and was at the trailer before the prisoner regained consciousness.

Behind them, a passing motorist saw the policeman on the shoulder and pulled over to assist him. The man was in agony, with a bloody wound to his face and nine missing teeth. The motorist ran to the police car and put out a radio call. It took a minute before the dispatcher got things straight, but three minutes after that a second radio car was there, then five more in as many minutes. The wounded officer was unable to speak, but handed up his clipboard, which had the car's description and tag number written down. He also still had 'Bob Taylor's' driver's license. That was message enough for the other officers. An immediate call was put out over all local police frequencies. Someone had shot a police officer. The actual crime that had been committed was far more serious than that, but the police did not know, nor would they have cared.

Candi was surprised to see that Al wasn't home. Her jaw was still numb from the Xylocaine shots, and she decided on soup. *But where's Al? Maybe he had to stay late for something.* She knew that she could call, but it wasn't that big a deal, and with the way her mouth felt, there wasn't much in the way of talking she could have done anyway.

At police headquarters on Cerrillos Road, the computers were already humming. A telex was dispatched at once to Oklahoma, where brother police officers took immediate note of the magnitude of the crime and punched up their own computer records. They learned at once that there was no license for Robert J. Taylor of 1353 NW 108th Street, Oklahoma City, OK 73210, nor was there a Plymouth Reliant with tag number XSW-498. The tag number, in fact, did not exist. The sergeant who ran the computer section was more than surprised. To be told that there was no record of a tag wasn't all that unusual, but to get a no-hit on a tag and a license, *and* in a case with an officer-involved shooting was pushing the laws of probability too hard. He lifted the phone for the senior watch officer.

'Captain, we have something really crazy here on the Mendez shooting.'

The state of New Mexico is filled with areas belonging to the federal government, and has a long history of highly sensitive activities. The Captain didn't know what had happened, but he knew at once that this wasn't a traffic incident. One minute after that, he was on the phone to the local FBI office.

Jennings and Perkins were there before Officer Mendez came out of surgery. The waiting room was so crowded with policemen that it was fortunate the hospital had no other surgical patients at the moment. The Captain running the investigation was there, as were the state police chaplain and half a dozen other officers who worked the same watch as Mendez, plus Mrs Mendez, who was seven months pregnant. Presently the doctor came out and announced that he'd be fine. The only major blood vessel damaged had been easily repaired. The officer's jaw and teeth had taken most of the damage, and a maxillary surgeon would start repairing that damage in a day or two. The officer's wife cried a bit, then was taken to see her husband before two of his fellows drove her home. Then it was time for everyone to get to work.

'He must have had the gun in the poor bastard's back,' Mendez said slowly, his words distorted by the wires holding his jaw together. He'd already refused a pain medication. He wanted to get the information out quickly, and was willing to suffer a little to do it. The state police officer was a very angry man. 'Only way he coulda got it out so fast.'

'The photo on the license, is it accurate?' Agent Jennings asked.

'Yes, ma'am.' Pete Mendez was a young officer, and managed to make Jennings feel her age with that remark. He next got out rough descriptions of the other two. Then came the victim: 'Maybe thirty, skinny, glasses. He was wearing a jacket – like a uniform jacket. I didn't see any insignia, but I didn't get much of a look. He had his hair cut like he was in the service, too. Don't know the eye color, either, but there was something funny . . . his eyes were shiny, like – oh, the Mace smell. Maybe that was it. Maybe they Maced him. He didn't say anything, but, like, he mouthed the words, you know? I thought that was funny, but the guy in the right-front reacted real strong to that. I was slow. I shoulda reacted faster. Too damned slow.'

'You said that one of them said something?' Perkins asked.

'The bastard who shot me. I don't know what it was. Not English, not Spanish. I just remember the last word . . . *maht*, something like that.'

'*Yob' tvoyu mat*'!' Jennings said at once.

'Yeah, that's it.' Mendez nodded. 'What's it mean?'

'It means "fuck your mother." Excuse me,' Perkins said, his Mormon face fairly glowing scarlet. Mendez went rigid on his bed. One doesn't say such things to an angry man with an Hispanic name.

'What?' the state police Captain asked.

'It's Russian, one of their favorite curses.' Perkins looked at Jennings.

'Oh, boy,' she breathed, scarcely able to believe it. 'We're calling Washington right now.'

'We have to identify the – wait a minute! – Gregory?' Perkins said. 'God almighty. You call Washington. I'll call the project office.'

It turned out that the state police could move the fastest. Candi answered a knock on the door and was surprised to see a policeman standing there. He asked politely if he could see Major Al Gregory, and was told that he wasn't home by a young woman whose numbed jaw was coming back to normal as the world around her began to shatter. She'd scarcely gotten the news when Tea Clipper's security chief pulled up. She was a mere spectator as a radio call was sent out to look for Al's car, too shocked even to cry.

The license photo of "Bob Taylor" was already in Washington, being examined by members of the FBI's counterintelligence branch, but it wasn't in their file of identified Soviet officers. The Assistant Director who ran counterintel ops was called in from his Alexandria home by the senior watch officer. The AD in turn called FBI Director Emil Jacobs, who arrived at the Hoover Building at two in the morning. They could scarcely believe it, but the wounded police officer positively identified the photograph of Major Alan T. Gregory. The Soviets had never committed a violent crime in the United States. This rule was so well established that the most senior Soviet defectors, if they wished, were able to live openly and without protection.

476

But this was even worse than the elimination of a person who was, under Soviet law, a condemned traitor. An American citizen had been kidnapped; to the FBI, kidnapping is a crime hardly different from murder.

There was, of course, a plan. Even though it had never happened, the operations experts whose job it was to think about unthinkable happenings had a pre-set protocol of things that had to be done. Before dawn thirty senior agents were taking off from Andrews Air Force Base, among them members of the elite Hostage Rescue Team. Agents from field offices throughout the Southwest briefed Border Patrol officers on the case.

Bob/Leonid sat by himself, drinking tepid coffee. *Why didn't I just keep going and make a U-turn down the street?* he asked himself. *Why was I in a hurry? Why was I excited when I didn't have to be?*

It was time to be excited now. His car had three bullet holes in it, two on the left side and one in the trunk lid. His driver's license was in the hands of the police, and that carried his photograph.

You won't get a teaching post at the academy this way, Tovarishch. He smiled to himself grimly.

He was in a safe house. He had that much consolation. It might even be safe for a day or two. This was clearly Captain Bisyarina's bolt-hole, never intended to be any more than a place where the officer could hide out if forced to run. Because of that, it had no telephone, and he had no way of communicating with the local resident officer. *What if she doesn't come back?* That was clear enough. He'd have to risk driving a car with known license tags – and bullet holes! – far enough to steal another. He had visions of thousands of police officers patrolling the roads with a single thought: find the maniacs who shot their comrade. How could he have let things go so bad, so fast!

He heard a car approach. Lenny was still guarding their prisoner. Bob and Bill picked up their pistols and peered around the edge of the single window that faced on the dirt road to the trailer. Both breathed easier when they saw it was Bisyarina's Volvo. She got out and made the proper all-clear gesture, then came toward the trailer, holding a large bag.

'Congratulations: you've made the television news,' she said on entering. *Idiot*. That part didn't need to be said. It hung in the air like a thundercloud.

'It's a long story,' he said, knowing it to be a lie.

'I'm sure.' She set the bag on the table. 'Tomorrow I'll rent you a new car. It's too dangerous to move yours. Where did you –'

'Two hundred meters up the road, in the thickest trees we could squeeze it into, covered with branches. It will be hard to spot, even from the air.'

'Yes, keep that in mind. The police here have some helicopters. Here.' She tossed Bob a black wig. Next came some glasses, one pair set with clear lenses, and the other, a pair of mirror-type sunglasses. 'Are you allergic to makeup?'

'What?'

'*Makeup*, you fool –'

'Captain . . .' Bob began with some heat. Bisyarina cut him off with a look.

'Your skin is pale. In case you haven't noticed, a large number of the people in this area are Spanish. This is my territory and you will now do exactly as I say.' She paused for a beat. 'I'll get you out of here.'

'The American woman, she knows you by sight –'

'Obviously. I suppose you want her eliminated? After all, we've broken one rule, why not another? What fucking *madman* ordered this operation?'

'The orders came from very high,' Leonid replied.

'*How* high?' she demanded, and got only a raised eyebrow that spoke volumes. 'You're joking.'

'The nature of the order, the "immediate action" prefix – what do you think?'

'I think all of our careers are ruined, and that assumes that we – well, we will. But I will not agree to the murder of

478

my agent. We have as yet not killed anyone, and I do not think that our orders contemplated –'

'That is correct,' Bob said aloud, while his head shook emphatically from side to side. Bisyarina's mouth dropped open.

'This could start a war,' she said quietly, in Russian. She didn't mean a real war, but rather something almost as bad, open conflict between KGB and CIA officers, something that almost never happened, even in third-world countries, where it usually involved surrogates killing other surrogates, and for the most part never knowing why – and even that was rare enough. The business of intelligence services was to gather information. Violence, both sides tacitly agreed, got in the way of the real mission. But if both sides began killing the strategic assets of their opponents . . .

'You should have refused the order,' she said after a moment.

'Certainly,' Bob observed. 'I understand that the Kolyma camps are lovely this time of year, all glistening white with their blanket of snow.' The odd thing – at least it would seem so to a Westerner – was that neither officer bothered considering surrendering with a request of political asylum. Though it would have ended their personal dangers, it would mean betraying their country.

'What you do here is your account, but I will not kill my agent,' 'Ann' said, ending discussion of the issue. 'I'll get you out.'

'How?'

'I don't know yet. By car, I think, but I will have to come up with something new. Perhaps not a car. Perhaps a truck,' she mused. There were lots of trucks out here, and it was not the least unusual for a woman to drive one. Take a van across the border, perhaps? A van with boxes in it . . . Gregory in a box, drugged or gagged . . . perhaps all of them . . . what are customs procedures like for such things? She'd never had to worry about that before. With a week's warning, as she would have had for a proper operation, she'd have had time to answer a lot of questions.

Take your time, she told herself. *We've had enough of hurrying, haven't we?*

'Two days, perhaps three.'

'That's a long time,' Leonid observed.

'I may need that long to evaluate the countermeasures that we are likely to face. For the moment, don't bother shaving.'

Bob nodded after a moment. 'It is your territory.'

'When you get back, you can write this up as a case study in why operations need proper preparation,' Bisyarina said. 'Anything else you need?'

'No.'

'Very well. I will see you again tomorrow afternoon.'

'No,' Beatrice Taussig told the agents. 'I saw Al this afternoon. I' – she glanced uneasily at Candi – 'I wanted him to help me with – well, with picking up a birthday present for Candace tomorrow. I saw him in the parking lot, too, but that was it. You really think – I mean, the *Russians* . . .?'

'That's what it looks like,' Jennings said.

'My God.'

'Does Major Gregory know enough that –' Jennings was surprised that Taussig answered instead of Dr Long.

'Yes, he does. He's the only one who really understands the whole project. Al's a very bright guy. And a friend,' she added. That earned her a warm smile from Candi. There were real tears in Bea's eyes now. It hurt her to see her friend in pain, even though she knew that it was all for the best.

'Ryan, you're going to love this.' Jack had just gotten back from the latest round of negotiations at the Foreign Ministry building, twenty stories of Stalinesque wedding cake on Smolenskiy Bul'var. Candela handed over the dispatch.

'That son of a bitch,' Ryan breathed.

'You didn't expect him to cooperate, did you?' the officer asked sardonically, then changed his mind. 'I beg your pardon, doc. I wouldn't have expected this either.'

'I know this kid. I've driven him around Washington myself, when he came east to brief us . . .' *It's your fault, Jack. It was your move that caused this to happen . . . wasn't it?* He asked a few questions.

'Yeah, that's a virtual certainty,' Candela said. 'They screwed things up, looks like. That sounds like an over-nighter. Hey, the KGB officers aren't supermen either, pal, but they follow their orders, just like we do.'

'You have some ideas?'

'Not much we can do from this end but hope the local cops can straighten things out.'

'But if it goes public –'

'Show me some evidence. You don't accuse a foreign government of something like this without evidence. Hell, there's half a dozen engineers in Europe who've been murdered by left-wing terrorist gangs in the last two years, all working on the fringes of the SDI program, not to mention a few "suicides". We haven't made a public issue of that, either.'

'But this breaks the *rules*, damn it!'

'When you get down to it, there's only one rule, doc: Win.'

'Does USIA still have that global TV operation going?'

'Worldnet, you mean? Sure. It's a hell of a program.'

'If we don't get him back, I will personally break the *Red October* story world-wide, and fuck the consequences!' Ryan swore. 'If it costs my career, I'll do it.'

'*Red October?*' Candela had no idea what he was talking about.

'Trust me, it's a good one.'

'Tell your KGB friends – hell, it might even work.'

'Even if it doesn't,' Ryan said, more in control now. *It's your fault, Jack*, he told himself again. Candela agreed; Jack could see it.

*

The funny part, the state police thought, was that the press wasn't given the real meat of the case. As soon as the FBI team arrived, the rules were established. For the moment, this was a simple case of a police shooting. The federal involvement was to be kept secret, and if it broke, the word would be that an international drug-trafficker was on the loose and that federal assistance had been requested. The Oklahoma authorities were told to tell any inquiring journalist that they'd merely provided identification help to a fellow police force. Meanwhile, the FBI took over the case, and federal assets began to flood the area. Citizens were told that nearby military bases were conducting routine exercises – special search-and-rescue drills – which explained the abnormal helicopter activity. People at Project Tea Clipper were briefed on what had happened and told to keep this secret as close as all of the others.

Gregory's car was located in a matter of hours. No fingerprints were found – Bisyarina had worn gloves, of course – nor was any other useful evidence, though the placement of his car and the location of the shooting merely confirmed the professionalism of the event.

Gregory had been the Washington guest of men more important than Ryan. The President's first appointment of the morning was with General Bill Parks, FBI Director Emil Jacobs, and Judge Moore.

'Well?' the President asked Jacobs.

'These things take time. I've got some of our best investigative minds out there, Mr President, but looking over their shoulder only slows things down.'

'Bill,' the President asked next, 'how important is the boy?'

'He's priceless,' Parks answered simply. 'He's one of my top three men, sir. People like that cannot be replaced very easily.'

The President took this information seriously. Next he turned to Judge Moore. 'We caused this, didn't we?'

'Yes, Mr President, in a manner of speaking. Obviously, we hit Gerasimov in a very tender spot. My estimate agrees with the general's. They want what Gregory knows. Gerasimov probably thinks that if he can get information of this magnitude, he can overcome the political consequences of the *Red October* disclosure. That's a hard call to make from this side of the ocean, but certainly there's a good chance that his evaluation is correct.'

'I knew we shouldn't have done this . . .' the President said quietly, then shook his head. 'Well, that's my responsibility. I authorized it. If the press. . . .'

'Sir, if the press gets wind of this, it sure as hell won't be from CIA. Second, we can always say that this was a desperate – I'd prefer to say "vigorous" – attempt to save the life of our agent. It doesn't have to go any further than that, and such action is expected of intelligence services. They go to great lengths to protect their agents. So do we. That's one of the rules of the game.'

'Where does Gregory fit into the rules?' Parks asked. 'What if they think we might have a chance of rescuing him?'

'I don't know,' Moore admitted. 'If Gerasimov succeeds in saving himself, he'll probably get word to us that we forced him into it, he's sorry, and it won't happen again. He'd expect us to retaliate once or twice, but it would probably stop at that, because neither KGB nor CIA wants to start a war. To answer your question directly, General, my opinion is that they may have orders to eliminate the asset entirely.'

'You mean murder him?' the President asked.

'That is a possibility. Gerasimov must have ordered this mission very quickly. Desperate men make for desperate orders. It would be incautious of us to assume otherwise.'

The President considered that for a minute. He leaned back in his chair and sipped at his coffee. 'Emil, if we can find where he is . . .?'

'The Hostage Rescue Team is standing by. I have the men in place. Their vehicles are being flown out by the

Air Force, but for the moment all they can do is sit and wait.'

'If they move in, what are the chances that they'll save him?'

'Pretty good, Mr President,' Jacobs replied.

'"Pretty good" doesn't cut it,' Parks said. 'If the Russians have orders to take him out –'

'My people are as well trained as anyone in the world,' the FBI Director said.

'What are their rules of engagement?' Parks demanded.

'They are trained to use deadly force in the protection of themselves or any innocent person. If any subject appears to be threatening a hostage, he's a dead man.'

'That's not good enough,' Parks said next.

'What do you mean?' the President asked.

'How long does it take to turn around and blow somebody's head off? What if they're willing to die to accomplish their mission? We expect our people to be, don't we?'

'Arthur?' Heads turned to Judge Moore.

The DCI shrugged. 'I can't predict the dedication of Soviets. Is it possible? Yes, I suppose it is. Is it certain? I don't know that. Nobody does.'

'I used to drive fighter planes for a living. I know what human reaction times are,' Parks said. 'If a guy does decide to turn and shoot, even if your man has a gun on him, he might not be fast enough to keep Al alive.'

'What do you want me to do, tell my people just to kill everybody in sight?' Jacobs asked quietly. 'We don't do that. We *can't* do that.'

Parks turned to the President next. 'Sir, even if the Russians don't get Gregory, if we lose him, they win. It might be years before we can replace him. I submit, sir, that Mr Jacobs' people are trained to deal with criminals, not folks like this, and not for this situation. Mr President, I recommend that you call in the Delta Force from Fort Bragg.'

'They don't have jurisdiction,' Jacobs noted at once.

'They have the right kind of training,' the General said.

The President was quiet for another minute. 'Emil, how good are your people at following orders?'

'They will do what you say, sir. But it will have to be your order, in writing.'

'Can you get me in touch with them?'

'Yes, Mr President.' Jacobs picked up the phone and routed a call through his own office in the Hoover Building. Along the way it was scrambled.

'Agent Werner, please . . . Agent Werner, this is Director Jacobs. I have a special message for you. Stand by.' He handed the phone over. 'This is Gus Werner. He's been the team leader for five years. Gus passed on a promotion to stay with the HRT.'

'Mr Werner, this is the President. Do you recognize my voice? Good. Please listen closely. In the event that you are able to attempt the rescue of Major Gregory, your only mission is to get him out. All other considerations are secondary to that objective. The arrest of the criminals in question is not, I repeat, not a matter of concern. Is that clear? Yes, even the possibility of a threat to the hostage is sufficient grounds for the use of deadly force. Major Gregory is an irreplaceable national asset. His survival is your only mission. I will put that in writing and hand it to the Director. Thank you. Good luck.' The President replaced the phone. 'He says that they've considered this possibility.'

'He would.' Jacobs nodded. 'Gus has a good imagination. Now the note, sir.'

The President took a small sheet of writing paper from his desk and made the order official. It wasn't until he was finished that he realized what he'd done. This was not an intellectual exercise. He'd just handwritten a death warrant. It turned out to be a depressingly easy thing to do.

'General, are you satisfied?'

'I hope these people are as good as the Director says,' was all Parks was willing to say.

'Judge, any repercussions from the other side?'

'No, Mr President. Our Soviet colleagues understand this sort of thing.'

'Then that's it.' *And may God have mercy on my soul*.

No one had slept. Candi hadn't gone to work, of course. With the arrival of the investigative team from Washington, Jennings and Perkins were baby-sitting her. There was the remote possibility that Gregory would escape, and in this event, it was deemed that he'd call here first. There was another reason, of course, but that wasn't official yet.

Bea Taussig was a veritable tornado of energy. She'd spent the night straightening the house and brewing coffee for everyone. Odd as it seemed, it gave her something to do besides sitting with her friend. She did a lot of that, too, which no one thought especially odd. It was one of the things friends do.

Jennings took several hours to note that she was wearing an outfit that actually looked feminine. She had, in fact, gone to the trouble the previous day to make herself look rather nice. Most of that was wreckage now. Once or twice she'd shed tears herself when she and Candi cried together, and what had been a properly decorated face now showed streaks. Her clothes were wrinkled and the paisley scarf was in the closet, wrapped around the same hanger that held her coat. But the most interesting thing about Taussig, Jennings thought from her chair, was her mental state. There was tenseness there. The bustling activity of the long night had alleviated it to some degree, but . . . there was more to it than just being helpful, the agent thought. She didn't say this to Perkins.

Taussig didn't notice or care about what the agent thought. She looked out the window, expecting to see the sun rising for the second time since she'd last slept, and wondered where all her energy was coming from. Maybe the coffee, she thought to herself with an inward smile. It was always funny when you lied to yourself. She wondered at the danger that she herself might face, but put that worry aside. She trusted Ann's professionalism. One of the first thing she'd been told on starting her second career was that she would be protected, even to the death. Such promises had to be real, Ann had said, because they had a practical dimension. It was a business, Bea thought, and she felt confident that those in it knew how to handle themselves. The worst thing that could happen was that the police and FBI would rescue Al, but they were probably already gone, she told herself. Or maybe they'd kill him, despite what Ann had told her the previous night. That would be too bad. She wanted him out of the way. Not dead, just out of the way. She remembered the table talk at the project about how some German, Italian, and British people working in SDI-related projects had died mysteriously. So there was a precedent, wasn't there? If Al got back alive . . . well, that was that, wasn't it? She had to trust her controller to run things. Too late now. She turned her attention to her friend.

Candi was staring blankly at the far wall. There was a picture there, a laser-print of the space shuttle lifting off from Cape Canaveral. Not a proper picture, but something Al had picked up for free from one contractor or another and decided to hang on the wall. Bea's thoughts returned to Candace. Her eyes were puffy from all the tears.

'You have to get some rest,' Bea told her. Candace didn't even turn her head, hardly reacted at all, but Bea put her arm around her friend's shoulder and lifted her from the couch. 'Come on.'

Candi rose as though in a dream, and Bea guided her out of the living room and up the steps toward the bedroom. Once inside, she closed the door.

'Why, Bea? Why did they do it?' Candi sat on the bed, and her stare was merely at a different wall.

'I don't know,' Bea said, more honestly than she knew. She really didn't know, but then, she really didn't care.

The tears started again, and the gasping breaths, and the running nose as she watched her friend contemplate a world that someone else had torn apart. She felt momentary guilt that she was one of those who'd done it, but knew that she would make it whole again. A timid person despite all her flamboyance, Bea had found unexpected courage in herself by working for a foreign government, and more courage still in doing something that she had never expected them to ask. One more thing remained. She sat down next to her friend and held her close, bringing her head down on the offered shoulder. It was so hard for Bea. Her previous experiences had been passing college affairs. She'd tried to find in herself something different, but the men she'd dated had not satisfied. Her first sexual experience at the clumsy hands of a teenage football player had been so awful . . . but she wasn't one to psychoanalyze herself. With strangers or mere acquaintances it was one thing, but now she had to face herself, to face her own image in the eyes of a friend. A friend in pain. A friend who needed. A friend, she reminded herself coldly, whom she'd betrayed. It wasn't that she hated Gregory any the less, but she could not ignore the fact that he meant something to her friend, and in that sense he was still between them even here, alone in the bedroom. That worthless little caricature of a man who had on this very bed . . .

Will you ever replace him? she asked herself.

Will you even try?

If you were willing to remove him, and hurt her, and then not even take the risk . . . what does that make you?

She wrapped her arms tightly around her friend, and was rewarded with a returning grasp. Candi was merely trying to hold on to part of her shattering world, but Bea didn't know that. She kissed her friend on the cheek, and Candi's grip grew stronger still.

She needs you.

It took all of Bea's courage. Already her heart was beating fast, and she ridiculed herself as she had for years. Bea the Confident. Bea the Tough, who snarled back at whomever she wished, who drove her kind of car, and wore her kind of clothes, and to hell with what anyone thought. Bea the Coward, who even after she had risked everything lacked the courage to reach out to the one person in all the world who mattered. One more hesitant step. She kissed her friend again, tasting the salt of her tears and feeling the desperate need in the arms that wrapped around her chest. Taussig took a deep breath and moved one hand down to her friend's breast.

Jennings and Perkins came through the door less than five seconds after hearing the scream. They saw the horror on Long's face, and something both similar and very different on Taussig's.

23

Best-Laid Plans

'It is the position of the United States government,' Ernest Allen said from his side of the table, 'that systems designed to defend innocent civilians from weapons of mass destruction are neither threatening nor destabilizing, and that restrictions on the development of such systems serve no useful purpose. This position has been consistently stated for the past eight years, and we have absolutely no reason to change it. We welcome the initiative of the government of the Union of Soviet Socialist Republics to reduce offensive weapons by as much as fifty percent, and we will examine the details of this proposal with interest, but a reduction of offensive weapons is not relevant to defensive weapons, which are not an issue for negotiation beyond their applicability to existing agreements between our two countries.

'On the question of on-site inspections, we are disappointed to note that the remarkable progress made only so recently should be . . .'

You had to admire the man, Ryan thought. He didn't agree with what he was saying, but it was the position of his country, and Ernie Allen was never one to let personal feelings out of whatever secret compartment he locked up before beginning these sessions.

The meeting officially adjourned when Allen finished his discourse, which had just been delivered for the third time today. The usual courtesies were exchanged. Ryan shook hands with his Soviet counterpart. In doing so, he passed over a note, as he'd been taught to do at Langley. Golovko gave no reaction at all, which earned him a friendly nod at the conclusion of the handshake. Jack had no particular choice. He had to continue with the plan. He knew that he'd learn in the next few days just how much of a high-roller Gerasimov was. For him to run the risk of the CIA disclosures, especially with the threat of a few even more spectacular than Jack had promised . . . But Ryan could not admire the man. His view was that Gerasimov was the chief thug in the main thug agency of a country that allowed itself to be controlled by thugs. He knew that it was a simplistic, dangerous way to think, but he was not a field officer, though he was now acting like one, and hadn't yet learned that the world which he ordinarily viewed from the air-conditioned safety of his desk on CIA's seventh floor was not so well defined as his reports about it. He'd expected that Gerasimov would cave in to his demand – after taking time to evaluate his position, of course, but still cave in. It hit him that he'd thought like a chess master because that's how he'd expected the KGB Chairman to think, only to be confronted with a man who was willing to throw the dice – as Americans were wont to do. The irony should have been entertaining, Jack told himself in the marble lobby of the Foreign Ministry. But it wasn't.

Jennings had never seen anyone so thoroughly destroyed as Beatrice Taussig had been. Beneath the brittle, confident exterior had beaten what was after all a lonely human heart, consumed by solitary rage at a world that hadn't treated her in the way that she desired, but was unable to make happen. She almost felt sorry for the woman in handcuffs, but sympathy did not extend to treason, and certainly not to kidnapping, the highest – or lowest – crime in the FBI's institutional pantheon.

Her collapse was agreeably complete, however, and that's what mattered right now, that and the fact that she and Will Perkins had gotten the information out of her. It was still dark when they took her outside to a waiting FBI car. They left her Datsun in the driveway to suggest that she was still there, but fifteen minutes later she came in the back door of the Santa Fe FBI office and gave her information to the newly arrived investigators. It wasn't all that much, really, just a name, an address, and a type of car, but it was the beginning the agents needed. A Bureau car drove by the house soon thereafter and noted that the Volvo was in place. Next, a crisscross telephone directory enabled them to call the family directly across the street, giving them one minute's warning that two FBI agents were about to knock on their back door. The two agents set up surveillance in the family's living room, which was both frightening and exciting to the young couple who owned the tract house. They told the agents that 'Ann', as she was known, was a quiet lady whose profession was unknown to the family, but who had caused no trouble in the neighborhood, though she did occasionally keep eccentric hours, like quite a few single people. Last night, for example, she hadn't gotten home until rather late, the husband noted, about twenty minutes before the Carson show ended. A heavy date, he thought. Odd that they'd never seen her bring anyone home, though . . .

'She's up. There go some lights.' One agent picked up binoculars, hardly needed to see across the street. The other one had a long-lens camera and high-speed film. Neither man could see anything more than a moving shadow through the drawn curtains. Outside, they watched a man in a tubular bicycle helmet ride past her car on his ten-speed, getting his morning exercise. From their vantage point they could see him place the radio beeper on the inside surface of the Volvo's rear bumper, but only because they knew what to look for.

'Who teaches them to do that,' the man with the camera asked, 'David Copperfield?'

'Stan something – works at Quantico. I played cards with him once,' the other chuckled. 'He gave the money back and showed me how it's done. I haven't played poker for money since.'

'Can you tell us what this is all about?' the homeowner asked.

'Sorry. You'll find out, but no time for it now. Bingo!'

'Got it.' The camera started clicking and winding.

'We timed that one close!' The man with the binoculars lifted his radio. 'Subject is moving, getting in the car.'

'We're ready,' the radio replied.

'There she goes, heading south, about to lose visual contact. That's it. She's yours now.'

'Right. We got her. Out.'

No fewer than eleven cars and trucks were assigned to the surveillance, but more important were the helicopters orbiting four thousand feet above the ground. One more helicopter was on the ground at Kirtland Air Force Base. A UH-1N, the two-engine variant of the venerable Huey of Vietnam fame, it had been borrowed from the Air Force and was now being fitted with rappelling ropes.

Ann drove her Volvo in what appeared to be a grossly ordinary fashion, but behind her sunglasses her eyes returned to her mirrors every few seconds. She needed all her skills now, all her training, and despite a mere five hours of sleep she kept to her professional standards. Next to her on the seat was a thermos of coffee. She'd already had two cups for herself, and would give the rest to her three colleagues.

Bob was moving too. Dressed in work clothes and boots, he was jogging cross-country through the woods, pausing only to look at a compass on a two-mile path through the pines. He'd given himself forty minutes to make the trip, and realized that he needed all of it. The high altitude and thin air had him gasping for breath even before he had to deal with the slopes here. He had put all the recriminations behind. All that mattered now was the mission. Things had gone wrong for field operations before, though not any of his, and the mark of a real field officer was the ability to deal with adversity and fulfil his task. At ten minutes after seven he could see the road, and on the near side of it was the convenience store. He stopped twenty yards inside the woodline and waited.

*

Ann's path was a random one, or seemingly so. Her driving took her on and off the main road twice before she settled down to the final part of the trip. At seven-fifteen she pulled into the parking lot of the small store and went inside.

The FBI was down to two cars now, so skilful had the subject been at evading the surveillance. Every random turn she made had forced a car off her tail – it was assumed that she could identify any car seen more than once – and a frantic call had been sent out for additional vehicles. She'd even chosen the convenience store with care. It could not be watched from anyplace on the road itself; traffic flow would not permit it. Car number ten went into the same parking lot. One of its two occupants went inside, while the other stayed with the vehicle.

The inside man got the Bureau's first real look at Ann, while she bought some donuts, and decided to get some more coffee in large, styrofoam cups, plus some soft-drinks, all of them high in caffeine content, though the agent didn't take note of that. He checked out right behind her with a paper and two large coffees. He watched her go out the door, and saw that a man joined her, getting into the car as naturally as the fiancé of a woman who liked to drive her own car. He hustled out of the door to his own car, but still they almost lost her.

'Here.' Ann handed over a paper. Bob's picture was on the front page. It had even been done in color, though the picture quality from the tiny license frame was not exciting. 'I'm glad you remembered to wear the wig,' she observed.

'What is the plan?' Leonid asked.

'First I will rent you a new car to get you back to the safe house. Next I will purchase some makeup so that all of you can alter your complexions. After that, I think we will get a small truck for the border crossing. We'll need some packing crates also. I don't know about those yet, but I will by the end of the day.'

'And the crossing?'

494

'Tomorrow. We'll leave before noon and make the crossing about dinnertime.'

'So fast?' Bob asked.

'*Da*. The more I think about it – they will flood the area with assets if we linger too much.' They drove the rest of the way in silence. She went back into the city and parked her car in a public lot, leaving Leonid there as she crossed the street and walked half a block to a rental car agency right across the street from a large hotel. There she went through the proper procedures in less than fifteen minutes, and soon thereafter parked a Ford beside her Volvo. She tossed the keys to Bob and told him to follow her to the interstate, after which he'd be on his own.

By the time they got to the freeway, the FBI was nearly out of cars. A decision had to be made, and the agent in charge of the surveillance guessed right. An unmarked state police vehicle took up the coverage on the Volvo while the last FBI car followed the Ford onto the highway. Meanwhile five cars from the early part of the morning's surveillance of 'Ann' raced to catch up with 'Bob' and his Ford. Three of them took the same exit, then followed him along the secondary road leading to the safe house. As he matched his driving to the posted speed limit, two of the cars were forced to pass him, but the third was able to lay back – until the Ford pulled to the shoulder and stopped. This section of the road was as straight as an arrow for over a mile, and he'd stopped right in the middle of it.

'I got him, I got him,' a helicopter observer reported, watching the car from three miles away through a pair of stabilized binoculars. He saw the minuscule figure of a man open the hood, then bend down and wait for several minutes before closing it and driving on. 'This boy is a pro,' the observer told the pilot.

'Not pro enough,' the pilot thought, his own eyes locked on the distant white dot of a car's roof. He could see the Ford turn off the road onto a dirt track that disappeared in the trees.

'Bingo!'

*

495

It had been expected that the safe house would be isolated. The geography of the area easily lent itself to this. As soon as the site was identified, an RF-4C Phantom of the 67th Tactical Reconnaisance Wing lifted off from Bergstrom Air Force Base in Texas. The two-man crew of the aircraft thought it was all something of a joke, but they didn't mind the trip, which took less than an hour. As a mission it was simple enough that anyone could have done it. The Phantom made a total of four high-altitude passes over the area, and after shooting several hundred feet of film through its multiple camera systems, the Phantom landed at Kirtland Air Force Base, just outside Albuquerque. A cargo plane had brought additional ground crew and equipment a few hours earlier. While the pilot shut down his engines, two groundcrewmen removed the film cannister and drove it to the trailer that served as an air-portable photolab. Automatic processing equipment delivered the damp frames to the photo-interpreters half an hour after the plane had stopped moving.

'There you go,' the pilot said when the right frame came up. 'Good conditions for it: clear, cold, low humidity, good sun angle. We didn't even leave any contrails.'

'Thank you, Major,' the sergeant said as she examined the film from the KA-91 panoramic camera. 'Looks like we have a dirt road coming off this highway here, snakes over the little ridge . . . and looks like a house-trailer, car parked about fifty yards – another one, covered up some. Two cars, then. Okay, what else . . . ?'

'Wait a minute – I don't see the second car,' an FBI agent said.

'Here, sir. The sun's reflecting off something, and it's too big to be a Coke bottle. Car windshield, probably. Maybe a back window, but I think it's the front end.'

'Why?' the agent asked. He just had to know.

She didn't look up. 'Well, sir, if it was me, and I was hiding a car, like, I'd back it in so's I could get out quick, y'know?'

It was all the man could do not to laugh. 'That's all right, sarge.'

She cranked to a new frame. 'There we go – here's a flash off the bumper, and that's probably the grille, too. See how they covered it up? Look by the trailer. That might be a man there in the shadows . . .' She went to the next frame. 'Yep, that's a person.' The man was about six feet, athletic, with dark hair and a shadow on his face suggesting that he'd neglected to shave today. No gun was visible.

There were thirty usable frames of the site, eight of which were blown up to poster size. These went to the hangar with the UH-1N. Gus Werner was there. He didn't like rush jobs any more than the people in that trailer did, but his choices were as limited as theirs had been.

'So, Colonel Filitov, we now have you to 1976.'

'Dmitri Fedorovich brought me with him when he became Defense Minister. It simplified things, of course.'

'And increased your opportunities,' Vatutin observed.

'Yes, it did.'

There were no recriminations now, no accusations, no comments on the nature of the crime that Misha had committed. They were past that for the moment. The admission had come first as it always did, and that was always hard, but after that, once they'd been broken or tricked into confessing, then came the easy part. It could last for weeks, and Vatutin had no idea where this one would end. The initial phase was aimed at outlining what he'd done. The detailed examination of each episode would follow, but the two-phase nature of the interrogation was crucial to establishing a cross-referencing index, lest the subject later try to change or deny particular things. Even this phase, glossing over the details as they went, horrified Vatutin and his men. Specifications for every tank and gun in the Soviet Army, including the variations never sent to the Arabs – which was as good as giving them to the Israelis, therefore as good as giving them to the Americans – or even the other Warsaw Pact countries, had gone out to the West even before the design prototypes had entered full production. Aircraft specifications. Performance on both conventional and nuclear warheads of every description. Reliability figures for strategic missiles. Inside squabbling in the Defense Ministry, and now, entering the time when Ustinov had become a full voting member of the Politburo, political disputes at the highest level. Most damaging of all, Filitov had given the West everything he knew of Soviet strategy – and he knew all there was to know. As sounding board and confidant for Dmitri Ustinov, and in his capacity as a legendary combat soldier, he'd been the bureaucrat's eyepiece onto the world of actual war-fighting.

And so, Misha, what do you think of this . . .? Ustinov must have asked that same question a thousand times, Vatutin realized, but he'd never suspected . . .

'What sort of man was Ustinov?' the Colonel of 'Two' asked.

'Brilliant,' Filitov said at once. 'His administrative talents were unparalleled. His instincts for manufacturing processes, for example, were like nothing I've seen before or since. He could smell a factory and tell if it was doing proper work or not. He could see five years in the future and determine which weapons would be needed and which would not. His only weakness was in understanding how they were actually used in combat, and as a result we fought occasionally when I tried to change things to make them easier to use. I mean, he looked for easier manufacturing methods to speed production while I looked at the ease with which the end product could be used on the battlefield. Usually I won him over, but sometimes not.'

Amazing, Vatutin thought as he made a few notes. *Misha never stopped fighting to make the weapons better even though he was giving everything to the West . . . why?* But he couldn't ask that now, nor for a very long time. He couldn't let Misha see himself as a patriot again until all of his treason was fully documented. The details of this confession, he knew now, would take months.

'What time is it in Washington?' Ryan asked Candela.

'Coming up on ten in the morning. You had a short session today.'

'Yeah. The other side wanted an early recess for something or other. Any word from DC on the Gregory matter?'

'Nothing,' Candela replied gloomily.

'You told us they would put their defense systems on the table,' Narmonov said to his KGB chief. The Foreign Minister had just reported otherwise. They'd actually learned that the day before, but now they were totally sure that it wasn't mere gamesmanship. The Soviets had hinted at reneging on the verification section of the proposal that had already been settled in principle, hoping this would shake the Americans loose, even a little, on the SDI question. That gambit had met a stone wall.

'It would seem that our source was incorrect,' Gerasimov admitted. 'Or perhaps the expected concession will take more time.'

'They have not changed their position, nor will they change it. You've been misinformed, Nikolay Borissovich,' the Foreign Minister said, defining his position to be in firm alliance with the Party's General Secretary.

'Is this possible?' Alexandrov inquired.

'One of the problems gathering intelligence on the Americans is that they themselves often do not know what their position is. Our information came from a well-placed source, and this report coincided with that from another agent. Perhaps Allen wished to do this, but was forbidden to.'

'That is possible,' the Foreign Minister allowed, unwilling to push Gerasimov too hard. 'I've long felt that he has his own thoughts on the issue. But that does not matter now. We will have to change our approach somewhat. Might this signal that the Americans have made another technical breakthrough?'

'Possibly. We're working on that right now. I have a team trying to bring out some rather sensitive material.' Gerasimov didn't dare to go further. His operation to

499

snatch the American Major was more desperate than Ryan himself guessed. If it became public, he'd stand accused within the Politburo of trying to destroy important negotiations – and to have done so without first consulting his peers. Even Politburo members were supposed to discuss what they did, but he couldn't do that. His ally Alexandrov would want to know why, and Gerasimov could not risk revealing his entrapment to anyone. On the other hand, he was certain that the Americans would not do anything to reveal the kidnapping. For them to do so would run an almost identical risk – political elements in Washington would try to accuse conservatives of using the incident to scuttle the talks for reasons of their own. The game was as grand as it had ever been, and the risks Gerasimov was running, though grave, merely added spice to the contest. It was too late to be careful. He was beyond that, and even though his own life was on the line, the scope of the contest was worthy of its goal.

'We don't know that he's there, do we?' Paulson asked. He was the senior rifleman on the Hostage Rescue Team. A member of the Bureau's 'Quarter-Inch Club', he could place three aimed shots within a circle less than half an inch in diameter at two hundred yards – and of that half-inch, .308 inches was the diameter of the bullet itself.

'No, but it's the best we got,' Gus Werner admitted. 'There's three of them. We know for sure that two of them are there. They wouldn't leave one man guarding the hostage while they were someplace else – that's unprofessional.'

'It all makes sense, Gus,' Paulson agreed. 'But we don't *know*. We go with this, then.' That part wasn't a question.

'Yeah, and fast.'

'Okay.' Paulson turned and looked at the wall. They were using a pilot's ready room. The cork on the walls, put there for sound-absorption, was also perfect for hanging maps and photos. The trailer, they all saw, was a cheap-o.

Only a few windows, and of the two original doors, one had been boarded over. They assumed that the room near the remaining door was occupied by the 'bad guys' while the other held the hostage. The one good thing about the case was that their opponents were professionals, and therefore somewhat predictable. They'd do the sensible thing in most cases, unlike common criminals, who only did things that occurred to them at the time.

Paulson switched his gaze to a different photo, then to the topographical map, and started picking his approach route. The high-resolution photographs were a godsend. They showed one man outside, and he was watching the road, the most likely route of approach. He'd walk around some, Paulson thought, but mostly he'd watch the road. So, the observer/sniper team would approach overland from the other side.

'You think they're city folks?' he asked Werner.

'Probably.'

'I'll come in this way. Marty and I can approach to within four hundred yards or so behind this ridge, then come down along here parallel to the trailer.'

'Where's your spot?'

'There.' Paulson tapped the best of the photos. 'I'd say we should bring the machine gun in with us.' He explained why, and everyone nodded.

'One more change,' Werner announced. 'We have new Rules of Engagement. If anybody even thinks that the hostage might be in danger, the bad guys go down. Paulson, if there's one near him when we make the move, you take him down with the first shot, whether he's got a weapon out or not.'

'Hold it, Gus,' Paulson objected. 'There's sure as hell going to be –'

'The hostage is important, and there is reason to suspect that any attempt to rescue him will result in his death –'

'Somebody's been watching too many movies,' another team member observed.'

'Who?' Paulson asked both quietly and pointedly.

'The President. Director Jacobs was on the phone, too. He's got it in writing.'

'I don't like it,' the rifleman said. 'They will have somebody in there baby-sitting him, and you want me to blow him away whether he is threatening the hostage or not.'

'That's exactly right,' Werner agreed. 'If you can't do it, tell me now.'

'I have to know why, Gus.'

'The President called him a priceless national asset. He's the key man in a project important enough that he briefed the President himself. That's why they kidnapped him, and the thinking is that if they see that they can't have him, they won't want us to have him either. Look at what they've done already,' the team leader concluded.

Paulson weighed this for a moment and nodded agreement. He turned to his backup man, Marty, who did the same.

'Okay. We have to go through a window. It's a two-rifle job.'

Werner moved to a blackboard and sketched out the assault plan in as much detail as he could. The interior arrangement of the trailer was unknown, and much would depend on last-minute intelligence to be gathered on the scene by Paulson's ten-power gunsight. The details of the plan were no different from a military assault. First of all, Werner established the chain of command – everyone knew it, but it was precisely defined anyway. Next came the composition of the assault teams and their parts of the mission. Doctors and ambulances would be standing by, as would an evidence team. They spent an hour, and still the plan was not as complete as any of them would like, but their training allowed for this. Once committed, the operation would depend on the expertise and judgment of the individual team members, but in the final analysis, such things always did. When they were finished, everyone started moving.

*

502

She decided on a small U-Haul van, the same-size vehicle as that used for mini-buses or small business deliveries. A larger truck, she thought, would take too long to fill with the proper boxes. These she picked up an hour later from a business called the Box Barn. It was something she'd never had to do before – all of her information transfers had been done with film cassettes that fitted easily into one's pocket – but all she'd needed to do was look through the Yellow Pages and make a few calls. She purchased ten shipping crates made with wood edges and plastic-covered cardboard sides, all neatly broken down for easy assembly. The same place sold her labels to indicate what was inside, and polystyrene shipping filler to protect her shipment. The salesperson insisted on the latter. Tania watched as two men loaded her truck, and drove off.

'What do you suppose that is all about?' an agent asked.

'I suppose she wants to take something someplace.' The driver followed her from several hundred yards back while his partner called in agents to talk to the shipping company. The U-Haul van was far easier to track than a Volvo.

Paulson and three other men stepped out of the Chevy Suburban at the far end of a housing development about two thousand yards from the trailer. A child in the front yard stared at the men – two carrying rifles, a third carrying an M-60 machine gun as they walked into the woods. Two police cars stayed there after the Suburban drove off, and officers knocked on doors to tell people not to discuss what they had – or in most cases, hadn't – seen.

One nice thing about pine trees, Paulson thought one hundred yards into the treeline, was that they dropped needles, not the noisy leaves that coated the western Virginia hills which he trudged every autumn looking for deer. He hadn't gotten one this year. He'd had two good opportunities, but the bucks he'd seen were smaller than what he preferred to bring home, and he'd decided to leave them for next year while waiting for another chance that had never presented itself.

Paulson was a woodsman, born in Tennessee, who was never happier than when in the back country, making his way quietly through ground decorated with trees and carpeted with the fallen vegetation that covered the untended ground. He led the other three, slowly and carefully, making as little noise as possible – like the revenuers who'd finally convinced his grandfather to discontinue the production of mountain-brewed White Lightning, he thought without smiling. Paulson had never killed anyone in his fifteen years of service. The Hostage Rescue Team had the best-trained snipers in the world, but they'd never actually applied their craft. He himself had come close half a dozen times, but always before, he'd had a reason not to shoot. It would be different today. He was almost certain of that, and that made his mood different. It was one thing to go into a job knowing that a shooting was possible. In the Bureau that chance was always there. You planned for it, always hoping that it would not be necessary – he knew all too well what happened when a cop killed someone, the nightmares, the depression that rarely seemed to appear on TV cop shows. The doc was already flying out, he thought. The Bureau kept a psychiatrist on retainer to help agents through the time after a shooting, because even when you knew that there'd been no choice at all, the human psyche quails before the reality of unnecessary death and punishes the survivor for being alive when his victim is not. That was one price of progress, Paulson thought. It hadn't always been so, and with criminals in most cases it still wasn't. That was the difference between one community and the other. But what community did his target belong to? Criminal? No, they'd be trained professionals, patriots after the fashion of their society. People doing a job. *Just like me.*

He heard a sound. His left hand went up, and all four men dropped behind cover. Something was moving . . . over to the left. It kept going left, away from their path.

Maybe a kid, he thought, a kid playing in the woods. He waited to be sure it was heading away, then started moving again. The shooter team wore standard military camouflage clothing over their protective gear, the woodland pattern's blend of greens and browns. After half an hour, Paulson checked his map.

'Checkpoint One,' he said into his radio.

'Roger,' Werner answered from three miles away. 'Any problems?'

'Negative. Ready to move over the first ridge. Should have the objective in sight in fifteen minutes.'

'Roger. Move in.'

'Okay. Out.' Paulson and his team formed line abreast to get to the first ridge. It was a small one, with the second two hundred yards beyond it. From there they'd be able to see the trailer, and now things went very slowly. Paulson handed his rifle to the fourth man. The agent moved forward alone, looking ahead to pick out the path that promised the quietest passage. It was mainly a question of looking where you walked rather than how, after all, something lost on city people who thought a forest floor was an invariably noisy place. Here there were plenty of rocky outcroppings, and he snaked his way among them and reached the second ridge in five minutes of nearly silent travel. Paulson snuggled up next to a tree and pulled out his binoculars – even these were coated with green plastic.

''Afternoon, folks,' he said to himself. He couldn't see anyone yet, but the trailer blocked his view of where he expected the outside man to be, and there were also plenty of trees in the way. Paulson searched his immediate surroundings for movement. He took several minutes to watch and listen before waving for his fellow agents to come forward. They took ten minutes. Paulson checked his watch. They'd been in the woods for ninety minutes, and were slightly ahead of schedule.

'Seen anyone?' the other rifleman asked when he came down at Paulson's side.

'Not yet.'

'Christ, I hope they haven't moved,' Marty said. 'Now what?'

'We'll move over to the left, then down the gully over there. That's our spot.' He pointed.

'Just like on the pictures.'

'Everybody ready?' Paulson asked. He decided to wait a minute before setting off, allowing everyone a drink of water. The air was thin and dry here, and throats were getting raspy. They didn't want anyone to cough. *Cough drops*, the lead sniper thought. *We ought to include those in the gear* . . .

It took another half hour to get to their perches. Paulson selected a damp spot next to a granite boulder that had been deposited by the last glacier to visit the area. He was about twenty feet above the level of the trailer, about what he wanted for the job, and not quite at a ninety-degree angle to it. He had a direct view of the large window on its back end. If Gregory were there, this was where they expected him to be kept. It was time to find out. Paulson unfolded the bipod legs on his rifle, flipped off the scope covers, and went to work. He grabbed for his radio again, fitting the earpiece. He spoke in a whisper lower than that of the wind in the pine branches over his head.

'This is Paulson. We're in place, looking now. Will advise.'

'Acknowledged,' the radio replied.

'Jeez,' Marty said first. 'There he is. Right side.'

Al Gregory was sitting in an armchair. He had little choice in the matter. His wrists were cuffed in his lap – that concession had been made to his comfort – but his upper arms and lower legs were roped in place. His glasses had been taken away, and every object in the room had a fuzzy edge. That included the one who called himself Bill. They were taking turns guarding him. Bill sat at the far end of the room, just beyond the window. There was an automatic pistol tucked in his belt, but Gregory couldn't tell the type, merely the unmistakable angular shape.

'What –'

'– will we do with you?' Bill completed the question. 'Damned if I know, Major. Some people are interested in what you do for a living, I suppose.'

'I won't –'

'I'm sure,' Bill said with a smile. 'Now, we told you to be quiet or I'll have to put the gag back. Just relax, kid.'

'What did she say the crates were for?' the agent asked.

'She said that her company was shipping a couple of statues. Some local artist, she said – a show in San Francisco, I think.'

There's a Soviet consulate in San Francisco, the agent thought at once. *But they can't be doing that . . . could they?*

'Man-sized crates, you said?'

'You could put two people in the big ones, easy, and a bunch of little ones.'

'How long?'

'You don't need special tools. Half an hour, tops.'

Half an hour . . . ? One of the agents left the room to make a phone call. The information was relayed by radio to Werner.

'Heads up,' the radio earpiece announced. 'We got a U-Haul truck – make that a small van – coming in off the main road.'

'We can't see it from here,' Paulson groused quietly to Marty at his left. One problem with their location was that they couldn't see all of the trailer, and could only catch glimpses of the road that led to it. The trees were too thick for that. To get a better view meant moving forward, but that meant a risk that they were unwilling to run. The laser rangefinder placed them six hundred and eleven feet from the trailer. The rifles were optimized for two-hundred-yard range, and their camouflage clothing made them invisible, so long as they didn't move. Even with binoculars, the trees so cluttered the view that there were simply too many things for the human eye to focus on.

He heard the van. Bad muffler, he thought. Then he heard a metal door slam and the squeak of another opening. Voices came next, but though he could tell that people were talking, he couldn't make out a single word.

'This should be big enough,' Captain Bisyarina told Leonid. 'I have two of these and three of the smaller ones. We'll use these to stack on top.'

'What are we shipping?'

'Statuary. There's an art show three days from now, and we're even going to make the crossing at the point nearest to it. If we leave in two hours, we'll hit the border at about the right time.'

'You're sure —'

'They search parcels coming north, not going south,' Bisyarina assured him.

'Very well. We'll assemble the boxes inside. Tell Oleg to come out.'

Bisyarina went inside. Lenny was stationed outside since he knew more about working in the wilderness than the other two officers. While Oleg and Leonid carried the crates inside, she went into the back of the trailer to check on Gregory.

'Hello, Major. Comfortable?'

'I got another one,' Paulson said the moment she came into view. 'Female, that's the one from the photos — the Volvo one,' he said into the radio. 'She's talking to the hostage.'

'Three men now visible,' the radio said next. Another agent had a perch on the far side of the trailer. 'They're carrying crates inside the trailer. Say again, three male subjects. Female subject inside and out of sight.'

'That should be all of the subjects. Tell me about the crates.' Werner stood by the helicopter in a field several miles away, holding a diagram of the trailer.

'They're broken down, not assembled. I guess they're going to put 'em together.'

'Four's all we know about,' Werner said to his men. 'And the hostage is there . .'

'That ought to tie up two of them, assembling the crates,' one of the assault team said. 'One outside, one with the hostage . . . sounds good to me, Gus.'

'Attention, this is Werner. We're moving. Everybody stand by.' He gestured to the helicopter pilot, who began the engine-start sequence. The HRT leader made his own mental check while his men boarded the helicopter. If the Russians tried to drive him away, his men could try to take them on the move, but that kind of van had windows only for the driver and passenger . . . that meant that two or three of them would be out of sight . . . and perhaps able to kill the hostage before his men could prevent it. His first instinct was right: They had to go now. The team's Chevy Suburban with four men pulled onto the main road leading to the site.

Paulson flipped the safety off his rifle, and Marty did the same. They agreed on what would happen next. Ten feet from them, the machine-gunner and his loader readied their weapon slowly, to mute the metallic sounds of the gun's action.

'Never goes according to plan,' the number-two rifleman noted quietly.

'That's why they train us so much.' Paulson had his crosshairs on the target. It wasn't easy because the glass window reflected much light from the surrounding woods. He could barely make out her head, but it was a woman, and it was someone positively identified as a target. He estimated the wind to be about ten knots from his right. Applied over two hundred yards, that would move his bullet about two inches to the left, and he'd have to allow for that. Even with a ten-power scope, a human head is not a large target at two hundred yards, and Paulson swiveled the rifle slightly to keep her head transfixed on the crosshairs of his sight as she walked about. He wasn't so much watching his target as the crosshair reticle of the sight itself, keeping it aligned with the target rather than the other way around. The drill he followed was automatic. He controlled his breathing, positioned himself on his elbows, and snugged the rifle in tight.

'Who are you?' Gregory asked.

'Tania Bisyarina.' She walked about to work the stiffness out of her legs.

'Are your orders to kill me?' Tania admired the way he'd asked that. Gregory wasn't exactly the image of a soldier, but the important part was always hidden from view.

'No, Major. You will be taking a little trip.'

'There's the truck,' Werner said. *Sixty seconds from the road to the trailer.* He lifted his radio. 'Go go go!' The doors on the helicopter slid back and coiled ropes were readied. Werner crashed his fist down on the pilot's shoulder hard enough to hurt, but the flyer was too busy to notice. He pushed down on the collective and dove the helicopter toward the trailer, now less than a mile away.

They heard it before they saw it, the distinctive *whop-whop-whop* of the twin-bladed rotor. There was enough helicopter traffic over the area that the danger it brought was not immediately obvious. The one outside came to the edge of the trailer and looked through the treetops, then turned when he thought he heard the sound of an approaching vehicle. Inside, Leonid and Oleg looked up from their half-assembled crate in irritation rather than concern, but that changed in an instant when the sound of the helicopter became a roar as the chopper came into a hover directly overhead. In the back of the trailer, Bisyarina went to the window and saw it first. It was the last thing she would ever see.

*

'On target,' Paulson said.

'On target,' the other rifleman agreed.

'Shoot!'

They fired at nearly the same moment, but Paulson knew the other shot had gone first. That one broke the thick window, and the bullet went wild, deflected by the breaking glass. The second hollow-point match bullet was a split-second behind it, and struck the Soviet agent in the face. Paulson saw it, but it was the instant of firing that was locked in his mind, the crosshairs on the target. To their left, the machine-gunner was already firing when Paulson called his shot: 'Center-head.'

'Target is down,' the second rifleman said into the radio. 'Female target is down. Hostage in view.' Both reloaded their rifles and searched for new targets.

Weighted ropes dropped from the helicopter, and four men rappelled down. Werner was in front, and swung his way through the broken window, his MP-5 submachine gun in hand. Gregory was there, shouting something. Werner was joined by another team member, who threw the chair on its side and knelt between it and the rest of the structure. Then a third man came through, and all three trained their weapons the other way.

Outside, the Chevy Suburban arrived in time to see one of the KGB men firing a pistol at an agent who'd landed atop the trailer and was caught on something, unable to bring his weapon around. Two agents leaped from the vehicle and fired three rounds each, dropping the man in his tracks. The agent atop the trailer freed himself and waved.

Inside, Leonid and Oleg were reaching for their weapons. One looked back to see a constant stream of machine-gun bullets chewing through the metal sides of the trailer, clearly to keep them from approaching Gregory. But those were their orders.

'Hostage is safe, hostage is safe. Female target is down,' Werner called over the radio.

'Outside target is down,' another agent called. From the

outside. He watched another team member put a small explosive charge on the door. The man backed up and nodded. 'Ready!'

'Machine-gunner, cease fire, cease fire,' Werner ordered.

The two KGB officers inside heard it stop and went toward the back. The front door of the trailer was blown off its hinges as they did so. The blast was supposed to be sufficient to disorient, but both men were too alert for that. Oleg turned, bringing his weapon up in two hands to cover Leonid. He fired at the first figure through the door, hitting the man in the arm. That agent fell, trying to bring his weapon around. He fired and missed, but drew Oleg's attention to himself. The second man in the door had his MP-5 cradled in his arm. His gun fired two rounds. Oleg's last impression was one of surprise: he hadn't heard them shoot. He understood when he saw the canlike silencers.

'Agent wounded and bad guy down. Another bad guy heading back. Lost him turning the corner.' The agent ran after him, but tripped on a packing case.

They let him come through the door. One agent, his torso protected with a bullet-resistant vest, was between the door and the hostage. They could take the chance now. It was the one who'd gotten the rent-a-car, Werner knew at once, and his weapon wasn't pointed at anybody yet. The man saw three HRT members dressed in black Nomex jump suits and obviously protected with body armor. His face showed the beginnings of hesitation.

'*Drop the gun!*' Werner screamed. '*Don't –*'

Leonid saw where Gregory was and remembered his orders. The pistol started coming around.

Werner did what he'd always told his people not to do, but would never remember why. He loosed half a dozen rounds at the man's arm, going for the gun – and miraculously enough, it worked. The gun hand jerked like a puppet's and the pistol fell free in a cloud of spraying blood. Werner leaped forward, knocking the subject down and placing the muzzle of his silenced gun right on his forehead.

'Number three is down! Hostage safe! Team: check in!'

'Outside, number one down and dead.'

'Trailer, number two down and dead! One agent hit in the arm, not serious.'

'Female down and dead,' Werner called. 'One subject wounded and in custody. Secure the area! Ambulances, now!' From the time of the sniper shots, it had taken a total of twenty-nine seconds.

Three agents appeared at the window through which Werner and the other two had arrived. One of the agents inside pulled out his combat knife and cut through the ropes that held Gregory, then practically threw him out the window, where he was caught and carried off like a rag doll. Al was put in the back of the HRT truck and rushed off. On the highway, an Air Force helicopter landed. As soon as Gregory was tossed inside, it lifted off.

All HRT members have medical training, and two on the assault team had trained with firemen-paramedics. One of them was wounded in the arm, and directed the bandaging done by the man who'd shot Oleg. The other trained paramedic came back and started working on Leonid.

'He'll make it. The arm's gonna need some surgery, though. Radius, ulna, and humerus all fractured, boss.'

'You should have dropped the gun,' Werner told him. 'You didn't have much of a chance.'

'Jesus.' It was Paulson. He stood at the window and looked to see what his single bullet had done. An agent was searching the body, looking for a weapon. He stood up, shaking his head. That told the rifleman something he would have preferred not to know. In that moment, he knew that he'd never hunt again. The bullet had entered just below the left eye. Most of the rest of her head was on the wall opposite the window. Paulson told himself that he should never have looked. The rifleman turned away after five long seconds and unloaded his weapon.

*

The helicopter took Gregory directly to the project. Six armed security people were waiting when it landed, and hustled him inside. He was surprised when someone snapped some pictures. Someone else tossed Al a can of Coke, and he anointed himself with carbonated spray when he worked the pop-top. After taking a drink, he spoke: 'What the hell was all that?'

'We're not even sure ourselves,' the chief of project security replied. It took a few more seconds for Gregory's mind to catch up with what had happened. That's when he started shaking.

Werner and his people were outside the trailer while the evidence team took over. A dozen New Mexico State Police officers were there also. The wounded agent and the wounded KGB officer were loaded into the same ambulance, though the latter was handcuffed to his stretcher and doing his best not to scream with the pain of three shattered bones in his arm.

'Where you taking him?' a state police captain asked.

'The base hospital at Kirtland – both of them,' Werner replied.

'Long ways.'

'Orders are to keep this one under wraps. For what it's worth, the guy who popped your officer is that one over there – from the description he gave us, it's him anyway.'

'I'm surprised you took one alive.' That earned the Captain a curious look. 'I mean, they were all armed, right?'

'Yeah,' Werner agreed. He smiled in an odd sort of way. 'I'm surprised, too.'

24

The Rules of the Game

The amazing thing was that it didn't make the news. Only a handful of unmuffled shots had been fired, and gunfire is not all that unusual a thing in the American West. An inquiry to the New Mexico State Police had gotten the reply that the investigation into the shooting of Officer Mendez was still continuing, with a break expected at any time, but that the helicopter activity was merely part of a routine search-and-rescue exercise conducted jointly by the state police and Air Force personnel. It wasn't all that good a story, but good enough to keep reporters off everyone's back for a day or two.

The evidence team sifted through the trailer and not surprisingly found little of note. A police photographer took the requisite pictures of all the victims – he called himself a professional ghoul – and handed over the film to the senior FBI agent on the scene. The bodies were bagged and driven to Kirtland, from which they were flown to Dover Air Force Base, where there was a special receiving center staffed by forensic pathologists. The developed photos of the dead KGB officers were sent electronically to Washington. The local police and FBI began talking about how the case against the surviving KGB agent would be handled. It was determined that he'd broken at least a dozen statutes, evenly divided between federal and state jurisdiction, and various attorneys would have to sort that mess out, even though they knew that the real decision would be made in Washington. They were wrong in that assessment, however. Part of it would be decided elsewhere.

*

It was four in the morning when Ryan felt a hand on his shoulder. He rolled over and looked in time to see Candela flip on the bedstand light.

'What?' Ryan asked as coherently as he could manage.

'The Bureau pulled it off. They have Gregory and he's fine,' Candela said. He handed over some photos. Ryan's eyes blinked a few times before going very wide.

'That's a hell of a thing to wake up to,' Jack said, even before seeing what had happened to Tania Bisyarina. 'Holy shit!' He dropped the photos on the bed and walked into the bathroom. Candela heard the sound of running water, then Ryan emerged and walked to the refrigerator. He pulled out a can of soda and popped it open.

'Excuse me. You want one?' Jack gestured at the refrigerator.

'It's a little early for me. You made the pass to Golovko yesterday?'

'Yeah. The session starts this afternoon. I want to see our friend about eight. I was planning to get up about five-thirty.'

'I thought you'd want to see these right away,' Candela said. That elicited a grunt.

'Sure. It beats the morning paper . . . We got his ass,' Ryan noted, staring at the carpet. 'Unless . . .'

'Unless he wants to die real bad,' the CIA officer agreed.

'What about his wife and daughter?' Jack asked. 'If you got opinions, I sure as hell want to hear them.'

'The meet's where I suggested?'

'Yep.'

'Push him as hard as you can.' Candela lifted the pictures off the bed and tucked them in an envelope. 'Make sure you show him these. I don't think it'll trouble his conscience much, but it'll damned well show him we're serious. If you want an opinion, I thought you were crazy before. Now' – he grinned – 'I think you're just about crazy enough. I'll be back when you're all woke up.'

Ryan nodded and watched him leave before heading

into the shower. The water was hot, and Jack took his time, in the process filling the small room with steam that he had to wipe off the mirror. When he shaved, he made a conscious effort to stare at his beard rather than his eyes. It wasn't a time for self-doubt.

It was dark outside his windows. Moscow was not lit the same way as an American city. Perhaps it was the near-total absence of cars at this hour. Washington always had people moving about. There was always the unconscious certainty that somewhere people were up and about their business, whatever that might be. The concept didn't translate here. Just as the words of one language never exactly, never quite correspond to those of another, so Moscow was to Ryan just similar enough to other major cities he'd visited to seem all the more alien in its differences. People didn't go about *their* business here. For the most part they went about the business assigned to them by someone else. The irony was that he would soon be one of the people giving orders, to a person who'd forgotten how to take them.

Morning came slowly to Moscow. The traffic sounds of trolley cars and the deeper rumble of truck diesels were muted by the snow cover, and Ryan's window didn't face in the proper direction to catch the first light of dawn. What had been gray began to acquire color, as though a child were playing with the controls on a color television. Jack finished his third cup of coffee, and set down the book he'd been reading at seven-thirty. Timing was everything on occasions like this, Candela told him. He made a final trip to the bathroom before dressing for his morning walk.

The sidewalks had been swept clean of the Sunday-night snowstorm, though there were still piles at the curbs. Ryan nodded to the security guards, Australian, American, and Russian, before turning north on Chaykovskogo. The bitter northerly wind made his eyes water, and he adjusted the scarf around his neck slightly as he walked toward Vosstaniya Square. This was Moscow's embassy district.

The previous morning he'd turned right at the far side of the square and seen half a dozen legations mixed together randomly, but this morning he turned left on Kudrinskiy Pereulok – the Russians had at least nine ways of saying 'street', but the nuances were lost on Jack – then right, then left again on Barrikadnaya.

'Barricade' seemed an odd name for both a street and a movie theater. It looked odder still in Cyrillic lettering. The B was recognizable, though the Cyrillic 'B' is actually a V, and the Rs in the word looked like Roman Ps. Jack altered his course somewhat, walking as close to the buildings as possible as he approached. Just as expected, a door opened and he turned into it. Again he was patted down. The security man found the sealed envelope in the coat pocket, but didn't open it, to Ryan's relief.

'Come.' The same thing he'd said the first time, Jack noted. Perhaps he had a limited vocabulary.

Gerasimov was sitting on an aisle seat, his back confidently to Ryan as Jack walked down the slope to see the man.

'Good morning,' he said to the back of the man's head.

'How do you like our weather?' Gerasimov asked, waving the security man away. He stood and led Jack down toward the screen.

'Wasn't this cold where I grew up.'

'You should wear a hat. Most Americans prefer not to, but here it is a necessity.'

'It's cold in New Mexico, too,' Ryan said.

'So I'm told. Did you think I would do nothing?' the KGB Chairman asked. He did so without emotion, like a teacher to a slow student. Ryan decided to let him enjoy the feeling for a moment.

'Am I supposed to negotiate with you for Major Gregory's freedom?' Jack asked neutrally – or tried to. The extra morning coffee had put an edge on his emotions.

'If you wish,' Gerasimov replied.

'I think you will find this to be of interest.' Jack handed over the envelope.

The KGB Chairman opened it and took out the photographs. He didn't display any reaction as he flipped through the three frames, but when he turned to look at Ryan his eyes made the morning's wind seem like the breath of spring.

'One's alive,' Jack reported. 'He's hurt, but he'll recover. I don't have his picture. Somebody screwed up on that end. We have Gregory back, unhurt.'

'I see.'

'You should also see that your options are now those which we intended. I need to know which choice you will make.'

'It is obvious, is it not?'

'One of the things I have learned in studying your country is that nothing is as obvious as we would like.' That drew something that was almost a smile.

'How will I be treated?'

'Quite well.' *A hell of a lot better than you deserve.*

'My family?'

'Them also.'

'And how do you propose to get the three of us out?'

'I believe your wife is Latvian by birth, and that she often travels to her home. Have them there Friday night,' Ryan said, continuing with some details.

'Exactly what –'

'You do not need that information, Mr Gerasimov.'

'Ryan, you cannot –'

'Yes, sir, I can,' Jack cut him off, wondering why he'd said 'sir'.

'And for me?' the Chairman asked. Ryan told him what he'd have to do. Gerasimov agreed. 'I have one question.'

'Yes?'

'How did you fool Platonov? He's a very clever man.'

'There really was a minor flap with the SEC, but that wasn't the important part.' Ryan got ready to leave. 'We couldn't have done it without you. We had to stage a really good scene, something that you don't fake. Congressman

519

Trent was over here six months ago, and he met a fellow named Valeriy. They got to be very close friends. He found out later that you gave Valeriy five years for "antisocial activity". Anyway, he wanted to get even. We asked for his help and he jumped at it. So I suppose you could say that we used your own prejudices against you.'

'What would you have us do with such people, Ryan?' the Chairman demanded. 'Do you –'

'I don't make laws, Mr Gerasimov.' Ryan walked out. It was nice, he thought on the return to the embassy compound, to have the wind at his back for a change.

'Good morning, Comrade General Secretary.'

'You need not be so formal, Ilya Arkadyevich. There are Politburo members more senior to you who do not have the vote, and we have been comrades too . . . long. What is troubling you?' Narmonov asked cautiously. The pain in his colleague's eyes was evident. They were scheduled to talk about the winter wheat crop, but –

'Andrey Il'ych, I do not know how to begin.' Vaneyev nearly choked on the words, and tears began to stream from his eyes. 'It is my daughter . . .' He went on for ten fitful minutes.

'And?' Narmonov asked, when it seemed that he'd finally stopped – but as was obvious, there had to be more. There was.

'Alexandrov and Gerasimov, then.' Narmonov leaned back in his chair and stared at the wall. 'It took great courage indeed for you to come to me with this, my friend.'

'I cannot let them – even if it means my career, Andrey, I cannot let them stop you now. You have too many things to do, we – you have too many things to change. I must leave. I know that. But you must stay, Andrey. The people need you here if we are to accomplish anything.'

It was noteworthy that he'd said *people* rather than *Party*, Narmonov thought. The times really were changing. No. He shook his head. It wasn't that, not yet. All he had accomplished was to create the atmosphere within which the times might have the possibility of change. Vaneyev was one who understood that the problem was not so much goals as process. Every Politburo member knew – had known for years – the things that needed to be changed. It was the method of change that no one could agree on. It was like turning a ship to a new course, he thought, but knowing that the rudder might break if you did so. Continuing in the same path would allow the ship to plow on into . . . what? Where was the Soviet Union heading? They didn't even know that. But to change course meant risk, and if the rudder broke – if the Party lost its ascendancy – then there would be only chaos. That was a choice that no rational man would wish to face, but it was a choice whose necessity no rational man could deny.

We don't even know what our country is doing, Narmonov thought to himself. For at least the past eight years all figures on economic performance had been false in one way or another, each compounding itself on the next until the economic forecasts generated by the GOSPLAN bureaucracy were as fictitious as the list of Stalin's virtues. The ship he commanded was running deeper and deeper into an enveloping fog of lies told by functionaries whose careers would be destroyed by the truth. That was how he spoke of it at the weekly Politburo meetings. Forty years of rosy goals and predictions had merely plotted a course on a meaningless chart. Even the Politburo itself didn't know the state of the Soviet Union – something the West hardly suspected.

The alternative? That was the rub, wasn't it? In his darker moments, Narmonov wondered if he or anyone else could really change things. The goal of his entire political life had been to achieve the power that he now held, and only now did he fully understand how circumscribed that power was. All the way up the ladder of his career he'd noted things that had to change, never fully appreciating how difficult that would be. The power he wielded wasn't the same as Stalin's had been. His more immediate predecessors had seen to that. Now the Soviet Union wasn't so much a ship to be guided, as a huge bureaucratic spring that absorbed and dissipated energy and vibrated only to its own inefficient frequency. Unless that changed . . . the West was racing into a new industrial age while the Soviet Union still could not feed itself. China was adopting the economic lessons of Japan, and in two generations might become the world's third economy: *a billion people with a strong, driving economy, right on our border, hungry for land, and with a racial hatred of all Russians that could make Hitler's fascist legions seem like a flock of football hooligans.* That was a strategic threat to his country that made the nuclear weapons of America and NATO shrivel to insignificance – and still the Party bureaucracy didn't see that it had to change or risk being the agent of its own doom!

Someone has to try, and that someone is me.

But in order to try, he first had to survive himself, survive long enough to communicate his vision of national goals, first to the Party, then to the people – or perhaps the other way around? Neither would be easy. The Party had its ways, resistant to change, and the people, the *narod*, no longer gave a moment's thought to what the Party and its leader said to them. That was the amusing part. The West – the enemies of his nation – held him in higher esteem than his own countrymen.

And what does that mean? he asked himself. *If they are enemies, does their favor mean that I am proceeding on the right path – right for whom?* Narmonov wondered if the American President were as lonely as he. But before facing that impossible task, he still had the day-to-day tactical problem of personal survival. Even now, even at the hands of a trusted colleague. Narmonov sighed. It was a very Russian sound.

'So, Ilya, what will you do?' he asked a man who could not commit an act of treason more heinous than his daughter's.

'I will support you if it means my disgrace. My Svetlana will have to face the consequences of her action.' Vaneyev sat upright and wiped his eyes. He looked like a man about to face a firing squad, assembling his manhood for one last act of defiance.

'I may have to denounce you myself,' Narmonov said.

'I will understand, Andruska,' Vaneyev replied, his voice laden with dignity.

'I would prefer not to do this. I need you, Ilya. I need your counsel. If I can save your place, I will.'

'I can ask for no more than that.'

It was time to build the man back up. Narmonov stood and walked around his desk to take his friend's hand. 'Whatever they tell you, agree to it without reservation. When the time comes, you will show them what kind of *man* you are.'

'As will you, Andrey.'

Narmonov walked him to the door. He had another five minutes till his next scheduled appointment. His day was full of economic matters, decisions that came to him because of indecision in men with ministerial rank, seeking him for his blessing as though from the village priest . . . *As though I don't have troubles enough*, the General Secretary of the Communist Party of the Soviet Union told himself. He spent his five minutes counting votes. It should have been easier for him than for his American counterpart – in the Soviet Union only full Politburo members had the right to vote, and there were only thirteen of them – but each man represented a collection of interests, and Narmonov was asking each of them to do things never before contemplated. In the final analysis, power still counted for more than anything else, he told himself, and he could still count on Defense Minister Yazov.

'I think you will like it here,' General Pokryshkin said as they walked the perimeter fence. The KGB guards saluted as they passed, and both men returned the halfhearted gestures. The dogs were gone now, and Gennady thought that a mistake, food problems or no.

'My wife will not,' Bondarenko replied. 'She's followed me from one camp to another for almost twenty years, and finally to Moscow. She likes it there.' He turned to look outside the fence and smiled. *Could a man ever tire of this view? But what will my wife say when I tell her this?* But it was not often that a Soviet soldier had the chance to make this sort of choice, and she would understand that, wouldn't she?

'Perhaps general's stars will change her mind – and we are working to make the place more hospitable. Do you have any idea how hard I had to fight for that? Finally I told them that my engineers were like dancers, and that they had to be happy to perform. I think that Central Committeeman is a devotee of the Bolshoy, and that finally made him understand. That's when the theater was authorized, and that's when we started getting decent food trucked in. By next summer the school will be finished, and all the children will be here. Of course' – he laughed – 'we'll have to put up another block of apartments, and the next Bright Star commander will also have to be a schoolmaster.'

'In five years we may not have room for the lasers. Well, you left the highest point for them, I see.'

'Yes, that argument lasted nine months. Just to convince them that we might eventually want to build something more powerful than the one we already have.'

'The real Bright Star,' Bondarenko noted.

'You will build it, Gennady Iosifovich.'

'Yes, Comrade General, I will build it. I will accept the appointment if you still want me.' He turned to survey the terrain again. *Someday this will all be mine* . . .

'Allah's will,' the Major said with a shrug.

He was getting tired of hearing that. The Archer's patience and even his faith were being tested by the forced change in plans. The Soviets had been running troops along the valley road on and off for the last thirty-six hours. He'd gotten half his force across when it had begun, then suffered while his men had been divided, each side watching the rolling trucks and personnel carriers and wondering if the Russians would halt and hop out, and climb the hills to find their visitors. There would be a bloody fight if they tried that, and many Russians would die – but he wasn't here merely to kill Russians. He was here to hurt them in a way that the simple loss of soldiers could never do.

But there was a mountain to climb, and he was now grossly behind schedule, and all the consolation anyone could offer was Allah's will. *Where was Allah when the bombs fell on my wife and daughter? Where was Allah when they took my son away? Where was Allah when the Russians bombed our refugee camp . . .? Why must life be so cruel?*

'It is hard to wait, isn't it?' the Major observed. 'Waiting is the hardest thing. The mind has nothing to occupy it, and the questions come.'

'And your questions?'

'When will the war end? There is talk . . . but there has been talk for years. I am tired of this war.'

'You spent much of it on the other –'

The Major's head snapped around. 'Do not say that. I have been giving your band information for years! Didn't your leader tell you this?'

'No. We knew that he was getting something, but –'

'Yes, he was a good man, and he knew that he had to protect me. Do you know how many times I sent my troops on useless patrols so that they'd miss you, how many times I was shot at by my own people – knowing that they wanted to kill me, knowing how they cursed my name?' The sudden flood of emotion amazed both men. 'Finally I could bear it no more. Those of my troops who wanted to work for the Russians – well, it was not hard to send them into your ambushes, but I couldn't merely send those, could I? Do you know, my friend, how many of my troops – my good men – I consigned to death at your hands? Those I had left were loyal to me, and loyal to Allah, and it was time to join the freedom fighters once and for all. May God forgive me for all those who did not live long enough for this.' Each man had his tale to tell, the Archer reflected, and the only consistent thread made but a single sentence:

'Life is hard.'

'It will be harder still for those atop this mountain.' The Major looked around. 'The weather is changing. The wind blows from the south now. The clouds will bring moisture with them. Perhaps Allah has not deserted us after all. Perhaps He will let us continue this mission. Perhaps we are His instrument, and He will show them through us that they should leave our country lest we come to visit them.'

The Archer grunted and looked up the mountain. He could no longer see the objective, but that didn't matter because, unlike the Major, he couldn't see the end to the war either.

'We'll bring the rest across tonight.'

'Yes. They will all be well rested, my friend.'

'Mr Clark?' He'd been on the treadmill for nearly an hour. Mancuso could tell from the sweat when he flipped the off switch.

'Yes, Captain?' Clark took off the headphones.

'What sort of music?'

'That sonar kid, Jones, lent me his machine. All he has is Bach, but it does keep the brain occupied.'

'Message for you.' Mancuso handed it over. The slip of paper merely had six words. They were code words, had to be, since they didn't actually mean anything.

'It's a go.'

'When?'

'It doesn't say that. That'll be the next message.'

'I think it's time you tell me how this thing goes,' the Captain observed.

'Not here,' Clark said quietly.

'My stateroom is this way.' Mancuso waved. They went forward past the submarine turbine engines, then through the reactor compartment with its annoyingly noisy door, and finally through the Attack Center and into Mancuso's cabin. It was about as far as anyone could walk on a submarine. The Captain tossed Clark a towel to wipe the sweat from his face.

'I hope you didn't wear yourself out,' he said.

'It's the boredom. All your people have jobs to do. Me, I just sit around and wait. Waiting is a bitch. Where's Captain Ramius?'

'Asleep. He doesn't have to be in on the thing this soon, does he?'

'No,' Clark agreed.

'What exactly is the job? Can you tell me now?'

'I'm bringing two people out,' Clark replied simply.

'Two Russians? You're not picking up a *thing*? Two *people*?'

'That's right.'

'And you're going to say that you do it all the time?' Mancuso asked.

'Not exactly *all* the time,' Clark admitted. 'I did one three years ago, another one a year before that. Two others never came off, and I never found out why. "Need-to-know," you know.'

'I've heard the phrase before.'

'It's funny,' Clark mused. 'I bet the people who make those decisions have never had their ass hanging out in the breeze . . .'

'The people you're picking up – do they know?'

'Nope. They know to be at a certain place at a certain time. My worry is that they're going to be surrounded by the KGB version of a SWAT team.' Clark lifted a radio. 'Your end is real easy. I don't say the right thing in the right way, on the right schedule, you and your boat get the hell out of here.'

'Leave you behind.' It wasn't a question.

'Unless you'd prefer to join me at Lefortovo Prison. Along with the rest of the crew, of course. It might look bad in the papers, Captain.'

'You struck me as a sensible man, too.'

Clark laughed. 'It's a real long story.'

'Colonel Eich?'

'Von Eich,' the pilot corrected Jack. 'My ancestors were Prussians. You're Dr Ryan, right? What can I do for you?' Jack took a seat. They were sitting in the Defense Attaché's office. The attaché, an Air Force general, was letting them use it.

'You know who I work for?'

'I seem to recall you're one of the intel guys, but I'm just your driver, remember? I leave the important stuff to the folks in soft clothes,' the Colonel said.

'Not anymore. I have a job for you.'

'What do you mean, a job?'

'You'll love it.' Jack was wrong. He didn't.

It was hard to keep his mind on his official job. Part of that was the mind-numbing boredom of the negotiating process, but the largest part was the heady wine of his unofficial job, and his mind was locked on that while he fiddled with his earpiece to get all of the simultaneous translation of the Soviet negotiator's second rendition of his current speech. The hint of the previous day, that on-site inspections would be more limited than previously agreed, was gone now. Instead they were asking for broader authority to inspect American sites. That would make the Pentagon happy, Jack thought with a concealed smile. Russian intelligence officers climbing over factories and descending into silos to get looks at American missiles, all under the watchful eyes of American counterintel officers and Strategic Air Command guards – who'd be fingering their new Beretta pistols all the while. And the submarine boys, who often regarded the rest of their *own* Navy as potential enemies, what would they think of having Russians aboard? It sounded as though they wouldn't get any further than standing on the deck while the technicians inside opened the tube doors under the watchful eyes of the boats' crews and the Marines who guarded the boomer bases. The same would happen on the Soviet side. Every officer sent to be on the inspection teams would be a spook, perhaps with the odd line-officer thrown in to take note of things that only an operator would notice. It was amazing. After thirty years of US demands, the Soviets had finally accepted the idea that both sides should allow officially recognized spying. When that happened, during the previous round of talks on intermediate weapons, the American reaction had been stunned suspicion – *Why were the Russians agreeing to our terms? Why did they say yes? What are they really trying to do?*

But it was progress, once you got used to the idea. Both sides would have a way of knowing what the other did and what the other had. Neither side would trust the other. Both intelligence communities would see to that. Spies would still be prowling about, looking for indications that the other side was cheating, assembling missiles at a secret location, hiding them in odd places for a surprise attack. They'd find such indications, write interim warning reports, and try to run the information down. Institutional paranoia would last longer than the weapons themselves. Treaties wouldn't change that, despite all the euphoria in the papers. Jack shifted his eyes to the Soviet who was doing the talking.

Why? Why did you guys change your mind? Do you know what I said in my National Intelligence Estimate? It hasn't made the papers yet, but you might have seen it. I said that you finally realized (1) how much the goddamned things cost, (2) that ten thousand warheads was enough to fry all of America eight times over when three or four times was probably enough, and (3) that you'd save money by eliminating all your old missiles, the ones that you can't maintain very well anymore. It's just business, I told them, not a change in your outlook. Oh, yes: (4) it's very good public relations, and you still love to play PR games, even though you screw it up every time.

Not that we mind, of course.

Once the agreement went through – and Jack thought it would – both sides would save about three percent of their defense outlays; maybe as much as five percent for the Russians because of their more diverse missile systems, but it was hard to be sure. A small fraction of total defense outlays, it would be enough for the Russians to finance a few new factories, or maybe build some roads, which was what they really needed. How would they reallocate their savings? For that matter, how would America? Jack was supposed to make an assessment of that, too, another Special National Intelligence Estimate. Rather a high-sounding title for what was, after all, nothing more than an official guess, and at the moment, Ryan didn't have a clue.

The Russian speech concluded, and it was time for a coffee break. Ryan closed his leather-bound folder and trooped out of the room with everyone else. He selected a cup of tea, just to be different, and decorated his saucer with finger food.

'So, Ryan, what do you think?' It was Golovko.

'Is this business or socializing?' Jack asked.

'The latter, if you wish.'

Jack walked to the nearest window and looked out. *One of these days*, he promised himself, *I will see something of Moscow. They must have something here that's worth snapping a few pictures. Maybe peace will break out someday and I'll be able to bring the family over . . .* He turned. *But not today, not this year, nor the year after that. Too bad.*

'Sergey Nikolayevich, if the world made sense, people like you and me would sit down and hammer all this crap out in two or three days. Hell, you and I know that both sides want to cut inventories by half. The issue we've been fighting over all week is how many hours of notice there'll be before the surprise-inspection team arrives, *but* because neither side can get its act together on the answer, we're talking about stuff that we've *already* come to terms on instead of getting on with it. If it was just between you and me, I'd say one hour, and you'd say eight, and we'd eventually talk down to three or four –'

'Four or five.' Golovko laughed.

'Four, then.' Jack did, too. 'You see? We'd *settle* the son of a bitch, wouldn't we?'

'But we are not diplomats,' Golovko pointed out. 'We know how to strike bargains, but not in the accepted way. We are too direct, you and I, too practical. Ah, Ivan

Emmetovich, we will make a Russian of you yet.' He'd just Russianized Jack's name. Ivan Emmetovich. John, son of Emmet.

Business time again, Ryan thought. He changed gears and decided to yank the other man's chain in turn. 'No, I don't think so. It gets a little too cool here. Tell you what, you go to your chief talker, and I'll go to Uncle Ernie, and we'll tell them what we decided on inspection-warning time – four hours. Right now. How 'bout it?'

That rattled him, Jack saw. For the briefest fraction of a second, Golovko thought that he was serious. The GRU/KGB officer recovered his composure in a moment, and even Jack barely noticed the lapse. The smile was hardly interrupted, but while the expression remained fixed around the mouth, it faded momentarily about the man's eyes, then returned. Jack didn't know the gravity of the mistake he had just made.

You should be very nervous, Ivan Emmetovich, but you are not. Why? You were before. You were so tense at the reception the other night that I thought you would explode. And yesterday when you passed the note, I could feel the sweat on your palm. But today, you make jokes. You try to unnerve me with your banter. Why the difference, Ryan? You are not a field officer. Your earlier nervousness proved that, but now you are acting like one. Why? he asked himself as everyone filed back into the conference room. Everyone sat for the next round of monologues, and Golovko kept an eye on his American counterpart.

Ryan wasn't fidgeting now, he noted with some surprise. On Monday and Tuesday he had been. He merely looked bored, no more uncomfortable than that. *You should be uncomfortable, Ryan*, Golovko thought.

Why did you need to meet with Gerasimov? Why twice? Why were you nervous before and after the first . . . and before but not after the second?

It didn't make much sense. Golovko listened to the droning words in his earpiece – it was the American's turn to ramble on about things that had already been decided –

but his mind was elsewhere. His mind was in Ryan's KGB file. Ryan, John Patrick. Son of Emmet William Ryan and Catherine Burke Ryan, both deceased. Married, two children. Degrees in economics and history. Wealthy. Brief service in US Marine Corps. Former stockbroker and history teacher. Joined CIA on a part-time basis four years before after a consulting job the year before that. Soon thereafter became a full-time officer-analyst. Never trained at the CIA's field school at Camp Peary, Virginia. Ryan had been involved in two violent incidents, and in both cases deported himself well – the Marine training, Golovko supposed, plus his innate qualities as a man, which the Russian respected. Very bright, brave when he had to be: a dangerous enemy. Ryan worked directly for the DDI, and was known to have prepared numerous special intelligence evaluations . . . but a special intelligence mission . . . ? He had no training for that. He was probably the wrong sort of personality. Too open, Golovko thought: there was little guile in the man. When he was hiding something, you would never know what, but you would know that he was hiding something . .

You were hiding something before, but not now, are you?

And what does that mean, Ivan Emmetovich? What the hell kind of name is Emmet? Golovko wondered irrelevantly.

Jack saw the man looking at him and saw the question in his eyes. The man was no dummy, Jack told himself, as Ernest Allen spoke on about some technical issue or other. We thought he was GRU, and he really turned out to be KGB – or so it would seem, Jack corrected himself. Is there something else about him that we don't know?

At parking position number nine at Sheremetyevo Airport, Colonel von Eich was standing at the aft passenger door of his aircraft. In front of him, a sergeant was fiddling with the door seal, an impressive array of tools spread out before him. Like most airliner doors, it opened outward only after opening inward, allowing the airtight seal to unseat itself and slide out of the way so that it would not be damaged. Faulty door seals had killed aircraft before, the most spectacular being the DC-10 crash outside Paris a decade before. Below them, a uniformed KGB guard stood with loaded rifle outside the aircraft. His own flight crew had to pass security checks. All Russians took security very seriously indeed, and the KGB were outright fanatics on the subject.

'I don't know why you're getting the warning light, Colonel,' the sergeant said after twenty minutes. 'The seal's perfect, the switch that goes to the light seems to be in good shape – anyway, the door is fine, sir. I'll check the panel up front next.'

You get that? Paul von Eich wanted to ask the KGB guard fifteen feet below, but couldn't.

His crew was already readying the plane for its return trip. They'd had a couple of days to see the sights. This time it had been an old monastery about forty miles outside the city – the last ten miles of which had been over roads that were probably dirt in summertime but were a mixture of mud and snow now. They'd had their guided, guarded tour of Moscow, and now the airmen were ready to go home. He hadn't briefed his men on what Ryan had told him yet. The time for that would come tomorrow evening. He wondered how they would react.

The session ended on schedule, with a hint from the Soviets that they'd be willing to talk over inspection times tomorrow. They'd have to talk fast, Ryan thought, because the delegation would be leaving tomorrow night, and they had to have something to take back home from this round of talks. After all, the summit meeting was already scheduled informally. This one would be in Moscow. Moscow in the spring, Jack thought. I wonder if they'll bring me along for the signing ceremony? I wonder if there'll be a treaty to sign? There had better be, Ryan concluded.

Golovko watched the Americans leave, then waved for his own car, which took him to KGB headquarters. He walked directly to the Chairman's office.

'So what did our diplomats give away today?' Gerasimov asked without preamble.

'I think tomorrow we'll make our amended proposal for inspection timing.' He paused before going on. 'I spoke with Ryan today. He seems to have changed somewhat and I thought I should report it.'

'Go on,' the Chairman said.

'Comrade Chairman, I do not know what the two of you discussed, but the change in his demeanor is such that I thought you should know of it.' Golovko went on to explain what he'd seen.

'Ah, yes. I cannot discuss our conversations because you are not cleared for that compartment, but I would not be concerned, Colonel. I am handling this matter personally. Your observation is noted. Ryan will have to learn to control his emotions better. Perhaps he is not Russian enough.' Gerasimov was not a man who made jokes, but this was an exception. 'Anything else on the negotiations?'

'My notes will be written up and on your desk tomorrow morning.'

'Good. Dismissed.' Gerasimov watched the man leave. His face didn't change until the door clicked shut. Bad enough to lose, he thought, and to lose to a nonprofessional . . . But he had lost, and, he reminded himself, he wasn't a professional either, merely the Party man who gave them orders. That decision was behind him. It was too bad about his officers in – wherever the place was – but they had failed, and earned their fates. He lifted his phone and ordered his private secretary to arrange for his wife and daughter to fly the following morning to Talinn, the capital of the Estonian Soviet Socialist Republic. Yes, they would need a car and a driver also. No, just one. The driver would double as their security guard. Not many people knew who his wife was, and the trip was unscheduled, just to see old friends. Very good. Gerasimov hung up his phone and looked around his office. He'd miss it. Not so much the office itself: the power. But he knew that he'd miss his life more.

*

534

'And this Colonel Bondarenko?' Vatutin asked.

'A fine young officer. Very bright. He'll make a good general when the time comes.'

Vatutin wondered how his final report would handle that issue. There was no suspicion about the man, except for his association with Filitov. But there had been no suspicion about Filitov, despite his connection with Oleg Penkovskiy. Colonel Vatutin shook his head in amazement. That fact would be talked about in security classes for a generation. Why didn't they see? the young officer-trainees would demand. How could anyone be so stupid? Because only the most trusted people can be spies – you don't give classified information to someone you cannot trust. The lesson was as it had always been: Trust no one. Coming back to Bondarenko, he wondered what would happen to him. If he were the loyal and exceptional officer he seemed to be, then he should not be tainted by this affair. But – there was always a *but*, wasn't there? – there were also some additional questions to ask, and Vatutin went to the bottom of his list. His initial interrogation report was due on Gerasimov's desk the following day.

The climb took all night in total darkness. The clouds that had swept in from the south covered both moon and stars, and the only illumination was from the perimeter lights of their objective, reflected off the clouds. Now they were within easy sight of it. Still a sizable march, they were close enough that the individual units could be briefed on their tasks, and could see what they had to do. The Archer picked for himself a high spot and rested his binoculars on a rock to steady them as he surveyed the site. There seemed to be three encampments. Only two of them were fenced, though at the third he could make out piles of posts and fencing material near an orange-white light atop the sort of pole used in cities to illuminate the streets. The extent of the construction surprised him. To do all this – on the top of a mountain! How important could such a place be to deserve all the effort, all the expense? Something that sent a laser beam into the sky . . . to what end? The Americans had asked him if he'd seen what the light-beam had hit. They knew it had hit something, then? Something in the sky. Whatever it was, it had frightened the Americans, had frightened the same people who made the missiles with which he had killed so many Russian pilots . . . What could frighten people so clever as that? The Archer could see the place, but did not see anything more frightening than the guard towers that held machine guns. One of those buildings held armed soldiers who would have heavy weapons. That was something to be frightened about. Which building? He had to know that, because that building had to be attacked first. His mortars would put their shells on that one first of all. But which one was it?

After that . . . ? He'd deploy his men into two sections of almost a hundred each. The Major would take one and go left. He'd take the other and go right. The Archer had selected his objective as soon as he saw the mountaintop. That building, he told himself, was where the people were. That was where the Russians lived. Not the soldiers, but those the soldiers guarded. Some of the windows were lighted. An apartment building built atop a mountain, he thought. What sort of people would they be that the Russians would put up a building of the sort found only in cities? People who needed comfort. People who had to be guarded. People who worked on something the Americans were afraid of. People he would kill without mercy, the Archer told himself.

The Major came down to lie at his side.

'All the men are well hidden,' the man said. He trained his own binoculars on the objective. It was so dark that the Archer barely saw the man's outline, only the contours of his face and the vague shadow of his bristling mustache. 'We misjudged the ground from the other hilltop. It will take three hours to close in.'

'Closer to four, I think.'

'I don't like those guard towers,' the Major noted. Both men shivered with the cold. The wind had picked up, and they no longer were sheltered from it by the bulk of the mountain. It would be a difficult night for all of the men. 'One or two machine guns in each of them. They can sweep us off the mountainside as we make the final assault.'

'No searchlights,' the Archer noted.

'Then they'll be using night-vision devices. I've used them myself.'

'How good?'

'Their range is limited because of the way they work. They can see large things, like trucks, out to this distance. A man on a broken background like this one . . . perhaps three thousand meters. Far enough for their purposes, my friend. The towers must go first. Use the mortars on them.'

'No.' The Archer shook his head. 'We have less than a hundred shells. They must go on the guard barracks. If we can kill all of the sleeping soldiers, so much the easier for us when we get inside.'

'If the machine-gunners in those towers see us coming, half of our men will be dead before the guards wake up,' the Major pointed out.

The Archer grunted. His comrade was right. Two of the towers were sited in a way that would allow the men in them to sweep the steep slope that they'd have to climb before getting to the mountain's flat summit. He could counter that with his own machine guns . . . but duels of that sort were usually won by the defender. The wind gusted at them, and both men knew that they'd have to find shelter soon or risk frostbite.

'Damn this cold!' the Major swore.

'Do you think the towers are cold also?' the Archer asked after a moment.

'Even worse. They are more exposed than we.'

'How will the Russian soldiers be dressed?'

The Major chuckled. 'The same as we – after all, we're all wearing their clothing, are we not?'

The Archer nodded, searching for the thought that hovered at the edge of his consciousness. It came to him through his cold-numbed brain, and he left his perch, telling the Major to remain. He came back carrying a Stinger missile launcher. The metal tube was cold to the touch as he assembled it. The acquisition units were all carried inside his men's clothing, to protect the batteries from the cold. He expertly assembled and activated the weapon, then rested his cheek on the metal conductance bar and trained it on the nearest guard tower . . .

'Listen,' he said, and handed the weapon over. The officer took it and did as he was directed.

'Ah.' His teeth formed a Cheshire-cat grin in the black night.

Clark was busy, too. Obviously a careful man, Mancuso noted as he watched, he was laying out and checking all of his equipment. The man's clothing looked ordinary, though shabby and not well made.

'Bought in Kiev,' Clark explained. 'You can't exactly wear Hart, Schaffner, and Marx and expect to look like a local.' He also had a coverall to put over it, with camouflage stripes. There was a complete set of identity papers – in Russian, which Mancuso couldn't read – and a pistol. It was a small one, barely larger than the silencer that sat next to it.

'Never seen one of these before,' the Captain said.

'Well, that's a Qual-A-Tec baffle-type silencer with no wipes and a slide-lock internal to the can,' Clark said.

'What –'

Mr Clark chuckled. 'You guys have been hitting me with subspeak ever since I got aboard, skipper. Now it's my turn.'

Mancuso lifted the pistol. 'This is only a twenty-two.'

'It's damned near impossible to silence a big round unless you want a silencer as long as your forearm, like the FBI guys have on their toys. I have to have something that'll fit in a pocket. This is the best Mickey can do, and he's the best around.'

'Who?'

'Mickey Finn. That's his real name. He does the design work for Qual-A-Tec, and I wouldn't use anybody else's silencer. It isn't like TV, Cap'n. For a silencer to work right, it has to be a small caliber, you have to use a subsonic round, and you have to have a sealed breech. And it helps if you're out in the open. In here, you'd hear it 'cause of the steel walls. Outside, you'd hear something out to thirty feet or so, but you wouldn't know what it was. The silencer goes on the pistol like this, and you twist it' – he demonstrated – 'and now the gun's a single shot. The silencer locks the action. To get off another round, you have to twist it back and cycle the action manually.'

'You mean you're going in there with a twenty-two single-shot?'

'That's how it's done, Captain.'

'Have you ever –'

'You really don't want to know. Besides, I can't talk about it.' Clark grinned. 'I'm not cleared for that myself. If it makes you feel any better, yeah, I'm scared, too, but this is what they pay me for.'

'But if –'

'You get the hell out of here. I have the authority to give you that order, Captain, remember? It hasn't happened yet. Don't worry about it. I do enough worrying for the both of us.'

25

Convergence

Maria and Katryn Gerasimov always got the sort of VIP treatment that they deserved as the immediate family of a Politburo member. A KGB car took them from their guarded eight-room apartment on Kutuzovskiy Prospekt to Vnukovo Airport, which was used mainly for domestic flights, where they waited in the lounge reserved for the *vlasti*. It was staffed by more people than ever seemed to use the facility at any one time, and this morning the only others present kept to themselves. An attendant took their hats and coats while another walked them to a couch, where a third asked if they wanted anything to eat or drink. Both ordered coffee and nothing more. The lounge staff eyed their clothing with envy. The cloak-room attendant ran her hands over the silky texture of their furs, and it struck her that her ancestors might have looked upon the czarist nobility with the same degree of envy that she felt toward these two. They sat in regal isolation, with only the distant company of their bodyguards as they sipped at their coffee and gazed out the plate-glass windows at the parked airliners.

Maria Ivanovna Gerasimova was not actually an Estonian, though she'd been born there fifty years before. Her family was composed entirely of ethnic Russians, since the small Baltic state had been part of the Russian Empire under the czars, only to experience a brief 'liberation' – as the trouble-makers called it – between the world wars, during which the Estonian nationalists had not made life overly easy for ethnic Russians. Her earliest childhood memories of Talinn were not all that pleasant, but like all children she had made friends who would be friends forever. They'd even survived her marriage to a young Party man who had, to everyone's surprise – most especially hers – risen to command the most hated organ of the Soviet government. Worse, he'd made his career on repressing dissident elements. That her childhood friendships had withstood this fact was testimony to her intelligence. Half a dozen people had been spared sentences in labor camps, or been transferred from one of strict regime to a milder place due to her intercession. The children of her friends had attended universities because of her influence. Those who had taunted her Russian name as a child did less well, though she'd helped one of them a little, enough to appear merciful. Such behavior was enough to keep her part of the small Talinn suburb despite her long-past move to Moscow. It also helped that her husband had only once accompanied her to her childhood home. She was not an evil person, merely one who used her vicarious power as a princess of an earlier age might have done, arbitrarily but seldom maliciously. Her face had the sort of regal composure that fitted the image. A beautiful catch twenty-five years ago, she was still a handsome woman, if somewhat more serious now. As an ancillary part of her husband's official identity, she had to play her part in the game – not as much as the wife of a Western politician, of course, but her behavior had to be proper. The practice stood her in good stead now. Those who watched her could never have guessed her thoughts.

She wondered what was wrong, knowing only that it was gravely serious. Her husband had told her to be at a specific place at a specific time, to ask no questions of him, only to promise that she would do exactly as she was told, regardless of consequences. The order, delivered in a quiet, emotionless monotone while the water was running in their kitchen, was the most frightening thing she had heard since the German tanks had rumbled into Talinn in 1941. But one legacy of the German occupation was that she knew just how important survival was.

Her daughter knew nothing of what they were doing. Her reactions could not be trusted. Katryn had never known danger in her life as her mother had, only the rare inconvenience. Their only child was in her first year at Moscow State University, where she majored in economics and traveled with a crowd of similarly important children of similarly important people, all of ministerial rank at least. Already a Party member – eighteen is the earliest age permitted – she played her role, too. The previous fall she'd traveled with some of her classmates and helped harvest wheat, mainly for a photograph that had been displayed on the second page of *Komsomolskaya Pravda*, the paper of the Young Communist League. Not that she'd liked it, but the new rules in Moscow 'encouraged' the children of the powerful at least to appear to be doing their fair share. It could have been worse. She'd returned from the ordeal with a new boyfriend, and her mother wondered if they'd been intimate, or had the young man been frightened off by the bodyguards and the knowledge of who her father was? Or did he see her as a chance to enter the KGB? Or was he one of the new generation that simply didn't care? Her daughter was one of these. The Party was something you joined to secure your position, and her father's post put her on the inside track for a comfortable job. She sat beside her mother in silence, reading a West German fashion magazine that was now sold in the Soviet Union and deciding what new Western fashions she would like to wear to classes. She would have to learn, her mother thought, remembering that at eighteen the world is a place with horizons both near and far, depending on one's mood.

About the time they finished their coffee, the flight was called. They waited. The plane wouldn't leave without them. Finally, when the last call came, the attendant brought their coats and hats, and another led them and their guards down the stairs to their car. The other passengers had already ridden out to the aircraft on a bus – the Russians haven't quite discovered jetways yet – and when their car arrived, they were able to walk right up the stairs. The stewardess guided them solicitously to their first-class seats in the forward cabin. They weren't called first class, of course, but they were wider, they had greater leg room, and they were reserved. The airliner lifted off at ten o'clock, Moscow time, stopped first at Leningrad, then proceeded to Talinn, where it landed just after one.

'So, Colonel, you have your summary of the subject's activity?' Gerasimov asked casually. He seemed preoccupied, Vatutin noted at once. He should have been more interested, particularly with a Politburo meeting only an hour away.

'Books will be written about this one, Comrade Chairman. Filitov had access to virtually all of our defense secrets. He even helped make defense policy. I needed thirty pages merely to summarize what he's done. The full interrogation will require several months.'

'Speed is less important than thoroughness,' Gerasimov said offhandedly.

Vatutin did not react. 'As you wish, Comrade Chairman.'

'If you will excuse me, the Politburo is meeting this morning.'

Colonel Vatutin came to attention, pivoted on his heels, and left. He found Golovko in the anteroom. The two knew each other casually. They'd been a year apart at the KGB Academy, and their careers had advanced at roughly the same rate.

'Colonel Golovko,' the Chairman's secretary said. 'The Chairman must leave now, and suggests that you return tomorrow morning at ten.'

'But –'

'He's leaving now,' the secretary said.

'Very well,' Golovko replied and stood. He and Vatutin left the room together.

'The Chairman is busy,' Vatutin observed on the way out.

'Aren't we all?' the other man replied after the door closed. 'I thought he wanted this. I arrived here at four to write this goddamned report! Well, I think I'll have some

543

breakfast. How go things in "Two", Klementi Vladimirovich?'

'Also busy – the people do not pay us to sit on our backsides.' He'd also arrived early to complete his paperwork, and his stomach was growling audibly.

'You must be hungry, too. Care to join me?'

Vatutin nodded, and both men made for the canteen. Senior officers – colonel and above – had a separate dining room and were served by white-coated waiters. The room was never empty. The KGB worked round the clock, and odd schedules made for irregular meals. Besides, the food was good, especially for senior officers. The room was a quiet place. When people talked here, even if they were discussing sports, they did so almost in whispers.

'Aren't you attached to the arms negotiations now?' Vatutin asked as he sipped his tea.

'Yes – nursemaiding diplomats. You know, the Americans think I'm GRU.' Golovko arched his eyebrows, partly in amusement at the Americans, partly to show his not-quite classmate how important his cover was.

'Really?' Vatutin was surprised. 'I would have thought that they were better informed – at least . . . well . . .' He shrugged to indicate that he couldn't go any further. *I, too, have things that I cannot discuss, Sergey Nikolayevich.*

'I suppose the Chairman is preoccupied by the Politburo meeting. The rumors –'

'He's not ready yet,' Vatutin said with the quiet confidence of an insider.

'You're sure?'

'Quite sure.'

'Where do you stand?' Golovko asked.

'Where do *you* stand?' Vatutin replied. Both traded a look of amusement, but then Golovko turned serious.

'Narmonov needs a chance. The arms agreement – if the diplomats ever get their thumbs out and execute it – will be a good thing for us.'

'You really think so?' Vatutin didn't know one way or the other.

'Yes, I do. I've had to become an expert on the arms of both camps. I know what we have, and I know what they have. Enough is enough. Once a man is dead, you do not need to shoot him again and again. There are better ways to spend the money. There are things that need changing.'

'You should be careful saying that,' Vatutin cautioned. Golovko had traveled too much. He had seen the West, and many KGB officers came back with tales of wonder – if only the Soviet Union could do this, or that, or the other thing . . . Vatutin sensed the truth of that, but was inherently a more cautious man. He was a 'Two' man, who looked for dangers, while Golovko, of the First Chief Directorate, looked for opportunities.

'Are we not the guardians? If we cannot speak, who can?' Golovko said, then backed off. 'Carefully, of course, with the guidance of the Party at all times – but even the Party sees the need for change.' They had to agree on that. Every Soviet newspaper proclaimed the need for a new approach, and every such article had to be approved by someone important, and of political purity. The Party was never wrong, both men knew, but it certainly did change its *kollektiv* mind a lot.

'A pity that the Party does not see the importance of rest for its guardians. Tired men make mistakes, Sergey Nikolayevich.'

Golovko contemplated his eggs for a moment, then lowered his voice even further. 'Klementi . . . let us assume for a moment I know that a senior KGB officer is meeting with a senior CIA officer.'

'How senior?'

'Higher than directorate head,' Golovko replied, telling Vatutin exactly who it was without using a name or a title. 'Let us assume that I arrange the meetings, and that he tells me I do not need to know what the meetings are about. Finally, let us assume that this senior officer is acting . . . strangely. What am I to do?' he asked, and was rewarded with an answer right from the book:

'You should write up a report for the Second Directorate, of course.'

Golovko nearly choked on his breakfast. 'A fine idea. Immediately afterwards I can slash my throat with a razor and save everyone the time and trouble of an interrogation. Some people are above suspicion – or have enough power that no one dares to suspect them.'

'Sergey, if there is anything I have learned in the past few weeks, it is that there is no such thing as "above suspicion". We've been working a case so high in the Defense Ministry . . . you would not believe it. I scarcely do.' Vatutin waved for a waiter to bring a fresh pot of tea. The pause gave the other man a chance to think. Golovko had intimate knowledge of that ministry because of his work on strategic arms. Who could it be? There were not many men whom the KGB was unable to suspect – that was hardly a condition the agency encouraged – and fewer still high in the Ministry of Defense, which the KGB is supposed to regard with the utmost suspicion. But . . .

'Filitov?'

Vatutin blanched, and made a mistake: 'Who told you?'

'My God, he briefed *me* last year on intermediate arms. I heard he was sick. You're not joking, are you?'

'There is nothing the least bit amusing about this. I cannot say much, and it may not go beyond this table, but – yes, Filitov was working for . . . for someone outside our borders. He's confessed, and the first phase of the interrogation is complete.'

'But he knows everything! The arms-negotiation team should know of this. It alters the whole basis for the talks,' Golovko said.

Vatutin hadn't considered that, but it wasn't his place to make policy decisions. He was, after all, nothing more than a policeman with a very special beat. Golovko might have been right in his assessment, but rules were rules.

'The information is being closely held for the moment, Sergey Nikolayevich. Remember that.'

'Compartmentalization of information can work both for

and against us, Klementi,' Golovko warned, wondering if he should warn the negotiators.

'That's true enough,' Vatutin agreed.

'When did you arrest your subject?' Golovko asked, and got his reply. *The timing* . . . He took a breath, and forgot about the negotiations. 'The Chairman has met at least twice with a senior CIA officer –'

'Who, and when?'

'Sunday night and yesterday morning. His name is Ryan. He's my counterpart on the American team, but he's an intelligence type, not a field officer as I once was. What do you make of that?'

'You're sure he's not an operations man?'

'Positive. I can even tell you the room he works in. This is not a matter of uncertainty. He's an analyst, a senior one, but only a desk man. Special assistant to their Deputy Director for Intelligence, before that he was part of a high-level liaison team in London. He's never been in the field.'

Vatutin finished his tea and poured another cup. Next he buttered a piece of bread. He took his time thinking about this. There was ample opportunity to delay a response, but –

'All we have here is unusual activity. Perhaps the Chairman has something going that is so sensitive –'

'Yes – or perhaps that is how it's supposed to appear,' Golovko observed.

'For a "One" man, you seem to have our way of thinking, Sergey. Very well. What we would do ordinarily – not that a case like this is ordinary, but you know what I mean – is that we assemble information and take it to the Director of the Second Chief Directorate. The Chairman has bodyguards. They would be taken aside and questioned. But such a thing would have to be handled very, very carefully. My chief would have to go to – who?' Vatutin asked rhetorically. 'A Politburo member, I suppose, or perhaps the Secretary of the Central Committee, but . . . the Filitov matter is being handled very quietly. I believe the Chairman may wish to use it as political leverage against both the Defense Minister and Vaneyev . . .'

'*What?*'

'Vaneyev's daughter was acting as a spy for the West – well, a courier to be precise. We broke her, and –'

'Why has this not become public knowledge?'

'The woman is back at her job, by order of the Chairman,' Vatutin replied.

'Klementi, do you have any idea what the hell is going on here?'

'No, not now. I assumed that the Chairman was seeking to strengthen his political position, but the meetings with a CIA man . . . you're *sure* of this?'

'I arranged the meetings myself,' Golovko repeated. 'The first must have been agreed upon before the Americans arrived, and I merely handled the details. Ryan requested the second. He passed a note to me – about as well as a trainee-officer on his first job. They met at the Barricade Theater yesterday, as I told you. Klementi, something very strange is happening.'

'It would seem so. But we have nothing –'

'What do you mean –'

'Sergey, investigation is *my* job. We have nothing but disparate bits of information that might easily be explained. Nothing queers an investigation like moving too rapidly. Before we can act, we must assemble and analyze what we have. Then we can go to see my chief, and *he* can authorize further action. Do you think two colonels can act on this without clearing it with higher authority? You have to write up everything you know and bring it to me. How soon can you do that?'

'I have to be at the negotiating session in' – he checked his watch – 'two hours. That will last until sixteen hours, followed by a reception. The Americans leave at twenty-two hours.'

'Can you skip the reception?'

'It will be awkward, but yes.'

'Be in my office at sixteen-thirty,' Vatutin said formally. Golovko, who was the senior officer by a year, smiled for the first time.

'By your order, Comrade Colonel.'

'Marshal Yazov, what is the position of the Ministry?' Narmonov asked.

'No less than six hours,' the Defense Minister said. 'In that time we should be able to conceal most of the highly sensitive items. As you know, we would prefer not to have our sites inspected at all, though examining American facilities does offer some intelligence advantages.'

The Foreign Minister nodded. 'The Americans will ask for less, but I think we can settle on that number.'

'I disagree.' Heads of the Politburo members turned to Alexandrov's chair. The ideologue's florid complexion was displaying itself again. 'It is bad enough to reduce our arsenals at all, but to have Americans examine the factories, to get all our secrets, this is madness.'

'Mikhail Petrovich, we have been through this,' General Secretary Narmonov said patiently. 'Further discussion?' He looked around the table. Heads nodded. The General Secretary checked off the item on his note pad. He waved to the Foreign Minister.

'Six hours, nothing less.'

The Foreign Minister whispered instruction to an aide, who left the room at once to call the chief negotiator. Next he leaned forward. 'That leaves only the question of which arms will be eliminated – the hardest question of all, of course. That will require another session – a long one.'

'We are scheduled to have our summit in three months . . .' Narmonov observed.

'Yes. It should be decided by then. Preliminary excursions into this question have not met any serious obstacles.'

'And the American defensive systems?' Alexandrov asked. 'What of them?' Heads turned again, now to the KGB Chairman.

'Our efforts to penetrate the American Tea Clipper program continue. As you know, it corresponds very closely to our Project Bright Star, though it would seem that we are further along in the most important areas,' Gerasimov said, without looking up from his scratch pad.

'We cut our missile force in half while the Americans learn to shoot our missiles down,' Alexandrov groused.

'And they will cut their force in half while we work to the same end,' Narmonov went on. 'Mikhail Petrovich, we've been working along these lines for over thirty years, and much harder than they have.'

'We are also further along in testing,' Yazov pointed out. 'And –'

'They know of it,' Gerasimov said. He referred to the test the Americans had observed from the Cobra Belle aircraft, but Yazov didn't know about that, and even the KGB hadn't discovered how the test had been observed, merely that the Americans knew of it. 'They have intelligence services too, remember.'

'But they haven't said anything about it,' Narmonov observed.

'The Americans have occasionally been reticent to discuss such things. They complain about some technical aspects of our defense activity, but not all of them, for fear of compromising their intelligence-gathering methods,' Gerasimov explained casually. 'Possibly they have conducted similar tests, though we have not learned of it. The Americans, too, are able to maintain secrecy when they wish.' Taussig had never gotten that information out either. Gerasimov leaned back to let others speak.

'In other words, both sides will continue as before,' Narmonov concluded.

'Unless we are able to win a concession,' the Foreign Minister said. 'Which is unlikely to happen. Is there anyone at this table who thinks we should restrict our missile-defense programs?' There wasn't. 'Then why should we realistically expect the Americans to feel any differently?'

'But what if they get ahead of us!' Alexandrov demanded.

'An excellent point, Mikhail Petrovich,' Narmonov seized the opportunity. 'Why do the Americans always seem to get ahead of us?' he asked the assembled chieftains of his country.

'They do so not because they are magicians, but because we allow them to – because we cannot make our economy perform as it should. That denies Marshal Yazov the tools our men in uniform need, denies our people the good things of life that they are coming to expect, and denies us the ability to face the West as equals.'

'Our weapons make us equals!' Alexandrov objected.

'But what advantage do they give us when the West has weapons, too? Is there anyone around this table who is content to be equal to the West? Our rockets do that for us,' Narmonov said, 'but there is more to national greatness than the ability to kill. If we are to defeat the West, it cannot be with nuclear bombs – unless you want the Chinese to inherit our world.' Narmonov paused. 'Comrades, if we are to prevail we have to get our economy moving!'

'It is moving,' Alexandrov said.

'Where? Do any of us know that?' Vaneyev asked, igniting the room's atmosphere.

The discussion turned boisterous for several minutes before settling down to the collegial sort of discussion normal to the Politburo. Narmonov used it to measure the strength of his opposition. He deemed his faction more than equal to that of Alexandrov's. Vaneyev hadn't tipped his hand – Alexandrov expected him to *pretend* to be on the Secretary's side, didn't he? And the General Secretary still had Yazov. Narmonov had also used the session to defuse the political dimension of his country's economic problems by couching the need for reforms as a means of improving the country's military power – which was true, of course, but was also an issue difficult for Alexandrov and his clique to deny. By taking the initiative, Narmonov judged, he'd been able to evaluate the other side's strength yet again, and by putting the argument in the open, he'd put them on the psychological defensive at least temporarily. It was all he could hope for at the moment. He'd lived to fight another day, Narmonov told himself. Once the arms-control treaty went through, his power at this table would increase another notch. The *people* would like that – and for the first time in Soviet history, the feelings of the people were beginning to matter. Once it had been decided which arms would be eliminated, and over what sort of schedule, they'd know how much additional money there would be to spend. Narmonov could control that discussion from his seat, using the funds to barter for additional power in the Politburo as members vied for it in pursuit of their own pet projects. Alexandrov could not interfere with that, since his power base was ideological rather than economic. It occurred to Narmonov that he would probably win out. With Defense at his back, and with Vaneyev in his pocket, he would win the confrontation, break KGB to his will, and put Alexandrov out to pasture. It was only a matter of deciding when to force the issue. There had to be agreement on the treaty, and he would gladly trade away small advantages on that score in order to secure his position at home. The West would be surprised by that, but someday it would be more surprised to see what a viable economy would do for its principal rival. Narmonov's immediate concern was his political survival. After that came the task of bringing life back into his country's economy. There was a further objective, one that hadn't changed in three generations, though the West was always discovering new ways to ignore it. Narmonov's eyes weren't fixed on it, but it was still there.

Last session, Ryan told himself. *Thank God*. The nervousness was back. There was no reason that everything shouldn't go well – the odd part was that Ryan had no idea what would happen with Gerasimov's family. 'Need-to-know' had again raised its wearisome head on that score, but the part about getting Gerasimov and CARDINAL out was so breathtakingly simple that he would never have come up with it. That part was Ritter's doing, and the crusty old bastard did have a flair.

The Russians spoke first this time, and five minutes into the speech, they proposed a warning time for surprise on-site inspections. Jack would have preferred zero-time, but that was unreasonable. It wasn't necessary to see what the insides of the birds looked like, desirable as that would be. It was enough to count the launchers and the warheads, and anything under ten hours was probably enough for that – especially if the snap visits were coordinated with satellite passes to catch any attempt at sleight-of-hand. The Russians offered ten hours. Ernest Allen, in his reply, demanded three. Two hours later the respective figures were seven and five. Two hours after that, much to everyone's surprise, the Americans said *six*, and the chief Russian delegate nodded consent. Both men rose and leaned across the table to shake hands. Jack was glad it was all over, but would have held out for five. After all, he and Golovko had agreed on four, hadn't they?

Four and a half hours to settle on one damned number, Jack thought. *And that may be an all-time record.* There was even some applause when everyone stood, and Jack joined the line for the nearest men's room. A few minutes later he returned. Golovko was there.

'Your people let us off easy,' the KGB officer said.

'I guess you're lucky it wasn't my job,' Jack agreed. 'This is a hell of a lot of work for two or three little things.'

'You think them little?'

'In the Great Scheme of Things . . . well, they're significant, but not overly so. Mainly what this means is that we can fly home,' Jack observed, and some unease crept into his voice. *It isn't over yet.*

'You look forward to this?' Golovko asked.

'Not exactly, but there you are.' *It isn't the flight that makes me nervous this time, sport.*

*

The flight crew had stayed at the Hotel Ukrania, just on the Moscow River, doubling up in the huge rooms, shopping in the 'friendship store' for souvenirs, and generally seeing what they could while maintaining a guard team on the aircraft. Now they checked out together and boarded a fifty-passenger tourist bus that crossed over the river and headed east on Kalinina Prospekt on its way to the airport, a half-hour drive in the light traffic.

When Colonel von Eich arrived, the British Airways ground crew that provided maintenance support was finishing up the fueling under the watchful eyes of his crew chief – the chief master sergeant who 'owned' the aircraft – and the Captain who'd serve as copilot in the VC-137's right seat. The members of the crew checked through the KGB control point, whose officers were assiduously thorough in verifying everyone's identity. Finished, the crew filed aboard, stowed its gear, and began getting the converted 707 ready for its flight back to Andrews Air Force Base. The pilot gathered five of his people together in the cockpit, and under the covering noise of somebody's boomer-box, informed them of what they'd be doing tonight that was 'a little different'.

'Christ, sir,' the crew chief noted, 'that's different all right.'

'What's life without a little excitement?' von Eich asked. 'Everybody clear on your duties?' He got nods. 'Then let's get to work, people.' The pilot and copilot picked up their checklists and went outside with the crew chief to pre-flight the aircraft. It would be good to get back home, they all agreed – assuming that they could unstick the tires from the pavement. It was, the crew chief observed, as cold as a witch's tit. Their hands gloved, and dressed now in Air Force-issue parkas, they took their time as they walked around the aircraft. The 89th Military Airlift Wing had a spotless safety record ferrying 'DVs' all over the world, and the way they maintained that was through uncompromising attention to every detail. Von Eich wondered if their 700,000 hours of accident-free flying would be undone tonight.

*

Ryan was already packed. They'd be leaving right from the reception to the airport. He decided to shave and brush his teeth again before putting his shaving kit in one of the pockets of his two-suiter. He was wearing one of his English suits. It was almost warm enough for the local climate, but Jack promised himself that if he ever again came to Moscow in the winter, he'd remember to bring long johns. It was almost time when a knock came at the door. It was Tony Candela.

'Enjoy the flight home,' he said.

'Yeah.' Ryan chuckled.

'Thought I'd give you a hand.' He hefted the two-suiter, and Jack merely had to grab his briefcase. Together they walked to the elevator, which took them from the seventh floor up to the ninth, where they waited for another elevator to take them down to the lobby.

'Do you know who designed this building?'

Obviously someone with a sense of humor,' Candela replied. 'They hired the same fellow to handle construction of the new embassy.' Both men laughed. That story was worthy of a Hollywood disaster epic. There were enough electronic devices in that building to cobble up a mainframe computer. The elevator came a minute later, taking both men to the lobby. Candela handed Ryan his suitcase.

'Break a leg,' he said before walking away.

Jack walked out to where the cars were waiting and dropped his case in the open trunk. The night was clear. There were stars in the sky, and the hint of the aurora borealis on the northern horizon. He'd heard that this natural phenomenon was occasionally seen from Moscow, but it was something that he'd never witnessed.

The motorcade left ten minutes later and made its way south to the Foreign Ministry, repeating the route that nearly encapsulated Ryan's slim knowledge of this city of eight million souls. One by one the cars curved onto the small traffic circle and their occupants were guided into the building. This reception was not nearly as elaborate as the last one in the Kremlin had been, but this session had not accomplished quite as much. The next one would be a bear, as the summit deadline approached, but the next session was scheduled to be in Washington. The reporters were already waiting, mainly print, with a few TV cameras present. Someone approached Jack as soon as he handed off his topcoat.

'Dr Ryan?'

'Yeah?' He turned.

'Mike Paster, *Washington Post*. There's a report in Washington that your SEC problems have been settled.'

Jack laughed. 'God, it's nice not to talk about the arms business for a change! As I said earlier, I didn't do anything wrong. I guess those – jerks, but don't quote me on that – folks finally figured it out. Good. I didn't want to have to hire a lawyer.'

'There's talk that CIA had a hand in –' Ryan cut him off.

'Tell you what. Tell your Washington bureau that if they give me a couple of days to unwind from this business, I'll show them everything I did. I do all my transactions by computer, and I keep hard copies of everything. Fair enough?'

'Sure – but why didn't –'

'You tell me,' Jack said, reaching for a glass of wine as a waiter went past. He had to have one, but tonight it would be one only. 'Maybe some people in DC have a hard-on for the Agency. For Christ's sake don't quote me on that, either.'

'So how'd the talks go?' the reporter asked next.

'You can get the details from Ernie, but off the record, pretty good. Not as good as last time, and there's a lot left to handle, but we settled a couple of tough ones, and that's about all we expected for this trip.'

'Will the agreement go through in time for the summit?' Paster inquired next.

'Off the record,' Jack said immediately. The reporter nodded. 'I'd call the chances better than two out of three.'

'How's the Agency feel about it?'

'We're not supposed to be political, remember? From a technical point of view, the fifty-percent reduction is something I think we can live with. It doesn't really change anything, does it? But it is "nice". I grant you that.'

'How do you want me to quote this?' Paster asked.

'Call me a Very Junior Administration Official.' Jack grinned. 'Fair enough? Uncle Ernie can speak on the record, but I'm not allowed to.'

'What about the effect this will have on Narmonov's remaining in power?'

'Not my turf,' Ryan lied smoothly. 'My opinions on that are private, not professional.'

'So . . .'

'So ask somebody else about that,' Jack suggested. 'Ask me the really important things, like who the 'Skins ought to draft in the first round.'

'Olson, the quarterback at Baylor,' the reporter said at once.

'I like that defensive end at Penn State myself, but he'll probably go too early.'

'Good trip,' the reporter said as he closed his note pad.

'Yeah, you enjoy the rest of the winter, pal.' The reporter made to go away, then paused. 'Can you say anything, completely off the record, about the Foley couple that the Russians sent home last –'

'Who? Oh, the ones they accused of spying? Off the record, and you never heard this from me, it's bullshit. Any other way, no comment.'

'Right.' The reporter walked off with a smile.

Jack was left standing alone. He looked around for Golovko, but couldn't find him. He was disappointed. Enemy or not, they could always talk, and Ryan had come to enjoy their conversations. The Foreign Minister showed up, then Narmonov. All the other fixtures were there: the violins, the tables laden with snacks, the circulating waiters with silver trays of wine, vodka, and champagne. The State Department people were knotted in conversation with their Soviet colleagues. Ernie Allen was laughing with his

Soviet counterpart. Only Jack was standing alone, and that wouldn't do. He walked over to the nearest group and hung on the periphery, scarcely noticed as he checked his watch from time to time and took tiny sips of the wine.

'Time,' Clark said.

Getting to this point had been difficult enough. Clark's equipment was already set in the watertight trunk that ran from the Attack Center to the top of the sail. It had hatches at both ends and was completely watertight, unlike the rest of the sail, which was free-flooding. One more sailor had volunteered to go in with him, and then the bottom hatch was closed and dogged down tight. Mancuso lifted a phone.

'Communications check.'

'Loud and clear, sir,' Clark replied. 'Ready whenever you are.'

'Don't touch the hatch until I say so.'

'Aye aye, Cap'n.'

The Captain turned around. 'I have the conn,' he announced.

'Captain has the conn,' the officer of the deck agreed.

'Diving Officer, pump out three thousand pounds. We're taking her off the bottom. Engine room, stand by to answer bells.'

'Aye.' The diving officer, who was also Chief of the Boat, gave the necessary orders. Electric trim pumps ejected a ton and a half of saltwater, and *Dallas* slowly righted herself. Mancuso looked around. The submarine was at battle stations. The fire-control tracking party stood ready. Ramius was with the navigator. The weapons-control panels were manned. Below in the torpedo room, all four tubes were loaded, and one was already flooded.

'Sonar, conn. Anything to report?' Mancuso asked next.

'Negative, conn. Nothing at all, sir.'

'Very well. Diving Officer, make your depth nine-zero feet.'

'Nine-zero feet, aye.'

They had to get off the bottom before giving the submarine any forward movement. Mancuso watched the depth gauge change slowly as the Chief of the Boat, also known as the Cob, slowly and skilfully adjusted the submarine's trim.

'Depth nine-zero feet, sir. It'll be very hard to hold.'

'Maneuvering, give me turns for five knots. Helm, right fifteen degrees rudder, come to new heading zero-three-eight.'

'Right fifteen degrees rudder, aye, coming to new heading zero-three-eight,' the helmsman acknowledged. 'Sir, my rudder is right fifteen degrees.'

'Very well.' Mancuso watched the gyrocompass click around to the northeasterly course. It took five minutes to get out from under the ice. The Captain ordered periscope depth. Another minute.

'Up 'scope!' Mancuso said next. A quartermaster twisted the control wheel, and the Captain met the rising instrument as the eyepiece cleared the deck. 'Hold!'

The periscope stopped a foot below the surface. Mancuso looked for shadows and possible ice, but saw nothing. 'Up two feet.' He was on his knees now. 'Two more and hold.'

He used the slender attack periscope, not the larger search one. The search periscope had better light-gathering capacity, but he didn't want to risk the larger radar cross-section, and the submarine for the past twelve hours had been using red internal lights only. It made the food look odd, but it also gave everyone better night vision. He made a slow sweep of the horizon. There was nothing to be seen but drifting ice on the surface.

'Clear,' he announced. 'All clear. Raise the ESM.' There was the hiss of hydraulics as the electronic-sensor mast went up. The thin reed of fiberglass was only half an inch wide, and nearly invisible on radar. 'Down 'scope.'

'I got that one surface-surveillance radar, bearing zero-three-eight,' the ESM technician announced, giving frequency and pulse characteristics. 'Signal is weak.'

'Here we go, people.' Mancuso lifted a phone to the bridge tube. 'You ready?'

'Yes, sir,' Clark replied.

'Stand by. Good luck.' The Captain replaced the phone and turned. 'Put her on the roof and stand by to take her down fast.'

It took a total of four minutes. The top of *Dallas*' black sail broached the surface, pointing directly at the nearest Soviet radar to minimize its radar cross-section. It was more than tricky to hold depth.

'Clark, go!'

'Right.'

With all the drifting ice on the water, the screen for that radar should be heavily cluttered, Mancuso thought. He watched the indicator light for the hatch change from a dash, meaning closed, to a circle, meaning open.

The bridge trunk ended on a platform a few feet below the bridge itself. Clark wrenched open the hatch and climbed up. Next he hauled out his raft with the help of the seaman below on the ladder. Alone now in the submarine's tiny bridge – the control station atop the sail – he set the thing athwart the top of the sail and pulled the rope that inflated it. The high-pitched rasp of the rushing air seemed to scream into the night, and Clark winced to hear it. As soon as the rubberized fabric became taut, he called to the sailor to close the trunk hatch, then grabbed the bridge phone.

'All ready here. The hatch is closed. See you in a couple of hours.'

'Right. Good luck,' Mancuso said again.

Aloft, Clark climbed smoothly into the raft as the submarine sank beneath him, and started the electric motor. Below, the bottom hatch of the bridge tube was opened only long enough for the sailor to leap down, then he and the Captain levered it shut.

'Straight board shut, we are rigged for dive,' the Cob reported when the last indicator light changed back to a dash.

'That's it,' Mancuso noted. 'Mr Goodman, you have the conn, you have the conn, and you know what to do.'

'I have the conn,' the OOD replied as the Captain went forward to the sonar room. Lieutenant Goodman immediately dived the boat, heading her for the bottom.

It was like old times, Mancuso thought, with Jones as lead sonarman. The submarine came right, pointing her bow-mounted sonar array at the path that Clark was taking. Ramius arrived a minute later to observe.

'How come you didn't want to use the 'scope?' Mancuso asked.

'A hard thing to see one's home and know that one cannot –'

'There he goes.' Jones tapped his finger on the video display. 'Doing turns for eighteen knots. Pretty quiet for an outboard. Electric, eh?'

'Right.'

'I sure hope he's got good batteries, skipper.'

'Rotating-anode lithium. I asked.'

'Cute.' Jones grunted. He tapped a cigarette out of his pack and offered one to the Captain, who forgot for the moment that he'd quit, again. Jones lit it and took on a contemplative expression.

'You know, sir, now I remember why I retired . . .' His voice trailed off as Jonesy watched the sonar trail stretch off in the distance. Aft, the fire-control party updated the range, just to have something to do. Jones craned his neck and listened. *Dallas* was about as quiet as she ever got, and the tension filled the air far more thickly than cigarette smoke ever could.

Clark lay nearly flat in the boat. Made of rubberized nylon, its color scheme was green and gray stripes, not very different from the sea. They'd thought of some white patches because of the ice to be found in the area in winter, but then it was realized that the channel here was always tended by an icebreaker, and a rapidly moving white spot on a dark surface might not be a terribly good idea. Mainly

Clark was concerned about radar. The submarine's sail might not have been picked up through all the clutter, but if the Russian radar sets had a moving-target-indicator setting, the simple computer that monitored the returning signals might well lock in on something traveling at twenty miles per hour. The boat itself was only a foot out of the water, the motor a foot higher than that and coated with radar-absorbing material. Clark kept his head level with the motor and wondered again if the half-dozen metal fragments that decorated his anatomy were large enough to be seen. He knew that this was irrational – they didn't even set off an airport metal-detector – but lonely men in dangerous places tended to develop unusually active minds. It was better, really, to be stupid, he told himself. Intelligence only allowed you to realize how dangerous things like this were. After such missions were over, after the shakes went away, after the hot shower, you could bask in the glow of how brave and clever you were, but not now. Now it just seemed dangerous, not to say crazy, to be doing something like this.

The coastline was clearly visible, a clean series of dots that covered the visible horizon. It seemed ordinary enough, but it was enemy territory. That knowledge was far more chilling than the clean night air.

At least the seas were calm, he told himself. Actually a few feet of chop would have made for more favorable radar conditions, but the smooth, oily surface made for speed, and speed always made him feel better. He looked aft. The boat didn't make much of a wake, and he'd reduce it further by slowing when he got close to the harbor.

Patience, he told himself uselessly. He hated the idea of patience. Who likes to wait for anything? Clark asked himself. *If it has to happen, let it happen and be done with it.* That wasn't the safe way, rushing into things, but at least when you were up and moving, you were doing something. But when he taught people how to do this sort of thing, which was his normal occupation, he always told them to be patient. *You friggin' hypocrite!* he observed silently.

The harbor buoys told him the distance from the coast. He cut his speed to ten knots, then to five, and finally to three. The electric motor made a barely audible hum. Clark turned the handle and steered the boat to a ramshackle pier. It had to have been an old one; its piles had been splintered and abraded by the harbor ice of many winters. Ever so slowly, he pulled out a low-light 'scope and examined the area. There was no movement he could see. He could hear things now, mainly traffic sounds that carried across the water to him, along with some music. It was Friday night, after all, and even in the Soviet Union there were parties going on at restaurants. People were dancing. In fact his plan depended on the presence of nightlife here – Estonia is livelier than most of the country – but the pier was derelict, as his briefers said it would be. He moved in, tying the boat off to a piling with considerable care – if it drifted away, he'd have real problems. Next to the pile was a ladder. Clark slipped out of his coverall and climbed up, pistol in hand. For the first time he noted the harbor smell. It was little different from its American equivalent, heavy with bilge oil and decorated with rotting wood from the piers. To the north, a dozen or so fishing boats were tied to another pier. To the south was yet another, that one piled up with lumber. So the harbor was being rebuilt. That explained the condition of this one, Clark thought. He checked his watch – it was a battered Russian 'Pilot' – and looked around for a place to wait. Forty minutes until he had to move. He'd allowed for choppier seas for his trip in, and all the calm had really done for him was to give him the additional time to meditate on how much a lunatic he was for taking on another of these extraction jobs.

Boris Filipovich Morozov walked outside the barracks where he still lived, staring upward. The lights at Bright Star made the sky into a feathery dome of descending flakes. He loved moments like this.

'Who's there?' a voice asked. It had authority in it.

'Morozov,' the young engineer answered as the figure came into the light. He saw the wide-brimmed hat of a senior Army officer.

'Good evening, Comrade Engineer. You're on the mirror-control team, aren't you?' Bondarenko asked.

'Have we met?'

'No.' The Colonel shook his head. 'Do you know who I am?'

'Yes, Comrade Colonel.'

Bondarenko gestured at the sky. 'Beautiful, isn't it? I suppose that's one consolation for being at the far end of nothing.'

'No, Comrade Colonel, we are at the leading edge of something very important,' Morozov pointed out.

'That is good for me to hear! Do all of your team feel that way?'

'Yes, Comrade Colonel. I asked to come here.'

'Oh? And how did you know of this place?' the Colonel wondered.

'I was here last fall with the Komsomol. We assisted the civil engineers in the blasting, and siting the mirror-pillars. I was a graduate student in lasers, and I guessed what Bright Star was. I did not tell anyone, of course,' Morozov added. 'But I knew this was the place for me.'

Bondarenko regarded the youngster with visible approval. 'How goes the work?'

'I had hoped to join the laser team, but my section chief press-ganged me into joining his group.' Morozov laughed.

'You are unhappy with this?'

'No – no, please excuse me. You misunderstand. I didn't know how important the mirror group was. I've learned. Now we're trying to adapt the mirror systems to more precise computer control – I may soon be an assistant section leader,' Morozov said proudly. 'I am also familiar with computer systems, you see.'

'Who's your section chief – Govorov, isn't it?'

'Correct. A brilliant field engineer, if I may say so. May I ask a question?'

564

'Certainly.'

'It is said that you – you're the new Army colonel they've been talking about, correct? They say that you may be the new deputy project officer.'

'There may be some substance to those rumors,' Bondarenko allowed.

'Then may I make a suggestion, Comrade?' Morozov asked.

'Certainly.'

'There are many single men here . . .'

'And not enough single women?'

'There *is* a need for laboratory assistants.'

'Your observation is noted, Comrade Engineer,' Bondarenko replied with a chuckle. 'We also plan a new apartment block to relieve the crowding. How are the barracks?'

'The atmosphere is comradely. The astronomy and chess clubs are very active.'

'Ah. It has been time since I played chess seriously. How tough is the competition?' the Colonel asked.

The younger man laughed. 'Murderous – even savage.'

Five thousand meters away, the Archer blessed his God's name. Snow was falling, and the flakes gave the air the magical quality so beloved by poets . . . and soldiers. You could hear – you could *feel* the hushed silence as the snow absorbed all sound. All round them, as far up and down as they could see, was the curtain of white that cut visibility to under two hundred meters. He assembled his subunit commanders and began organizing the assault. They moved out in a few minutes. They were in tactical formation. The Archer was with the lead section of the first company, while his second-in-command stayed with the other.

The footing was surprisingly good. The Russians had dumped the spoil from their blasting all over the area, and even though coated with snow, the rock chips were not slippery. This was well, since their path took them perilously close to a sheer wall at least a hundred meters high. Navigating was difficult. The Archer was going from memory, but he'd spent hours examining the objective and knew every curve of the mountain – or so he'd thought. The doubts came now, as they always did, and it took all his concentration to keep his mind on the mission. He had mapped out a dozen checkpoints in his memory before setting out. A boulder here, a dip there, this the place where the path turned to the left, and that one where it went to the right. At first progress seemed maddeningly slow, but the closer they came to the objective, the more rapid became the pace. They were guided at all times by the glow of the lights. How confident the Russians were, to have lights here, he thought. There was even a moving vehicle, a bus, by the sound of it, with its headlights lit. The small, moving points of light shone through the enveloping white cloud. Within the larger bubble of light, those on guard duty would be at a disadvantage now. Ordinarily the outwardly aimed spotlights would serve to dazzle and blind an intruder, but now the reverse was true. Little of their glow penetrated the snow, and much was reflected back, ruining the night vision of the armed troops. Finally the lead party reached the last checkpoint. The Archer deployed his men and waited for the rest to catch up. It took half an hour. His men were grouped in knots of three or four, and the *mudjaheddin* took the time to drink some water and commit their souls to Allah, preparing both for the battle and for its possible aftermath. Theirs was the warrior's creed. Their enemy was also the enemy of their God. Whatever they did to the people who had offended Allah would be forgiven them, and every one of the Archer's men reminded himself of friends and family who had died at Russian hands.

'This is amazing,' the Major whispered as he arrived.

'Allah is with us, my friend,' the Archer replied.

'He must be.' They were now only five hundred meters from the site, and still unseen. *We might actually survive . . .*

'How much closer can we –'

'One hundred meters. The low-light equipment they have will penetrate snow to about four hundred. The nearest tower is six hundred meters that way.' He pointed unnecessarily. The Archer knew exactly where it was, and the next one, two hundred meters farther down.

The Major checked his watch and thought for a moment.

'The guard will change in another hour if they follow the same pattern here as in Kabul. Those on duty will be tired and cold, and the relief troops aren't yet awake. This is the time.'

'Good luck,' the Archer said simply. Both men embraced.

'"Why should we refuse to fight for the cause of Allah, when we and our children have been driven from our dwellings?"'

'"When they met Goliath and his warriors they cried: 'Lord fill our hearts with steadfastness. Make us firm of foot and help us against the unbelievers.'"'

The quote was from the Koran, and neither man thought it strange that the passage actually referred to the Israelites' battle against the Philistines. David and Saul were known to the Muslims, too, as was their cause. The Major smiled one last time before running off to join his men.

The Archer turned and waved to his missile team. Two of them shouldered their Stingers and followed the leader as he continued his way across the mountain. One more knoll and they were looking down at the guard towers. He was surprised that he could actually see three of them from here, and a third missile was brought out. The Archer gave his instructions and left them to rejoin the main body. On the knoll, the target-acquisition units sang their deadly song to each missileer. The guard towers were heated – and the Stinger searches only for heat.

Next the Archer ordered his mortar team in close – closer than he would have preferred, but the miserable visibility was not entirely on the side of the *mudjaheddin*. He watched the Major's company slide down to the left, disappearing into the snow. They would assault the laser test facility itself, while he and his eighty men went for the place where most of the people lived. Now it was their turn. The Archer led them forward as far as he dared, just to the edge of where the floodlights penetrated the snow. He was rewarded with the sight of a sentry, bundled up for the cold, his breath left behind in a series of small white clouds that drifted in the wind. Ten more minutes. The Archer pulled out his radio. They had only four of them, and hadn't dared to use them until now for fear of being detected by the Russians.

We should never have gotten rid of the dogs, Bondarenko told himself. *First thing I do when I get settled here, get the dogs back*. He was walking around the camp, enjoying the cold and the snow and using the quiet atmosphere to order his thoughts. There were things that needed changing here. They needed a real soldier. General Pokryshkin was too confident in the security scheme, and the KGB troops were too lazy. For example, they did not have night patrols out. Too dangerous on this terrain, their commander said, our day patrols will detect anyone who tries to get close, the guard towers have low-light scanners, and the rest of the site is floodlit. But low-light devices had their effectiveness cut eighty percent by this sort of weather. What if there was a group of Afghans out there right now? he wondered. *First thing*, Bondarenko told himself, *I'll call Colonel Nikolayev at Spetsnaz headquarters, and I'll lead a practice assault on this place to show those KGB idiots how vulnerable they are*. He looked up the hill. There was a KGB sentry, flapping his arms to keep warm, rifle slung over his shoulder – it would take him four seconds to get it unslung, aimed, and taken off safety. *Four seconds, for the last three of which he'd be dead if there were anyone competent out there right now* . . . Well, he told himself, the assistant commander of any post is supposed to be a ruthless son of a bitch, and if those *chekisti* want to play at soldiers they'll damned

568

well have to act like soldiers. The Colonel turned to walk back to the apartment block.

Gerasimov's car pulled up to Lefortovo Prison's administrative entrance. His driver stayed with the car while the bodyguard followed him in. The KGB Chairman showed his ID card to the guard and walked by without breaking stride. The KGB was careful with security, but all its members knew the face of the Chairman and knew even better the power that it represented. Gerasimov turned left and headed for the administration offices. The prison superintendent wasn't there, of course, but one of his deputies was. Gerasimov found him filling out some forms.'

'Good evening.' The man's eyes were saved from bugging out by the glasses he wore.

'Comrade Chairman! I was not –'

'You weren't supposed to be.'

'How may I –'

'The prisoner Filitov. I need him immediately,' Gerasimov said gruffly. 'Immediately,' he repeated for effect.

'At once!' The second deputy prison superintendent leaped to his feet and ran to another room. He was back in under a minute. 'It will take five minutes.'

'He must be properly dressed,' Gerasimov said.

'His uniform?' the man asked.

'Not that, you idiot!' the Chairman snarled. 'Civilian clothes. He must be presentable. You have all his personal effects here, don't you?'

'Yes, Comrade Chairman, but –'

'I do not have all night,' he said quietly. There was nothing more dangerous than a quiet KGB Chairman. The second deputy superintendent fairly flew from the room. Gerasimov turned to his bodyguard, who smiled in amusement. Nobody liked jailers. 'How long do you think?'

'Less than ten minutes. Comrade Chairman, even though they have to find his clothes. After all, that pipsqueak knows what a wonderful place this is to live in. I know him.'

'Oh?'

'He was originally a "One" man, but he performed poorly on his first assignment and has been a jailer ever since.' The bodyguard checked his watch.

It took eight minutes. Filitov appeared with his suit most of the way on, though his shirt was not buttoned, and his tie merely draped around his neck. The second deputy superintendent was holding a threadbare topcoat. Filitov never had been one to buy a lot of civilian clothes. He was a Colonel of the Red Army, and was never comfortable out of his uniform. The old man's eyes were confused at first, then he saw Gerasimov.

'What is this?' he asked.

'You are coming with me, Filitov. Button your shirt. At least try to look like a man!'

Misha nearly said something, but bit it off. The look he gave the Chairman was enough to make the bodyguard move his hand a centimeter. He buttoned his shirt and tied his tie. It ended up crooked in his collar because he didn't have a mirror.

'Now, Comrade Chairman, if you will sign this –'

'You give me custody of a criminal like this?'

'What –'

'*Handcuffs, man!*' Gerasimov boomed.

Unsurprisingly, the second deputy superintendent had a pair in his desk. He got them, put them on Filitov, and nearly pocketed the key before he saw Gerasimov's outstretched hand.

'Very good. I'll have him back to you tomorrow night.'

'But I need you to sign –' The second deputy superintendent found that he was talking to a receding back.

'Well, with all the people under me,' Gerasimov observed to his bodyguard, 'there have to be a few . . .'

'Indeed, Comrade Chairman.' The bodyguard was an immensely fit man of forty-two, a former field officer who was an expert in all forms of armed and unarmed combat. His firm grip on the prisoner told Misha all of these things.

'Filitov,' the Chairman observed over his shoulder, 'we are taking a brief trip, a flight that is. You will not be harmed. If you behave yourself, we might even allow you a decent meal or two. If you do not behave, Vasiliy here will make you wish you did. Is that clear?'

'Clear, Comrade *Chekist*.'

The guard snapped to attention, then pushed open the door. The outside guards saluted and were rewarded with nods. The driver held open the back door. Gerasimov stopped and turned.

'Put him in back with me, Vasiliy. You should be able to cover things from the front seat.'

'As you wish, Comrade.'

'Sheremetyevo,' Gerasimov told the driver. 'The cargo terminal on the south side.'

There was the airport, Ryan thought. He stifled a belch that tasted of wine and sardines. The motorcade entered the airport ground, then curved to the right, bypassing the regular entrance to the terminal and heading out onto the aircraft parking area. Security, he noted, was *tight*. You could always depend on the Russians for that. Everywhere he looked were rifle-toting soldiers in KGB uniforms. The car drove right past the main terminal, then past a recent addition. It was unused, but looked like the alien spaceship in Spielberg's *Close Encounters*. He'd meant to ask somebody why it had been built, but wasn't yet in use. Maybe next time, Ryan thought.

The formal goodbyes had been made at the Foreign Ministry. A few junior officials stood at the bottom of the stairs to shake hands, and nobody was in a hurry to leave the heated comfort of the limousines. Progress was correspondingly slow. His car lurched forward and stopped, and the man to Ryan's right opened the door as the driver popped the trunk open. He didn't want to go outside either. It had taken most of the drive to get the car warm.

Jack got his bag and his briefcase and headed for the stairs.

'I hope you enjoyed your visit,' the Soviet official said.

'I would like to come back and see the city sometime,' Jack replied as he shook the man's hand.

'We would be delighted.'

Sure you would, Jack thought as he went up the stairs. Once in the aircraft, he looked forward. A Russian officer was in the cockpit jump seat to assist with traffic control. His eyes were on the curtained-off communications console. Ryan nodded at the pilot through the door and got a wink.

'The political dimension scares the hell out of me,' Vatutin said. At 2 Dzerzhinskiy Square, he and Golovko were comparing their written notes.

'This isn't the old days. They can't shoot us for following our training and procedures.'

'Really? What if Filitov was being run with the knowledge of the Chairman?'

'Ridiculous,' Golovko observed.

'Oh? What if his early work on the dissidents put him in contact with the West? We know that he personally intervened in some cases – mainly from the Baltic region, but some others, too.'

'You're really thinking like a "Two" man now!'

'Think for a minute. We arrest Filitov and immediately thereafter the Chairman meets personally with a CIA man. Has that ever happened before?'

'I've heard stories about Philby, but – no, that was only after he came over.'

'It's one hell of a coincidence,' Vatutin said as he rubbed his eyes. 'They do not train us to believe in coincidences, and –'

'*Tvoyu mat'!*' Golovko said. Vatutin looked up in annoyance to see the other man roll his eyes. 'The last time the Americans were over – how could I forget this! Ryan spoke with Filitov – they collided as though by accident, and –'

Vatutin lifted his phone and dialed. 'Give me the night superintendent . . . This is Colonel Vatutin. Wake up the prisoner Filitov. I want to see him within the hour . . . What was that? Who? Very well. Thank you.' The Colonel of the Second Chief Directorate stood. 'Chairman Gerasimov just took Filitov out of Lefortovo fifteen minutes ago. He said that they were taking a special trip.'

'Where's your car?'

'I can order –'

'No,' Golovko said. 'Your personal car.'

26

Black Operations

There was no hurry, yet. While the cabin crew got everybody settled in, Colonel von Eich ran down the preflight checklist. The VC-137 was taking electrical power from a generator truck that would also allow them to start their engines more easily than internal systems allowed. He checked his watch and hoped everything would go as planned.

Aft, Ryan walked past his normal place, just forward of Ernie Allen's midships cabin, and took a seat in the back row of the after part of the aircraft. It looked much like part of a real airliner, though the seating was five-across, and this space handled the overflow from the 'distinguished visitor' areas forward. Jack picked one on the left side, where the seats were in pairs, while ten or so others entered the cabin and kept as far forward as possible for the smoother ride, as advised by another crew member. The aircraft's crew chief would be across the aisle to his right instead of in the crew quarters forward. Ryan wished for another man to help, but they couldn't be too obvious. They had a Soviet officer aboard. That was part of the regular routine, and diverging from it would attract attention. The whole point of this was that everyone would be comfortably secure in the knowledge that everything was exactly as it should be.

Forward, the pilot got to the end of the checklist page.
'Everybody aboard?'
'Yes, sir. Ready to close the doors.'
'Keep an eye on the indicator light for the crew door. It's been acting funny,' von Eich told the flight engineer.
'A problem?' the Soviet pilot asked from the jump seat.

Sudden depressurization is something every flyer takes seriously.

'Every time we check the door it looks fine. Probably a bad relay in the panel, but we haven't found the sucker yet. I've checked the goddamned door-seal myself,' he assured the Russian. 'It has to be an electrical fault.'

'Ready to start,' the flight engineer told him next.

'Okay.' The pilot looked to make sure the stairs were away while the flight crew donned their headsets. 'All clear left.'

'All clear right,' the copilot said.

'Turning one.' Buttons were pushed, switches were goggled, and the left-outboard engine began to rotate its turbine blades. The needles on several indicator dials started moving and were soon in normal idling range. The generator truck withdrew now that the plane could supply its own electric power.

'Turning four,' the pilot said next. He toggled his microphone to the cabin setting. 'Ladies and gentlemen, this is Colonel von Eich. We're getting the engines started, and we should be moving in about five minutes. Please buckle your seat belts. Those of you who smoke, try to hang in there another few minutes.'

At his seat in the back row, Ryan would have killed for a smoke. The crew chief glanced over to him and smiled. He certainly seemed tough enough to handle it, Jack thought. The chief master sergeant looked to be pushing fifty, but he also looked like a man who could teach manners to an NFL linebacker. He was wearing leather work gloves with the adjustment straps pulled in tight.

'All ready?' Jack asked. There was no danger of being heard. The engine noise was hideous back here.

'Whenever you say, sir.'

'You'll know when.'

'Hmph,' Gerasimov noted. 'Not here yet.' The cargo terminal was closed, and dark except for the security floodlights.

'Should I make a call?' the driver asked.

'No hurry. What –' A uniformed guard waved for them to stop. They'd already come through one checkpoint. 'Oh, that's right. The Americans are getting ready to leave. That must be screwing things up.'

The guard came to the driver's window and asked for passes. The driver just waved to the back.

'Good evening, Corporal,' Gerasimov said. He held up his identification card. The youngster snapped to attention. 'A plane will be here in a few minutes for me. The Americans must be holding things up. Is the security force out?'

'Yes, Comrade Chairman! A full company.'

'While we're here, why don't we do a fast inspection? Who is your commander?'

'Major Zarudin, Com –'

'What the hell is –' A lieutenant came over. He got as far as the corporal before he saw who was in the car.

'Lieutenant, where is Major Zarudin?'

'In the control tower, Comrade Chairman. That is the best place to –'

'I'm sure. Get him on your radio and tell him that I am going to inspect the guard perimeter, then I will come to see him and tell him what I think. Drive on,' he told the driver. 'Go right.'

'Sheremetyevo Tower, this is niner-seven-one requesting permission to taxi to runway two-five-right,' von Eich said into his microphone.

'Nine-seven-one, permission granted. Turn left onto main taxiway one. Wind is two-eight-one at forty kilometers.'

'Roger, out,' the pilot said. 'Okay, let's get this bird moving.' The copilot advanced the throttles and the aircraft started to roll. On the ground in front of them, a man with two lighted wands gave them unneeded directions to the taxiway – but the Russians always assumed that everyone needed to be told what to do. Von Eich left the parking pad and headed south on taxiway nine, then turned left. The small wheel that controlled the steerable nose-gear was stiff, as always, and the aircraft came around slowly, pushed by the outboard engine. He always took things easy here. The taxiways were so rough that there was always the worry of damaging something. He didn't want that to happen tonight. It was the best part of a mile to the end of the number-one main taxiway, and the bumps and rolls were enough to make one motion-sick. He finally turned right onto taxiway five.

'The men seem alert,' Vasiliy observed as they crossed runway twenty-five-left. The driver had his lights off and kept to the edge. There was an airplane coming, and both driver and bodyguard were keeping their eyes on that hazard. They didn't see Gerasimov take the key from his pocket and unlock the handcuffs of an amazed prisoner Filitov. Next the Chairman pulled an automatic pistol from inside his coat.

'Shit – there's a car there,' Colonel von Eich said. 'What the hell is a car doing here?'

'We'll clear it easy,' the copilot said. 'He's way over on the edge.'

'Great.' The pilot turned right again to the end of the runway. 'Fucking Sunday drivers.'

'You're not going to like this either, Colonel,' the flight engineer said. 'I got a light on the rear door again.'

'God damn it!' von Eich swore over the intercom. He flipped his mike to the cabin setting again, but had to adjust his voice before speaking. 'Crew chief, check the rear door.'

'Here we go,' the sergeant said. Ryan flipped off his seat belt and moved a few feet as he watched the sergeant work the door handle.

'We got a short in here someplace,' the flight engineer said on the flight deck, forward. 'Just lost the aft cabin lights. The breaker just popped and I can't get it to reset.'

'Maybe it's a bad breaker?' Colonel von Eich asked.

'I can try a spare,' the engineer said.

'Go ahead. I'll tell the folks in back why the lights just went out.' It was a lie, but a good enough one, and with everyone buckled in, it wasn't all that easy to turn around and see the back of the cabin.

'Where's the Chairman?' Vatutin asked the Lieutenant.

'He's conducting an inspection – who are you?'

'Colonel Vatutin – this is Colonel Golovko. Where's the fucking Chairman, you young idiot!'

The Lieutenant sputtered for a few seconds, then pointed.

'Vasiliy,' the Chairman said. It was too bad really. His bodyguard turned to see the muzzle of a pistol. 'Your gun, please.'

'But –'

'No time for talking.' He took the gun and pocketed it. Next he handed over the cuffs. 'Both of you, and put your hands through the steering wheel.'

The driver was aghast, but both men did as they were told. Vasiliy snapped one ring on his left wrist and reached through the steering wheel to attach the other to the driver. While they did so, Gerasimov detached the receiver from his car's radiophone and pocketed that.

'The keys?' Gerasimov asked. The driver handed them over with his free left hand. The nearest uniformed guard was a hundred meters away. The airplane was a mere twenty. The Chairman of the Committee for State Security opened the car door himself. He hadn't done that in months. 'Colonel Filitov, will you come with me, please?'

Misha was as surprised as everyone else, but did as he was told. In full view of everyone at the airport – at least, those few who were bothering to watch the routine departure – Gerasimov and Filitov walked towards the VC-137's red, white, and blue tail. As though on command, the after door opened.

'Let's hustle, people.' Ryan tossed out a rope ladder.

Filitov's legs betrayed him. The wind and blast from the jet engines made the ladder flutter like a flag in the breeze, and he couldn't get both feet on it despite help from Gerasimov.

'My God, look!' Golovko pointed. 'Move!'

Vatutin didn't say anything. He floored his car and flipped on the high-beam lights.

'Trouble,' the crew chief said when he saw the car. There was a man with a rifle running this way, too. '*Come on, pop!*' he urged the Cardinal of the Kremlin.

'Shit!' Ryan pushed the sergeant aside and jumped down. It was too far, and he landed badly, twisting his right ankle and ripping his pants at his left knee. Jack ignored the pain and leaped to his feet. He took one of Filitov's shoulders while Gerasimov took the other, and together they got him up the ladder far enough that the sergeant at the door was able to haul him aboard. Gerasimov went next, with Ryan's help. Then it was Jack's turn – but he had the same problem Filitov had. His left knee was already stiff, and when he tried to climb up on his sprained ankle, his right leg simply refused to work. He swore loudly enough to be heard over the sound of the engines and tried to do it hand over hand, but he lost his grip and fell to the pavement.

'*Stoi, stoi!*' somebody with a gun shouted from ten feet away. Jack looked up at the aircraft door.

'*Go!*' he screamed. 'Close the fucking door and go!'

The crew chief did exactly that without a moment's hesitation. He reached around to pull the door shut, and Jack watched it seal itself in a matter of seconds. Inside, the sergeant lifted the interphone and told the pilot that the door was properly sealed.

'Tower, this is niner-seven-one, rolling now. Out.' The pilot advanced the throttles to takeoff power.

The force of the engine blast hurled all four men – the rifleman had just arrived at the scene, too – right off the end of the icy runway. Jack watched from flat on his belly as the blinking red light atop the aircraft's tall rudder diminished in the distance, then rose. His last view of it was the glow of the infrared jammers that protected the VC-137 against surface-to-air missiles. He almost started laughing, when he was rolled over and saw a pistol against his face.

'Hello, Sergey,' Ryan said to Colonel Golovko.

'Ready,' the radio told the Archer. He raised a flare pistol and fired a single star-shell round that burst directly over one of the shops.

Everything happened at once. To his left, three Stinger missiles were launched after a long and boring wait. Each streaked toward a guard tower – or more precisely, to the electric heaters inside them. The paired sentries in each had time enough only to see and be surprised by the signal round over the central region of the installation, and only one of the six saw an inbound streak of yellow, too fast to permit a reaction. All three of the missiles hit – they could hardly miss a stationary target – and in each case the six-pound warhead functioned as designed. Less than five seconds after the first round had been fired, the towers were eliminated, and with them also the machine guns that protected the laser facility.

The sentry to the Archer's front died next. He hadn't a chance. Forty rifles fired on him at once, with half of the bursts connecting. Next the mortars fired ranging rounds, and the Archer used his radio to adjust the fire onto what he thought was the guards' barracks.

The sound of automatic-weapons fire cannot be mistaken for anything else. Colonel Bondarenko had just decided that he'd spent enough time communing with a cold though beautiful nature and was walking back to his quarters when the sound stopped him in his tracks. His first thought was that one of the KGB guards had accidentally discharged his weapon, but that impression lasted less than a second. He heard a *crack!* overhead and looked up to see the star shell, then heard the explosions from the laser site, and as though a switch had been thrown, he changed from a startled man to a professional soldier under attack. The KGB barracks were two hundred meters to his right, and he ran there as fast as he could.

Mortar rounds were falling, he saw. They were falling on the big new machine shop just beyond the barracks. Men were stumbling out the door of the latter when he arrived, and he had to stop and hold up his arms to avoid being shot.

'I am Colonel Bondarenko! Where is your officer?'

'Here!' A lieutenant came out. 'What –' Someone had just learned of his mistake. The next mortar round hit the back of the barracks.

'Follow me!' Bondarenko screamed, leading them away from the most obvious target in sight. All around them was the deadly chatter of rifles – Soviet rifles; the colonel noted at once that he couldn't use sound to identify who was who. *Wonderful!* 'Form up!'

'What is –'

'We're under attack, Lieutenant! How many men do you have?'

He turned and counted. Bondarenko did it faster still. There were forty-one, all with rifles, but there were no heavy weapons, and no radios. The machine guns he could do without, but radios were vital.

The dogs, he told himself stupidly, *they should have kept the dogs . . .*

The tactical situation was appallingly bad, and he knew that it would only get worse. A series of explosions sundered the night.

'The lasers, we must –' the Lieutenant said, but the Colonel grabbed his shoulder.

'We can rebuild the machines,' Bondarenko said urgently, 'but we cannot rebuild the scientists. We're going to get to the apartment building and hold that until relieved. Send a good sergeant to the bachelor quarters and get them to the apartments.'

'No, Comrade Colonel! My orders are to protect the lasers, and I must –'

581

'I am ordering you to get your men –'

'*No!*' the Lieutenant screamed back at him.

Bondarenko knocked him down, took his rifle, flipped off the safety, and fired two rounds into his chest. He turned. 'Who's the best sergeant?'

'I am, Colonel,' a young man said shakily.

'I am Colonel Bondarenko, and I am in command!' the officer announced as forcefully as a command from God. 'You take four men, get to the bachelor barracks, and bring everyone up the hill to the apartment building. Fast as you can!' The sergeant pointed to four others and ran off. 'The rest of you, follow me!' He led them into the falling snow. There wasn't time for him or them to wonder what awaited. Before they'd gone ten meters, every light in the camp went out.

At the gate of the laser site a GAZ jeep sat, with a heavy machine gun aboard. General Pokryshkin ran from the control building when he heard the explosions, and was stunned to see that only blazing stumps remained of his three guard towers. The commander of the KGB detachment raced down to him on his vehicle.

'We're under attack,' the officer said unnecessarily.

'Get your men together – right here.' Pokryshkin looked up to see running men. They were dressed in Soviet uniforms, but somehow he knew that they were not Russians. The General climbed into the back of the jeep and brought the machine gun around over the head of the astonished KGB officer. The first time he pressed the trigger nothing happened, and he had to ratchet a round into the chamber. The second time, Pokryshkin had the satisfaction of watching three men fall. The guard force commander needed no further encouragement. He barked rapid orders into his radio. The battle under way degenerated at once into confusion, as it had to – both sides were wearing identical uniforms and using identical weapons. But there were more Afghans than Russians.

*

582

Morozov and several of his unmarried friends had stepped outside when they heard the noise. Most of them had military experience, though he did not. It didn't matter – nobody had the first idea what they should do. Five men came running out of the darkness. They were wearing uniforms and carrying rifles.

'Come! All of you come, follow us!' More weapons started firing close by, and two of the KGB troops went down, one dead, one wounded. He fired back, emptying his rifle in one long burst. There was a scream in the darkness, followed by shouts. Morozov ran inside and called for people to make for the door. The engineers needed little prompting.

'Up the hill,' the sergeant said. 'To the apartment block. Fast as you can!' The four KGB troops waved them along, looking for targets, but seeing only flashes. Bullets were flying everywhere now. Another of the troops went down screaming out his last breath, but the sergeant got the one who killed him. When the last engineer left the room, he and a private grabbed the spare rifles and helped their comrade back up the hill.

It was too big a mission for eighty men, the Archer realized too late. Too much ground to cover, too many buildings, but there were many unbelievers running around, and that was why he'd brought his men here. He watched one of them explode a bus with an RPG-7 antitank round. It burst into flames and slid off the road, rolling down the side of the mountain while those inside screamed. Teams of men with explosives went into the buildings. They found machine tools bathed in oil and set their charges quickly, running out before the explosions could begin the fires. The Archer had realized a minute too late which building was the guard barracks, and now that was ablaze as he led his section in to mop up the men who'd been kept there. He was too late, but didn't know it yet. A stray mortar round had cut the power line that handled all of the site's lighting, and all of his men were robbed of their night vision by the flashes of their own weapons.

'Well done, Sergeant!' Bondarenko told the boy. He'd already ordered the engineers upstairs. 'We'll set our perimeter around the building. They may force us back. If so, we'll make our stand on the first floor. The walls are concrete. RPGs can hurt us, but the roof and walls will stop bullets. Pick one man to go inside and find men with military experience. Give them those two rifles. Whenever a man goes down, retrieve his weapon and get it to someone who knows how to use it. I'm going inside for a moment to see if I can get a telephone to work –'

'There's a radiotelephone in the first-floor office,' the sergeant said. 'All the buildings have them.'

'Good! Hold the perimeter, Sergeant. I'll be back to you in two minutes.' Bondarenko ran inside. The radio-telephone was hanging on a wall hook, and he was relieved to see it was a military type, powered by its own battery. The Colonel shouldered it and ran back outside.

The attackers – who were they? he wondered – had planned their attack poorly. First they had failed to identify the KGB barracks before launching their assault; second, they hadn't hit the residential area as quickly as they should have. They were moving in now, but they found a line of Border Guards lying in the snow. They were only KGB troops, Bondarenko knew, but they did have basic training, and most of all they knew that there was no place to run. That young sergeant was a good one, he saw. He moved from point to point along the perimeter, not using his weapon but encouraging the men and telling them what to do. The Colonel activated the radio.

'This is Colonel G. I. Bondarenko at Project Bright Star. We are under attack. I repeat, Bright Star is under attack. Any unit on this net respond at once, over.'

'Gennady, this is Pokryshkin at the laser site. We're in the control building. What is your situation?'

'I'm at the apartments. I have all the civilians we could find inside. I have forty men, and we're going to try to hold this place. What about help?'

'I'm trying. Gennady, we cannot get you any help from here. Can you hold?'

'Ask me in twenty minutes.'

'Protect my people, Colonel. Protect my people!' Pokryshkin shouted into the microphone.

'To the death, Comrade General. Out.' Bondarenko kept the radio on his back and hefted his rifle. 'Sergeant!'

'Here, Colonel!' The young man appeared. 'They're probing now, not really attacking yet –'

'Looking for weaknesses.' Bondarenko got back down to his knees. The air seemed alive with gunfire, but it was not yet concentrated. Above and behind the two, windows were shattering. Bullets pounded into the pre-cast concrete sections that formed the building wall, spraying everyone outside with chips. 'Position yourself at the corner opposite this one. You'll command the north and east walls. I'll handle these two. Tell your men to fire only when they have targets –'

'Already done, Comrade.'

'Good!' Bondarenko punched the young man on the shoulder. 'Don't fall back until you have to, but tell me if you do. The people in this building are priceless assets. They must survive. Go!' The Colonel watched the sergeant run off. Perhaps the KGB did train some of its people. He ran to his corner of the building.

He now had twenty – no, he counted eighteen men. Their camouflage clothing made them hard to spot. He ran from man to man, his back bowed by the weight of the radio, spacing them out, telling them to husband their rounds. He was just finishing the line on the west side when there came a chorus of human voices from the darkness.

'Here they come!' a private screamed.

'*Hold your fire!*' the Colonel bellowed.

The running figures appeared as though by magic. One

moment the scene was empty of anything but falling snow – the next, there was a line of men firing Kalashnikov rifles from the hip. He let them get to within fifty meters.

'*Fire!*' He saw ten of them go down in an instant. The rest wavered and stopped, then fell back, leaving two more bodies behind. There was more firing from the opposite side of the building. Bondarenko wondered if the sergeant had held, but that was not in his hands. Some nearby screams told him that his men had taken casualties, too. On checking the line he found that one had made no noise at all. He was down to fifteen men.

The climb-out was routine enough, Colonel von Eich thought. A few feet behind him, the Russian in the jump seat was giving the electrical panel an occasional look.

'How's the electricity doing?' the pilot asked in some irritation.

'No problem with engine and hydraulic power. Seems to be in the lighting system,' the engineer replied, quietly turning off the tail and wingtip anticollision lights.

'Well . . .' The cockpit instrument lights were all on, of course, and there was no additional illumination for the flight crew. 'We'll fix it when we get to Shannon.'

'Colonel.' It was the voice of the crew chief in the pilot's headset.

'Go ahead,' the engineer said, making sure that the Russian's headset was not on that channel.

'Go ahead Sarge.'

'We have our two . . . our two new passengers, sir, but Mr Ryan – he got left behind, Colonel.'

'Repeat that?' von Eich said.

'He said to move out, sir. Two guys with guns, sir, they – he said to move out, sir,' the crew chief said again.

Von Eich let out a breath. 'Okay. How are things back there?'

'I got them in the back row, sir. I don't think anybody noticed, even, what with the engine noise and all.'

'Keep it that way.'

'Yes, sir. I have Freddie keeping the rest of the passengers forward. The aft can is broke, sir.'

'Pity,' the pilot observed. 'Tell 'em to go forward if they gotta go.'

'Right, Colonel.'

'Seventy-five minutes,' the navigator advised.

Christ, Ryan, the pilot thought. *I hope you like it there . . .*

'I should kill you here and now!' Golovko said.

They were in the Chairman's car. Ryan found himself facing four very irate KGB officers. The maddest seemed to be the guy in the right-front seat. Gerasimov's bodyguard, Jack thought, the one who worked close in. He looked like the physical type, and Ryan was glad that there was a seatback separating them. He had a more immediate problem. He looked at Golovko and thought it might be a good idea to calm him down.

'Sergey, that would set off an international incident like you would not believe,' Jack said calmly. The next conversations he heard were in Russian. He couldn't understand what they were saying, but the emotional content was clear enough. They didn't know what to do. That suited Ryan just fine.

Clark was walking along a street three blocks from the waterfront when he saw them. It was eleven forty-five. They were right on time, thank God. This part of the city had restaurants and, though he scarcely believed it, some discos. They were walking out of one when he spotted them. Two women, dressed as he'd been told to expect, with a male companion. The bodyguard. Only one, also as per orders. It was an agreeable surprise that so far everything had gone according to plan. Clark counted another dozen or so other people on the sidewalk, some in loud groups, some in quiet couples, many of them weaving from too much drink. But it was a Friday night, and that's what people all over the world did on Friday night. He maintained visual contact with the three people who concerned him, and closed in.

The bodyguard was a pro. He stayed on their right, keeping his gun hand free. He was ahead of them, but that didn't keep his head from scanning in all directions. Clark adjusted the scarf on his neck, then reached in his pocket. The pistol was there as he increased his pace to catch up. It wasn't hard. The two women seemed to be in no hurry as they approached the corner. The older one seemed to be looking around at the city. The buildings looked old, but weren't. The Second World War had swept through Talinn in two explosive waves, leaving behind nothing but scorched stones. But whoever made such decisions had opted to rebuild the city much as it had been, and the town had a feel very different from the Russian cities Clark had visited before. It made him think of Germany somehow, though he couldn't imagine why. That was his last frivolous thought of the night. He was now thirty feet behind them, just another man walking home on a cold February night, his face lowered to avoid the wind and a fur hat pulled down over his head. He could hear their voices now, and they were speaking Russian. Time.

'*Russkiy*,' Clark said with a Moscow accent. 'You mean not everyone in this city is an arrogant Balt?'

'This is an old and lovely city, Comrade,' the older woman answered. 'Show some respect.'

Here we go . . . Clark told himself. He walked forward with the curving steps of a man in his cups.

'Your pardon, lovely lady. Have a good evening,' he said as he passed. He moved around the women and bumped into the bodyguard. 'Excuse me, Comrade –' The man found that there was a pistol aimed at his face. 'Turn left and go into the alley. Hands out where I can see them, Comrade.'

The shock on the poor bastard's face was amusing as hell, Clark thought, reminding himself that this was a skilled man with a gun in *his* pocket. He grabbed the back of the man's collar and kept him out at arm's length, with his gun held in tight.

'Mother . . .' Katryn said in quiet alarm.

'Hush and do as I say. Do as this man says.'

'But –'

'Against the wall,' Clark told the man. He kept the gun aimed at the center of the bodyguard's head while he switched hands, then he chopped hard on the side of his neck with his right hand. The man fell stunned, and Clark put handcuffs on his wrists. Next he gagged him, tied up his ankles, and dragged him to the darkest spot he could find.

'Ladies, if you will come with me, please?'

'What is this?' Katryn asked.

'I don't know,' her mother admitted. 'Your father told me to –'

'Miss, your father has decided that he wants to visit America, and he wants you and your mother to join him,' Clark said in flawless Russian.

Katryn did not reply. The lighting in the alley was very poor, but he could see her face lose all of the color it had. Her mother looked little better.

'But,' the young girl said finally. 'But that's treason . . . I don't believe it.'

'He told me . . . he told me to do whatever this man says,' Maria said. 'Katryn – we must.'

'But –'

'Katryn,' her mother said. 'What will happen to your life if your father defects and you remain behind? What will happen to your friends? What will happen to you? They will use you to get him back, anything they have to do, Katusha . . .'

'Time to leave, folks.' Clark took both women by the arm.

'But –' Katryn gestured at the bodyguard.

'He'll be fine. We don't kill people. It's bad for business.' Clark led them back to the street, turning left toward the harbor.

*

The Major had divided his men into two groups. The smaller one was setting explosive charges on everything they could find. A light pole or a laser, it didn't matter to them. The large group had cut down most of the KGB troops who'd tried to come here, and was arrayed around the control bunker. It wasn't actually a bunker, but whoever had made the construction plans for the place had evidently thought that the control room should have the same sort of protection as those at the Leninsk Cosmodrome, or maybe he'd thought that the mountain might someday be subjected to a nuclear airburst attack. Most likely was that someone had decided the manual prescribed this sort of structure for this sort of place. What had resulted was a building with reinforced-concrete walls fully a meter thick. His men had killed the KGB commander and taken his vehicle, with the heavy machine gun, and were pouring fire into the vision slits cut in the structure. In fact, no one used them for looking, and their rounds had long since pounded through the thick glass and were chewing into the room's computers and control gear.

Inside, General Pokryshkin had taken command by default. He had thirty or so KGB troops, armed only with light weapons and what little ammunition they'd been carrying when the attack had begun. A lieutenant was handling the defense as best he could, while the General was trying to get help by radio.

'It will take an hour,' a regimental commander was saying. 'My men are moving out right now!'

'Fast as you can!' Pokryshkin said. 'People are dying here.' He'd already thought of helicopters, but in this weather they'd accomplish nothing at all. A helicopter assault would not even have been a gamble, just suicide. He set down the radio and picked up his service automatic. He could hear the noise from the outside. All the site's equipment was being blown up. He could live with that now. As great a catastrophe as that was, the people mattered more. Nearly a third of his engineers were in the bunker. They'd been finishing up a lengthy conference when the attack began. Had that not been the case, fewer would be here, but those would have been out working on the equipment. At least here they had a chance.

On the other side of the bunker's concrete walls, the Major was still trying to figure this one out. He'd hardly expected to find this sort of structure. His RPG antitank rounds merely chipped the wall, and aiming them at the narrow slits was difficult in the darkness. His machine-gun rounds could be guided to them with tracers, but that wasn't good enough.

Find the weak points, he told himself. *Take your time and think it out.* He ordered his men to maintain a steady rate of fire and started moving around the building. Whoever was inside had his weapons equally dispersed, but buildings like this one always had at least one blind spot . . . The Major merely had to find it.

'What is happening?' his radio squawked.

'We have killed perhaps fifty. The rest are in a bunker and we're trying to get them, too. What of your target?'

'The apartment building,' the Archer replied. 'They're all in there, and –' The radio transmitted the sound of gunfire. 'We will have them soon.'

'Thirty minutes and we must leave, my friend,' the Major said.

'Yes!' The radio went silent.

The Archer was a good man, and a brave one, the Major thought as he examined the bunker's north face, but with just a week's formal training he'd be so much more effective . . . just a week to codify the things that he was learning on his own . . . and to pass on the lessons that others had shed blood for . . .

There was the place. There was a blind spot.

The last mortar rounds were targeted on the roof of the apartment block. Bondarenko smiled as he watched. Finally the other side had done something really foolish. The 82-millimeter shells didn't have a chance of breaking through the concrete roof slabs, but if they'd spread them around the building's periphery he'd have lost many of his men. He was down to ten, two of them wounded. The rifles of the fallen were inside the building now, being fired from the second floor. He counted twenty bodies outside his perimeter, and the attackers – they were Afghans, he was sure of that now – were milling about beyond his vision, trying to decide what to do. For the first time Bondarenko felt that they just might survive after all. The General had radioed to say that a motorized regiment was on the way down the road from Nurek, and though he shuddered to think what it would be like driving BTR infantry carriers over snow-covered mountain roads, the loss of a few infantry squads was as nothing compared to the corporate expertise that he was trying to protect now.

The incoming rifle fire was sporadic now, just harassment fire while they decided what to do next. With more people he'd try a counterattack, just to throw them off balance, but the colonel was tied to his post. He couldn't risk it, not with a mere squad left to cover two sides of the building.

Do I pull back now? The longer I can keep them away from the building, the better, but should I do my withdrawal now? His thoughts wavered at that decision. Inside the building his troops would have far better protection, but he'd lose the ability to control them when each man was separated from the next by the interior walls. If they pulled inside and withdrew to the upper floors, they'd allow the Afghan sappers to drop the building with explosive charges – no, that was the counsel of despair. Bondarenko listened to the scattered rifle shots that punctuated the sounds of wounded and dying men and couldn't make up his mind.

Two hundred meters away, the Archer was about to do that for him. Mistaking the casualties he'd taken here to mean that this part of the building was the most heavily defended, he was leading what was left of his men to the other side. It required five minutes to do so, while those he left behind kept up a steady drumbeat of fire into the Russian perimeter. Out of mortar rounds, out of RPG projectiles, the only thing left to him besides rifles were a few grenades and six satchel charges. All around him fires blazed into the night, separate orange-red flames reaching upward to melt the falling snow. He heard the cries of his own wounded as he formed up the fifty men he had left. They'd attack as one mass, behind the leader who'd brought them here. The Archer flipped the safety off his AK-47, and remembered the first three men he'd killed with it.

Bondarenko's head snapped around when he heard the screams from the other side of the building. He turned back and saw that nothing was happening. It was time to do something, and he hoped that it was the right thing:

'Everyone back to the building. Move!' Two of his remaining ten were wounded, and each had to be helped. It took over a minute as the night shattered yet again with volleys of rifle fire. Bondarenko took five and ran down the building's main first-floor corridor and out of the other side.

He couldn't tell if there'd been a breakthrough, or if the men here were also falling back – again he had to hold fire because both sides were identically uniformed. Then one of those running toward the building fired, and the Colonel went to one knee and dropped him with a five-round burst. More appeared, and he nearly fired until he heard their shouts.

'*Nashi, nashi!*' He counted eight. The last of them was the sergeant, wounded in both legs.

'Too many, we couldn't –'

'Get inside,' Bondarenko told him. 'Can you still fight?'

'Fuck, yes!' Both men looked around. They couldn't fight from the individual rooms. They'd have to make their stand in the corridors and stairwells.

'Help is on the way. A regiment is coming down from Nurek if we can hold on!' Bondarenko told his men. He didn't tell them how long it was supposed to take. It was the first good news in over half an hour. Two civilians came downstairs. Both carried rifles.

'You need help?' Morozov asked. He'd avoided military service, but he had just learned that a rifle wasn't all that hard to use.

'How are things up there?' Bondarenko asked.

'My section chief is dead. I took this from him. Many people are hurt, and the rest are as terrified as I am.'

'Stay with the sergeant,' the Colonel told him. 'Keep your head, Comrade Engineer, and we may yet live through this. Help's on the way.'

'I hope the bastards hurry.' Morozov helped the sergeant – who was even younger than the engineer – go to the far end of the corridor.

Bondarenko put half of his men at the stairwell and the other half by the elevators. It was quiet again. They could hear the jabbering of voices outside, but the shooting had died down for the moment.

'Down the ladder. Carefully,' Clark said. 'There's a cross-member at the bottom. You can stand on that.'

Maria looked with disgust at the slimy wood, doing as she was told like a person in a dream. Her daughter followed. Clark went last, stepped around them, and got into the boat. He untied the ropes and moved the boat by hand underneath where the women were standing. It was a three-foot drop.

'One at a time. You first, Katryn. Step down slowly and I'll catch you.' She did so, her knees wobbling with doubt and fear. Clark grabbed her ankle and pulled it toward him. She fell into the boat as elegantly as a sack of beans. Maria came next. He gave the same instructions, and she followed them, but Katryn tried to help, and in doing so moved the boat. Maria lost her grip and fell into the water with a scream.

'What is that?' someone called from the landside end of the pier.

Clark ignored it, grabbing the woman's splashing hands and pulling her aboard. She was gasping from the cold, but there wasn't much Clark could do about that. He heard the sound of running feet along the pier as he turned on the boat's electric motor and headed straight out.

'*Stoi!*' a voice called. It was a cop, Clark realized, it would have to be a damned cop. He turned to see the glimmer of a flashlight. It couldn't reach the boat, but it was fixed on the wake he'd left behind. Clark lifted his radio.

'Uncle Joe, this is Willy. On the way. The sun is out!'

'They may have been spotted,' the communications officers told Mancuso.

'Great.' The Captain went forward. 'Goodman, come right to zero-eight-five. Move her in toward the coast at ten knots.'

'Conn, sonar, contact bearing two-nine-six. Diesel engine,' Jones's voice announced. 'Twin screws.'

'Will be KGB patrol frigate – Grisha, probably,' Ramius said. 'Routine patrol.'

Mancuso didn't say anything, but he pointed to the fire-control tracking party. They'd work up a position on the seaward target while *Dallas* moved into the coast at periscope depth, keeping her radio antenna up.

'Nine-seven-one, this is Velikiye Luki Center. Turn right to new course one-zero-four,' the Russian voice told Colonel von Eich. The pilot squeezed the microphone trigger on his wheel.

'Say again, Luki. Over.'

'Nine-seven-one, you are ordered to turn right to new heading one-zero-four and return to Moscow. Over.'

'Ah, thank you, Luki, negative, we are proceeding on a heading of two-eight-six per our flight plan. Over.'

'Nine-seven-one, you are ordered to return to Moscow!' the controller insisted.

'Roger. Thank you. Out.' Von Eich looked down to see that his autopilot was on the proper heading, then resumed his outside scanning for other aircraft.

'But you are not turning back,' the Russian said over the intercom.

'No.' Von Eich turned to look at the man. 'We didn't leave anything behind that I know of.' *Well* . . .

'But they ordered you –'

'Son, I am in command of this aircraft, and my orders are to fly to Shannon,' the pilot explained.

'But –' The Russian unsnapped his straps and started to stand up.

'Sit down!' the pilot ordered. 'Nobody leaves my flight deck without my permission, mister! You are a guest on my airplane, and you'll goddamned well do what I say!' *Damn, it was supposed to be easier than this!* He gestured to the engineer, who toggled off another switch. That shut off all the cabin lights in the aircraft. The VC-137 was now totally blacked out. Von Eich keyed his radio again. 'Luki, this is niner-seven-one. We have some electrical problems aboard. I don't want to make any radical course changes until we have them figured out. Do you copy? Over.'

'What is your problem?' the controller asked. The pilot wondered what he'd been told as he gave out the next set of lies.

'Luki, we don't know yet. We're losing electrical power. All our lights have gone bad. The bird is blacked out at the moment, say again we are running without lights. I'm a little worried, and I don't need any distractions right now.' That bought him two minutes of silence, and twenty miles of westward progress.

'Nine-seven-one, I have notified Moscow of your problems. They advise that you return at once. They will clear you for an emergency approach,' the controller offered.

'Roger, thank you, Luki, but I don't want to risk a course change right now, if you know what I mean. We're working to fix the problem. Please stand by. Will advise. Out.' Colonel von Eich checked the clock in his instrument panel. Thirty more minutes to the coast.

'What?' Major Zarudin asked. 'Who got on the airplane?'

'Chairman Gerasimov and an arrested enemy spy,' Vatutin said.

'On an American airplane? You tell me that the *Chairman* is defecting on an American airplane!' The officer commanding the airport security detail had taken charge of the situation, as his orders allowed him to do. He found that he had two colonels, a lieutenant colonel, a driver, and an American in the office he used here – along with the craziest damned story he'd ever heard. 'I must call for instructions.'

'I am senior to you!' Golovko said.

'You are not senior to my commander!' Zarudin pointed out as he reached for the phone. He'd been able to have the air traffic controllers try to recall the American plane, but it had not come as a surprise to his visitors that it had decided not to turn.

Ryan sat perfectly still, barely breathing, not even moving his head. He told himself that as long as they didn't get too excited he would be completely safe. Golovko was too smart to do anything crazy. He knew who Jack was, and he knew what would happen if an accredited member of a diplomatic mission to his country was so much as scratched. Ryan had been scratched, of course. His ankle hurt like hell, and his knee was oozing blood, but he'd done that to himself. Golovko glared at him from five feet away. Ryan didn't return the look. He swallowed his fear and tried to look exactly as harmless as he was right now.

'Where's his family?' Vatutin asked.

'They flew to Talinn yesterday,' Vasiliy answered lamely. 'She wanted to see some friends . . .'

Time was running out for everyone. Bondarenko's men were down to less than half a magazine each. Two more were dead from grenades that had been tossed in. The Colonel had watched a private leap on one, ripped to shreds to save his comrades. The boy's blood covered the tile floor like paint. Six Afghans were piled up at the door. It had been like this at Stalingrad, the Colonel told himself. No one excelled the Russian soldier at house-to-house fighting. How far away was that motorized regiment? An hour was such a short period of time. Half a movie, a television show, a pleasant night's stroll . . . such a short time, unless people were shooting at you. Then every second stretched before your eyes, and the hands of your watch seemed frozen, and the only thing that went fast was your heart. It was only his second experience with close combat. He'd been decorated after the first, and he wondered if he'd be buried after the second. But he couldn't let that happen. On the floors above him were several hundred people, engineers and scientists, their wives and their children, all of whose lives rested on his ability to hold the Afghan invaders off for less than an hour.

Go away, he wished at them. *Do you think that we wanted to come and be shot at in that miserable rockpile you call a country? If you want to kill those who are responsible, why don't you go to Moscow?* But that wasn't the way things were in war, was it? The politicians never seemed to come close enough to see what they had wrought. They never really knew what they did, and now the bastards had nuclear-tipped missiles. They had the power to kill millions, but they didn't even have the courage to see the horror on a simple, old-fashioned battlefield.

The nonsense you think at times like this! he raged at himself.

He'd failed. His men had trusted him with command, and he'd failed them, the Archer told himself. He looked around at the bodies in the snow and each seemed to accuse him. He could kill individuals, could pluck aircraft from the sky, but he'd never learned how to lead a large body of men. Was this Allah's curse on him for torturing the Russian flyers? No! There were still enemies to kill. He gestured to his men to enter the building through several broken, ground-floor windows.

The Major was leading from the front, as the *mudjaheddin* expected. He had gotten ten of them right up to the side of the bunker, then led them along the wall toward the main door, covered by fire from the rest of his company. It was going well, he thought. He'd lost five men, but that was not very many for a mission like this . . . *Thank you for all the training you gave me, my Russians friends* . . .

The main door was steel. He personally set a pair of satchel charges at both lower corners and set the fuses before crawling back around the corner. Russian rifles blazed over his head, but those inside the building didn't know where he was. That would change. He set the charges, pulled the fuse cords, and dashed back around the corner.

Pokryshkin cringed as he heard it happen. He turned to see the heavy steel door flying across the room and smashing into a control console. The KGB Lieutenant was killed instantly by the blast, and as Pokryshkin's men raced to cover the breach in the wall, three more explosive packs flew in. There was nowhere to run. The Border Guards kept firing, killing one of the attackers at the door, but then the charges went off.

It was a strangely hollow sound, the Major thought. The force of the explosions was contained by the stout concrete walls. He led his men in a second later. Electrical circuits were sparking, and fires would soon begin in earnest, but everyone he could see inside was down. His men moved swiftly from one to another, seizing weapons and killing those merely unconscious. The Major saw a Russian officer with general's stars. The man was bleeding from his nose and ears, trying to bring up his pistol when the Major cut him down. In another minute they were all dead. The building was rapidly filling with thick, acrid smoke. He ordered his men out.

'We're finished here,' he said into his radio. There was no answer. 'Are you there?'

The Archer was against a wall next to a half-open door. His radio was switched off. Just outside his room was a soldier, facing down the corridor. It was time. The freedom fighter threw the door aside with the barrel of his rifle and shot the Russian before the man had had a chance to turn. He screamed a command, and five other men emerged from their rooms, but two were killed before they got a chance to shoot. He looked up and down the corridor and saw nothing but gun flashes and half-hidden silhouettes.

Fifty meters away, Bondarenko reacted to the new threat. He shouted an order for his men to stay under cover, and then with murderous precision, the Colonel identified and engaged the targets moving in the open, identified by the emergency lighting in the corridor. The corridor was exactly like a shooting gallery, and he got two men with as many bursts. Another ran toward him, screaming something unintelligible and firing his weapon in a single extended burst. Bondarenko's shots missed, to his amazement, but someone else got him. There was more shooting, and the sound of it reverberating off the concrete walls completely deafened everyone. Then, he saw, there was only one man left. The Colonel watched two more of his men fall, and the last Afghan chipped concrete only centimeters from his face. Bondarenko's eyes stung from it, and the right side of his face recoiled at the sudden pain. The Colonel pulled back from the line of fire, flipped his weapon to full automatic, took a deep breath, and jumped into the corridor. The man was less than ten meters away.

The moment stretched into eternity as both men brought their weapons to bear. He saw the man's eyes. It was a young face there, immediately below the emergency light, but the eyes . . . the rage there, the hatred, nearly stopped the Colonel's heart. But Bondarenko was a soldier before all things. The Afghan's first shot missed. His did not.

The Archer felt shock, but not pain in his chest as he fell. His brain sent a message to his hands to bring the weapon to the left, but they ignored the command and dropped it. He fell in stages, first to his knees, then on his back, and at last he was staring up at a ceiling. It was finally over. Then the man stood by his side. It was not a cruel face, the Archer thought. It was the enemy, and it was an infidel, but he was a man, too, wasn't he? There was curiosity there. He wants to know who I am; the Archer told him with his last breath.

'*Allahu akhbar!*' God is great.

Yes, I suppose He is, Bondarenko told the corpse. He knew the phrase well enough. *Is that why you came?* He saw that the man had a radio. It started to make noise, and the Colonel bent down to grab it.

'Are you there?' the radio asked a moment later. The question was in Pashtu, but the answer was delivered in Russian.

'It is all finished here,' Bondarenko said.

The Major looked at his radio for a moment, then blew his whistle to assemble what was left of his men. The Archer's company knew the way to the assembly point, but all that mattered now was getting home. He counted his men. He'd lost eleven and had six wounded. With luck he'd get to the border before the snow stopped. Five minutes later his men were heading off the mountain.

'Secure the area!' Bondarenko told his remaining six men. 'Collect weapons and get them handed out.' It was probably over, he thought, but 'over' would not truly come until that motor-rifle regiment got here.

'Morozov!' he called next. The engineer appeared a moment later.

'Yes, Colonel?'

'Is there a physician upstairs?'

'Yes, several – I'll get one.'

The Colonel found that he was sweating. The building still held some warmth. He dropped the field radio off his back and was stunned to see that two bullets had hit it – and even more surprised to see blood on one of the straps. He'd been hit and hadn't known it. The sergeant came over and looked at it.

'Just a scratch, Comrade, like those on my legs.'

'Help me off with this coat, will you?' Bondarenko shrugged out of the knee-length greatcoat, exposing his uniform blouse. With his right hand he reached inside, while his left removed the ribbon that designated the Red Banner. This he pinned to the young man's collar. 'You deserve better, Sergeant, but this is all I can do for the present.'

'Up 'scope!' Mancuso used the search periscope now, with its light-amplifying equipment. 'Still nothing . . .' He turned to look west. 'Uh-oh, I got a masthead light at two-seven-zero –'

'That's our sonar contact,' Lieutenant Goodman noted unnecessarily.

'Sonar, conn, do you have an ident on the contact?' Mancuso asked.

'Negative,' Jones replied. 'We're getting reverbs from the ice, sir. Acoustic conditions are pretty bad. It's twin screw and diesel, but no ident.'

Mancuso turned on the 'scope television camera. Ramius needed only one look at the picture. 'Grisha.'

Mancuso looked at the tracking party. 'Solution?'

'Yes, but it's a little shaky,' the weapons officer replied. 'The ice isn't going to help,' he added. What he meant was that the Mark 48 torpedo in surface-attack mode could be confused by floating ice. He paused for a moment. 'Sir, if that's a Grisha, how come no radar?'

'New contact! Conn, sonar, new contact bearing zero-eight-six – sounds like our friend, sir,' Jones called. 'Something else near that bearing, high-speed screw . . . definitely something new there, sir, call it zero-eight-three.'

'Up two feet,' Mancuso told the quartermaster. The periscope came up. 'I see him, just on the horizon . . . call it three miles. There's a light behind them!' He slapped the handles up and the 'scope went down at once. 'Let's get there fast. All ahead two-thirds.'

'All ahead two-thirds, aye.' The helmsman dialed up the engine order.

The navigator plotted the position of the inbound boat and ticked off the yards.   *

Clark was looking back toward the shore. There was a light sweeping left and right across the water. Who was it? He didn't know if the local cops had boats, but there had to be a detachment of KGB Border Guards: they had their own little navy, *and* their own little air force. But how alert were they on a Friday night? Probably better than they were when that German kid decided to fly into Moscow . . . right through this sector, Clark remembered. *This area's probably pretty alert . . . where are you*, Dallas? He lifted his radio.

'Uncle Joe, this is Willy. The sun is rising, and we're far from home.'

'He says he's close, sir,' communications reported.

''Gator?' Mancuso asked.

'The navigator looked up from his table. 'I gave him fifteen knots. We should be within five hundred yards now.'

'All ahead one-third,' the Captain ordered. 'Up 'scope!' The oiled steel tube hissed up again – all the way up.

'Captain, I got a radar emitter astern, bearing two-six-eight. It's a Don-2,' the ESM technician said.

'Conn, sonar, both the hostile contacts have increased speed. Blade count looks like twenty knots and coming up on the Grisha, sir,' Jones said. 'Confirm target ident is Grisha-class. Easterly contact still unknown, one screw, probably a gas engine, doing turns for twenty or so.'

'Range about six thousand yards,' the fire-control party said next.

'This is the fun part,' Mancuso observed. 'I have them. Bearing – *mark!*'

'Zero-nine-one.'

'Range.' Mancuso squeezed the trigger for the 'scope's laser-rangefinder. '*Mark!*'

'Six hundred yards.'

'Nice call, 'Gator. Solution on the Grisha?' he asked fire control.

'Set for tubes two and four. Outer doors are still closed, sir.'

'Keep 'em that way.' Mancuso went to the bridge trunk's lower hatch. 'XO, you have the conn. I'm going to do the recovery myself. Let's get it done.'

'All stop,' the executive officer said. Mancuso opened the hatch and went up the ladder to the bridge. The lower hatch was closed behind him. He heard the water rushing around him in the sail, then the splashes of surface waves. The intercom told him he could open the bridge hatch. Mancuso spun the locking wheel and heaved against the heavy steel cover. He was rewarded with a faceful of cold, oily saltwater, but ignored it and got to the bridge.

He looked aft first. There was the Grisha, its masthead light low on the horizon. Next he looked forward and pulled the flashlight from his hip pocket. He aimed directly at the raft and tapped out the Morse letter D.

'A light, a light!' Maria said. Clark turned back forward, saw it, and steered for it. Then he saw something else.

The patrol boat behind Clark was a good two miles off, its searchlight looking in the wrong place. The Captain turned west to see the other contact. Mancuso knew in a distant sort of way that Grishas carried searchlights, but had allowed himself to disregard the fact. After all, why should searchlights concern a submarine? *When she's on the surface*, the Captain told himself. The ship was still too far away to see him, light or not, but that would change in a hurry. He watched it sweep the surface aft of his submarine, and realized too late that they probably had *Dallas* on radar now.

'Over here, Clark, move your ass!' he screamed across the water, swinging the light left and right. The next thirty seconds seemed to last into the following month. Then it was there.

'Help the ladies,' the man said. He held the raft against the submarine's sail with his motor. *Dallas* was still moving, had to be to maintain this precarious depth, not quite surfaced, not quite dived. The first one felt and moved like a young girl, the skipper thought as he brought her aboard. The second one was wet and shivering. Clark waited a moment, setting a small box atop the motor. Mancuso wondered how it stayed balanced there until he realized that it was either magnetic or glued somehow.

'Down the ladder,' Mancuso told the ladies.

Clark scrambled aboard and said something – probably the same thing – in Russian. To Mancuso he spoke in English. 'Five minutes before it blows.'

The women were already halfway down. Clark went behind them, and finally Mancuso, with a last look at the raft. The last thing he saw was the harbor patrol boat, now heading directly toward him. He dropped down and pulled the hatch behind himself. Then he punched the intercom button. 'Take her down and move the boat!'

The bottom hatch opened underneath them all, and he heard the executive officer. 'Make your depth ninety feet, all ahead two-thirds, left full rudder!'

A petty officer met the ladies at the bottom of the bridge tube. The astonishment on his face would have been funny at any other time. Clark took them by the arm and led them forward to his stateroom. Mancuso went aft.

'I have the conn,' he announced.

'Captain has the conn,' the XO agreed. 'ESM says they got some VHF radio traffic, close in, probably the Grisha talking to the other one.'

'Helm, come to new course three-five-zero. Let's get her under the ice. They probably know we're here – well, they know something's here. 'Gator, how's the chart look?'

'We'll have to turn soon,' the navigator warned. 'Shoal water in eight thousand yards. Recommend come to new course two-nine-one.' Mancuso ordered the change at once.

'Depth now eight-five feet, leveling out,' the diving officer said. 'Speed eighteen knots.' A small bark of sound announced the destruction of the raft and its motor.

'Okay, people, now all we have to do is leave,' Mancuso told his Attack Center crew. A high-pitched snap of sound told them that this would not be easy.

'Conn, sonar, we're being pinged. That's a Grisha death-ray,' Jones said, using the slang term for the Russian set. 'Might have us.'

'Under the ice now,' the nagivator said.

'Range to target?'

'Just under four thousand yards,' the weapons officer replied. 'Set for tubes two and four.'

The problem was, they couldn't shoot. *Dallas* was inside Russian territorial waters, and even if the Grisha shot at them, shooting back wasn't self-defense, but an act of war. Mancuso looked at the chart. He had thirty feet of water under his keel, and a bare twenty over his sail – minus the thickness of the ice . . .

'Marko?' the Captain said.

'They will request instructions first,' Ramius judged. 'The more time they have, the better chance they will shoot.'

'Okay. All ahead full,' Mancuso ordered. At thirty knots he'd be in international waters in ten minutes.

'Grisha is passing abeam on the portside,' Jones said. Mancuso went forward to the sonar room.

'What's happening?' the Captain asked.

'The high-frequency stuff works pretty good in the ice. He's searchlighting back and forth. He knows something's here, but not exactly where yet.'

Mancuso lifted a phone. 'Five-inch room, launch two noisemakers.'

A pair of bubble-making decoys was ejected from the portside of the submarine.

'Good, Mancuso,' Ramius observed. 'His sonar will fix on those. He cannot maneuver well with the ice.'

'We'll know for sure in the next minute.' Just as he said it, the submarine was rocked by explosions aft. A very feminine scream echoed through the forward portion of the submarine.

'All ahead flank!' the Captain called aft.

'The decoys,' Ramius said. 'Surprising that he fired so quickly . . .'

'Losing sonar performance, skipper,' Jones said as the screen went blank with flow noise. Mancuso and Ramius went aft. The navigator had their course track marked on the chart.

'Uh-oh, we have to transit this place right here where the ice stops. How much you want to bet he knows it?' Mancuso looked up. They were still being pinged, and he still couldn't shoot back. And that Grisha might get lucky.

'Radio – Mancuso, let me speak on radio!' Ramius said.

'We don't do things that way –' Mancuso said. American doctrine was to evade, never to let them be sure there was a submarine there at all.

'I know that. But we are not American submarine, Captain Mancuso, we are Soviet submarine,' Ramius suggested. Bart Mancuso nodded. He'd never played this card before.

'Take her to antenna depth!'

A radio technician dialed in the Soviet guard frequency, and the slender VHF antenna was raised as soon as the submarine cleared the ice. The periscope went up, too.

'There he is. Angle on the bow, zero. Down 'scope!'

'Radar contact bearing two-eight-one,' the speaker proclaimed.

The Captain of the Grisha was coming off a week's patrolling on the Baltic Sea, six hours late, and had been looking forward to four days off. Then first came a radio transmission from the Talinn harbor police about a strange craft seen leaving the docks, followed by something from the KGB, then a small explosion near the harbor police boat, next several sonar contacts. The twenty-nine-year-old senior lieutenant with all of three months in command had made his estimate of the situation and fired at what his sonar operator called a positive submarine contact. Now he was wondering if he'd made a mistake, and how ghastly it might be. All he knew was that he had not the smallest idea what was happening, but if he were chasing a submarine, it would be heading west.

And now he had a radar contact forward. The speaker for the guard radio frequency started chattering.

'Cease fire, you idiot!' a metallic voice screamed at him three times.

'Identify!' the Grisha's commander replied.

'This is *Novosibiirsk Komsomolets!* What the hell do you think you're doing firing live ammunition in a practice exercise! *You* identify!'

The young officer stared at his microphone and swore. *Novosibiirsk Komsomolets* was a special-ops boat based at Kronshtadt, always playing *Spetznaz* games . . .

'This is *Krepkiy*.'

'Thank you. We will discuss this episode the day after tomorrow. Out!'

The Captain looked around at the bridge crew. 'What exercise . . . ?'

'Too bad,' Marko said as he replaced the microphone. 'He reacted well. Now he will take several minutes to call his base, and . . .'

'And that's all we need. And they still don't know what happened.' Mancuso turned. ''Gator, shortest way out?'

'Recommend two-seven-five, distance is eleven thousand yards.'

At thirty-four knots, the remaining distance was covered quickly. Ten minutes later the submarine was back in international waters. The anticlimax was remarkable for all those in the control room. Mancuso changed course for deeper water and ordered speed reduced to one-third, then went back to sonar.

'That should be that,' he announced.

'Sir, what was this all about?' Jones asked.

'Well, I don't know that I can tell you.'

'What's her name?' From his seat Jones could see into the passageway.

'I don't even know that myself. But I'll find out.' Mancuso went across the passageway and knocked on the door of Clark's stateroom.

'Who is it?'

'Guess,' Mancuso said. Clark opened the door. The Captain saw a young woman in presentable clothes, but wet feet. Then an older woman appeared from the head. She was dressed in the khaki shirt and pants of *Dallas'* chief engineer, though she carried her own things, which were wet. These she handed to Mancuso with a phrase of Russian.

'She wants you to have them cleaned, skipper,' Clark translated, and started laughing. 'These are our new guests. Mrs Gerasimov, and her daughter, Katryn.'

'What's so special about them?' Mancuso asked.

'My father is head of KGB!' Katryn said.

The Captain managed not to drop the clothes.

'We got company,' the copilot said. They were coming in from the right side, the strobe lights of what had to be a pair of fighter planes. 'Closing fast.'

'Twenty minutes to the coast,' the navigator reported. The pilot had long since spotted it.

'Shit!' the pilot snapped. The fighters missed his aircraft by less than two hundred yards of vertical separation, little more in horizontal. A moment later, the VC-137 bounced through their wake turbulence.

'Engure Control, this is US Air Force flight niner-seven-one. We just had a near miss. What the hell is going on down there?'

'Let me speak to the Soviet officer!' the voice answered. It didn't sound like a controller.

'I speak for this aircraft,' Colonel von Eich replied. 'We are cruising on a heading of two-eight-six, flight level eleven thousand six hundred meters. We are on a correctly filed flight plan, in a designated air corridor, and we have electrical problems. We don't need to have some hardrock fighter jocks playing tag with us – this is an American aircraft with a diplomatic mission aboard. You want to start World War Three or something? Over!'

'Nine-seven-one, you are ordered to turn back!'

'Negative! We have electrical problems and cannot repeat cannot comply. This airplane is flying without lights, and those crazy MiG drivers damned near rammed us! Are you trying to kill us, over!'

'You have kidnapped a Soviet citizen and you must return to Moscow!'

'Repeat that last,' von Eich requested.

But the Captain couldn't. A fighter ground-intercept officer, he'd been rushed to Engure, the last air-traffic-control point within Soviet borders, quickly briefed by a local KGB officer, and told to force the American aircraft to turn back. He should not have said what he had just said in the clear.

'You must stop the aircraft!' the KGB General shouted.

'Simple, then. I order my MiGs to shoot it down!' the Captain replied in kind. 'Do you give me the order, Comrade General?'

'I do not have the authority. You have to make it stop.'

'It cannot be done. We can shoot it down, but we cannot make it *stop*.'

'Do you wish to be shot?' the General asked.

'Where the hell is it now?' the Foxbat pilot asked his wingman. They'd only seen it once, and that for a single ghastly instant. They could track the intruder – except that it was leaving, and wasn't really an intruder, they both knew – on radar, and kill it with radar-guided missiles, but to close on the target in darkness . . . Even in the relatively clear night, the target was running without lights, and trying to find it meant running the risk of what American fighter pilots jokingly called a Fox-Four: midair collision, a quick and spectacular death for all involved.

'Hammer Lead, this is Toolbox. You are ordered to close on the target and force it to turn,' the controller said. 'Target is now at your twelve o'clock and level, range three thousand meters.'

'I know that,' the pilot said to himself. He had the airliner on radar, but he did not have it visually, and his radar could not track precisely enough to warn him of an imminent collision. He also had to worry about the other MiG on his wing.

'Stay back,' he ordered his wingman. 'I'll handle this alone.' He advanced his throttles slightly and moved the stick a hair to the right. The MiG-25 was heavy and sluggish, not a very maneuverable fighter. He had a pair of air-to-air missiles hanging from each wing, and all he had to do to stop this aircraft was . . . But instead of ordering him to do something he was trained to do, some jackass of a KGB officer was –

There. He didn't so much see the aircraft, but saw something ahead disappear. *Ah!* He pulled back on the stick to gain a few hundred meters of altitude and . . . yes! He could pick the Boeing out against the sea. Slowly and carefully, he moved forward until he was abeam of the target and two hundred meters higher.

'I got lights on the right side,' the copilot said. 'Fighter, but I don't know what kind.'

'If you were him, what would you do?' von Eich asked.

'Defect!' *Or shoot us down . . .*

Behind them in the jump seat, the Russian pilot, whose only job was to talk Russian in case of an emergency, was strapped down in his seat and had not the first idea what to do. He'd been cut out of the radio conversations and had only intercom now. Moscow wanted them to turn the aircraft back. He didn't know why, but – but what? he asked himself.

'Here he comes, sliding over toward us.'

As carefully as he could, the MiG pilot maneuvered his fighter to the left. He wanted to get over the Boeing's cockpit, from which position he could gently reduce altitude and force it downward. To do this required as much skill as he could muster, and the pilot could only pray that the American was equally adept. He positioned himself so that he could see . . . but –

The MiG-25 was designed as an interceptor, and the cockpit gave the pilot very restricted visibility. He could no longer see the airplane with which he was flying formation. He looked ahead. The shore was only a few kilometers away. Even if he were able to make the American reduce altitude, he'd be over the Baltic before it would matter to anyone. The pilot pulled back on his stick and climbed off to the right. Once clear, he reversed course.

'Toolbox, this is Hammer Lead,' he reported. 'The American will not change course. I tried, but I will not collide with his airplane without orders.'

The controller had watched the two radar blips merge on his scope, and was now amazed that his heart hadn't stopped. What the hell was going on? This was an American plane. They couldn't force it to stop, and if there were an accident, who would be blamed for it? He made his decision.

'Return to base. Out.'

'You will pay for this!' the KGB General promised the ground-intercept officer. He was wrong.

'Thank God,' von Eich said as they passed over the coastline. He called up the chief cabin steward next. 'How are the folks in back?'

'Mainly asleep. They must have had a big party tonight. When are we getting the electricity back?'

'Flight engineer,' the pilot said, 'they want to know about the electrical problems.'

'Looks like it was a bad breaker, sir. I think . . . Yeah, I fixed it.'

The pilot looked out his window. The wingtip lights were back on, as were the cabin lights, except in back. Passing Ventspils, they turned left to a new heading two-five-nine. He let out a long breath. Two and a half hours to Shannon. 'Some coffee would be nice,' he thought aloud.

*

Golovko hung up the phone and spat out a few words that Jack didn't understand exactly, though their message seemed rather clear.

'Sergey, could I clean my knee up?'

'What exactly have you done, Ryan?' the KGB officer asked.

'I fell out of the airplane and the bastards left without me. I want to be taken to my embassy, but first, my knee hurts.'

Golovko and Vatutin stared at each other and both wondered several things. What had actually happened? What would happen to them? What to do with Ryan?

'Who do we even call?' Golovko asked.

27

Under Wraps

Vatutin decided to call his directorate chief, who called the
KGB's First Deputy Chairman, who called someone else,
and then called back to the airport office where they were
all waiting. Vatutin noted the instructions, took everyone
to Gerasimov's car, and gave directions that Jack didn't
understand. The car headed straight through Moscow's
empty early-morning streets – it was just after midnight,
and those who had been out to the movies or the opera or
the ballet were now at home. Jack was nestled between the
two KGB colonels, and hoped that they'd be taking him to
the embassy, but they kept going, crossing the city at a high
rate of speed, then up into the Lenin Hills and beyond to
the forests that surround the city. Now he was frightened.
Diplomatic immunity seemed a surer thing at the airport
than it did in the woods.

The car slowed after an hour, turning off the paved main
road onto a gravel path that meandered through trees.
There were uniforms about, he saw through the windows.
Men with rifles. That sight made him forget the pain from
his ankle and knee. Exactly where was he? Why was he
being brought here? Why the people with guns . . . ? The
phrase that came to him was a simple, ominous one: Take
him for a ride . . .

No! They can't be doing that, reason told him. *I have a
diplomatic passport. I was seen alive by too many people.
Probably the Ambassador is already* – But he wouldn't be.
He wasn't cleared for what had happened, and unless they
got word off the plane. . . . Regardless, they couldn't
possibly . . . But in the Soviet Union, the saying went,

things happened that simply *didn't* happen. The car's door flew open. Golovko got out and pulled Ryan with him. The only thing Jack was sure of now was that there was no point in resistance.

It was a house, a quite ordinary frame house in the woods. The windows glowed yellow from lights behind the curtains. Ryan saw a dozen or so people standing around, all with uniforms, all with rifles, all staring at him with the same degree of interest given a paper target. One, an officer, came over and frisked Ryan with considerable thoroughness, eliciting a grunt of pain when he got to the bloody knee and torn trousers. He surprised Ryan with what might have been a perfunctory apology. The officer nodded to Golovko and Vatutin, who handed over their automatics and led Ryan into the house.

Inside the door, a man took their coats. Two more men in civilian clothes were obvious police or KGB types. They wore unzipped jackets, and they had to be packing pistols from the way they stood, Jack knew. He nodded politely to them, and got no response other than another frisking from one while the other watched from a safe shooting distance. Ryan was astonished when the two KGB officers were frisked as well. When this was complete, the other one motioned them through a doorway.

General Secretary of the Communist Party of the Soviet Union Andrey Il'ych Narmonov was sitting in an over-stuffed chair in front of a newly built fire. He rose when the four men entered the room, and gestured for them to sit on the sofa opposite his place. The bodyguard took position standing behind the head of the Soviet government. Narmonov spoke in Russian. Golovko translated.

'You are?'

'John Ryan, sir,' Jack said. The General Secretary pointed him to a chair opposite his own, and noted that Ryan favored his leg.

'Anatoliy,' he said to the bodyguard, who took Ryan's arm and walked him to a first-floor bathroom. The man dampened a washcloth with warm water and handed it over. Back in the sitting room, he could hear people talking, but Ryan's knowledge of Russian was too thin to catch any of it. It was good to wash off the leg, but it looked as though the pants were finished, and the nearest change of clothes – he checked his watch – was probably near Denmark by now. Anatoliy watched him the whole time. The bodyguard pulled a gauze bandage from the medicine cabinet and helped Jack tape it in place, then walked him back as gracefully as Ryan's aches and pains allowed.

Golovko was still there, though Vatutin had left, and the empty chair was still waiting. Anatoliy took his former place behind Narmonov.

'The fire feels good,' Jack said. 'Thank you for letting me wash the knee off.'

'Golovko tells me that we did not do that to you. Is this correct?'

It seemed an odd question to Jack, since Golovko was handling the translating. *So Andrey Ily'ch speaks a little English, does he?*

'No, sir, I did it to myself. I have not been mistreated in any way.' *Just had the piss scared out of me,* Ryan thought to himself. *But that's my own damned fault.* Narmonov looked at him with silent interest for perhaps half a minute before speaking again.

'I did not need your help.'

'I do not know what you mean, sir,' Ryan lied.

'Did you really think that Gerasimov could remove me?'

'Sir, I don't know what you are talking about. My mission was to save the life of one of our agents. To do this meant compromising Chairman Gerasimov. It was just a matter of fishing with the proper bait.'

'And fishing for the proper fish,' Narmonov commented. The amusement in his voice did not show on his face. 'And your agent was Colonel Filitov?'

'Yes, sir. You know that.'

'I just learned it.'

Then you know that Yazov was compromised also. Just how close might they have come, Comrade General Secretary? Ryan did not say. Probably Narmonov didn't know either.

'Do you know why he turned traitor?'

'No, I don't. I was briefed only on what I needed to know.'

'And therefore you do not know about the attack on our Project Bright Star?'

'What?' Jack was very surprised, and showed it.

'Don't insult me, Ryan. You do know the name.'

'It's southeast of Dushanbe. I know it. Attacked?' he asked.

'As I thought. You know that was an act of war,' Narmonov observed.

'Sir, KGB officers kidnapped an American SDI scientist several days ago. That was ordered by Gerasimov himself. His name is Alan Gregory. He's a major in the US Army, and he was rescued.'

'I don't believe it,' Golovko said before translating. Narmonov was annoyed by the interruption, but shocked by the substance of Ryan's statement.

'One of your officers was captured. He's alive. It is true, sir,' Jack assured him.

Narmonov shook his head and rose to toss another log on the fire. He maneuvered it into place with a poker. 'It's madness, you know,' he said at the hearth. 'We have a perfectly satisfactory situation now.'

'Excuse me? I don't understand,' Ryan asked.

'The world is stable, is it not? Yet your country wishes to change this, and forces us to pursue the same goal.' That the ABM test site at Sary Shagan had been operating for over thirty years was, for the moment, beside the point.

'Mr Secretary, if you think the ability to turn every city, every home in my country into a fire like the one you have right there –'

'My country, too, Ryan,' Narmonov said.

'Yes, sir, your country, too, and a bunch of others. You

can kill most every civilian in my country, and we can murder almost every person in your country, in sixty minutes or less from the time you pick up the phone – or my President does. And what do we call that? We call it "*stability*".'

'It is stability, Ryan,' Narmonov said.

'No, sir, the technical name we use is MAD: Mutual Assured Destruction, which isn't even good grammar, but it's accurate enough. The situation we have now is mad, all right, and the fact that supposedly intelligent people have thought it up doesn't make it any more sensible.'

'It works, doesn't it?'

'Sir, why is it stabilizing to have several hundred million people less than an hour away from death? Why do we view weapons that might protect those people to be dangerous? Isn't that backwards?'

'But if we never use them . . . Do you think that I could live with such a crime on my conscience?'

'No, I don't think that any man could, but someone might screw up. He'd probably blow his brains out a week after the fact, but that might be a little late for the rest of us. The damned things are just too easy to use. You push a button, and they go, and they'll work, probably because there's nothing to stop them. Unless something stands in their way, there's no reason to think that they won't work. And as long as somebody thinks they might work, it's too easy to use them.'

'Be realistic, Ryan. Do you think that we'll ever rid ourselves of atomic arms?' Narmonov asked.

'No, we'll never get rid of all the weapons. I know that. We'll both always have the ability to hurt each other badly, but we can make that process more complicated than it is now. We can give everybody one more reason not to push the button. That's not destabilizing, sir. That's just good sense. That's just something more to protect your conscience.'

'You sound like your President.' This was delivered with a smile.

'He's right.' Ryan returned it.

'It is bad enough that I must argue with one American. I will not do so with another. What will you do with Gerasimov?' the General Secretary asked.

'It will be handled very quietly, for the obvious reason,' Jack said, hoping that he was right.

'It would be very damaging to my government if his defection became public. I suggest that he died in a plane crash . . .'

'I will convey that to my government if I am permitted to do so. We can also keep Filitov's name out of the news. We have nothing to gain by publicity. That would just complicate things for your country and mine. We both want the arms treaty to go forward – all that money to save, for both of us.'

'Not so much,' Narmonov said. 'A few percentage points of the defense budgets on both sides.'

'There is a saying in our government, sir. A billion here and a billion there, pretty soon you're talking about some real money.' That earned Jack a laugh. 'May I ask a question, sir?'

'Go on.'

'What will you do with the money on your side? I'm supposed to figure that one out.'

'Then perhaps you can offer me suggestions. What makes you think that I know?' Narmonov asked. He rose, and Ryan did the same. 'Back to your embassy. Tell your people that it is better for both sides if this never becomes public.'

Half an hour later Ryan was dropped off at the front door of the embassy. The first one to see him was a Marine sergeant. The second was Candela.

The VC-137 landed at Shannon ten minutes late, due to head-winds over the North Sea. The crew chief and another sergeant herded the passengers out the front way, and when all had left the aircraft, came back to open the rear door. While cameras flashed in the main terminal, steps were rolled to the Boeing's tail and four men left wearing the uniform parkas of US Air Force sergeants. They entered a car and were driven to a far end of the terminal, where they boarded another plane of the 89th Military Airlift Wing, a VC-20A, the military version of the Gulfstream-III executive jet.

'Hello, Misha.' Mary Pat Foley met him at the door and took him forward. She hadn't kissed him before. She made up for it now. 'We have food and drink, and another plane ride home. Come, Misha.' She took his arm and led him to his seat.

A few feet away, Robert Ritter greeted Gerasimov.

'My family?' the latter asked.

'Safe. We'll have them in Washington in two days. At this moment they are aboard a US Navy ship in international waters.'

'I am supposed to thank you?'

'We expect you to cooperate.'

'You were very lucky,' Gerasimov observed.

'Yes,' Ritter agreed. 'We were.'

The embassy car drove Ryan to Sheremetyevo the following day to catch the regular Pan Am 727 flight to Frankfurt. The ticket they provided him was tourist, but Ryan upgraded it to first class. Three hours later he connected with a 747 for Dulles, also Pan Am. He slept most of the way.

Bondarenko surveyed the carnage. The Afghans had left forty-seven bodies behind, with evidence of plenty more. Only two of the site's laser assemblies had survived. All of the machine shops were wrecked, along with the theater and bachelor quarters. The hospital was largely intact, and full of wounded people. The good news was that he'd saved three-quarters of the scientific and engineering personnel and nearly all of their dependents. Four general officers were there already to tell him what a hero he was, promising medals and promotion, but he'd already gotten the only reward that mattered. As soon as the relief force had arrived, he'd seen that the people were safe. Now, he just looked from the roof of the apartment block.

'There is much work to do,' a voice noted. The Colonel, soon to be a General, turned.

'Morozov. We still have two of the lasers. We can rebuild the shops and laboratories. A year, perhaps eighteen months.'

'That's about right,' the young engineer said. 'The new mirrors and their computer control equipment will take at least that long. Comrade Colonel, the people have asked me to –'

'That is my job, Comrade Engineer, and I had my own ass to save, remember? This will never happen again. We'll have a battalion of motorized infantry here from now on, from a guards regiment. I've already seen to that. By summer this installation will be as safe as any place in the Soviet Union.'

'Safe? What does that mean, Colonel?'

'That is my new job. And yours,' Bondarenko said. 'Remember?'

EPILOGUE

Common Ground

It didn't surprise Ortiz when the Major came in alone. The report of the battle took an hour, and again the CIA officer was given a few rucksacks of equipment. The Archer's band had fought its way out, and of the nearly two hundred who had left the refugee camp, fewer than fifty returned on this first day of spring. The Major went immediately to work making contact with other bands, and the prestige of the mission which his group had carried out enabled him to deal with older and more powerful chieftains as a near equal. Within a week he had made good his losses with eager new warriors, and the arrangement the Archer had made with Ortiz remained in force.

'You're going back already?' the CIA officer asked the new leader.

'Of course. We're winning now,' the Major said with a degree of confidence that even he did not understand.

Ortiz watched them leave at nightfall, a single file of small, ferocious warriors, led now by a trained soldier. He hoped it would make a difference.

Gerasimov and Filitov never saw each other again. The debriefings lasted for weeks, and were conducted at separate locations. Filitov was taken to Camp Peary, Virginia, where he met a spectacled US Army major and told what he remembered of the Russian breakthrough in laser power. It seemed curious to the old man that this boy could be so excited about things that he'd memorized but never fully understood.

After that came the routine explanations of the second

career that had joined and paralleled his first. A whole generation of field officers visited him for meals and walks, and drinking sessions that worried the doctors but which no one could deny the Cardinal. His living quarters were closely guarded, and even bugged. Those who listened to him were surprised that he occasionally spoke in his sleep.

One CIA officer who was six months from his retirement paused from reading the local paper when it happened again. He smiled at the noise in his headphones and set down the article he was reading about the President's visit to Moscow. *That sad, lonely old man*, he thought as he listened. *Most of his friends dead, and he only sees them in his sleep. Was that why he went to work for us?* The murmuring stopped, and in the quarters next door, the Cardinal's baby-sitter went back to his paper.

'Comrade Captain,' Romanov said.

'Yes, Corporal?' It seemed more real than most of his dreams, Misha noted. A moment later he knew why.

They were spending their honeymoon under the protection of security officers, all four days of it – which was as long as Al and Candi were willing to stay away from work. Major Gregory got the phone when it rang.

'Yeah – I mean, yes, sir,' Candi heard him say. A sigh. A shake of the head in the darkness. 'Not even anyplace to send flowers, is there? Can Candi and I – Oh . . . I understand. Thanks for calling, General.' She heard him replace the phone and let out another breath.

'Candi, you awake?'

'Yeah.'

'Our first kid, his name's going to be Mike.'

Major General Grigoriy Dalmatov's post of Defense Attaché at the Soviet Embassy in Washington carried a number of ceremonial duties that conflicted with his primary mission, intelligence gathering. He was slightly annoyed when the telephone call from the Pentagon had come, asking him to drive over to the American military headquarters – and to his great surprise, to do so in full uniform. His car dropped him off at the River entrance, and a young paratroop captain had escorted him inside, then to the office of General Ben Crofter, Chief of Staff, United States Army.

'May I ask what is going on?'

'Something that we thought you should see, Grigoriy,' Crofter answered cryptically. They walked across the building to the Pentagon's own helicopter pad, where to Dalmatov's astonishment they boarded a Marine helicopter of the Presidential Fleet. The Sikorsky lifted off at once, heading northwest into the Maryland hills. Twenty minutes later they were descending. Dalmatov's mind registered yet another surprise. The helicopter was landing at Camp David. A member of the Marine guard force in dress blues saluted at the foot of the stairs as they left the aircraft and escorted them into the trees. Several minutes later they came to a clearing. Dalmatov hadn't known there were birch trees here, perhaps half an acre of them, and the clearing was near a hilltop that offered a fine view of the surrounding country.

And there was a rectangular hole in the ground, exactly six feet deep. It seemed strange that there was no headstone, and that the sod had been carefully cut and set aside for replacement.

Around the scene, Dalmatov could make out more Marines in the treeline. These wore camouflage fatigues and pistol belts. Well, it was no particular surprise that there was heavy security here, and the General found it rather comforting that in the past hour one unsurprising thing had taken place.

A jeep appeared first. Two Marines – in dress blues again – got out and erected a prefabricated stand around the hole. They must have practiced, the General thought, since it took them only three minutes by his watch. Then a three-quarter-ton truck came through the trees, followed by some more jeeps. Cradled in the back of the truck was a polished oak coffin. The truck pulled to within a few meters of the hole and stopped. An honor guard assembled.

'May I ask why I am here?' Dalmatov asked when he couldn't stand it any longer.

'You came up in tanks, right?'

'Yes, General Crofter, as did you.'

'That's why.'

The six men of the honor guard set the coffin on the stand. The gunnery sergeant in command of the detail removed the lid. Crofter walked toward it. Dalmatov gasped when he saw who was inside.

'Misha.'

'I thought you knew him,' a new voice said. Dalmatov spun around.

'You are Ryan.' Others were there, Ritter of CIA, General Parks, and a young couple, in their thirties, Dalmatov thought. The wife seemed to be pregnant, though rather early along. She was weeping silently in the gentle spring breeze.

'Yes, sir.'

The Russian gestured to the coffin. 'Where – how did you –'

'I just flew back from Moscow. The General Secretary was kind enough to give me the Colonel's uniform and decorations. He said that – he said that in the case of this man, he prefers to remember the reason he got those three gold stars. We hope that you will tell your people that Colonel Mikhail Semyonovich Filitov, three times Hero of the Soviet Union, died peacefully in his sleep.'

Dalmatov went red. 'He was a traitor to his country – I will not stand here and –'

'General,' Ryan said harshly, 'it should be clear that your General Secretary does not agree with that sentiment. That man may be a greater hero than you know, for your country and for mine. Tell me, General, how many battles have you fought? How many wounds have you received for your country? Can you really look at that man and call him traitor? In any case . . .' Ryan gestured to the sergeant, who closed the coffin. When he'd finished, another Marine draped a Soviet flag over it. A team of riflemen appeared and formed at the head of the grave. Ryan took a paper from his pocket and read off Misha's citations for bravery. The riflemen brought up their weapons and fired off their volleys. A trumpeter played Taps.

Dalmatov came to rigid attention and saluted. It seemed a pity to Ryan that the ceremony had to be secret, but its simplicity made for dignity, and that at least was fitting enough.

'Why here?' Dalmatov asked when it was finished.

'I would have preferred Arlington, but then someone might notice. Right over those hills is the Antietam battlefield. On the bloodiest day in our Civil War, the Union forces repelled Lee's first invasion of the North after a desperate battle. It just seemed like the right place,' Ryan said. 'If a hero must have an unmarked grave, it should at least be close to where his comrades fell.'

'Comrades?'

'One way or another we all fight for the things we believe in. Doesn't that give us some common ground?' Jack asked. He walked off to his car, leaving Dalmatov with the thought.